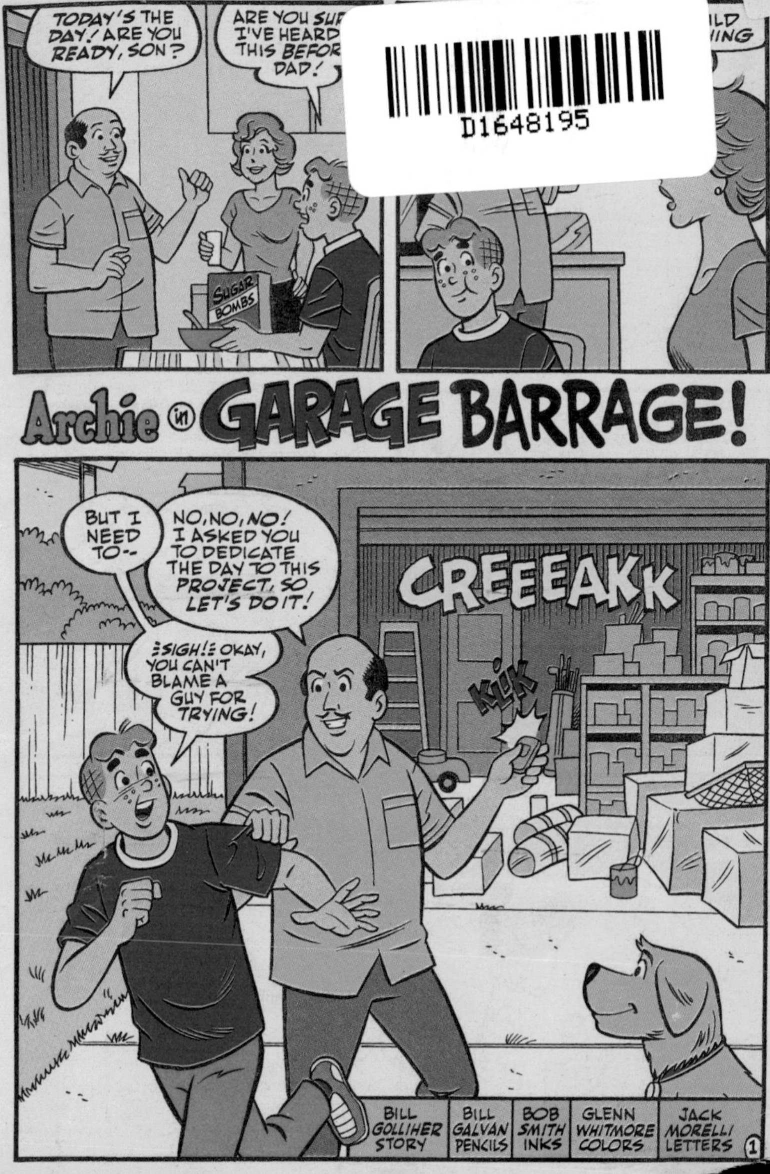
TODAY'S THE DAY! ARE YOU READY, SON?
ARE YOU SUR
I'VE HEARD
THIS BEFOR
DAD!
SUGAR BOMBS
Archie in GARAGE BARRAGE!
BUT I NEED TO--
NO, NO, NO! I ASKED YOU TO DEDICATE THE DAY TO THIS PROJECT, SO LET'S DO IT!
CREEEAKK
KLIK
:SIGH!: OKAY, YOU CAN'T BLAME A GUY FOR TRYING!
BILL GOLLIHER STORY
BILL GALVAN PENCILS
BOB SMITH INKS
GLENN WHITMORE COLORS
JACK MORELLI LETTERS
1

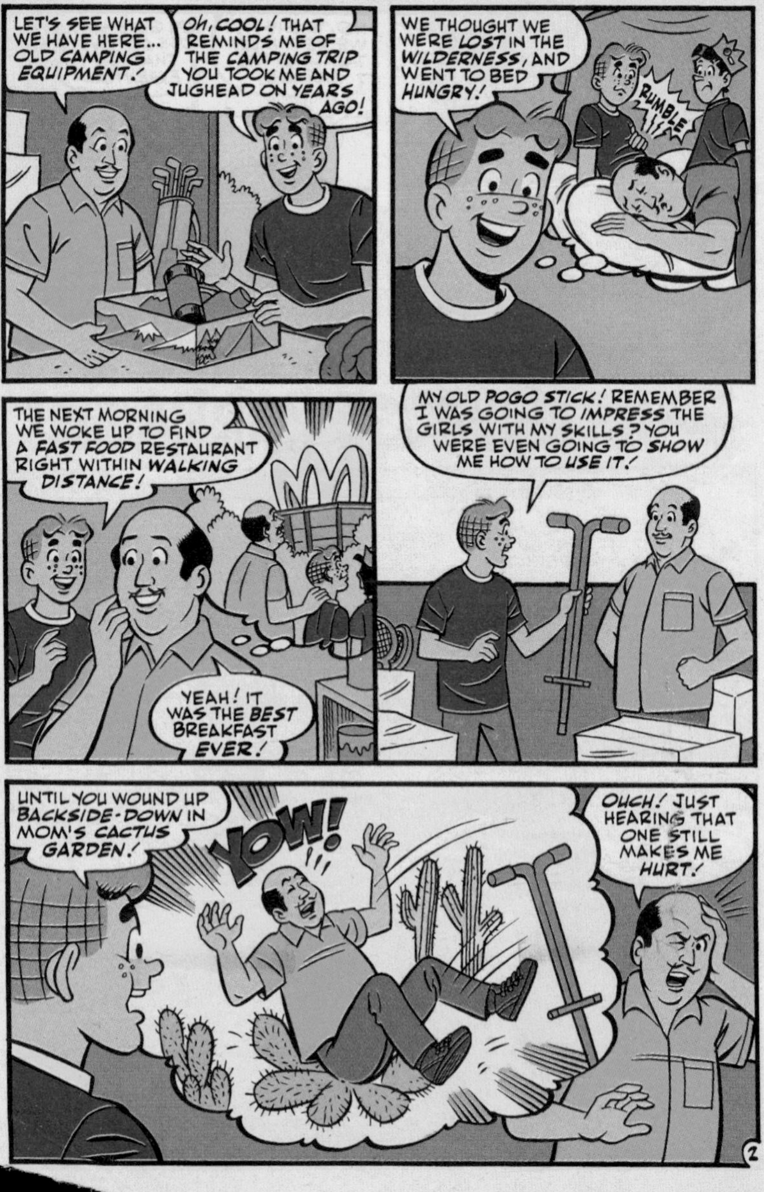
LET'S SEE WHAT WE HAVE HERE... OLD CAMPING EQUIPMENT!
OH, COOL! THAT REMINDS ME OF THE CAMPING TRIP YOU TOOK ME AND JUGHEAD ON YEARS AGO!
WE THOUGHT WE WERE LOST IN THE WILDERNESS, AND WENT TO BED HUNGRY!
RUMBLE
THE NEXT MORNING WE WOKE UP TO FIND A FAST FOOD RESTAURANT RIGHT WITHIN WALKING DISTANCE!
YEAH! IT WAS THE BEST BREAKFAST EVER!
MY OLD POGO STICK! REMEMBER I WAS GOING TO IMPRESS THE GIRLS WITH MY SKILLS? YOU WERE EVEN GOING TO SHOW ME HOW TO USE IT!
UNTIL YOU WOUND UP BACKSIDE-DOWN IN MOM'S CACTUS GARDEN!
YOW!
OUCH! JUST HEARING THAT ONE STILL MAKES ME HURT!

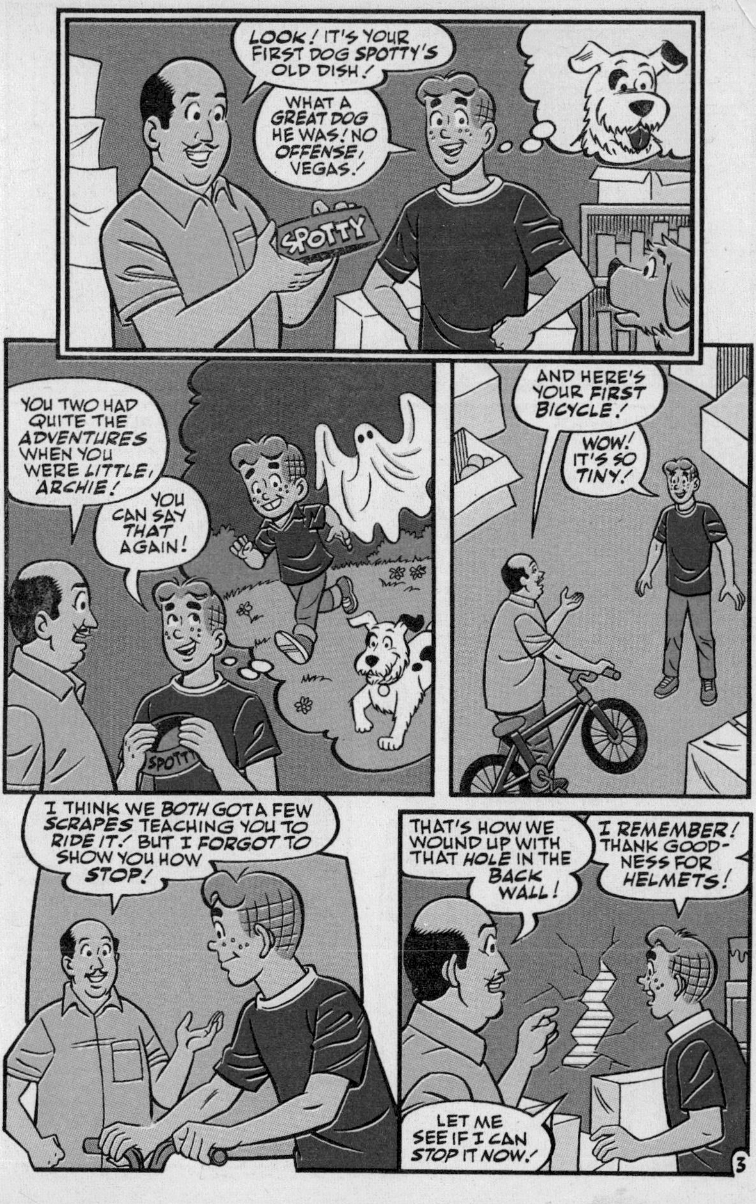
LOOK! IT'S YOUR FIRST DOG SPOTTY'S OLD DISH!
WHAT A GREAT DOG HE WAS! NO OFFENSE, VEGAS!
SPOTTY
YOU TWO HAD QUITE THE ADVENTURES WHEN YOU WERE LITTLE, ARCHIE!
YOU CAN SAY THAT AGAIN!
AND HERE'S YOUR FIRST BICYCLE!
WOW! IT'S SO TINY!
I THINK WE BOTH GOT A FEW SCRAPES TEACHING YOU TO RIDE IT! BUT I FORGOT TO SHOW YOU HOW STOP!
THAT'S HOW WE WOUND UP WITH THAT HOLE IN THE BACK WALL!
I REMEMBER! THANK GOODNESS FOR HELMETS!
LET ME SEE IF I CAN STOP IT NOW!

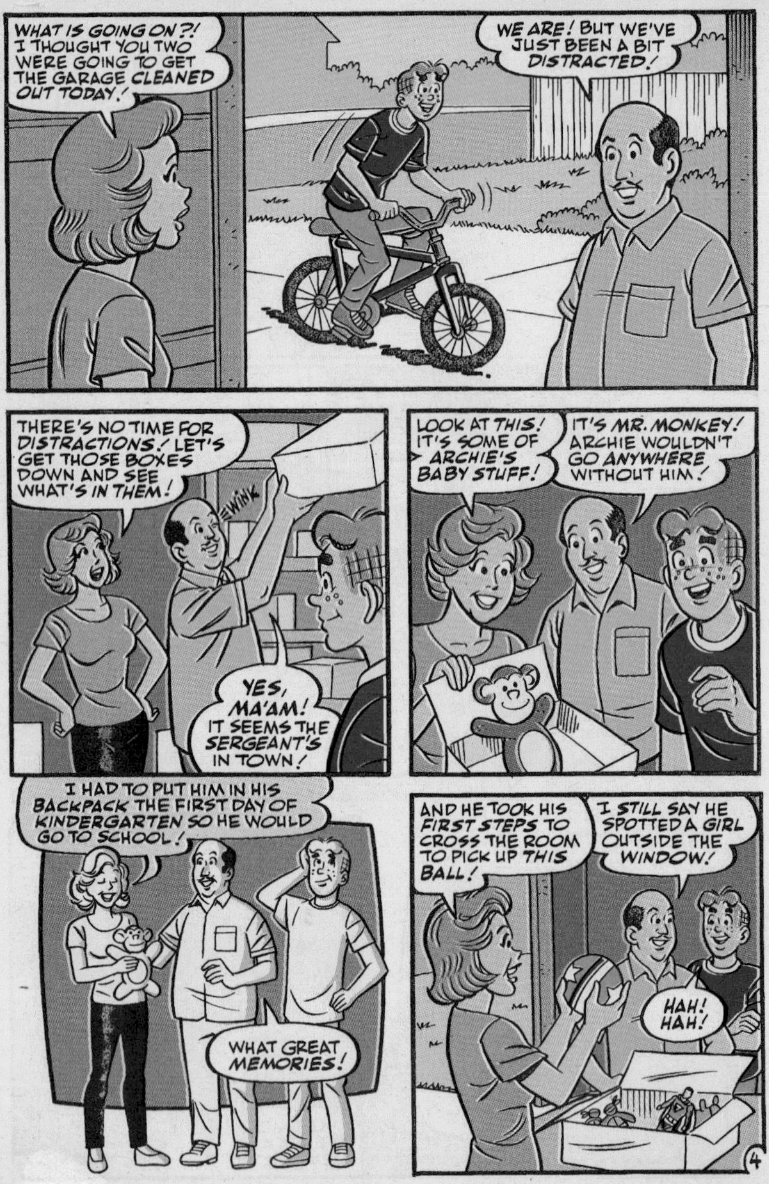
WHAT IS GOING ON?! I THOUGHT YOU TWO WERE GOING TO GET THE GARAGE CLEANED OUT TODAY!
WE ARE! BUT WE'VE JUST BEEN A BIT DISTRACTED!
THERE'S NO TIME FOR DISTRACTIONS! LET'S GET THOSE BOXES DOWN AND SEE WHAT'S IN THEM!
WINK
YES, MA'AM! IT SEEMS THE SERGEANT'S IN TOWN!
LOOK AT THIS! IT'S SOME OF ARCHIE'S BABY STUFF!
IT'S MR. MONKEY! ARCHIE WOULDN'T GO ANYWHERE WITHOUT HIM!
I HAD TO PUT HIM IN HIS BACKPACK THE FIRST DAY OF KINDERGARTEN SO HE WOULD GO TO SCHOOL!
WHAT GREAT MEMORIES!
AND HE TOOK HIS FIRST STEPS TO CROSS THE ROOM TO PICK UP THIS BALL!
I STILL SAY HE SPOTTED A GIRL OUTSIDE THE WINDOW!
HAH! HAH!
4

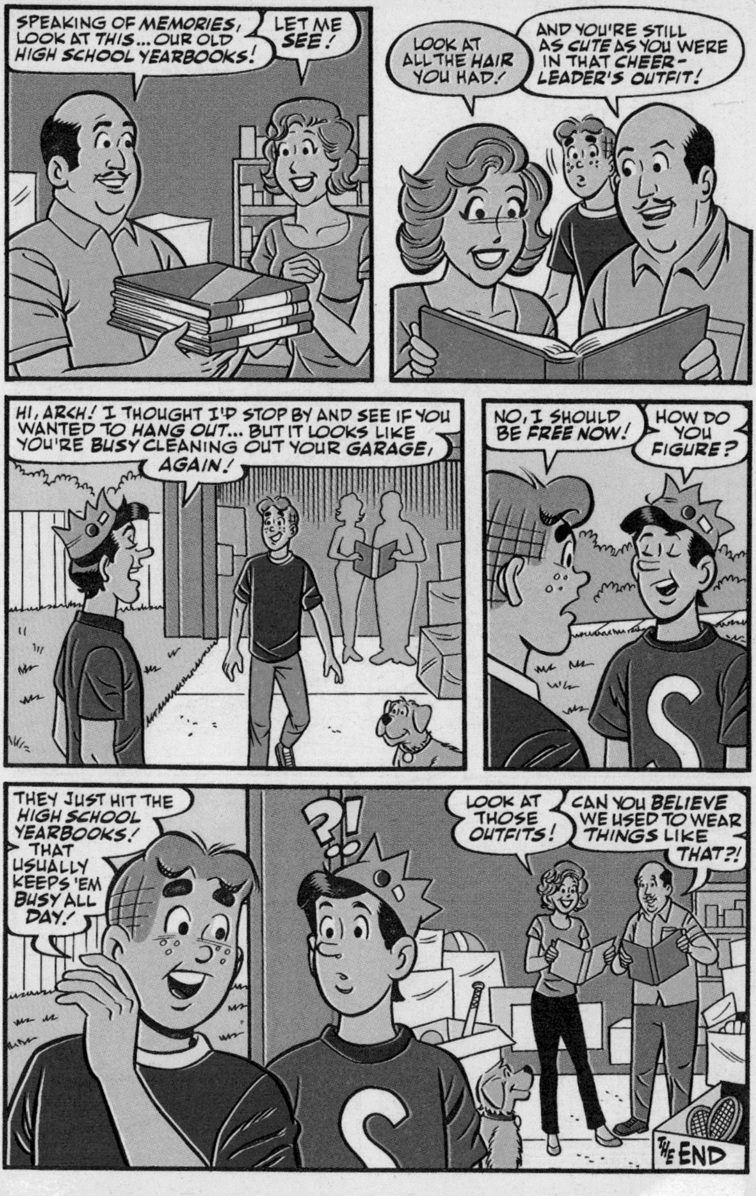
SPEAKING OF MEMORIES, LOOK AT THIS... OUR OLD HIGH SCHOOL YEARBOOKS!
LET ME SEE!
LOOK AT ALL THE HAIR YOU HAD!
AND YOU'RE STILL AS CUTE AS YOU WERE IN THAT CHEER-LEADER'S OUTFIT!
HI, ARCH! I THOUGHT I'D STOP BY AND SEE IF YOU WANTED TO HANG OUT... BUT IT LOOKS LIKE YOU'RE BUSY CLEANING OUT YOUR GARAGE, AGAIN!
NO, I SHOULD BE FREE NOW!
HOW DO YOU FIGURE?
THEY JUST HIT THE HIGH SCHOOL YEARBOOKS! THAT USUALLY KEEPS 'EM BUSY ALL DAY!
?!
LOOK AT THOSE OUTFITS!
CAN YOU BELIEVE WE USED TO WEAR THINGS LIKE THAT?!
THE END

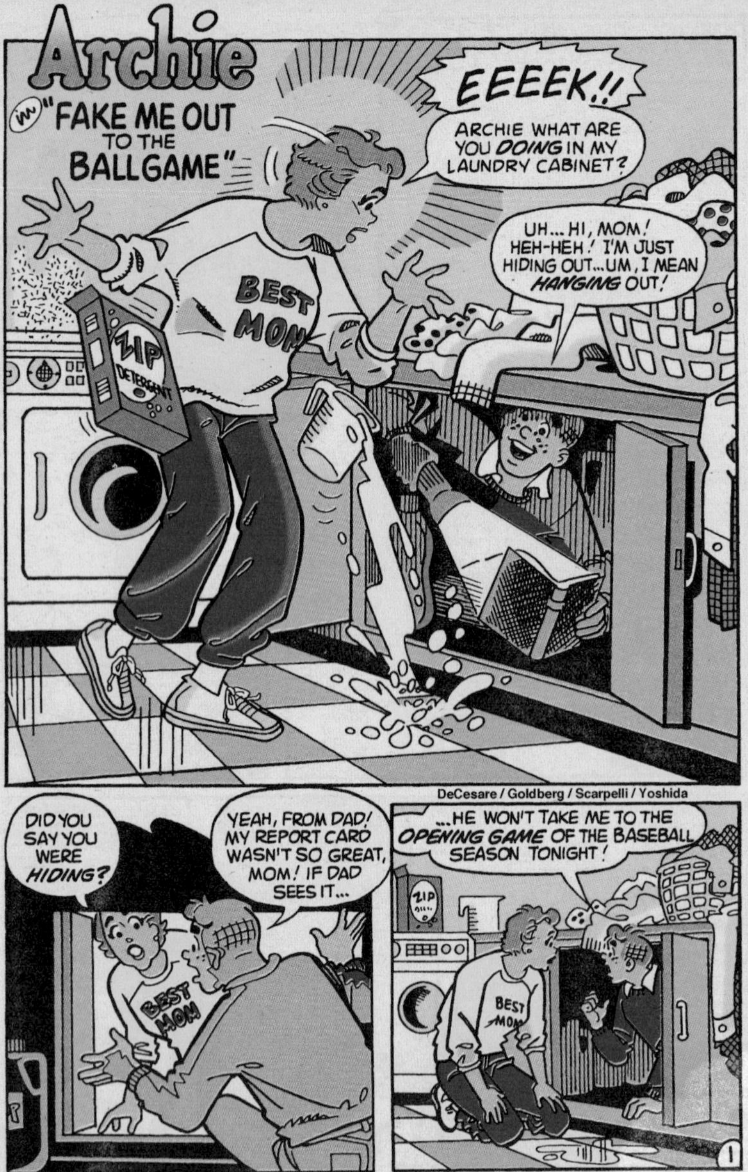
Archie
in "FAKE ME OUT TO THE BALLGAME"
EEEEK!!
ARCHIE WHAT ARE YOU DOING IN MY LAUNDRY CABINET?
UH... HI, MOM! HEH-HEH! I'M JUST HIDING OUT...UM, I MEAN HANGING OUT!
BEST MOM
ZIP DETERGENT
DID YOU SAY YOU WERE HIDING?
YEAH, FROM DAD! MY REPORT CARD WASN'T SO GREAT, MOM! IF DAD SEES IT...
...HE WON'T TAKE ME TO THE OPENING GAME OF THE BASEBALL SEASON TONIGHT!

DeCesare / Goldberg / Scarpelli / Yoshida

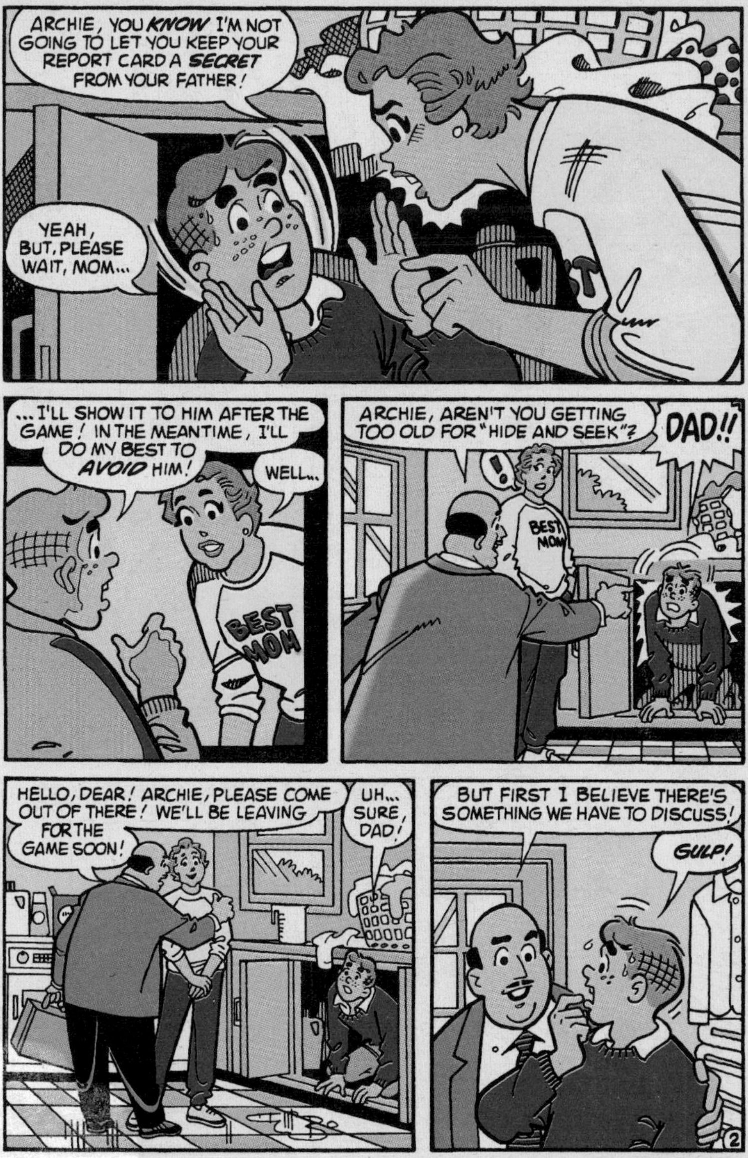
ARCHIE, YOU KNOW I'M NOT GOING TO LET YOU KEEP YOUR REPORT CARD A SECRET FROM YOUR FATHER!
YEAH, BUT, PLEASE WAIT, MOM...
...I'LL SHOW IT TO HIM AFTER THE GAME! IN THE MEANTIME, I'LL DO MY BEST TO AVOID HIM!
WELL...
BEST MOM
ARCHIE, AREN'T YOU GETTING TOO OLD FOR "HIDE AND SEEK"?
DAD!!
BEST MOM
HELLO, DEAR! ARCHIE, PLEASE COME OUT OF THERE! WE'LL BE LEAVING FOR THE GAME SOON!
UH... SURE, DAD!
BUT FIRST I BELIEVE THERE'S SOMETHING WE HAVE TO DISCUSS!
GULP!
2

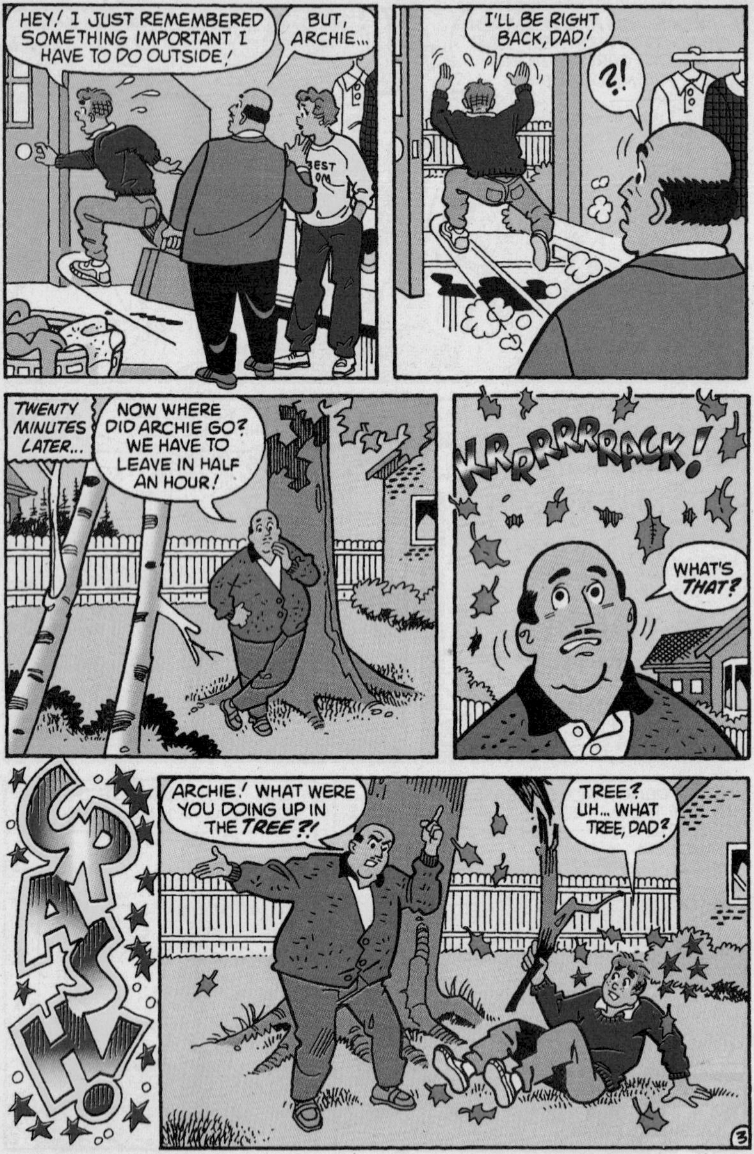
HEY! I JUST REMEMBERED SOMETHING IMPORTANT I HAVE TO DO OUTSIDE!
BUT, ARCHIE...
I'LL BE RIGHT BACK, DAD!
?!
TWENTY MINUTES LATER...
NOW WHERE DID ARCHIE GO? WE HAVE TO LEAVE IN HALF AN HOUR!
KRRRRRRACK!
WHAT'S THAT?
CRASH!
ARCHIE! WHAT WERE YOU DOING UP IN THE TREE?!
TREE? UH... WHAT TREE, DAD?
3

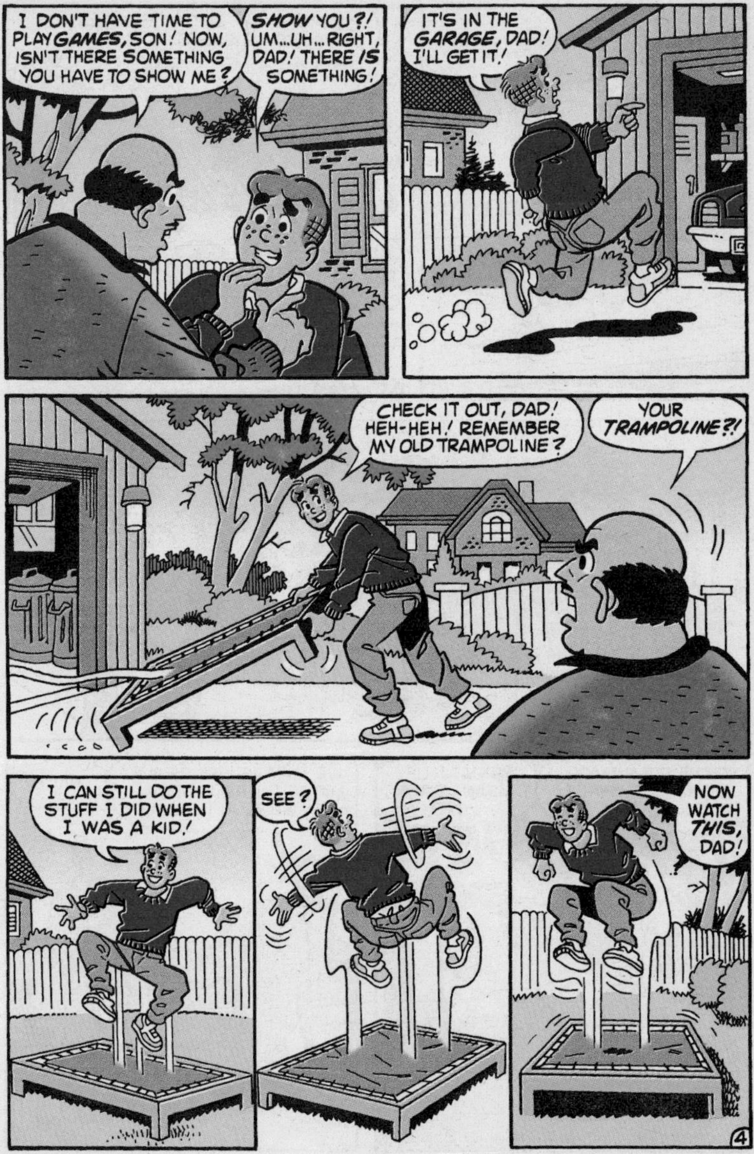
I DON'T HAVE TIME TO PLAY GAMES, SON! NOW, ISN'T THERE SOMETHING YOU HAVE TO SHOW ME?
SHOW YOU?! UM...UH... RIGHT, DAD! THERE IS SOMETHING!
IT'S IN THE GARAGE, DAD! I'LL GET IT!
CHECK IT OUT, DAD! HEH-HEH! REMEMBER MY OLD TRAMPOLINE?
YOUR TRAMPOLINE?!
I CAN STILL DO THE STUFF I DID WHEN I WAS A KID!
SEE?
NOW WATCH THIS, DAD!
4

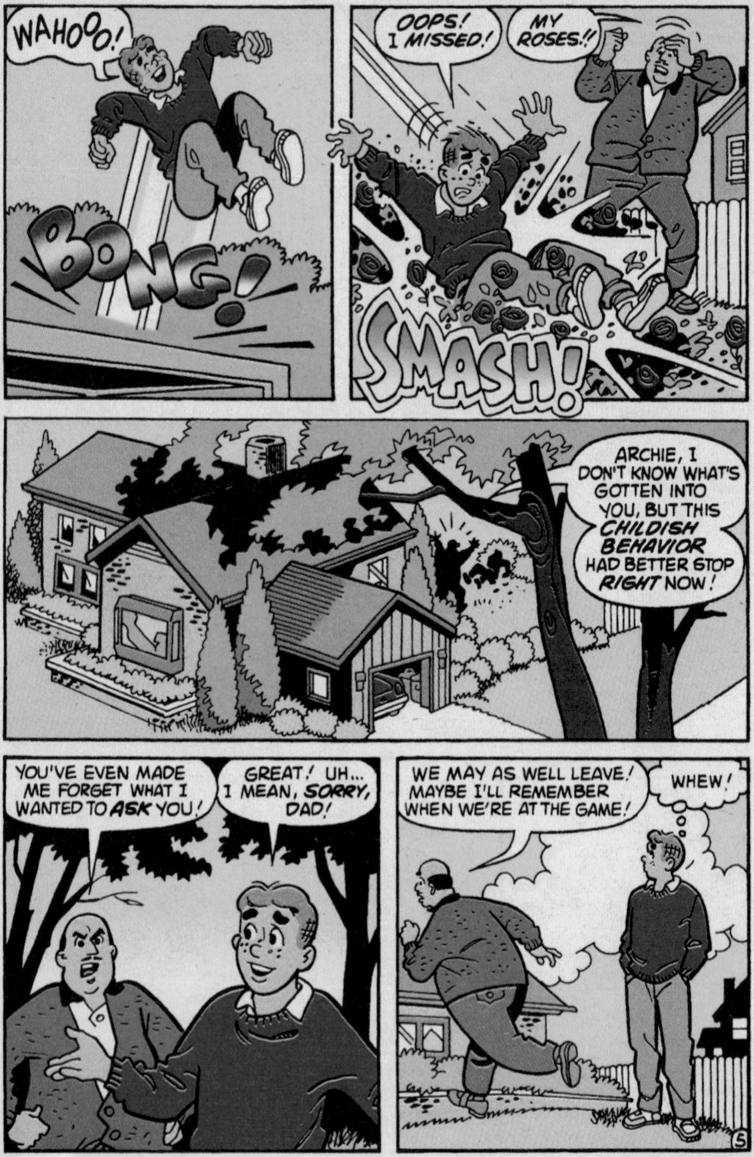
WAHOOOO!
BONG!
OOPS! I MISSED!
MY ROSES!!
SMASH!
ARCHIE, I DON'T KNOW WHAT'S GOTTEN INTO YOU, BUT THIS CHILDISH BEHAVIOR HAD BETTER STOP RIGHT NOW!
YOU'VE EVEN MADE ME FORGET WHAT I WANTED TO ASK YOU!
GREAT! UH... I MEAN, SORRY, DAD!
WE MAY AS WELL LEAVE! MAYBE I'LL REMEMBER WHEN WE'RE AT THE GAME!
WHEW!
5

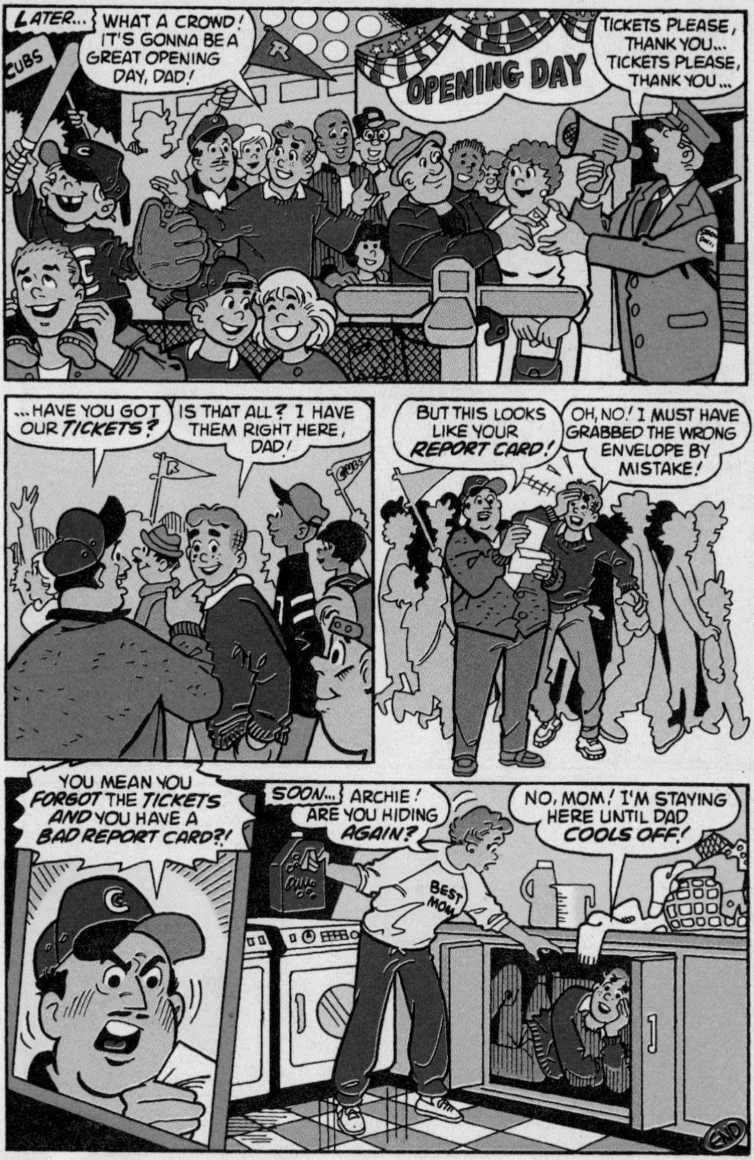
LATER...
WHAT A CROWD! IT'S GONNA BE A GREAT OPENING DAY, DAD!
CUBS
OPENING DAY
TICKETS PLEASE, THANK YOU... TICKETS PLEASE, THANK YOU...
...HAVE YOU GOT OUR TICKETS?
IS THAT ALL? I HAVE THEM RIGHT HERE, DAD!
BUT THIS LOOKS LIKE YOUR REPORT CARD!
OH, NO! I MUST HAVE GRABBED THE WRONG ENVELOPE BY MISTAKE!
YOU MEAN YOU FORGOT THE TICKETS AND YOU HAVE A BAD REPORT CARD?!
SOON...
ARCHIE! ARE YOU HIDING AGAIN?
BEST MOM
NO, MOM! I'M STAYING HERE UNTIL DAD COOLS OFF!
END

Archie in FOUNTAIN PEN

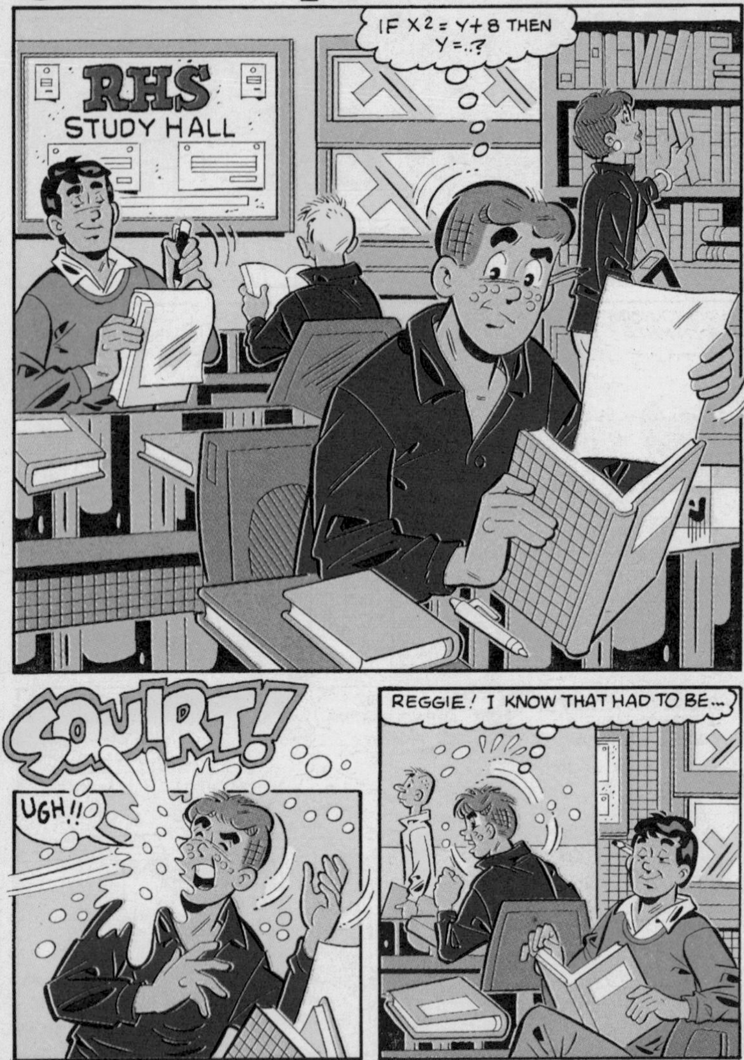
RHS
STUDY HALL
IF $X^2 = Y+8$ THEN $Y = ..?$
SQUIRT!
UGH!!
REGGIE! I KNOW THAT HAD TO BE...

Script: Mike Pellowski / Pencils: Tim Kennedy / Inks: Ken Selig / Letters: Bill Yoshida

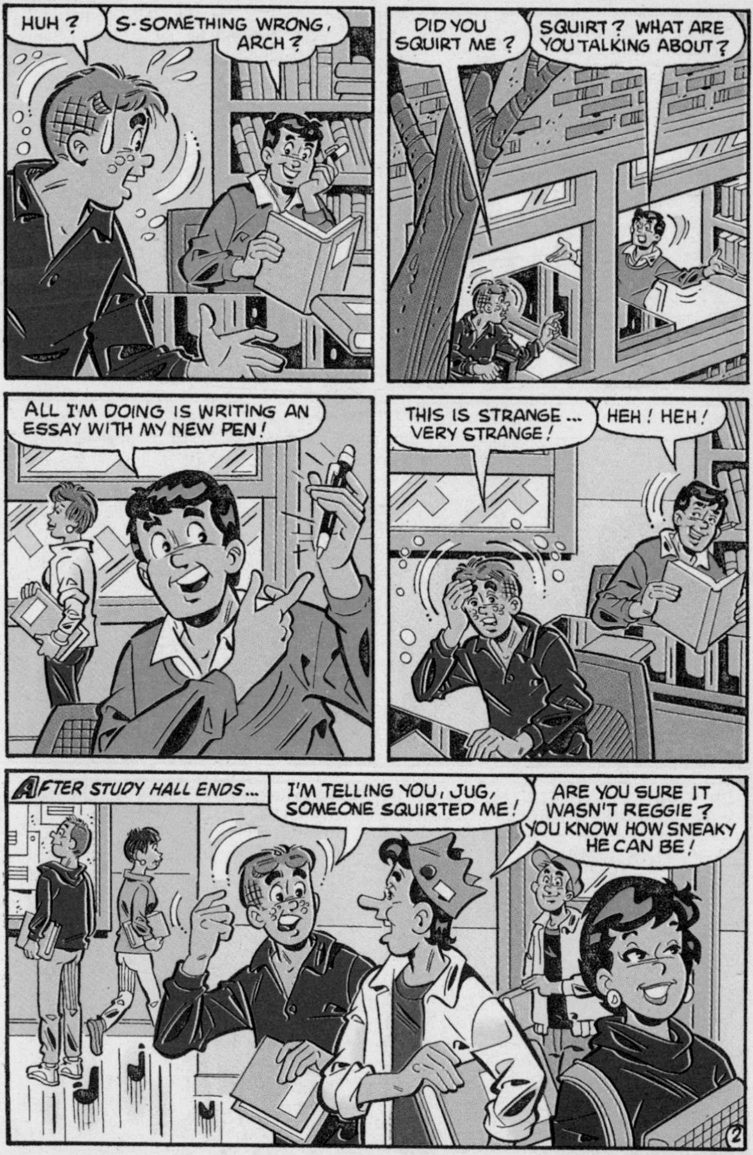
HUH ?
S-SOMETHING WRONG, ARCH ?
DID YOU SQUIRT ME ?
SQUIRT ? WHAT ARE YOU TALKING ABOUT ?
ALL I'M DOING IS WRITING AN ESSAY WITH MY NEW PEN !
THIS IS STRANGE ... VERY STRANGE !
HEH ! HEH !
AFTER STUDY HALL ENDS...
I'M TELLING YOU, JUG, SOMEONE SQUIRTED ME !
ARE YOU SURE IT WASN'T REGGIE ? YOU KNOW HOW SNEAKY HE CAN BE !
2

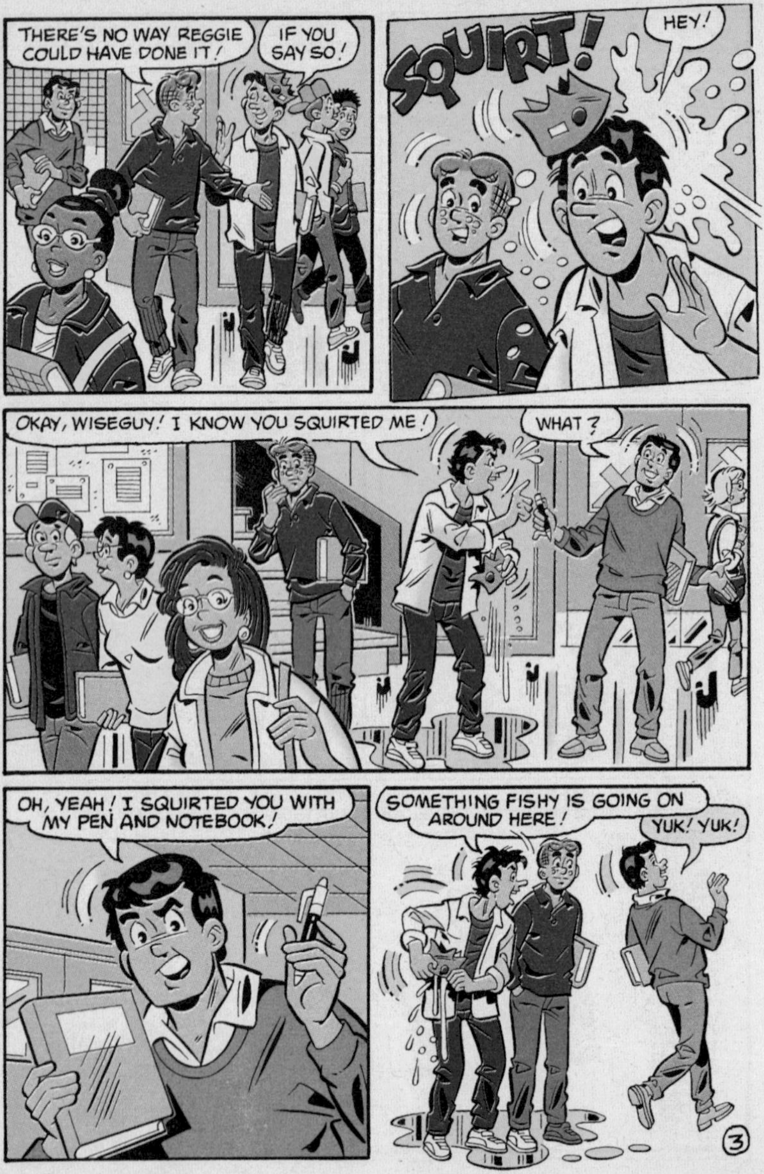
THERE'S NO WAY REGGIE COULD HAVE DONE IT!
IF YOU SAY SO!
SQUIRT!
HEY!
OKAY, WISEGUY! I KNOW YOU SQUIRTED ME!
WHAT?
OH, YEAH! I SQUIRTED YOU WITH MY PEN AND NOTEBOOK!
SOMETHING FISHY IS GOING ON AROUND HERE!
YUK! YUK!
3

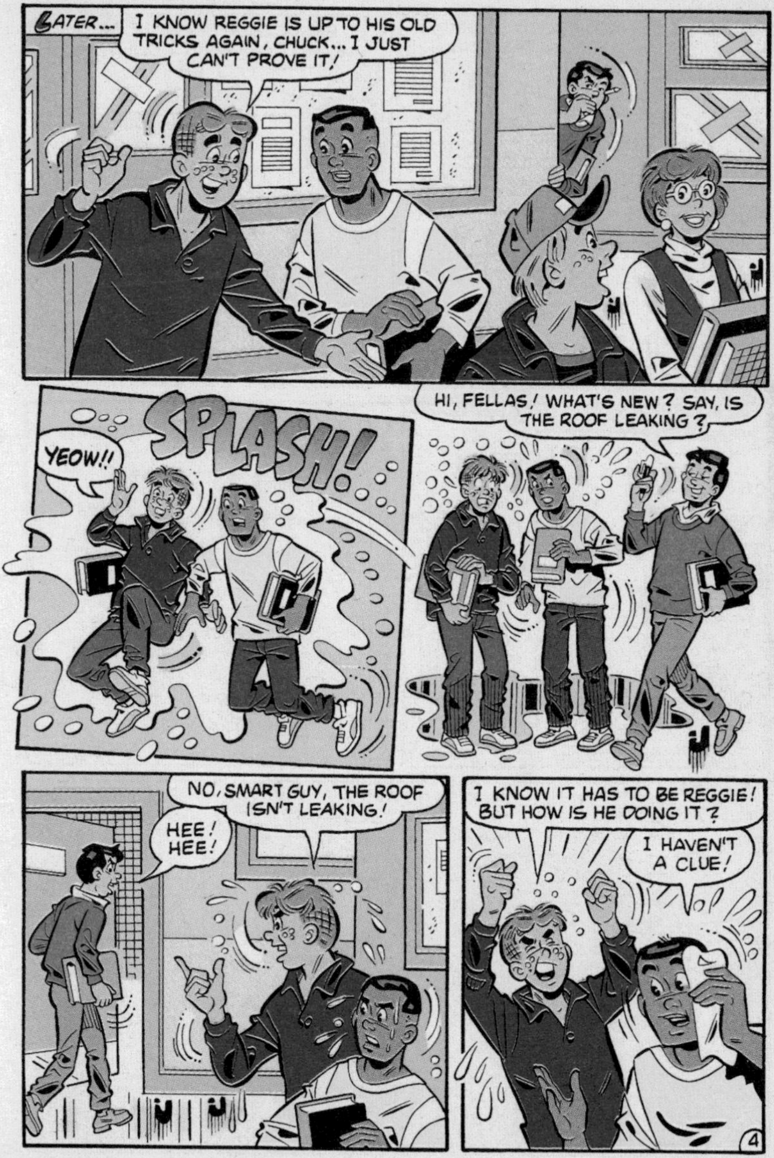
LATER...
I KNOW REGGIE IS UP TO HIS OLD TRICKS AGAIN, CHUCK... I JUST CAN'T PROVE IT!
SPLASH!
YEOW!!
HI, FELLAS! WHAT'S NEW? SAY, IS THE ROOF LEAKING?
NO, SMART GUY, THE ROOF ISN'T LEAKING!
HEE! HEE!
I KNOW IT HAS TO BE REGGIE! BUT HOW IS HE DOING IT?
I HAVEN'T A CLUE!
4

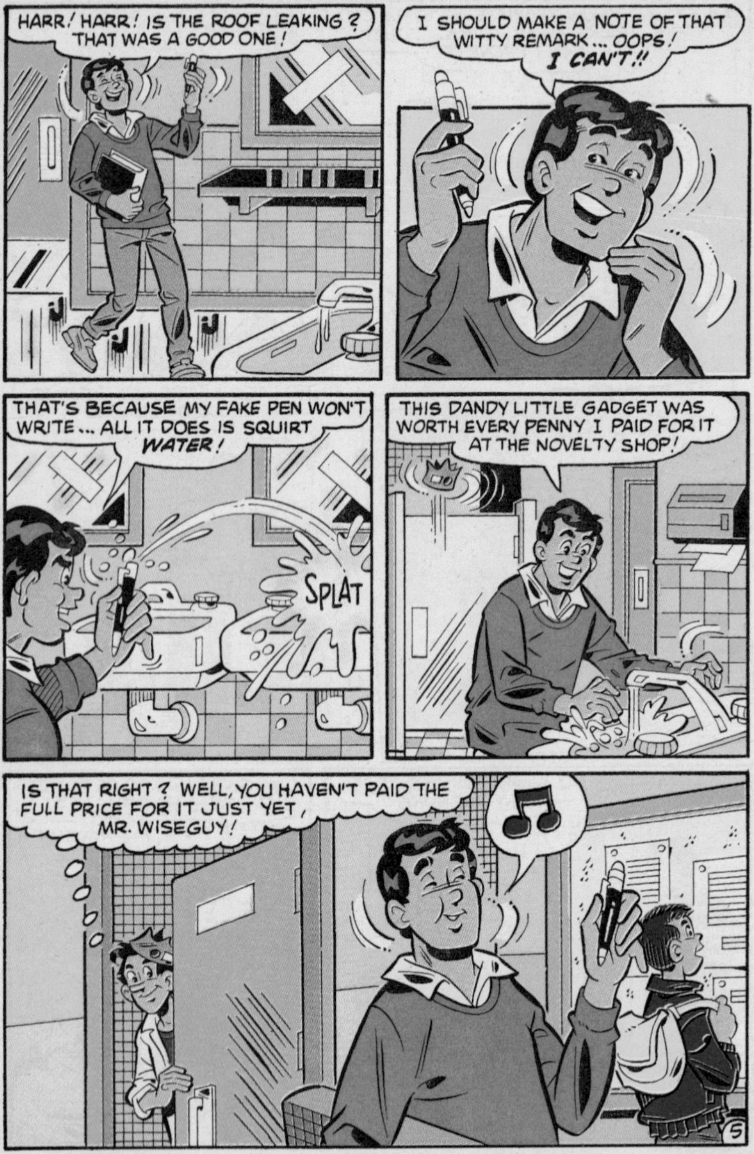
HARR! HARR! IS THE ROOF LEAKING? THAT WAS A GOOD ONE!
I SHOULD MAKE A NOTE OF THAT WITTY REMARK... OOPS! I CAN'T!!
THAT'S BECAUSE MY FAKE PEN WON'T WRITE... ALL IT DOES IS SQUIRT WATER!
SPLAT
THIS DANDY LITTLE GADGET WAS WORTH EVERY PENNY I PAID FOR IT AT THE NOVELTY SHOP!
IS THAT RIGHT? WELL, YOU HAVEN'T PAID THE FULL PRICE FOR IT JUST YET, MR. WISEGUY!
5

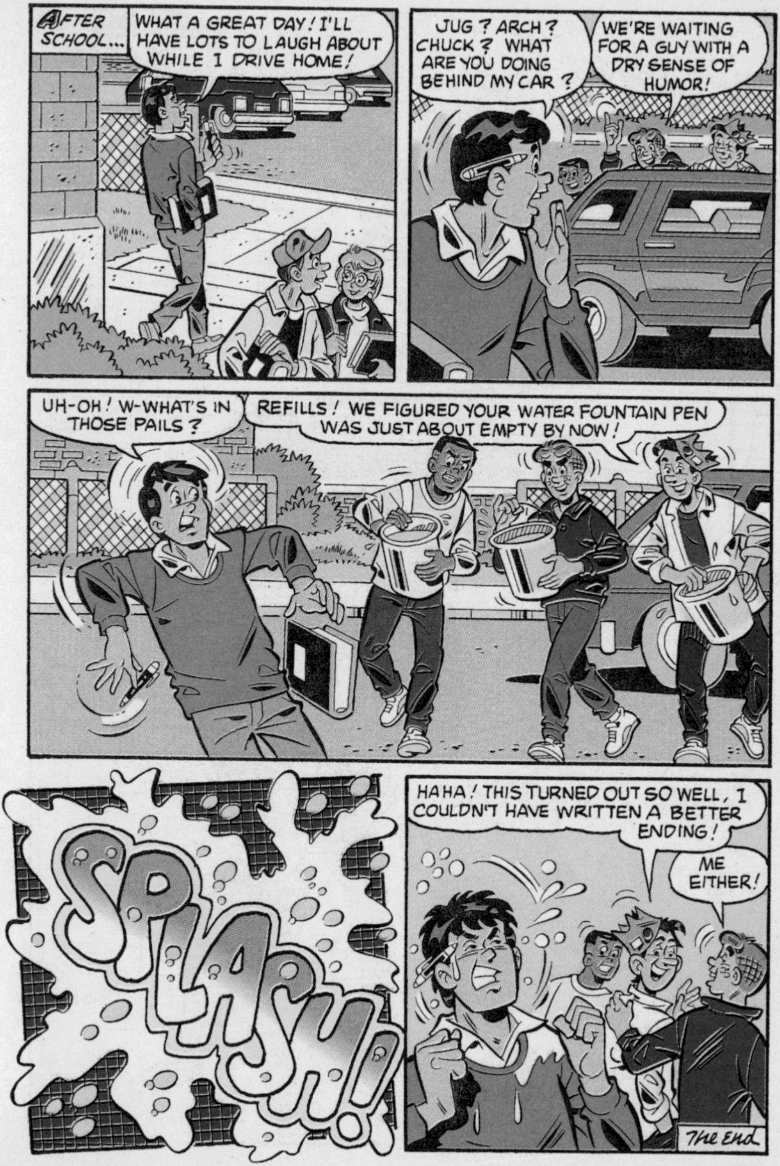
AFTER SCHOOL...
WHAT A GREAT DAY! I'LL HAVE LOTS TO LAUGH ABOUT WHILE I DRIVE HOME!
JUG? ARCH? CHUCK? WHAT ARE YOU DOING BEHIND MY CAR?
WE'RE WAITING FOR A GUY WITH A DRY SENSE OF HUMOR!
UH-OH! W-WHAT'S IN THOSE PAILS?
REFILLS! WE FIGURED YOUR WATER FOUNTAIN PEN WAS JUST ABOUT EMPTY BY NOW!
SPLASH!!
HA HA! THIS TURNED OUT SO WELL, I COULDN'T HAVE WRITTEN A BETTER ENDING!
ME EITHER!
The End

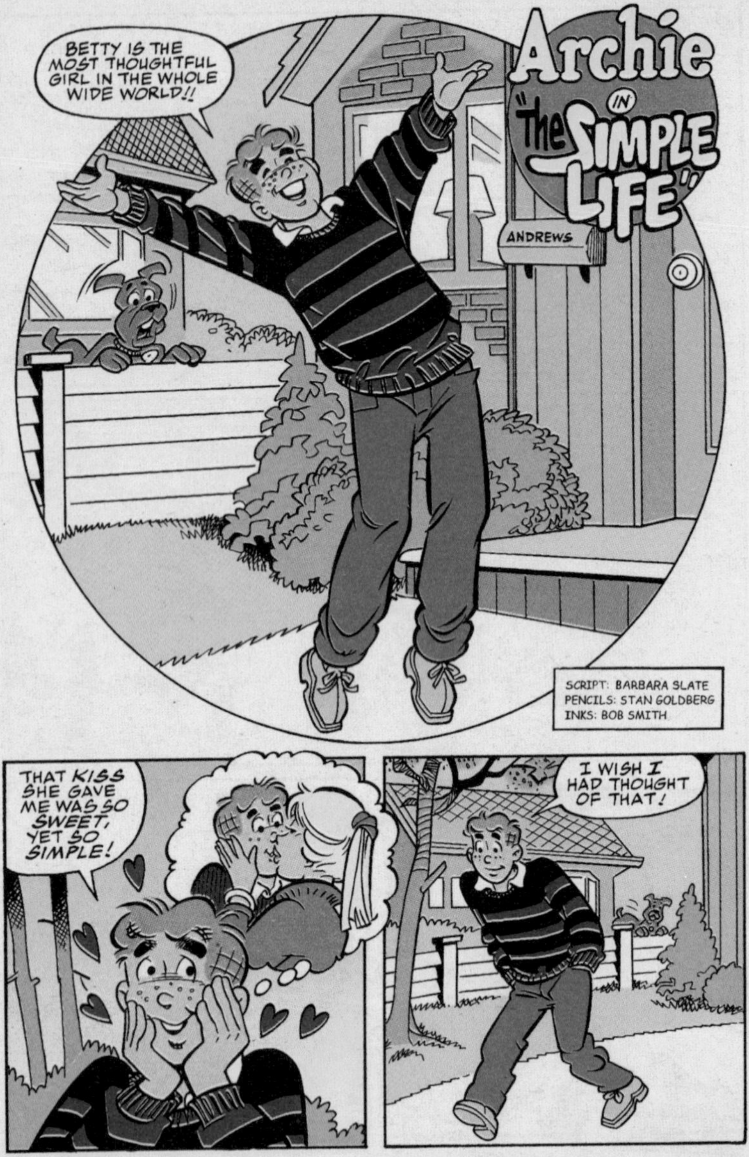
Archie IN "The SIMPLE LIFE"
BETTY IS THE MOST THOUGHTFUL GIRL IN THE WHOLE WIDE WORLD!!
ANDREWS
SCRIPT: BARBARA SLATE
PENCILS: STAN GOLDBERG
INKS: BOB SMITH
THAT KISS SHE GAVE ME WAS SO SWEET, YET SO SIMPLE!
I WISH I HAD THOUGHT OF THAT!

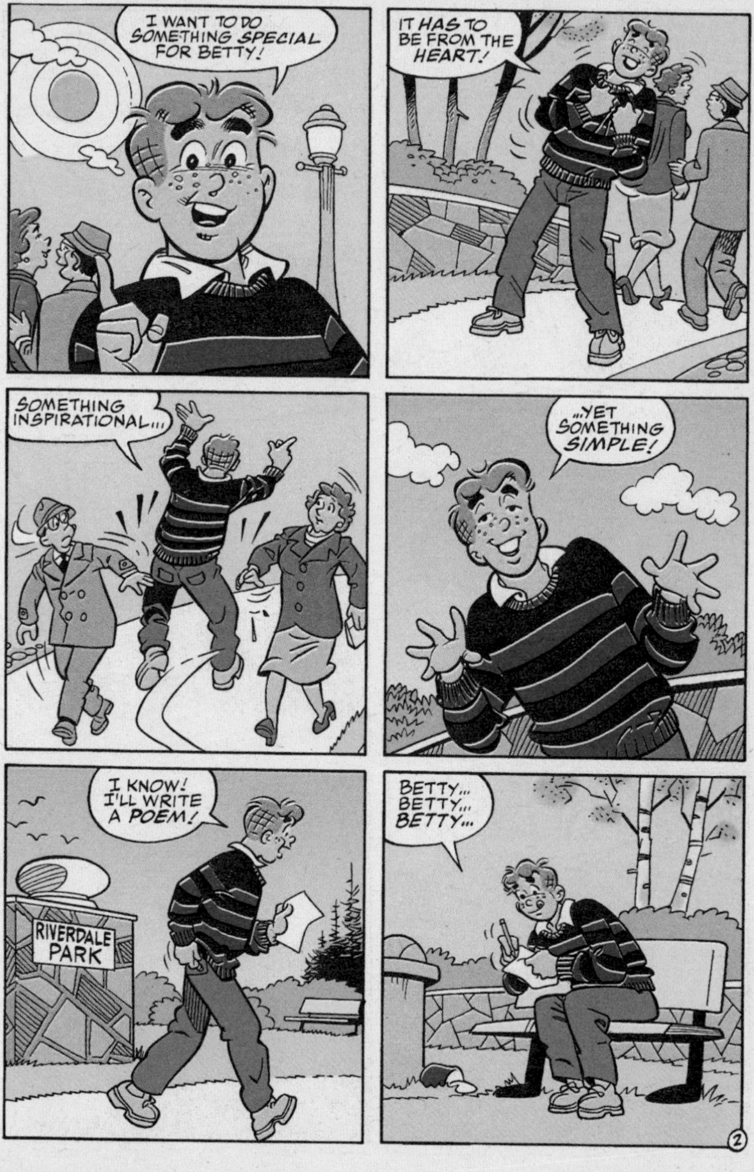

I WANT TO DO SOMETHING SPECIAL FOR BETTY!
IT HAS TO BE FROM THE HEART!
SOMETHING INSPIRATIONAL...
...YET SOMETHING SIMPLE!
I KNOW! I'LL WRITE A POEM!
RIVERDALE PARK
BETTY... BETTY... BETTY...
2

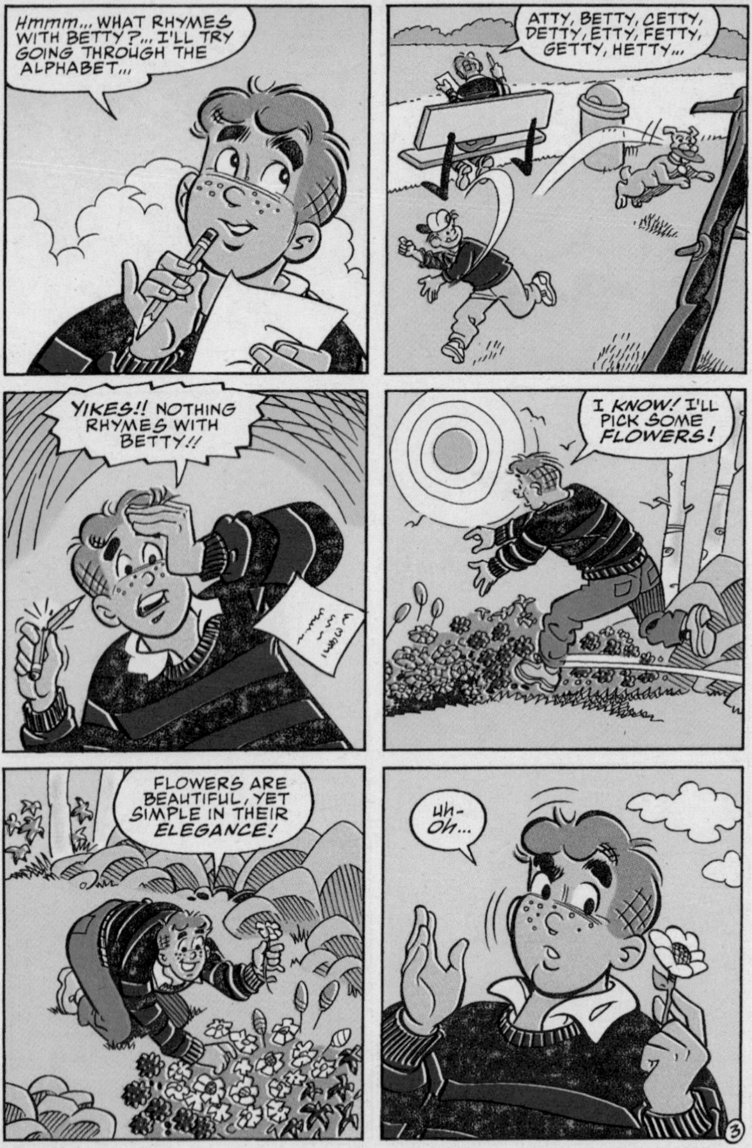
Hmmm... WHAT RHYMES WITH BETTY?... I'LL TRY GOING THROUGH THE ALPHABET...
ATTY, BETTY, CETTY, DETTY, ETTY, FETTY, GETTY, HETTY...
YIKES!! NOTHING RHYMES WITH BETTY!!
I KNOW! I'LL PICK SOME FLOWERS!
FLOWERS ARE BEAUTIFUL, YET SIMPLE IN THEIR ELEGANCE!
uh-Oh...
3

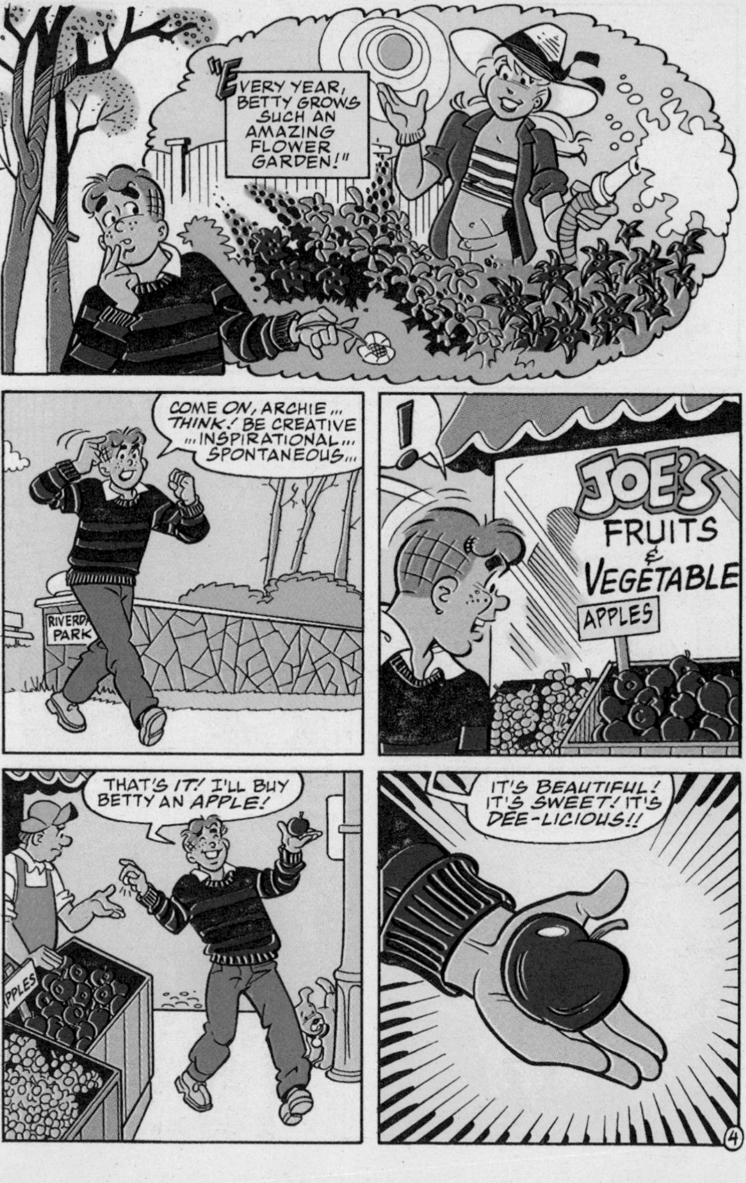
"EVERY YEAR, BETTY GROWS SUCH AN AMAZING FLOWER GARDEN!"
COME ON, ARCHIE... THINK! BE CREATIVE ...INSPIRATIONAL... SPONTANEOUS...
RIVERDA PARK
!
JOE'S FRUITS & VEGETABLE
APPLES
THAT'S IT! I'LL BUY BETTY AN APPLE!
APPLES
IT'S BEAUTIFUL! IT'S SWEET! IT'S DEE-LICIOUS!!

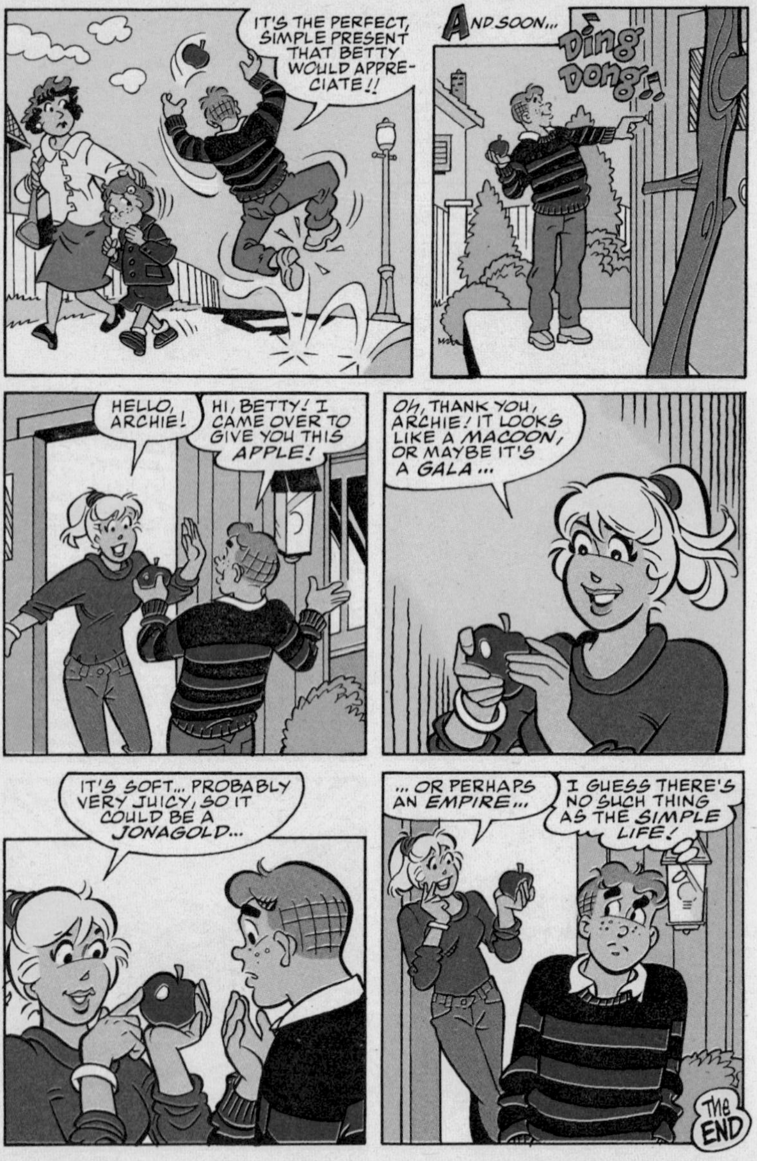
IT'S THE PERFECT, SIMPLE PRESENT THAT BETTY WOULD APPRE-CIATE!!
AND SOON...
DING DONG
HELLO, ARCHIE!
HI, BETTY! I CAME OVER TO GIVE YOU THIS APPLE!
Oh, THANK YOU, ARCHIE! IT LOOKS LIKE A MACOON, OR MAYBE IT'S A GALA...
IT'S SOFT... PROBABLY VERY JUICY, SO IT COULD BE A JONAGOLD...
... OR PERHAPS AN EMPIRE...
I GUESS THERE'S NO SUCH THING AS THE SIMPLE LIFE!
The END

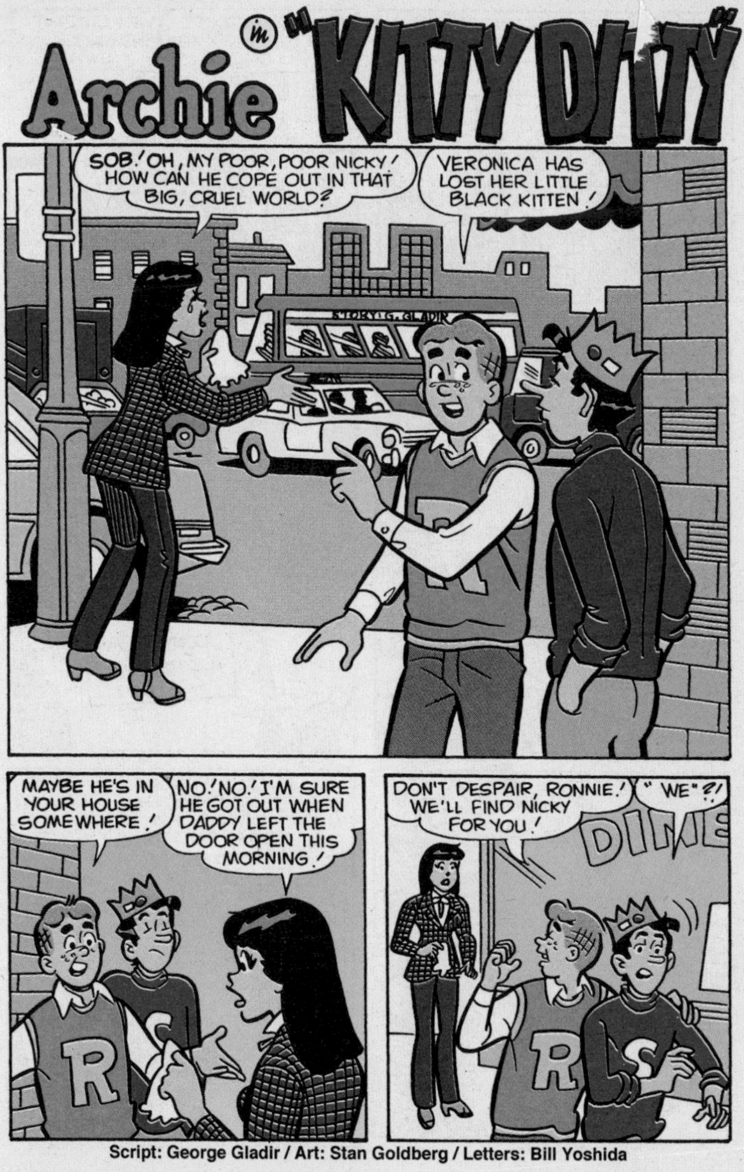
Archie in "KITTY DITTY"
SOB! OH, MY POOR, POOR NICKY! HOW CAN HE COPE OUT IN THAT BIG, CRUEL WORLD?
VERONICA HAS LOST HER LITTLE BLACK KITTEN!
MAYBE HE'S IN YOUR HOUSE SOMEWHERE!
NO! NO! I'M SURE HE GOT OUT WHEN DADDY LEFT THE DOOR OPEN THIS MORNING!
DON'T DESPAIR, RONNIE! WE'LL FIND NICKY FOR YOU!
"WE"?!

Script: George Gladir / Art: Stan Goldberg / Letters: Bill Yoshida

JUG, RONNIE'S MISSING KITTEN IS MY BIG CHANCE TO MAKE POINTS WITH HER!

AN OPPORTUNITY LIKE THIS KNOCKS ONLY ONCE!

WHY CAN'T IT GO KNOCK SOMEWHERE ELSE?

WE'LL MAKE POSTERS!

WE'LL CALL THE RADIO STATION!

WE'LL GET IN OVER OUR HEADS!

LOST CUTE B

HERE! I WANT YOU TO NAIL THESE POSTERS ALL OVER TOWN!

I WAS AFRAID OF THAT!

LOST CUTE, BLACK KITTEN ON STATE ST.

CONTACT - A. ANDREWS 543 - 607

YOU'RE DOING A NICE JOB, JUG!

LOS CUTE, B KITTEN ON STATE S CONTACT A. ANDREWS 543-607

YOU KNOW, IF SOME-ONE FOUND NICKY, THEY MIGHT'VE TAKEN HIM TO THE ANIMAL SHELTER!

GOOD THINKING!!

LOST CUTE, B KITTE. ON STATE

CO A.A 54

2

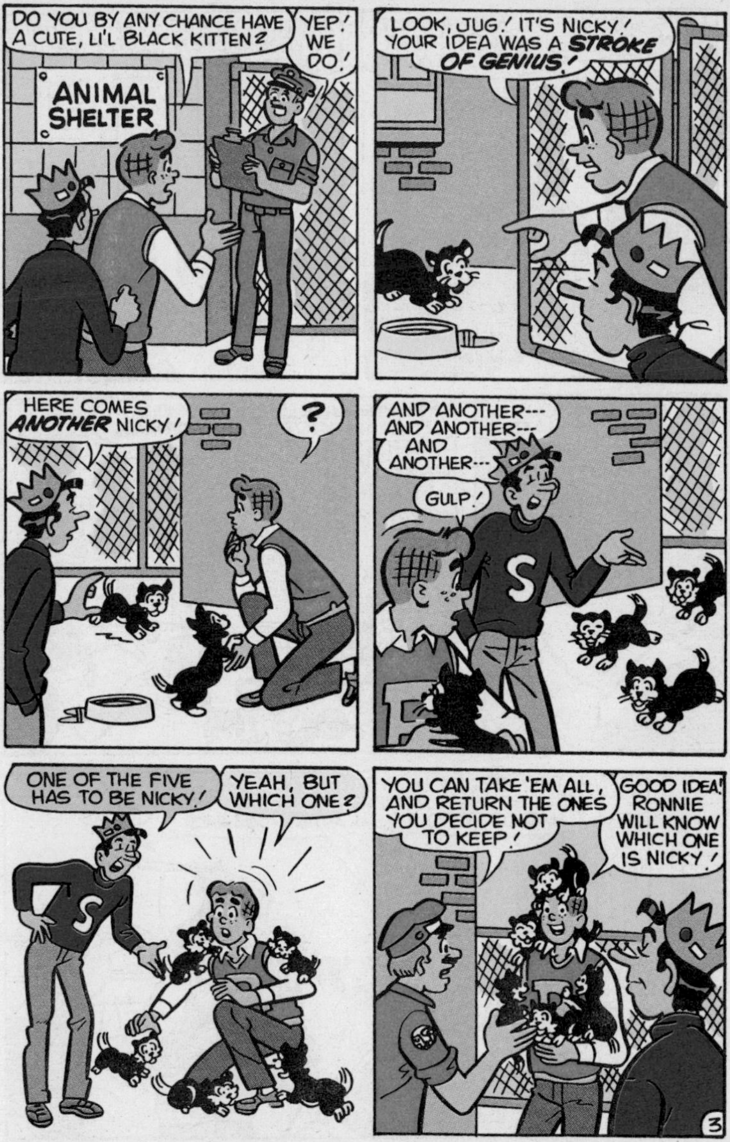
DO YOU BY ANY CHANCE HAVE A CUTE, LI'L BLACK KITTEN?
YEP! WE DO!
ANIMAL SHELTER
LOOK, JUG! IT'S NICKY! YOUR IDEA WAS A **STROKE OF GENIUS**!
HERE COMES **ANOTHER** NICKY!
?
AND ANOTHER--- AND ANOTHER--- AND ANOTHER---
GULP!
ONE OF THE FIVE HAS TO BE NICKY!
YEAH, BUT WHICH ONE?
YOU CAN TAKE 'EM ALL, AND RETURN THE ONES YOU DECIDE NOT TO KEEP!
GOOD IDEA! RONNIE WILL KNOW WHICH ONE IS NICKY!
3

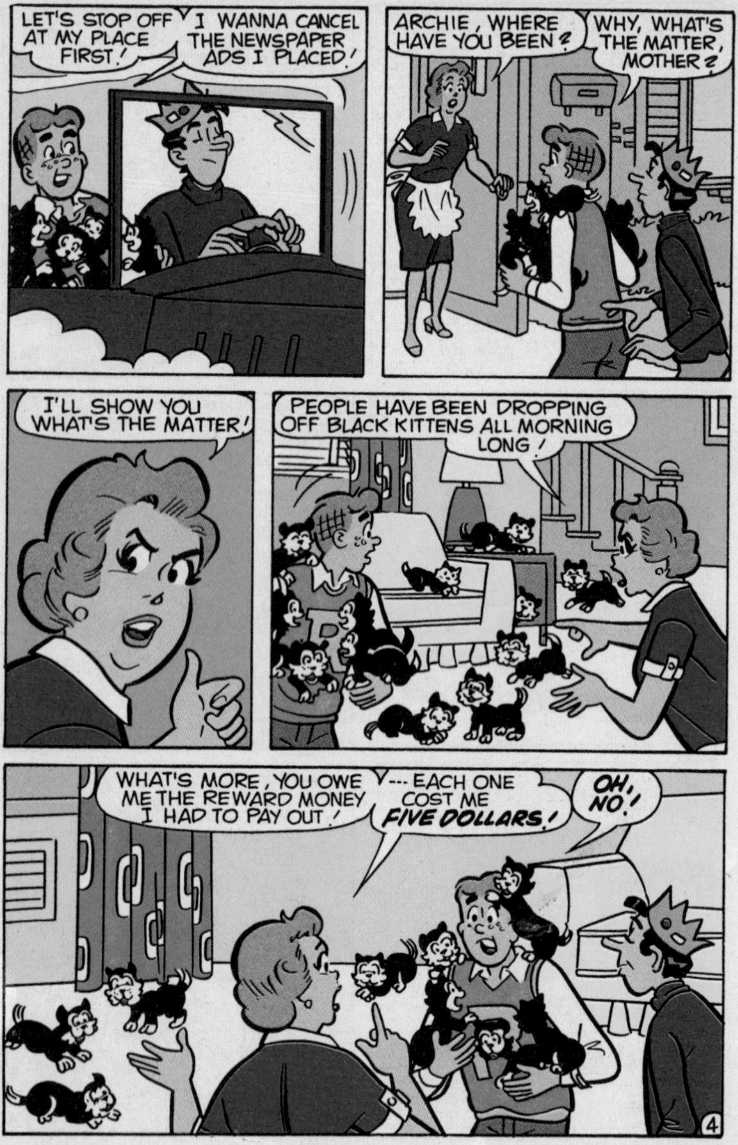

LET'S STOP OFF AT MY PLACE FIRST!
I WANNA CANCEL THE NEWSPAPER ADS I PLACED!
ARCHIE, WHERE HAVE YOU BEEN?
WHY, WHAT'S THE MATTER, MOTHER?
I'LL SHOW YOU WHAT'S THE MATTER!
PEOPLE HAVE BEEN DROPPING OFF BLACK KITTENS ALL MORNING LONG!
WHAT'S MORE, YOU OWE ME THE REWARD MONEY I HAD TO PAY OUT!
--- EACH ONE COST ME FIVE DOLLARS!
OH, NO!
4

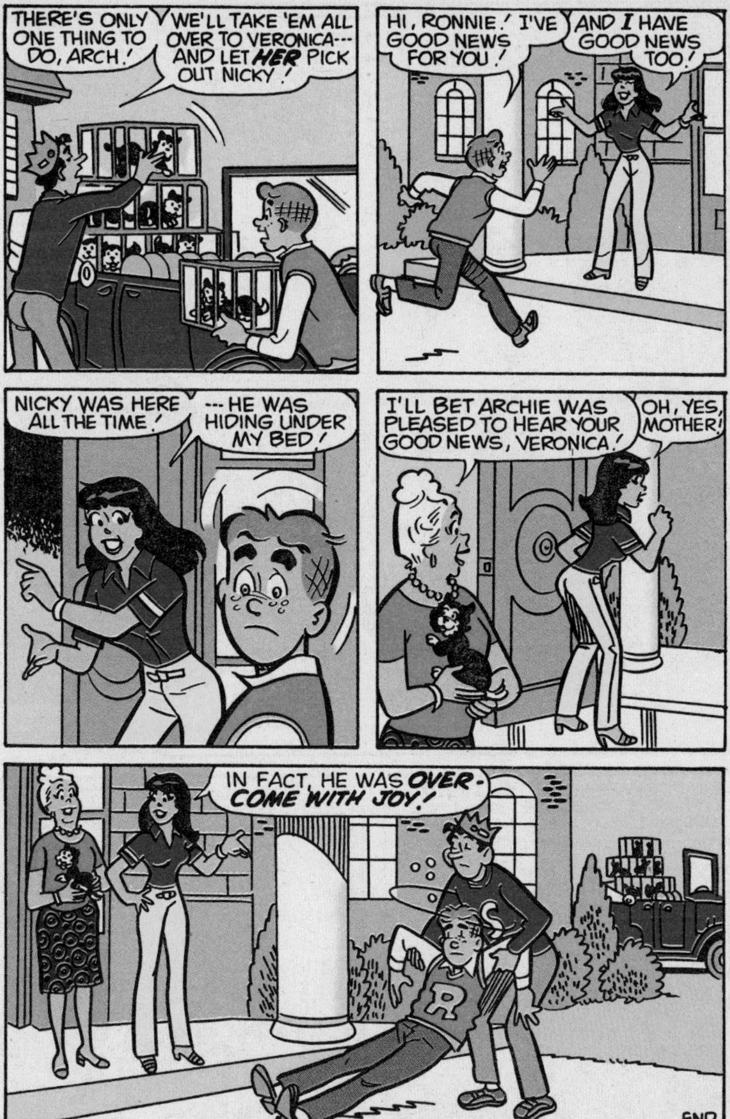
THERE'S ONLY ONE THING TO DO, ARCH.!
WE'LL TAKE 'EM ALL OVER TO VERONICA--- AND LET HER PICK OUT NICKY!
HI, RONNIE! I'VE GOOD NEWS FOR YOU!
AND I HAVE GOOD NEWS TOO!
NICKY WAS HERE ALL THE TIME!
--- HE WAS HIDING UNDER MY BED!
I'LL BET ARCHIE WAS PLEASED TO HEAR YOUR GOOD NEWS, VERONICA!
OH, YES, MOTHER!
IN FACT, HE WAS OVER-COME WITH JOY!
END

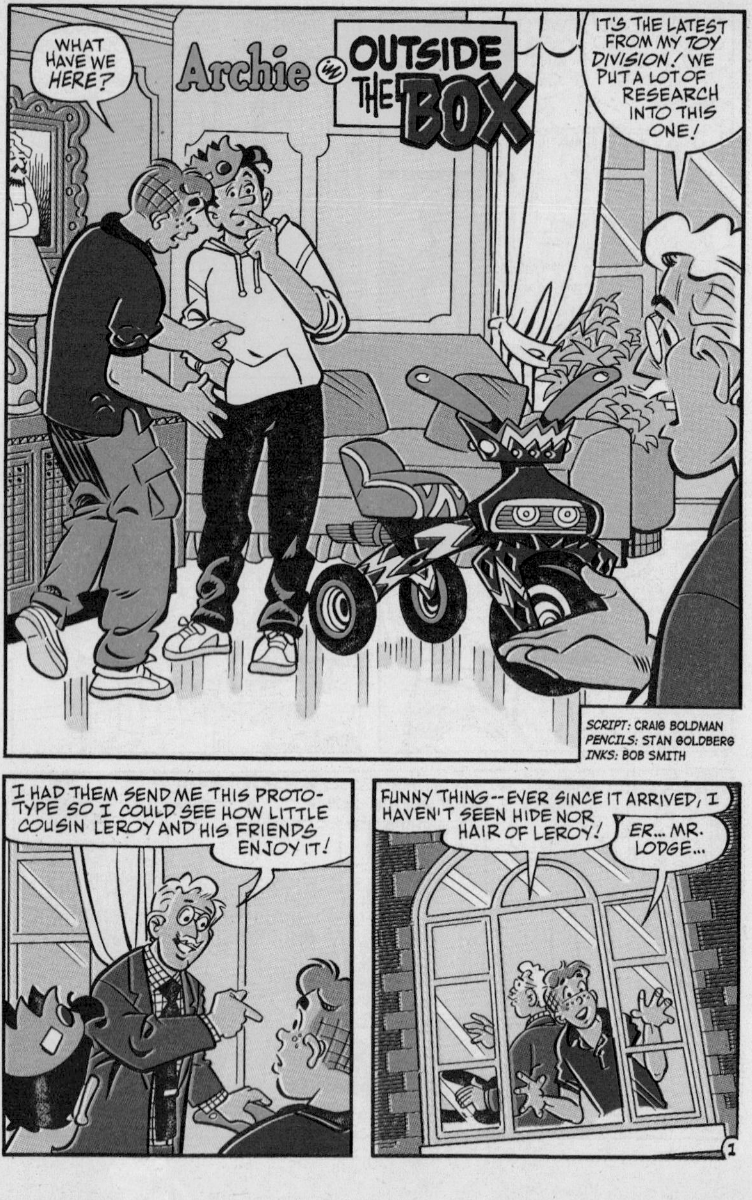
Archie in OUTSIDE THE BOX
WHAT HAVE WE HERE?
IT'S THE LATEST FROM MY TOY DIVISION! WE PUT A LOT OF RESEARCH INTO THIS ONE!
SCRIPT: CRAIG BOLDMAN
PENCILS: STAN GOLDBERG
INKS: BOB SMITH
I HAD THEM SEND ME THIS PROTOTYPE SO I COULD SEE HOW LITTLE COUSIN LEROY AND HIS FRIENDS ENJOY IT!
FUNNY THING -- EVER SINCE IT ARRIVED, I HAVEN'T SEEN HIDE NOR HAIR OF LEROY!
ER... MR. LODGE...

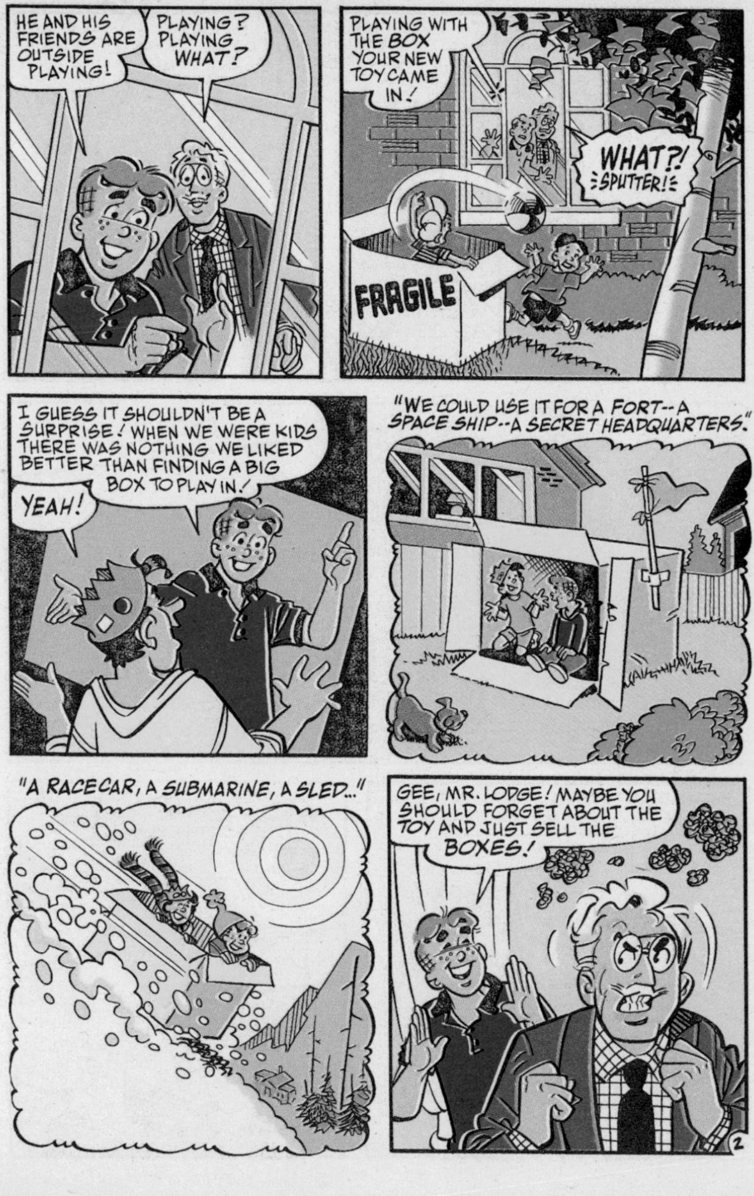
HE AND HIS FRIENDS ARE OUTSIDE PLAYING!
PLAYING? PLAYING WHAT?
PLAYING WITH THE BOX YOUR NEW TOY CAME IN!
WHAT?! SPUTTER!
FRAGILE
I GUESS IT SHOULDN'T BE A SURPRISE! WHEN WE WERE KIDS THERE WAS NOTHING WE LIKED BETTER THAN FINDING A BIG BOX TO PLAY IN!
YEAH!
"WE COULD USE IT FOR A FORT-- A SPACE SHIP--A SECRET HEADQUARTERS."
"A RACECAR, A SUBMARINE, A SLED..."
GEE, MR. LODGE! MAYBE YOU SHOULD FORGET ABOUT THE TOY AND JUST SELL THE BOXES!
2

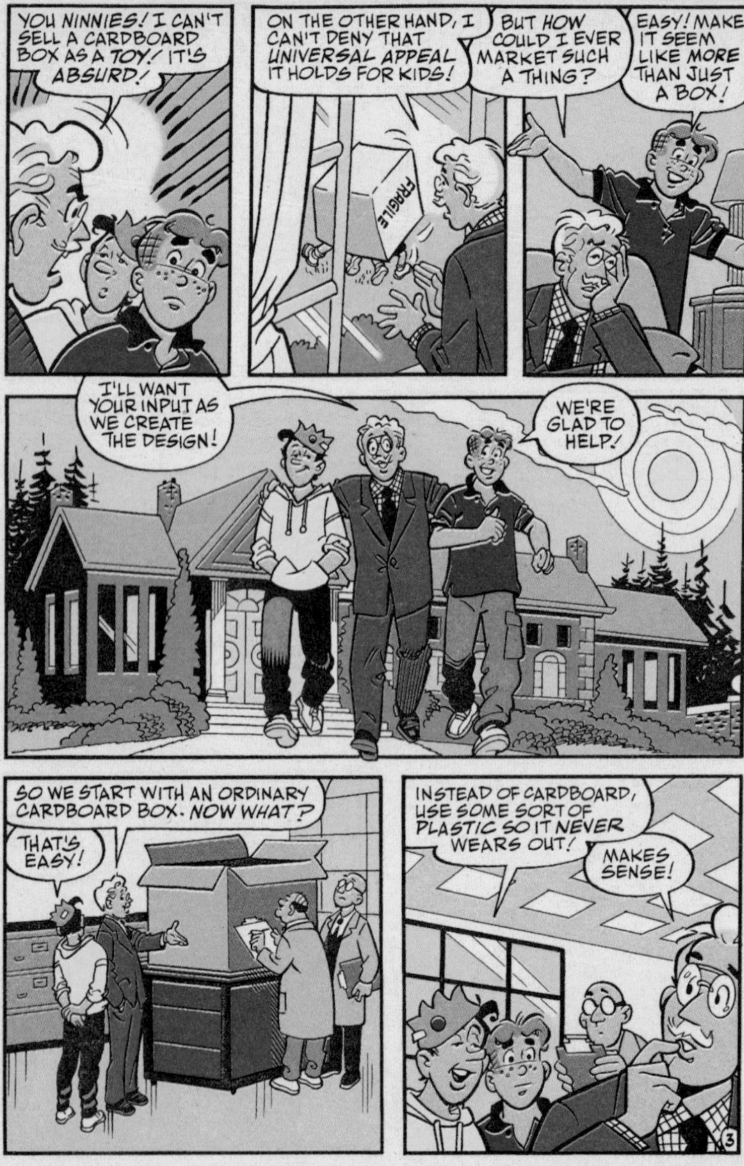
YOU NINNIES! I CAN'T SELL A CARDBOARD BOX AS A TOY! IT'S ABSURD!
ON THE OTHER HAND, I CAN'T DENY THAT UNIVERSAL APPEAL IT HOLDS FOR KIDS!
FRAGILE
BUT HOW COULD I EVER MARKET SUCH A THING?
EASY! MAKE IT SEEM LIKE MORE THAN JUST A BOX!
I'LL WANT YOUR INPUT AS WE CREATE THE DESIGN!
WE'RE GLAD TO HELP!
SO WE START WITH AN ORDINARY CARDBOARD BOX. NOW WHAT?
THAT'S EASY!
INSTEAD OF CARDBOARD, USE SOME SORT OF PLASTIC SO IT NEVER WEARS OUT!
MAKES SENSE!
3

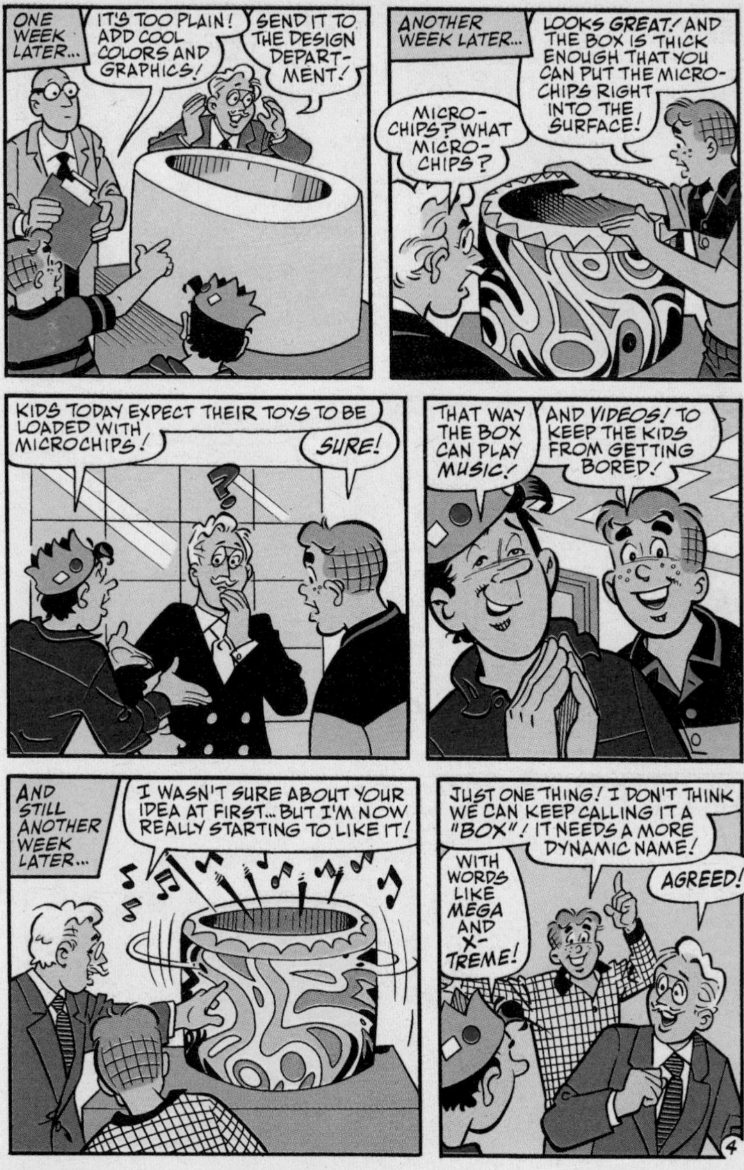
ONE WEEK LATER...
IT'S TOO PLAIN! ADD COOL COLORS AND GRAPHICS!
SEND IT TO THE DESIGN DEPARTMENT!
ANOTHER WEEK LATER...
LOOKS GREAT! AND THE BOX IS THICK ENOUGH THAT YOU CAN PUT THE MICROCHIPS RIGHT INTO THE SURFACE!
MICRO-CHIPS? WHAT MICRO-CHIPS?
KIDS TODAY EXPECT THEIR TOYS TO BE LOADED WITH MICROCHIPS!
SURE!
THAT WAY THE BOX CAN PLAY MUSIC!
AND VIDEOS! TO KEEP THE KIDS FROM GETTING BORED!
AND STILL ANOTHER WEEK LATER...
I WASN'T SURE ABOUT YOUR IDEA AT FIRST... BUT I'M NOW REALLY STARTING TO LIKE IT!
JUST ONE THING! I DON'T THINK WE CAN KEEP CALLING IT A "BOX"! IT NEEDS A MORE DYNAMIC NAME!
WITH WORDS LIKE MEGA AND X-TREME!
AGREED!
4

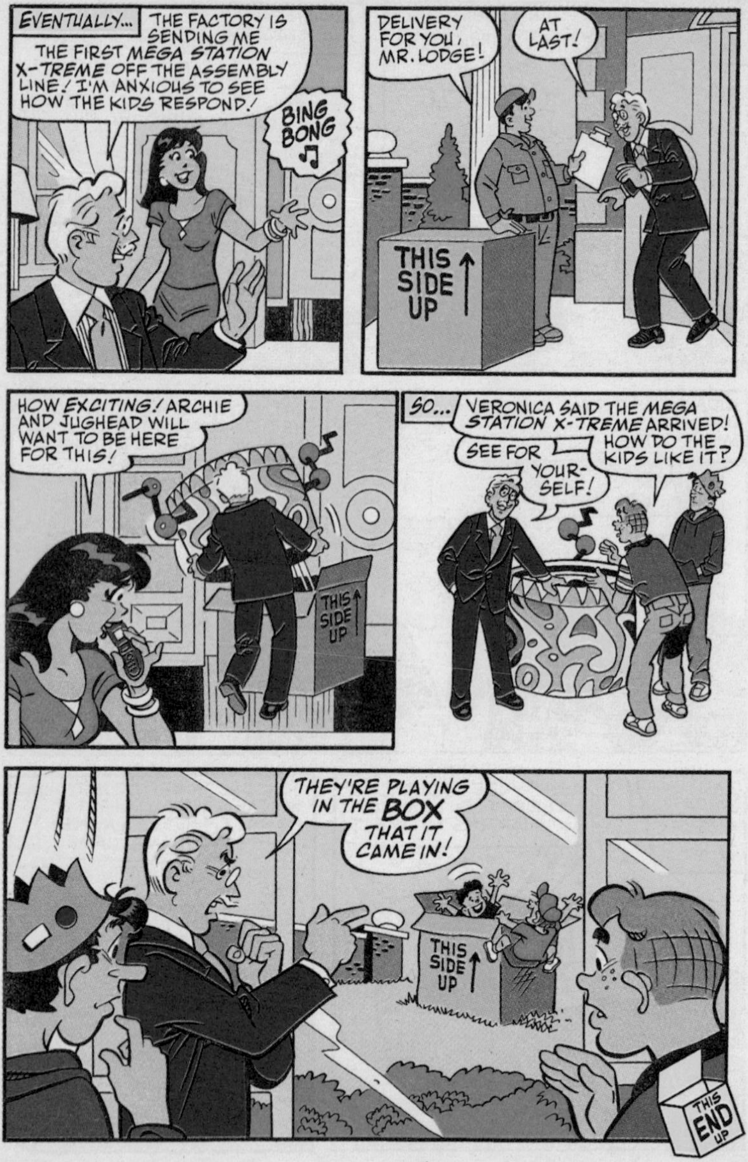
EVENTUALLY...
THE FACTORY IS SENDING ME THE FIRST MEGA STATION X-TREME OFF THE ASSEMBLY LINE! I'M ANXIOUS TO SEE HOW THE KIDS RESPOND!
BING BONG
DELIVERY FOR YOU, MR. LODGE!
AT LAST!
THIS SIDE UP
HOW EXCITING! ARCHIE AND JUGHEAD WILL WANT TO BE HERE FOR THIS!
THIS SIDE UP
SO...
VERONICA SAID THE MEGA STATION X-TREME ARRIVED! HOW DO THE KIDS LIKE IT?
SEE FOR YOURSELF!
THEY'RE PLAYING IN THE BOX THAT IT CAME IN!
THIS SIDE UP
THIS END UP

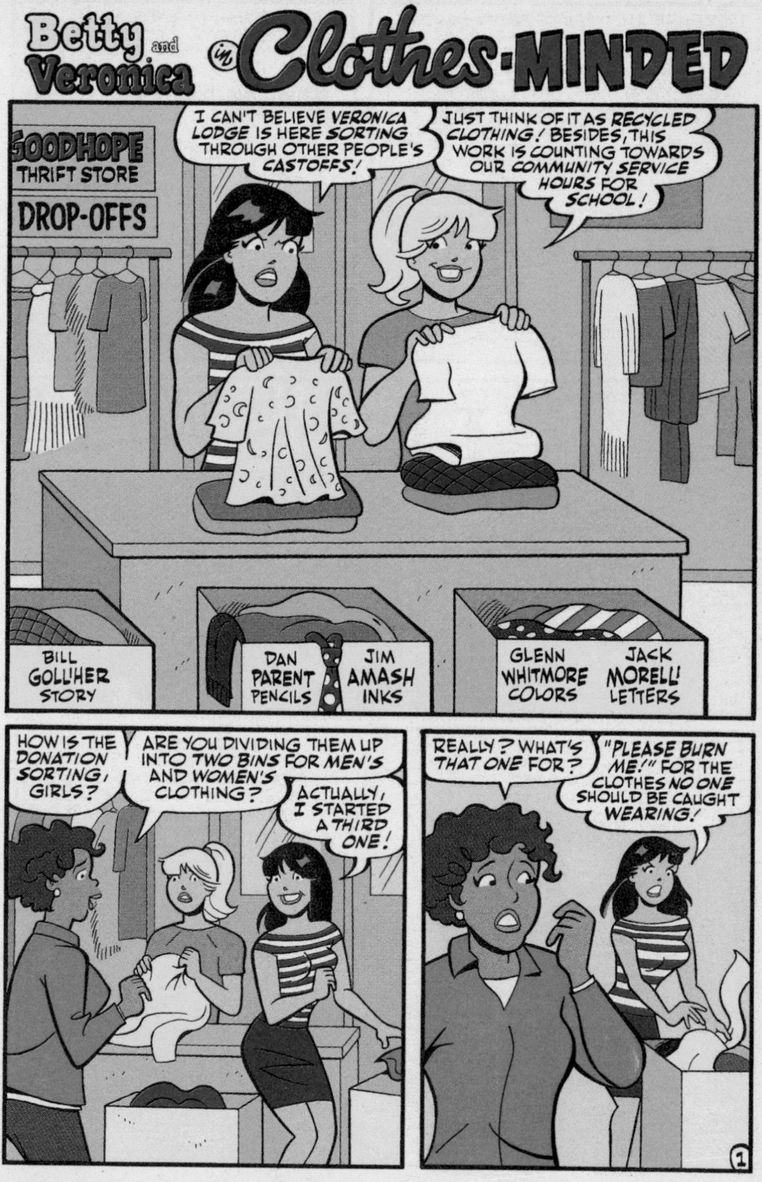

Betty and Veronica in Clothes-MINDED
GOODHOPE THRIFT STORE
DROP-OFFS
I CAN'T BELIEVE VERONICA LODGE IS HERE SORTING THROUGH OTHER PEOPLE'S CASTOFFS!
JUST THINK OF IT AS RECYCLED CLOTHING! BESIDES, THIS WORK IS COUNTING TOWARDS OUR COMMUNITY SERVICE HOURS FOR SCHOOL!
BILL GOLLIHER STORY
DAN PARENT PENCILS
JIM AMASH INKS
GLENN WHITMORE COLORS
JACK MORELLI LETTERS
HOW IS THE DONATION SORTING, GIRLS?
ARE YOU DIVIDING THEM UP INTO TWO BINS FOR MEN'S AND WOMEN'S CLOTHING?
ACTUALLY, I STARTED A THIRD ONE!
REALLY? WHAT'S THAT ONE FOR?
"PLEASE BURN ME!" FOR THE CLOTHES NO ONE SHOULD BE CAUGHT WEARING!
1

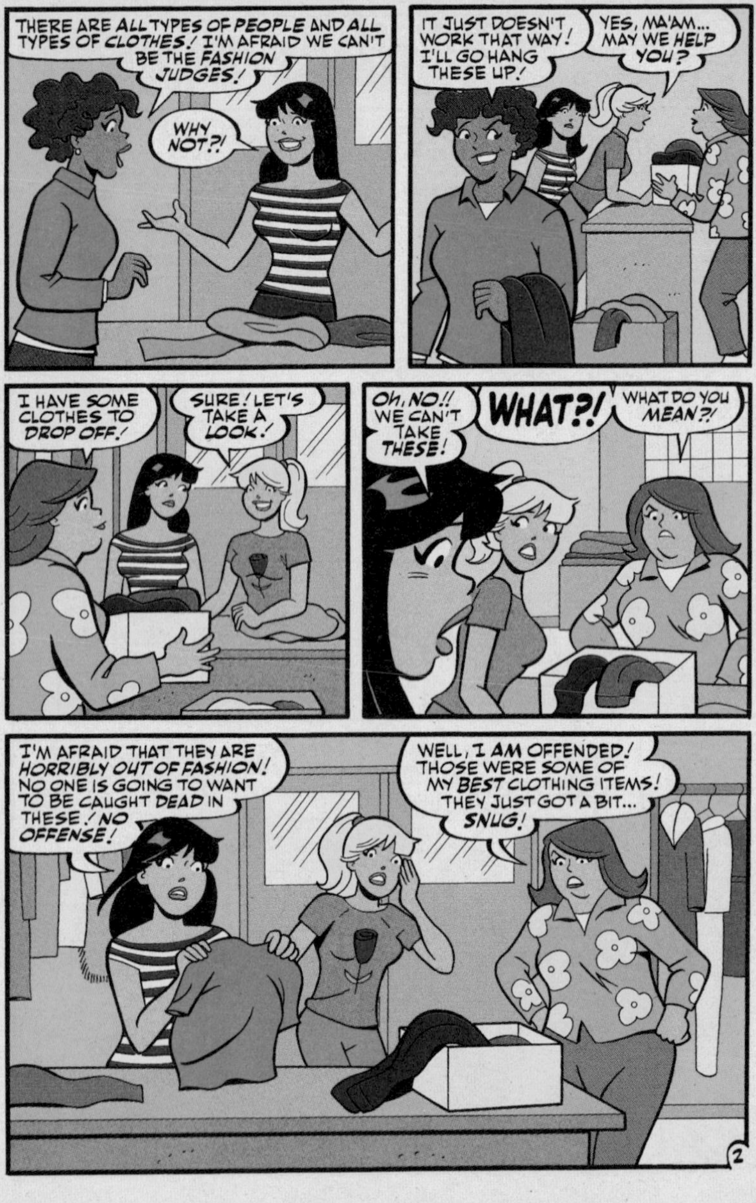
THERE ARE ALL TYPES OF PEOPLE AND ALL TYPES OF CLOTHES! I'M AFRAID WE CAN'T BE THE FASHION JUDGES!
WHY NOT?!
IT JUST DOESN'T WORK THAT WAY! I'LL GO HANG THESE UP!
YES, MA'AM... MAY WE HELP YOU?
I HAVE SOME CLOTHES TO DROP OFF!
SURE! LET'S TAKE A LOOK!
Oh, NO!! WE CAN'T TAKE THESE!
WHAT?!
WHAT DO YOU MEAN?!
I'M AFRAID THAT THEY ARE HORRIBLY OUT OF FASHION! NO ONE IS GOING TO WANT TO BE CAUGHT DEAD IN THESE! NO OFFENSE!
WELL, I AM OFFENDED! THOSE WERE SOME OF MY BEST CLOTHING ITEMS! THEY JUST GOT A BIT... SNUG!
2

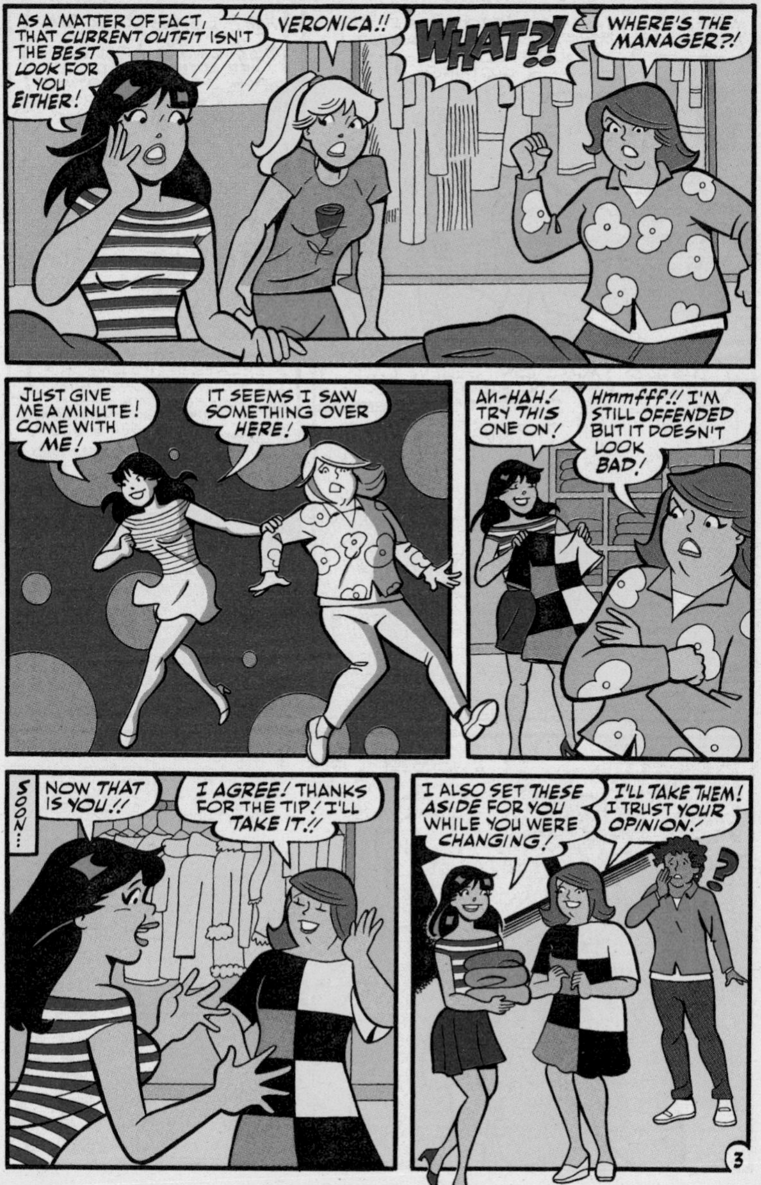

AS A MATTER OF FACT, THAT CURRENT OUTFIT ISN'T THE BEST LOOK FOR YOU EITHER!
VERONICA!!
WHAT?!
WHERE'S THE MANAGER?!
JUST GIVE ME A MINUTE! COME WITH ME!
IT SEEMS I SAW SOMETHING OVER HERE!
AH-HAH! TRY THIS ONE ON!
Hmmfff!! I'M STILL OFFENDED BUT IT DOESN'T LOOK BAD!
SOON...
NOW THAT IS YOU!!
I AGREE! THANKS FOR THE TIP! I'LL TAKE IT!!
I ALSO SET THESE ASIDE FOR YOU WHILE YOU WERE CHANGING!
I'LL TAKE THEM! I TRUST YOUR OPINION!
?

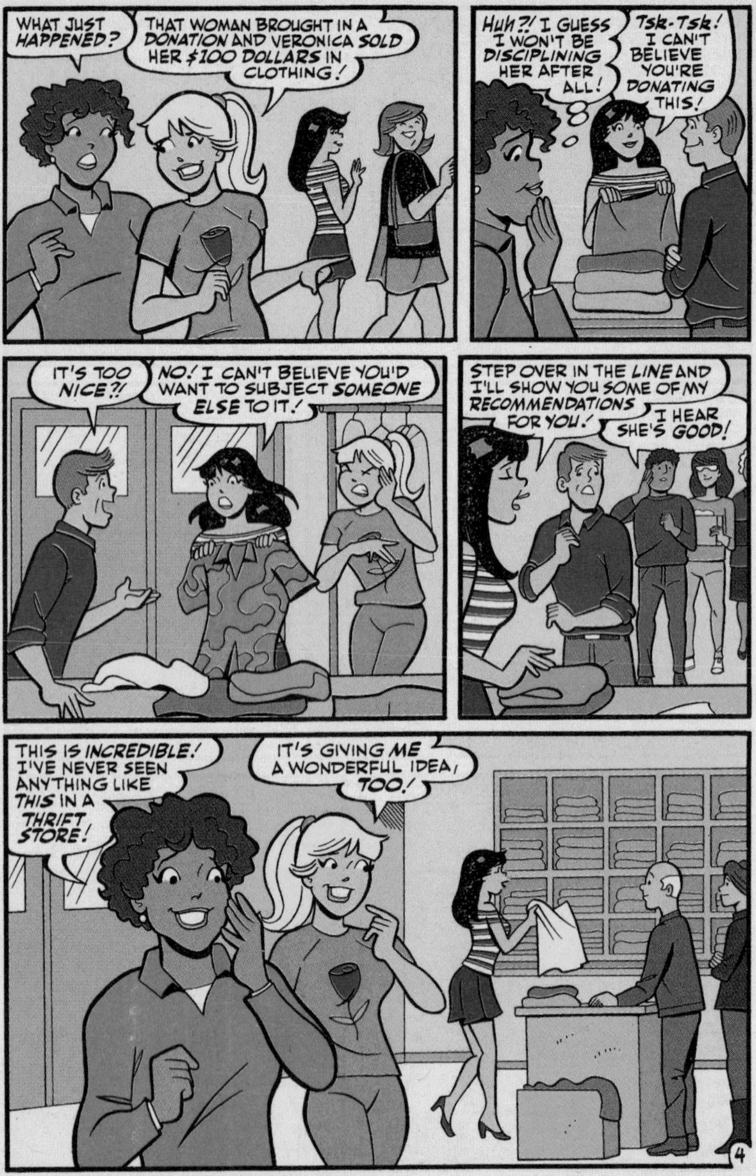
WHAT JUST HAPPENED?
THAT WOMAN BROUGHT IN A DONATION AND VERONICA SOLD HER $100 DOLLARS IN CLOTHING!
Huh?! I GUESS I WON'T BE DISCIPLINING HER AFTER ALL!
Tsk-Tsk! I CAN'T BELIEVE YOU'RE DONATING THIS!
IT'S TOO NICE?!
NO! I CAN'T BELIEVE YOU'D WANT TO SUBJECT SOMEONE ELSE TO IT!
STEP OVER IN THE LINE AND I'LL SHOW YOU SOME OF MY RECOMMENDATIONS FOR YOU!
I HEAR SHE'S GOOD!
THIS IS INCREDIBLE! I'VE NEVER SEEN ANYTHING LIKE THIS IN A THRIFT STORE!
IT'S GIVING ME A WONDERFUL IDEA, TOO!
4

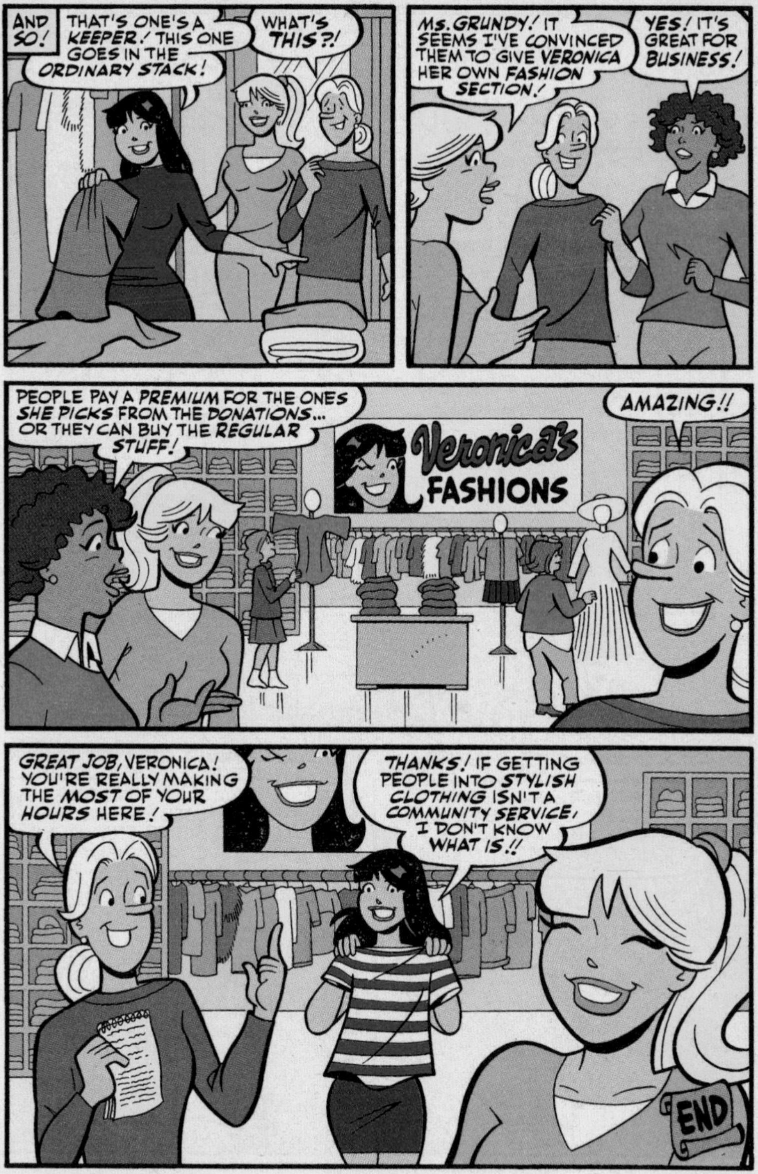
AND SO!
THAT'S ONE'S A KEEPER! THIS ONE GOES IN THE ORDINARY STACK!
WHAT'S THIS?!
Ms. GRUNDY! IT SEEMS I'VE CONVINCED THEM TO GIVE VERONICA HER OWN FASHION SECTION!
YES! IT'S GREAT FOR BUSINESS!
PEOPLE PAY A PREMIUM FOR THE ONES SHE PICKS FROM THE DONATIONS... OR THEY CAN BUY THE REGULAR STUFF!
Veronica's FASHIONS
AMAZING!!
GREAT JOB, VERONICA! YOU'RE REALLY MAKING THE MOST OF YOUR HOURS HERE!
THANKS! IF GETTING PEOPLE INTO STYLISH CLOTHING ISN'T A COMMUNITY SERVICE, I DON'T KNOW WHAT IS!!
END

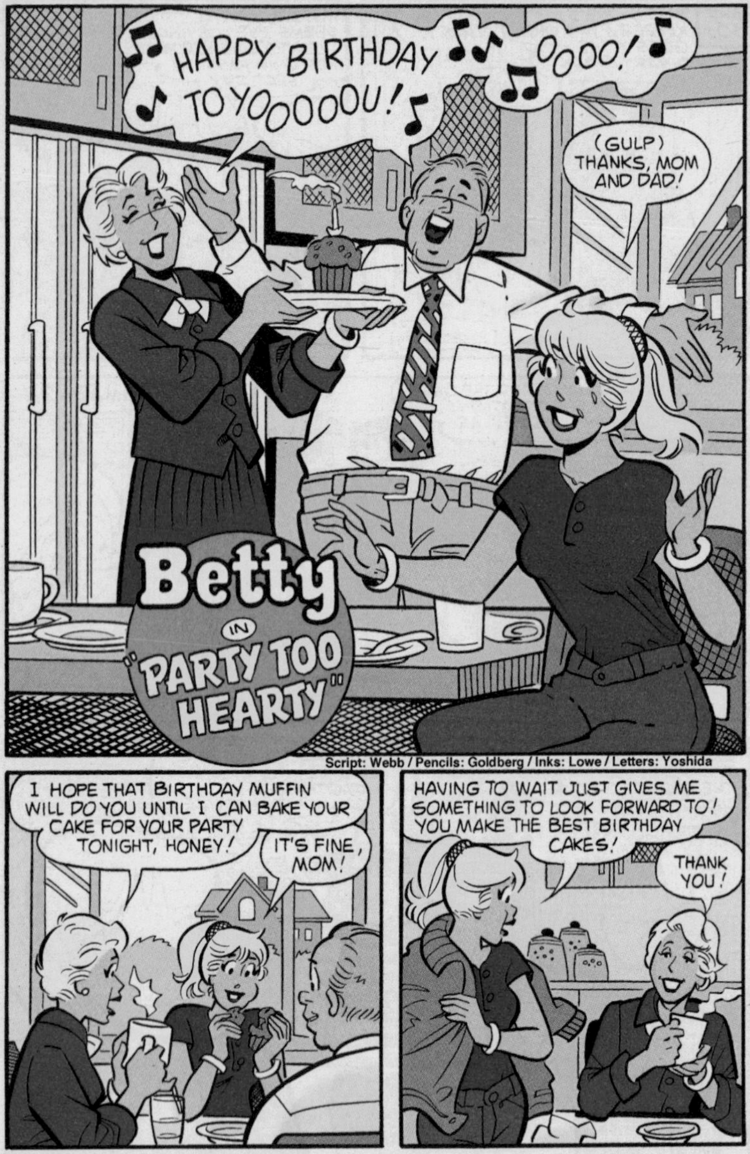
HAPPY BIRTHDAY TO YOOOOOOU! OOOO!
(GULP) THANKS, MOM AND DAD!
Betty
IN
"PARTY TOO HEARTY"
Script: Webb / Pencils: Goldberg / Inks: Lowe / Letters: Yoshida
I HOPE THAT BIRTHDAY MUFFIN WILL DO YOU UNTIL I CAN BAKE YOUR CAKE FOR YOUR PARTY TONIGHT, HONEY!
IT'S FINE, MOM!
HAVING TO WAIT JUST GIVES ME SOMETHING TO LOOK FORWARD TO! YOU MAKE THE BEST BIRTHDAY CAKES!
THANK YOU!

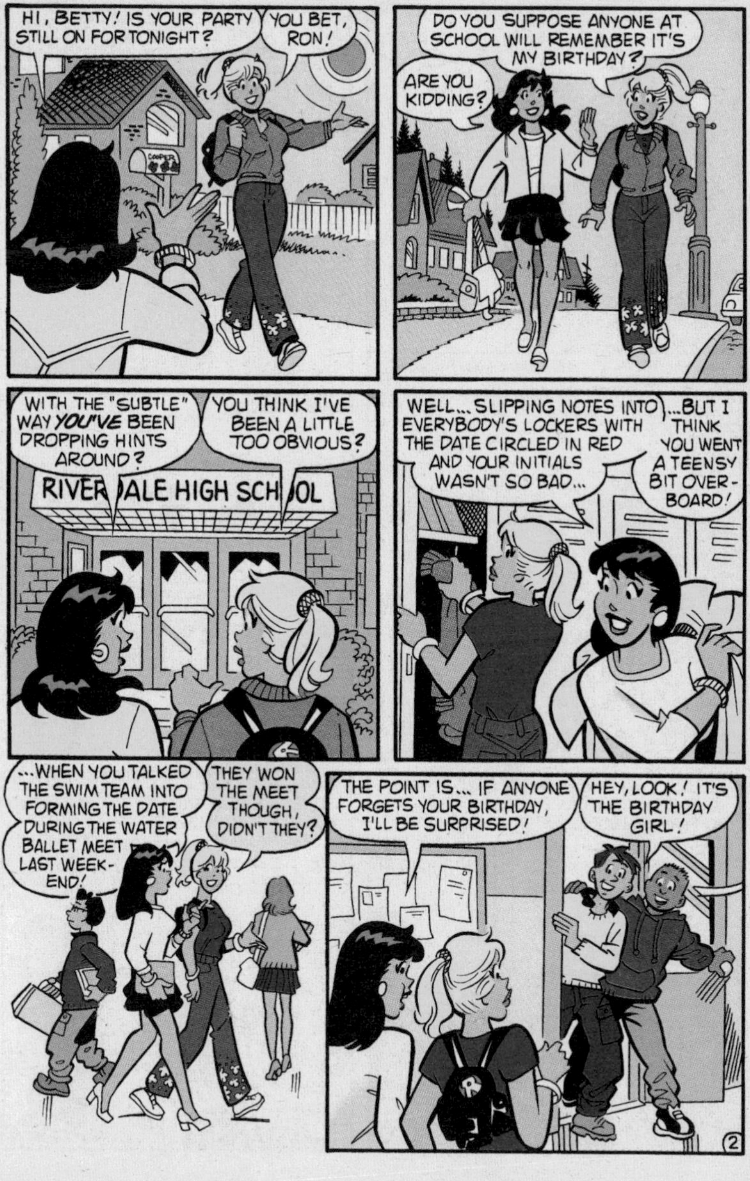

HI, BETTY! IS YOUR PARTY STILL ON FOR TONIGHT?
YOU BET, RON!
COOPER
DO YOU SUPPOSE ANYONE AT SCHOOL WILL REMEMBER IT'S MY BIRTHDAY?
ARE YOU KIDDING?
WITH THE "SUBTLE" WAY *YOU'VE* BEEN DROPPING HINTS AROUND?
YOU THINK I'VE BEEN A LITTLE TOO OBVIOUS?
RIVERDALE HIGH SCHOOL
WELL... SLIPPING NOTES INTO EVERYBODY'S LOCKERS WITH THE DATE CIRCLED IN RED AND YOUR INITIALS WASN'T SO BAD...
...BUT I THINK YOU WENT A TEENSY BIT OVER-BOARD!
...WHEN YOU TALKED THE SWIM TEAM INTO FORMING THE DATE DURING THE WATER BALLET MEET LAST WEEK-END!
THEY WON THE MEET THOUGH, DIDN'T THEY?
THE POINT IS... IF ANYONE FORGETS YOUR BIRTHDAY, I'LL BE SURPRISED!
HEY, LOOK! IT'S THE BIRTHDAY GIRL!
2

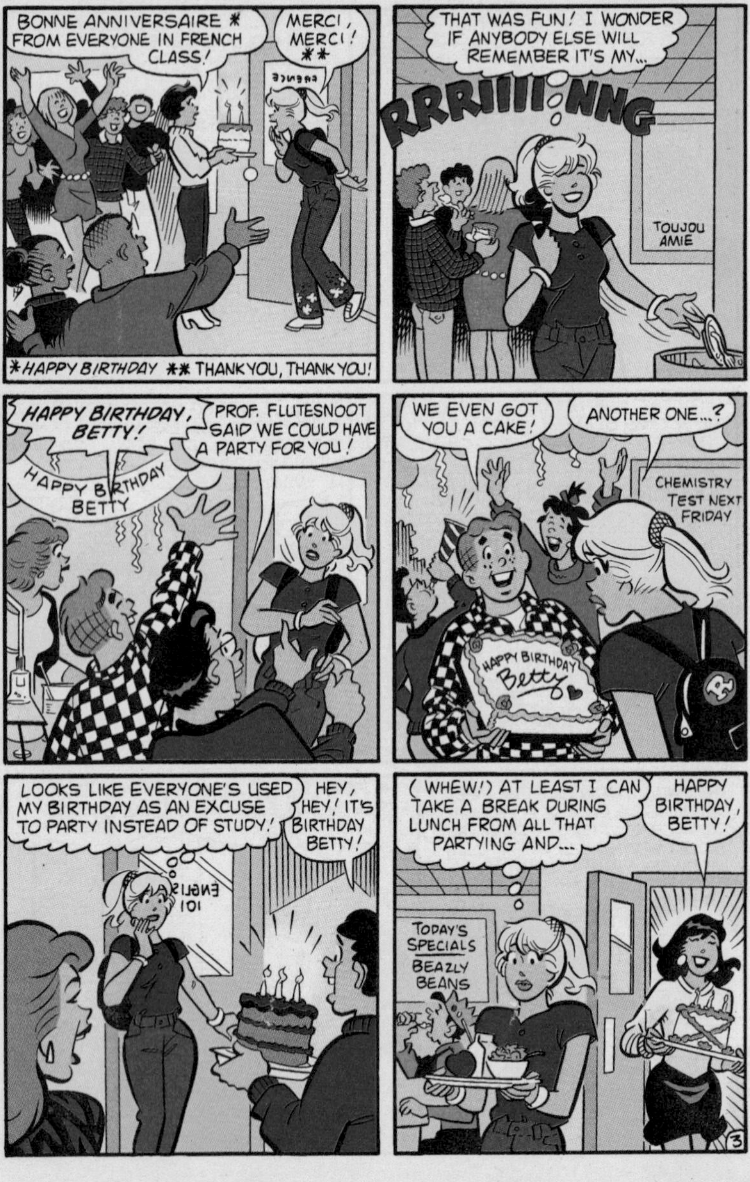

BONNE ANNIVERSAIRE * FROM EVERYONE IN FRENCH CLASS!
MERCI, MERCI! **
*HAPPY BIRTHDAY **THANK YOU, THANK YOU!
THAT WAS FUN! I WONDER IF ANYBODY ELSE WILL REMEMBER IT'S MY...
RRRIIIIINNG
TOUJOU AMIE
HAPPY BIRTHDAY, BETTY!
PROF. FLUTESNOOT SAID WE COULD HAVE A PARTY FOR YOU!
HAPPY BIRTHDAY BETTY
WE EVEN GOT YOU A CAKE!
ANOTHER ONE...?
CHEMISTRY TEST NEXT FRIDAY
HAPPY BIRTHDAY Betty
LOOKS LIKE EVERYONE'S USED MY BIRTHDAY AS AN EXCUSE TO PARTY INSTEAD OF STUDY!
HEY, HEY! IT'S BIRTHDAY BETTY!
(WHEW!) AT LEAST I CAN TAKE A BREAK DURING LUNCH FROM ALL THAT PARTYING AND...
HAPPY BIRTHDAY, BETTY!
TODAY'S SPECIALS
BEAZLY BEANS
3

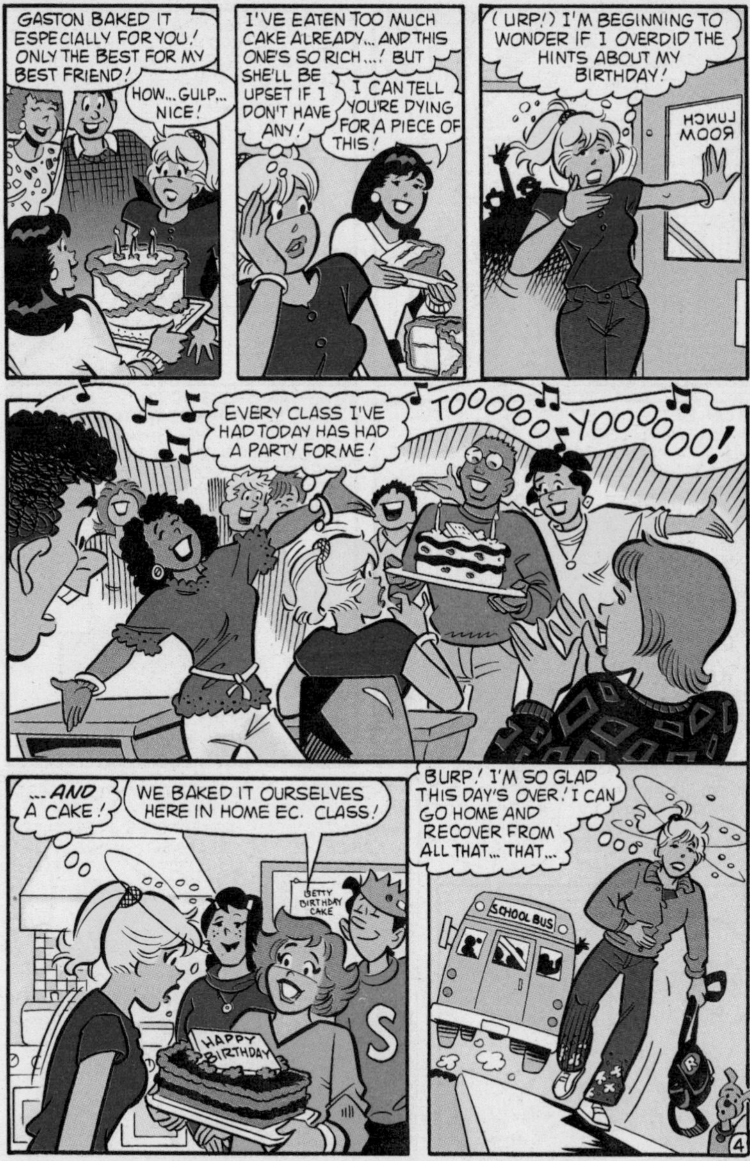
GASTON BAKED IT ESPECIALLY FOR YOU! ONLY THE BEST FOR MY BEST FRIEND!
HOW... GULP... NICE!
I'VE EATEN TOO MUCH CAKE ALREADY... AND THIS ONE'S SO RICH...! BUT SHE'LL BE UPSET IF I DON'T HAVE ANY!
I CAN TELL YOU'RE DYING FOR A PIECE OF THIS!
(URP!) I'M BEGINNING TO WONDER IF I OVERDID THE HINTS ABOUT MY BIRTHDAY!
LUNCH ROOM
EVERY CLASS I'VE HAD TODAY HAS HAD A PARTY FOR ME!
TOOOOOO-YOOOOOO!
...AND A CAKE!
WE BAKED IT OURSELVES HERE IN HOME EC. CLASS!
BETTY BIRTHDAY CAKE
HAPPY BIRTHDAY
BURP! I'M SO GLAD THIS DAY'S OVER! I CAN GO HOME AND RECOVER FROM ALL THAT... THAT...
SCHOOL BUS
4

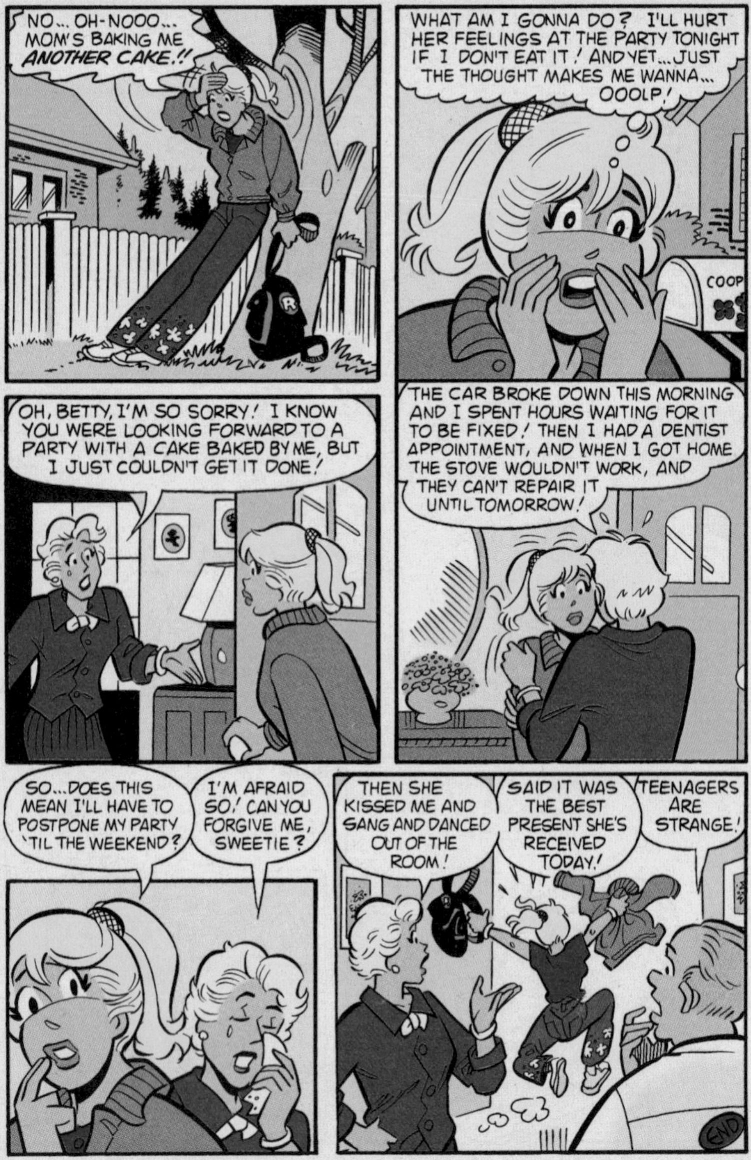
NO... OH-NOOO... MOM'S BAKING ME ANOTHER CAKE.!!
WHAT AM I GONNA DO? I'LL HURT HER FEELINGS AT THE PARTY TONIGHT IF I DON'T EAT IT! AND YET... JUST THE THOUGHT MAKES ME WANNA... OOOLP!
COOP
OH, BETTY, I'M SO SORRY! I KNOW YOU WERE LOOKING FORWARD TO A PARTY WITH A CAKE BAKED BY ME, BUT I JUST COULDN'T GET IT DONE!
THE CAR BROKE DOWN THIS MORNING AND I SPENT HOURS WAITING FOR IT TO BE FIXED! THEN I HAD A DENTIST APPOINTMENT, AND WHEN I GOT HOME THE STOVE WOULDN'T WORK, AND THEY CAN'T REPAIR IT UNTIL TOMORROW!
SO...DOES THIS MEAN I'LL HAVE TO POSTPONE MY PARTY 'TIL THE WEEKEND?
I'M AFRAID SO! CAN YOU FORGIVE ME, SWEETIE?
THEN SHE KISSED ME AND SANG AND DANCED OUT OF THE ROOM!
SAID IT WAS THE BEST PRESENT SHE'S RECEIVED TODAY!
TEENAGERS ARE STRANGE!
END

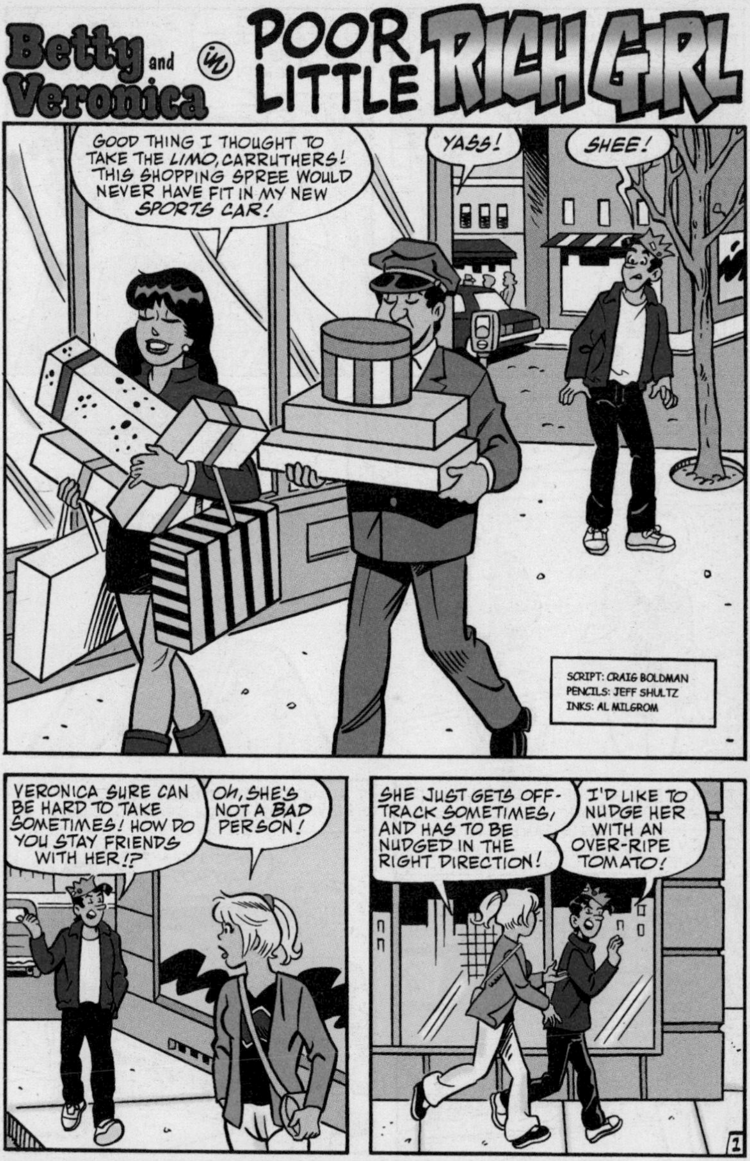
Betty and Veronica in POOR LITTLE RICH GIRL
GOOD THING I THOUGHT TO TAKE THE LIMO, CARRUTHERS! THIS SHOPPING SPREE WOULD NEVER HAVE FIT IN MY NEW SPORTS CAR!
YASS!
SHEE!
SCRIPT: CRAIG BOLDMAN
PENCILS: JEFF SHULTZ
INKS: AL MILGROM
VERONICA SURE CAN BE HARD TO TAKE SOMETIMES! HOW DO YOU STAY FRIENDS WITH HER!?
OH, SHE'S NOT A BAD PERSON!
SHE JUST GETS OFF-TRACK SOMETIMES, AND HAS TO BE NUDGED IN THE RIGHT DIRECTION!
I'D LIKE TO NUDGE HER WITH AN OVER-RIPE TOMATO!
1

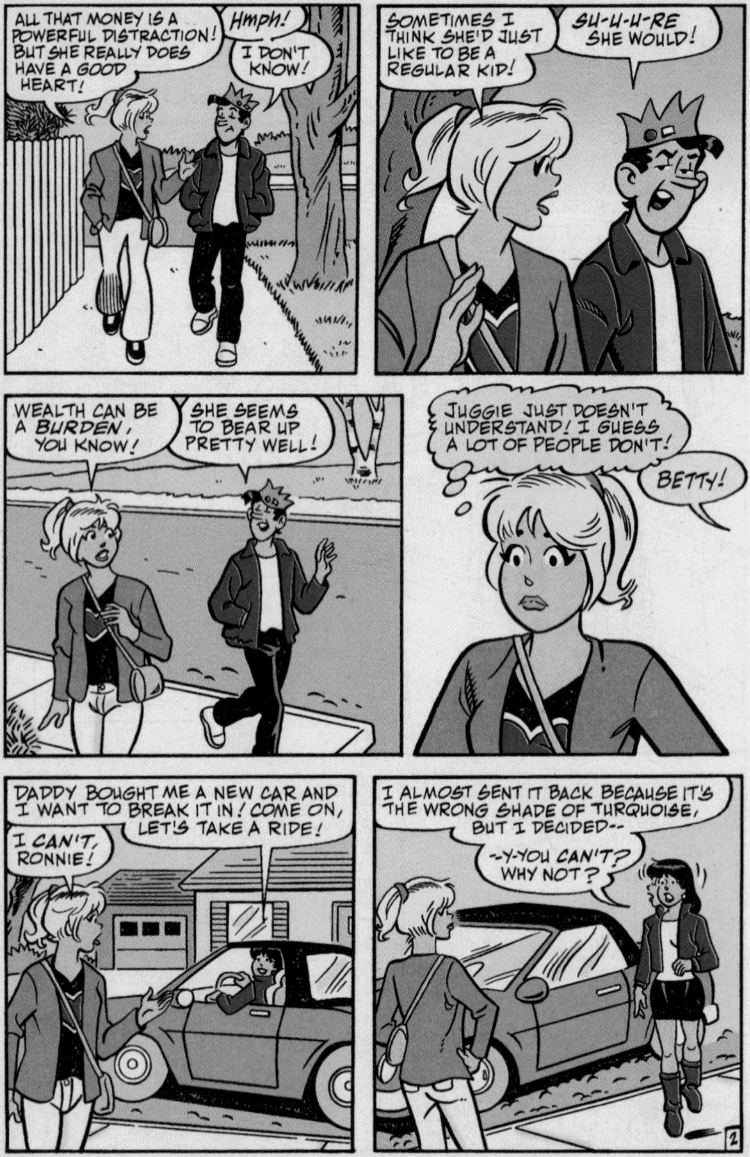
ALL THAT MONEY IS A POWERFUL DISTRACTION! BUT SHE REALLY DOES HAVE A GOOD HEART!
Hmph!
I DON'T KNOW!
SOMETIMES I THINK SHE'D JUST LIKE TO BE A REGULAR KID!
SU-U-U-RE SHE WOULD!
WEALTH CAN BE A BURDEN, YOU KNOW!
SHE SEEMS TO BEAR UP PRETTY WELL!
JUGGIE JUST DOESN'T UNDERSTAND! I GUESS A LOT OF PEOPLE DON'T!
BETTY!
DADDY BOUGHT ME A NEW CAR AND I WANT TO BREAK IT IN! COME ON, LET'S TAKE A RIDE!
I CAN'T, RONNIE!
I ALMOST SENT IT BACK BECAUSE IT'S THE WRONG SHADE OF TURQUOISE, BUT I DECIDED--
--Y-YOU CAN'T? WHY NOT?
2

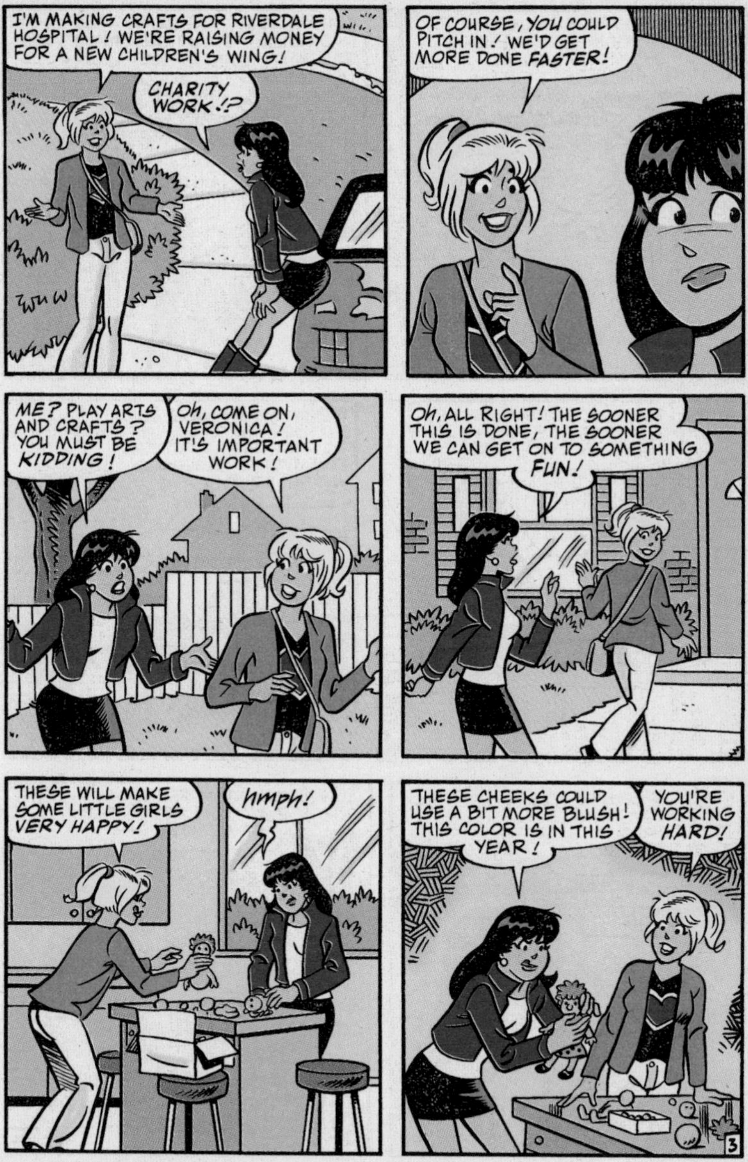

I'M MAKING CRAFTS FOR RIVERDALE HOSPITAL! WE'RE RAISING MONEY FOR A NEW CHILDREN'S WING!
CHARITY WORK!?
OF COURSE, YOU COULD PITCH IN! WE'D GET MORE DONE FASTER!
ME? PLAY ARTS AND CRAFTS? YOU MUST BE KIDDING!
Oh, COME ON, VERONICA! IT'S IMPORTANT WORK!
Oh, ALL RIGHT! THE SOONER THIS IS DONE, THE SOONER WE CAN GET ON TO SOMETHING FUN!
THESE WILL MAKE SOME LITTLE GIRLS VERY HAPPY!
hmph!
THESE CHEEKS COULD USE A BIT MORE BLUSH! THIS COLOR IS IN THIS YEAR!
YOU'RE WORKING HARD!
3

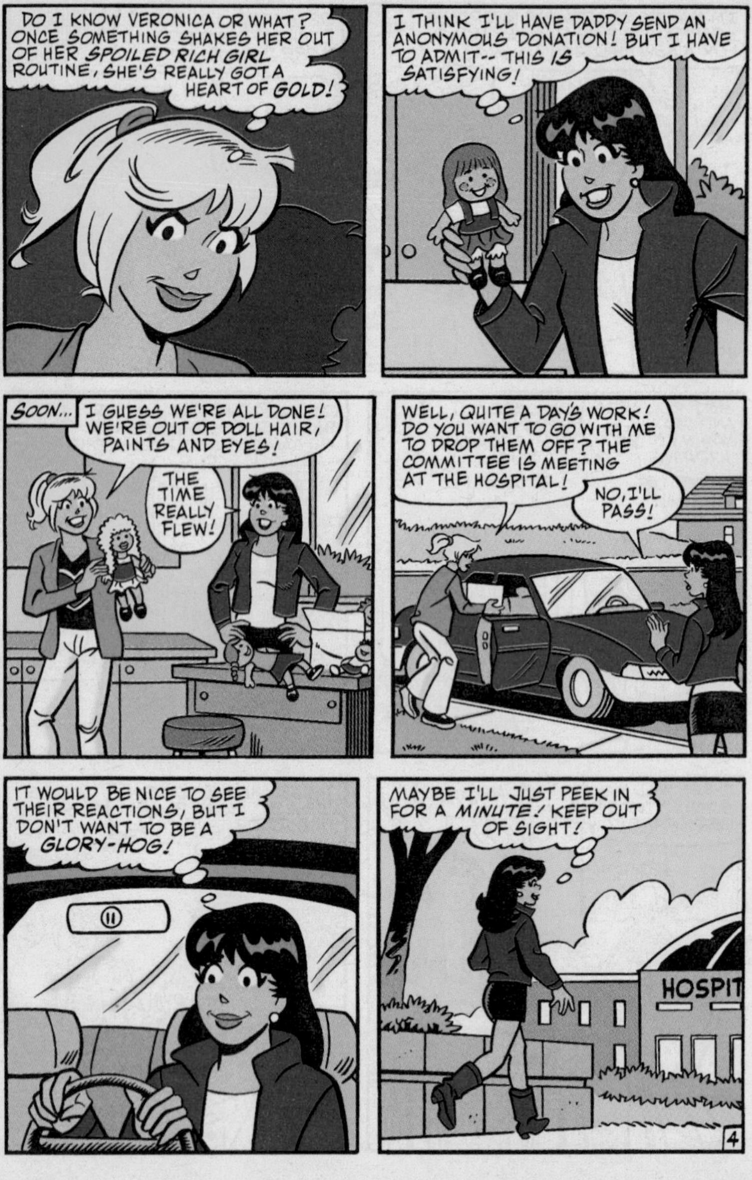
DO I KNOW VERONICA OR WHAT? ONCE SOMETHING SHAKES HER OUT OF HER SPOILED RICH GIRL ROUTINE, SHE'S REALLY GOT A HEART OF GOLD!
I THINK I'LL HAVE DADDY SEND AN ANONYMOUS DONATION! BUT I HAVE TO ADMIT-- THIS IS SATISFYING!
SOON...
I GUESS WE'RE ALL DONE! WE'RE OUT OF DOLL HAIR, PAINTS AND EYES!
THE TIME REALLY FLEW!
WELL, QUITE A DAY'S WORK! DO YOU WANT TO GO WITH ME TO DROP THEM OFF? THE COMMITTEE IS MEETING AT THE HOSPITAL!
NO, I'LL PASS!
IT WOULD BE NICE TO SEE THEIR REACTIONS, BUT I DON'T WANT TO BE A GLORY-HOG!
MAYBE I'LL JUST PEEK IN FOR A MINUTE! KEEP OUT OF SIGHT!
HOSPIT
4

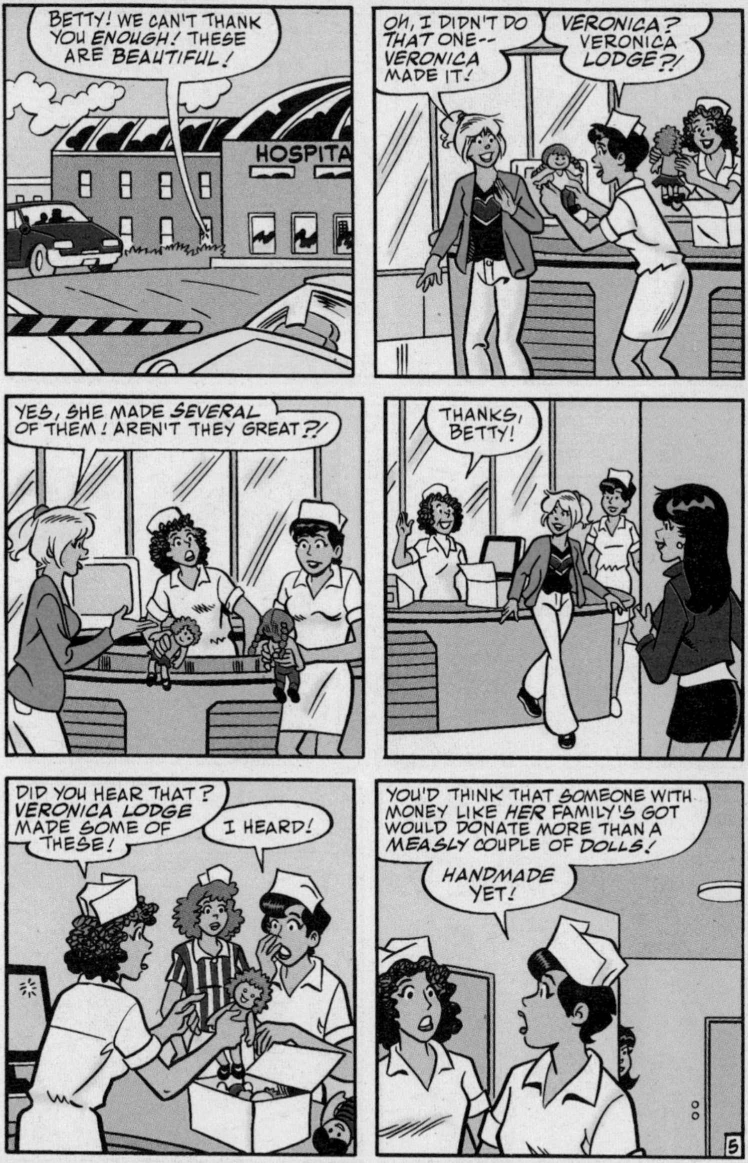

BETTY! WE CAN'T THANK YOU ENOUGH! THESE ARE BEAUTIFUL!
HOSPITA
OH, I DIDN'T DO THAT ONE-- VERONICA MADE IT!
VERONICA? VERONICA LODGE?!
YES, SHE MADE SEVERAL OF THEM! AREN'T THEY GREAT?!
THANKS, BETTY!
DID YOU HEAR THAT? VERONICA LODGE MADE SOME OF THESE!
I HEARD!
YOU'D THINK THAT SOMEONE WITH MONEY LIKE HER FAMILY'S GOT WOULD DONATE MORE THAN A MEASLY COUPLE OF DOLLS!
HANDMADE YET!
5

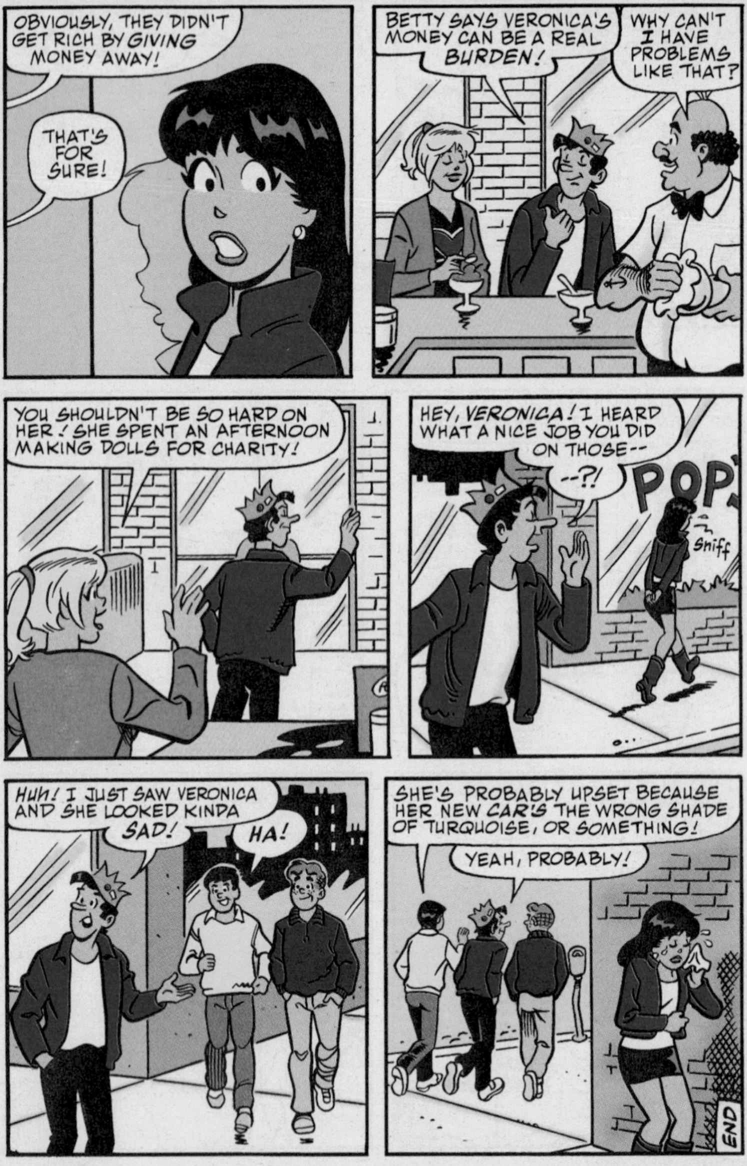
OBVIOUSLY, THEY DIDN'T GET RICH BY GIVING MONEY AWAY!
THAT'S FOR SURE!
BETTY SAYS VERONICA'S MONEY CAN BE A REAL BURDEN!
WHY CAN'T I HAVE PROBLEMS LIKE THAT?
YOU SHOULDN'T BE SO HARD ON HER! SHE SPENT AN AFTERNOON MAKING DOLLS FOR CHARITY!
HEY, VERONICA! I HEARD WHAT A NICE JOB YOU DID ON THOSE--
--?!
POP
Sniff
HUH! I JUST SAW VERONICA AND SHE LOOKED KINDA SAD!
HA!
SHE'S PROBABLY UPSET BECAUSE HER NEW CAR'S THE WRONG SHADE OF TURQUOISE, OR SOMETHING!
YEAH, PROBABLY!
END

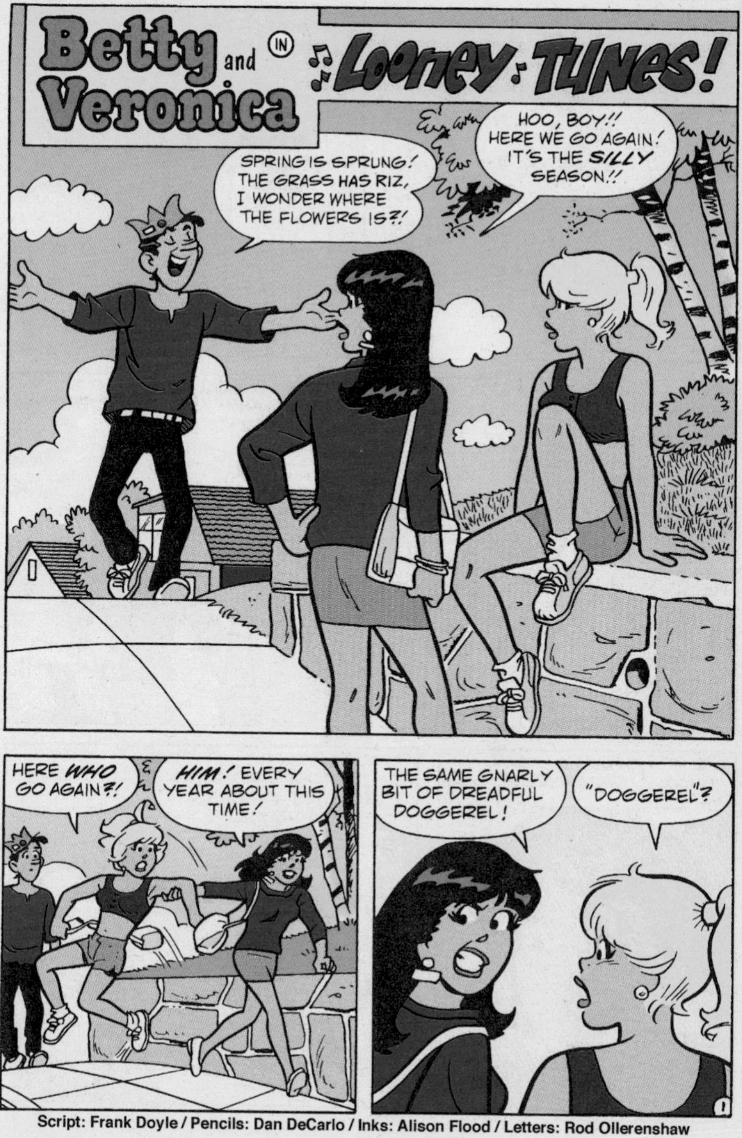
Betty and Veronica
IN
Looney Tunes!
SPRING IS SPRUNG! THE GRASS HAS RIZ, I WONDER WHERE THE FLOWERS IS?!
HOO, BOY!! HERE WE GO AGAIN! IT'S THE SILLY SEASON!!
HERE WHO GO AGAIN?!
HIM! EVERY YEAR ABOUT THIS TIME!
THE SAME GNARLY BIT OF DREADFUL DOGGEREL!
"DOGGEREL"?
1

Script: Frank Doyle / Pencils: Dan DeCarlo / Inks: Alison Flood / Letters: Rod Ollerenshaw

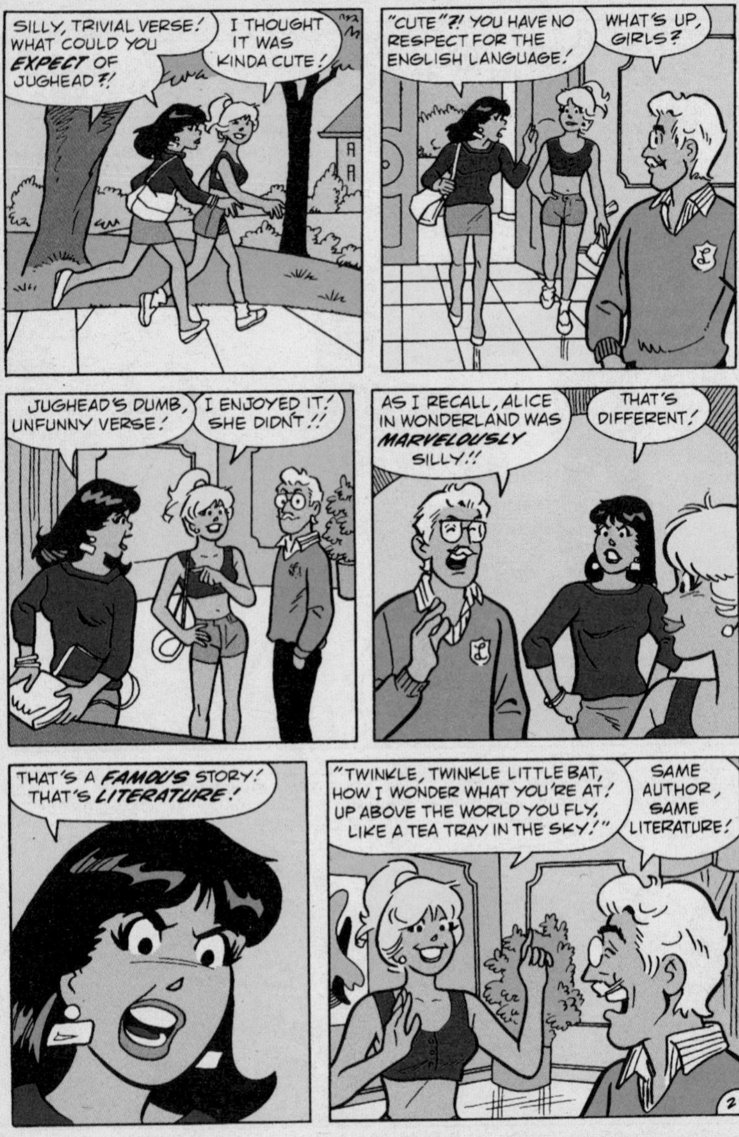
SILLY, TRIVIAL VERSE! WHAT COULD YOU EXPECT OF JUGHEAD?!
I THOUGHT IT WAS KINDA CUTE!
"CUTE"?! YOU HAVE NO RESPECT FOR THE ENGLISH LANGUAGE!
WHAT'S UP, GIRLS?
JUGHEAD'S DUMB, UNFUNNY VERSE!
I ENJOYED IT! SHE DIDN'T!!
AS I RECALL, ALICE IN WONDERLAND WAS MARVELOUSLY SILLY!!
THAT'S DIFFERENT!
THAT'S A FAMOUS STORY! THAT'S LITERATURE!
"TWINKLE, TWINKLE LITTLE BAT, HOW I WONDER WHAT YOU'RE AT! UP ABOVE THE WORLD YOU FLY, LIKE A TEA TRAY IN THE SKY!"
SAME AUTHOR, SAME LITERATURE!
2

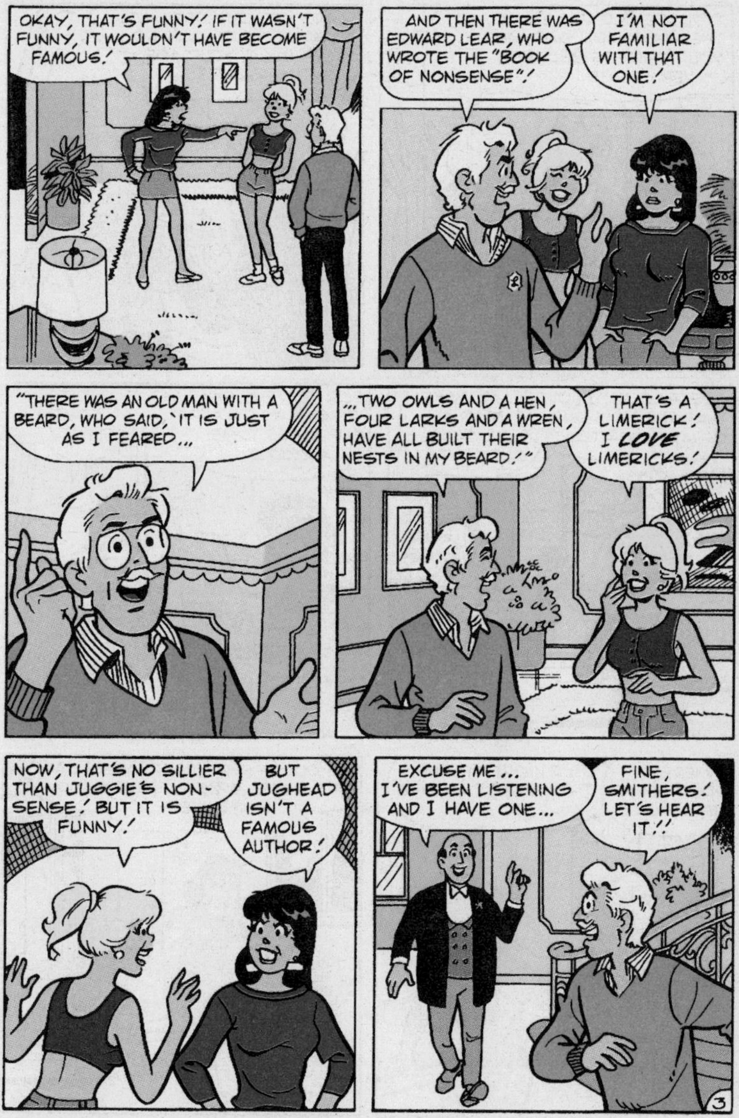

OKAY, THAT'S FUNNY! IF IT WASN'T FUNNY, IT WOULDN'T HAVE BECOME FAMOUS!
AND THEN THERE WAS EDWARD LEAR, WHO WROTE THE "BOOK OF NONSENSE"!
I'M NOT FAMILIAR WITH THAT ONE!
"THERE WAS AN OLD MAN WITH A BEARD, WHO SAID, 'IT IS JUST AS I FEARED...
...TWO OWLS AND A HEN, FOUR LARKS AND A WREN, HAVE ALL BUILT THEIR NESTS IN MY BEARD!'"
THAT'S A LIMERICK! I *LOVE* LIMERICKS!
NOW, THAT'S NO SILLIER THAN JUGGIE'S NON-SENSE! BUT IT IS FUNNY!
BUT JUGHEAD ISN'T A FAMOUS AUTHOR!
EXCUSE ME... I'VE BEEN LISTENING AND I HAVE ONE...
FINE, SMITHERS! LET'S HEAR IT!!
3

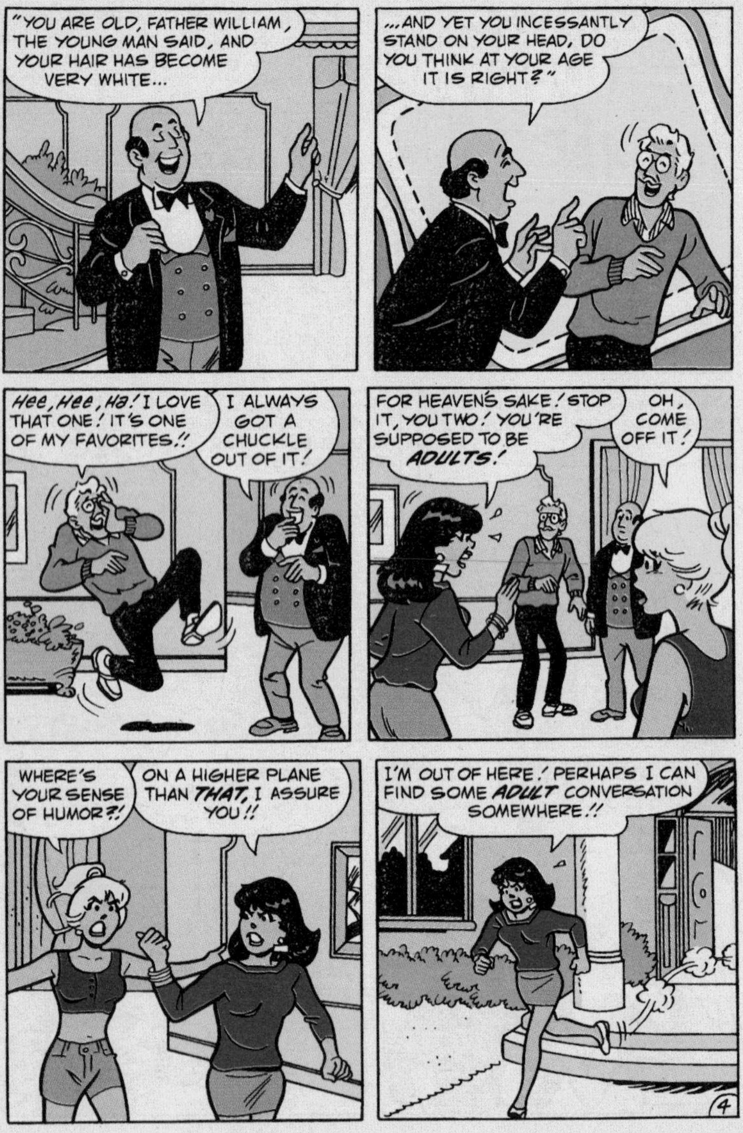
"YOU ARE OLD, FATHER WILLIAM, THE YOUNG MAN SAID, AND YOUR HAIR HAS BECOME VERY WHITE...
...AND YET YOU INCESSANTLY STAND ON YOUR HEAD, DO YOU THINK AT YOUR AGE IT IS RIGHT?"
HEE, HEE, HA! I LOVE THAT ONE! IT'S ONE OF MY FAVORITES!!
I ALWAYS GOT A CHUCKLE OUT OF IT!
FOR HEAVEN'S SAKE! STOP IT, YOU TWO! YOU'RE SUPPOSED TO BE ADULTS!
OH, COME OFF IT!
WHERE'S YOUR SENSE OF HUMOR?!
ON A HIGHER PLANE THAN THAT, I ASSURE YOU!!
I'M OUT OF HERE! PERHAPS I CAN FIND SOME ADULT CONVERSATION SOMEWHERE!!
4

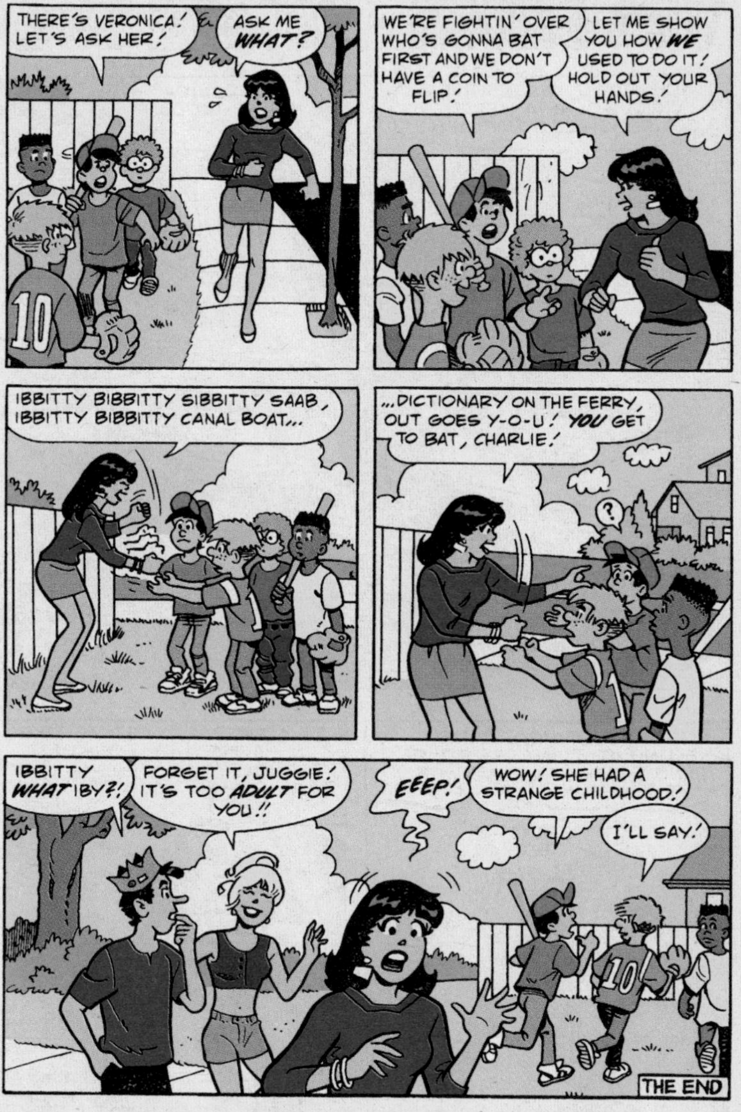
THERE'S VERONICA! LET'S ASK HER!
ASK ME WHAT?
WE'RE FIGHTIN' OVER WHO'S GONNA BAT FIRST AND WE DON'T HAVE A COIN TO FLIP!
LET ME SHOW YOU HOW WE USED TO DO IT! HOLD OUT YOUR HANDS!
IBBITTY BIBBITTY SIBBITTY SAAB, IBBITTY BIBBITTY CANAL BOAT...
...DICTIONARY ON THE FERRY, OUT GOES Y-O-U! YOU GET TO BAT, CHARLIE!
?
IBBITTY WHAT IBY?!
FORGET IT, JUGGIE! IT'S TOO ADULT FOR YOU!!
EEEP!
WOW! SHE HAD A STRANGE CHILDHOOD!
I'LL SAY!
10
THE END

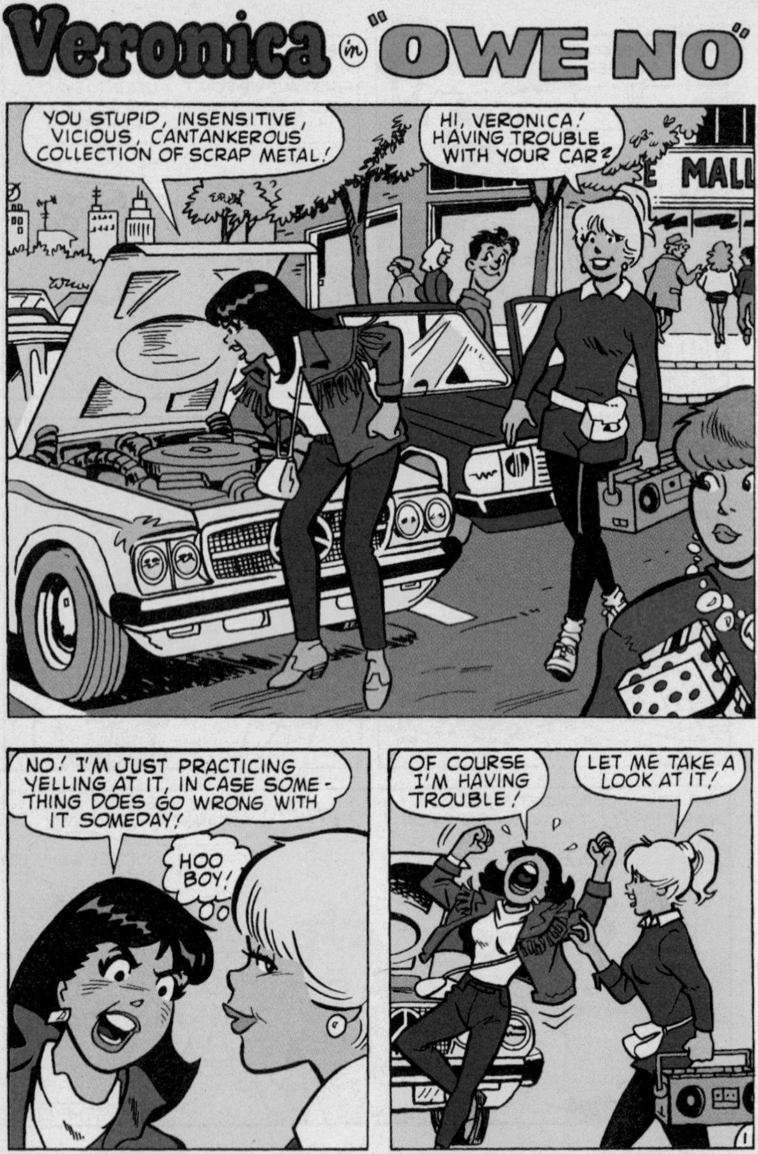
Veronica in "OWE NO"
YOU STUPID, INSENSITIVE, VICIOUS, CANTANKEROUS COLLECTION OF SCRAP METAL!
HI, VERONICA! HAVING TROUBLE WITH YOUR CAR?
E MALL
NO! I'M JUST PRACTICING YELLING AT IT, IN CASE SOME-THING DOES GO WRONG WITH IT SOMEDAY!
HOO BOY!
OF COURSE I'M HAVING TROUBLE!
LET ME TAKE A LOOK AT IT!
1

Script: Hal Smith / Pencils: Dan DeCarlo / Inks: Alison Flood / Letters: Bill Yoshida

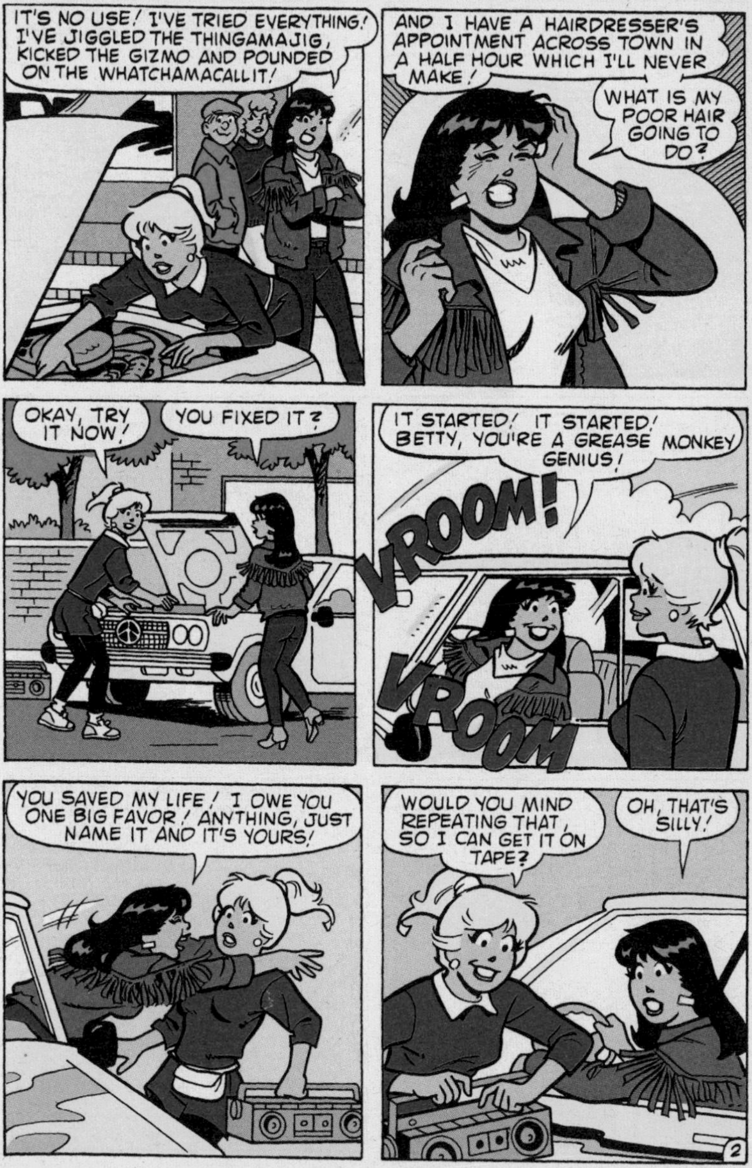
IT'S NO USE! I'VE TRIED EVERYTHING! I'VE JIGGLED THE THINGAMAJIG, KICKED THE GIZMO AND POUNDED ON THE WHATCHAMACALLIT!
AND I HAVE A HAIRDRESSER'S APPOINTMENT ACROSS TOWN IN A HALF HOUR WHICH I'LL NEVER MAKE!
WHAT IS MY POOR HAIR GOING TO DO?
OKAY, TRY IT NOW!
YOU FIXED IT?
IT STARTED! IT STARTED! BETTY, YOU'RE A GREASE MONKEY GENIUS!
VROOM!
VROOM
YOU SAVED MY LIFE! I OWE YOU ONE BIG FAVOR! ANYTHING, JUST NAME IT AND IT'S YOURS!
WOULD YOU MIND REPEATING THAT, SO I CAN GET IT ON TAPE?
OH, THAT'S SILLY!
2

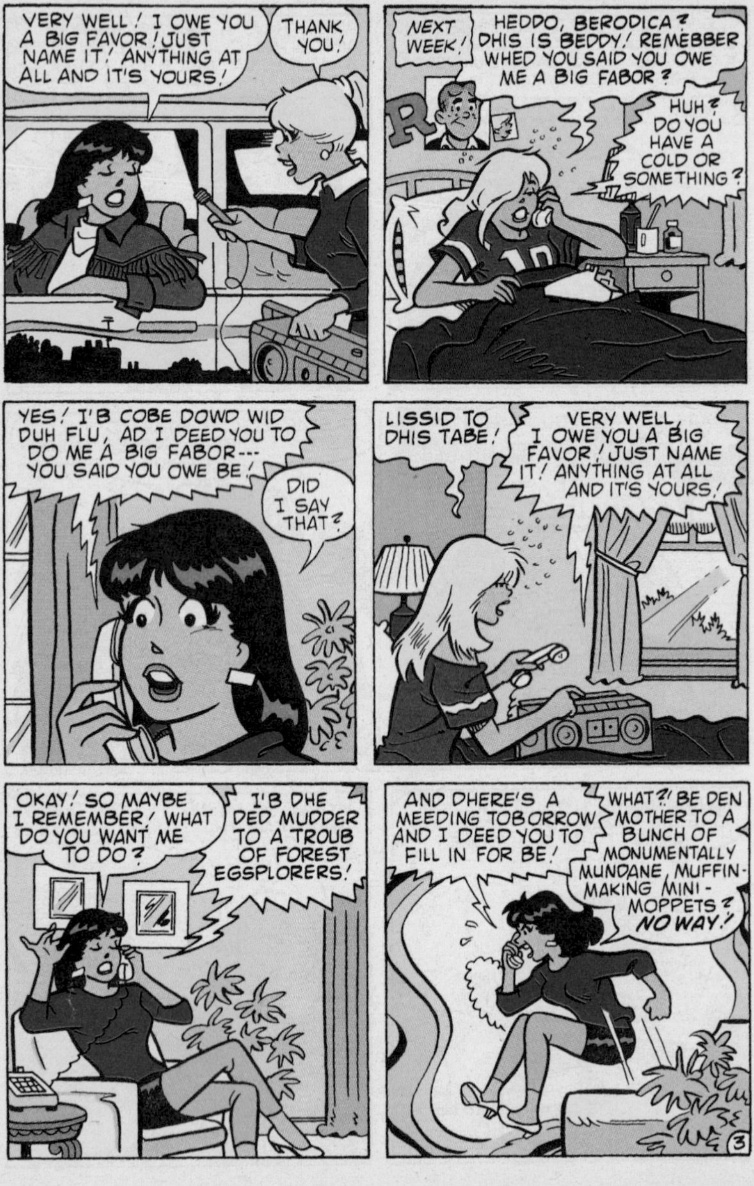
VERY WELL! I OWE YOU A BIG FAVOR! JUST NAME IT! ANYTHING AT ALL AND IT'S YOURS!
THANK YOU!
NEXT WEEK!
HEDDO, BERODICA? DHIS IS BEDDY! REMEBBER WHED YOU SAID YOU OWE ME A BIG FABOR?
HUH? DO YOU HAVE A COLD OR SOMETHING?
YES! I'B COBE DOWD WID DUH FLU, AD I DEED YOU TO DO ME A BIG FABOR--- YOU SAID YOU OWE BE!
DID I SAY THAT?
LISSID TO DHIS TABE!
VERY WELL, I OWE YOU A BIG FAVOR! JUST NAME IT! ANYTHING AT ALL AND IT'S YOURS!
OKAY! SO MAYBE I REMEMBER! WHAT DO YOU WANT ME TO DO?
I'B DHE DED MUDDER TO A TROUB OF FOREST EGSPLORERS!
AND DHERE'S A MEEDING TOBORROW AND I DEED YOU TO FILL IN FOR BE!
WHAT?! BE DEN MOTHER TO A BUNCH OF MONUMENTALLY MUNDANE, MUFFIN-MAKING MINI-MOPPETS? NO WAY!
3

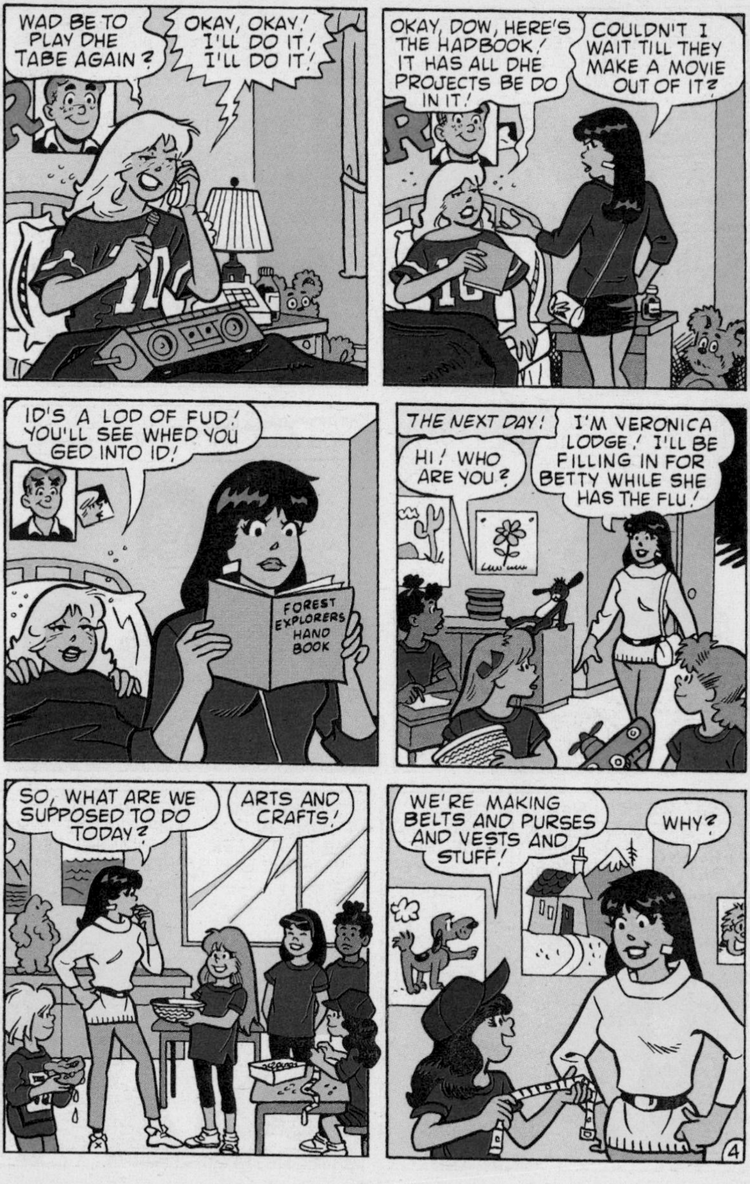
WAD BE TO PLAY DHE TABE AGAIN?
OKAY, OKAY! I'LL DO IT! I'LL DO IT!
OKAY, DOW, HERE'S THE HADBOOK! IT HAS ALL DHE PROJECTS BE DO IN IT!
COULDN'T I WAIT TILL THEY MAKE A MOVIE OUT OF IT?
ID'S A LOD OF FUD! YOU'LL SEE WHED YOU GED INTO ID!
FOREST EXPLORERS HAND BOOK
THE NEXT DAY!
HI! WHO ARE YOU?
I'M VERONICA LODGE! I'LL BE FILLING IN FOR BETTY WHILE SHE HAS THE FLU!
SO, WHAT ARE WE SUPPOSED TO DO TODAY?
ARTS AND CRAFTS!
WE'RE MAKING BELTS AND PURSES AND VESTS AND STUFF!
WHY?
4

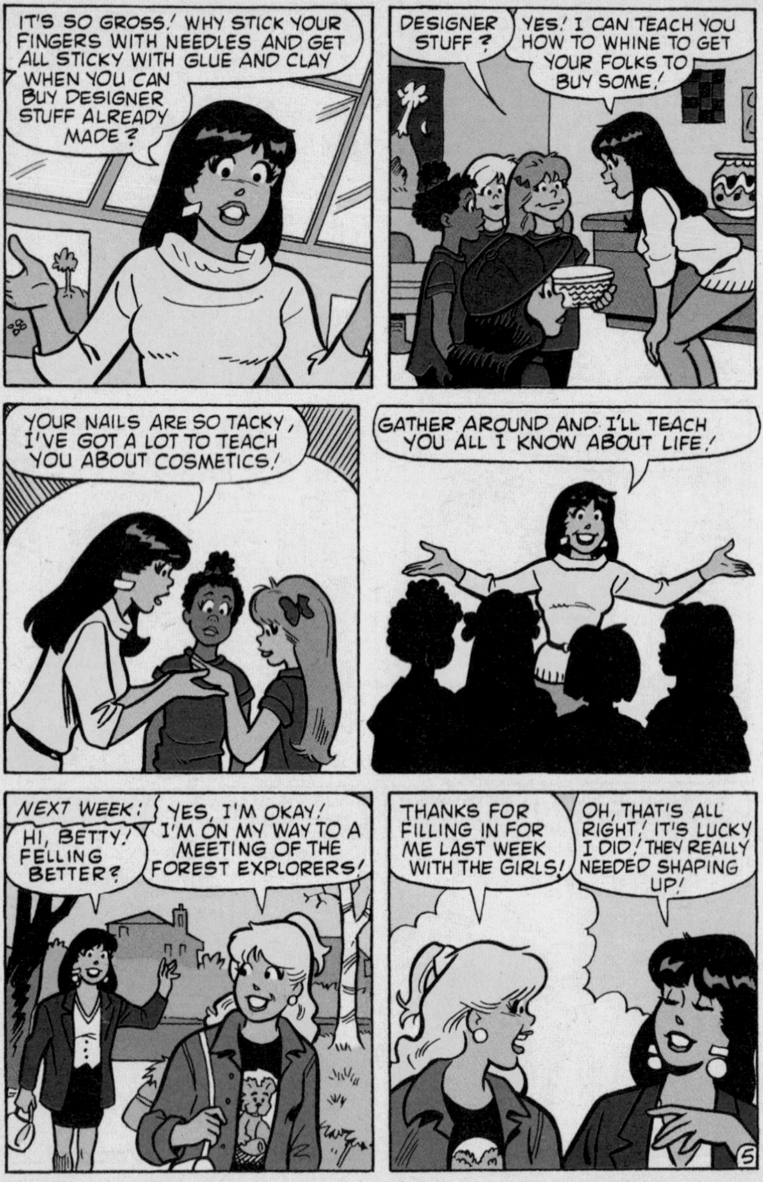
IT'S SO GROSS! WHY STICK YOUR FINGERS WITH NEEDLES AND GET ALL STICKY WITH GLUE AND CLAY WHEN YOU CAN BUY DESIGNER STUFF ALREADY MADE?
DESIGNER STUFF?
YES! I CAN TEACH YOU HOW TO WHINE TO GET YOUR FOLKS TO BUY SOME!
YOUR NAILS ARE SO TACKY, I'VE GOT A LOT TO TEACH YOU ABOUT COSMETICS!
GATHER AROUND AND I'LL TEACH YOU ALL I KNOW ABOUT LIFE!
NEXT WEEK:
HI, BETTY! FELLING BETTER?
YES, I'M OKAY! I'M ON MY WAY TO A MEETING OF THE FOREST EXPLORERS!
THANKS FOR FILLING IN FOR ME LAST WEEK WITH THE GIRLS!
OH, THAT'S ALL RIGHT! IT'S LUCKY I DID! THEY REALLY NEEDED SHAPING UP!
5

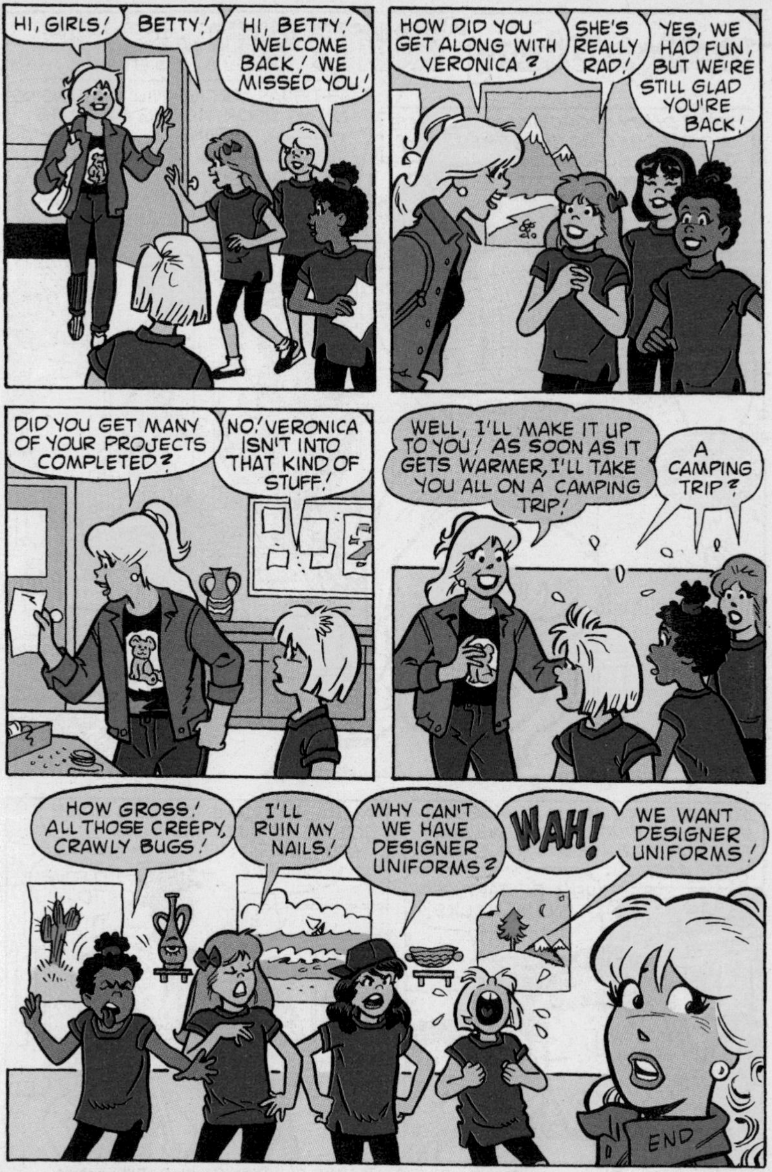
HI, GIRLS!
BETTY!
HI, BETTY! WELCOME BACK! WE MISSED YOU!
HOW DID YOU GET ALONG WITH VERONICA?
SHE'S REALLY RAD!
YES, WE HAD FUN, BUT WE'RE STILL GLAD YOU'RE BACK!
DID YOU GET MANY OF YOUR PROJECTS COMPLETED?
NO! VERONICA ISN'T INTO THAT KIND OF STUFF!
WELL, I'LL MAKE IT UP TO YOU! AS SOON AS IT GETS WARMER, I'LL TAKE YOU ALL ON A CAMPING TRIP!
A CAMPING TRIP?
HOW GROSS! ALL THOSE CREEPY, CRAWLY BUGS!
I'LL RUIN MY NAILS!
WHY CAN'T WE HAVE DESIGNER UNIFORMS?
WAH!
WE WANT DESIGNER UNIFORMS!
END

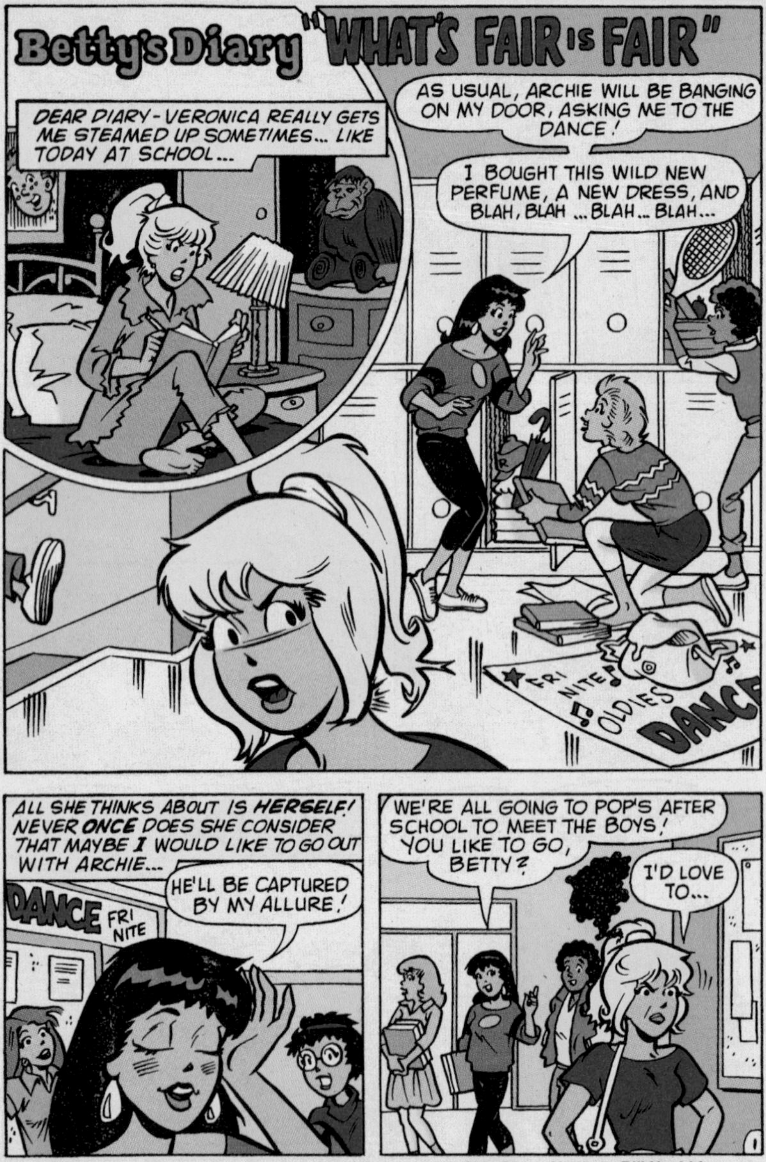
Betty's Diary
"WHAT'S FAIR IS FAIR"
DEAR DIARY - VERONICA REALLY GETS ME STEAMED UP SOMETIMES... LIKE TODAY AT SCHOOL...
AS USUAL, ARCHIE WILL BE BANGING ON MY DOOR, ASKING ME TO THE DANCE!
I BOUGHT THIS WILD NEW PERFUME, A NEW DRESS, AND BLAH, BLAH ... BLAH... BLAH...
FRI NITE OLDIES DANCE
ALL SHE THINKS ABOUT IS HERSELF! NEVER ONCE DOES SHE CONSIDER THAT MAYBE I WOULD LIKE TO GO OUT WITH ARCHIE...
HE'LL BE CAPTURED BY MY ALLURE!
DANCE FRI NITE
WE'RE ALL GOING TO POP'S AFTER SCHOOL TO MEET THE BOYS! YOU LIKE TO GO, BETTY?
I'D LOVE TO...
1

Script: Rod Ollerenshaw / Pencils: Doug Crane / Inks: Chic Stone / Letters: Bill Yoshida

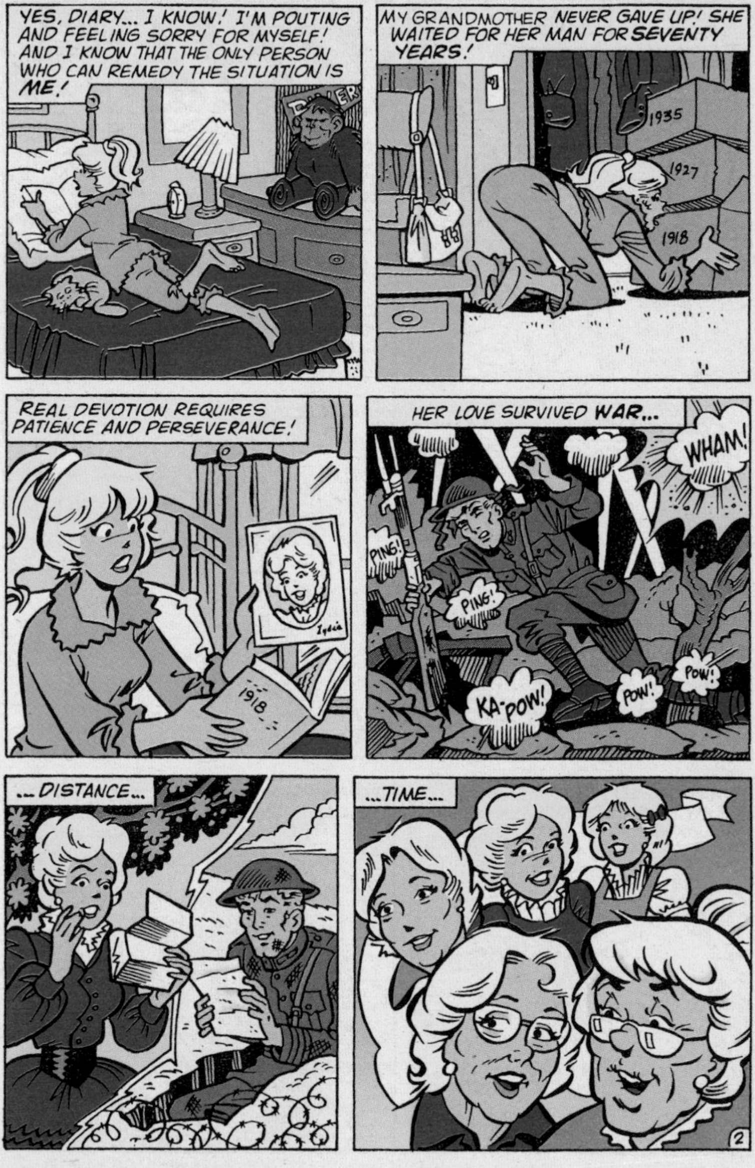
YES, DIARY... I KNOW! I'M POUTING AND FEELING SORRY FOR MYSELF! AND I KNOW THAT THE ONLY PERSON WHO CAN REMEDY THE SITUATION IS ME!
MY GRANDMOTHER NEVER GAVE UP! SHE WAITED FOR HER MAN FOR SEVENTY YEARS!
1935
1927
1918
REAL DEVOTION REQUIRES PATIENCE AND PERSEVERANCE!
1918
HER LOVE SURVIVED WAR...
WHAM!
PING!
PING!
KA-POW!
POW!
POW!
...DISTANCE...
...TIME...
2

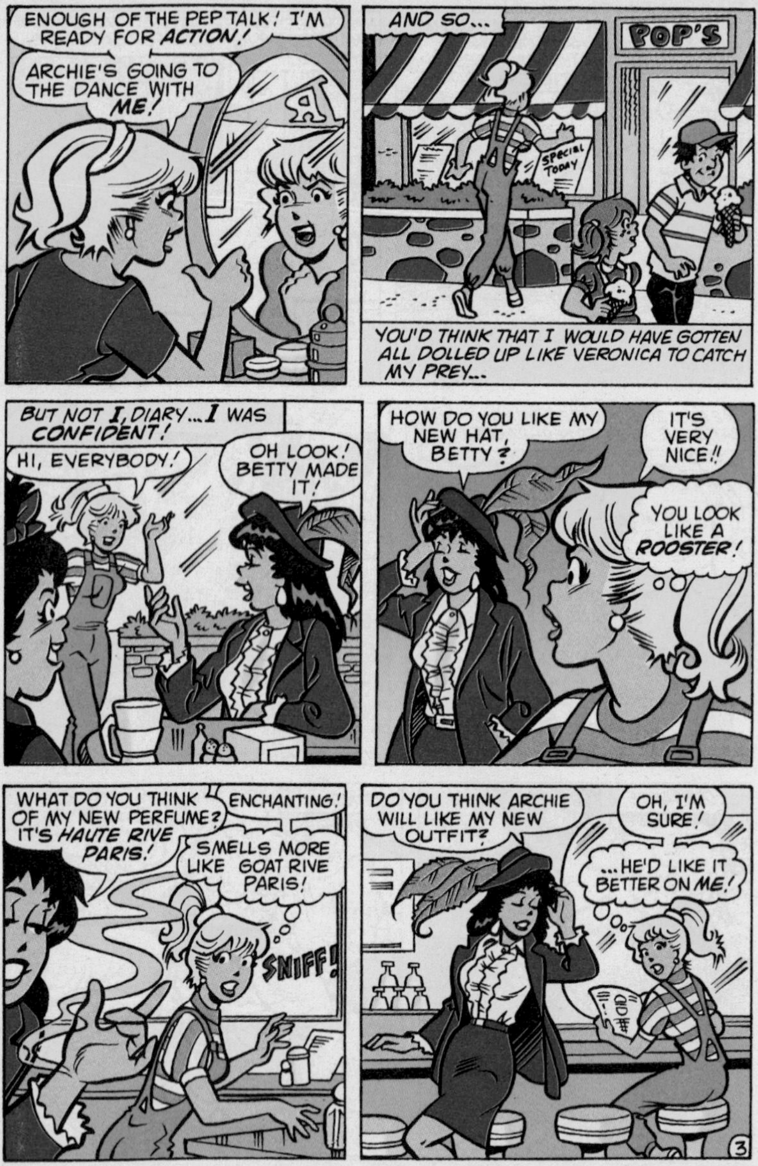
ENOUGH OF THE PEP TALK! I'M READY FOR ACTION!
ARCHIE'S GOING TO THE DANCE WITH ME!
AND SO...
POP'S
SPECIAL TODAY
YOU'D THINK THAT I WOULD HAVE GOTTEN ALL DOLLED UP LIKE VERONICA TO CATCH MY PREY...
BUT NOT I, DIARY... I WAS CONFIDENT!
HI, EVERYBODY!
OH LOOK! BETTY MADE IT!
HOW DO YOU LIKE MY NEW HAT, BETTY?
IT'S VERY NICE!!
YOU LOOK LIKE A ROOSTER!
WHAT DO YOU THINK OF MY NEW PERFUME? IT'S HAUTE RIVE PARIS!
ENCHANTING!
SMELLS MORE LIKE GOAT RIVE PARIS!
SNIFF!
DO YOU THINK ARCHIE WILL LIKE MY NEW OUTFIT?
OH, I'M SURE!
...HE'D LIKE IT BETTER ON ME!
3

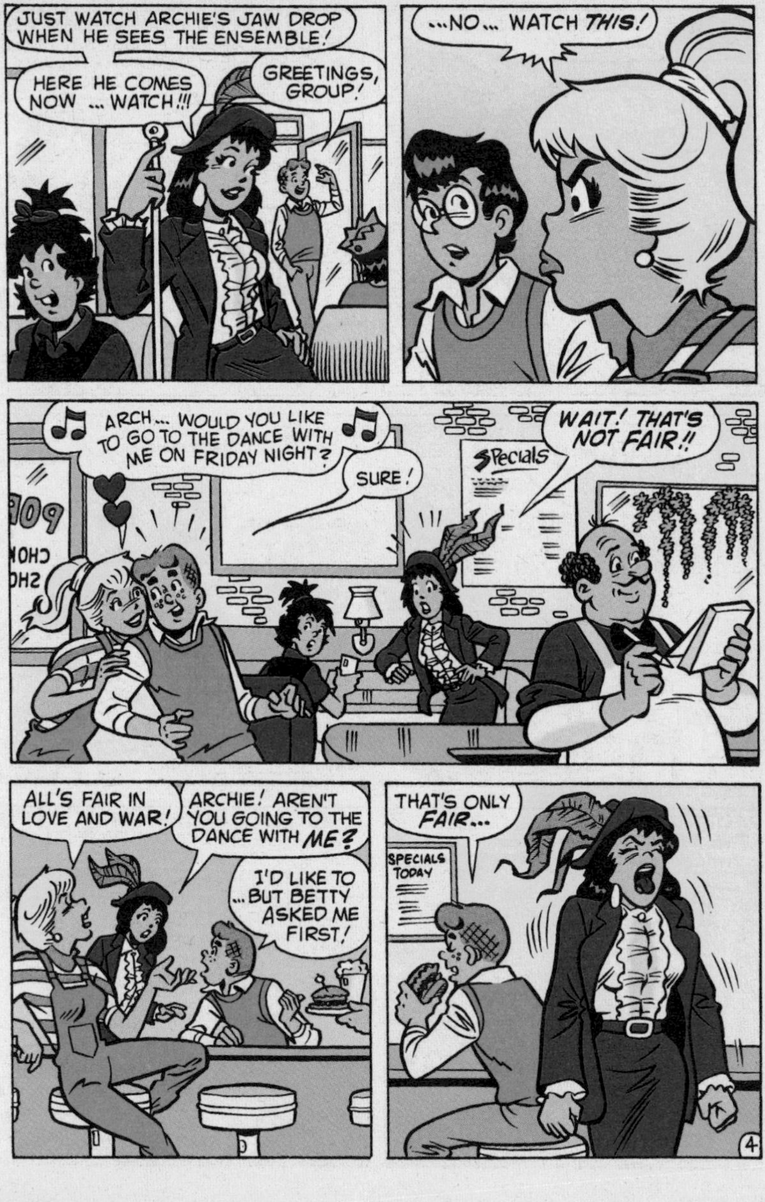
JUST WATCH ARCHIE'S JAW DROP WHEN HE SEES THE ENSEMBLE!
HERE HE COMES NOW ... WATCH!!!
GREETINGS, GROUP!
...NO... WATCH THIS!
ARCH... WOULD YOU LIKE TO GO TO THE DANCE WITH ME ON FRIDAY NIGHT?
SURE!
WAIT! THAT'S NOT FAIR!!
SPecials
ALL'S FAIR IN LOVE AND WAR!
ARCHIE! AREN'T YOU GOING TO THE DANCE WITH ME?
I'D LIKE TO ...BUT BETTY ASKED ME FIRST!
THAT'S ONLY FAIR...
SPECIALS TODAY
4

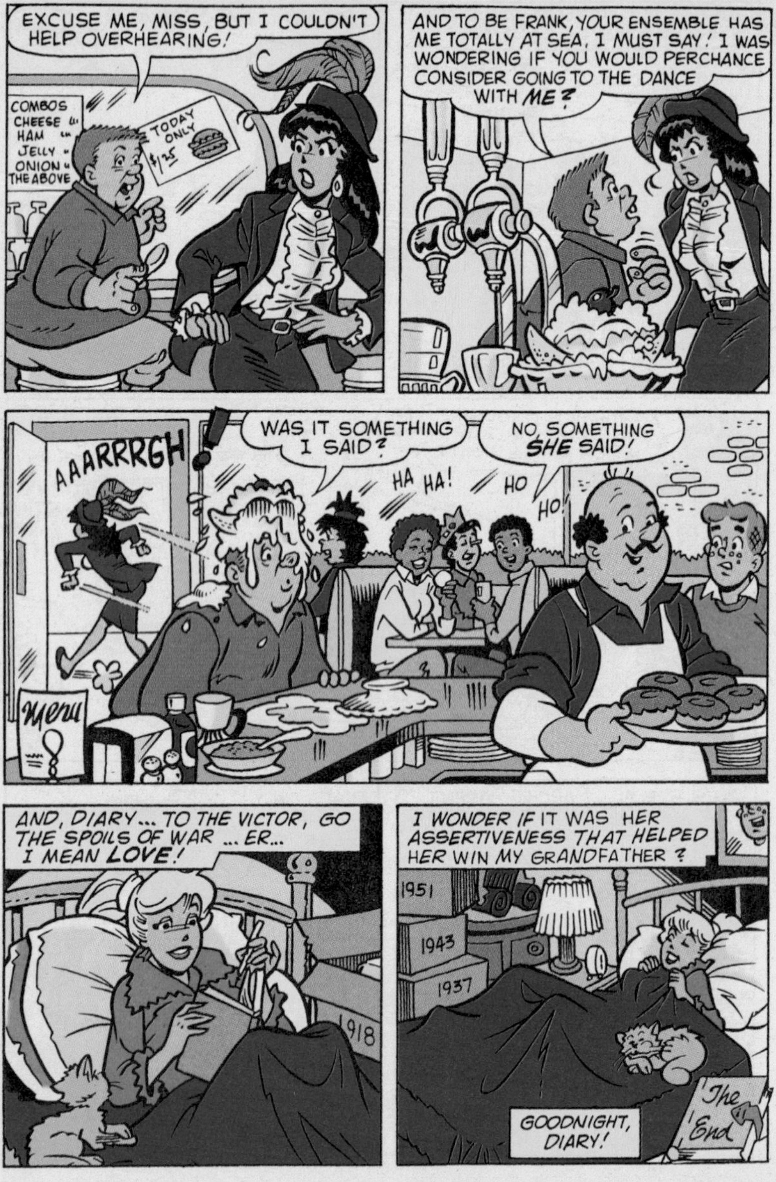
EXCUSE ME, MISS, BUT I COULDN'T HELP OVERHEARING!
COMBOS CHEESE HAM JELLY ONION THE ABOVE
TODAY ONLY $1.25
AND TO BE FRANK, YOUR ENSEMBLE HAS ME TOTALLY AT SEA, I MUST SAY! I WAS WONDERING IF YOU WOULD PERCHANCE CONSIDER GOING TO THE DANCE WITH ME?
AAARRRGH!
WAS IT SOMETHING I SAID?
NO, SOMETHING SHE SAID!
HA HA!
HO HO!
MENU
AND, DIARY... TO THE VICTOR, GO THE SPOILS OF WAR ... ER... I MEAN LOVE!
1918
I WONDER IF IT WAS HER ASSERTIVENESS THAT HELPED HER WIN MY GRANDFATHER?
1951
1943
1937
GOODNIGHT, DIARY!
The End

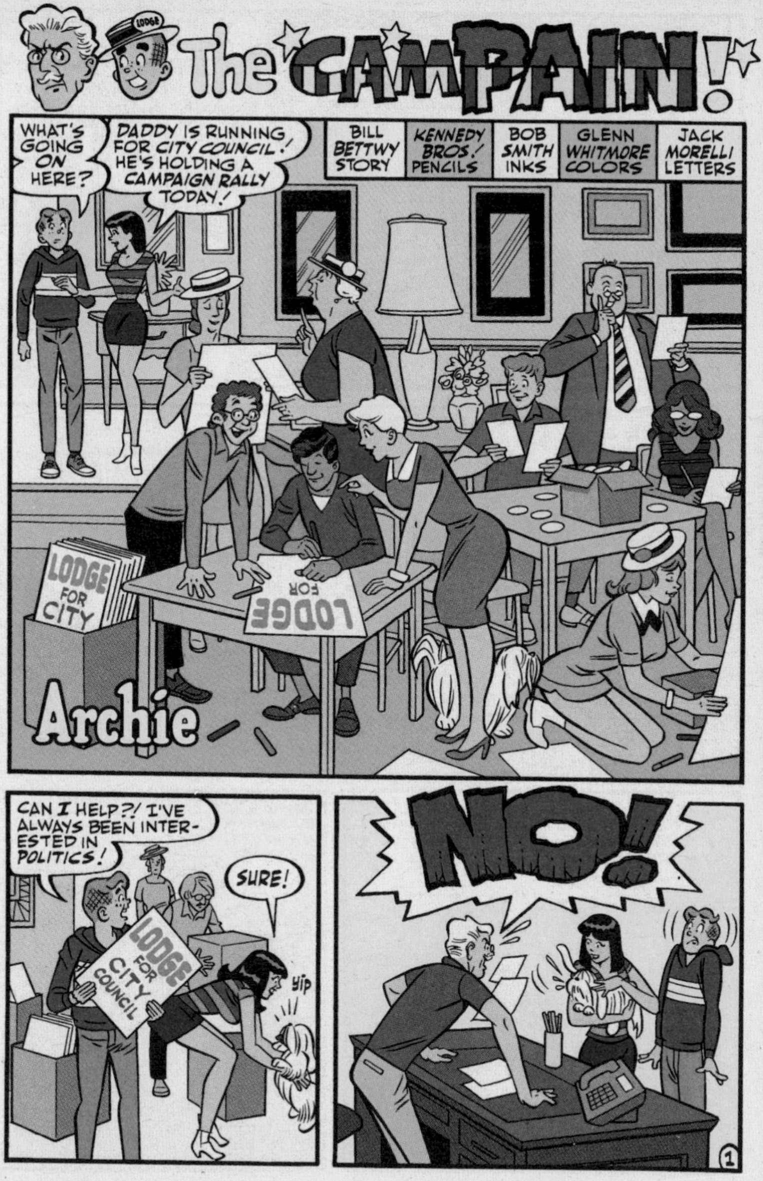
The CAMPAIN!
LODGE
WHAT'S GOING ON HERE?
DADDY IS RUNNING FOR CITY COUNCIL! HE'S HOLDING A CAMPAIGN RALLY TODAY!
BILL BETTWY STORY
KENNEDY BROS.! PENCILS
BOB SMITH INKS
GLENN WHITMORE COLORS
JACK MORELLI LETTERS
LODGE FOR CITY
LODGE FOR
Archie
CAN I HELP?! I'VE ALWAYS BEEN INTERESTED IN POLITICS!
SURE!
LODGE FOR CITY COUNCIL
YIP
NO!
1

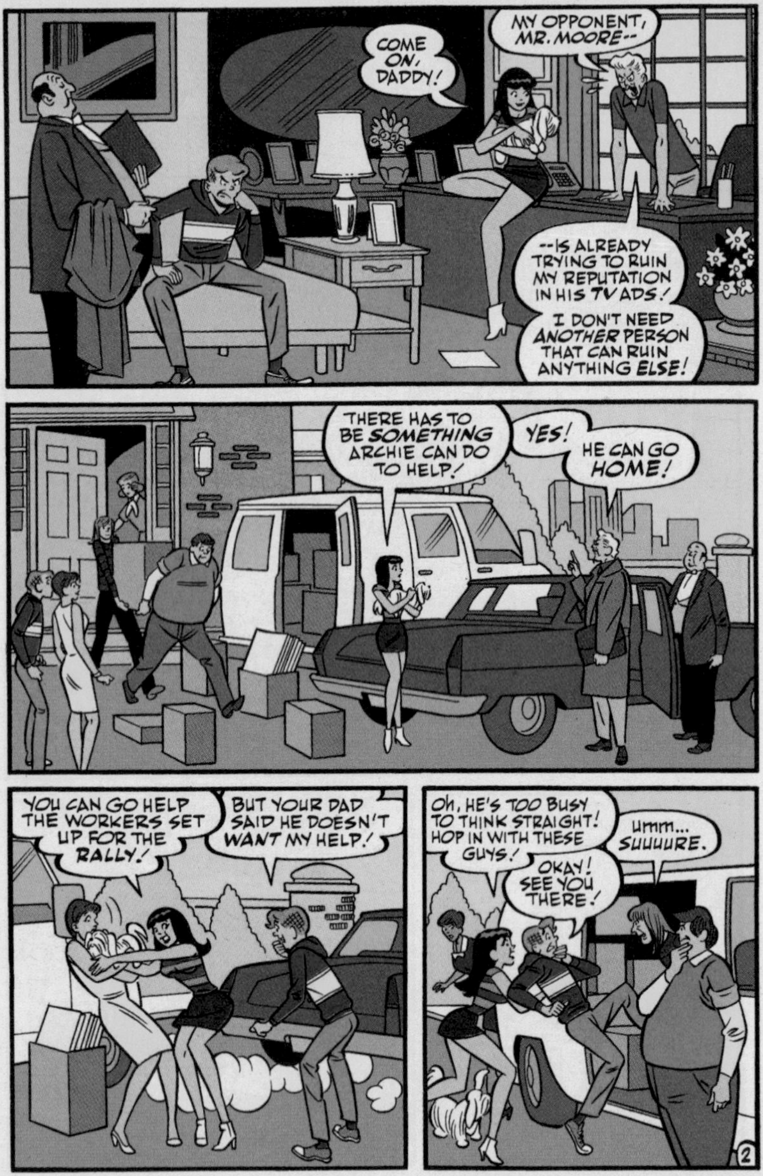
COME ON, DADDY!
MY OPPONENT, MR. MOORE--
--IS ALREADY TRYING TO RUIN MY REPUTATION IN HIS TV ADS!
I DON'T NEED ANOTHER PERSON THAT CAN RUIN ANYTHING ELSE!
THERE HAS TO BE SOMETHING ARCHIE CAN DO TO HELP!
YES!
HE CAN GO HOME!
YOU CAN GO HELP THE WORKERS SET UP FOR THE RALLY!
BUT YOUR DAD SAID HE DOESN'T WANT MY HELP!
Oh, HE'S TOO BUSY TO THINK STRAIGHT! HOP IN WITH THESE GUYS!
OKAY! SEE YOU THERE!
umm... SUUUURE.
2

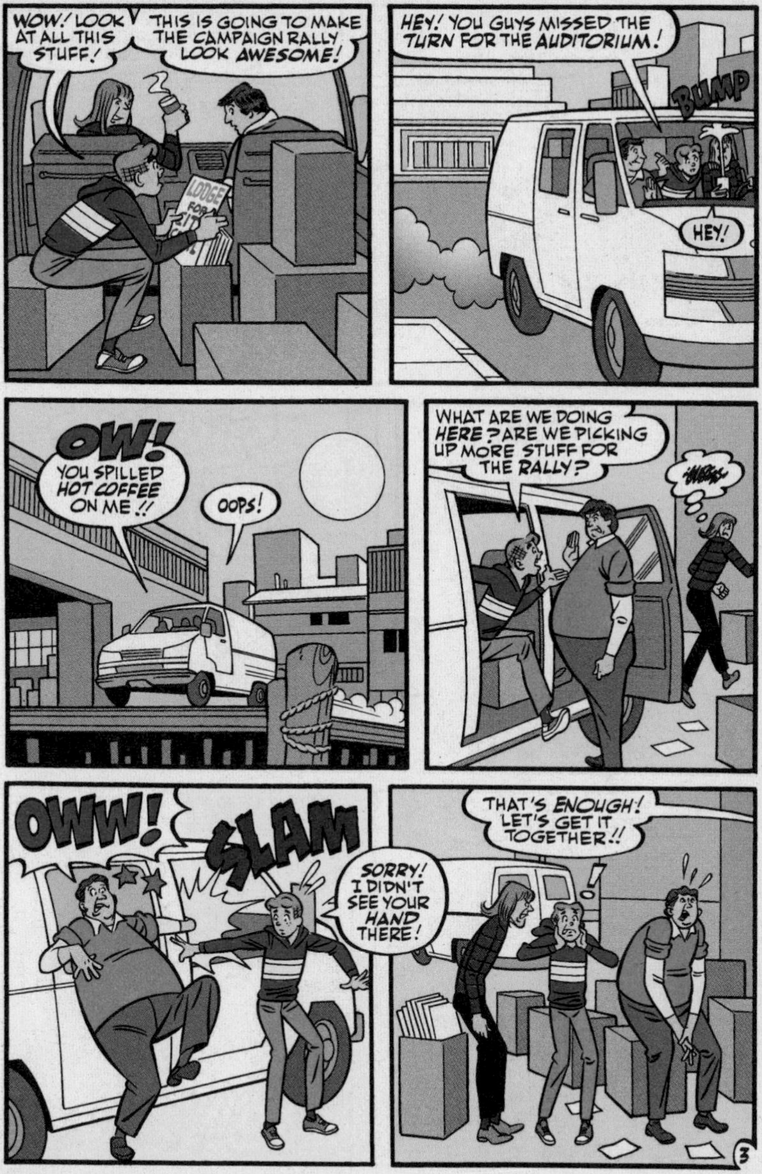
WOW! LOOK AT ALL THIS STUFF!
THIS IS GOING TO MAKE THE CAMPAIGN RALLY LOOK AWESOME!
HEY! YOU GUYS MISSED THE TURN FOR THE AUDITORIUM!
BUMP
HEY!
OW! YOU SPILLED HOT COFFEE ON ME!!
OOPS!
WHAT ARE WE DOING HERE? ARE WE PICKING UP MORE STUFF FOR THE RALLY?
OWW!
SLAM
SORRY! I DIDN'T SEE YOUR HAND THERE!
THAT'S ENOUGH! LET'S GET IT TOGETHER!!
3

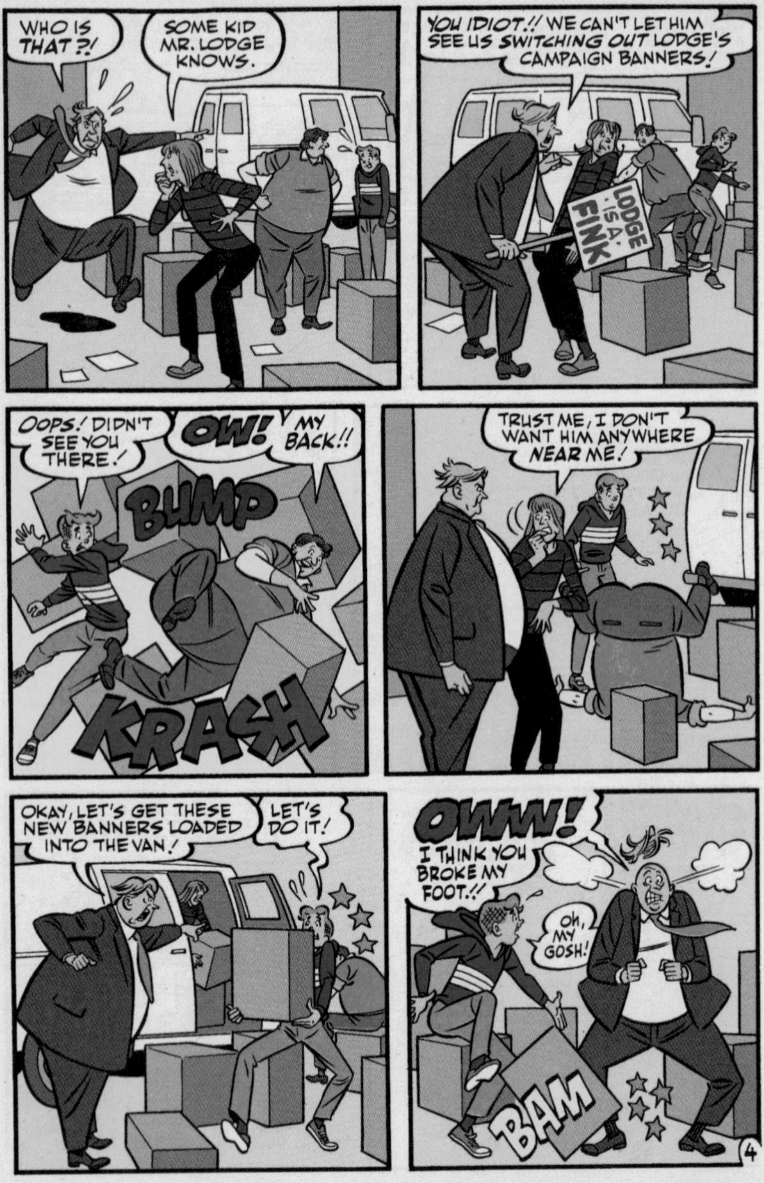
WHO IS THAT?!
SOME KID MR. LODGE KNOWS.
YOU IDIOT!! WE CAN'T LET HIM SEE US SWITCHING OUT LODGE'S CAMPAIGN BANNERS!
LODGE IS A FINK
OOPS! DIDN'T SEE YOU THERE!
OW! MY BACK!!
BUMP
KRASH
TRUST ME, I DON'T WANT HIM ANYWHERE NEAR ME!
OKAY, LET'S GET THESE NEW BANNERS LOADED INTO THE VAN!
LET'S DO IT!
OWW!
I THINK YOU BROKE MY FOOT!!
OH, MY GOSH!
BAM
4

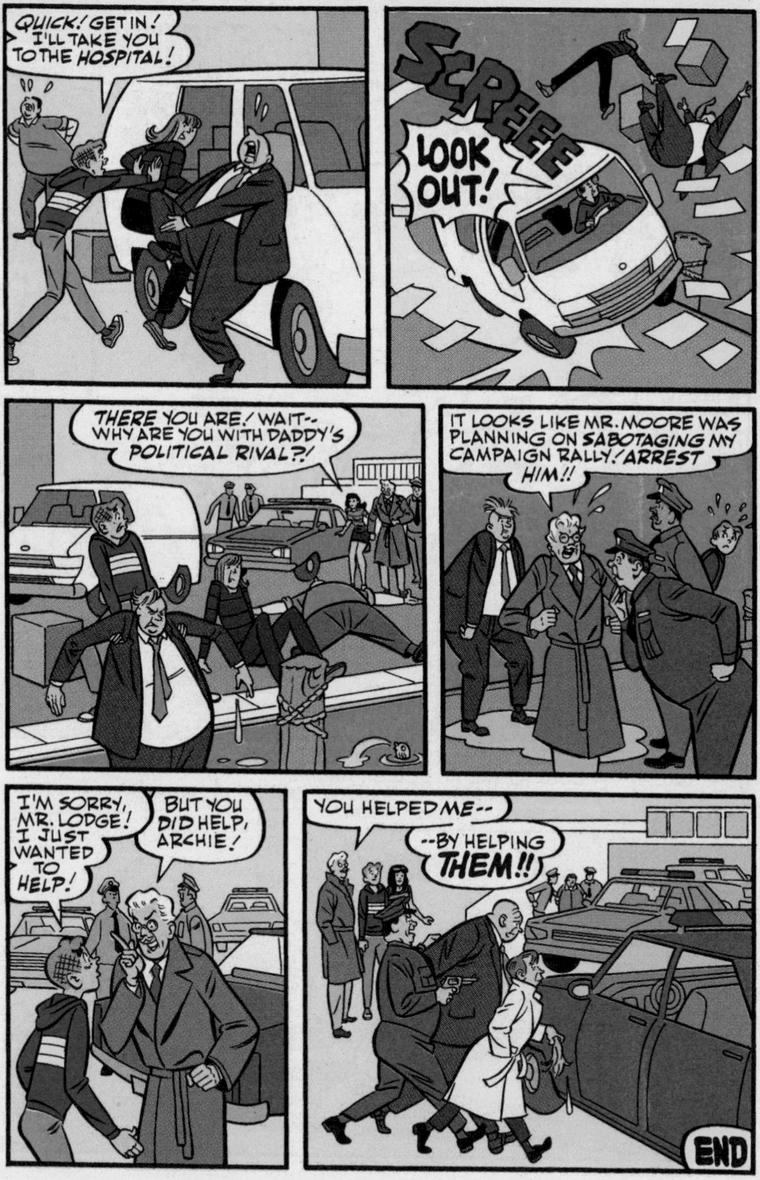
QUICK! GET IN! I'LL TAKE YOU TO THE HOSPITAL!
SCREEE
LOOK OUT!
THERE YOU ARE! WAIT-- WHY ARE YOU WITH DADDY'S POLITICAL RIVAL?!
IT LOOKS LIKE MR. MOORE WAS PLANNING ON SABOTAGING MY CAMPAIGN RALLY! ARREST HIM!!
I'M SORRY, MR. LODGE! I JUST WANTED TO HELP!
BUT YOU DID HELP, ARCHIE!
YOU HELPED ME--
--BY HELPING THEM!!
END

Archie in "NOTHING TO SNEEZE AT!"

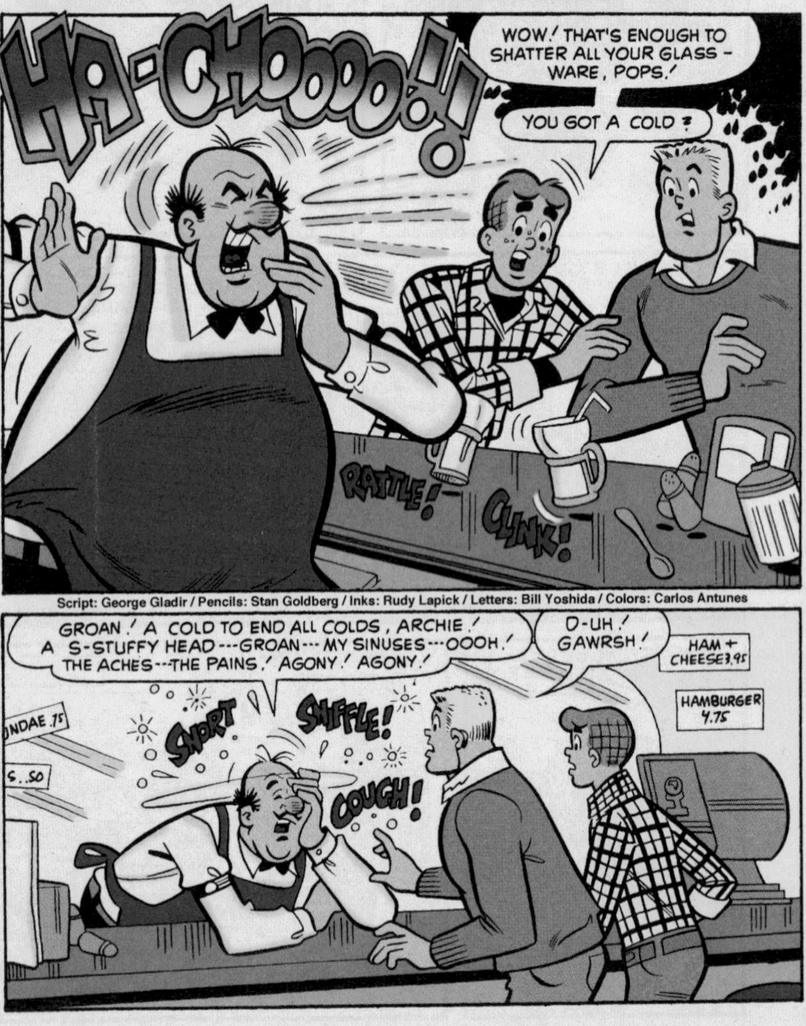
HA-CHOOOOO!!
WOW! THAT'S ENOUGH TO SHATTER ALL YOUR GLASS - WARE, POPS!
YOU GOT A COLD ?
RATTLE!
CLINK!
GROAN! A COLD TO END ALL COLDS, ARCHIE! A S-STUFFY HEAD---GROAN--- MY SINUSES---OOOH! THE ACHES--THE PAINS! AGONY! AGONY!
O-UH! GAWRSH!
HAM + CHEESE 3.95
HAMBURGER 4.75
NDAE .75
S..50
SNORT
SNIFFLE!
COUGH!

Script: George Gladir / Pencils: Stan Goldberg / Inks: Rudy Lapick / Letters: Bill Yoshida / Colors: Carlos Antunes

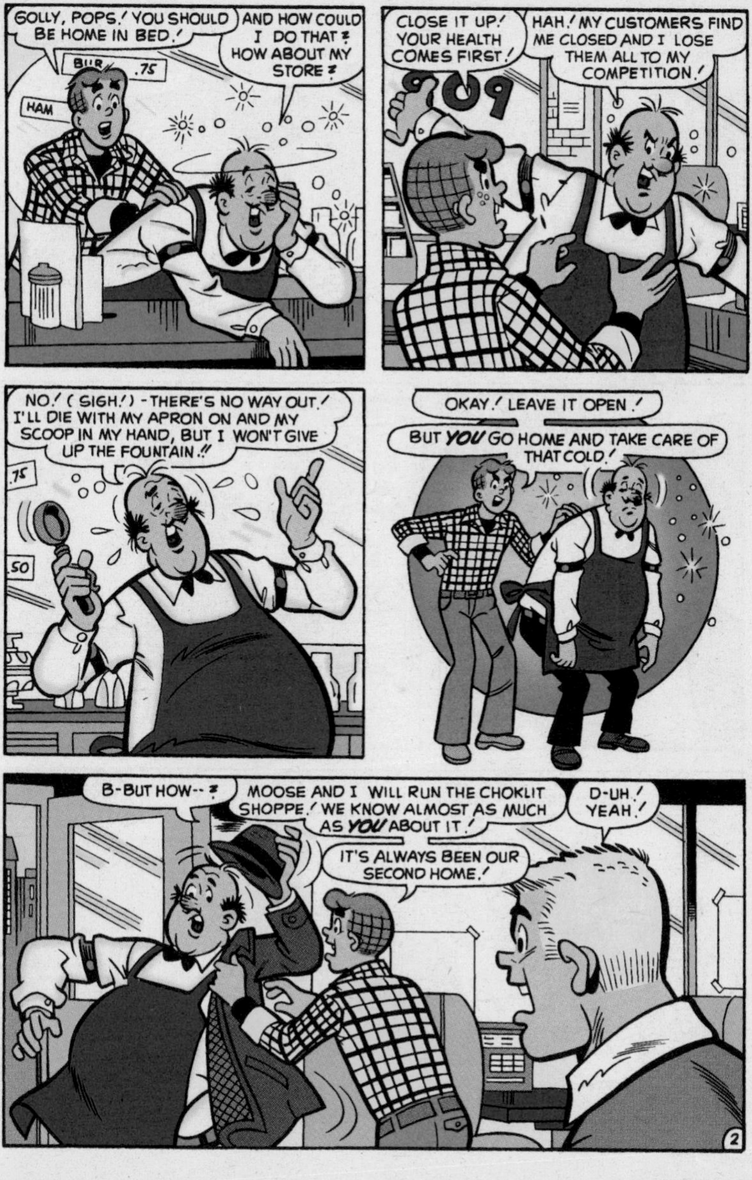
GOLLY, POPS! YOU SHOULD BE HOME IN BED!
AND HOW COULD I DO THAT? HOW ABOUT MY STORE?
BUR
.75
HAM
CLOSE IT UP! YOUR HEALTH COMES FIRST!
HAH! MY CUSTOMERS FIND ME CLOSED AND I LOSE THEM ALL TO MY COMPETITION!
POP
NO! (SIGH!) - THERE'S NO WAY OUT! I'LL DIE WITH MY APRON ON AND MY SCOOP IN MY HAND, BUT I WON'T GIVE UP THE FOUNTAIN!!
.75
.50
OKAY! LEAVE IT OPEN!
BUT YOU GO HOME AND TAKE CARE OF THAT COLD!
B-BUT HOW--?
MOOSE AND I WILL RUN THE CHOKLIT SHOPPE! WE KNOW ALMOST AS MUCH AS YOU ABOUT IT!
D-UH! YEAH!
IT'S ALWAYS BEEN OUR SECOND HOME!

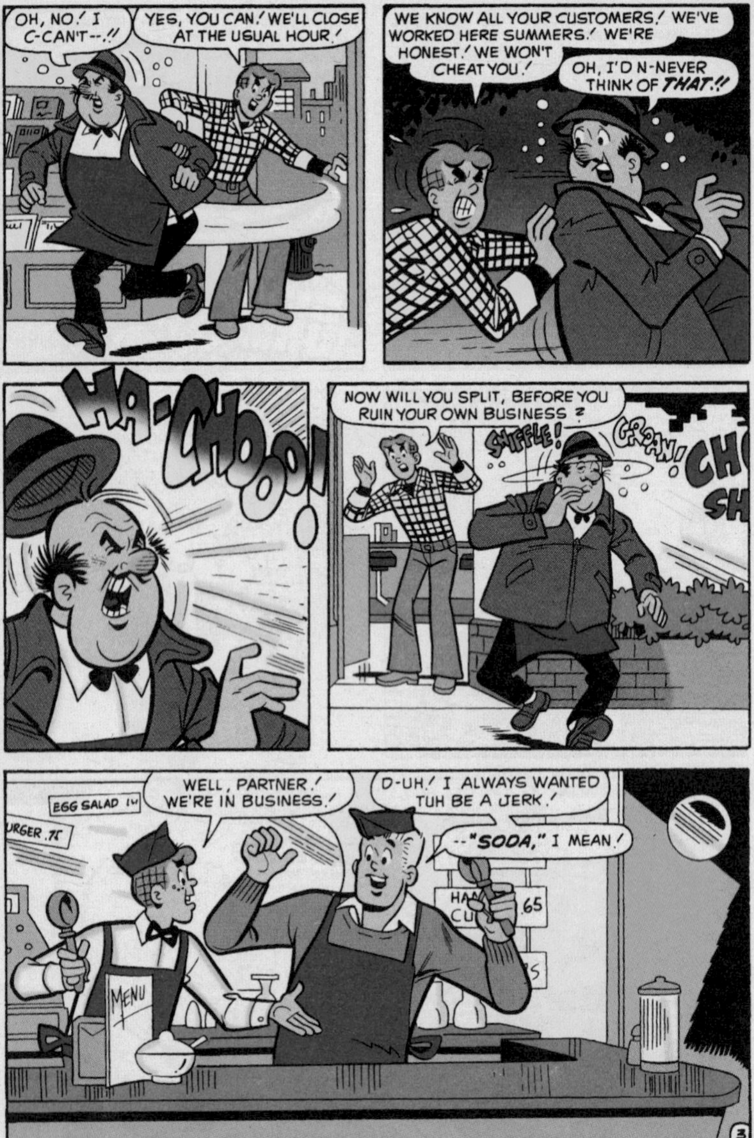
OH, NO! I C-CAN'T--!!
YES, YOU CAN! WE'LL CLOSE AT THE USUAL HOUR!
WE KNOW ALL YOUR CUSTOMERS! WE'VE WORKED HERE SUMMERS! WE'RE HONEST! WE WON'T CHEAT YOU!
OH, I'D N-NEVER THINK OF THAT!!
HA-CHOOO!
NOW WILL YOU SPLIT, BEFORE YOU RUIN YOUR OWN BUSINESS?
SNIFFLE!
GROAN!
EGG SALAD
WELL, PARTNER! WE'RE IN BUSINESS!
D-UH! I ALWAYS WANTED TUH BE A JERK!
--"SODA," I MEAN!
MENU
3

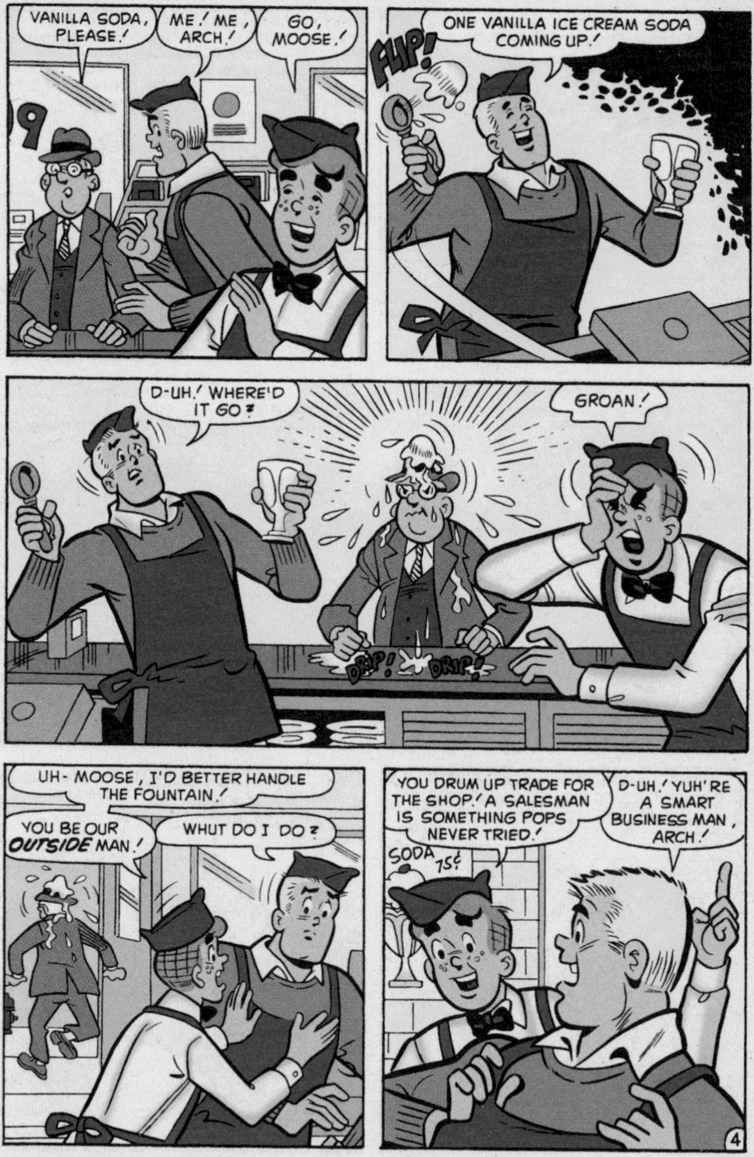
VANILLA SODA, PLEASE.!
ME.! ME, ARCH.!
GO, MOOSE.!
FLIP!
ONE VANILLA ICE CREAM SODA COMING UP.!
D-UH.! WHERE'D IT GO?
GROAN.!
DRIP! DRIP!
UH- MOOSE, I'D BETTER HANDLE THE FOUNTAIN.!
YOU BE OUR OUTSIDE MAN.!
WHUT DO I DO?
YOU DRUM UP TRADE FOR THE SHOP.! A SALESMAN IS SOMETHING POPS NEVER TRIED.!
D-UH.! YUH'RE A SMART BUSINESS MAN, ARCH.!
SODA 75¢
4

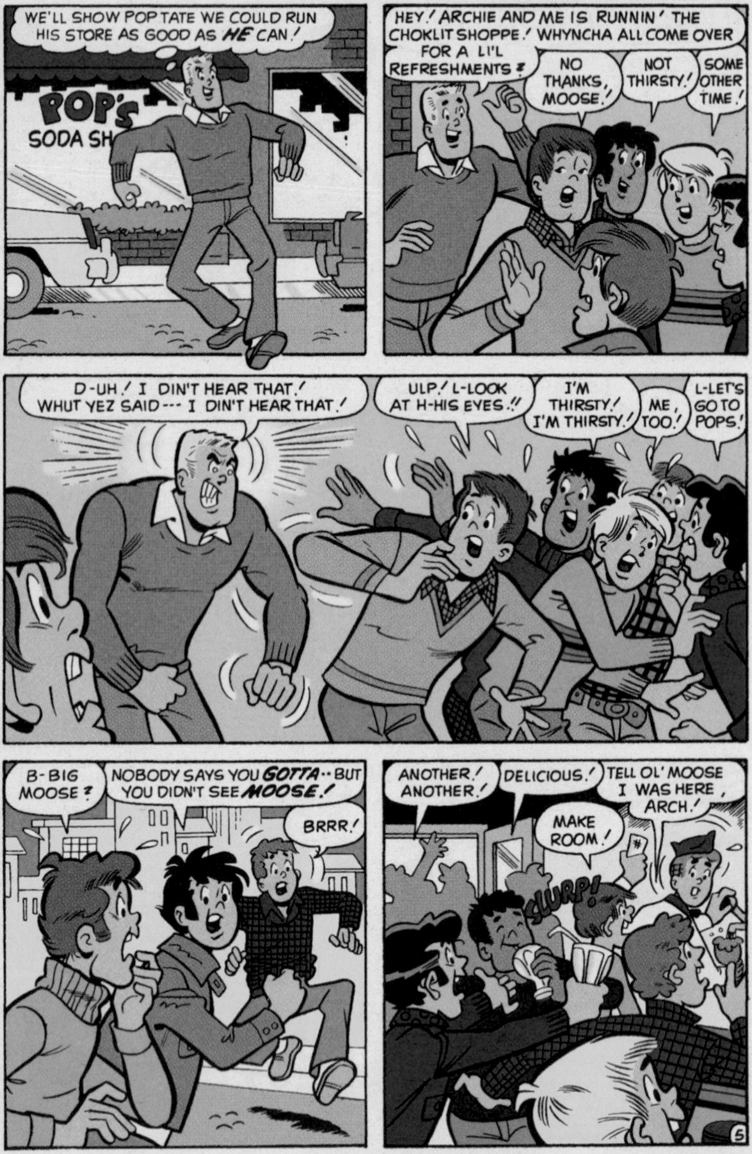
WE'LL SHOW POP TATE WE COULD RUN HIS STORE AS GOOD AS HE CAN!
POP'S SODA SH
HEY! ARCHIE AND ME IS RUNNIN' THE CHOKLIT SHOPPE! WHYNCHA ALL COME OVER FOR A LI'L REFRESHMENTS?
NO THANKS, MOOSE.
NOT THIRSTY!
SOME OTHER TIME!
D-UH! I DIN'T HEAR THAT! WHUT YEZ SAID --- I DIN'T HEAR THAT!
ULP! L-LOOK AT H-HIS EYES!!
I'M THIRSTY! I'M THIRSTY!
ME, TOO!
L-LET'S GO TO POPS!
B-BIG MOOSE?
NOBODY SAYS YOU GOTTA.. BUT YOU DIDN'T SEE MOOSE!
BRRR!
ANOTHER! ANOTHER!
DELICIOUS!
TELL OL' MOOSE I WAS HERE, ARCH!
MAKE ROOM!
SLURP!

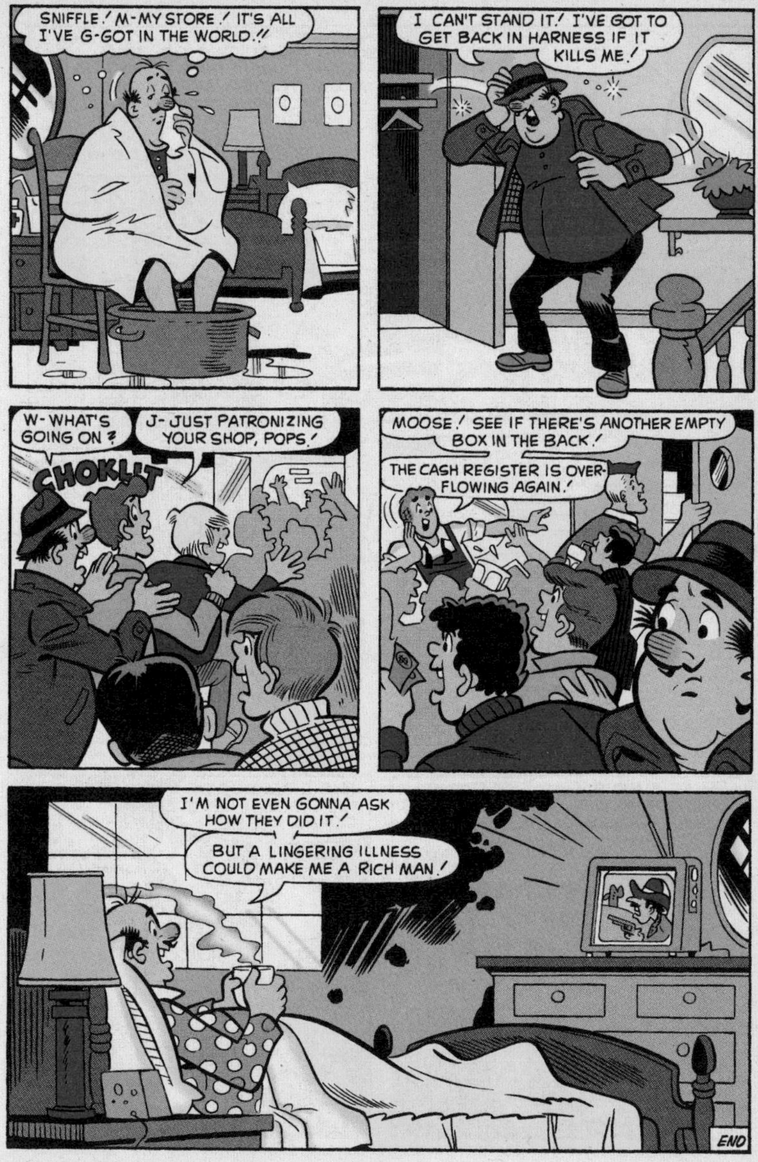

SNIFFLE! M-MY STORE! IT'S ALL I'VE G-GOT IN THE WORLD.!!
I CAN'T STAND IT! I'VE GOT TO GET BACK IN HARNESS IF IT KILLS ME!
W-WHAT'S GOING ON ?
J-JUST PATRONIZING YOUR SHOP, POPS!
CHOKLIT
MOOSE! SEE IF THERE'S ANOTHER EMPTY BOX IN THE BACK!
THE CASH REGISTER IS OVER-FLOWING AGAIN!
I'M NOT EVEN GONNA ASK HOW THEY DID IT!
BUT A LINGERING ILLNESS COULD MAKE ME A RICH MAN!
END

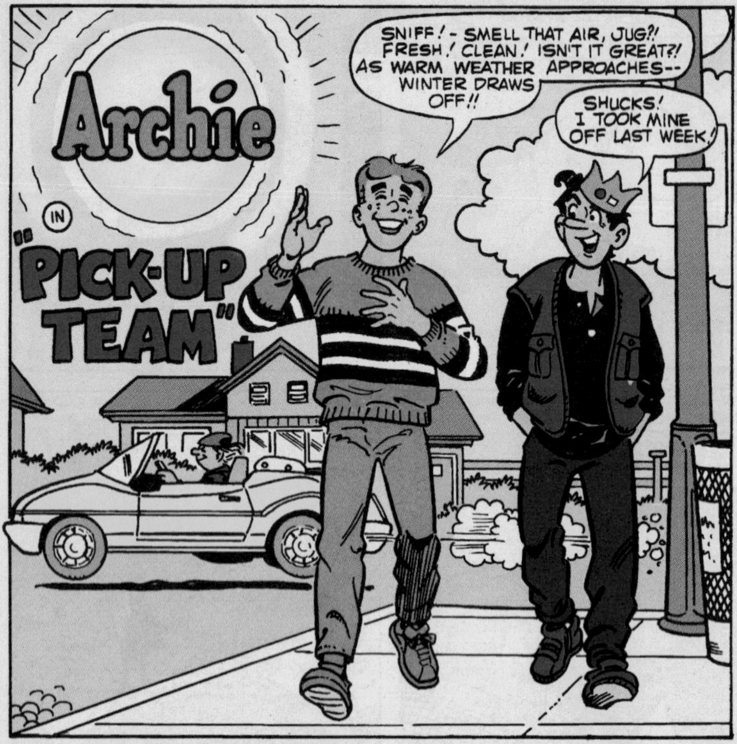
Archie
IN
"PICK-UP TEAM"
SNIFF! - SMELL THAT AIR, JUG?! FRESH! CLEAN! ISN'T IT GREAT?! AS WARM WEATHER APPROACHES-- WINTER DRAWS OFF!!
SHUCKS! I TOOK MINE OFF LAST WEEK!

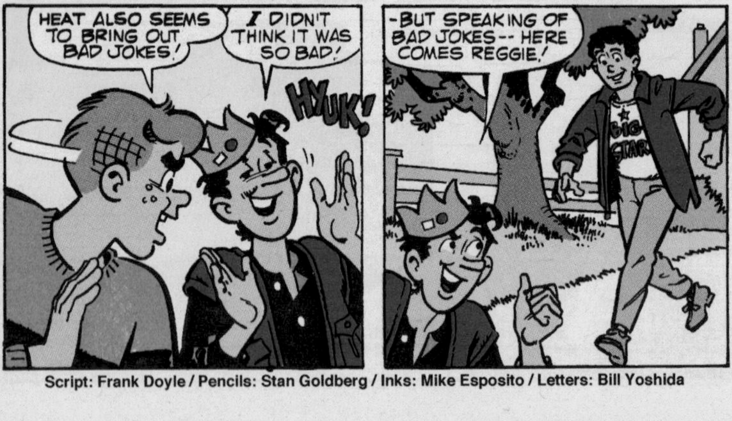
HEAT ALSO SEEMS TO BRING OUT BAD JOKES!
I DIDN'T THINK IT WAS SO BAD!
HYUK!
-BUT SPEAKING OF BAD JOKES-- HERE COMES REGGIE!
BIG STAR

Script: Frank Doyle / Pencils: Stan Goldberg / Inks: Mike Esposito / Letters: Bill Yoshida

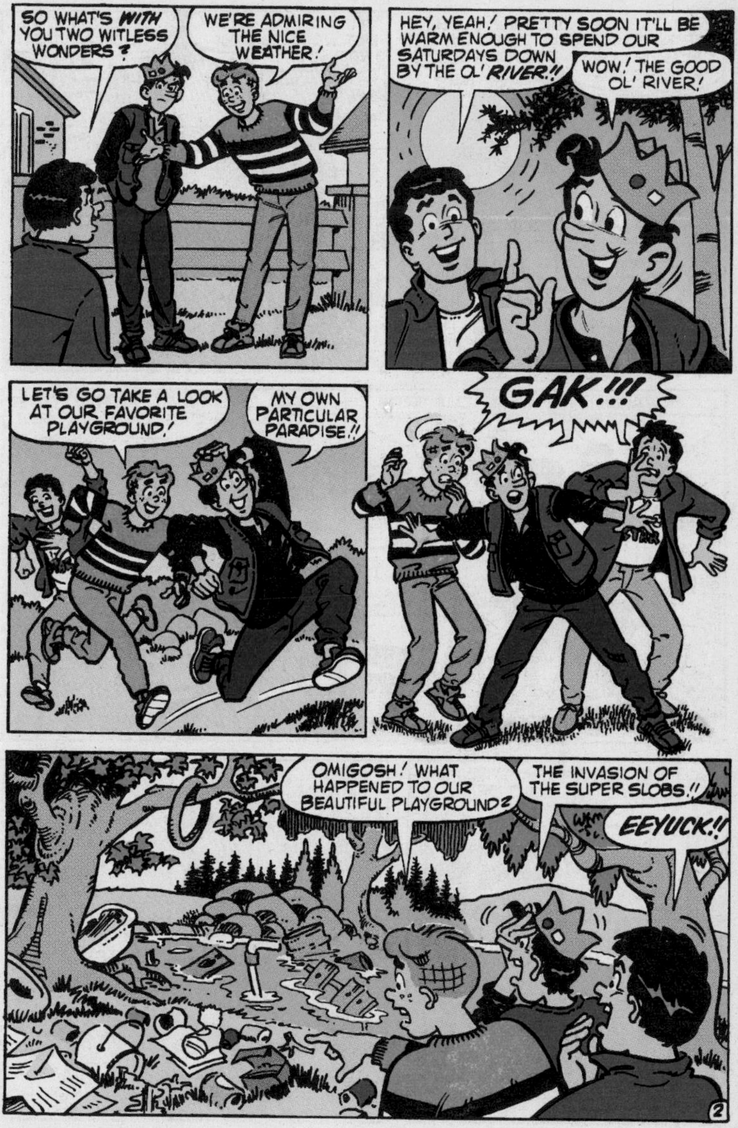
SO WHAT'S WITH YOU TWO WITLESS WONDERS?
WE'RE ADMIRING THE NICE WEATHER!
HEY, YEAH! PRETTY SOON IT'LL BE WARM ENOUGH TO SPEND OUR SATURDAYS DOWN BY THE OL' RIVER!!
WOW! THE GOOD OL' RIVER!
LET'S GO TAKE A LOOK AT OUR FAVORITE PLAYGROUND!
MY OWN PARTICULAR PARADISE!!
GAK!!!
OMIGOSH! WHAT HAPPENED TO OUR BEAUTIFUL PLAYGROUND?
THE INVASION OF THE SUPER SLOBS!!
EEYUCK!!
2

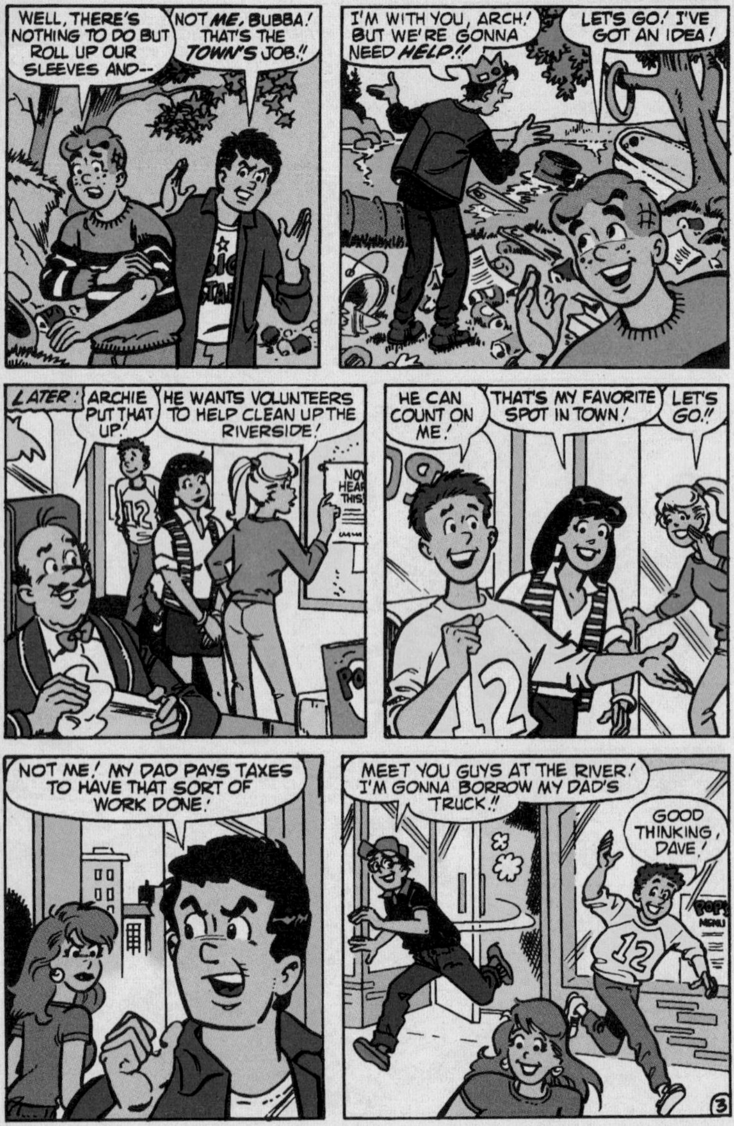
WELL, THERE'S NOTHING TO DO BUT ROLL UP OUR SLEEVES AND--
NOT ME, BUBBA! THAT'S THE TOWN'S JOB!!
I'M WITH YOU, ARCH! BUT WE'RE GONNA NEED HELP!!
LET'S GO! I'VE GOT AN IDEA!
LATER:
ARCHIE PUT THAT UP!
HE WANTS VOLUNTEERS TO HELP CLEAN UP THE RIVERSIDE!
HE CAN COUNT ON ME!
THAT'S MY FAVORITE SPOT IN TOWN!
LET'S GO!!
NOT ME! MY DAD PAYS TAXES TO HAVE THAT SORT OF WORK DONE!
MEET YOU GUYS AT THE RIVER! I'M GONNA BORROW MY DAD'S TRUCK!!
GOOD THINKING, DAVE!
3

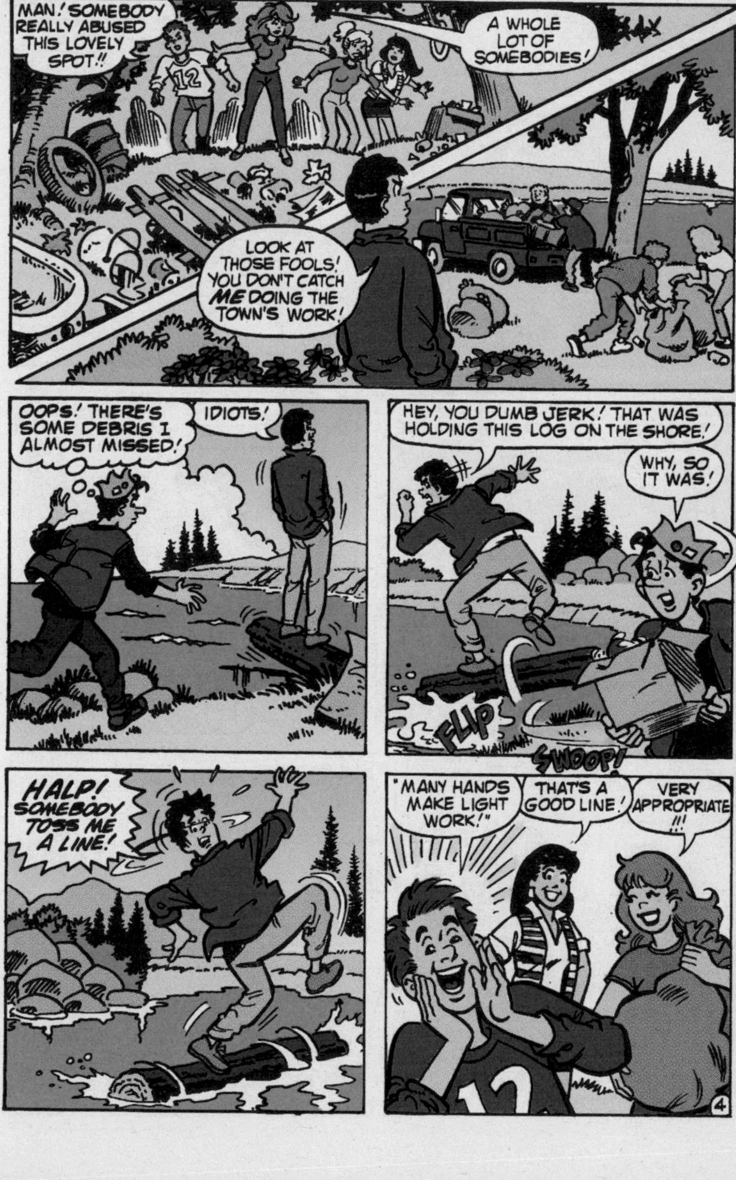
MAN! SOMEBODY REALLY ABUSED THIS LOVELY SPOT!!
A WHOLE LOT OF SOMEBODIES!
LOOK AT THOSE FOOLS! YOU DON'T CATCH ME DOING THE TOWN'S WORK!
OOPS! THERE'S SOME DEBRIS I ALMOST MISSED!
IDIOTS!
HEY, YOU DUMB JERK! THAT WAS HOLDING THIS LOG ON THE SHORE!
WHY, SO IT WAS!
FLIP
SWOOP!
HALP! SOMEBODY TOSS ME A LINE!
"MANY HANDS MAKE LIGHT WORK!"
THAT'S A GOOD LINE!
VERY APPROPRIATE !!!
4

ACK! I'M LOSING MY BALANCE!!
BIG STAR
REGGIE WAS UNBALANCED!
SO WHAT ELSE IS NEW?
SPLASH!
WELL, GUYS! WE DID A GOOD JOB! THE PLACE LOOKS GREAT!
JUST ONE MORE UGLY PIECE OF TRASH AND WE'RE DONE!
SOMETIMES I WONDER AT THE THINGS PEOPLE THROW AWAY - BUT THIS ONE I UNDERSTAND!
SPUT ..
GLUB! GLUB!
BRING ON THE SUMMERTIME! WE'RE READY!
PARADISE REGAINED!
HUMPH! THE WORLD IS FULL OF WISE GUYS!
END

Archie in "MATCH GAME"

Script: M. Pellowski / Pencils: T. Kennedy / Inks: K. Selig / Letters: B. Yoshida

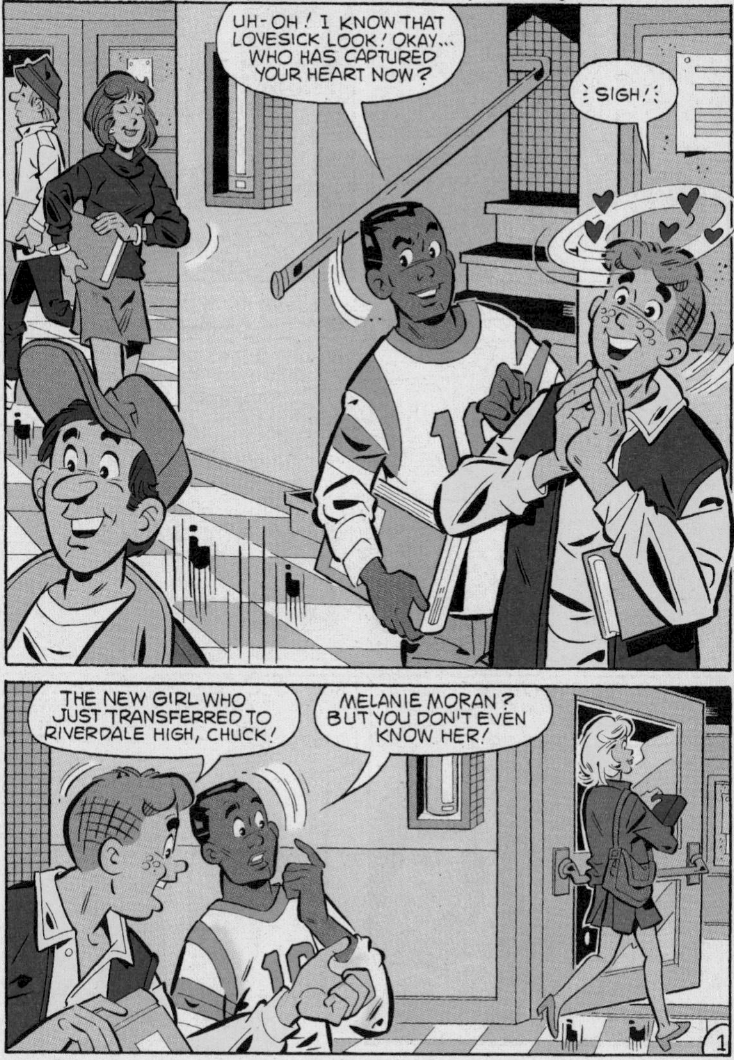

UH-OH! I KNOW THAT LOVESICK LOOK! OKAY... WHO HAS CAPTURED YOUR HEART NOW?
SIGH!
THE NEW GIRL WHO JUST TRANSFERRED TO RIVERDALE HIGH, CHUCK!
MELANIE MORAN? BUT YOU DON'T EVEN KNOW HER!

OH, YES I DO! I KNOW THAT SHE'S BEAUTIFUL, SHE'S WONDERFUL... AND SHE'S OUT OF MY REACH... ∫ SIGH! ∫

OUT OF YOUR REACH? WHAT DO YOU MEAN?

UNFORTUNATELY WE HAVE NOTHING IN COMMON!

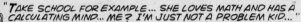

"TAKE SCHOOL FOR EXAMPLE... SHE LOVES MATH AND HAS A CALCULATING MIND... ME? I'M JUST NOT A PROBLEM KID..."

X = 28!

CORRECT! NOW, ANY QUESTIONS ABOUT 'Y'?

YES! WHY DID I TAKE THIS CLASS?

SO? THERE ARE OTHER THINGS YOU CAN TALK ABOUT BESIDES MATH!

TRUE!

HOW ABOUT MUSIC? WHY NOT ASK HER TO A CONCERT?

I THOUGHT ABOUT DOING THAT!

2

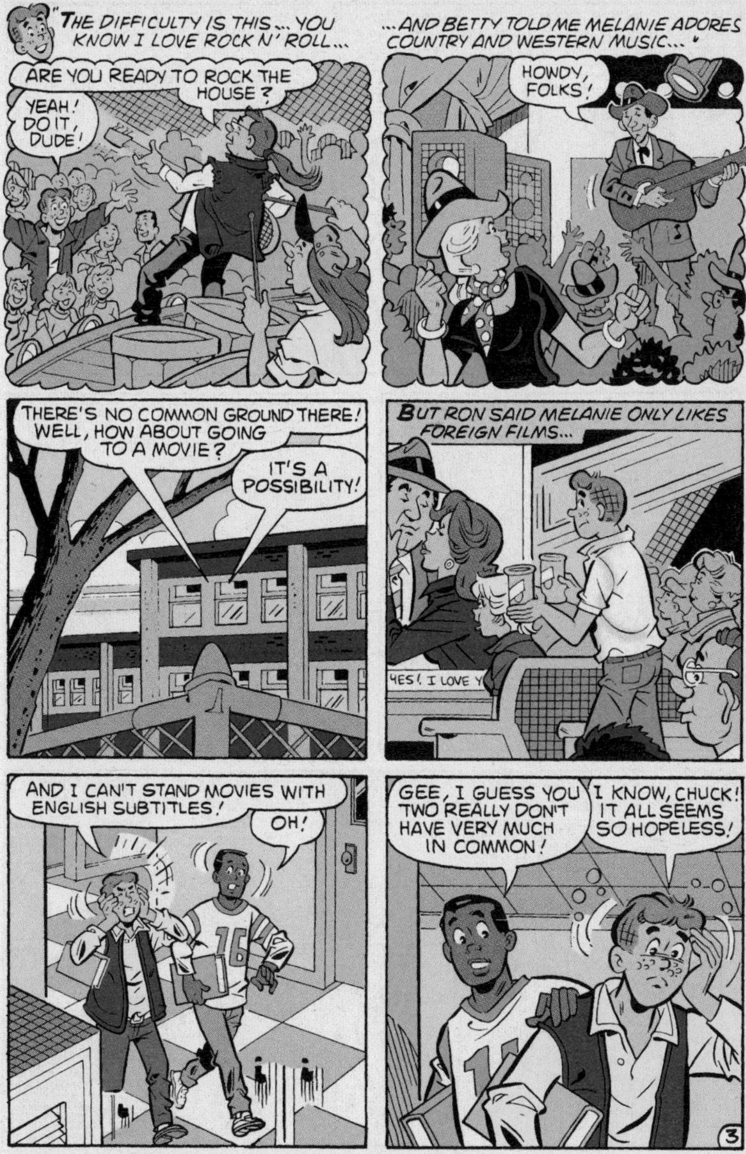
"THE DIFFICULTY IS THIS... YOU KNOW I LOVE ROCK N' ROLL...
ARE YOU READY TO ROCK THE HOUSE?
YEAH! DO IT, DUDE!
...AND BETTY TOLD ME MELANIE ADORES COUNTRY AND WESTERN MUSIC..."
HOWDY, FOLKS!
THERE'S NO COMMON GROUND THERE! WELL, HOW ABOUT GOING TO A MOVIE?
IT'S A POSSIBILITY!
BUT RON SAID MELANIE ONLY LIKES FOREIGN FILMS...
YES! I LOVE Y
AND I CAN'T STAND MOVIES WITH ENGLISH SUBTITLES!
OH!
16
GEE, I GUESS YOU TWO REALLY DON'T HAVE VERY MUCH IN COMMON!
I KNOW, CHUCK! IT ALL SEEMS SO HOPELESS!
3

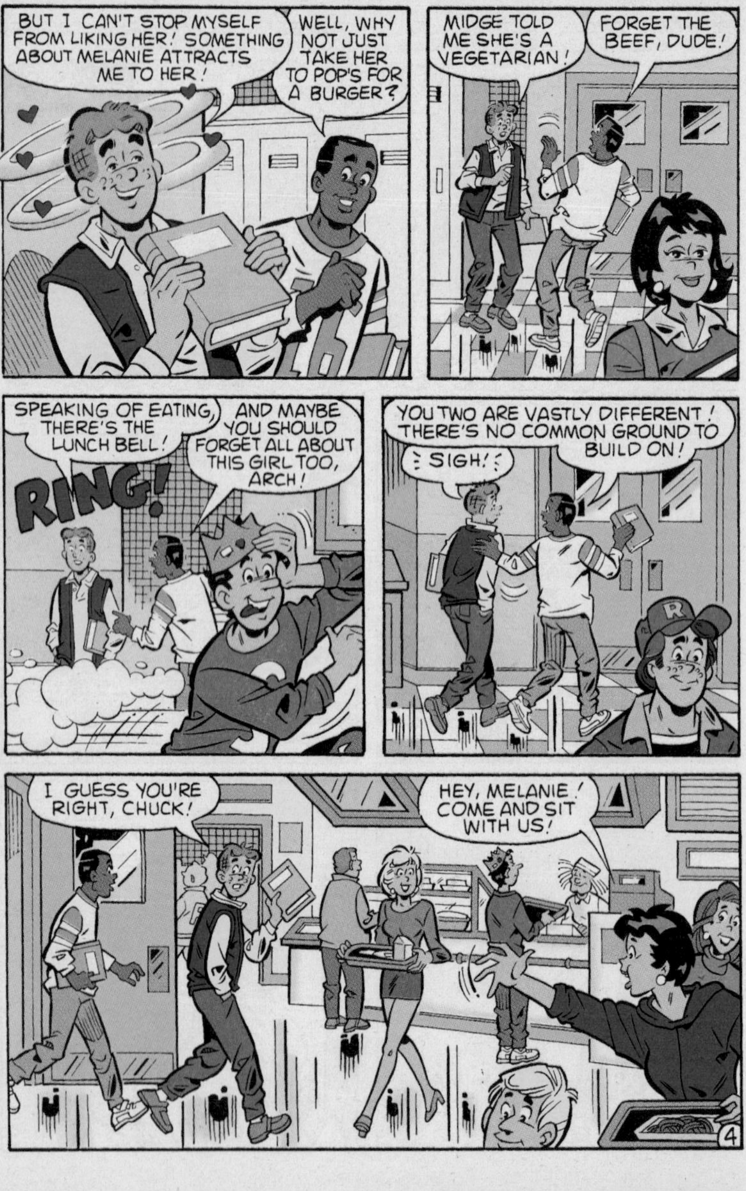
BUT I CAN'T STOP MYSELF FROM LIKING HER! SOMETHING ABOUT MELANIE ATTRACTS ME TO HER!
WELL, WHY NOT JUST TAKE HER TO POP'S FOR A BURGER?
MIDGE TOLD ME SHE'S A VEGETARIAN!
FORGET THE BEEF, DUDE!
SPEAKING OF EATING, THERE'S THE LUNCH BELL!
RING!
AND MAYBE YOU SHOULD FORGET ALL ABOUT THIS GIRL TOO, ARCH!
YOU TWO ARE VASTLY DIFFERENT! THERE'S NO COMMON GROUND TO BUILD ON!
SIGH!
I GUESS YOU'RE RIGHT, CHUCK!
HEY, MELANIE! COME AND SIT WITH US!
4

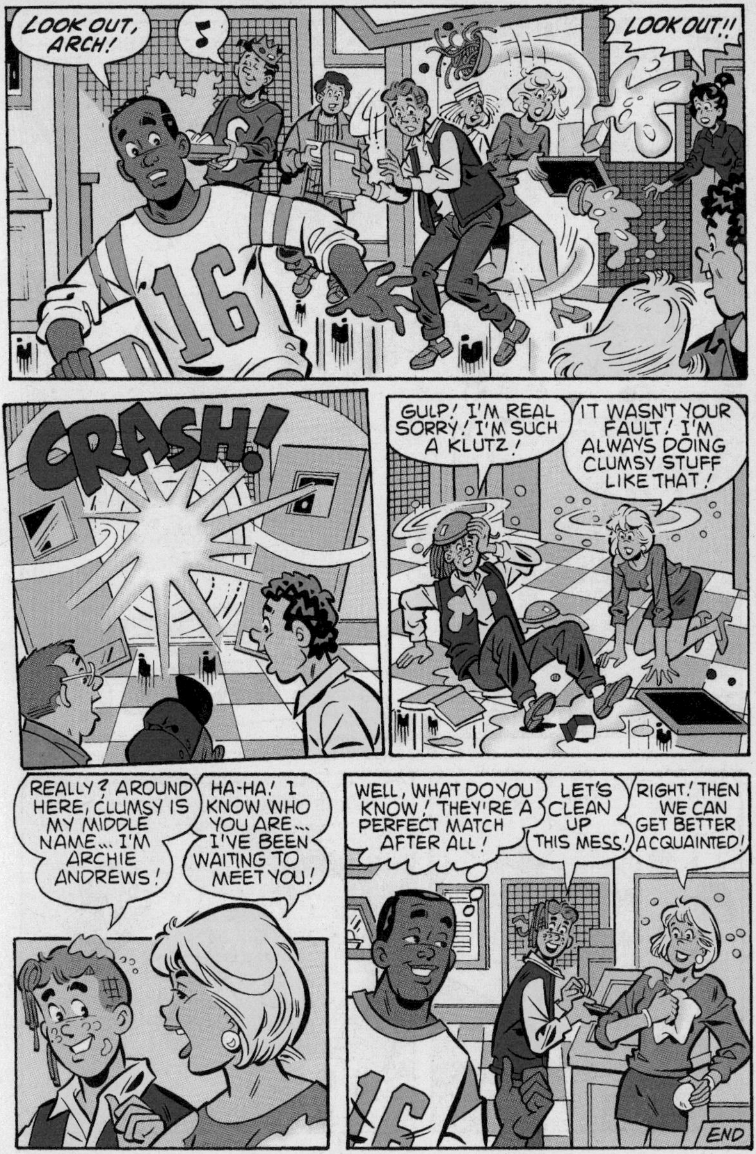
LOOK OUT, ARCH!
♪
LOOK OUT!!
CRASH!
GULP! I'M REAL SORRY! I'M SUCH A KLUTZ!
IT WASN'T YOUR FAULT! I'M ALWAYS DOING CLUMSY STUFF LIKE THAT!
REALLY? AROUND HERE, CLUMSY IS MY MIDDLE NAME... I'M ARCHIE ANDREWS!
HA-HA! I KNOW WHO YOU ARE... I'VE BEEN WAITING TO MEET YOU!
WELL, WHAT DO YOU KNOW! THEY'RE A PERFECT MATCH AFTER ALL!
LET'S CLEAN UP THIS MESS!
RIGHT! THEN WE CAN GET BETTER ACQUAINTED!
END

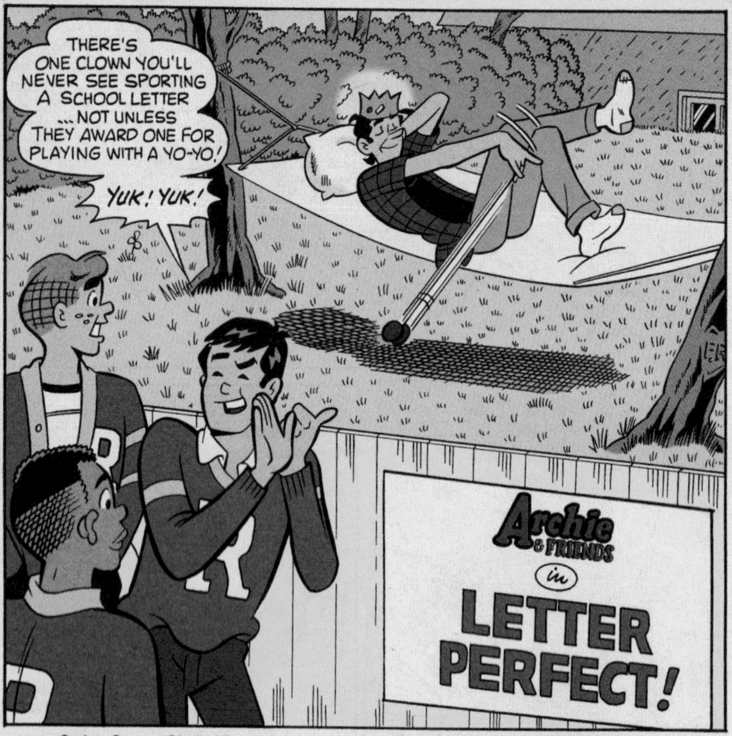
THERE'S ONE CLOWN YOU'LL NEVER SEE SPORTING A SCHOOL LETTER ...NOT UNLESS THEY AWARD ONE FOR PLAYING WITH A YO-YO!
YUK! YUK!
Archie & FRIENDS in
LETTER PERFECT!

Script: George Gladir / Pencils: Fernando Ruiz / Inks: Jim Amash / Letters: Bill Yoshida

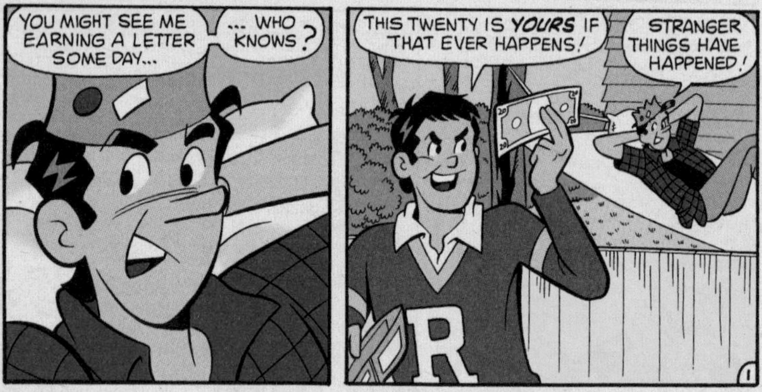
YOU MIGHT SEE ME EARNING A LETTER SOME DAY...
... WHO KNOWS?
THIS TWENTY IS YOURS IF THAT EVER HAPPENS!
STRANGER THINGS HAVE HAPPENED!
1

COACH, I THINK I COULD BE YOUR NEXT FIELD GOAL KICKER!
WE'LL GIVE YOU A SHOT AT IT, JUG!
GO IVERDALE!
FOOTBA TRY-OUT TODAY!
DENNY, HOLD THE BALL FOR HIM WHILE HE TRIES TO KICK A FIELD GOAL!
I'LL BE DARNED! IT'S SAILING RIGHT THROUGH THE UPRIGHTS!
GO CHAMPS
RIVERD
GO!
THAT WAS HIS SHOE, COACH!
THE BALL IS STILL HERE!
NEXT CANDIDATE!
2

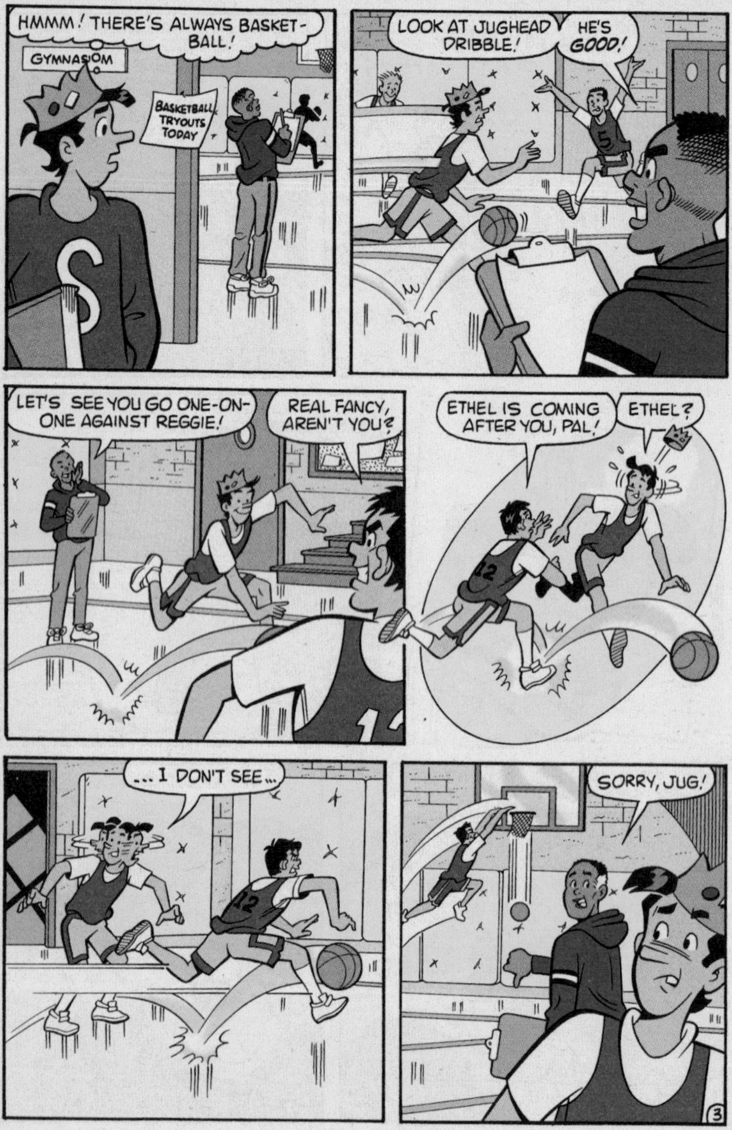
HMMM! THERE'S ALWAYS BASKET-BALL!
GYMNASIUM
BASKETBALL TRYOUTS TODAY
LOOK AT JUGHEAD DRIBBLE!
HE'S GOOD!
LET'S SEE YOU GO ONE-ON-ONE AGAINST REGGIE!
REAL FANCY, AREN'T YOU?
ETHEL IS COMING AFTER YOU, PAL!
ETHEL?
... I DON'T SEE...
SORRY, JUG!
3

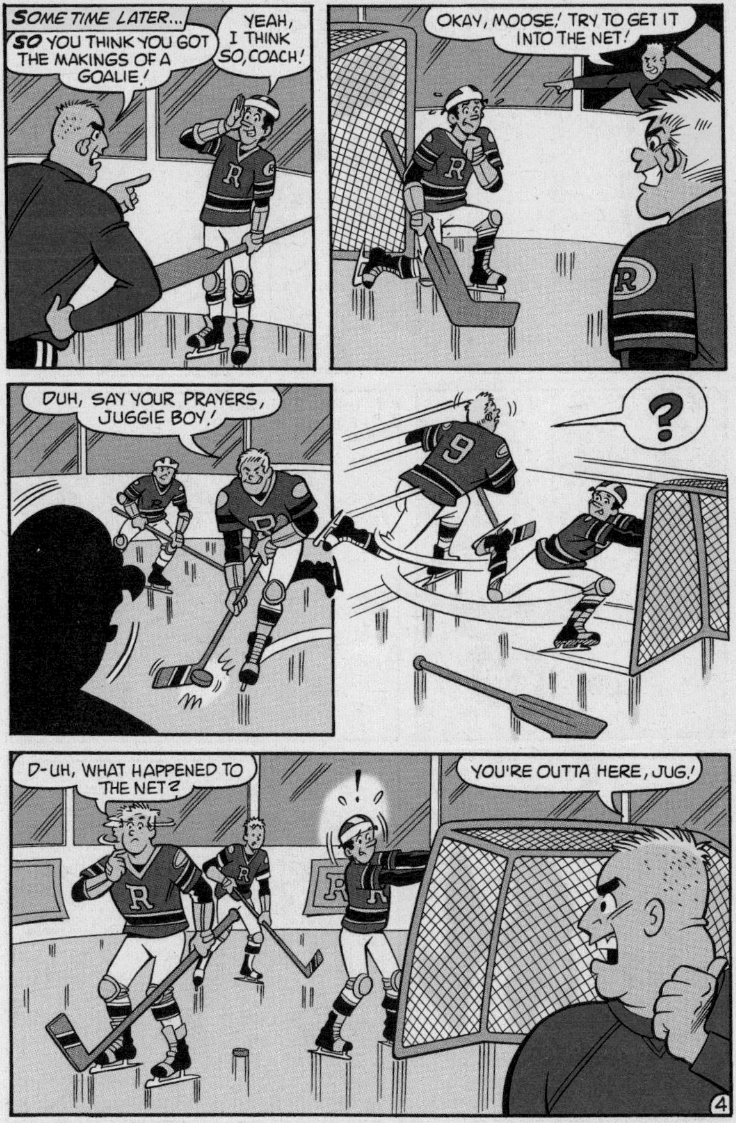

SOME TIME LATER...
SO YOU THINK YOU GOT THE MAKINGS OF A GOALIE!
YEAH, I THINK SO, COACH!
OKAY, MOOSE! TRY TO GET IT INTO THE NET!
DUH, SAY YOUR PRAYERS, JUGGIE BOY!
?
D-UH, WHAT HAPPENED TO THE NET?
!
YOU'RE OUTTA HERE, JUG!
4

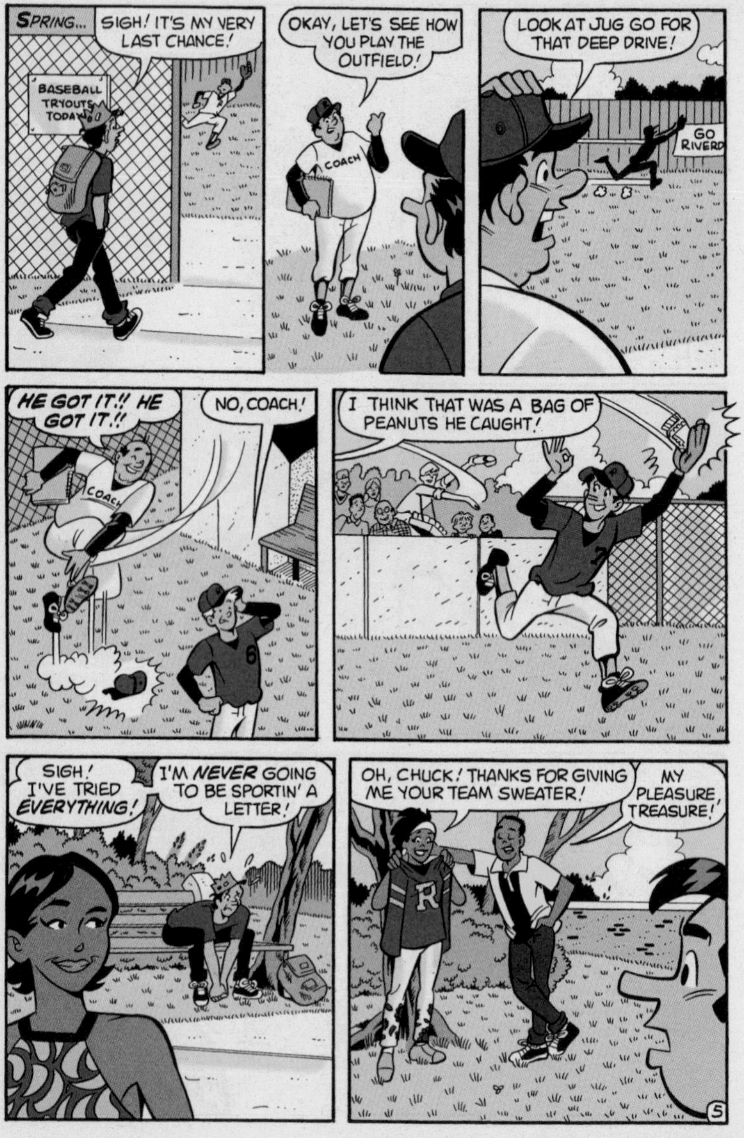
SPRING...
SIGH! IT'S MY VERY LAST CHANCE!
BASEBALL TRYOUTS TODAY
OKAY, LET'S SEE HOW YOU PLAY THE OUTFIELD!
COACH
LOOK AT JUG GO FOR THAT DEEP DRIVE!
GO RIVERD
HE GOT IT!! HE GOT IT!!
NO, COACH!
I THINK THAT WAS A BAG OF PEANUTS HE CAUGHT!
SIGH! I'VE TRIED EVERYTHING!
I'M NEVER GOING TO BE SPORTIN' A LETTER!
OH, CHUCK! THANKS FOR GIVING ME YOUR TEAM SWEATER!
MY PLEASURE, TREASURE!
5

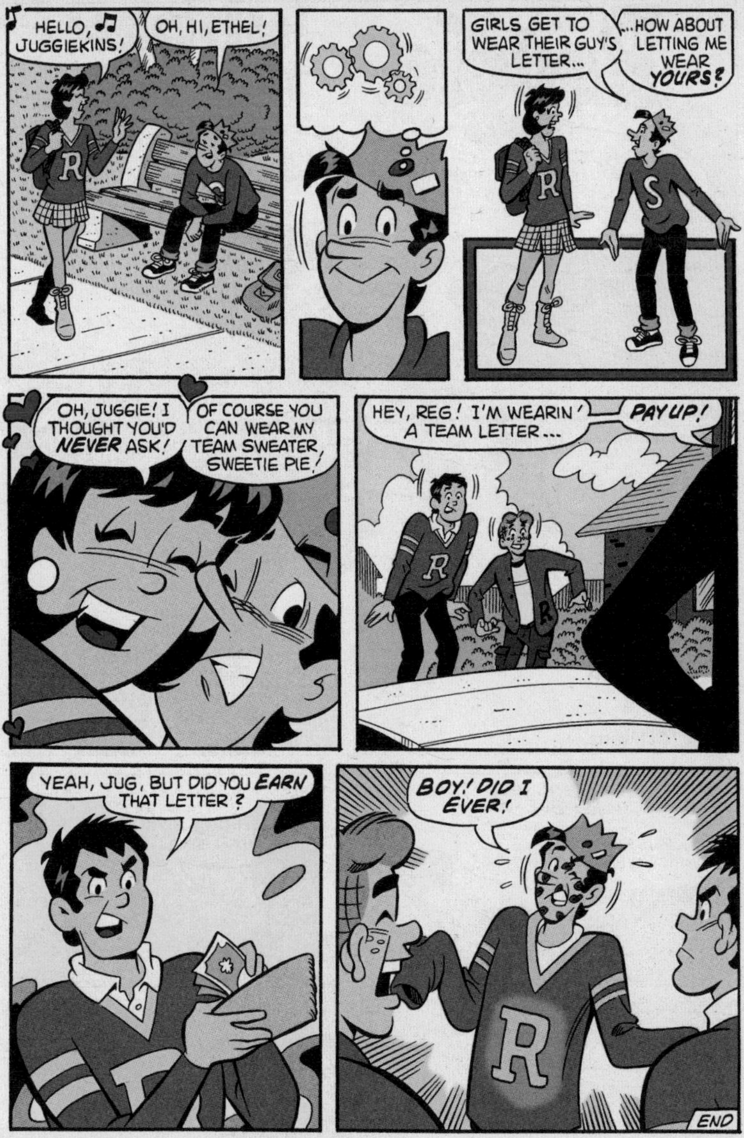
HELLO, ♫ JUGGIEKINS!
OH, HI, ETHEL!
GIRLS GET TO WEAR THEIR GUY'S LETTER...
...HOW ABOUT LETTING ME WEAR YOURS?
OH, JUGGIE! I THOUGHT YOU'D NEVER ASK!
OF COURSE YOU CAN WEAR MY TEAM SWEATER, SWEETIE PIE!
HEY, REG! I'M WEARIN' A TEAM LETTER...
PAY UP!
YEAH, JUG, BUT DID YOU EARN THAT LETTER?
BOY! DID I EVER!
END

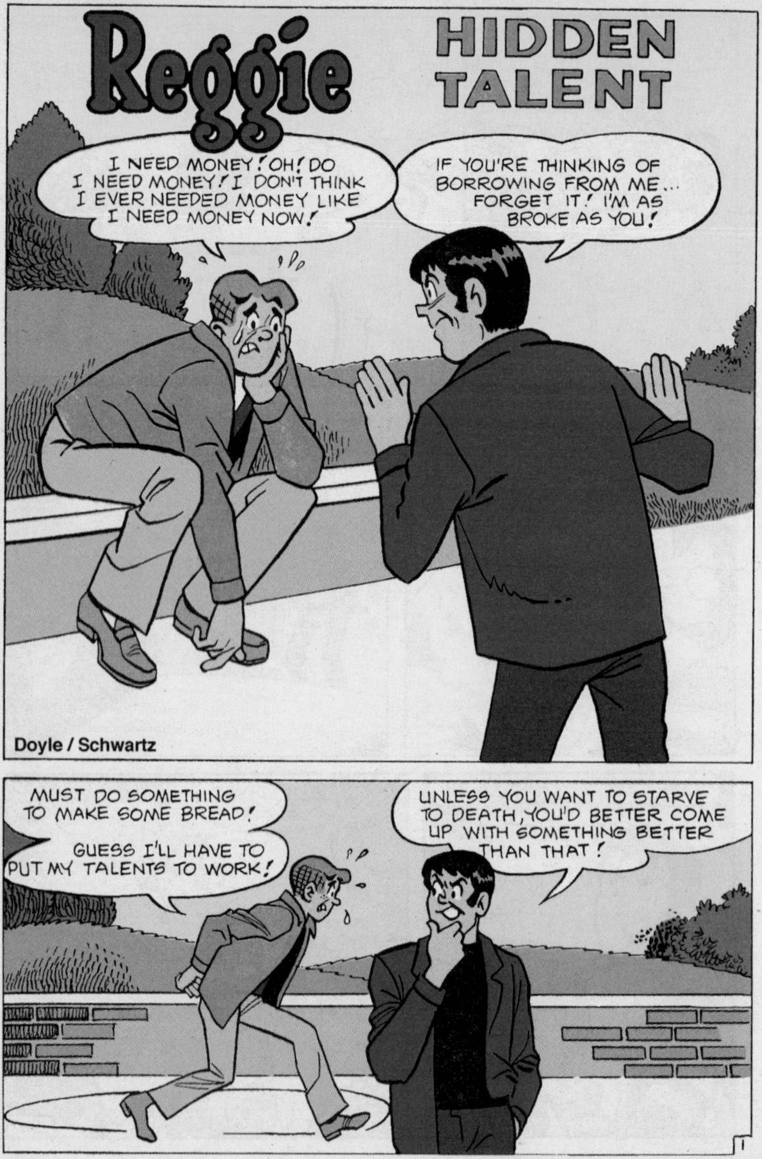
Reggie
HIDDEN TALENT
I NEED MONEY! OH! DO I NEED MONEY! I DON'T THINK I EVER NEEDED MONEY LIKE I NEED MONEY NOW!
IF YOU'RE THINKING OF BORROWING FROM ME... FORGET IT! I'M AS BROKE AS YOU!
Doyle / Schwartz
MUST DO SOMETHING TO MAKE SOME BREAD!
GUESS I'LL HAVE TO PUT MY TALENTS TO WORK!
UNLESS YOU WANT TO STARVE TO DEATH, YOU'D BETTER COME UP WITH SOMETHING BETTER THAN THAT!
1

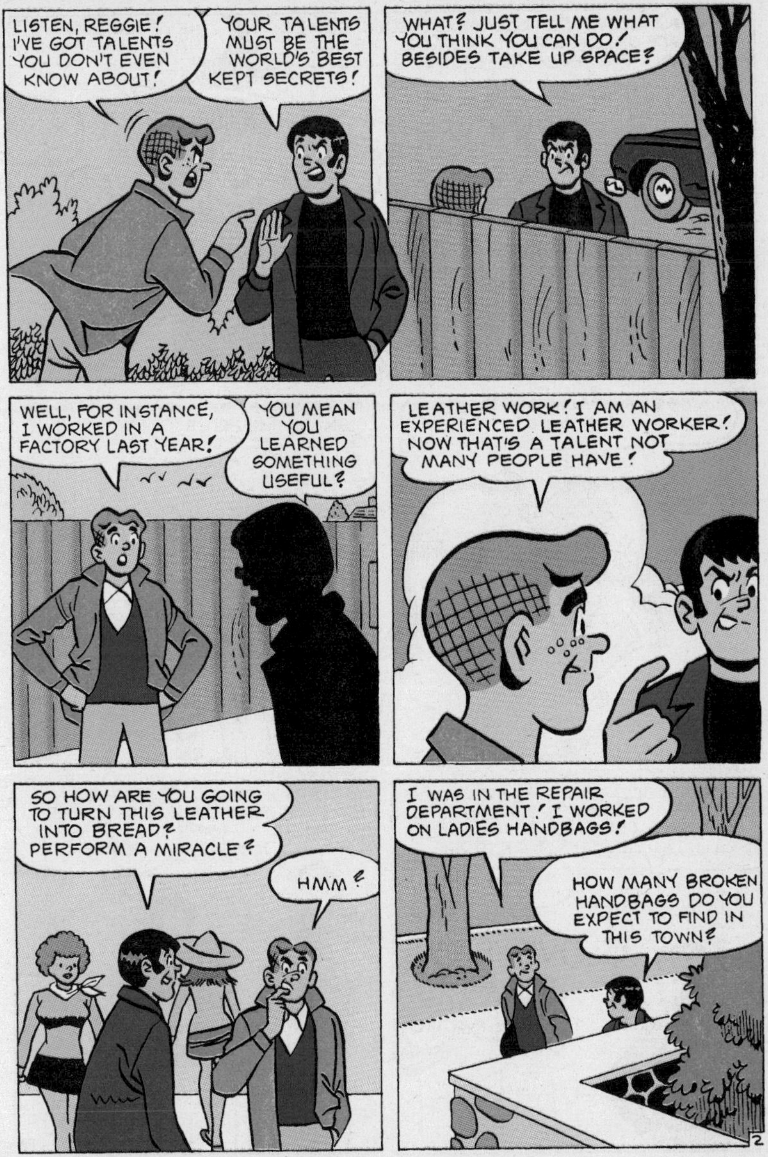
LISTEN, REGGIE! I'VE GOT TALENTS YOU DON'T EVEN KNOW ABOUT!
YOUR TALENTS MUST BE THE WORLD'S BEST KEPT SECRETS!
WHAT? JUST TELL ME WHAT YOU THINK YOU CAN DO! BESIDES TAKE UP SPACE?
WELL, FOR INSTANCE, I WORKED IN A FACTORY LAST YEAR!
YOU MEAN YOU LEARNED SOMETHING USEFUL?
LEATHER WORK! I AM AN EXPERIENCED LEATHER WORKER! NOW THAT'S A TALENT NOT MANY PEOPLE HAVE!
SO HOW ARE YOU GOING TO TURN THIS LEATHER INTO BREAD? PERFORM A MIRACLE?
HMM?
I WAS IN THE REPAIR DEPARTMENT! I WORKED ON LADIES HANDBAGS!
HOW MANY BROKEN HANDBAGS DO YOU EXPECT TO FIND IN THIS TOWN?
2

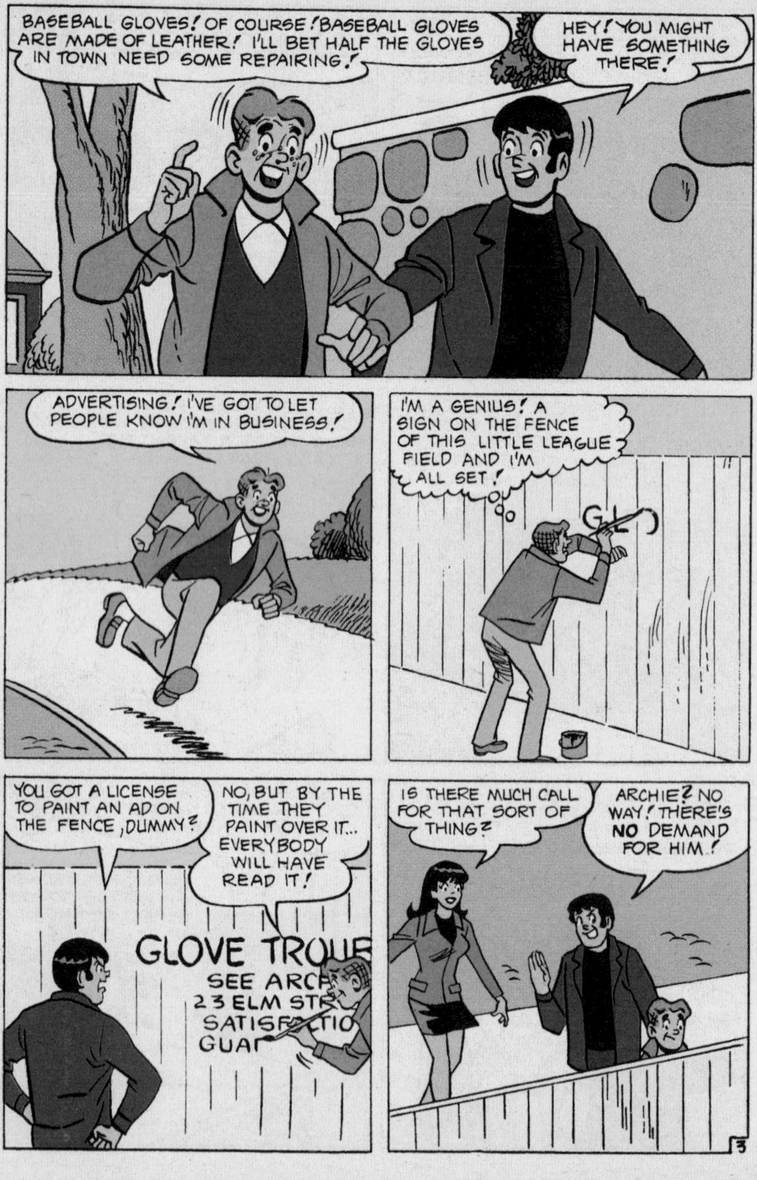

BASEBALL GLOVES! OF COURSE! BASEBALL GLOVES ARE MADE OF LEATHER! I'LL BET HALF THE GLOVES IN TOWN NEED SOME REPAIRING!
HEY! YOU MIGHT HAVE SOMETHING THERE!
ADVERTISING! I'VE GOT TO LET PEOPLE KNOW I'M IN BUSINESS!
I'M A GENIUS! A SIGN ON THE FENCE OF THIS LITTLE LEAGUE FIELD AND I'M ALL SET!
GL
YOU GOT A LICENSE TO PAINT AN AD ON THE FENCE, DUMMY?
NO, BUT BY THE TIME THEY PAINT OVER IT... EVERYBODY WILL HAVE READ IT!
GLOVE TROUB
SEE ARCH
23 ELM STR
SATISFACTIO
GUAI
IS THERE MUCH CALL FOR THAT SORT OF THING?
ARCHIE? NO WAY! THERE'S **NO** DEMAND FOR HIM!
3

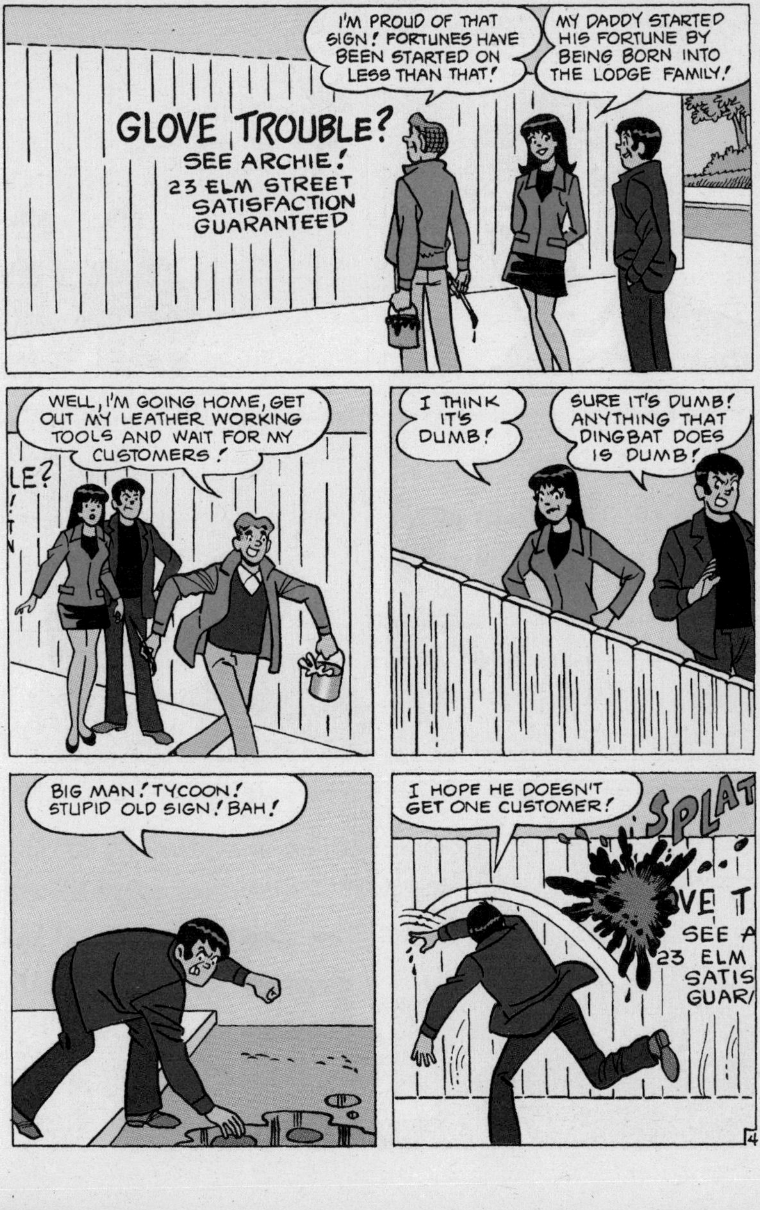
I'M PROUD OF THAT SIGN! FORTUNES HAVE BEEN STARTED ON LESS THAN THAT!
MY DADDY STARTED HIS FORTUNE BY BEING BORN INTO THE LODGE FAMILY!
GLOVE TROUBLE? SEE ARCHIE! 23 ELM STREET SATISFACTION GUARANTEED
WELL, I'M GOING HOME, GET OUT MY LEATHER WORKING TOOLS AND WAIT FOR MY CUSTOMERS!
I THINK IT'S DUMB!
SURE IT'S DUMB! ANYTHING THAT DINGBAT DOES IS DUMB!
BIG MAN! TYCOON! STUPID OLD SIGN! BAH!
I HOPE HE DOESN'T GET ONE CUSTOMER!
SPLAT
4

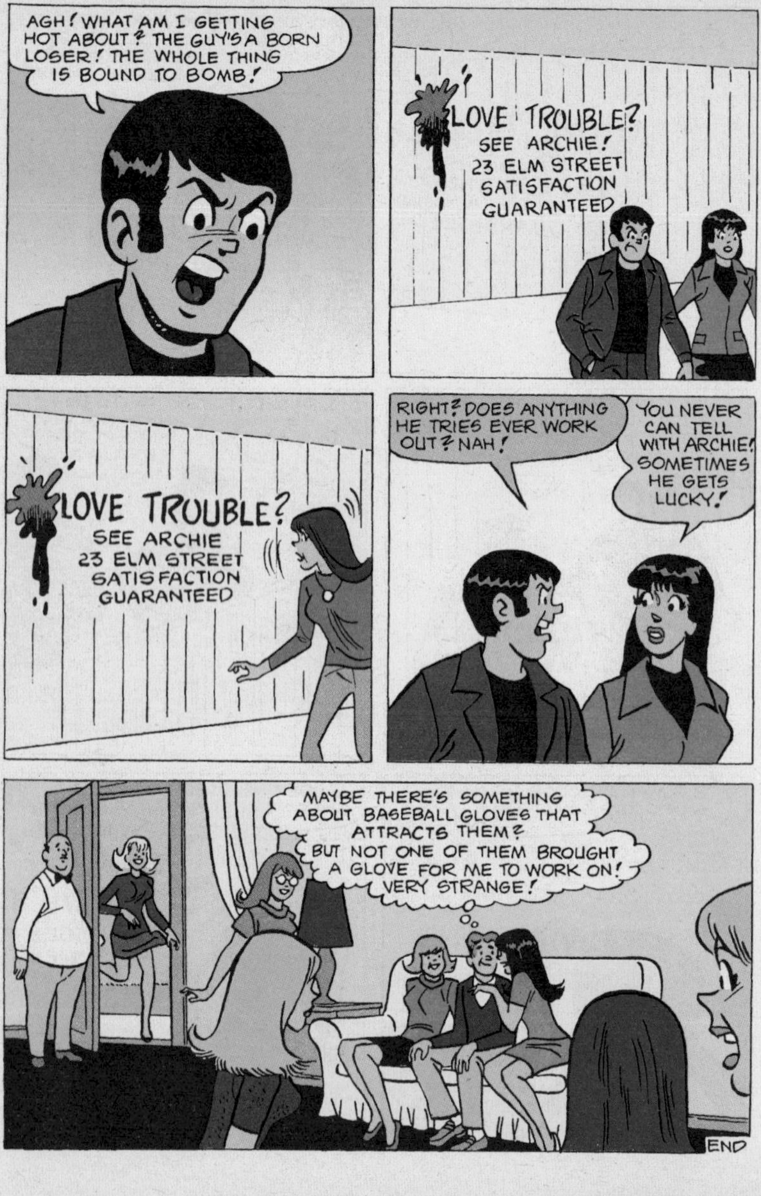
AGH! WHAT AM I GETTING HOT ABOUT? THE GUY'S A BORN LOSER! THE WHOLE THING IS BOUND TO BOMB!
LOVE TROUBLE? SEE ARCHIE! 23 ELM STREET SATISFACTION GUARANTEED
LOVE TROUBLE? SEE ARCHIE 23 ELM STREET SATISFACTION GUARANTEED
RIGHT? DOES ANYTHING HE TRIES EVER WORK OUT? NAH!
YOU NEVER CAN TELL WITH ARCHIE! SOMETIMES HE GETS LUCKY!
MAYBE THERE'S SOMETHING ABOUT BASEBALL GLOVES THAT ATTRACTS THEM? BUT NOT ONE OF THEM BROUGHT A GLOVE FOR ME TO WORK ON! VERY STRANGE!
END

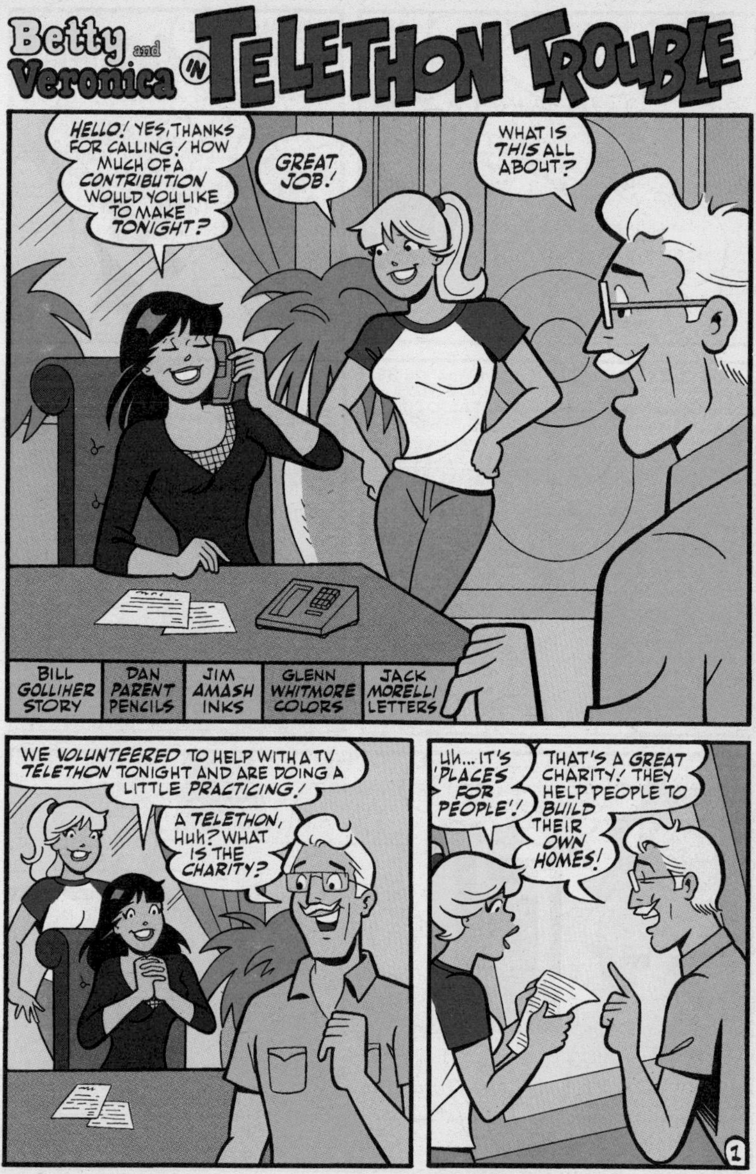
Betty and Veronica in TELETHON TROUBLE
HELLO! YES, THANKS FOR CALLING! HOW MUCH OF A CONTRIBUTION WOULD YOU LIKE TO MAKE TONIGHT?
GREAT JOB!
WHAT IS THIS ALL ABOUT?
BILL GOLLIHER STORY
DAN PARENT PENCILS
JIM AMASH INKS
GLENN WHITMORE COLORS
JACK MORELLI LETTERS
WE VOLUNTEERED TO HELP WITH A TV TELETHON TONIGHT AND ARE DOING A LITTLE PRACTICING!
A TELETHON, HUH? WHAT IS THE CHARITY?
UH... IT'S 'PLACES FOR PEOPLE'!
THAT'S A GREAT CHARITY! THEY HELP PEOPLE TO BUILD THEIR OWN HOMES!
1

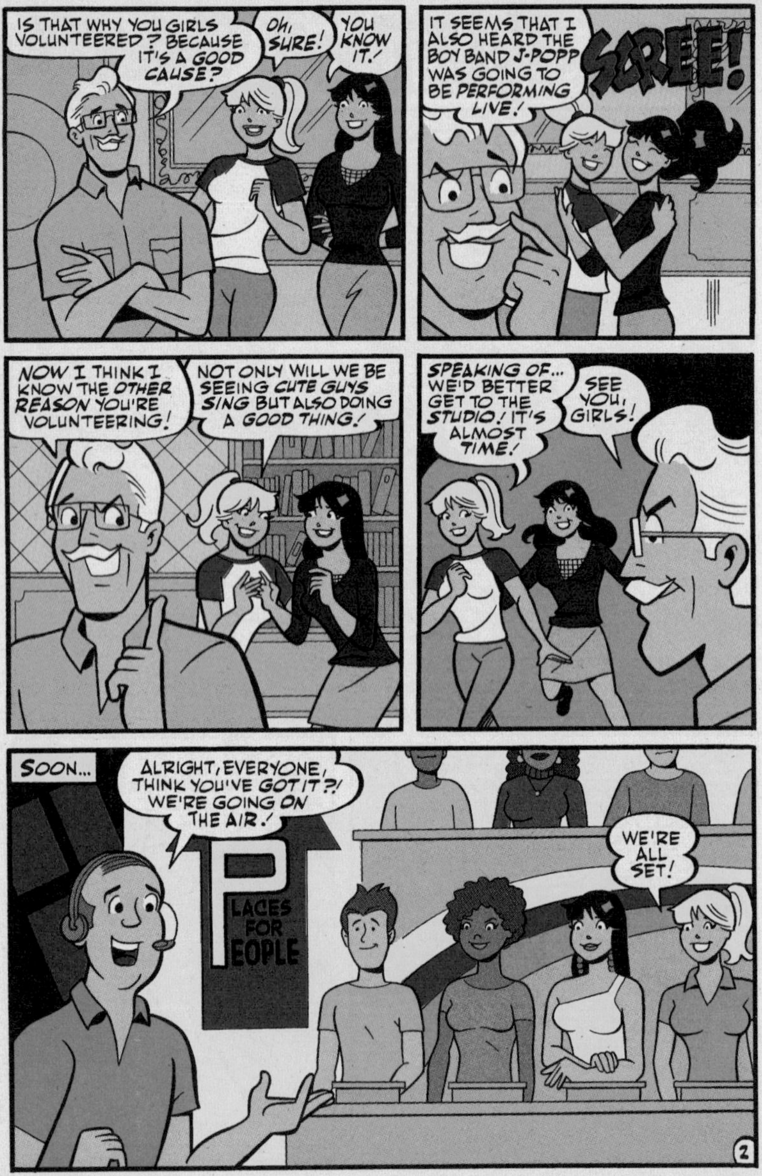
IS THAT WHY YOU GIRLS VOLUNTEERED? BECAUSE IT'S A GOOD CAUSE?
OH, SURE!
YOU KNOW IT.!
IT SEEMS THAT I ALSO HEARD THE BOY BAND J-POPP WAS GOING TO BE PERFORMING LIVE!
SCREE!
NOW I THINK I KNOW THE OTHER REASON YOU'RE VOLUNTEERING!
NOT ONLY WILL WE BE SEEING CUTE GUYS SING BUT ALSO DOING A GOOD THING!
SPEAKING OF... WE'D BETTER GET TO THE STUDIO! IT'S ALMOST TIME!
SEE YOU, GIRLS!
SOON...
ALRIGHT, EVERYONE, THINK YOU'VE GOT IT?! WE'RE GOING ON THE AIR!
PLACES FOR PEOPLE
WE'RE ALL SET!
2

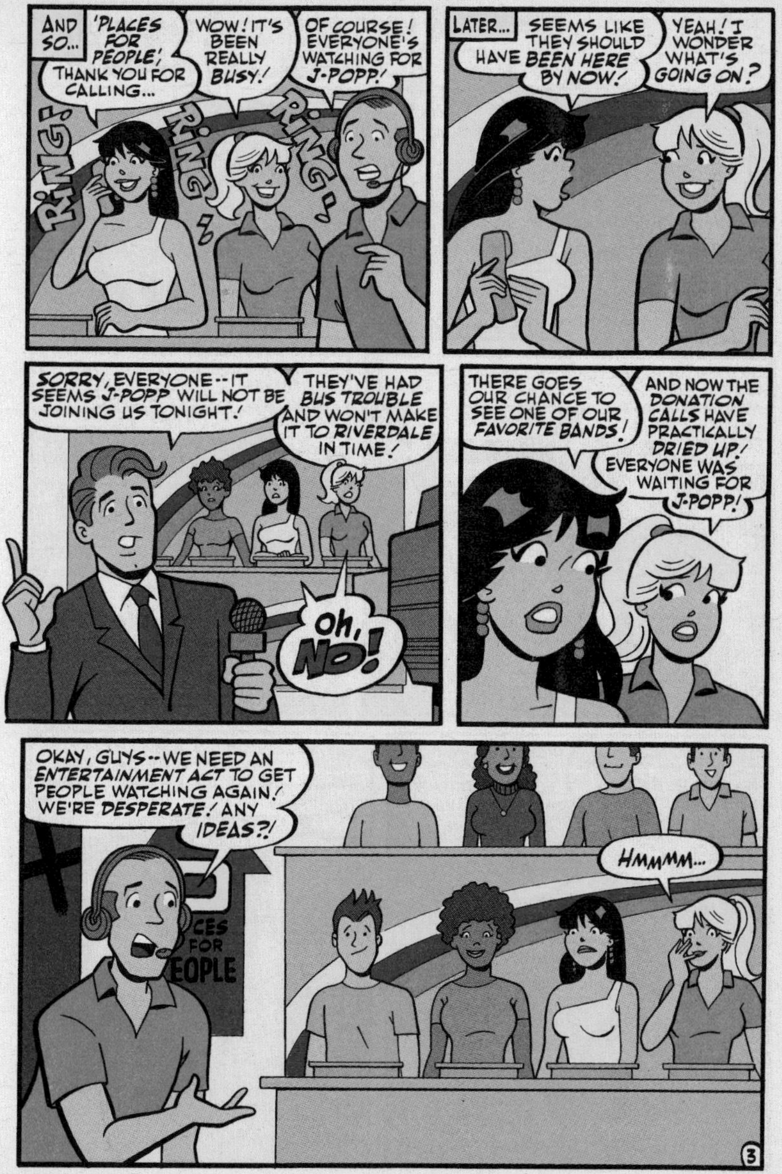

AND SO...
'PLACES FOR PEOPLE', THANK YOU FOR CALLING...
WOW! IT'S BEEN REALLY BUSY!
OF COURSE! EVERYONE'S WATCHING FOR J-POPP!
RING!
RING
RING
LATER...
SEEMS LIKE THEY SHOULD HAVE BEEN HERE BY NOW!
YEAH! I WONDER WHAT'S GOING ON?
SORRY, EVERYONE -- IT SEEMS J-POPP WILL NOT BE JOINING US TONIGHT!
THEY'VE HAD BUS TROUBLE AND WON'T MAKE IT TO RIVERDALE IN TIME!
OH, NO!
THERE GOES OUR CHANCE TO SEE ONE OF OUR FAVORITE BANDS!
AND NOW THE DONATION CALLS HAVE PRACTICALLY DRIED UP! EVERYONE WAS WAITING FOR J-POPP!
OKAY, GUYS -- WE NEED AN ENTERTAINMENT ACT TO GET PEOPLE WATCHING AGAIN! WE'RE DESPERATE! ANY IDEAS?!
CES FOR EOPLE
HMMMM...

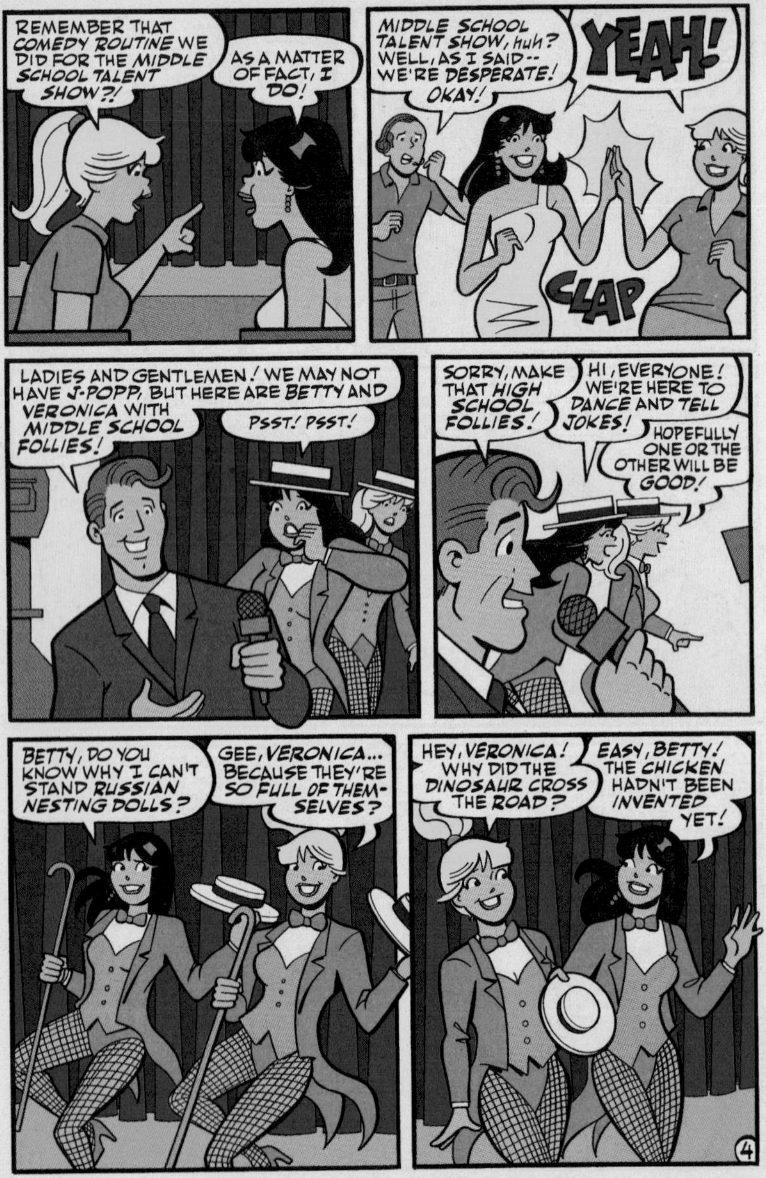

REMEMBER THAT COMEDY ROUTINE WE DID FOR THE MIDDLE SCHOOL TALENT SHOW?!
AS A MATTER OF FACT, I DO!
MIDDLE SCHOOL TALENT SHOW, huh? WELL, AS I SAID-- WE'RE DESPERATE! OKAY!
YEAH!
CLAP
LADIES AND GENTLEMEN! WE MAY NOT HAVE J-POPP, BUT HERE ARE BETTY AND VERONICA WITH MIDDLE SCHOOL FOLLIES!
PSST! PSST!
SORRY, MAKE THAT HIGH SCHOOL FOLLIES!
HI, EVERYONE! WE'RE HERE TO DANCE AND TELL JOKES!
HOPEFULLY ONE OR THE OTHER WILL BE GOOD!
BETTY, DO YOU KNOW WHY I CAN'T STAND RUSSIAN NESTING DOLLS?
GEE, VERONICA... BECAUSE THEY'RE SO FULL OF THEMSELVES?
HEY, VERONICA! WHY DID THE DINOSAUR CROSS THE ROAD?
EASY, BETTY! THE CHICKEN HADN'T BEEN INVENTED YET!
4

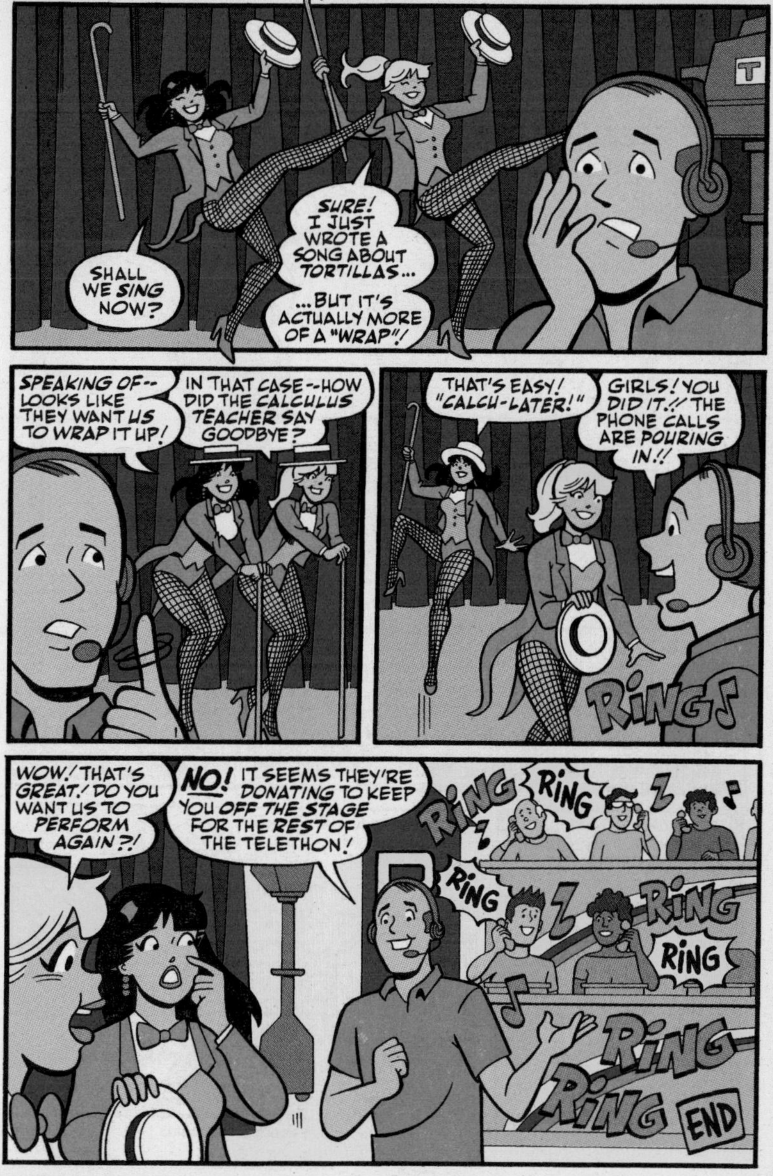
SHALL WE SING NOW?
SURE! I JUST WROTE A SONG ABOUT TORTILLAS...
...BUT IT'S ACTUALLY MORE OF A "WRAP"!
SPEAKING OF-- LOOKS LIKE THEY WANT US TO WRAP IT UP!
IN THAT CASE--HOW DID THE CALCULUS TEACHER SAY GOODBYE?
THAT'S EASY! "CALCU-LATER!"
GIRLS! YOU DID IT!! THE PHONE CALLS ARE POURING IN!!
RINGS
WOW! THAT'S GREAT! DO YOU WANT US TO PERFORM AGAIN?!
NO! IT SEEMS THEY'RE DONATING TO KEEP YOU OFF THE STAGE FOR THE REST OF THE TELETHON!
RING
RING
RING
RING
RING
RING
RING
END

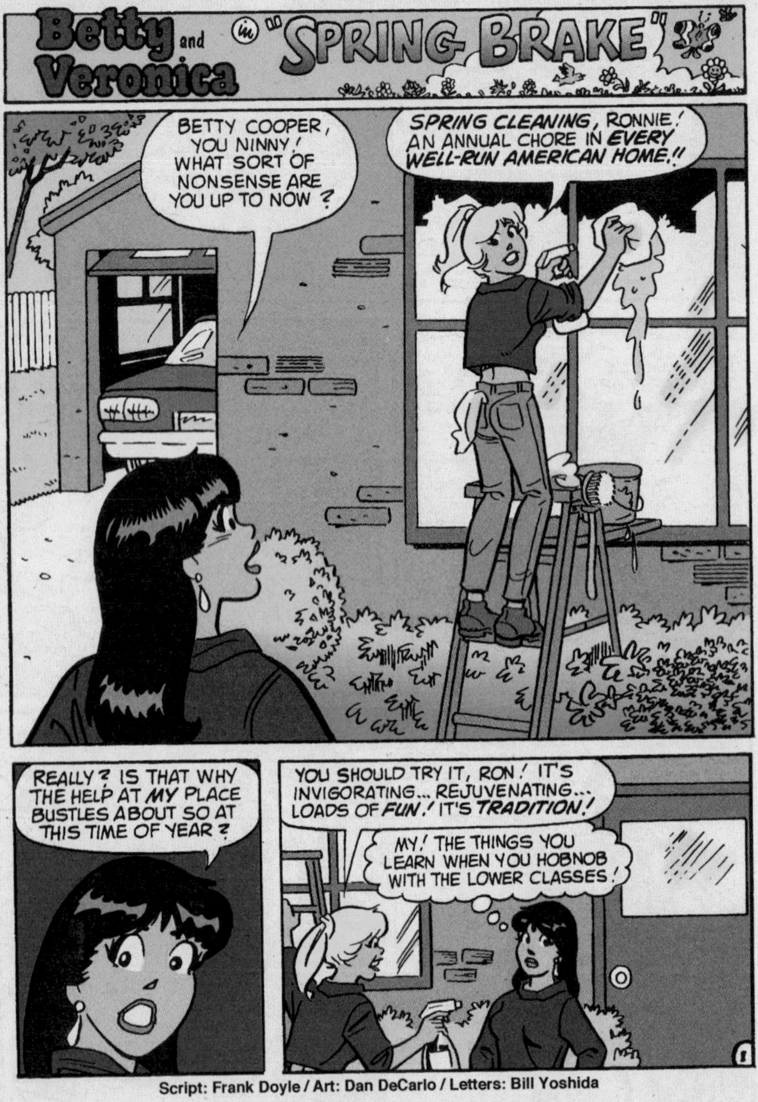
Betty and Veronica in "SPRING BRAKE"
BETTY COOPER, YOU NINNY! WHAT SORT OF NONSENSE ARE YOU UP TO NOW?
SPRING CLEANING, RONNIE! AN ANNUAL CHORE IN EVERY WELL-RUN AMERICAN HOME!!
REALLY? IS THAT WHY THE HELP AT MY PLACE BUSTLES ABOUT SO AT THIS TIME OF YEAR?
YOU SHOULD TRY IT, RON! IT'S INVIGORATING... REJUVENATING... LOADS OF FUN! IT'S TRADITION!
MY! THE THINGS YOU LEARN WHEN YOU HOBNOB WITH THE LOWER CLASSES!
1
Script: Frank Doyle / Art: Dan DeCarlo / Letters: Bill Yoshida

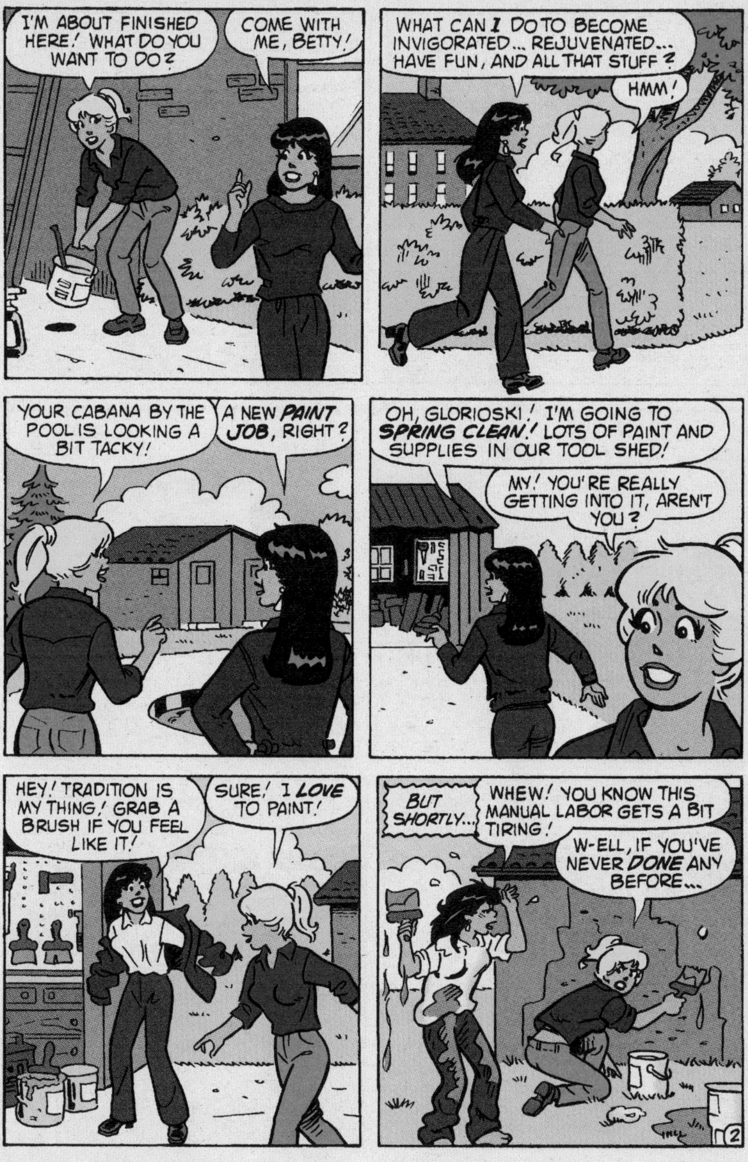
I'M ABOUT FINISHED HERE! WHAT DO YOU WANT TO DO?
COME WITH ME, BETTY!
WHAT CAN I DO TO BECOME INVIGORATED... REJUVENATED... HAVE FUN, AND ALL THAT STUFF?
HMM!
YOUR CABANA BY THE POOL IS LOOKING A BIT TACKY!
A NEW PAINT JOB, RIGHT?
OH, GLORIOSKI! I'M GOING TO SPRING CLEAN! LOTS OF PAINT AND SUPPLIES IN OUR TOOL SHED!
MY! YOU'RE REALLY GETTING INTO IT, AREN'T YOU?
HEY! TRADITION IS MY THING! GRAB A BRUSH IF YOU FEEL LIKE IT!
SURE! I LOVE TO PAINT!
BUT SHORTLY...
WHEW! YOU KNOW THIS MANUAL LABOR GETS A BIT TIRING!
W-ELL, IF YOU'VE NEVER DONE ANY BEFORE...
2

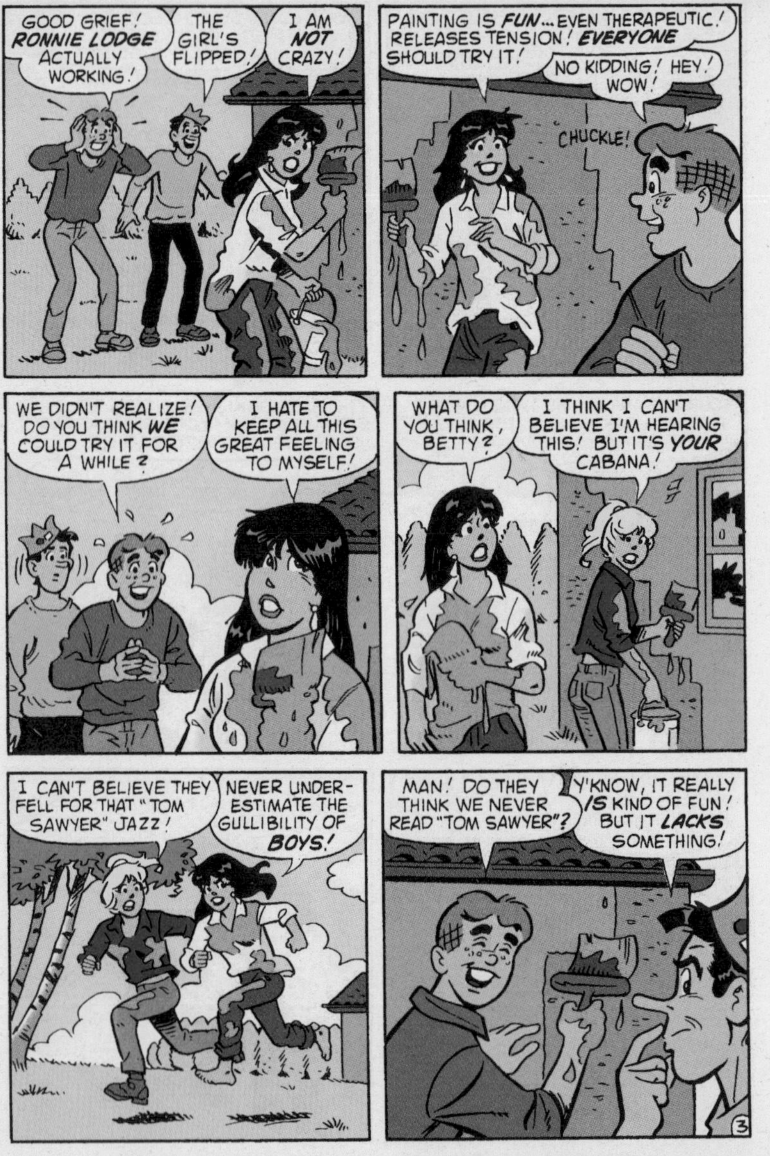
GOOD GRIEF! RONNIE LODGE ACTUALLY WORKING!
THE GIRL'S FLIPPED!
I AM NOT CRAZY!
PAINTING IS FUN... EVEN THERAPEUTIC! RELEASES TENSION! EVERYONE SHOULD TRY IT!
NO KIDDING! HEY! WOW!
CHUCKLE!
WE DIDN'T REALIZE! DO YOU THINK WE COULD TRY IT FOR A WHILE?
I HATE TO KEEP ALL THIS GREAT FEELING TO MYSELF!
WHAT DO YOU THINK, BETTY?
I THINK I CAN'T BELIEVE I'M HEARING THIS! BUT IT'S YOUR CABANA!
I CAN'T BELIEVE THEY FELL FOR THAT "TOM SAWYER" JAZZ!
NEVER UNDER-ESTIMATE THE GULLIBILITY OF BOYS!
MAN! DO THEY THINK WE NEVER READ "TOM SAWYER"?
Y'KNOW, IT REALLY IS KIND OF FUN! BUT IT LACKS SOMETHING!
3

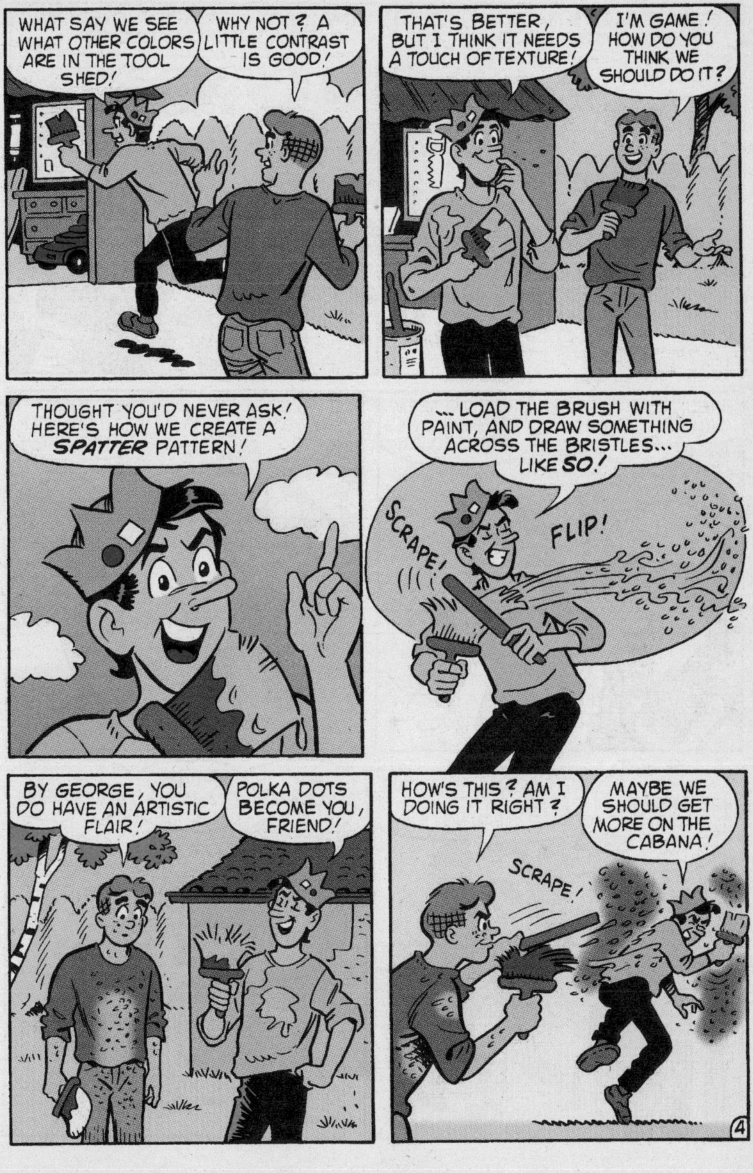

WHAT SAY WE SEE WHAT OTHER COLORS ARE IN THE TOOL SHED!
WHY NOT? A LITTLE CONTRAST IS GOOD!
THAT'S BETTER, BUT I THINK IT NEEDS A TOUCH OF TEXTURE!
I'M GAME! HOW DO YOU THINK WE SHOULD DO IT?
THOUGHT YOU'D NEVER ASK! HERE'S HOW WE CREATE A SPATTER PATTERN!
...LOAD THE BRUSH WITH PAINT, AND DRAW SOMETHING ACROSS THE BRISTLES... LIKE SO!
SCRAPE!
FLIP!
BY GEORGE, YOU DO HAVE AN ARTISTIC FLAIR!
POLKA DOTS BECOME YOU, FRIEND!
HOW'S THIS? AM I DOING IT RIGHT?
MAYBE WE SHOULD GET MORE ON THE CABANA!
SCRAPE!
4

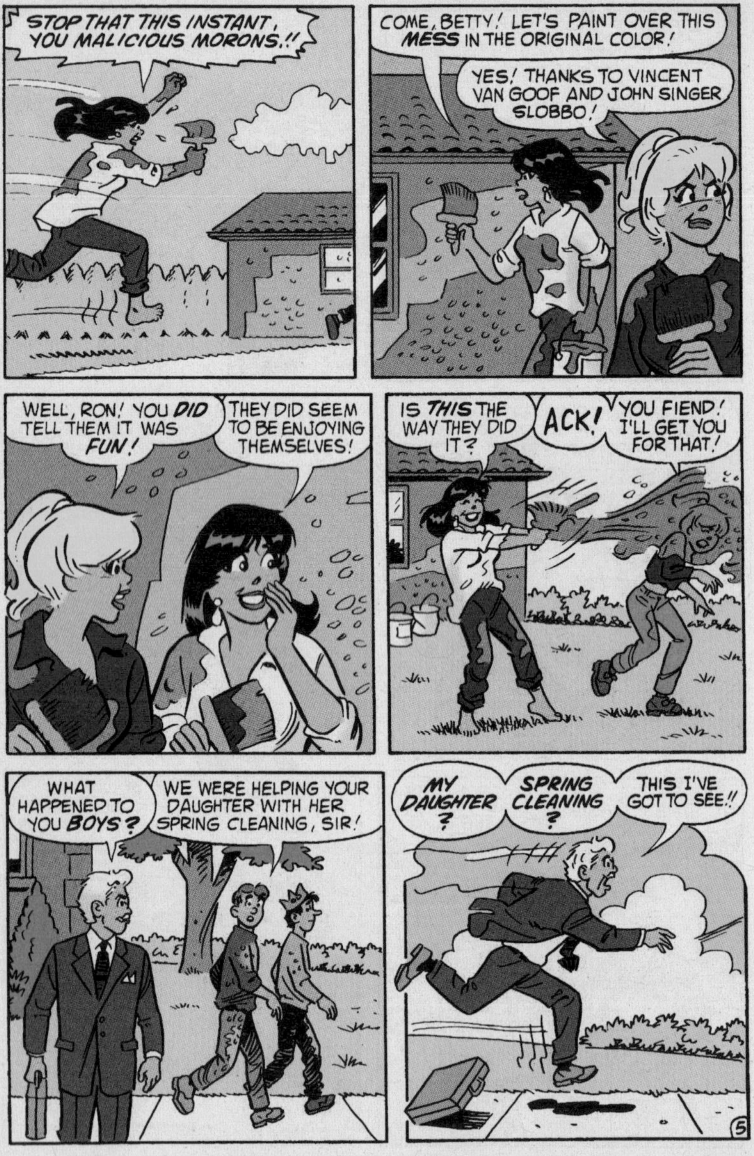

STOP THAT THIS INSTANT, YOU MALICIOUS MORONS!!
COME, BETTY! LET'S PAINT OVER THIS MESS IN THE ORIGINAL COLOR!
YES! THANKS TO VINCENT VAN GOOF AND JOHN SINGER SLOBBO!
WELL, RON! YOU DID TELL THEM IT WAS FUN!
THEY DID SEEM TO BE ENJOYING THEMSELVES!
IS THIS THE WAY THEY DID IT?
ACK!
YOU FIEND! I'LL GET YOU FOR THAT!
WHAT HAPPENED TO YOU BOYS?
WE WERE HELPING YOUR DAUGHTER WITH HER SPRING CLEANING, SIR!
MY DAUGHTER?
SPRING CLEANING?
THIS I'VE GOT TO SEE!!
5

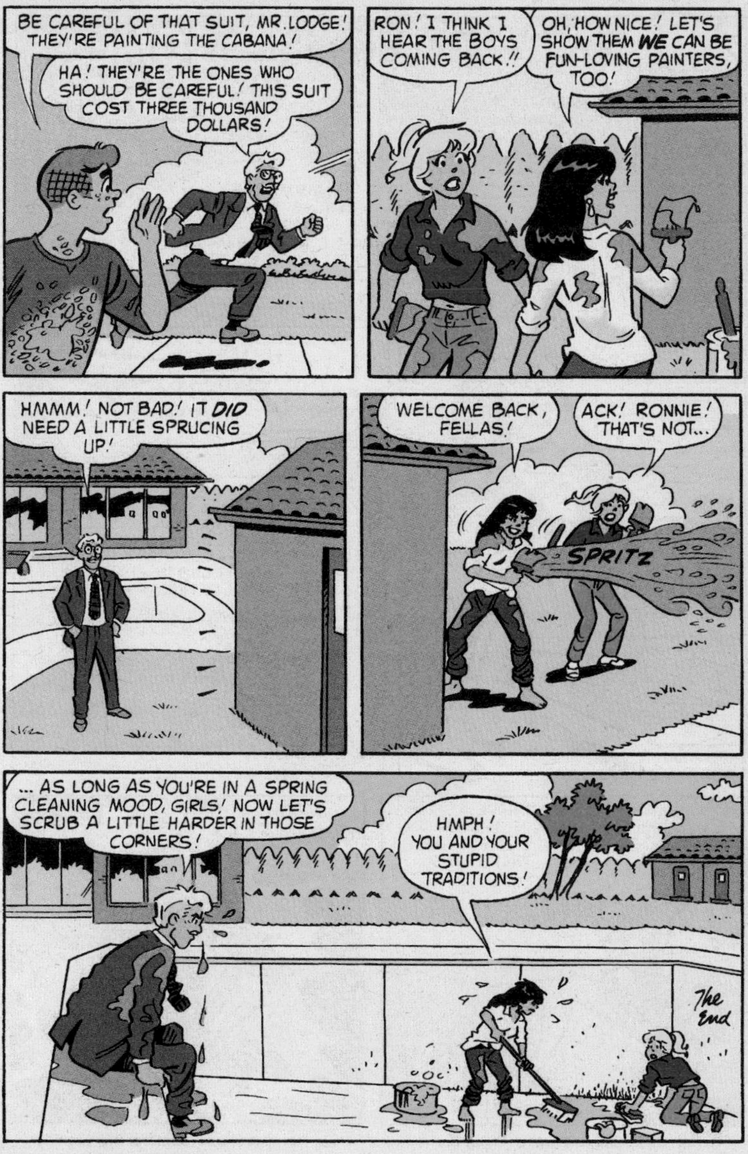
BE CAREFUL OF THAT SUIT, MR. LODGE! THEY'RE PAINTING THE CABANA!
HA! THEY'RE THE ONES WHO SHOULD BE CAREFUL! THIS SUIT COST THREE THOUSAND DOLLARS!
RON! I THINK I HEAR THE BOYS COMING BACK!!
OH, HOW NICE! LET'S SHOW THEM WE CAN BE FUN-LOVING PAINTERS, TOO!
HMMM! NOT BAD! IT DID NEED A LITTLE SPRUCING UP!
WELCOME BACK, FELLAS!
ACK! RONNIE! THAT'S NOT...
SPRITZ
... AS LONG AS YOU'RE IN A SPRING CLEANING MOOD, GIRLS! NOW LET'S SCRUB A LITTLE HARDER IN THOSE CORNERS!
HMPH! YOU AND YOUR STUPID TRADITIONS!
The End

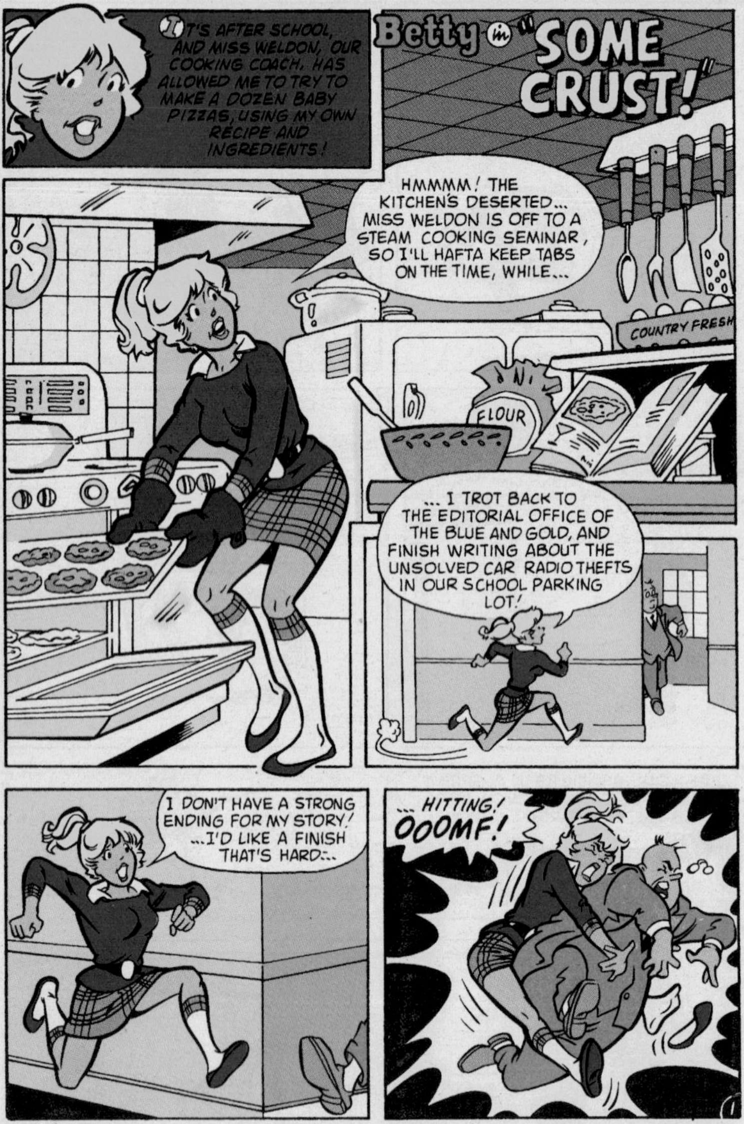
IT'S AFTER SCHOOL, AND MISS WELDON, OUR COOKING COACH, HAS ALLOWED ME TO TRY TO MAKE A DOZEN BABY PIZZAS, USING MY OWN RECIPE AND INGREDIENTS!
Betty in "SOME CRUST!"
HMMMM! THE KITCHEN'S DESERTED... MISS WELDON IS OFF TO A STEAM COOKING SEMINAR, SO I'LL HAFTA KEEP TABS ON THE TIME, WHILE...
COUNTRY FRESH
FLOUR
... I TROT BACK TO THE EDITORIAL OFFICE OF THE BLUE AND GOLD, AND FINISH WRITING ABOUT THE UNSOLVED CAR RADIO THEFTS IN OUR SCHOOL PARKING LOT!
I DON'T HAVE A STRONG ENDING FOR MY STORY! ...I'D LIKE A FINISH THAT'S HARD...
... HITTING! OOOMF!
1

Script: Bob Bolling / Pencils: Doug Crane / Inks: Harvey Mercadoocasio / Letters: Bill Yoshida

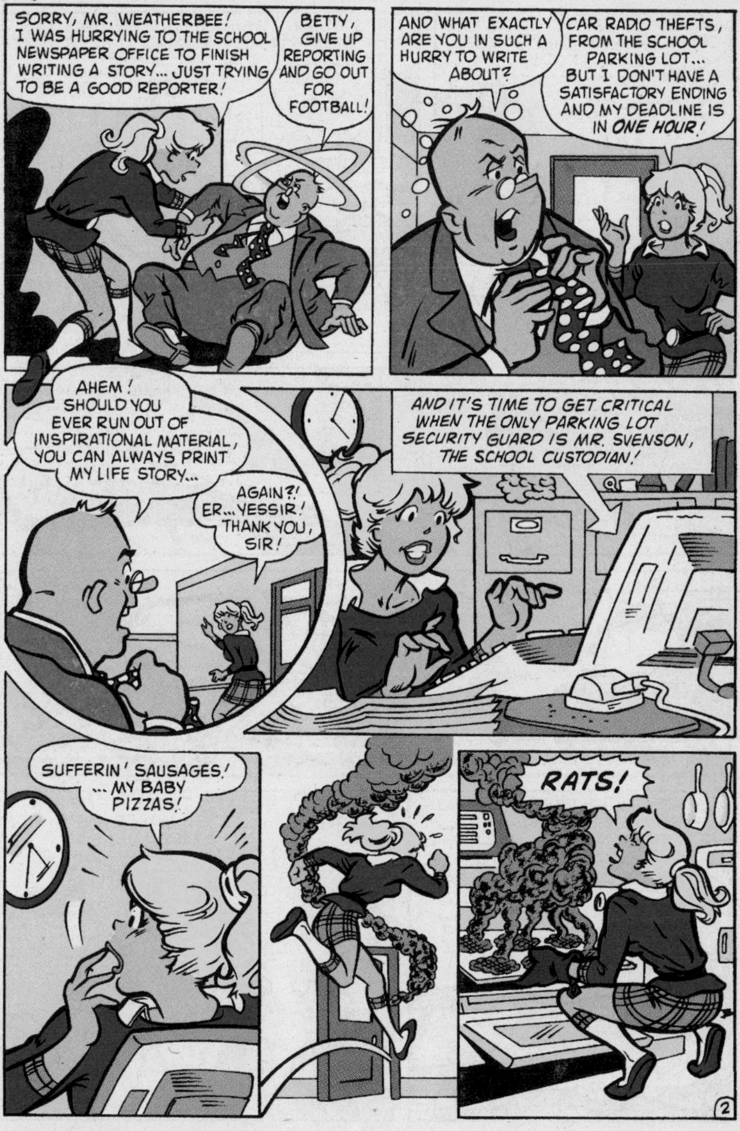
SORRY, MR. WEATHERBEE! I WAS HURRYING TO THE SCHOOL NEWSPAPER OFFICE TO FINISH WRITING A STORY... JUST TRYING TO BE A GOOD REPORTER!
BETTY, GIVE UP REPORTING AND GO OUT FOR FOOTBALL!
AND WHAT EXACTLY ARE YOU IN SUCH A HURRY TO WRITE ABOUT?
CAR RADIO THEFTS, FROM THE SCHOOL PARKING LOT... BUT I DON'T HAVE A SATISFACTORY ENDING AND MY DEADLINE IS IN ONE HOUR!
AHEM! SHOULD YOU EVER RUN OUT OF INSPIRATIONAL MATERIAL, YOU CAN ALWAYS PRINT MY LIFE STORY...
AGAIN?! ER...YESSIR! THANK YOU, SIR!
AND IT'S TIME TO GET CRITICAL WHEN THE ONLY PARKING LOT SECURITY GUARD IS MR. SVENSON, THE SCHOOL CUSTODIAN!
SUFFERIN' SAUSAGES! ...MY BABY PIZZAS!
RATS!
2

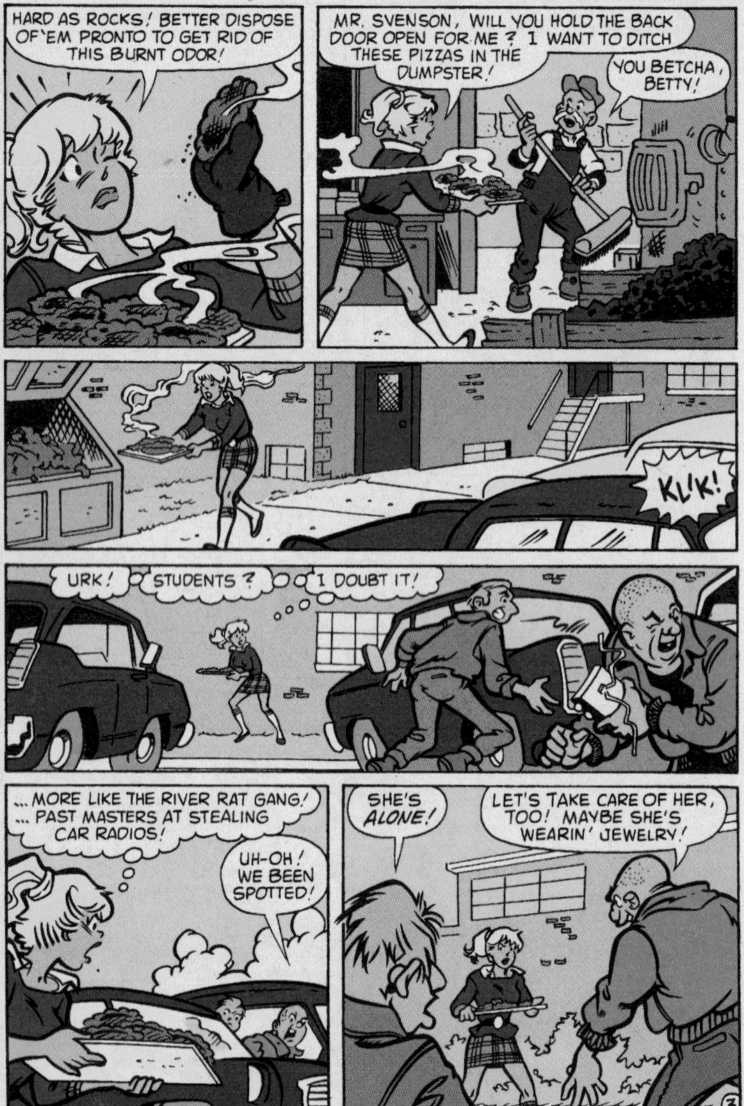

HARD AS ROCKS! BETTER DISPOSE OF'EM PRONTO TO GET RID OF THIS BURNT ODOR!
MR. SVENSON, WILL YOU HOLD THE BACK DOOR OPEN FOR ME? I WANT TO DITCH THESE PIZZAS IN THE DUMPSTER!
YOU BETCHA, BETTY!
KL'K!
URK!
STUDENTS?
I DOUBT IT!
... MORE LIKE THE RIVER RAT GANG! ... PAST MASTERS AT STEALING CAR RADIOS!
UH-OH! WE BEEN SPOTTED!
SHE'S *ALONE*!
LET'S TAKE CARE OF HER, TOO! MAYBE SHE'S WEARIN' JEWELRY!
3

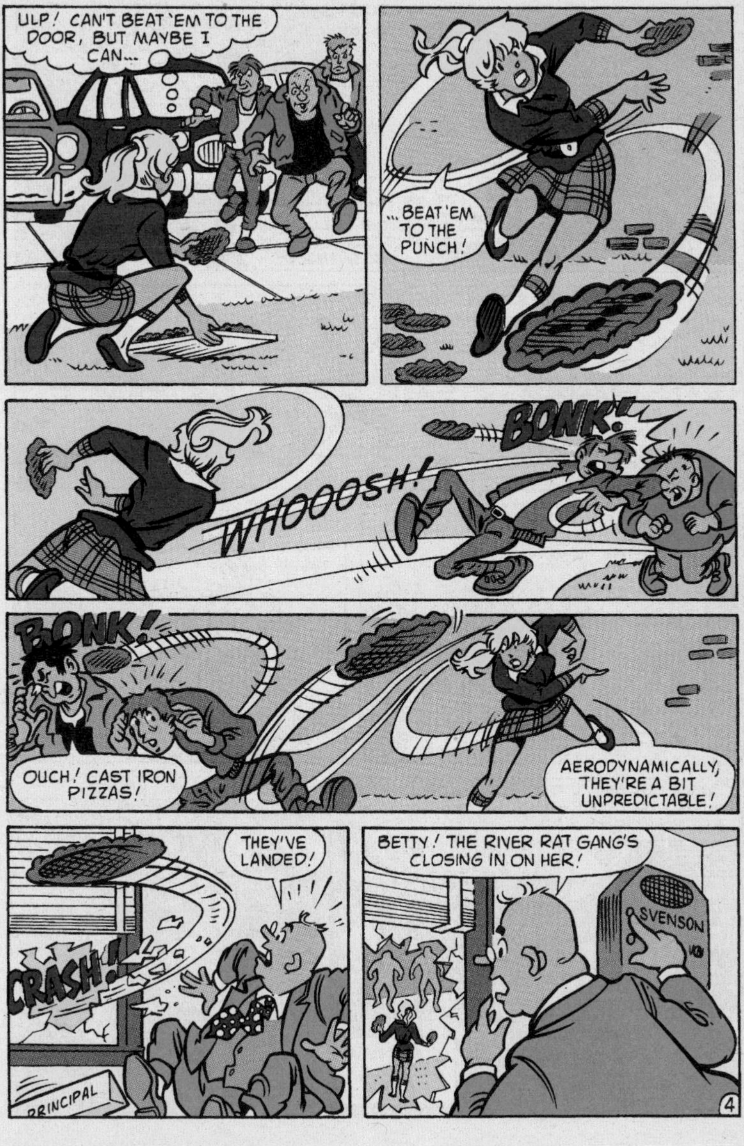
ULP! CAN'T BEAT 'EM TO THE DOOR, BUT MAYBE I CAN...
...BEAT 'EM TO THE PUNCH!
WHOOOOSH!
BONK!
BONK!
OUCH! CAST IRON PIZZAS!
AERODYNAMICALLY, THEY'RE A BIT UNPREDICTABLE!
THEY'VE LANDED!
CRASH!
PRINCIPAL
BETTY! THE RIVER RAT GANG'S CLOSING IN ON HER!
SVENSON
4

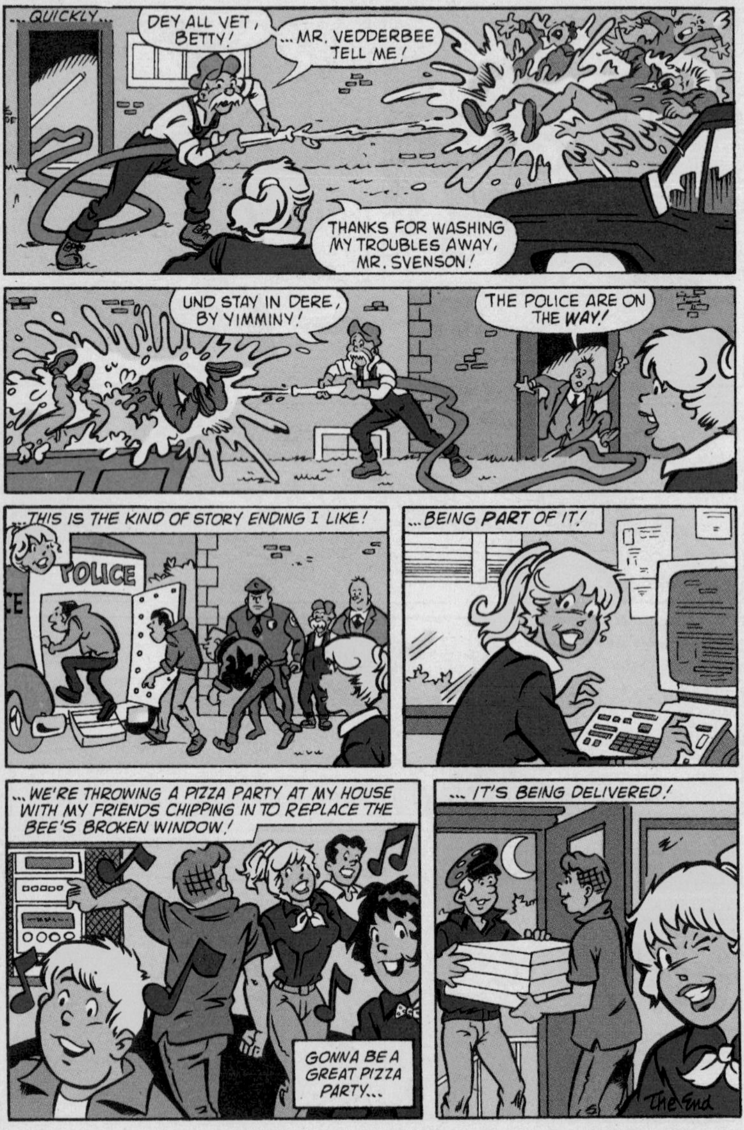
...QUICKLY...
DEY ALL VET, BETTY!
...MR. VEDDERBEE TELL ME!
THANKS FOR WASHING MY TROUBLES AWAY, MR. SVENSON!
UND STAY IN DERE, BY YIMMINY!
THE POLICE ARE ON THE WAY!
...THIS IS THE KIND OF STORY ENDING I LIKE!
POLICE
...BEING PART OF IT!
...WE'RE THROWING A PIZZA PARTY AT MY HOUSE WITH MY FRIENDS CHIPPING IN TO REPLACE THE BEE'S BROKEN WINDOW!
GONNA BE A GREAT PIZZA PARTY...
... IT'S BEING DELIVERED!
The End

GINGER LOPEZ in Toolbelt Diva!

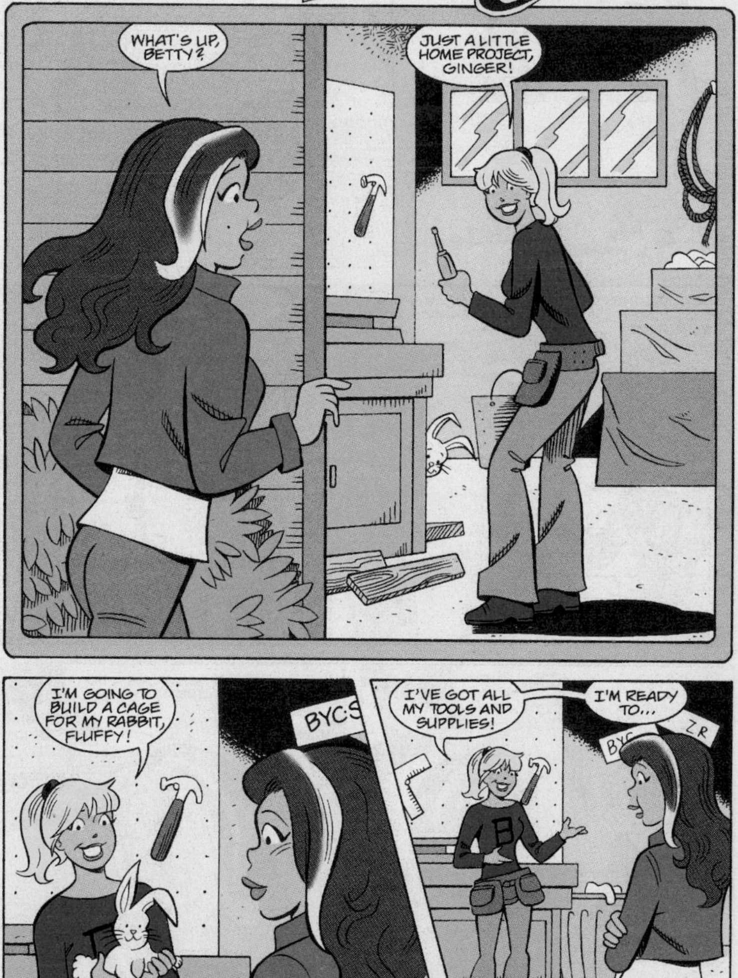
WHAT'S UP, BETTY?
JUST A LITTLE HOME PROJECT, GINGER!
I'M GOING TO BUILD A CAGE FOR MY RABBIT, FLUFFY!
I'VE GOT ALL MY TOOLS AND SUPPLIES!
I'M READY TO...

Script & Pencils: Dan Parent / Inks: Jim Amash / Letters: Vickie Williams

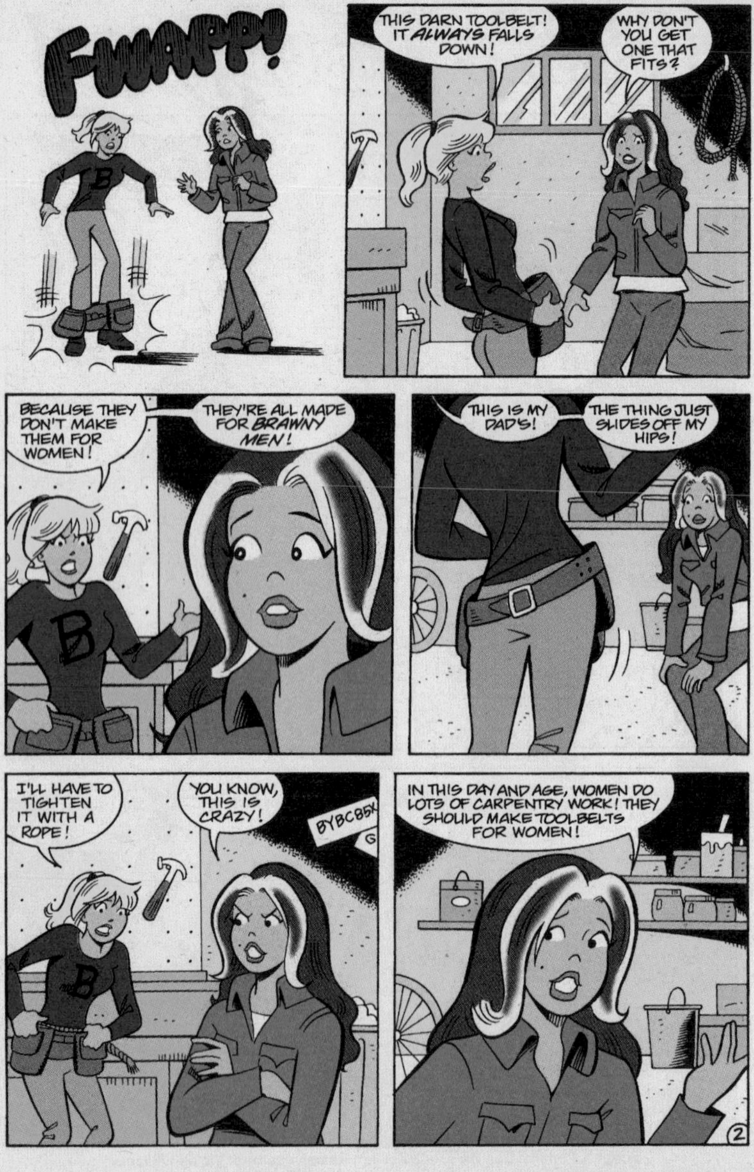

FWAPP!
THIS DARN TOOLBELT! IT *ALWAYS* FALLS DOWN!
WHY DON'T YOU GET ONE THAT FITS?
BECAUSE THEY DON'T MAKE THEM FOR WOMEN!
THEY'RE ALL MADE FOR *BRAWNY MEN*!
THIS IS MY DAD'S!
THE THING JUST SLIDES OFF MY HIPS!
I'LL HAVE TO TIGHTEN IT WITH A ROPE!
YOU KNOW, THIS IS CRAZY!
BYBC85X
G
IN THIS DAY AND AGE, WOMEN DO LOTS OF CARPENTRY WORK! THEY SHOULD MAKE TOOLBELTS FOR WOMEN!

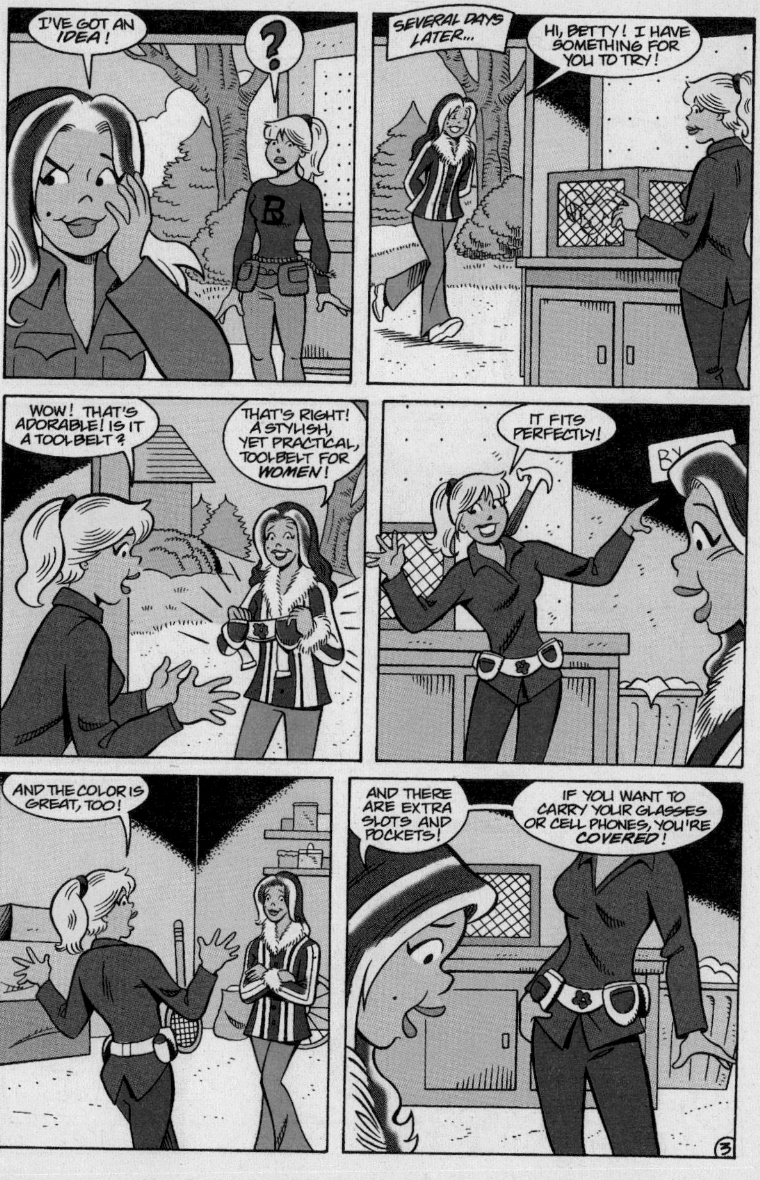

I'VE GOT AN IDEA!
?
SEVERAL DAYS LATER...
HI, BETTY! I HAVE SOMETHING FOR YOU TO TRY!
WOW! THAT'S ADORABLE! IS IT A TOOLBELT?
THAT'S RIGHT! A STYLISH, YET PRACTICAL, TOOLBELT FOR WOMEN!
IT FITS PERFECTLY!
AND THE COLOR IS GREAT, TOO!
AND THERE ARE EXTRA SLOTS AND POCKETS!
IF YOU WANT TO CARRY YOUR GLASSES OR CELL PHONES, YOU'RE COVERED!
3

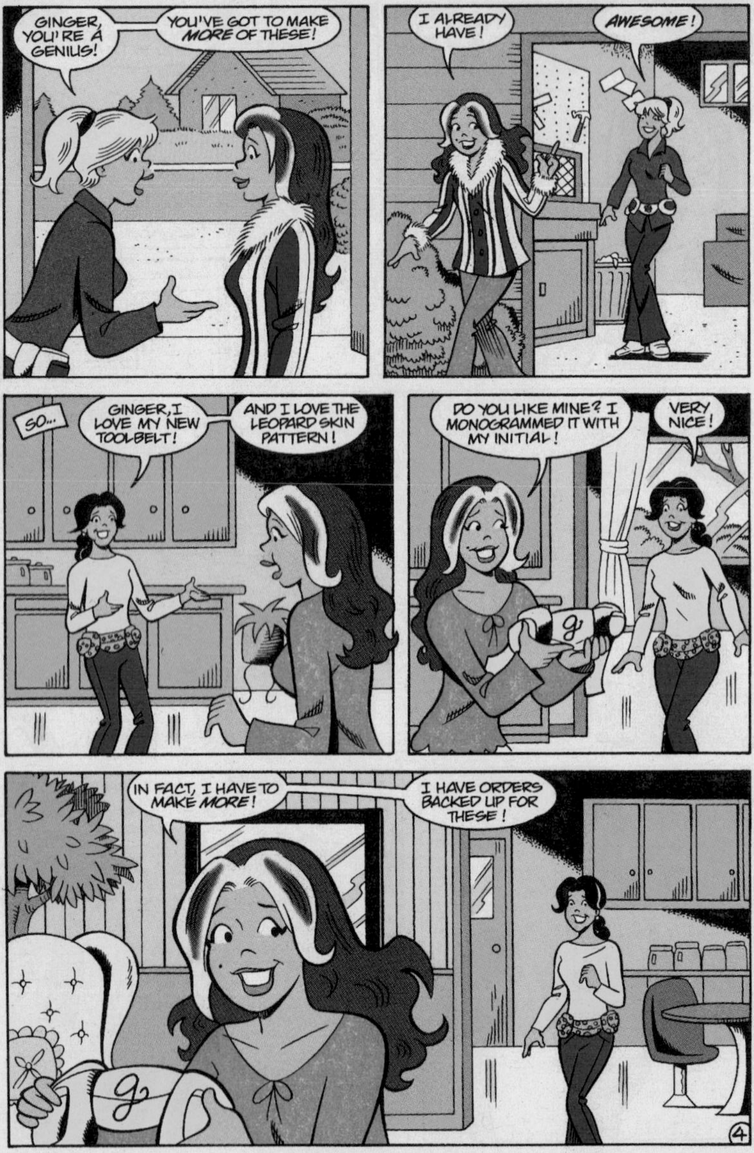

GINGER, YOU'RE A GENIUS!
YOU'VE GOT TO MAKE MORE OF THESE!
I ALREADY HAVE!
AWESOME!
SO...
GINGER, I LOVE MY NEW TOOLBELT!
AND I LOVE THE LEOPARD SKIN PATTERN!
DO YOU LIKE MINE? I MONOGRAMMED IT WITH MY INITIAL!
VERY NICE!
IN FACT, I HAVE TO MAKE MORE!
I HAVE ORDERS BACKED UP FOR THESE!
4

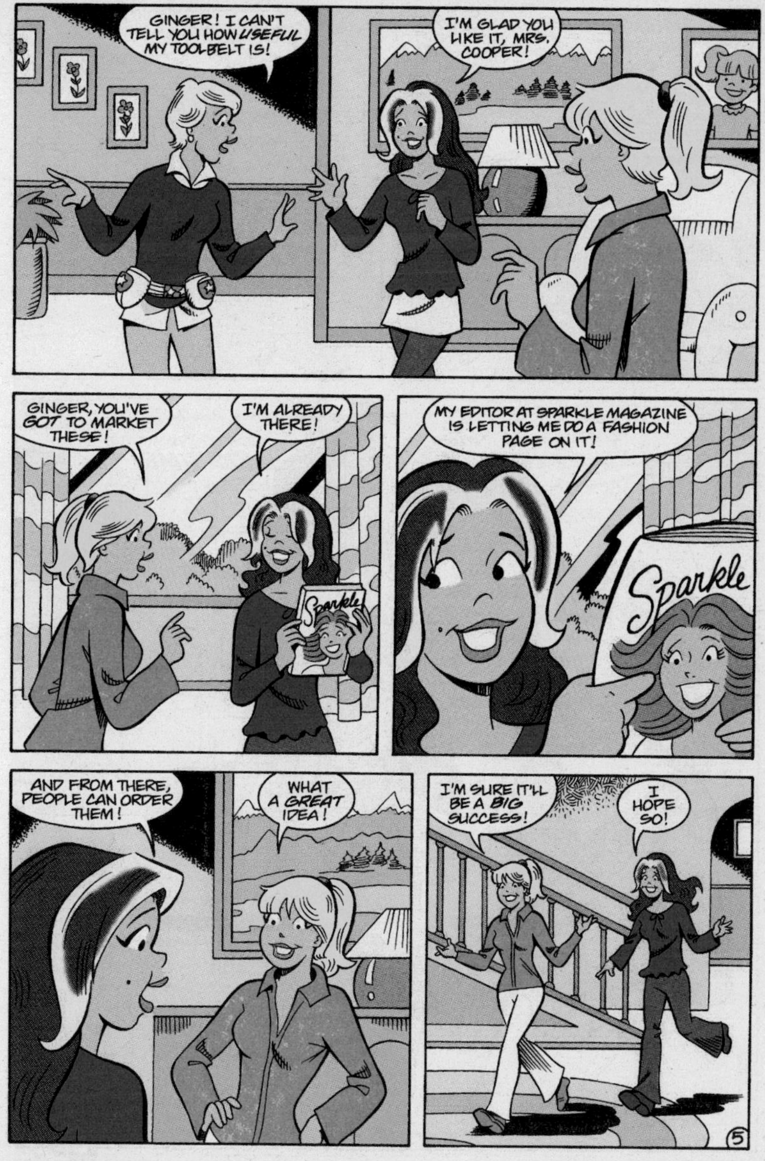

GINGER! I CAN'T TELL YOU HOW USEFUL MY TOOLBELT IS!
I'M GLAD YOU LIKE IT, MRS. COOPER!
GINGER, YOU'VE GOT TO MARKET THESE!
I'M ALREADY THERE!
Sparkle
MY EDITOR AT SPARKLE MAGAZINE IS LETTING ME DO A FASHION PAGE ON IT!
Sparkle
AND FROM THERE, PEOPLE CAN ORDER THEM!
WHAT A GREAT IDEA!
I'M SURE IT'LL BE A BIG SUCCESS!
I HOPE SO!
5

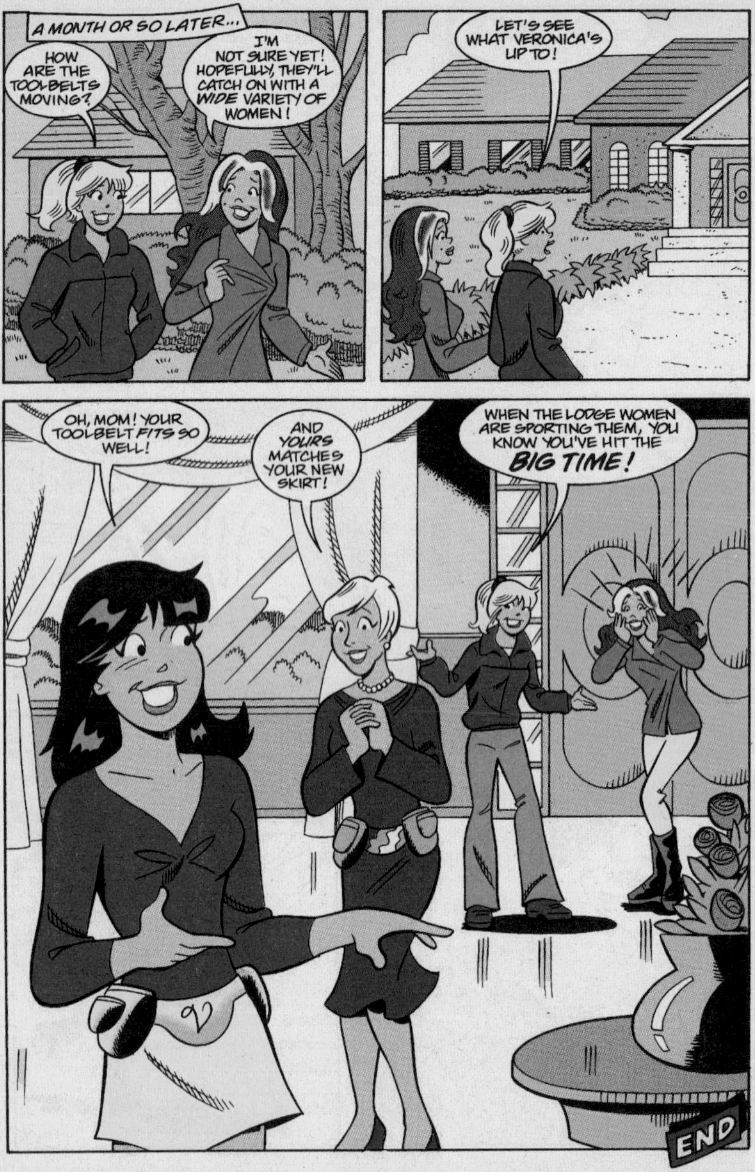
A MONTH OR SO LATER...
HOW ARE THE TOOLBELTS MOVING?
I'M NOT SURE YET! HOPEFULLY, THEY'LL CATCH ON WITH A *WIDE* VARIETY OF WOMEN!
LET'S SEE WHAT VERONICA'S UP TO!
OH, MOM! YOUR TOOLBELT *FITS* SO WELL!
AND *YOURS* MATCHES YOUR NEW SKIRT!
WHEN THE LODGE WOMEN ARE SPORTING THEM, YOU KNOW YOU'VE HIT THE **BIG TIME!**
END

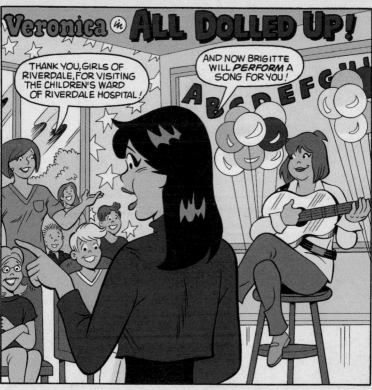

Veronica in ALL DOLLED UP!

THANK YOU, GIRLS OF RIVERDALE, FOR VISITING THE CHILDREN'S WARD OF RIVERDALE HOSPITAL!

AND NOW BRIGITTE WILL *PERFORM* A SONG FOR YOU!

WOW! BRIGITTE SOUNDS GREAT!!

AND THE KIDS LOVE HER!

HMMM! I WISH I HAD SOMETHING TO OFFER THESE KIDS!

YAY! BRAVO!!

Script & Pencils: Dan Parent / Inks: Jim Amash / Letters: Bill Yoshida

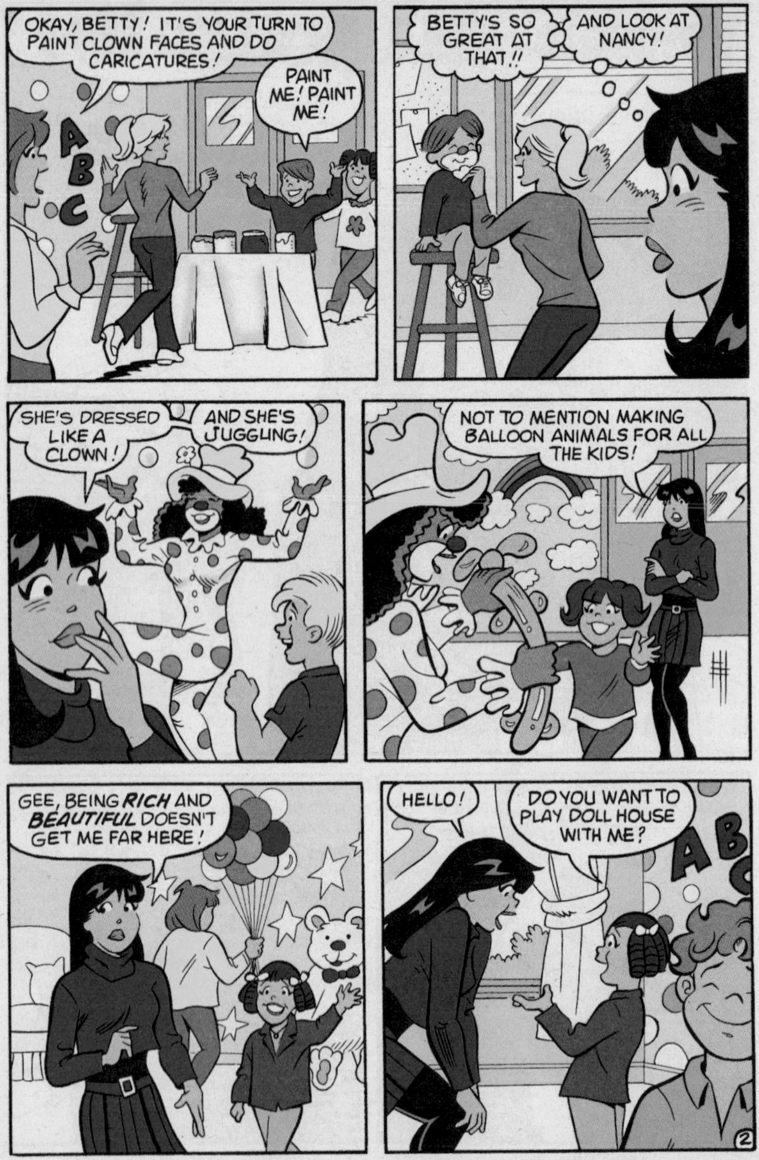
OKAY, BETTY! IT'S YOUR TURN TO PAINT CLOWN FACES AND DO CARICATURES!
PAINT ME! PAINT ME!
A B C
BETTY'S SO GREAT AT THAT!!
AND LOOK AT NANCY!
SHE'S DRESSED LIKE A CLOWN!
AND SHE'S JUGGLING!
NOT TO MENTION MAKING BALLOON ANIMALS FOR ALL THE KIDS!
GEE, BEING RICH AND BEAUTIFUL DOESN'T GET ME FAR HERE!
HELLO!
DO YOU WANT TO PLAY DOLL HOUSE WITH ME?
A B C
2

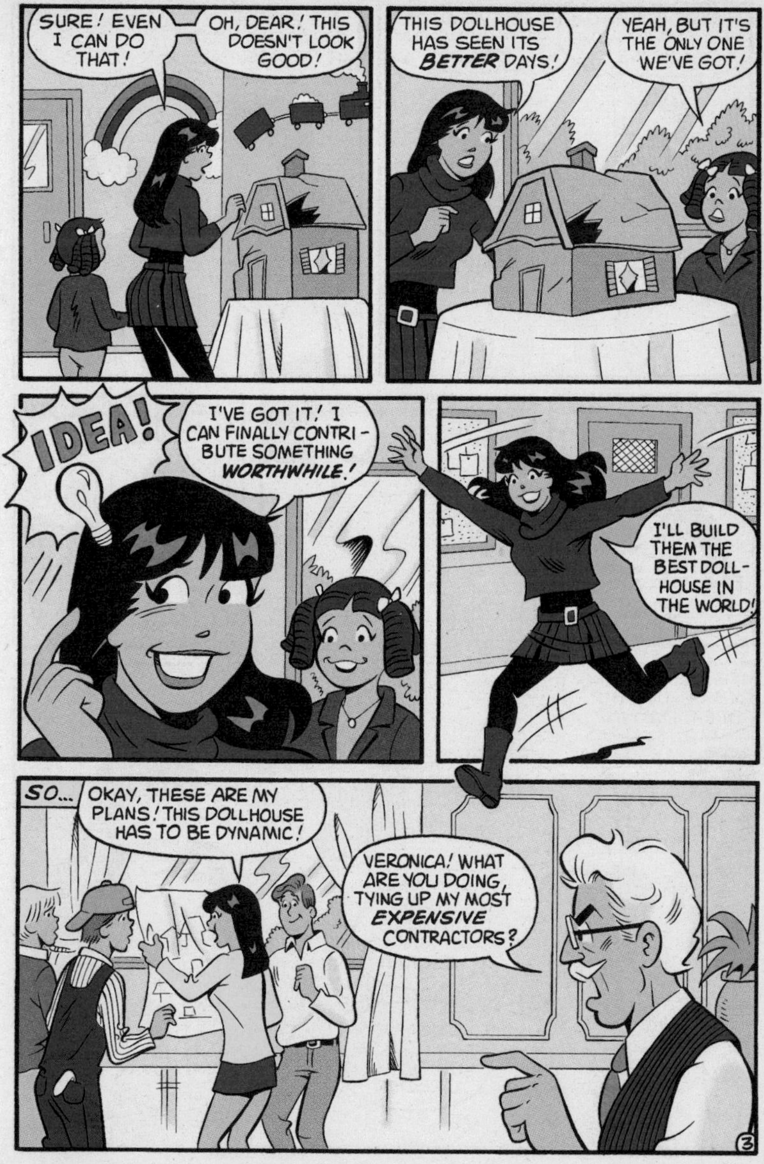
SURE! EVEN I CAN DO THAT!
OH, DEAR! THIS DOESN'T LOOK GOOD!
THIS DOLLHOUSE HAS SEEN ITS BETTER DAYS!
YEAH, BUT IT'S THE ONLY ONE WE'VE GOT!
IDEA!
I'VE GOT IT! I CAN FINALLY CONTRI-BUTE SOMETHING WORTHWHILE!
I'LL BUILD THEM THE BEST DOLL-HOUSE IN THE WORLD!
SO...
OKAY, THESE ARE MY PLANS! THIS DOLLHOUSE HAS TO BE DYNAMIC!
VERONICA! WHAT ARE YOU DOING, TYING UP MY MOST EXPENSIVE CONTRACTORS?
3

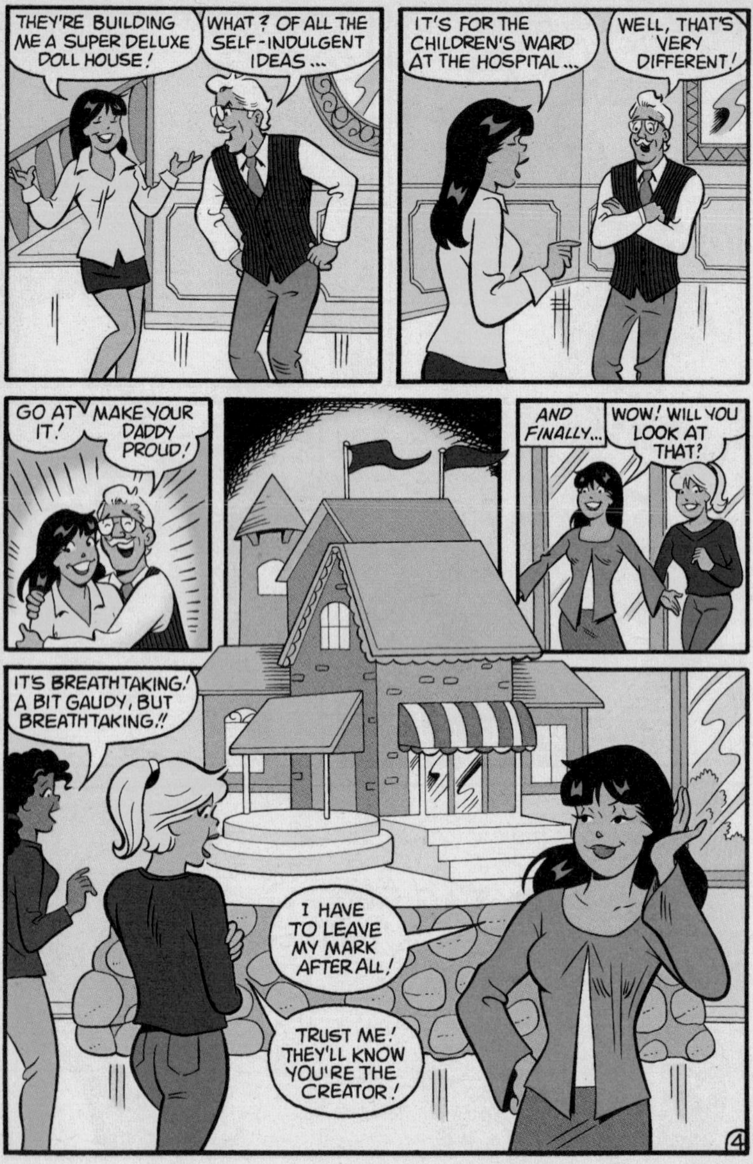
THEY'RE BUILDING ME A SUPER DELUXE DOLL HOUSE!
WHAT? OF ALL THE SELF-INDULGENT IDEAS ...
IT'S FOR THE CHILDREN'S WARD AT THE HOSPITAL ...
WELL, THAT'S VERY DIFFERENT!
GO AT IT!
MAKE YOUR DADDY PROUD!
AND FINALLY...
WOW! WILL YOU LOOK AT THAT?
IT'S BREATHTAKING! A BIT GAUDY, BUT BREATHTAKING!!
I HAVE TO LEAVE MY MARK AFTER ALL!
TRUST ME! THEY'LL KNOW YOU'RE THE CREATOR!
4

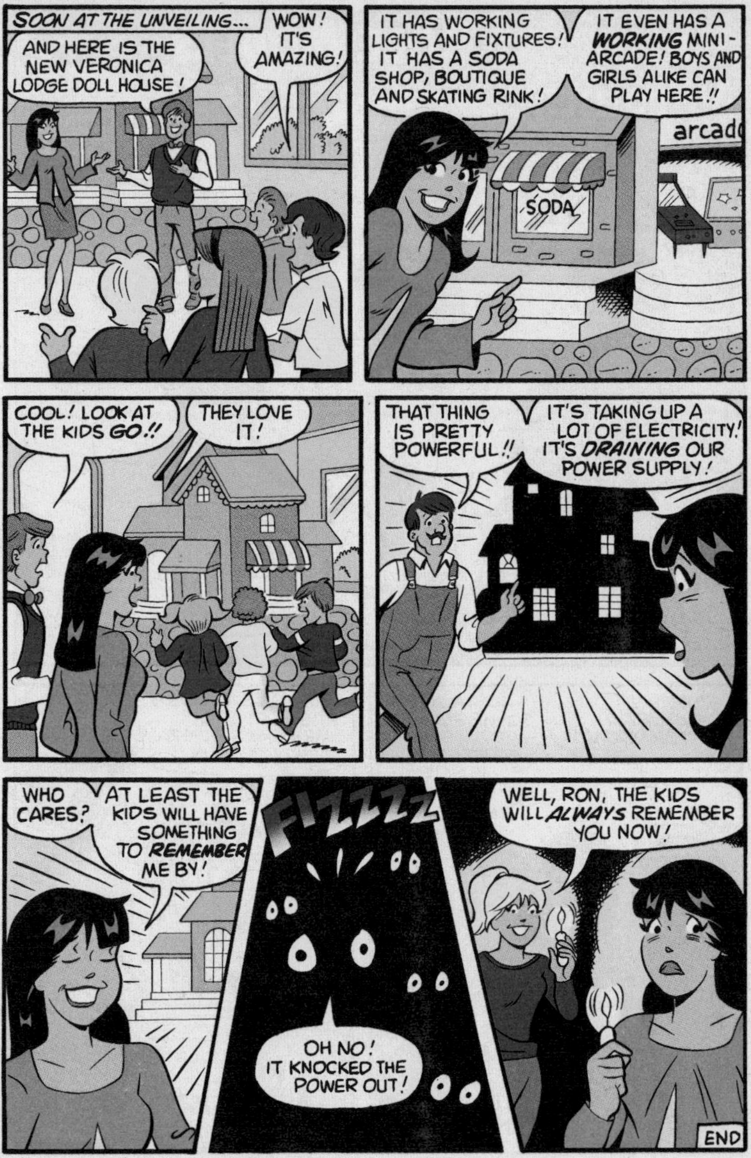
SOON AT THE UNVEILING...
AND HERE IS THE NEW VERONICA LODGE DOLL HOUSE!
WOW! IT'S AMAZING!
IT HAS WORKING LIGHTS AND FIXTURES! IT HAS A SODA SHOP, BOUTIQUE AND SKATING RINK!
IT EVEN HAS A WORKING MINI-ARCADE! BOYS AND GIRLS ALIKE CAN PLAY HERE!!
arcad
SODA
COOL! LOOK AT THE KIDS GO!!
THEY LOVE IT!
THAT THING IS PRETTY POWERFUL!!
IT'S TAKING UP A LOT OF ELECTRICITY! IT'S DRAINING OUR POWER SUPPLY!
WHO CARES?
AT LEAST THE KIDS WILL HAVE SOMETHING TO REMEMBER ME BY!
FIZZZZ
OH NO! IT KNOCKED THE POWER OUT!
WELL, RON, THE KIDS WILL ALWAYS REMEMBER YOU NOW!
END

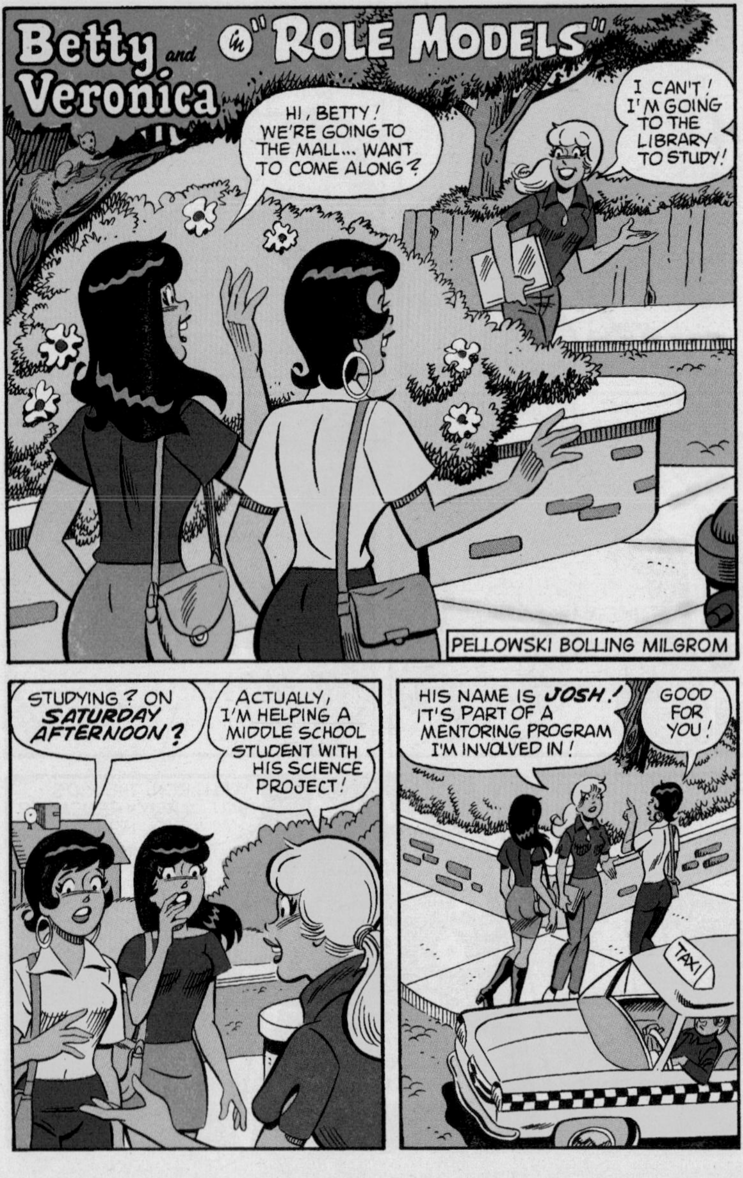
Betty and Veronica
in "ROLE MODELS"
HI, BETTY! WE'RE GOING TO THE MALL... WANT TO COME ALONG?
I CAN'T! I'M GOING TO THE LIBRARY TO STUDY!
PELLOWSKI BOLLING MILGROM
STUDYING? ON SATURDAY AFTERNOON?
ACTUALLY, I'M HELPING A MIDDLE SCHOOL STUDENT WITH HIS SCIENCE PROJECT!
HIS NAME IS JOSH! IT'S PART OF A MENTORING PROGRAM I'M INVOLVED IN!
GOOD FOR YOU!
TAXI

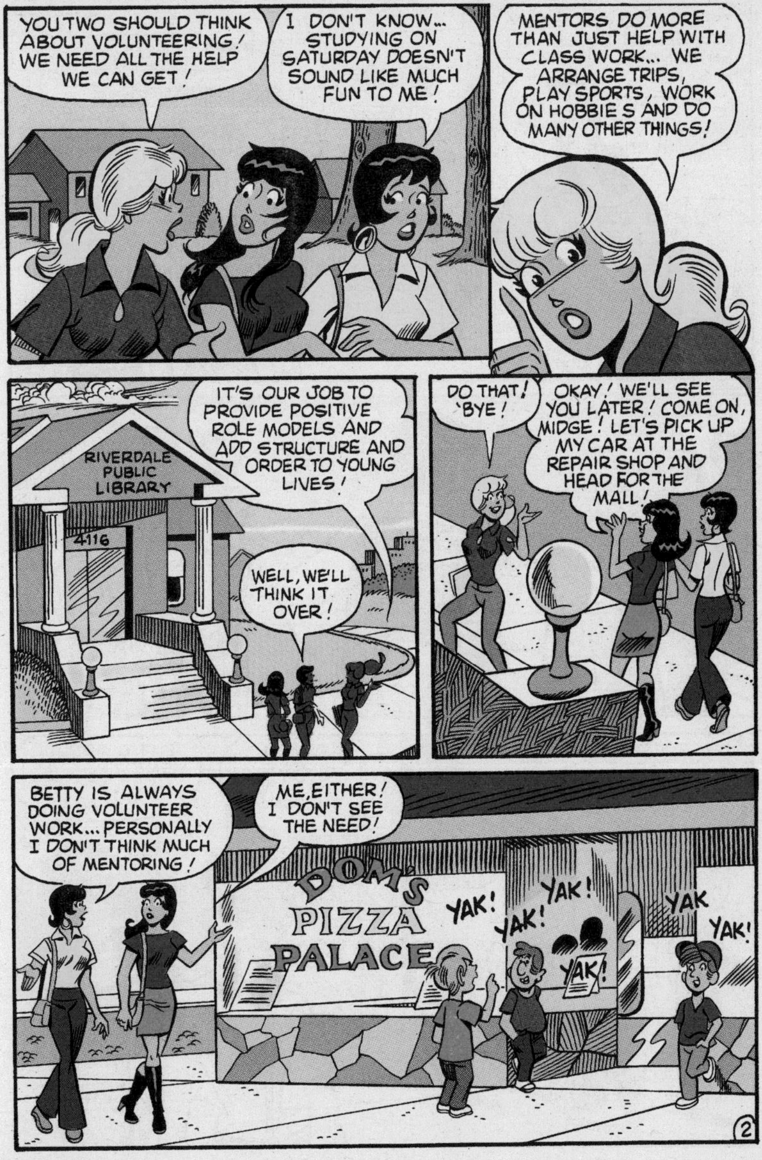
YOU TWO SHOULD THINK ABOUT VOLUNTEERING! WE NEED ALL THE HELP WE CAN GET!
I DON'T KNOW... STUDYING ON SATURDAY DOESN'T SOUND LIKE MUCH FUN TO ME!
MENTORS DO MORE THAN JUST HELP WITH CLASS WORK... WE ARRANGE TRIPS, PLAY SPORTS, WORK ON HOBBIE S AND DO MANY OTHER THINGS!
RIVERDALE PUBLIC LIBRARY
4116
IT'S OUR JOB TO PROVIDE POSITIVE ROLE MODELS AND ADD STRUCTURE AND ORDER TO YOUNG LIVES!
WELL, WE'LL THINK IT OVER!
DO THAT! 'BYE!
OKAY! WE'LL SEE YOU LATER! COME ON, MIDGE! LET'S PICK UP MY CAR AT THE REPAIR SHOP AND HEAD FOR THE MALL!
BETTY IS ALWAYS DOING VOLUNTEER WORK... PERSONALLY I DON'T THINK MUCH OF MENTORING!
ME, EITHER! I DON'T SEE THE NEED!
DOM'S PIZZA PALACE
YAK!
YAK!
YAK!
YAK!
YAK
YAK!
2

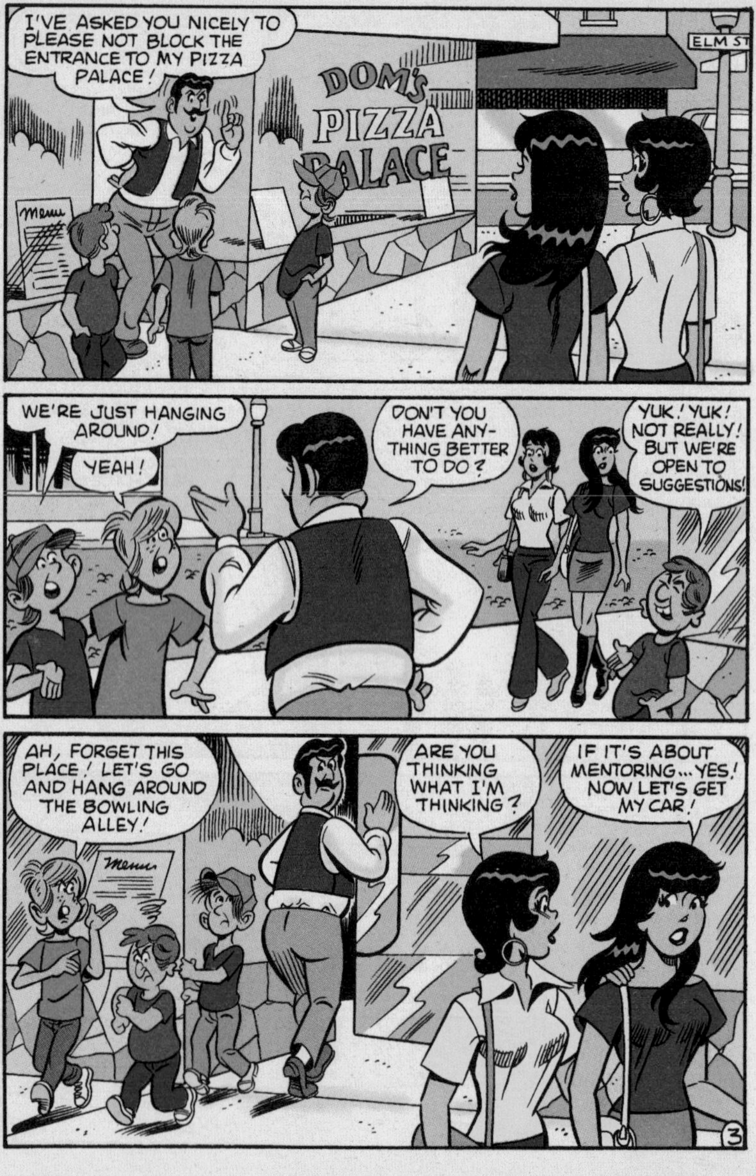

I'VE ASKED YOU NICELY TO PLEASE NOT BLOCK THE ENTRANCE TO MY PIZZA PALACE!
DOM'S PIZZA PALACE
ELM ST
WE'RE JUST HANGING AROUND!
YEAH!
DON'T YOU HAVE ANY-THING BETTER TO DO?
YUK! YUK! NOT REALLY! BUT WE'RE OPEN TO SUGGESTIONS!
AH, FORGET THIS PLACE! LET'S GO AND HANG AROUND THE BOWLING ALLEY!
ARE YOU THINKING WHAT I'M THINKING?
IF IT'S ABOUT MENTORING... YES! NOW LET'S GET MY CAR!
3

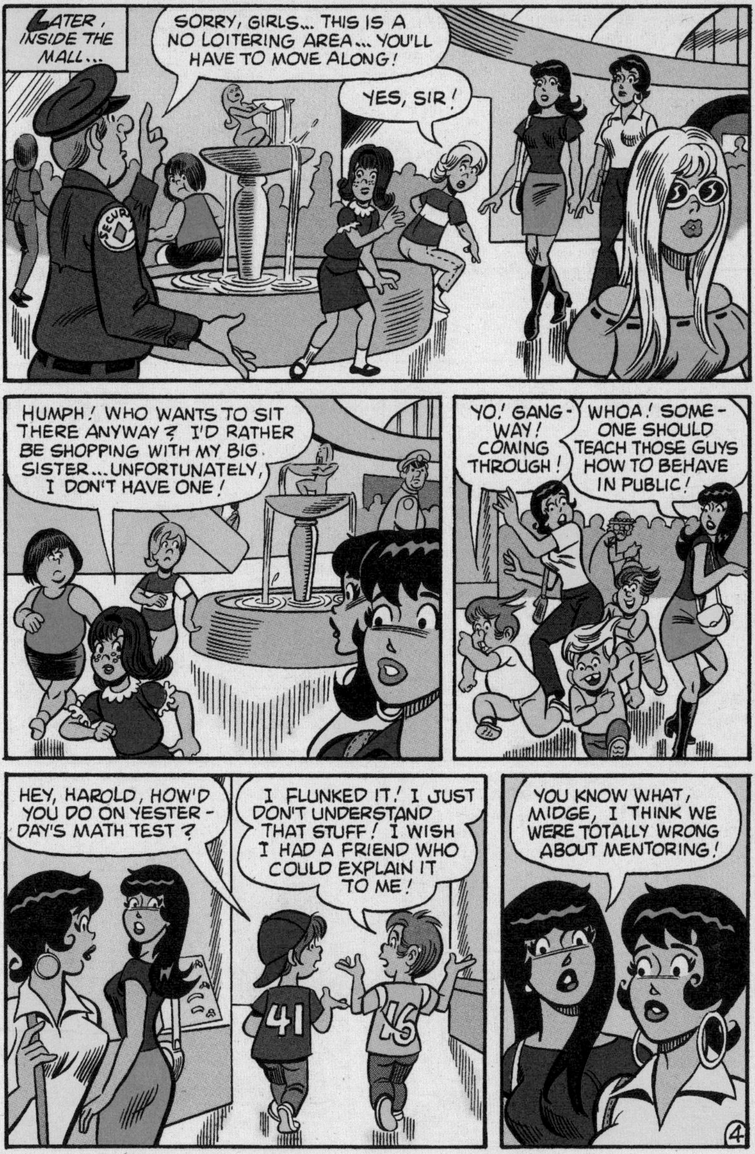
LATER, INSIDE THE MALL...
SORRY, GIRLS... THIS IS A NO LOITERING AREA... YOU'LL HAVE TO MOVE ALONG!
YES, SIR!
HUMPH! WHO WANTS TO SIT THERE ANYWAY? I'D RATHER BE SHOPPING WITH MY BIG SISTER... UNFORTUNATELY, I DON'T HAVE ONE!
YO! GANG-WAY! COMING THROUGH!
WHOA! SOME-ONE SHOULD TEACH THOSE GUYS HOW TO BEHAVE IN PUBLIC!
HEY, HAROLD, HOW'D YOU DO ON YESTER-DAY'S MATH TEST?
I FLUNKED IT! I JUST DON'T UNDERSTAND THAT STUFF! I WISH I HAD A FRIEND WHO COULD EXPLAIN IT TO ME!
YOU KNOW WHAT, MIDGE, I THINK WE WERE TOTALLY WRONG ABOUT MENTORING!
41
45
4

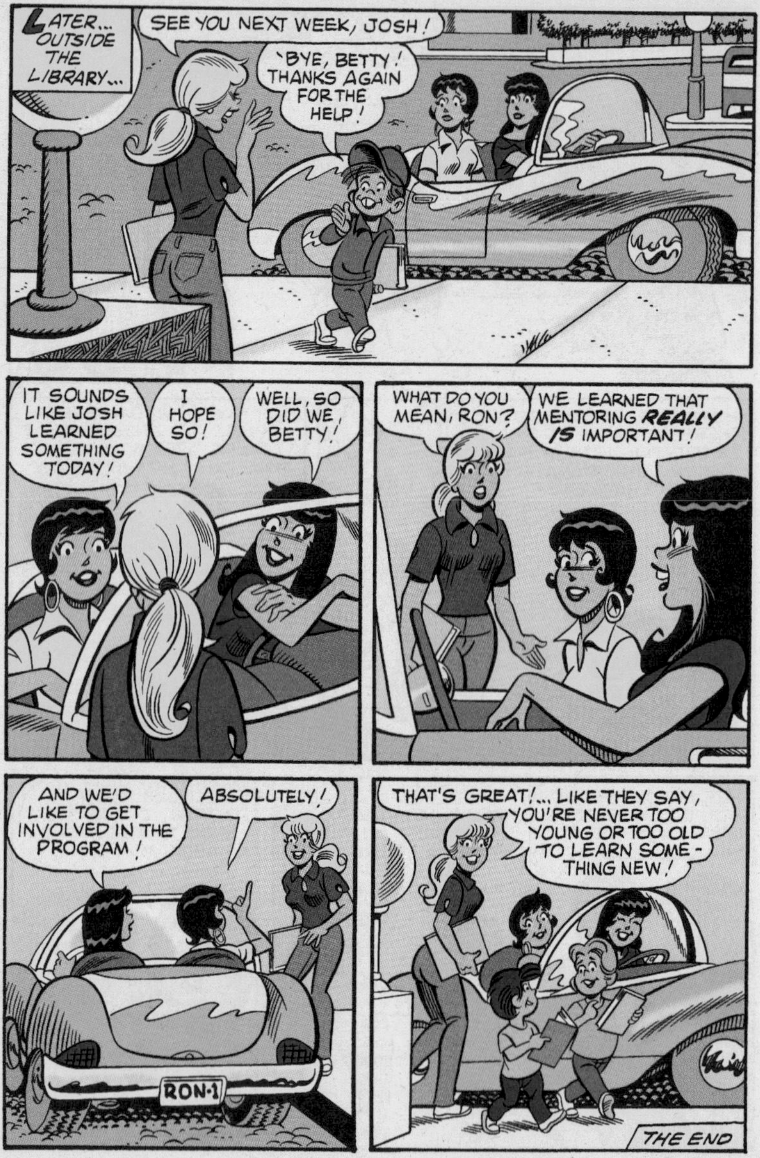
LATER... OUTSIDE THE LIBRARY...
SEE YOU NEXT WEEK, JOSH!
`BYE, BETTY! THANKS AGAIN FOR THE HELP!
IT SOUNDS LIKE JOSH LEARNED SOMETHING TODAY!
I HOPE SO!
WELL, SO DID WE, BETTY!
WHAT DO YOU MEAN, RON?
WE LEARNED THAT MENTORING REALLY IS IMPORTANT!
AND WE'D LIKE TO GET INVOLVED IN THE PROGRAM!
ABSOLUTELY!
RON-1
THAT'S GREAT!... LIKE THEY SAY, YOU'RE NEVER TOO YOUNG OR TOO OLD TO LEARN SOME-THING NEW!
THE END

Archie at Riverdale
"The Cost of Quality" Chapter One

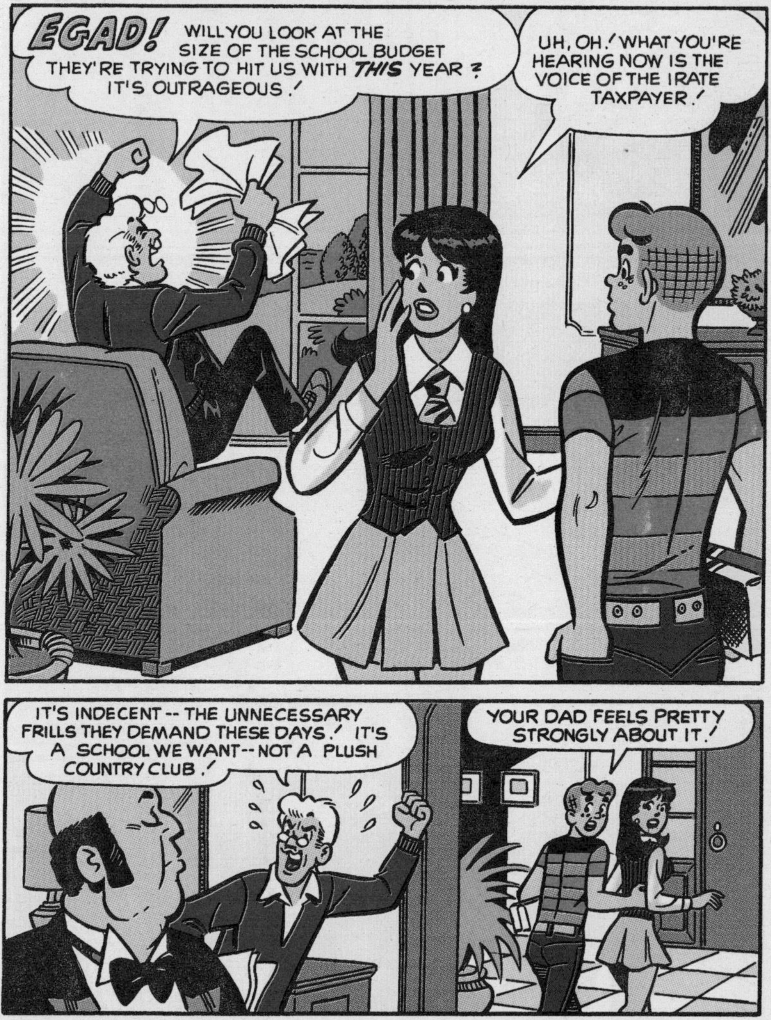
EGAD! WILL YOU LOOK AT THE SIZE OF THE SCHOOL BUDGET THEY'RE TRYING TO HIT US WITH THIS YEAR? IT'S OUTRAGEOUS!
UH, OH! WHAT YOU'RE HEARING NOW IS THE VOICE OF THE IRATE TAXPAYER!
IT'S INDECENT -- THE UNNECESSARY FRILLS THEY DEMAND THESE DAYS! IT'S A SCHOOL WE WANT -- NOT A PLUSH COUNTRY CLUB!
YOUR DAD FEELS PRETTY STRONGLY ABOUT IT!

Script: Frank Doyle / Pencils: Dan DeCarlo / Inks: Rudy Lapick / Letters: Bill Yoshida

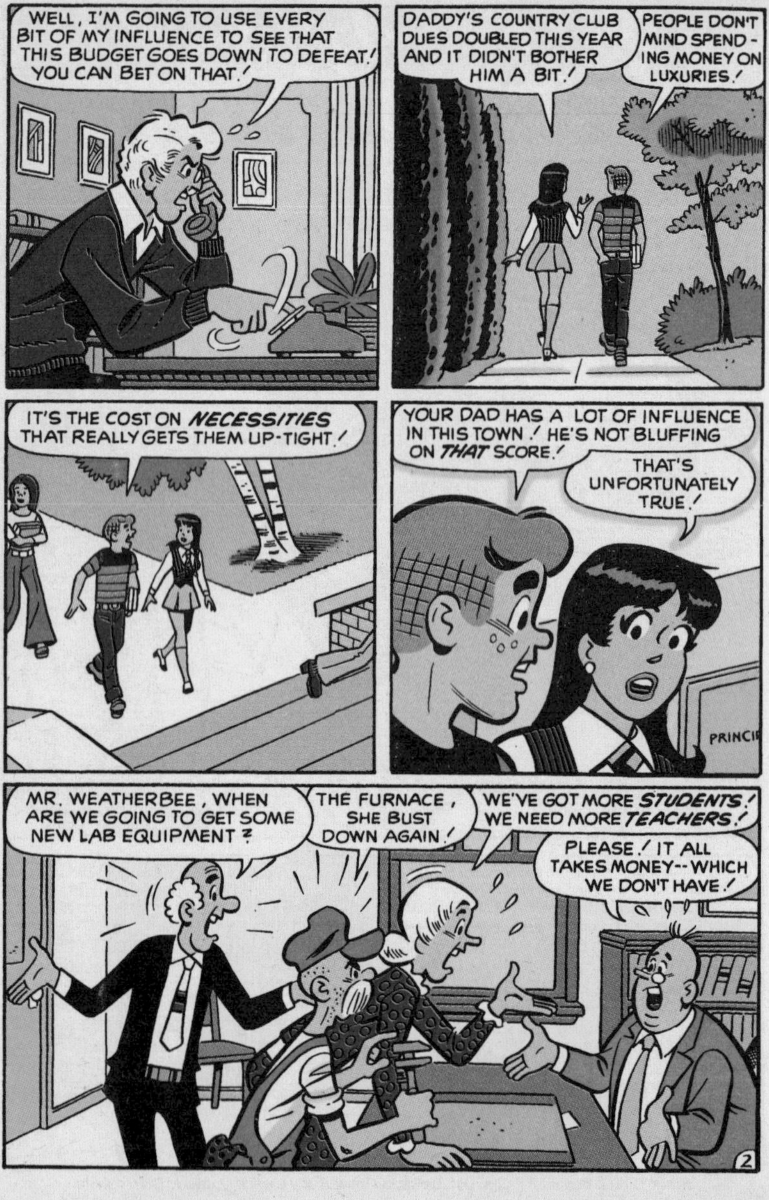

WELL, I'M GOING TO USE EVERY BIT OF MY INFLUENCE TO SEE THAT THIS BUDGET GOES DOWN TO DEFEAT! YOU CAN BET ON THAT!
DADDY'S COUNTRY CLUB DUES DOUBLED THIS YEAR AND IT DIDN'T BOTHER HIM A BIT!
PEOPLE DON'T MIND SPEND-ING MONEY ON LUXURIES!
IT'S THE COST ON *NECESSITIES* THAT REALLY GETS THEM UP-TIGHT!
YOUR DAD HAS A LOT OF INFLUENCE IN THIS TOWN! HE'S NOT BLUFFING ON *THAT* SCORE!
THAT'S UNFORTUNATELY TRUE!
PRINCIP
MR. WEATHERBEE, WHEN ARE WE GOING TO GET SOME NEW LAB EQUIPMENT?
THE FURNACE, SHE BUST DOWN AGAIN!
WE'VE GOT MORE *STUDENTS*! WE NEED MORE *TEACHERS*!
PLEASE! IT ALL TAKES MONEY-- WHICH WE DON'T HAVE!
2

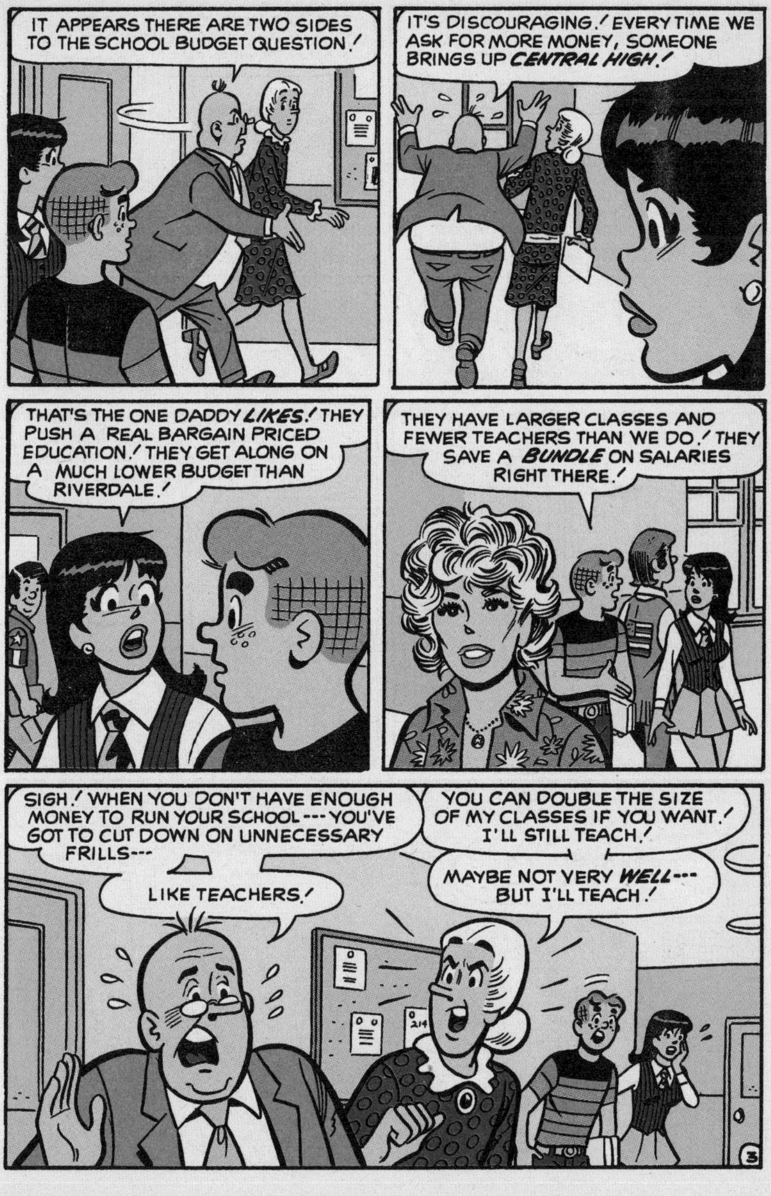

IT APPEARS THERE ARE TWO SIDES TO THE SCHOOL BUDGET QUESTION!
IT'S DISCOURAGING! EVERY TIME WE ASK FOR MORE MONEY, SOMEONE BRINGS UP CENTRAL HIGH!
THAT'S THE ONE DADDY LIKES! THEY PUSH A REAL BARGAIN PRICED EDUCATION! THEY GET ALONG ON A MUCH LOWER BUDGET THAN RIVERDALE!
THEY HAVE LARGER CLASSES AND FEWER TEACHERS THAN WE DO! THEY SAVE A BUNDLE ON SALARIES RIGHT THERE!
SIGH! WHEN YOU DON'T HAVE ENOUGH MONEY TO RUN YOUR SCHOOL --- YOU'VE GOT TO CUT DOWN ON UNNECESSARY FRILLS---
LIKE TEACHERS!
YOU CAN DOUBLE THE SIZE OF MY CLASSES IF YOU WANT! I'LL STILL TEACH!
MAYBE NOT VERY WELL--- BUT I'LL TEACH!
3

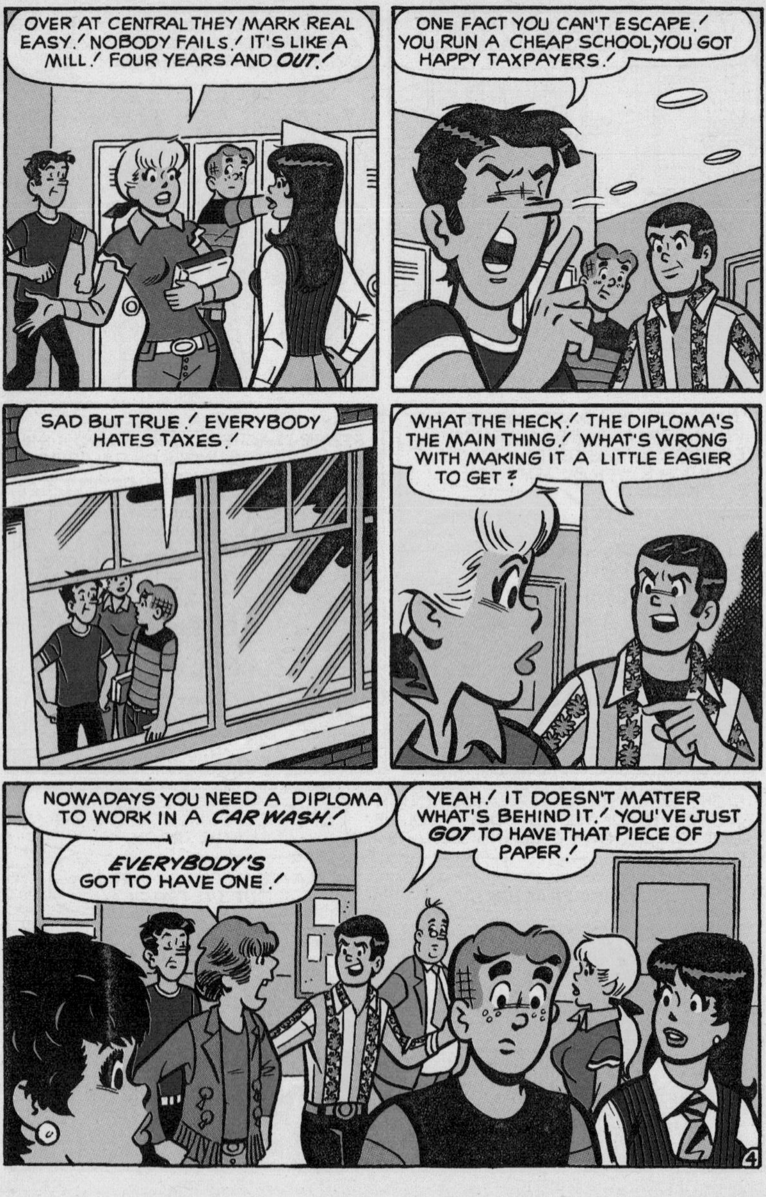
OVER AT CENTRAL THEY MARK REAL EASY! NOBODY FAILS! IT'S LIKE A MILL! FOUR YEARS AND OUT!
ONE FACT YOU CAN'T ESCAPE! YOU RUN A CHEAP SCHOOL, YOU GOT HAPPY TAXPAYERS!
SAD BUT TRUE! EVERYBODY HATES TAXES!
WHAT THE HECK! THE DIPLOMA'S THE MAIN THING! WHAT'S WRONG WITH MAKING IT A LITTLE EASIER TO GET?
NOWADAYS YOU NEED A DIPLOMA TO WORK IN A CAR WASH!
EVERYBODY'S GOT TO HAVE ONE!
YEAH! IT DOESN'T MATTER WHAT'S BEHIND IT! YOU'VE JUST GOT TO HAVE THAT PIECE OF PAPER!
4

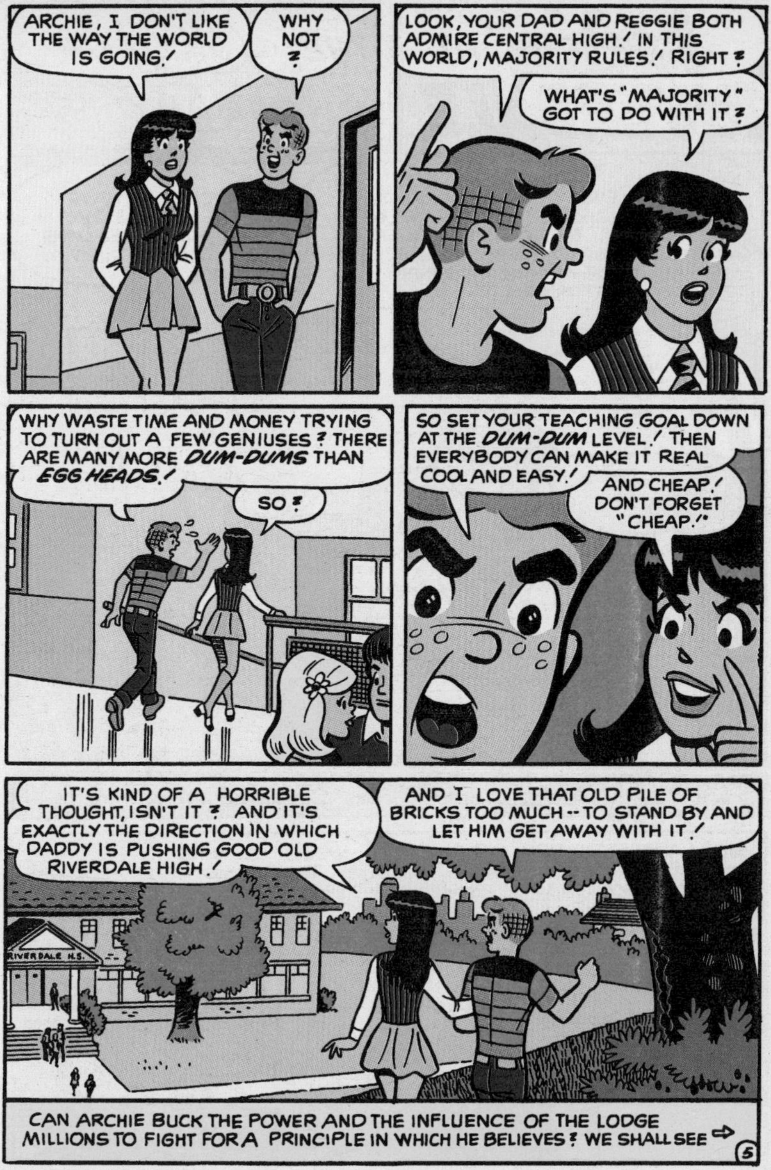
ARCHIE, I DON'T LIKE THE WAY THE WORLD IS GOING!
WHY NOT?
LOOK, YOUR DAD AND REGGIE BOTH ADMIRE CENTRAL HIGH! IN THIS WORLD, MAJORITY RULES! RIGHT?
WHAT'S "MAJORITY" GOT TO DO WITH IT?
WHY WASTE TIME AND MONEY TRYING TO TURN OUT A FEW GENIUSES? THERE ARE MANY MORE DUM-DUMS THAN EGG HEADS!
SO?
SO SET YOUR TEACHING GOAL DOWN AT THE DUM-DUM LEVEL! THEN EVERYBODY CAN MAKE IT REAL COOL AND EASY!
AND CHEAP! DON'T FORGET "CHEAP!"
IT'S KIND OF A HORRIBLE THOUGHT, ISN'T IT? AND IT'S EXACTLY THE DIRECTION IN WHICH DADDY IS PUSHING GOOD OLD RIVERDALE HIGH!
AND I LOVE THAT OLD PILE OF BRICKS TOO MUCH -- TO STAND BY AND LET HIM GET AWAY WITH IT!
RIVERDALE H.S.
CAN ARCHIE BUCK THE POWER AND THE INFLUENCE OF THE LODGE MILLIONS TO FIGHT FOR A PRINCIPLE IN WHICH HE BELIEVES? WE SHALL SEE ⇨
5

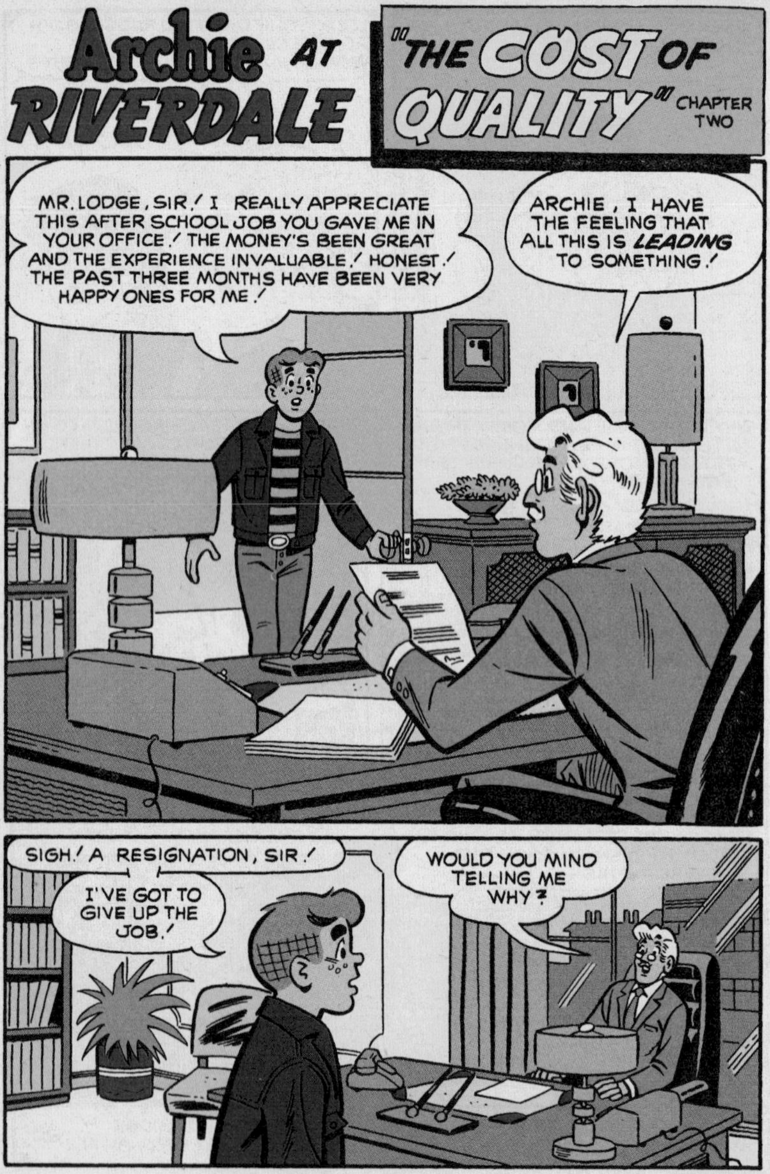
Archie AT RIVERDALE
"THE COST OF QUALITY" CHAPTER TWO
MR. LODGE, SIR! I REALLY APPRECIATE THIS AFTER SCHOOL JOB YOU GAVE ME IN YOUR OFFICE! THE MONEY'S BEEN GREAT AND THE EXPERIENCE INVALUABLE! HONEST! THE PAST THREE MONTHS HAVE BEEN VERY HAPPY ONES FOR ME!
ARCHIE, I HAVE THE FEELING THAT ALL THIS IS LEADING TO SOMETHING!
SIGH! A RESIGNATION, SIR!
I'VE GOT TO GIVE UP THE JOB!
WOULD YOU MIND TELLING ME WHY?

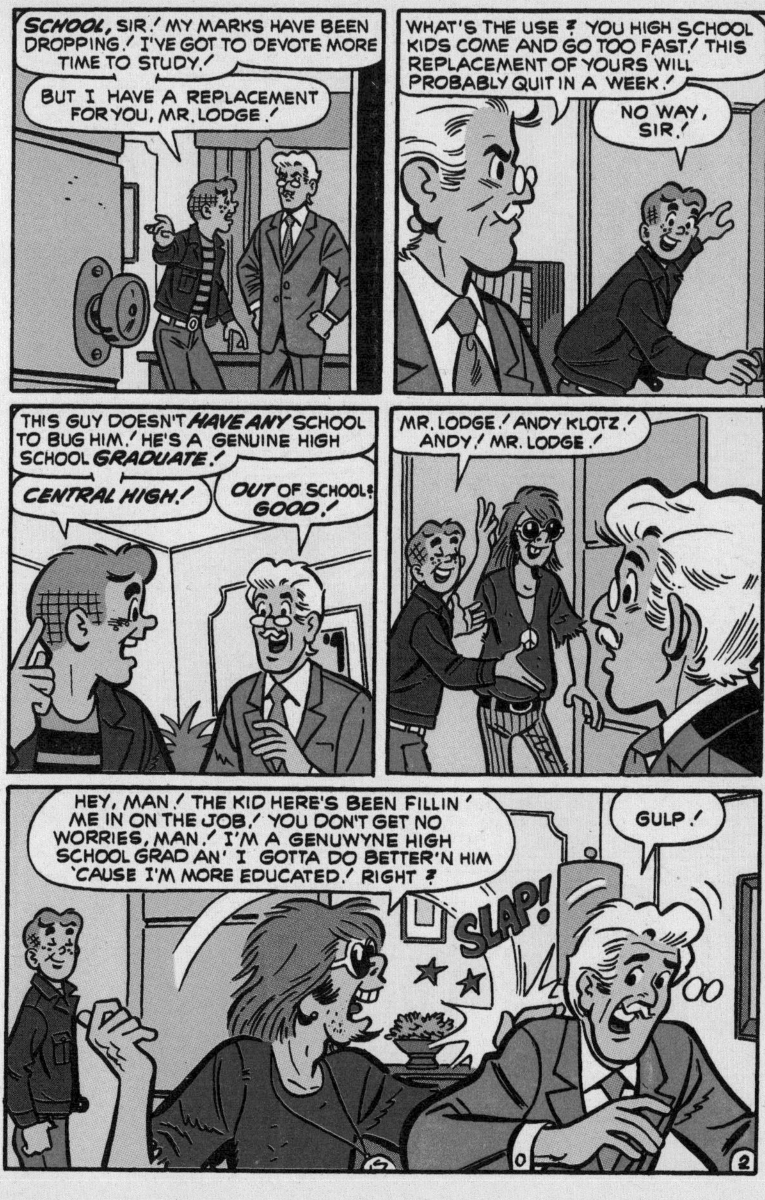
SCHOOL, SIR.! MY MARKS HAVE BEEN DROPPING.! I'VE GOT TO DEVOTE MORE TIME TO STUDY.!
BUT I HAVE A REPLACEMENT FOR YOU, MR. LODGE.!
WHAT'S THE USE ? YOU HIGH SCHOOL KIDS COME AND GO TOO FAST.! THIS REPLACEMENT OF YOURS WILL PROBABLY QUIT IN A WEEK.!
NO WAY, SIR.!
THIS GUY DOESN'T HAVE ANY SCHOOL TO BUG HIM.! HE'S A GENUINE HIGH SCHOOL GRADUATE.!
CENTRAL HIGH.!
OUT OF SCHOOL! GOOD.!
MR. LODGE.! ANDY KLOTZ.! ANDY.! MR. LODGE.!
HEY, MAN.! THE KID HERE'S BEEN FILLIN' ME IN ON THE JOB.! YOU DON'T GET NO WORRIES, MAN.! I'M A GENUWYNE HIGH SCHOOL GRAD AN' I GOTTA DO BETTER'N HIM 'CAUSE I'M MORE EDUCATED.! RIGHT ?
GULP.!
SLAP!
2

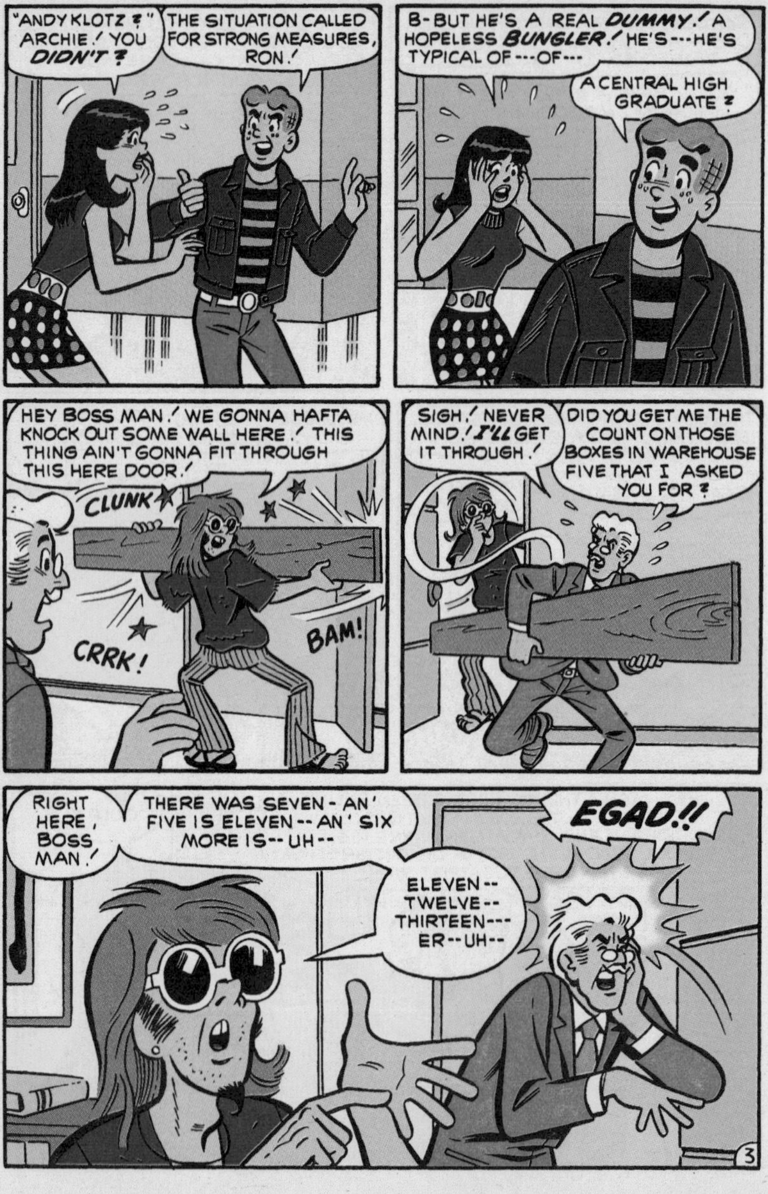
"ANDY KLOTZ ?" ARCHIE! YOU DIDN'T ?
THE SITUATION CALLED FOR STRONG MEASURES, RON!
B-BUT HE'S A REAL DUMMY! A HOPELESS BUNGLER! HE'S---HE'S TYPICAL OF---OF---
A CENTRAL HIGH GRADUATE ?
HEY BOSS MAN! WE GONNA HAFTA KNOCK OUT SOME WALL HERE! THIS THING AIN'T GONNA FIT THROUGH THIS HERE DOOR!
CLUNK
CRRK!
BAM!
SIGH! NEVER MIND! I'LL GET IT THROUGH!
DID YOU GET ME THE COUNT ON THOSE BOXES IN WAREHOUSE FIVE THAT I ASKED YOU FOR ?
RIGHT HERE, BOSS MAN!
THERE WAS SEVEN - AN' FIVE IS ELEVEN -- AN' SIX MORE IS -- UH --
ELEVEN -- TWELVE -- THIRTEEN --- ER -- UH --
EGAD!!
3

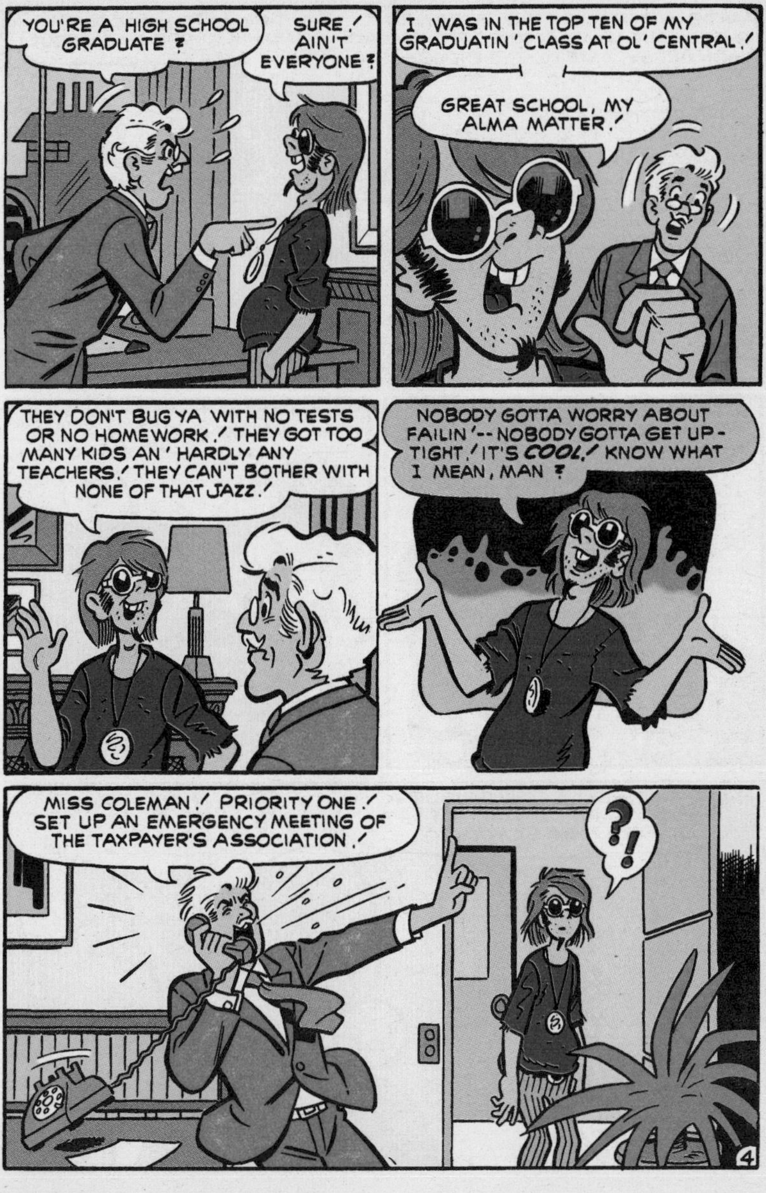
YOU'RE A HIGH SCHOOL GRADUATE ?
SURE ! AIN'T EVERYONE ?
I WAS IN THE TOP TEN OF MY GRADUATIN' CLASS AT OL' CENTRAL !
GREAT SCHOOL, MY ALMA MATTER !
THEY DON'T BUG YA WITH NO TESTS OR NO HOMEWORK ! THEY GOT TOO MANY KIDS AN' HARDLY ANY TEACHERS ! THEY CAN'T BOTHER WITH NONE OF THAT JAZZ !
NOBODY GOTTA WORRY ABOUT FAILIN' -- NOBODY GOTTA GET UP-TIGHT ! IT'S COOL ! KNOW WHAT I MEAN, MAN ?
MISS COLEMAN ! PRIORITY ONE ! SET UP AN EMERGENCY MEETING OF THE TAXPAYER'S ASSOCIATION !
?!
4

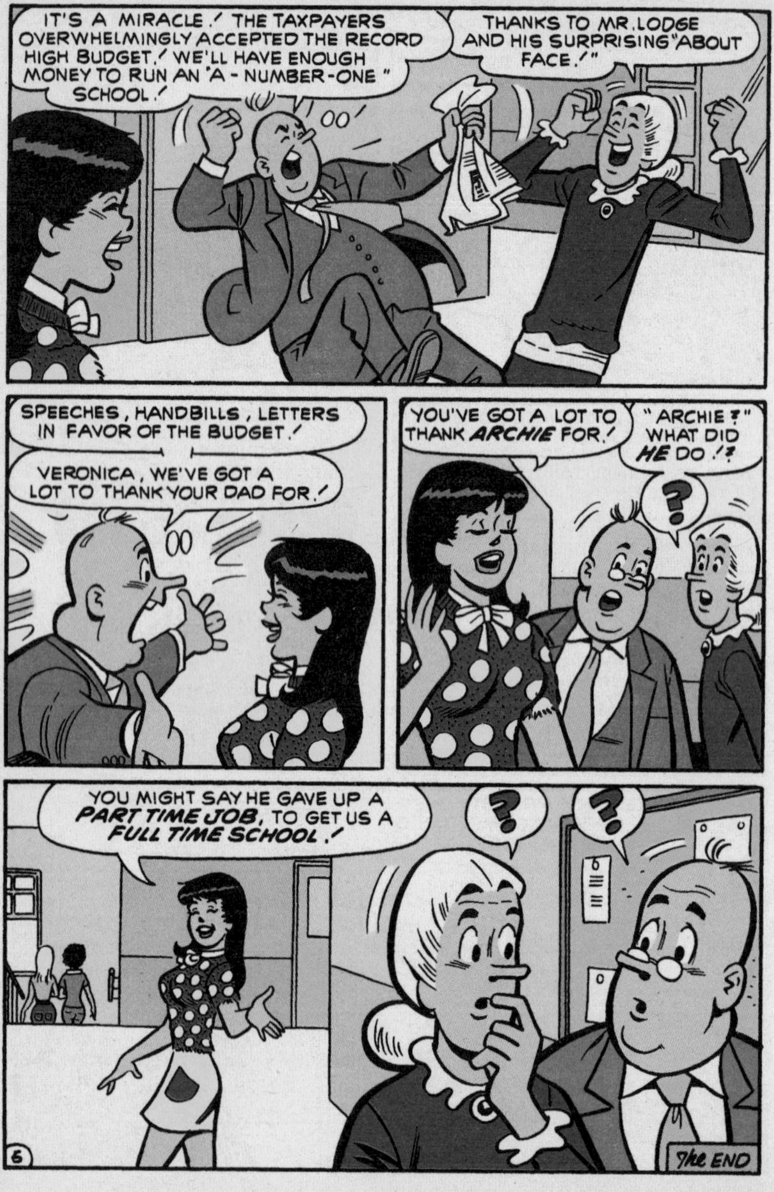
IT'S A MIRACLE! THE TAXPAYERS OVERWHELMINGLY ACCEPTED THE RECORD HIGH BUDGET! WE'LL HAVE ENOUGH MONEY TO RUN AN "A - NUMBER-ONE" SCHOOL!
THANKS TO MR. LODGE AND HIS SURPRISING "ABOUT FACE!"
SPEECHES, HANDBILLS, LETTERS IN FAVOR OF THE BUDGET!
VERONICA, WE'VE GOT A LOT TO THANK YOUR DAD FOR!
YOU'VE GOT A LOT TO THANK ARCHIE FOR!
"ARCHIE?" WHAT DID HE DO!?
?
YOU MIGHT SAY HE GAVE UP A PART TIME JOB, TO GET US A FULL TIME SCHOOL!
?
?
6
The END

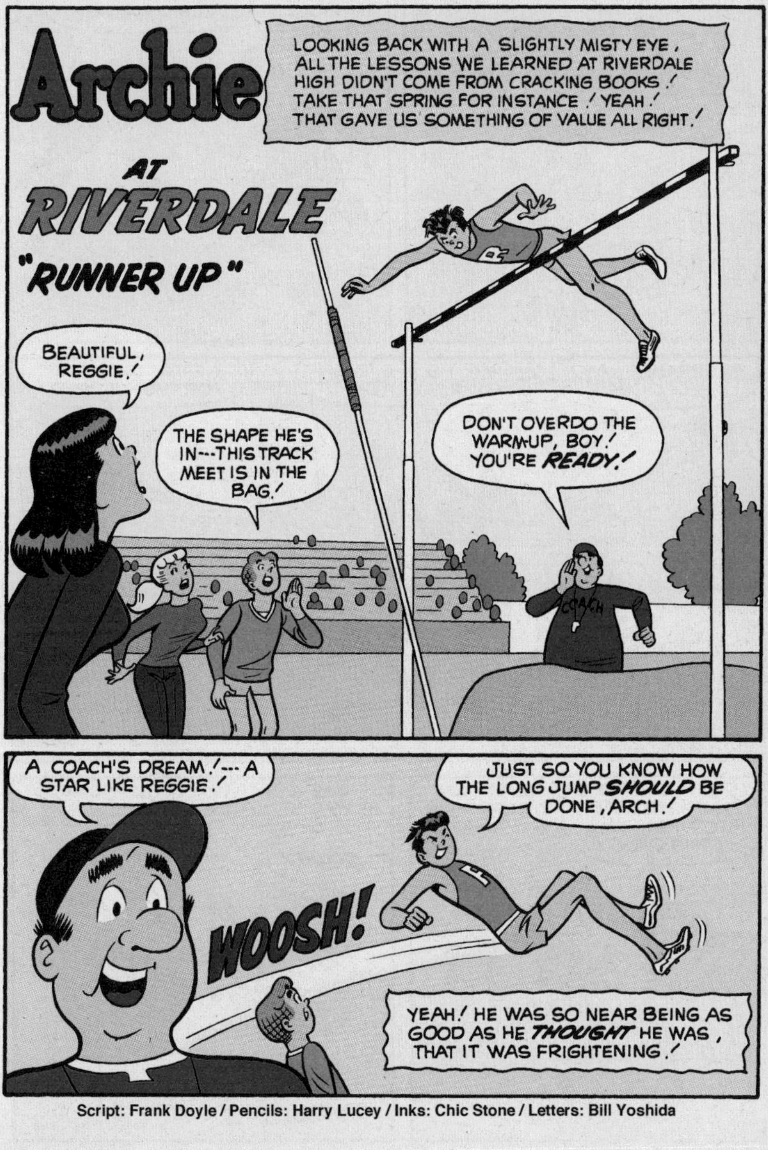
Archie
LOOKING BACK WITH A SLIGHTLY MISTY EYE, ALL THE LESSONS WE LEARNED AT RIVERDALE HIGH DIDN'T COME FROM CRACKING BOOKS! TAKE THAT SPRING FOR INSTANCE! YEAH! THAT GAVE US SOMETHING OF VALUE ALL RIGHT!
AT RIVERDALE
"RUNNER UP"
BEAUTIFUL, REGGIE!
THE SHAPE HE'S IN---THIS TRACK MEET IS IN THE BAG!
DON'T OVERDO THE WARM-UP, BOY! YOU'RE READY!
COACH
A COACH'S DREAM!--- A STAR LIKE REGGIE!
JUST SO YOU KNOW HOW THE LONG JUMP SHOULD BE DONE, ARCH!
WOOSH!
YEAH! HE WAS SO NEAR BEING AS GOOD AS HE THOUGHT HE WAS, THAT IT WAS FRIGHTENING!

Script: Frank Doyle / Pencils: Harry Lucey / Inks: Chic Stone / Letters: Bill Yoshida

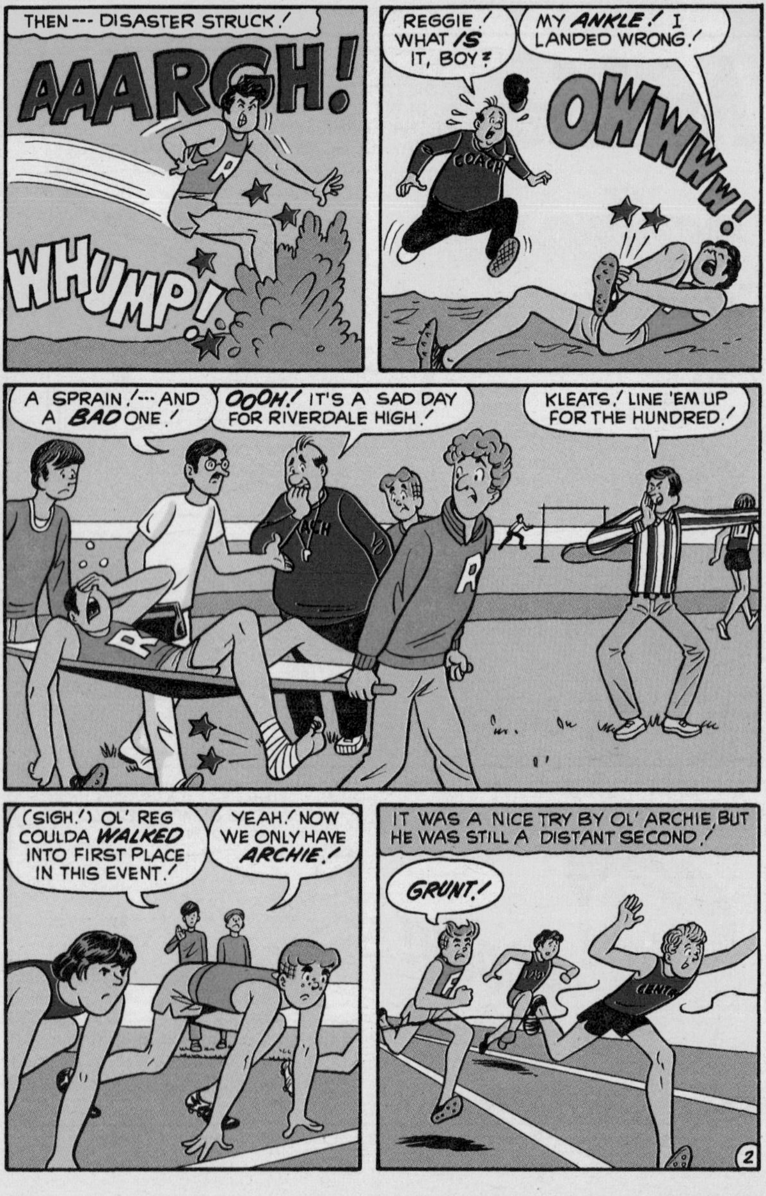
THEN --- DISASTER STRUCK!
AAARGH!
WHUMP!
REGGIE! WHAT IS IT, BOY?
MY ANKLE! I LANDED WRONG!
OWWWW!
A SPRAIN! --- AND A BAD ONE!
OOOH! IT'S A SAD DAY FOR RIVERDALE HIGH!
KLEATS! LINE 'EM UP FOR THE HUNDRED!
(SIGH!) OL' REG COULDA WALKED INTO FIRST PLACE IN THIS EVENT!
YEAH! NOW WE ONLY HAVE ARCHIE!
IT WAS A NICE TRY BY OL' ARCHIE, BUT HE WAS STILL A DISTANT SECOND!
GRUNT!
2

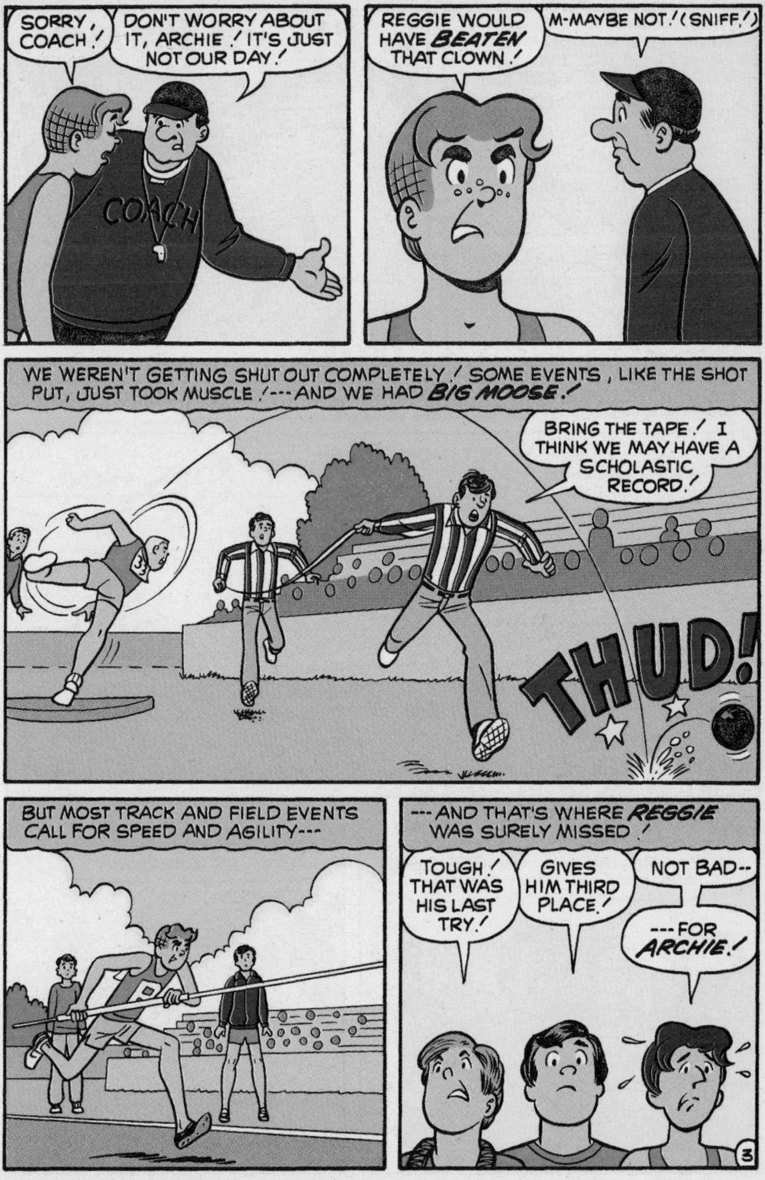
SORRY, COACH!
DON'T WORRY ABOUT IT, ARCHIE! IT'S JUST NOT OUR DAY!
COACH
REGGIE WOULD HAVE BEATEN THAT CLOWN!
M-MAYBE NOT! (SNIFF!)
WE WEREN'T GETTING SHUT OUT COMPLETELY! SOME EVENTS, LIKE THE SHOT PUT, JUST TOOK MUSCLE!---AND WE HAD BIG MOOSE!
BRING THE TAPE! I THINK WE MAY HAVE A SCHOLASTIC RECORD!
THUD!
BUT MOST TRACK AND FIELD EVENTS CALL FOR SPEED AND AGILITY---
---AND THAT'S WHERE REGGIE WAS SURELY MISSED!
TOUGH! THAT WAS HIS LAST TRY!
GIVES HIM THIRD PLACE!
NOT BAD--
---FOR ARCHIE!
3

C'MON, LADY LUCK! GIVE ME A LITTLE PUSH!

I'VE GOTTA WIN THIS! I'VE JUST *GOT* TO!

EEE - YAAGH!

BUT THE PRAYERS DIDN'T SEEM TO HELP! LADY LUCK TURNED HER BACK! ARCHIE'S FIERCE DETERMINATION WAS OF NO AVAIL!

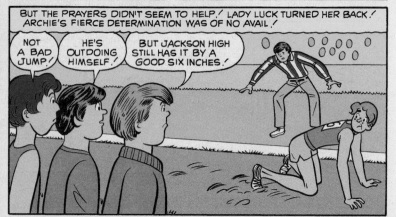

NOT A BAD JUMP!

HE'S OUTDOING HIMSELF!

BUT JACKSON HIGH STILL HAS IT BY A GOOD SIX INCHES!

SECOND! MAYBE HE SHOULD OPEN A CAR RENTAL AGENCY!

ARCH! HE'S ALWAYS WALKED IN *REGGIE'S* SHADOW!

YOU MAY TRY HARDER IF YOU'RE SECOND, BUT YOU DON'T WIN MANY MEETS THAT WAY!

④

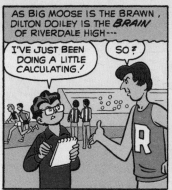

AS BIG MOOSE IS THE BRAWN, DILTON DOILEY IS THE *BRAIN* OF RIVERDALE HIGH---

I'VE JUST BEEN DOING A LITTLE CALCULATING!

SO?

EACH SCHOOL HAS AT LEAST ONE FIRST PLACE PLUS A LOT OF *FOURTHS* AND A FEW *THIRDS!*

OL' REG WOULD HAVE TAKEN FIRST IN AT LEAST *FIVE* EVENTS!

WELL GUESS *WHO* HAS BEEN TAKING CONSISTENT *SECONDS* AND A COUPLE OF *THIRDS?* AND GUESS *WHICH* SCHOOL IS ABOUT TO *WIN* THIS MEET ON *TOTAL POINTS?*

HUH?

Y- YOU M-MEAN--- *ARCHIE?*

WE'RE *AHEAD?*

MEANWHILE THE GAME LITTLE RED-HEAD WAS POURING HIS HEART OUT IN ANOTHER EVENT---

--- AND EATING MORE DUST---

CHOKE!

5

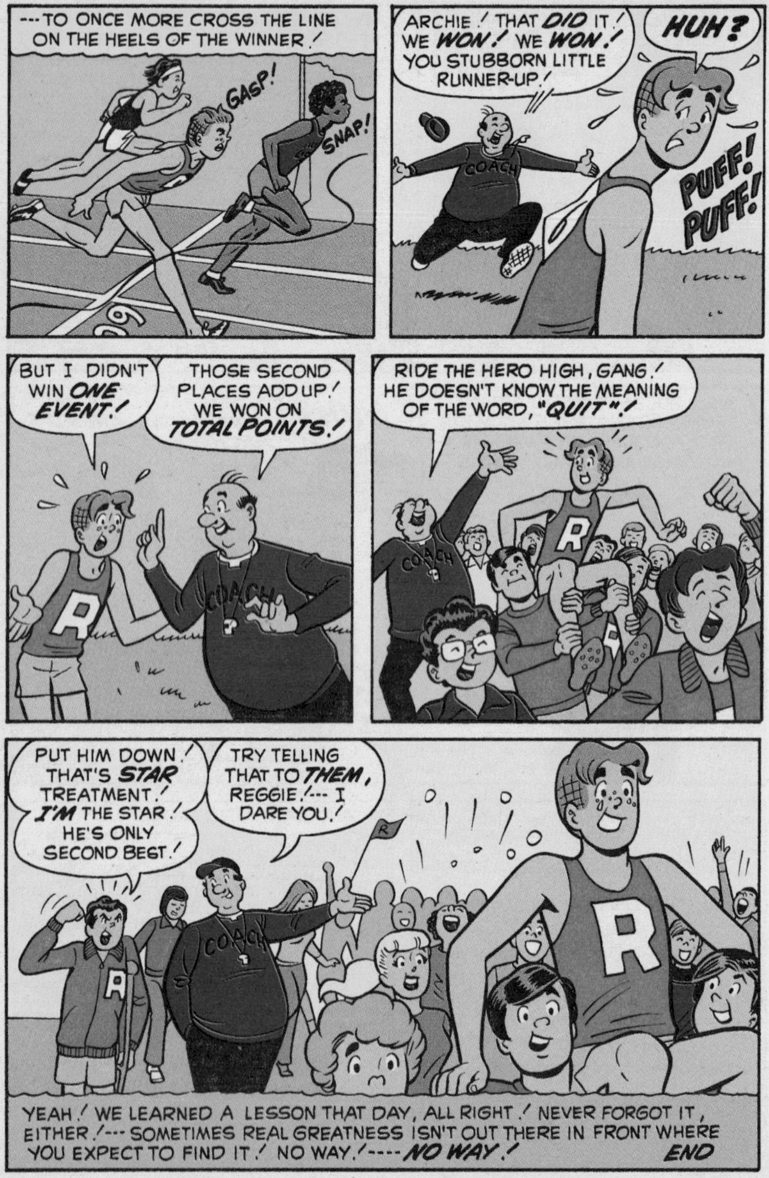
---TO ONCE MORE CROSS THE LINE ON THE HEELS OF THE WINNER!
GASP!
SNAP!
ARCHIE! THAT DID IT! WE WON! WE WON! YOU STUBBORN LITTLE RUNNER-UP!
HUH?
COACH
PUFF! PUFF!
BUT I DIDN'T WIN ONE EVENT!
THOSE SECOND PLACES ADD UP! WE WON ON TOTAL POINTS!
COACH
RIDE THE HERO HIGH, GANG! HE DOESN'T KNOW THE MEANING OF THE WORD, "QUIT"!
COACH
PUT HIM DOWN! THAT'S STAR TREATMENT! I'M THE STAR! HE'S ONLY SECOND BEST!
TRY TELLING THAT TO THEM, REGGIE!--- I DARE YOU!
COACH
YEAH! WE LEARNED A LESSON THAT DAY, ALL RIGHT! NEVER FORGOT IT, EITHER!--- SOMETIMES REAL GREATNESS ISN'T OUT THERE IN FRONT WHERE YOU EXPECT TO FIND IT! NO WAY!---- NO WAY!
END

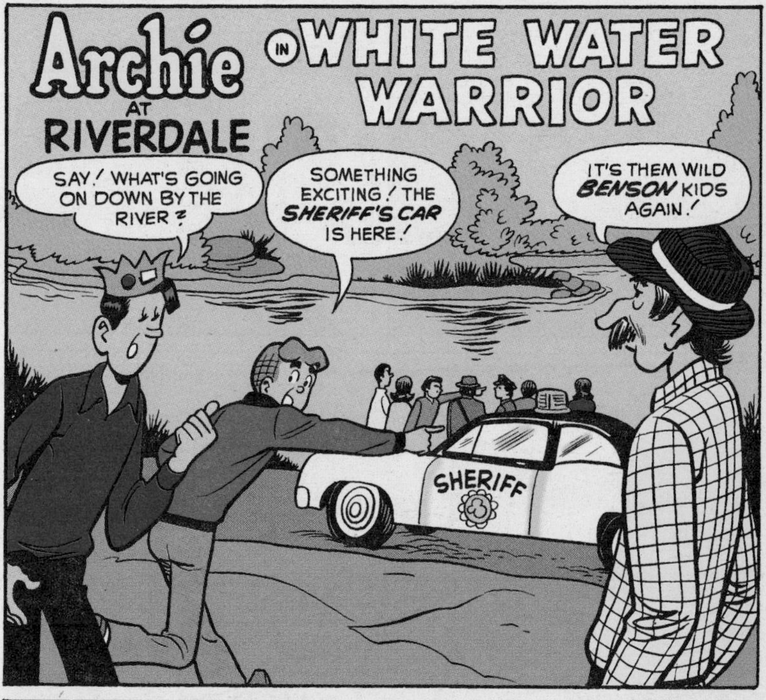
Archie AT RIVERDALE
IN WHITE WATER WARRIOR
SAY! WHAT'S GOING ON DOWN BY THE RIVER?
SOMETHING EXCITING! THE SHERIFF'S CAR IS HERE!
IT'S THEM WILD BENSON KIDS AGAIN!
SHERIFF

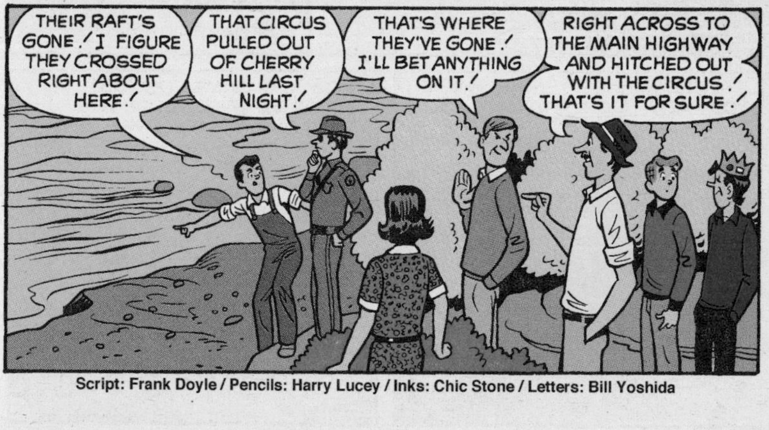
THEIR RAFT'S GONE! I FIGURE THEY CROSSED RIGHT ABOUT HERE!
THAT CIRCUS PULLED OUT OF CHERRY HILL LAST NIGHT!
THAT'S WHERE THEY'VE GONE! I'LL BET ANYTHING ON IT!
RIGHT ACROSS TO THE MAIN HIGHWAY AND HITCHED OUT WITH THE CIRCUS! THAT'S IT FOR SURE!

Script: Frank Doyle / Pencils: Harry Lucey / Inks: Chic Stone / Letters: Bill Yoshida

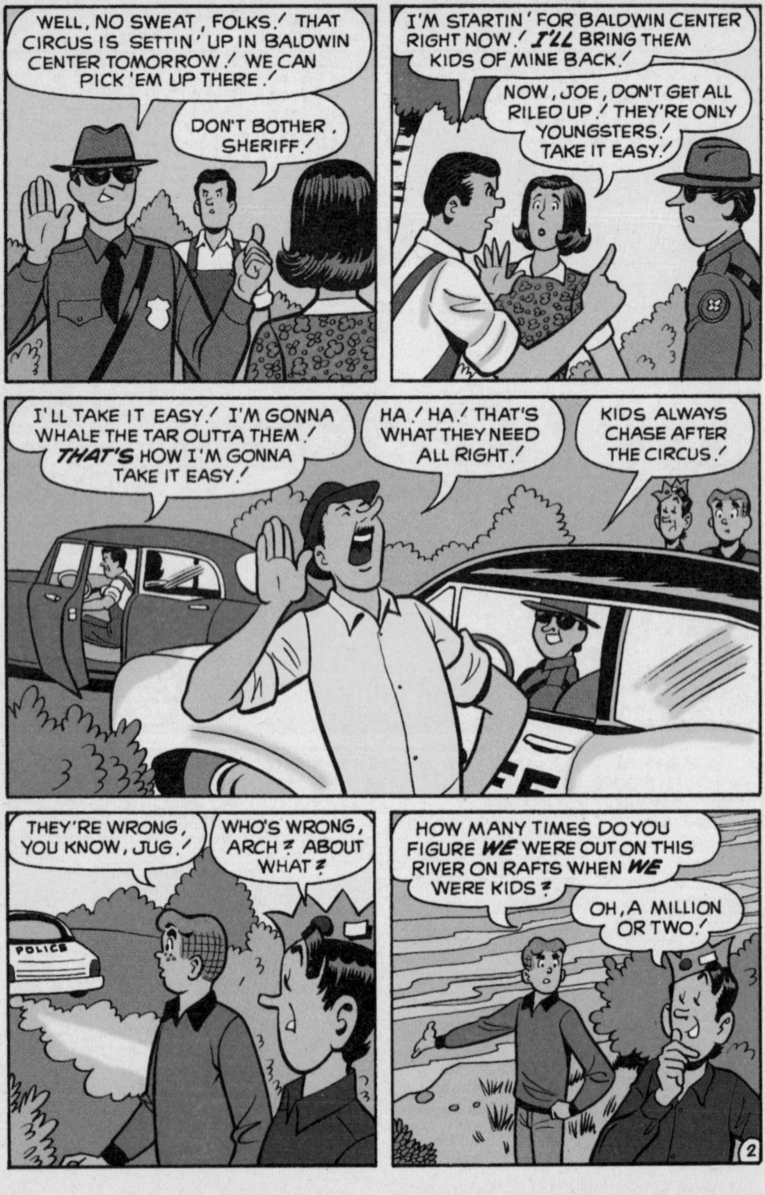
WELL, NO SWEAT, FOLKS! THAT CIRCUS IS SETTIN' UP IN BALDWIN CENTER TOMORROW! WE CAN PICK 'EM UP THERE!
DON'T BOTHER, SHERIFF!
I'M STARTIN' FOR BALDWIN CENTER RIGHT NOW! I'LL BRING THEM KIDS OF MINE BACK!
NOW, JOE, DON'T GET ALL RILED UP! THEY'RE ONLY YOUNGSTERS! TAKE IT EASY!
I'LL TAKE IT EASY! I'M GONNA WHALE THE TAR OUTTA THEM! THAT'S HOW I'M GONNA TAKE IT EASY!
HA! HA! THAT'S WHAT THEY NEED ALL RIGHT!
KIDS ALWAYS CHASE AFTER THE CIRCUS!
THEY'RE WRONG, YOU KNOW, JUG!
WHO'S WRONG, ARCH? ABOUT WHAT?
POLICE
HOW MANY TIMES DO YOU FIGURE WE WERE OUT ON THIS RIVER ON RAFTS WHEN WE WERE KIDS?
OH, A MILLION OR TWO!
2

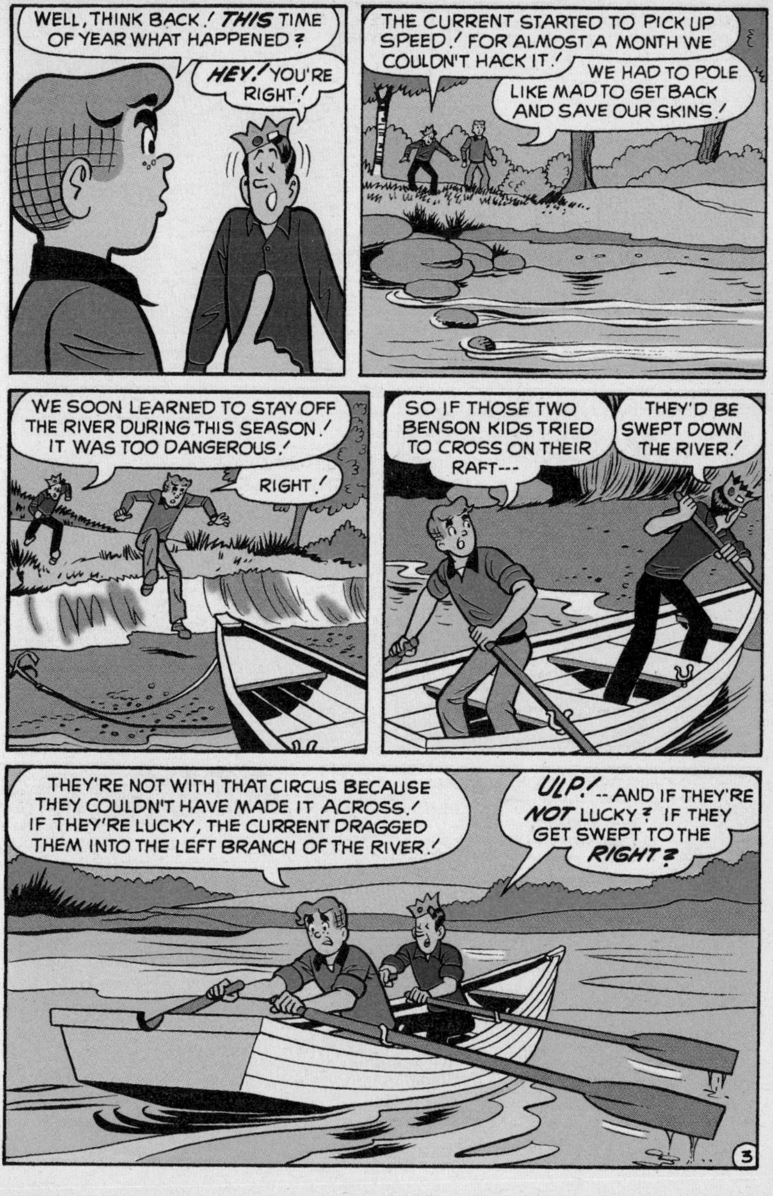

WELL, THINK BACK! THIS TIME OF YEAR WHAT HAPPENED?
HEY! YOU'RE RIGHT!
THE CURRENT STARTED TO PICK UP SPEED! FOR ALMOST A MONTH WE COULDN'T HACK IT!
WE HAD TO POLE LIKE MAD TO GET BACK AND SAVE OUR SKINS!
WE SOON LEARNED TO STAY OFF THE RIVER DURING THIS SEASON! IT WAS TOO DANGEROUS!
RIGHT!
SO IF THOSE TWO BENSON KIDS TRIED TO CROSS ON THEIR RAFT---
THEY'D BE SWEPT DOWN THE RIVER!
THEY'RE NOT WITH THAT CIRCUS BECAUSE THEY COULDN'T HAVE MADE IT ACROSS! IF THEY'RE LUCKY, THE CURRENT DRAGGED THEM INTO THE LEFT BRANCH OF THE RIVER!
ULP! -- AND IF THEY'RE NOT LUCKY? IF THEY GET SWEPT TO THE RIGHT?
3

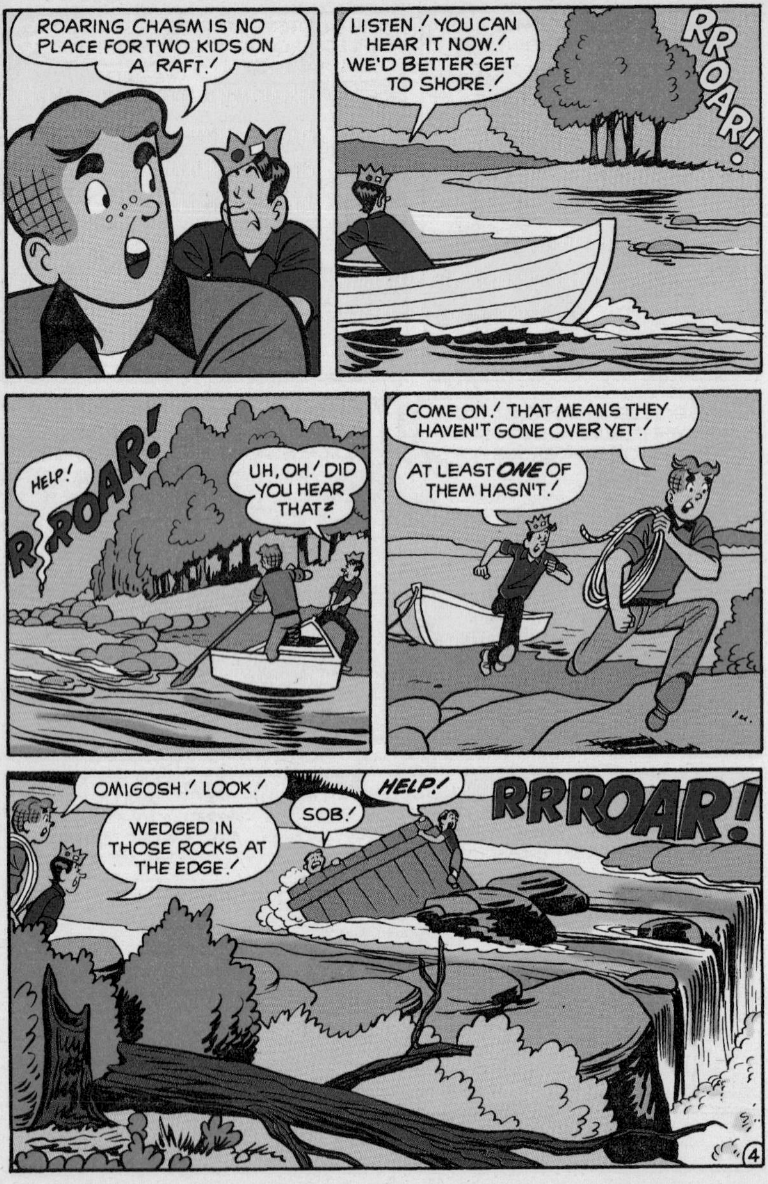

ROARING CHASM IS NO PLACE FOR TWO KIDS ON A RAFT!
LISTEN! YOU CAN HEAR IT NOW! WE'D BETTER GET TO SHORE!
RRROAR!
HELP!
RRROAR!
UH, OH! DID YOU HEAR THAT?
COME ON! THAT MEANS THEY HAVEN'T GONE OVER YET!
AT LEAST ONE OF THEM HASN'T!
OMIGOSH! LOOK!
WEDGED IN THOSE ROCKS AT THE EDGE!
SOB!
HELP!
RRROAR!
4

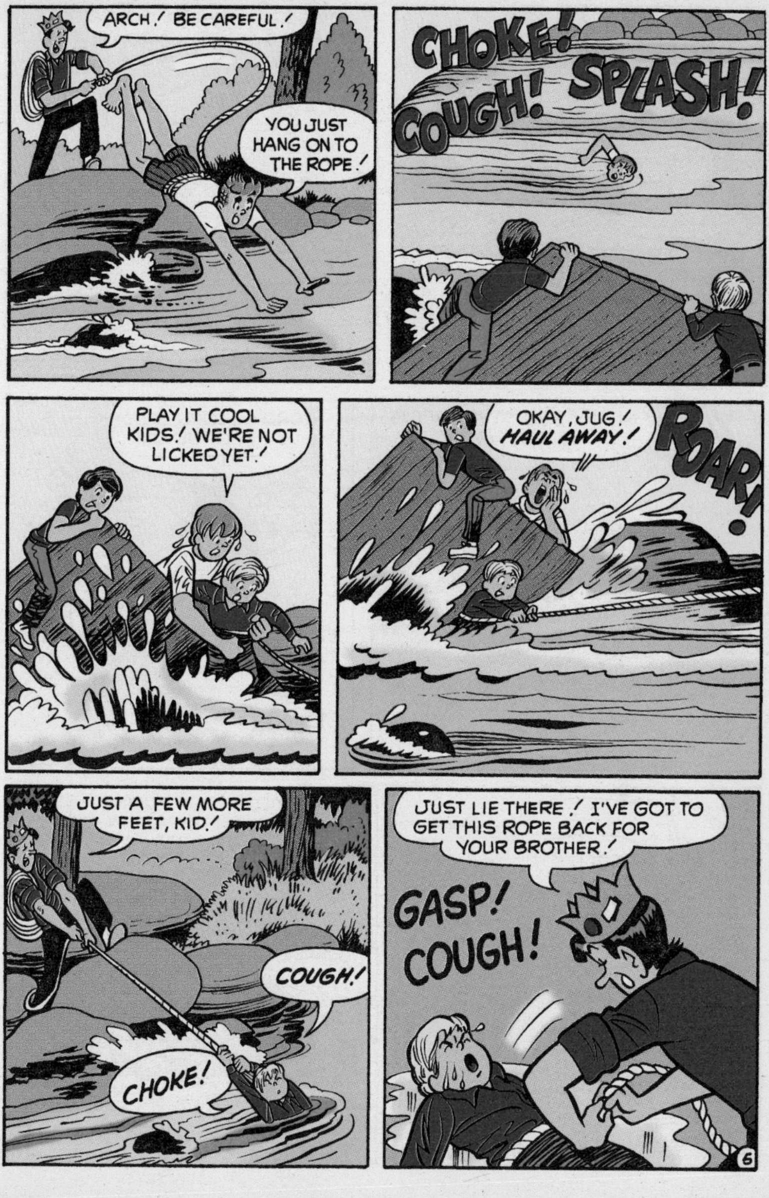

ARCH! BE CAREFUL!
YOU JUST HANG ON TO THE ROPE!
CHOKE!
COUGH!
SPLASH!
PLAY IT COOL KIDS! WE'RE NOT LICKED YET!
OKAY, JUG! HAUL AWAY!
ROAR!
JUST A FEW MORE FEET, KID!
COUGH!
CHOKE!
JUST LIE THERE! I'VE GOT TO GET THIS ROPE BACK FOR YOUR BROTHER!
GASP! COUGH!

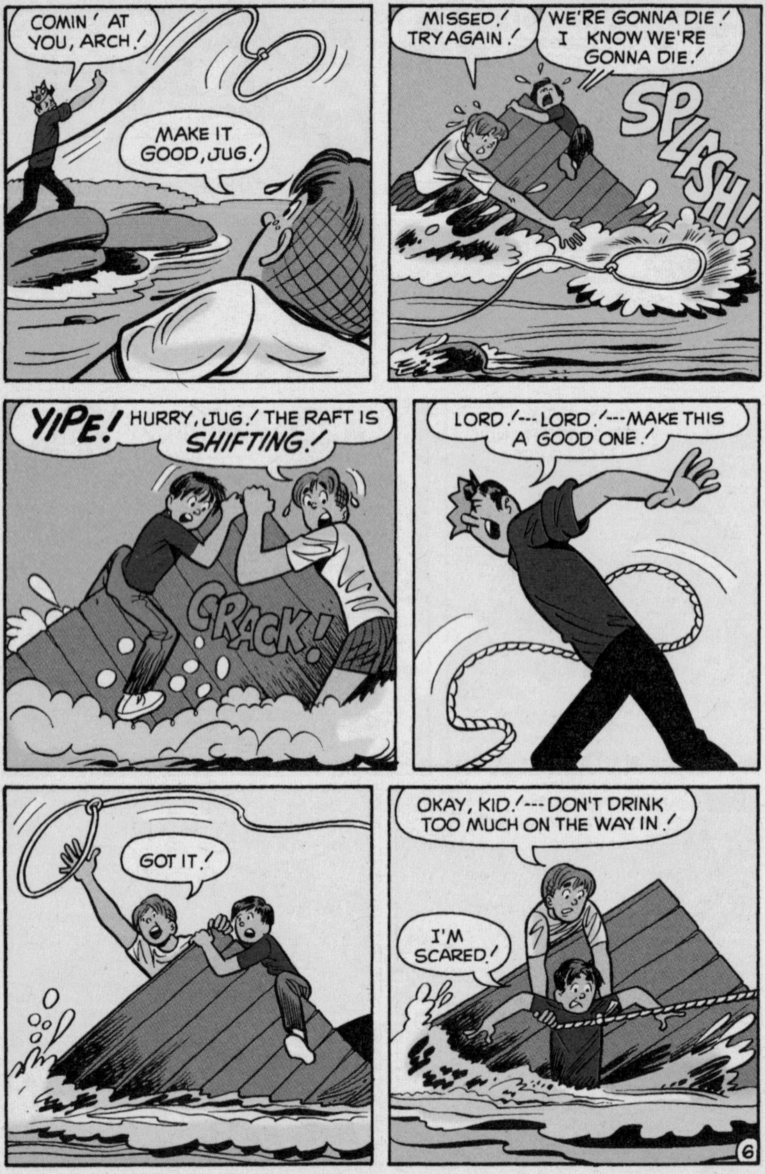
COMIN' AT YOU, ARCH!
MAKE IT GOOD, JUG!
MISSED! TRY AGAIN!
WE'RE GONNA DIE! I KNOW WE'RE GONNA DIE!
SPLASH!
YIPE! HURRY, JUG! THE RAFT IS SHIFTING!
CRACK!
LORD!---LORD!---MAKE THIS A GOOD ONE!
GOT IT!
OKAY, KID!---DON'T DRINK TOO MUCH ON THE WAY IN!
I'M SCARED!
6

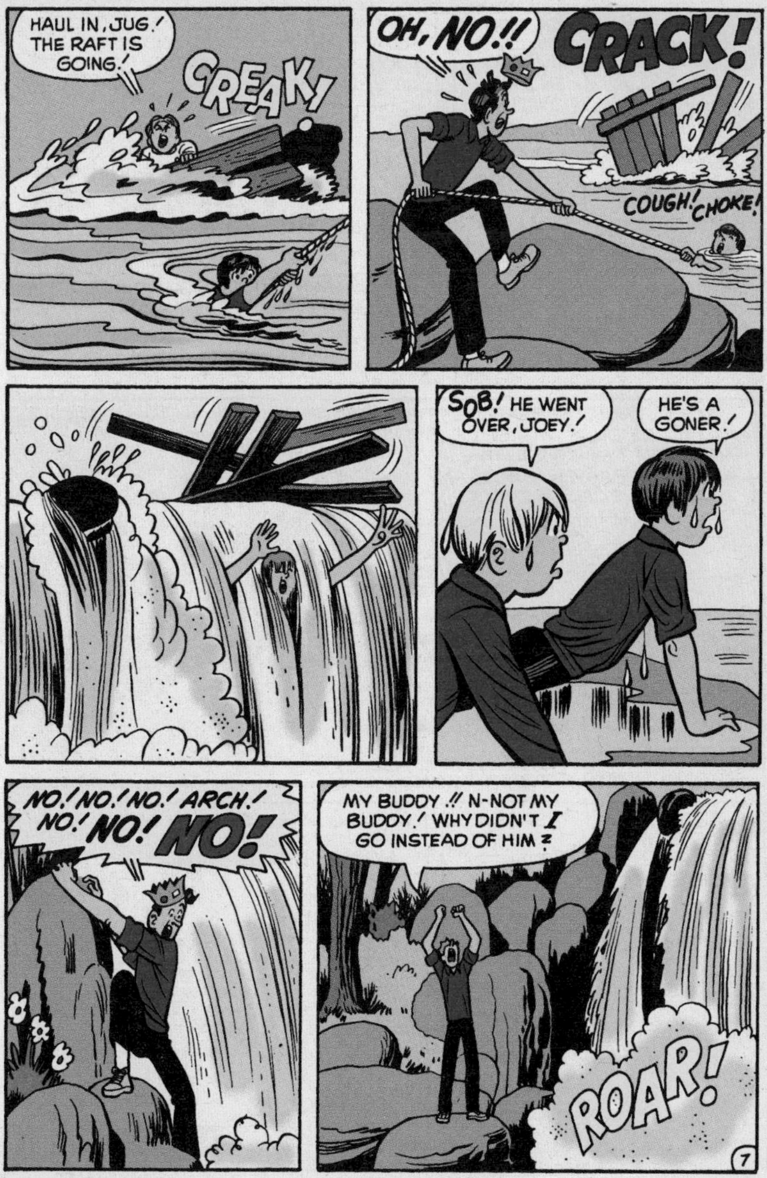
HAUL IN, JUG! THE RAFT IS GOING!
CREAK!
OH, NO!!
CRACK!
COUGH! CHOKE!
SOB! HE WENT OVER, JOEY!
HE'S A GONER!
NO! NO! NO! ARCH! NO! NO! NO!
MY BUDDY!! N-NOT MY BUDDY! WHY DIDN'T I GO INSTEAD OF HIM?
ROAR!

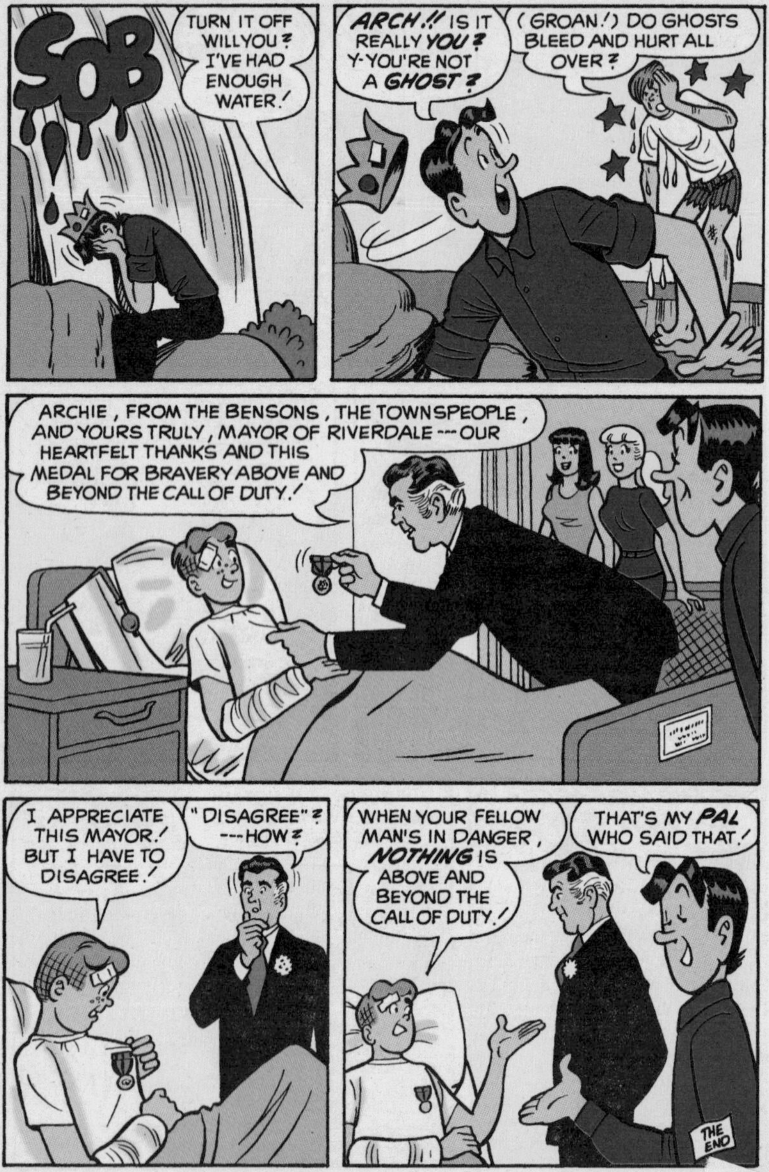
SOB
TURN IT OFF WILLYOU? I'VE HAD ENOUGH WATER!
ARCH!! IS IT REALLY YOU? Y-YOU'RE NOT A GHOST?
(GROAN!) DO GHOSTS BLEED AND HURT ALL OVER?
ARCHIE, FROM THE BENSONS, THE TOWNSPEOPLE, AND YOURS TRULY, MAYOR OF RIVERDALE --- OUR HEARTFELT THANKS AND THIS MEDAL FOR BRAVERY ABOVE AND BEYOND THE CALL OF DUTY!
I APPRECIATE THIS MAYOR! BUT I HAVE TO DISAGREE!
"DISAGREE"? ---HOW?
WHEN YOUR FELLOW MAN'S IN DANGER, NOTHING IS ABOVE AND BEYOND THE CALL OF DUTY!
THAT'S MY PAL WHO SAID THAT!
THE END

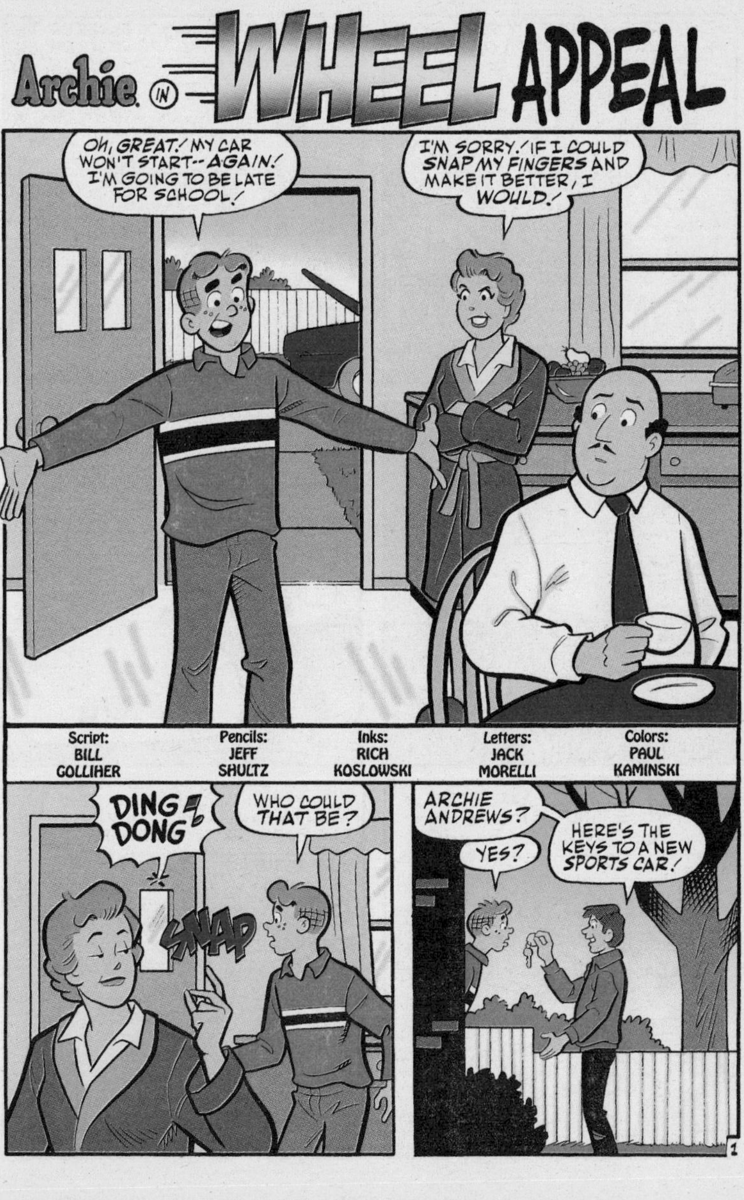
Archie in WHEEL APPEAL
Oh, GREAT! MY CAR WON'T START-- AGAIN! I'M GOING TO BE LATE FOR SCHOOL!
I'M SORRY! IF I COULD SNAP MY FINGERS AND MAKE IT BETTER, I WOULD!
Script: BILL GOLLIHER
Pencils: JEFF SHULTZ
Inks: RICH KOSLOWSKI
Letters: JACK MORELLI
Colors: PAUL KAMINSKI
DING DONG
WHO COULD THAT BE?
SNAP
ARCHIE ANDREWS?
YES?
HERE'S THE KEYS TO A NEW SPORTS CAR!

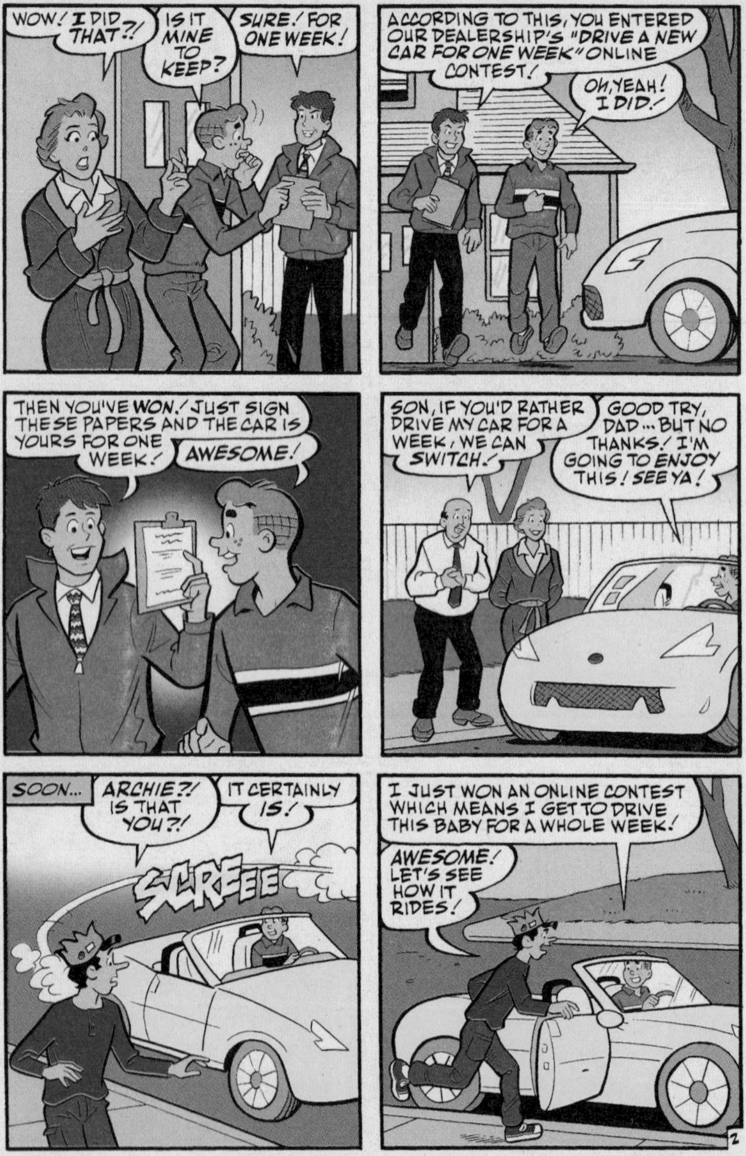
WOW! I DID THAT?!
IS IT MINE TO KEEP?
SURE! FOR ONE WEEK!
ACCORDING TO THIS, YOU ENTERED OUR DEALERSHIP'S "DRIVE A NEW CAR FOR ONE WEEK" ONLINE CONTEST!
OH, YEAH! I DID!
THEN YOU'VE WON! JUST SIGN THESE PAPERS AND THE CAR IS YOURS FOR ONE WEEK!
AWESOME!
SON, IF YOU'D RATHER DRIVE MY CAR FOR A WEEK, WE CAN SWITCH!
GOOD TRY, DAD... BUT NO THANKS! I'M GOING TO ENJOY THIS! SEE YA!
SOON...
ARCHIE?! IS THAT YOU?!
IT CERTAINLY IS!
SCREEE
I JUST WON AN ONLINE CONTEST WHICH MEANS I GET TO DRIVE THIS BABY FOR A WHOLE WEEK!
AWESOME! LET'S SEE HOW IT RIDES!
2

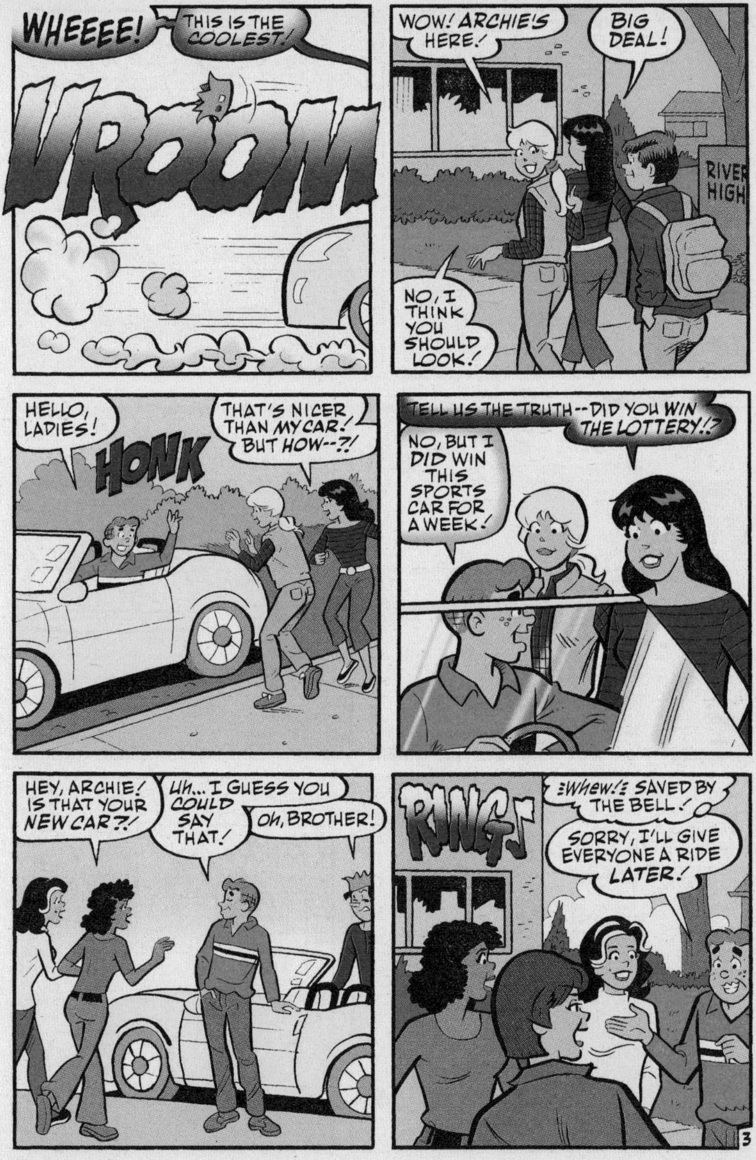
WHEEEEE!
THIS IS THE COOLEST!
VROOM
WOW! ARCHIE'S HERE!
BIG DEAL!
NO, I THINK YOU SHOULD LOOK!
RIVER HIGH
HELLO, LADIES!
HONK
THAT'S NICER THAN MY CAR! BUT HOW--?!
TELL US THE TRUTH--DID YOU WIN THE LOTTERY!?
NO, BUT I DID WIN THIS SPORTS CAR FOR A WEEK!
HEY, ARCHIE! IS THAT YOUR NEW CAR?!
UH... I GUESS YOU COULD SAY THAT!
OH, BROTHER!
RING
WHEW! SAVED BY THE BELL!
SORRY, I'LL GIVE EVERYONE A RIDE LATER!

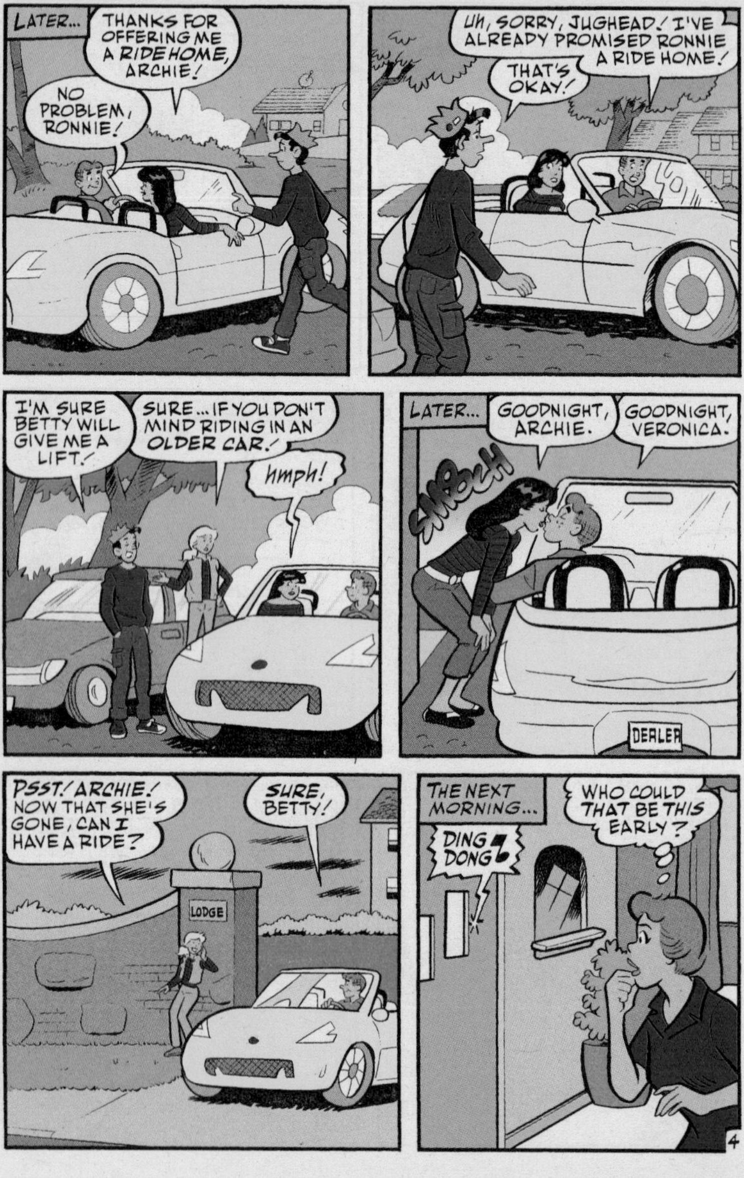
LATER...
THANKS FOR OFFERING ME A RIDE HOME, ARCHIE!
NO PROBLEM, RONNIE!
UH, SORRY, JUGHEAD! I'VE ALREADY PROMISED RONNIE A RIDE HOME!
THAT'S OKAY!
I'M SURE BETTY WILL GIVE ME A LIFT!
SURE... IF YOU DON'T MIND RIDING IN AN OLDER CAR!
hmph!
LATER...
GOODNIGHT, ARCHIE.
GOODNIGHT, VERONICA.
SMOOCH
DEALER
PSST! ARCHIE! NOW THAT SHE'S GONE, CAN I HAVE A RIDE?
SURE, BETTY!
LODGE
THE NEXT MORNING...
DING DONG
WHO COULD THAT BE THIS EARLY?

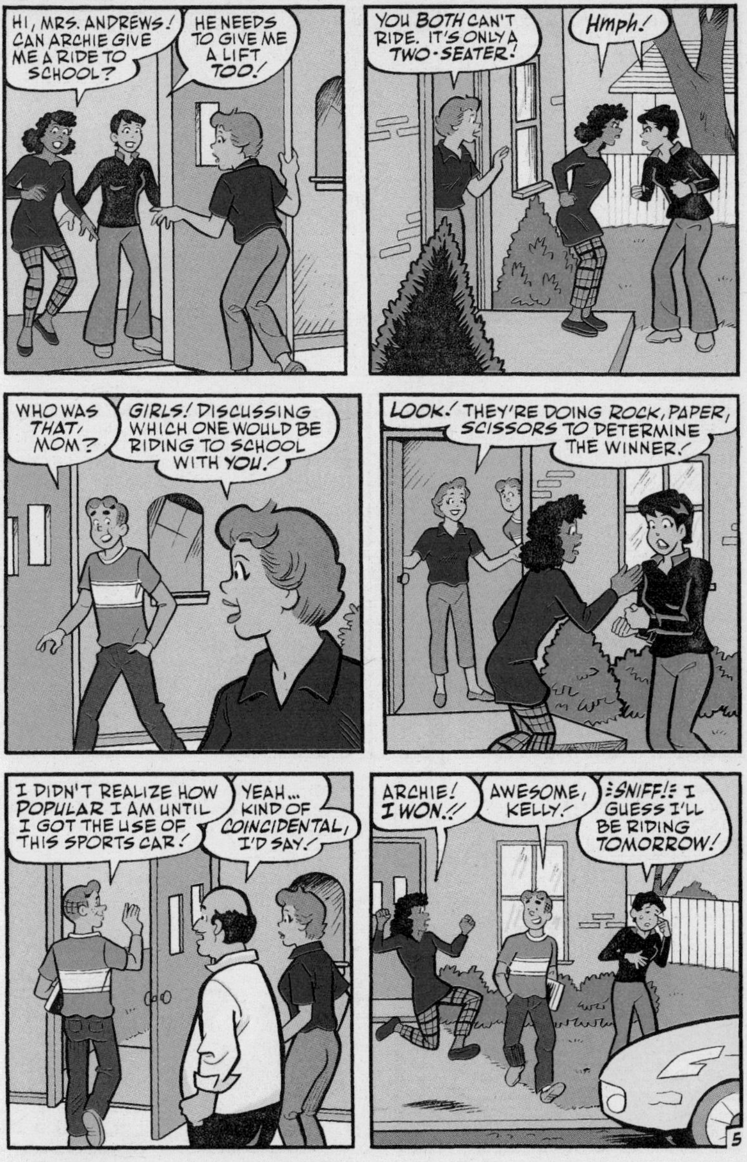
HI, MRS. ANDREWS! CAN ARCHIE GIVE ME A RIDE TO SCHOOL?
HE NEEDS TO GIVE ME A LIFT TOO!
YOU BOTH CAN'T RIDE. IT'S ONLY A TWO-SEATER!
Hmph!
WHO WAS THAT, MOM?
GIRLS! DISCUSSING WHICH ONE WOULD BE RIDING TO SCHOOL WITH YOU!
LOOK! THEY'RE DOING ROCK, PAPER, SCISSORS TO DETERMINE THE WINNER!
I DIDN'T REALIZE HOW POPULAR I AM UNTIL I GOT THE USE OF THIS SPORTS CAR!
YEAH... KIND OF COINCIDENTAL, I'D SAY!
ARCHIE! I WON!!
AWESOME, KELLY!
SNIFF! I GUESS I'LL BE RIDING TOMORROW!

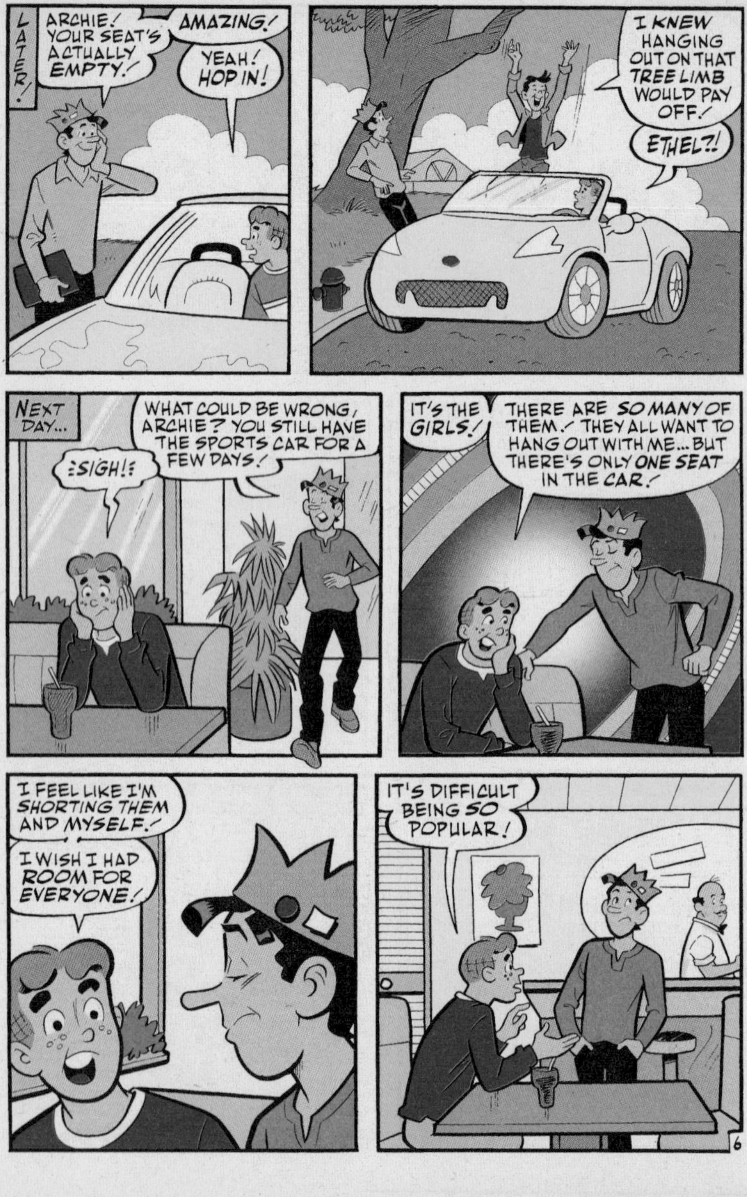
LATER!
ARCHIE! YOUR SEAT'S ACTUALLY EMPTY!
AMAZING!
YEAH! HOP IN!
I KNEW HANGING OUT ON THAT TREE LIMB WOULD PAY OFF!
ETHEL?!
NEXT DAY...
WHAT COULD BE WRONG, ARCHIE? YOU STILL HAVE THE SPORTS CAR FOR A FEW DAYS!
SIGH!
IT'S THE GIRLS!
THERE ARE SO MANY OF THEM! THEY ALL WANT TO HANG OUT WITH ME... BUT THERE'S ONLY ONE SEAT IN THE CAR!
I FEEL LIKE I'M SHORTING THEM AND MYSELF!
I WISH I HAD ROOM FOR EVERYONE!
IT'S DIFFICULT BEING SO POPULAR!
6

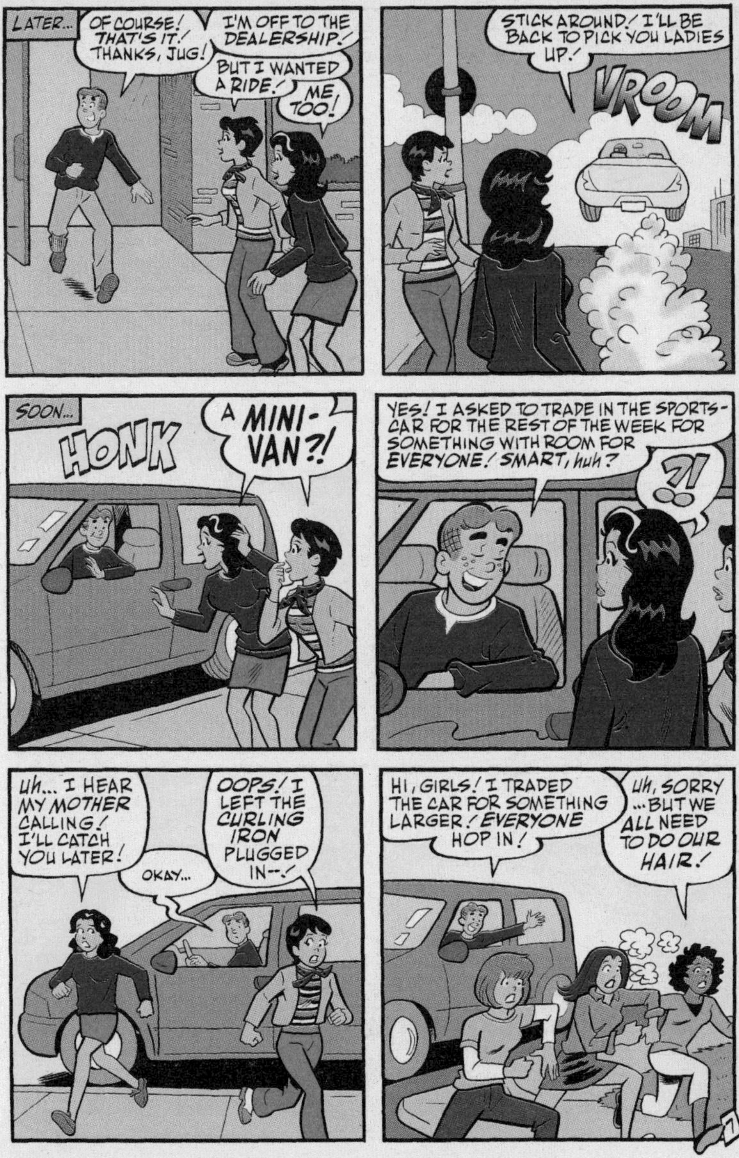
LATER...
OF COURSE! THAT'S IT! THANKS, JUG!
I'M OFF TO THE DEALERSHIP!
BUT I WANTED A RIDE!
ME TOO!
STICK AROUND! I'LL BE BACK TO PICK YOU LADIES UP!
VROOM
SOON...
HONK
A MINI-VAN?!
YES! I ASKED TO TRADE IN THE SPORTS-CAR FOR THE REST OF THE WEEK FOR SOMETHING WITH ROOM FOR EVERYONE! SMART, huh?
?!
uh... I HEAR MY MOTHER CALLING! I'LL CATCH YOU LATER!
OKAY...
OOPS! I LEFT THE CURLING IRON PLUGGED IN--!
HI, GIRLS! I TRADED THE CAR FOR SOMETHING LARGER! EVERYONE HOP IN!
uh, SORRY ...BUT WE ALL NEED TO DO OUR HAIR!
7

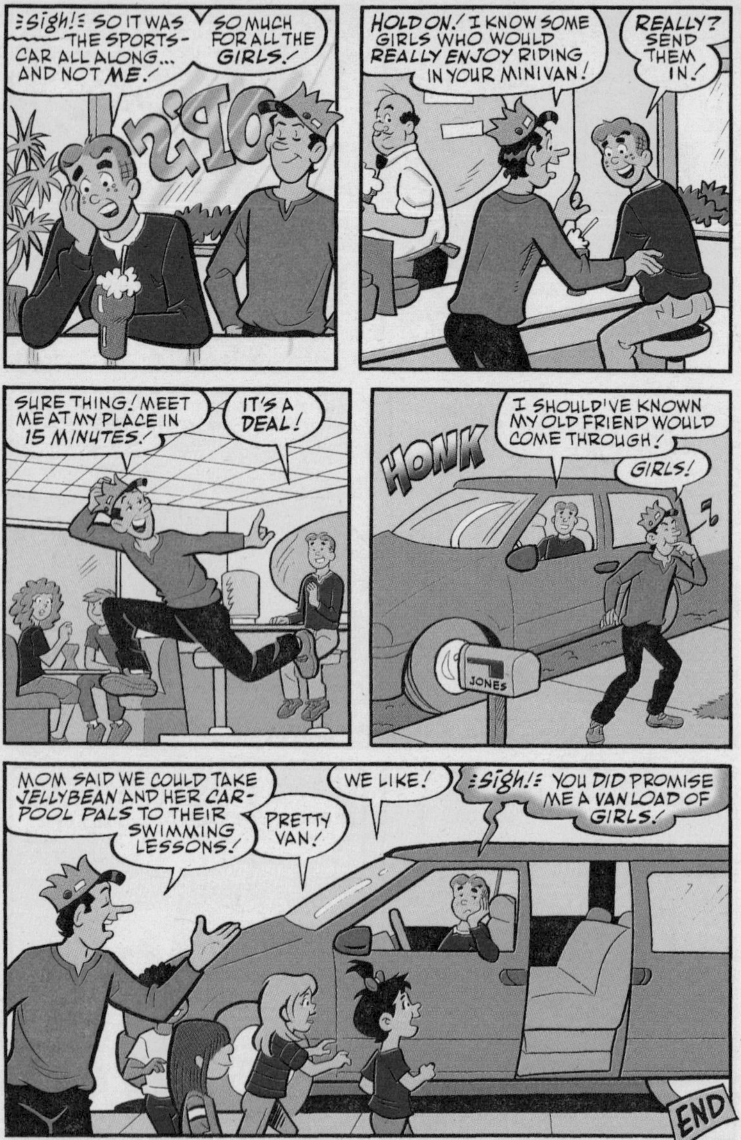

SIGH! SO IT WAS THE SPORTS-CAR ALL ALONG... AND NOT ME!
SO MUCH FOR ALL THE GIRLS!
HOLD ON! I KNOW SOME GIRLS WHO WOULD REALLY ENJOY RIDING IN YOUR MINIVAN!
REALLY? SEND THEM IN!
POP'S
SURE THING! MEET ME AT MY PLACE IN 15 MINUTES!
IT'S A DEAL!
HONK
I SHOULD'VE KNOWN MY OLD FRIEND WOULD COME THROUGH!
GIRLS!
JONES
MOM SAID WE COULD TAKE JELLYBEAN AND HER CAR-POOL PALS TO THEIR SWIMMING LESSONS!
PRETTY VAN!
WE LIKE!
SIGH! YOU DID PROMISE ME A VAN LOAD OF GIRLS!
END

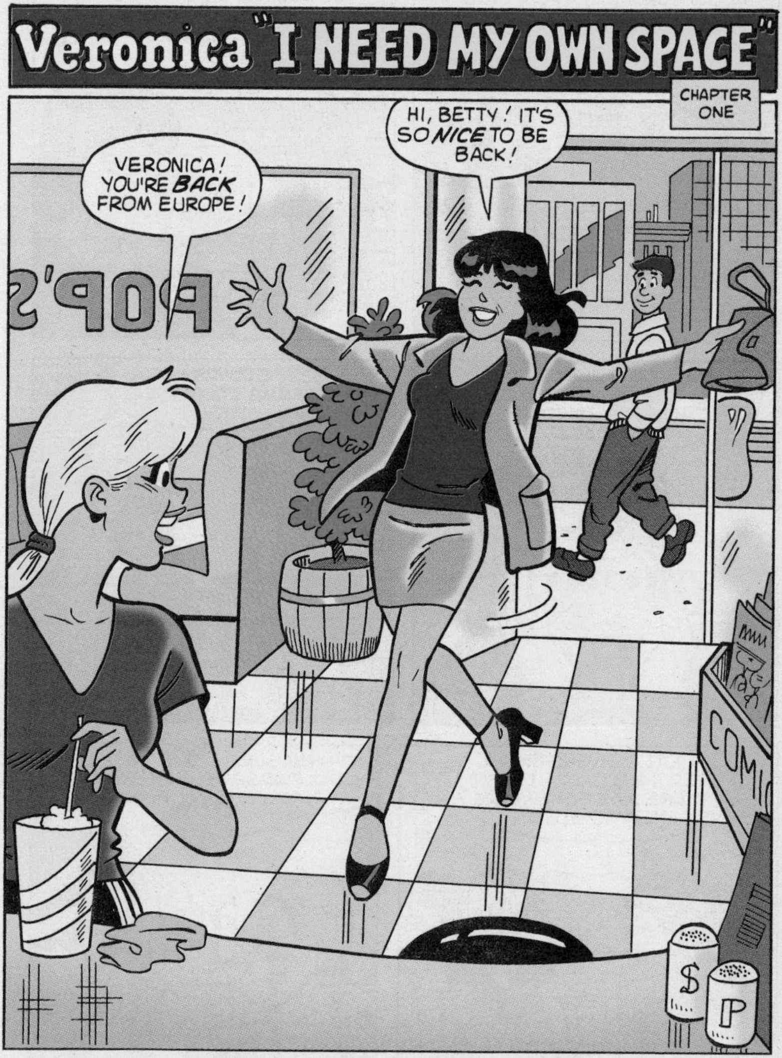
Veronica "I NEED MY OWN SPACE"
CHAPTER ONE
VERONICA! YOU'RE BACK FROM EUROPE!
HI, BETTY! IT'S SO NICE TO BE BACK!
POP'S
COMIC

SCRIPT: DAN PARENT
PENCILS: DAN DECARLO
INKING: HENRY SCARPELLI
LETTERING: BILL YOSHIDA

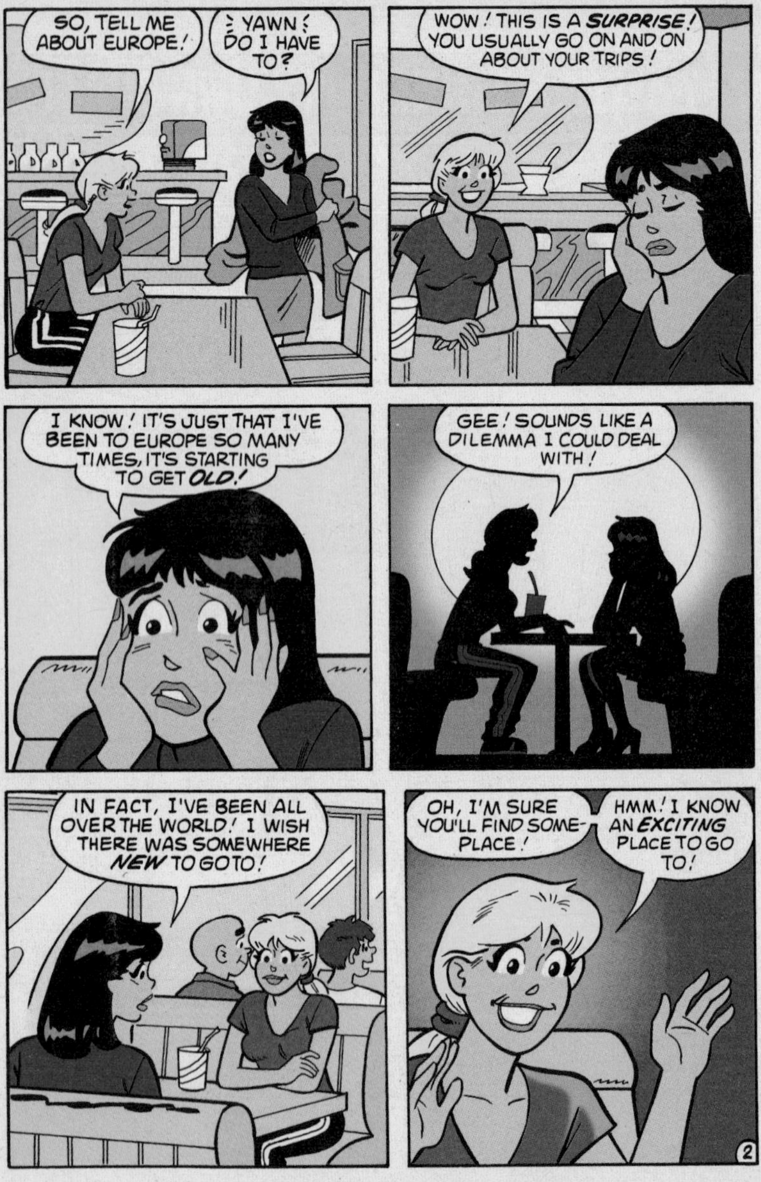
SO, TELL ME ABOUT EUROPE!
YAWN DO I HAVE TO?
WOW! THIS IS A SURPRISE! YOU USUALLY GO ON AND ON ABOUT YOUR TRIPS!
I KNOW! IT'S JUST THAT I'VE BEEN TO EUROPE SO MANY TIMES, IT'S STARTING TO GET OLD!
GEE! SOUNDS LIKE A DILEMMA I COULD DEAL WITH!
IN FACT, I'VE BEEN ALL OVER THE WORLD! I WISH THERE WAS SOMEWHERE NEW TO GO TO!
OH, I'M SURE YOU'LL FIND SOME-PLACE!
HMM! I KNOW AN EXCITING PLACE TO GO TO!
2

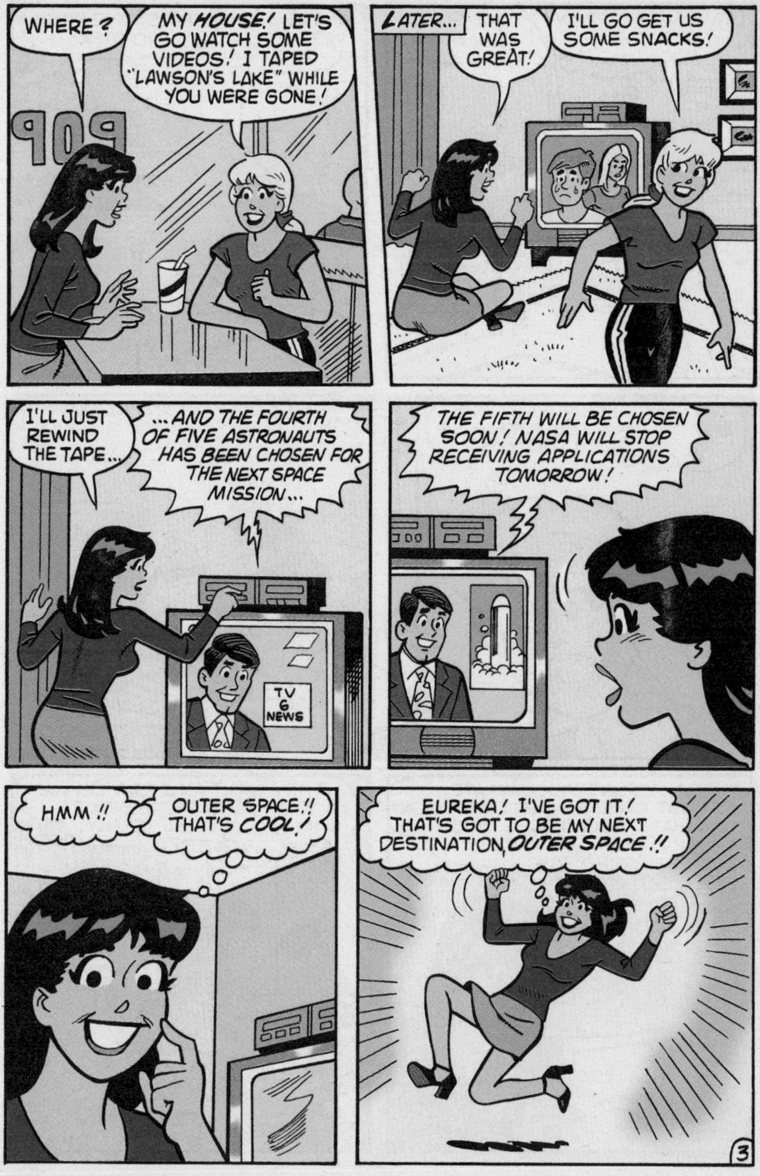
WHERE ?
MY HOUSE! LET'S GO WATCH SOME VIDEOS! I TAPED "LAWSON'S LAKE" WHILE YOU WERE GONE!
POP
LATER...
THAT WAS GREAT!
I'LL GO GET US SOME SNACKS!
I'LL JUST REWIND THE TAPE...
...AND THE FOURTH OF FIVE ASTRONAUTS HAS BEEN CHOSEN FOR THE NEXT SPACE MISSION...
TV 6 NEWS
THE FIFTH WILL BE CHOSEN SOON! NASA WILL STOP RECEIVING APPLICATIONS TOMORROW!
HMM !!
OUTER SPACE!! THAT'S COOL!
EUREKA! I'VE GOT IT! THAT'S GOT TO BE MY NEXT DESTINATION, OUTER SPACE.!!
3

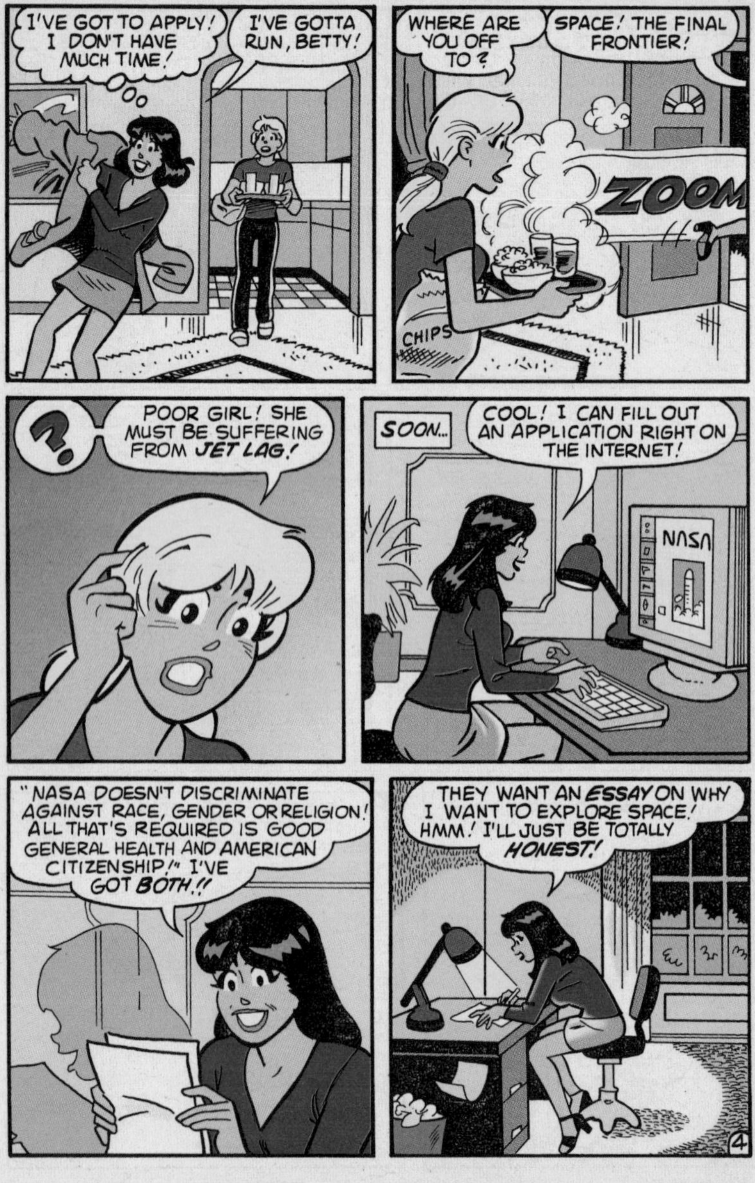
I'VE GOT TO APPLY! I DON'T HAVE MUCH TIME!
I'VE GOTTA RUN, BETTY!
WHERE ARE YOU OFF TO?
SPACE! THE FINAL FRONTIER!
ZOOM
CHIPS
POOR GIRL! SHE MUST BE SUFFERING FROM JET LAG!
SOON...
COOL! I CAN FILL OUT AN APPLICATION RIGHT ON THE INTERNET!
NASA
"NASA DOESN'T DISCRIMINATE AGAINST RACE, GENDER OR RELIGION! ALL THAT'S REQUIRED IS GOOD GENERAL HEALTH AND AMERICAN CITIZENSHIP!" I'VE GOT BOTH!!
THEY WANT AN ESSAY ON WHY I WANT TO EXPLORE SPACE! HMM! I'LL JUST BE TOTALLY HONEST!
4

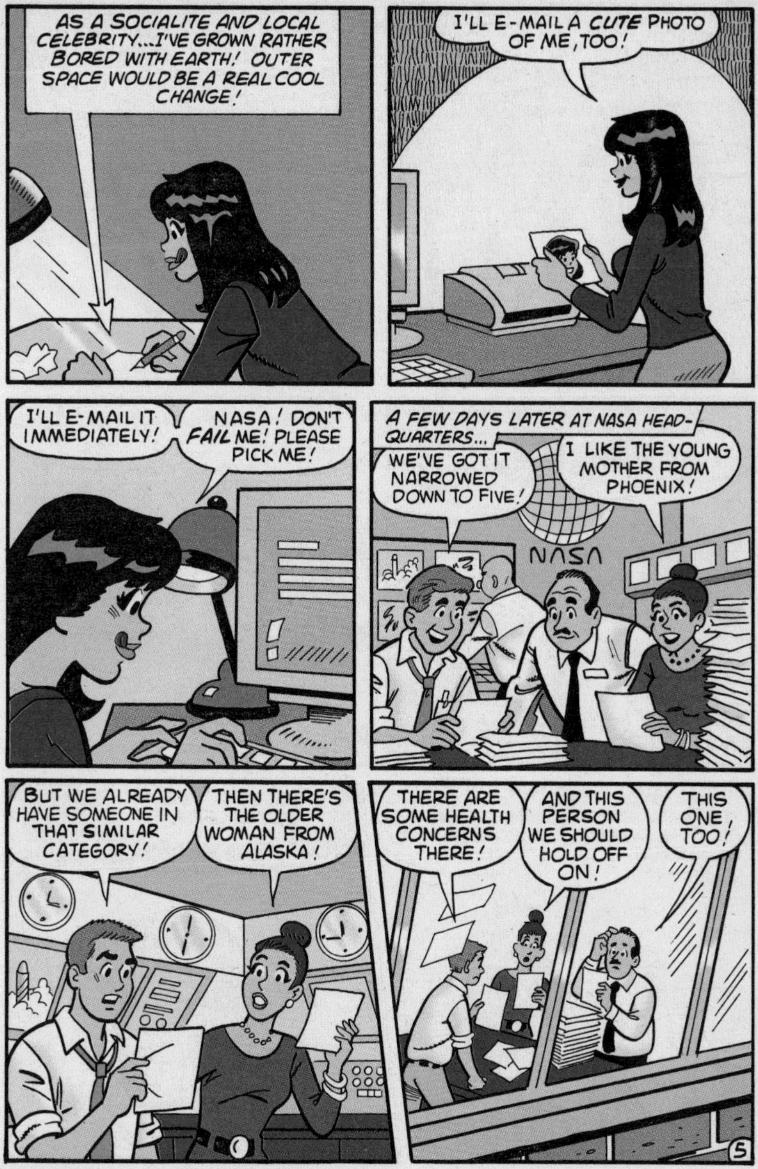
AS A SOCIALITE AND LOCAL CELEBRITY...I'VE GROWN RATHER BORED WITH EARTH! OUTER SPACE WOULD BE A REAL COOL CHANGE!
I'LL E-MAIL A CUTE PHOTO OF ME, TOO!
I'LL E-MAIL IT IMMEDIATELY!
NASA! DON'T FAIL ME! PLEASE PICK ME!
A FEW DAYS LATER AT NASA HEAD-QUARTERS...
WE'VE GOT IT NARROWED DOWN TO FIVE!
I LIKE THE YOUNG MOTHER FROM PHOENIX!
NASA
BUT WE ALREADY HAVE SOMEONE IN THAT SIMILAR CATEGORY!
THEN THERE'S THE OLDER WOMAN FROM ALASKA!
THERE ARE SOME HEALTH CONCERNS THERE!
AND THIS PERSON WE SHOULD HOLD OFF ON!
THIS ONE, TOO!
5

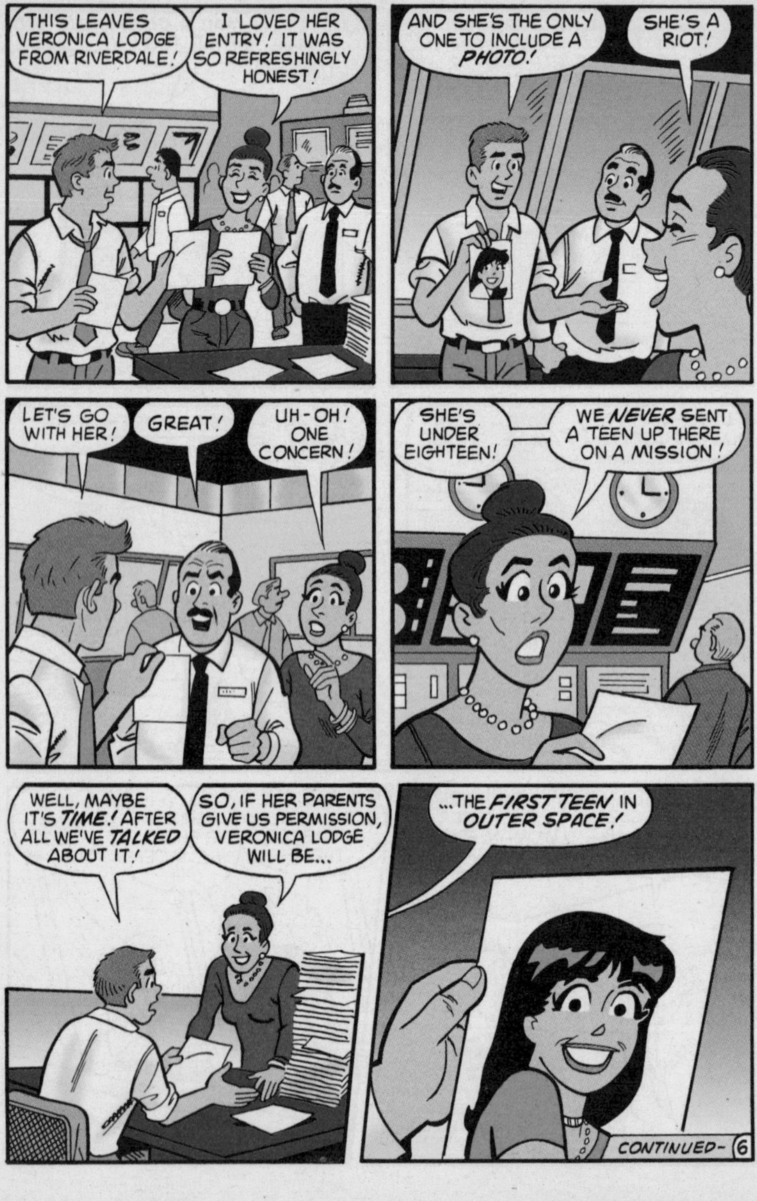
THIS LEAVES VERONICA LODGE FROM RIVERDALE!
I LOVED HER ENTRY! IT WAS SO REFRESHINGLY HONEST!
AND SHE'S THE ONLY ONE TO INCLUDE A *PHOTO*!
SHE'S A RIOT!
LET'S GO WITH HER!
GREAT!
UH-OH! ONE CONCERN!
SHE'S UNDER EIGHTEEN!
WE *NEVER* SENT A TEEN UP THERE ON A MISSION!
WELL, MAYBE IT'S *TIME!* AFTER ALL WE'VE *TALKED* ABOUT IT!
SO, IF HER PARENTS GIVE US PERMISSION, VERONICA LODGE WILL BE...
...THE *FIRST TEEN* IN *OUTER SPACE!*
CONTINUED-

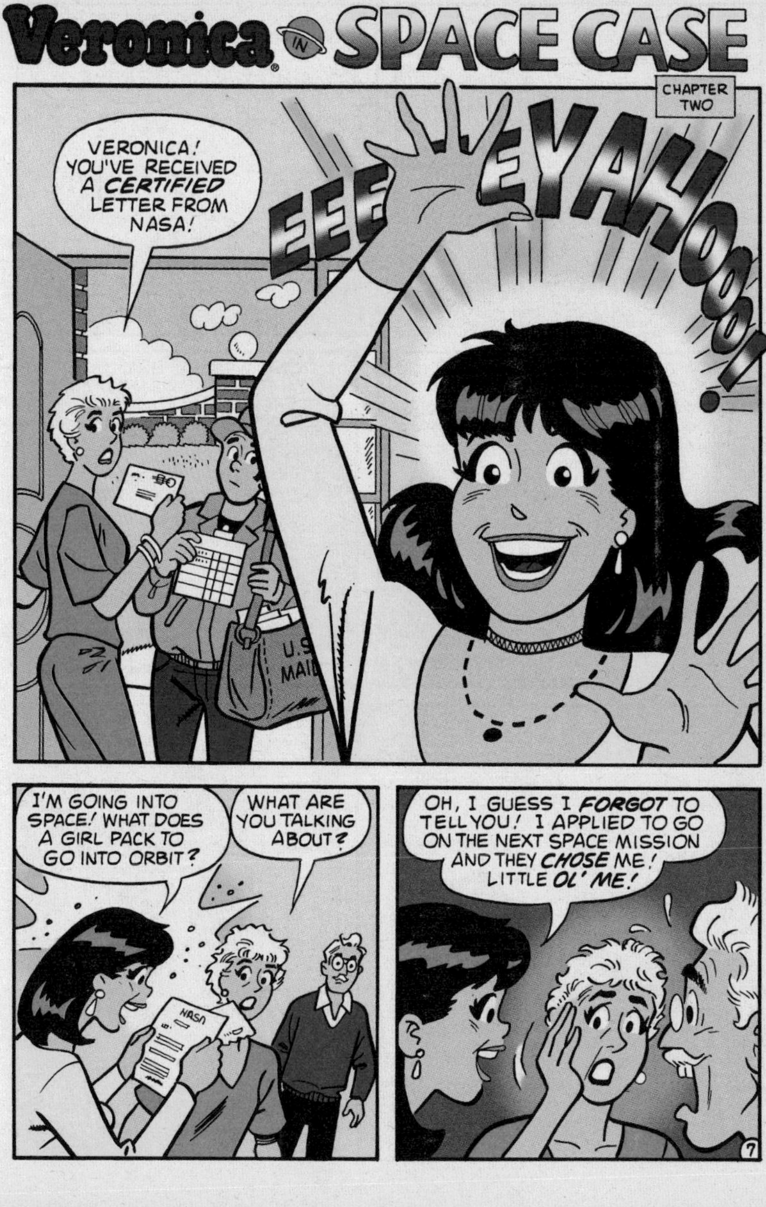
Veronica IN SPACE CASE
CHAPTER TWO
VERONICA! YOU'VE RECEIVED A CERTIFIED LETTER FROM NASA!
EEEEYAHOOOO!
U.S. MAIL
I'M GOING INTO SPACE! WHAT DOES A GIRL PACK TO GO INTO ORBIT?
WHAT ARE YOU TALKING ABOUT?
NASA
OH, I GUESS I FORGOT TO TELL YOU! I APPLIED TO GO ON THE NEXT SPACE MISSION AND THEY CHOSE ME! LITTLE OL' ME!

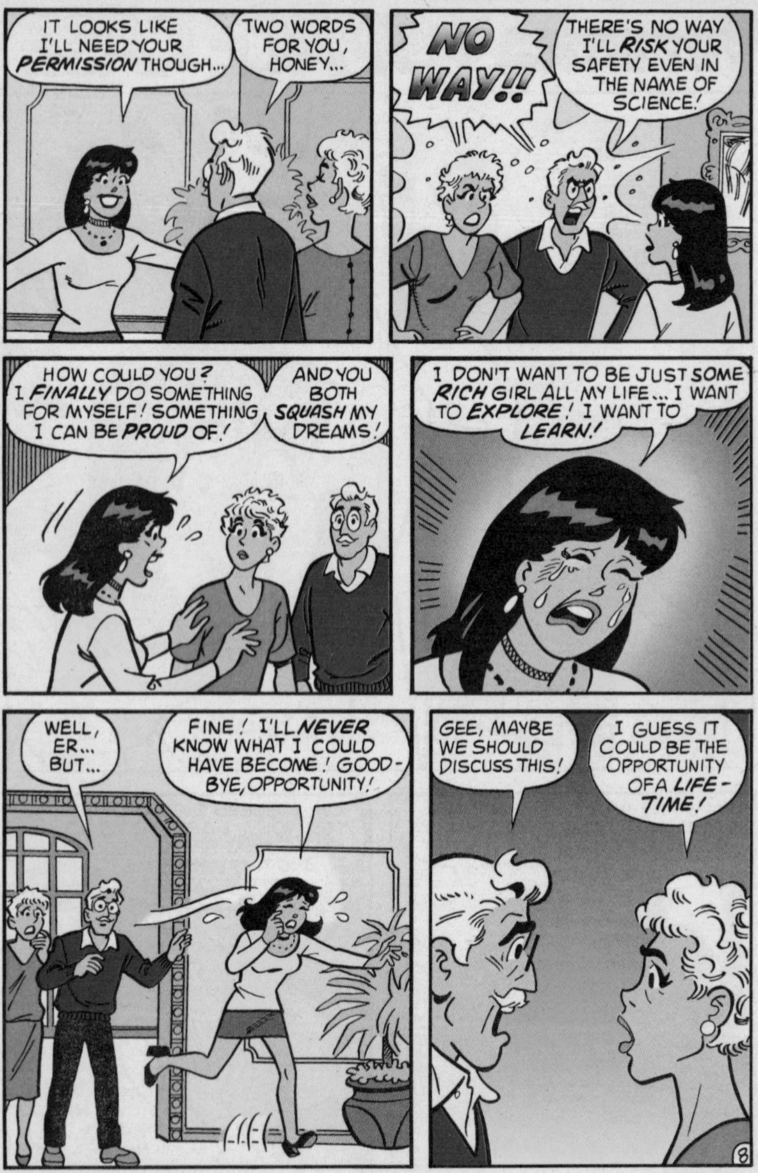
IT LOOKS LIKE I'LL NEED YOUR PERMISSION THOUGH...
TWO WORDS FOR YOU, HONEY...
NO WAY!!
THERE'S NO WAY I'LL RISK YOUR SAFETY EVEN IN THE NAME OF SCIENCE!
HOW COULD YOU? I FINALLY DO SOMETHING FOR MYSELF! SOMETHING I CAN BE PROUD OF!
AND YOU BOTH SQUASH MY DREAMS!
I DON'T WANT TO BE JUST SOME RICH GIRL ALL MY LIFE... I WANT TO EXPLORE! I WANT TO LEARN!
WELL, ER... BUT...
FINE! I'LL NEVER KNOW WHAT I COULD HAVE BECOME! GOOD-BYE, OPPORTUNITY!
GEE, MAYBE WE SHOULD DISCUSS THIS!
I GUESS IT COULD BE THE OPPORTUNITY OF A LIFE-TIME!
8

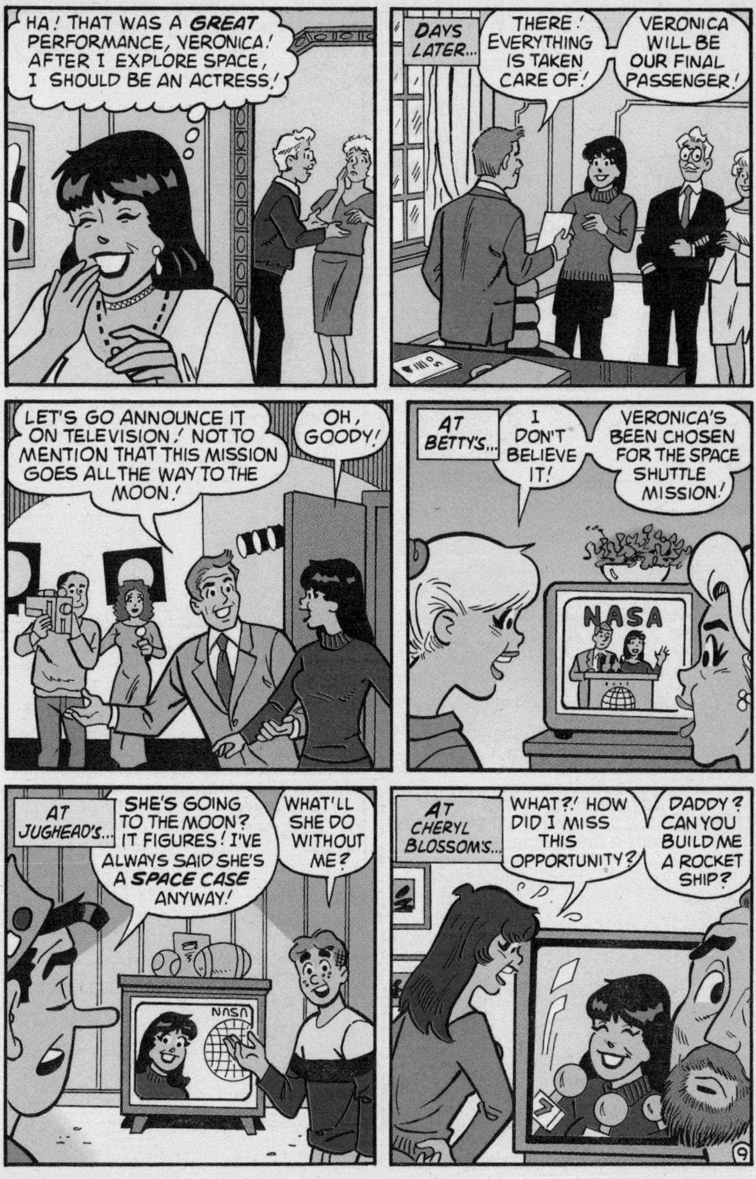
HA! THAT WAS A GREAT PERFORMANCE, VERONICA! AFTER I EXPLORE SPACE, I SHOULD BE AN ACTRESS!
DAYS LATER...
THERE! EVERYTHING IS TAKEN CARE OF!
VERONICA WILL BE OUR FINAL PASSENGER!
LET'S GO ANNOUNCE IT ON TELEVISION! NOT TO MENTION THAT THIS MISSION GOES ALL THE WAY TO THE MOON!
OH, GOODY!
AT BETTY'S...
I DON'T BELIEVE IT!
VERONICA'S BEEN CHOSEN FOR THE SPACE SHUTTLE MISSION!
NASA
AT JUGHEAD'S...
SHE'S GOING TO THE MOON? IT FIGURES! I'VE ALWAYS SAID SHE'S A SPACE CASE ANYWAY!
WHAT'LL SHE DO WITHOUT ME?
NASA
AT CHERYL BLOSSOM'S...
WHAT?! HOW DID I MISS THIS OPPORTUNITY?
DADDY? CAN YOU BUILD ME A ROCKET SHIP?
9

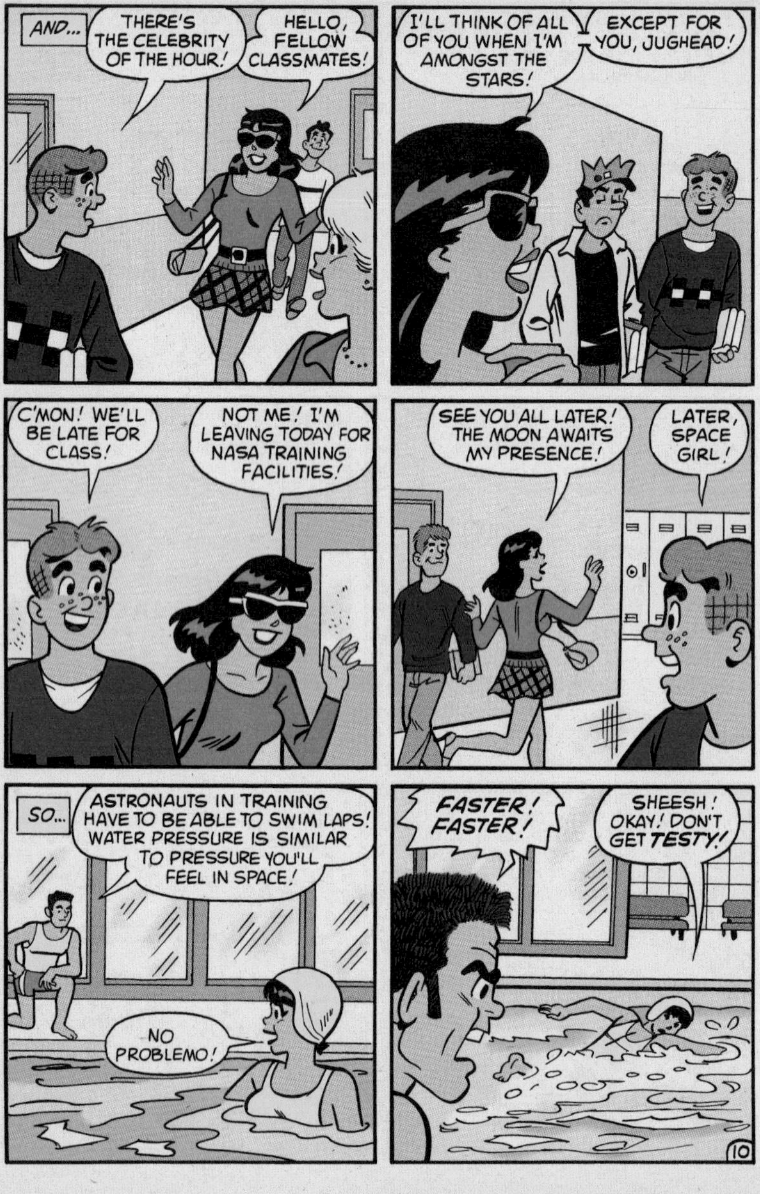
AND...
THERE'S THE CELEBRITY OF THE HOUR!
HELLO, FELLOW CLASSMATES!
I'LL THINK OF ALL OF YOU WHEN I'M AMONGST THE STARS!
EXCEPT FOR YOU, JUGHEAD!
C'MON! WE'LL BE LATE FOR CLASS!
NOT ME! I'M LEAVING TODAY FOR NASA TRAINING FACILITIES!
SEE YOU ALL LATER! THE MOON AWAITS MY PRESENCE!
LATER, SPACE GIRL!
SO...
ASTRONAUTS IN TRAINING HAVE TO BE ABLE TO SWIM LAPS! WATER PRESSURE IS SIMILAR TO PRESSURE YOU'LL FEEL IN SPACE!
NO PROBLEMO!
FASTER! FASTER!
SHEESH! OKAY! DON'T GET TESTY!
10

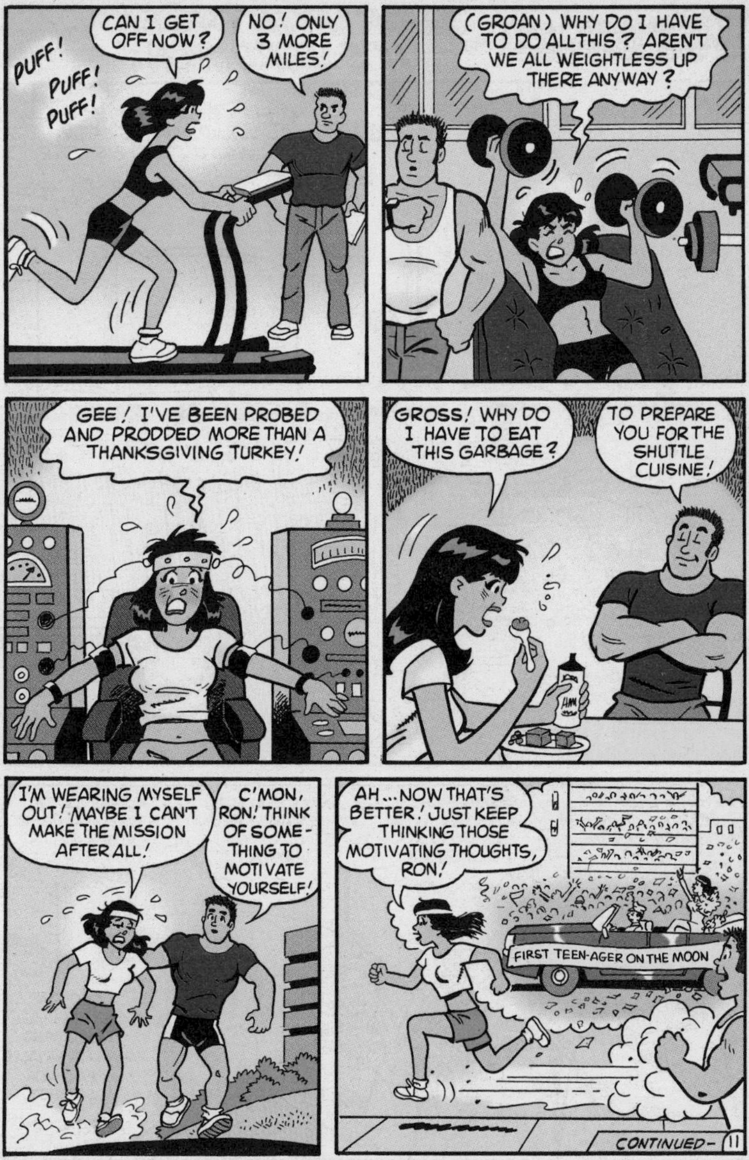
PUFF! PUFF! PUFF!
CAN I GET OFF NOW?
NO! ONLY 3 MORE MILES!
(GROAN) WHY DO I HAVE TO DO ALL THIS? AREN'T WE ALL WEIGHTLESS UP THERE ANYWAY?
GEE! I'VE BEEN PROBED AND PRODDED MORE THAN A THANKSGIVING TURKEY!
GROSS! WHY DO I HAVE TO EAT THIS GARBAGE?
TO PREPARE YOU FOR THE SHUTTLE CUISINE!
I'M WEARING MYSELF OUT! MAYBE I CAN'T MAKE THE MISSION AFTER ALL!
C'MON, RON! THINK OF SOMETHING TO MOTIVATE YOURSELF!
AH... NOW THAT'S BETTER! JUST KEEP THINKING THOSE MOTIVATING THOUGHTS, RON!
FIRST TEEN-AGER ON THE MOON
CONTINUED-
11

Veronica in "LOOK UP IN THE SKY... IT'S VERONICA"

CHAPTER THREE

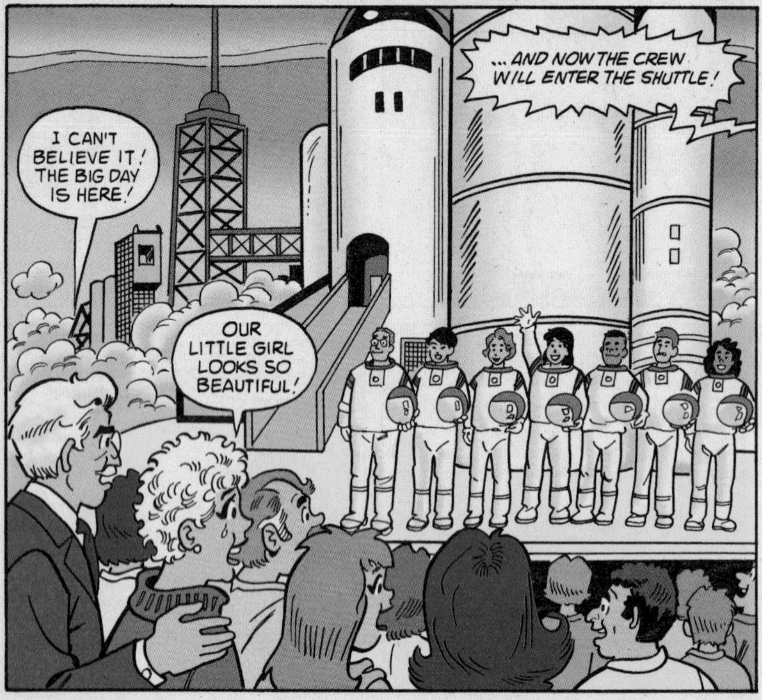

... AND NOW THE CREW WILL ENTER THE SHUTTLE!
I CAN'T BELIEVE IT! THE BIG DAY IS HERE!
OUR LITTLE GIRL LOOKS SO BEAUTIFUL!

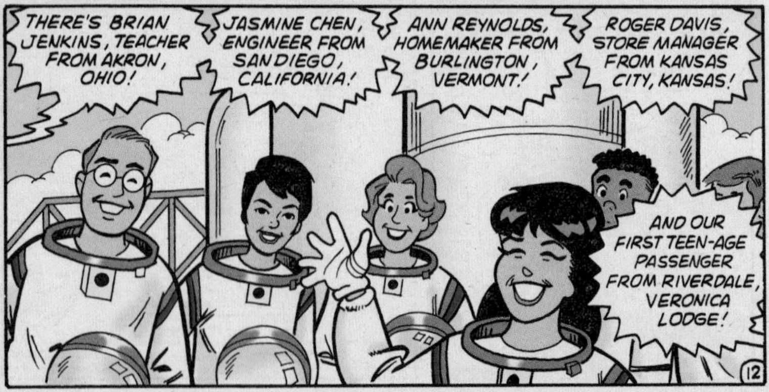

THERE'S BRIAN JENKINS, TEACHER FROM AKRON, OHIO!
JASMINE CHEN, ENGINEER FROM SAN DIEGO, CALIFORNIA!
ANN REYNOLDS, HOMEMAKER FROM BURLINGTON, VERMONT!
ROGER DAVIS, STORE MANAGER FROM KANSAS CITY, KANSAS!
AND OUR FIRST TEEN-AGE PASSENGER FROM RIVERDALE, VERONICA LODGE!

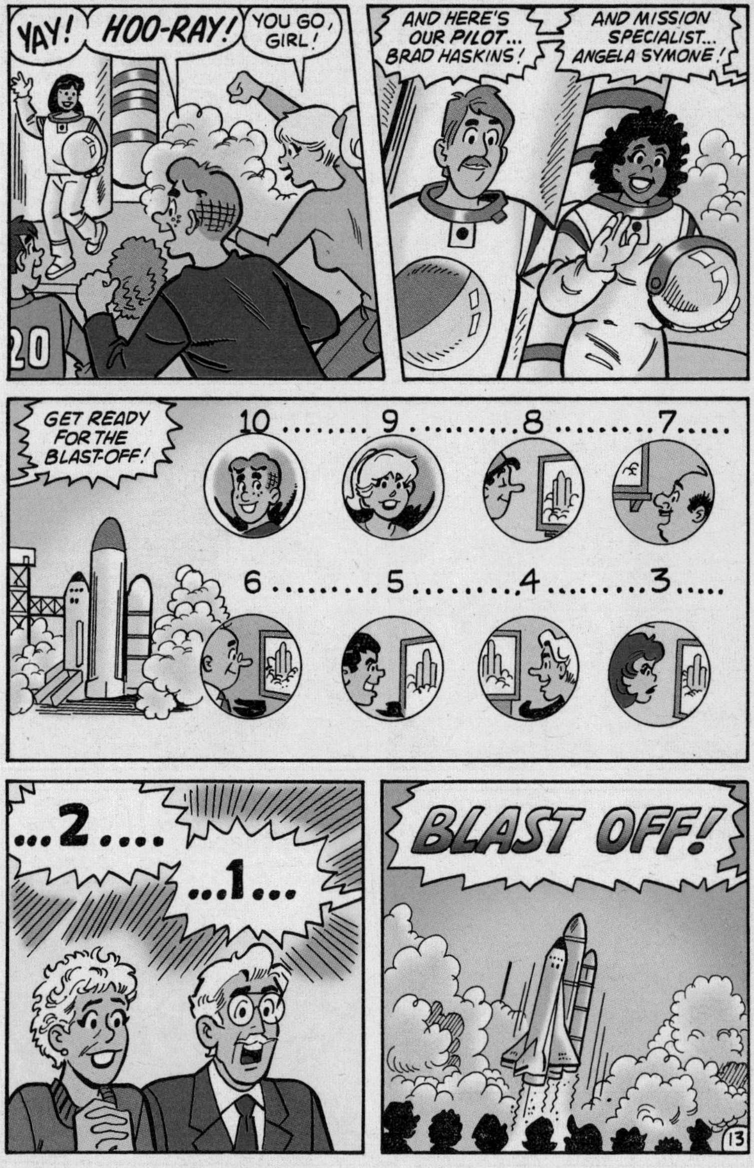
YAY!
HOO-RAY!
YOU GO, GIRL!
20
AND HERE'S OUR PILOT... BRAD HASKINS!
AND MISSION SPECIALIST... ANGELA SYMONE!
GET READY FOR THE BLAST-OFF!
10........9..........8..........7.....
6..........5..........4..........3.....
...2....
...1...
BLAST OFF!
13

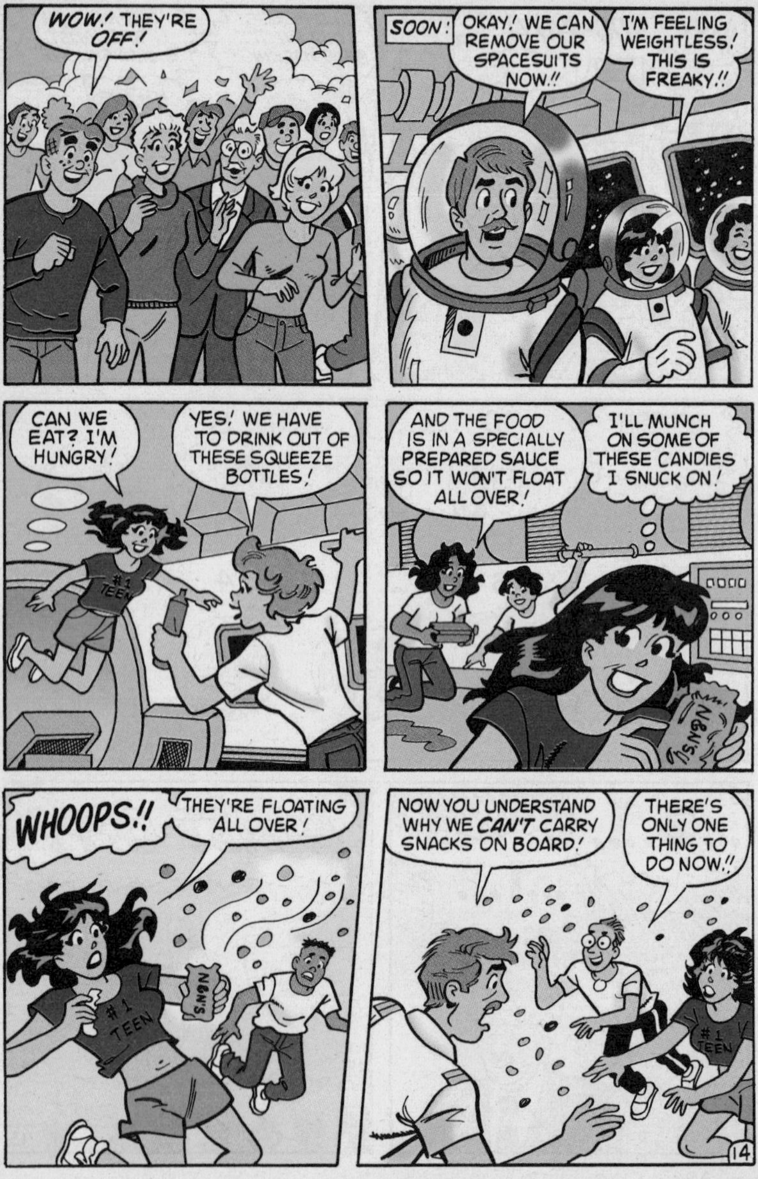
WOW! THEY'RE OFF!
SOON:
OKAY! WE CAN REMOVE OUR SPACESUITS NOW!!
I'M FEELING WEIGHTLESS! THIS IS FREAKY!!
CAN WE EAT? I'M HUNGRY!
YES! WE HAVE TO DRINK OUT OF THESE SQUEEZE BOTTLES!
#1 TEEN
AND THE FOOD IS IN A SPECIALLY PREPARED SAUCE SO IT WON'T FLOAT ALL OVER!
I'LL MUNCH ON SOME OF THESE CANDIES I SNUCK ON!
N&N'S
WHOOPS!!
THEY'RE FLOATING ALL OVER!
#1 TEEN
N&N'S
NOW YOU UNDERSTAND WHY WE CAN'T CARRY SNACKS ON BOARD!
THERE'S ONLY ONE THING TO DO NOW!!
#1 TEEN
14

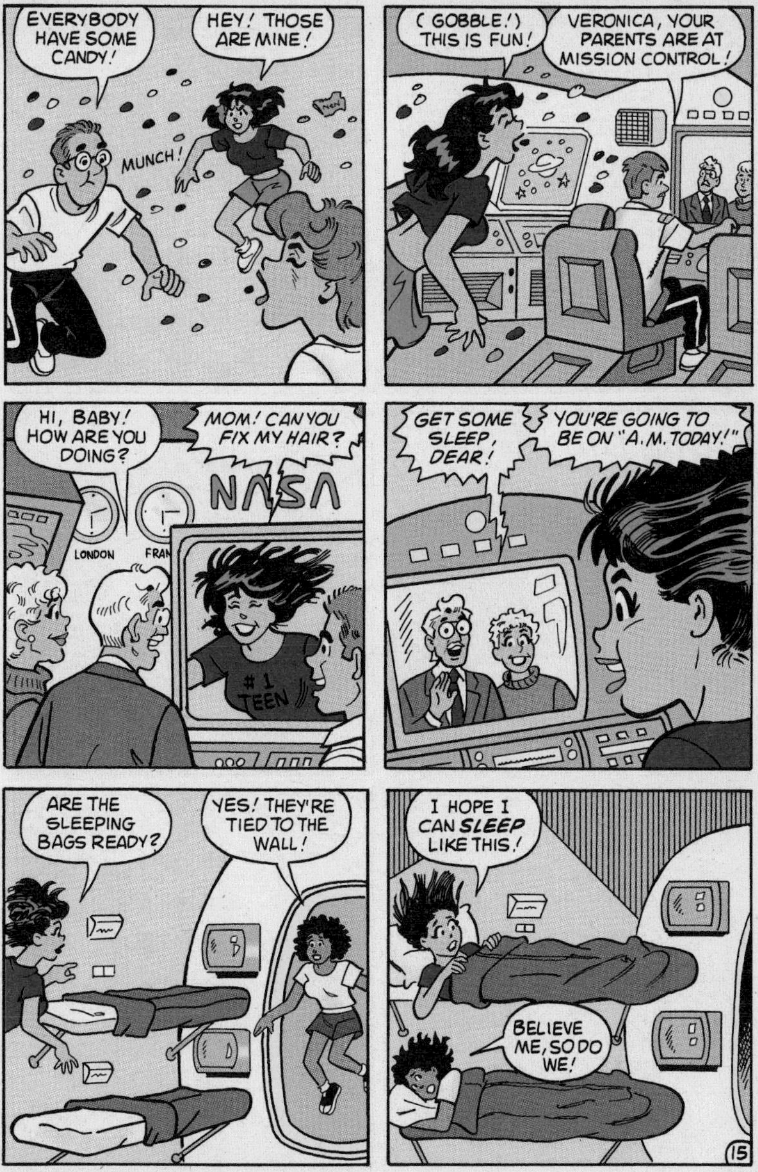
EVERYBODY HAVE SOME CANDY!
HEY! THOSE ARE MINE!
MUNCH!
(GOBBLE!) THIS IS FUN!
VERONICA, YOUR PARENTS ARE AT MISSION CONTROL!
HI, BABY! HOW ARE YOU DOING?
MOM! CAN YOU FIX MY HAIR?
NASA
LONDON
#1 TEEN
GET SOME SLEEP, DEAR!
YOU'RE GOING TO BE ON "A.M. TODAY!"
ARE THE SLEEPING BAGS READY?
YES! THEY'RE TIED TO THE WALL!
I HOPE I CAN SLEEP LIKE THIS!
BELIEVE ME, SO DO WE!

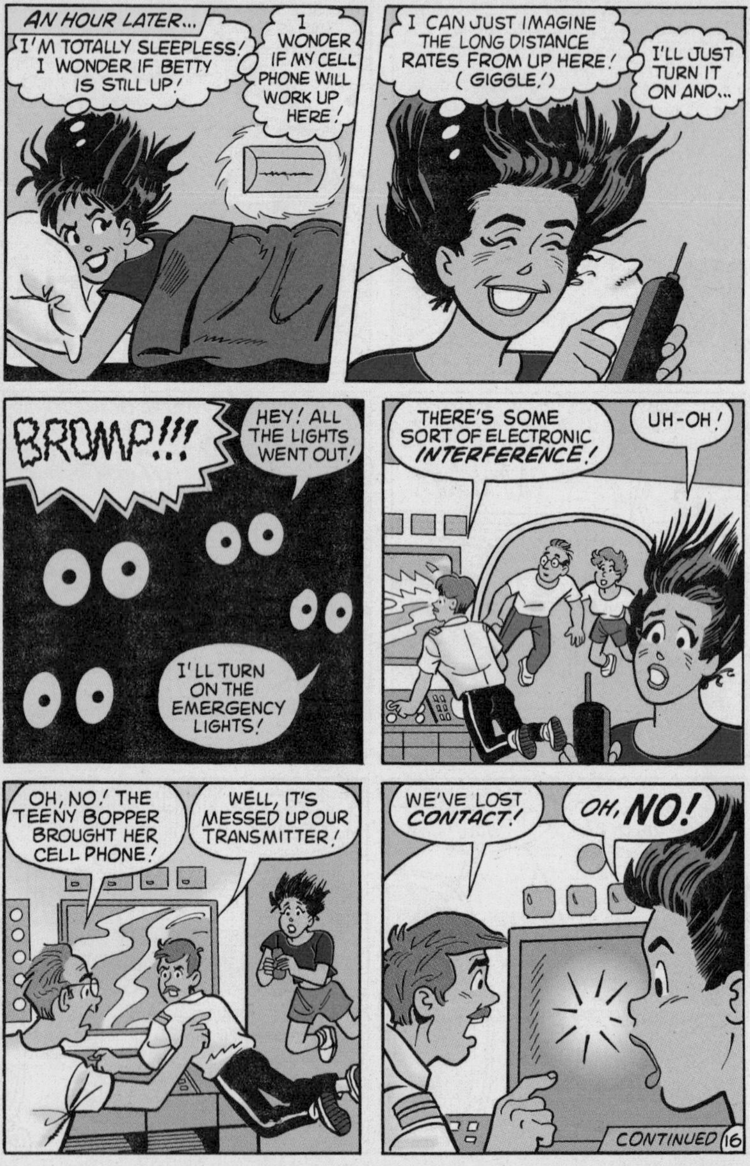
AN HOUR LATER...
I'M TOTALLY SLEEPLESS! I WONDER IF BETTY IS STILL UP!
I WONDER IF MY CELL PHONE WILL WORK UP HERE!
I CAN JUST IMAGINE THE LONG DISTANCE RATES FROM UP HERE! (GIGGLE!)
I'LL JUST TURN IT ON AND...
BROMP!!!
HEY! ALL THE LIGHTS WENT OUT!
I'LL TURN ON THE EMERGENCY LIGHTS!
THERE'S SOME SORT OF ELECTRONIC INTERFERENCE!
UH-OH!
OH, NO! THE TEENY BOPPER BROUGHT HER CELL PHONE!
WELL, IT'S MESSED UP OUR TRANSMITTER!
WE'VE LOST CONTACT!
OH, NO!
CONTINUED
16

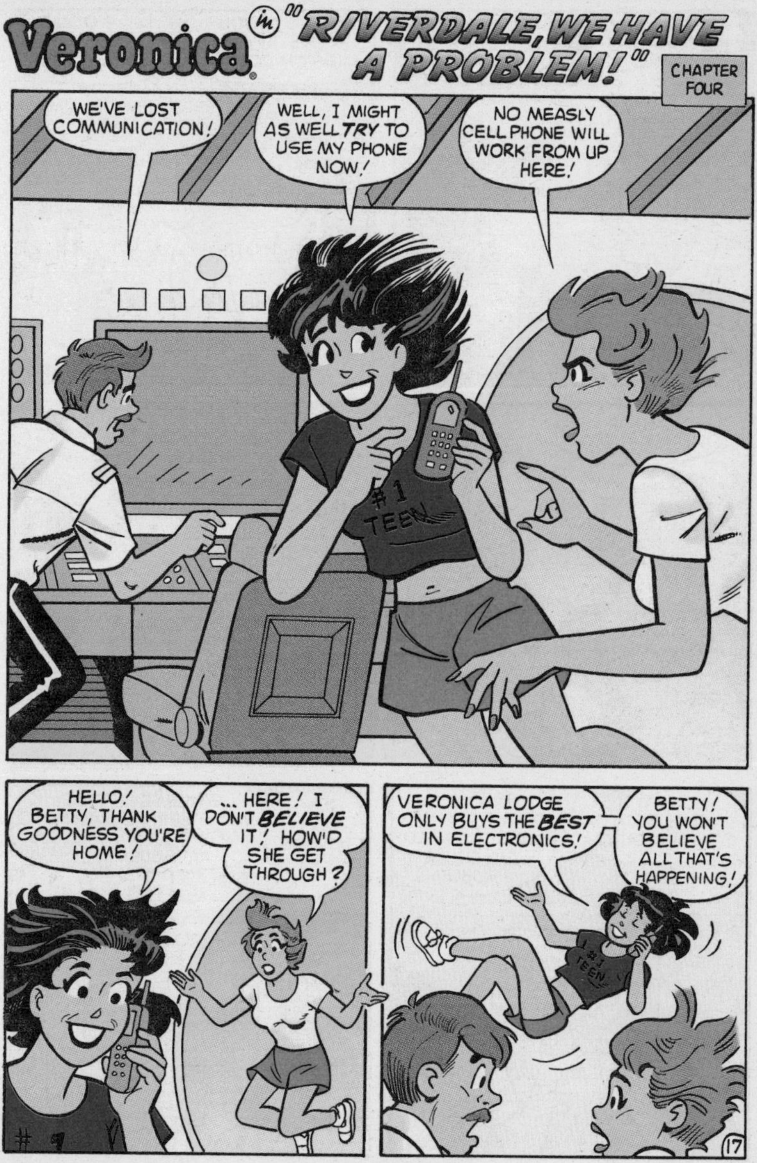
Veronica
in
"RIVERDALE, WE HAVE A PROBLEM!"
CHAPTER FOUR
WE'VE LOST COMMUNICATION!
WELL, I MIGHT AS WELL TRY TO USE MY PHONE NOW!
NO MEASLY CELL PHONE WILL WORK FROM UP HERE!
#1 TEEN
HELLO! BETTY, THANK GOODNESS YOU'RE HOME!
... HERE! I DON'T BELIEVE IT! HOW'D SHE GET THROUGH?
VERONICA LODGE ONLY BUYS THE BEST IN ELECTRONICS!
BETTY! YOU WON'T BELIEVE ALL THAT'S HAPPENING!
17

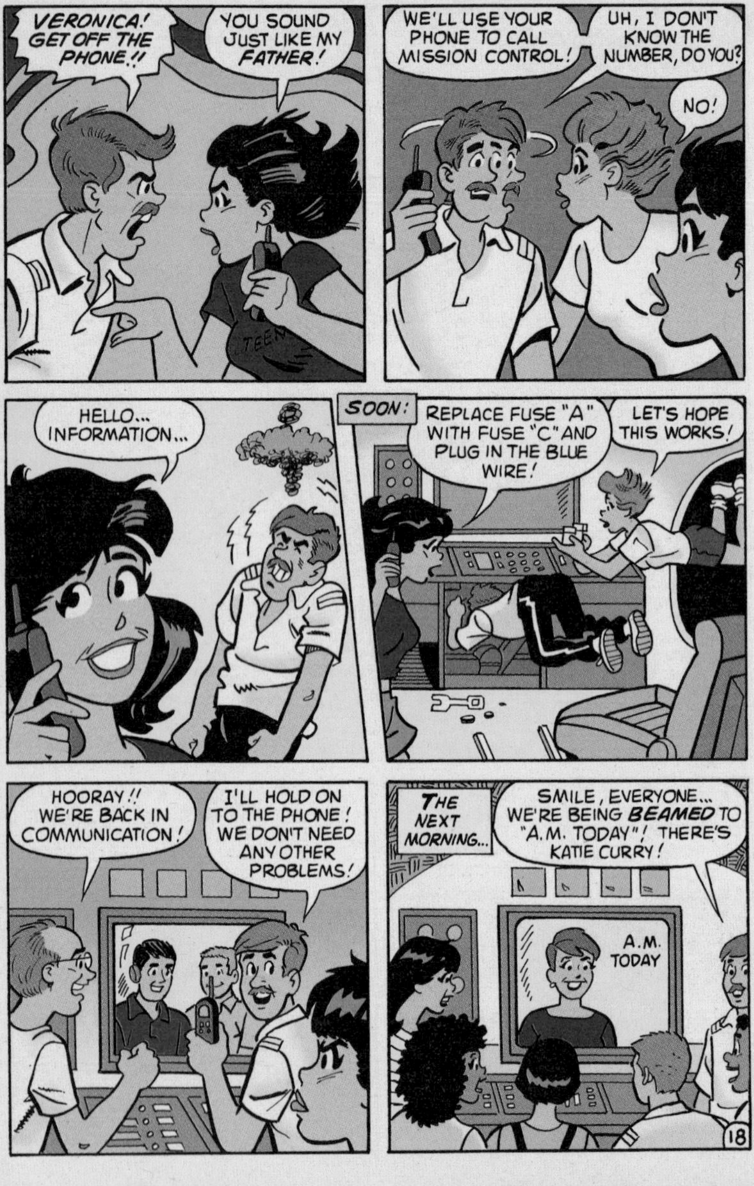

VERONICA! GET OFF THE PHONE!!
YOU SOUND JUST LIKE MY FATHER!
TEEN
WE'LL USE YOUR PHONE TO CALL MISSION CONTROL!
UH, I DON'T KNOW THE NUMBER, DO YOU?
NO!
HELLO... INFORMATION...
SOON:
REPLACE FUSE "A" WITH FUSE "C" AND PLUG IN THE BLUE WIRE!
LET'S HOPE THIS WORKS!
HOORAY!! WE'RE BACK IN COMMUNICATION!
I'LL HOLD ON TO THE PHONE! WE DON'T NEED ANY OTHER PROBLEMS!
THE NEXT MORNING...
SMILE, EVERYONE... WE'RE BEING BEAMED TO "A.M. TODAY"! THERE'S KATIE CURRY!
A.M. TODAY

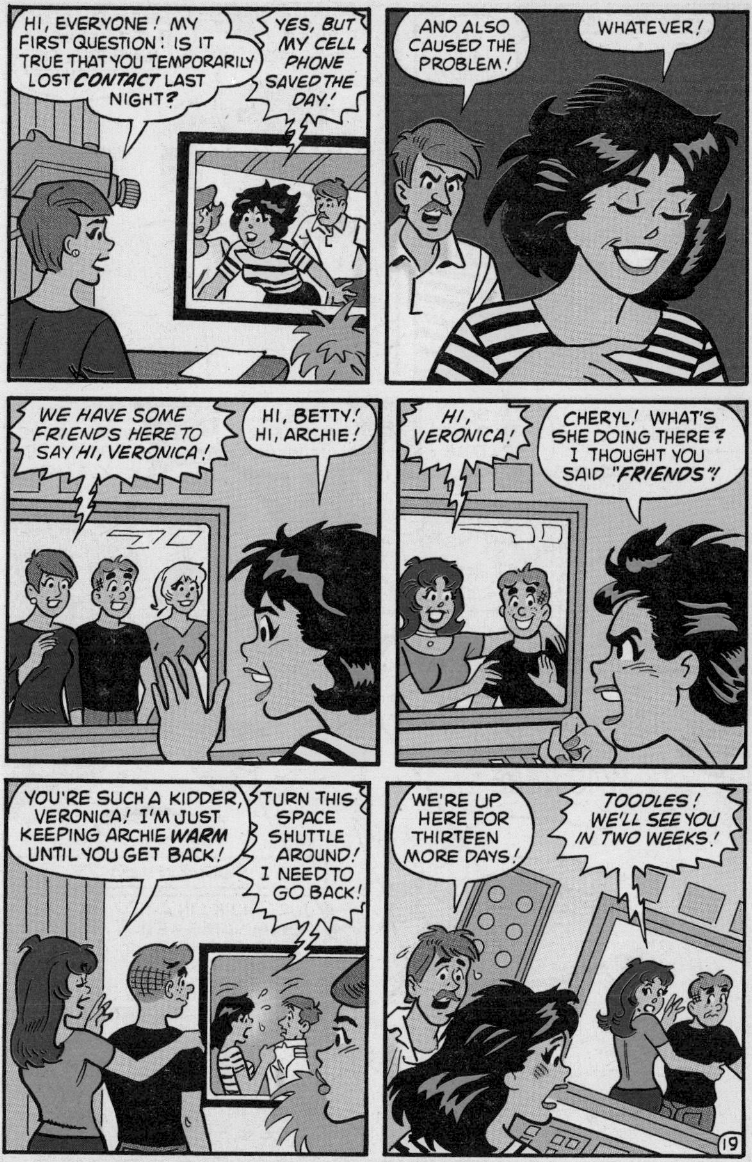
HI, EVERYONE! MY FIRST QUESTION: IS IT TRUE THAT YOU TEMPORARILY LOST CONTACT LAST NIGHT?
YES, BUT MY CELL PHONE SAVED THE DAY!
AND ALSO CAUSED THE PROBLEM!
WHATEVER!
WE HAVE SOME FRIENDS HERE TO SAY HI, VERONICA!
HI, BETTY! HI, ARCHIE!
HI, VERONICA!
CHERYL! WHAT'S SHE DOING THERE? I THOUGHT YOU SAID "FRIENDS"!
YOU'RE SUCH A KIDDER, VERONICA! I'M JUST KEEPING ARCHIE WARM UNTIL YOU GET BACK!
TURN THIS SPACE SHUTTLE AROUND! I NEED TO GO BACK!
WE'RE UP HERE FOR THIRTEEN MORE DAYS!
TOODLES! WE'LL SEE YOU IN TWO WEEKS!
19

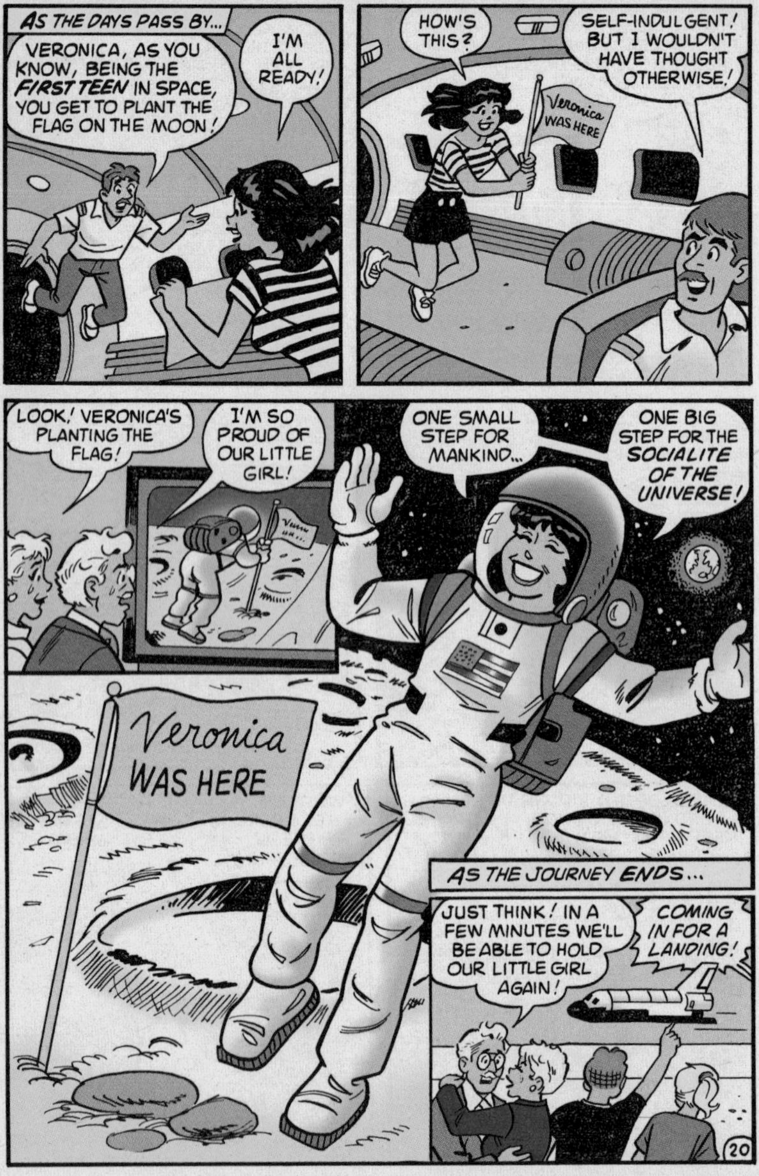

AS THE DAYS PASS BY...
VERONICA, AS YOU KNOW, BEING THE FIRST TEEN IN SPACE, YOU GET TO PLANT THE FLAG ON THE MOON!
I'M ALL READY!
HOW'S THIS?
Veronica WAS HERE
SELF-INDULGENT! BUT I WOULDN'T HAVE THOUGHT OTHERWISE!
LOOK! VERONICA'S PLANTING THE FLAG!
I'M SO PROUD OF OUR LITTLE GIRL!
ONE SMALL STEP FOR MANKIND...
ONE BIG STEP FOR THE SOCIALITE OF THE UNIVERSE!
Veronica WAS HERE
AS THE JOURNEY ENDS...
JUST THINK! IN A FEW MINUTES WE'LL BE ABLE TO HOLD OUR LITTLE GIRL AGAIN!
COMING IN FOR A LANDING!
20

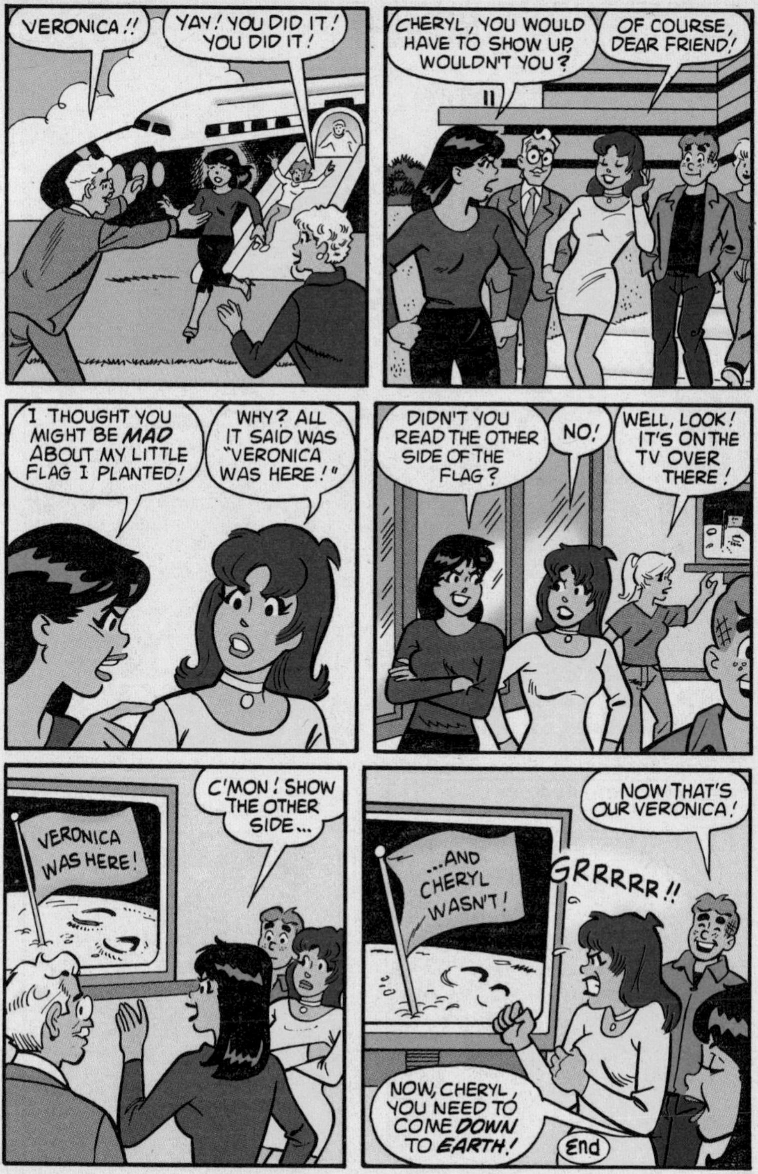
VERONICA!!
YAY! YOU DID IT! YOU DID IT!
CHERYL, YOU WOULD HAVE TO SHOW UP, WOULDN'T YOU?
OF COURSE, DEAR FRIEND!
I THOUGHT YOU MIGHT BE MAD ABOUT MY LITTLE FLAG I PLANTED!
WHY? ALL IT SAID WAS "VERONICA WAS HERE!"
DIDN'T YOU READ THE OTHER SIDE OF THE FLAG?
NO!
WELL, LOOK! IT'S ON THE TV OVER THERE!
VERONICA WAS HERE!
C'MON! SHOW THE OTHER SIDE...
...AND CHERYL WASN'T!
NOW THAT'S OUR VERONICA!
GRRRRRR!!
NOW, CHERYL, YOU NEED TO COME DOWN TO EARTH!
End

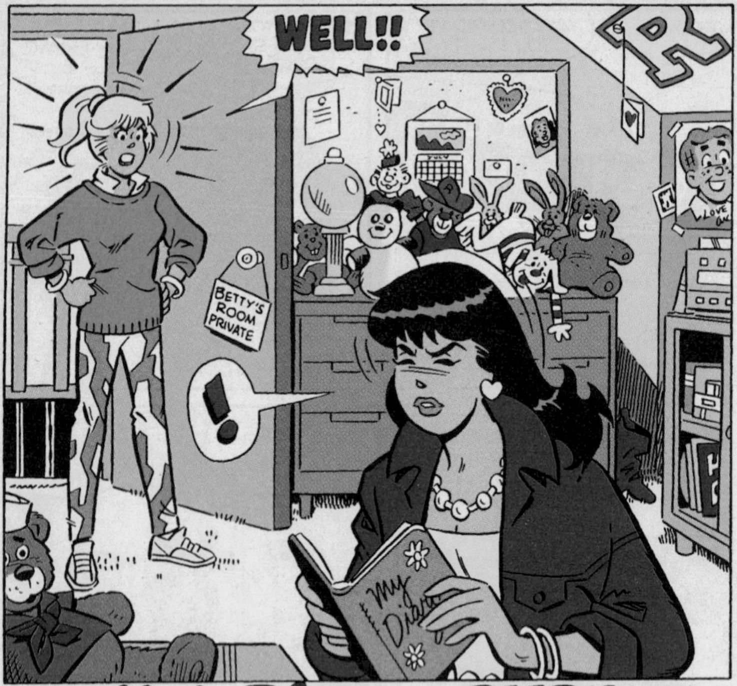
WELL!!
BETTY'S ROOM PRIVATE
!
My Diary

Betty's Diary DIARY X 3

Script: Kathleen Webb / Pencils: Stan Goldberg / Inks: Rudy Lapick / Letters: Bill Yoshida

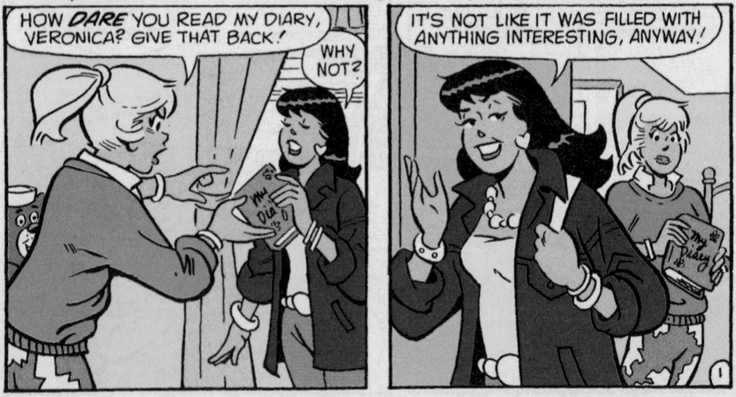
HOW *DARE* YOU READ MY DIARY, VERONICA? GIVE THAT BACK!
WHY NOT?
IT'S NOT LIKE IT WAS FILLED WITH ANYTHING INTERESTING, ANYWAY!
My Diary

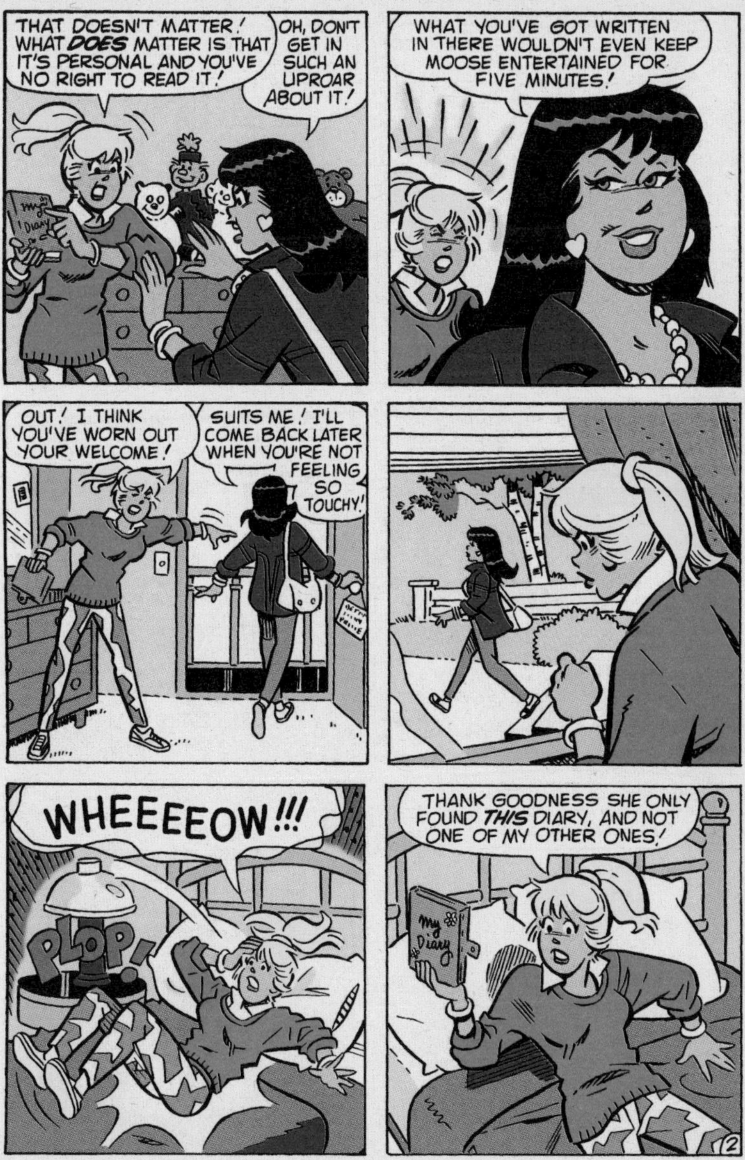
THAT DOESN'T MATTER! WHAT DOES MATTER IS THAT IT'S PERSONAL AND YOU'VE NO RIGHT TO READ IT!
OH, DON'T GET IN SUCH AN UPROAR ABOUT IT!
My Diary
WHAT YOU'VE GOT WRITTEN IN THERE WOULDN'T EVEN KEEP MOOSE ENTERTAINED FOR FIVE MINUTES!
OUT! I THINK YOU'VE WORN OUT YOUR WELCOME!
SUITS ME! I'LL COME BACK LATER WHEN YOU'RE NOT FEELING SO TOUCHY!
WHEEEEOW!!!
PLOP!
THANK GOODNESS SHE ONLY FOUND THIS DIARY, AND NOT ONE OF MY OTHER ONES!
My Diary
2

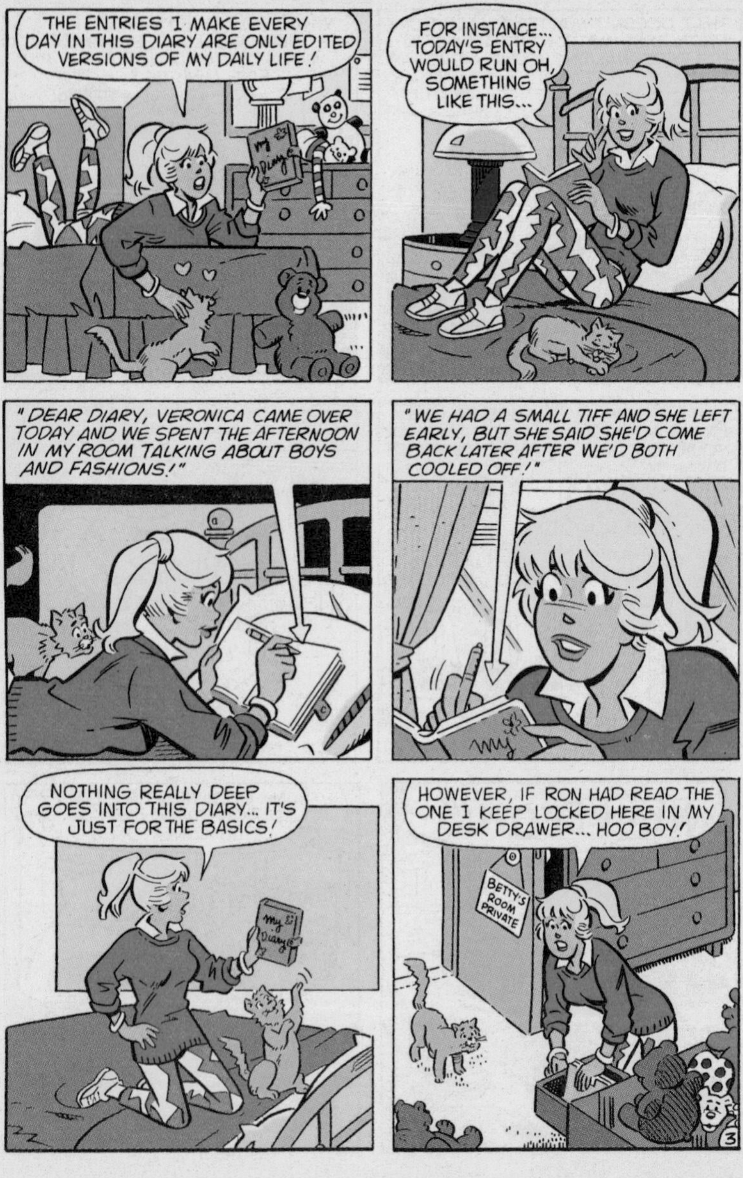
THE ENTRIES I MAKE EVERY DAY IN THIS DIARY ARE ONLY EDITED VERSIONS OF MY DAILY LIFE!
MY DIARY
FOR INSTANCE... TODAY'S ENTRY WOULD RUN OH, SOMETHING LIKE THIS...
"DEAR DIARY, VERONICA CAME OVER TODAY AND WE SPENT THE AFTERNOON IN MY ROOM TALKING ABOUT BOYS AND FASHIONS!"
"WE HAD A SMALL TIFF AND SHE LEFT EARLY, BUT SHE SAID SHE'D COME BACK LATER AFTER WE'D BOTH COOLED OFF!"
NOTHING REALLY DEEP GOES INTO THIS DIARY... IT'S JUST FOR THE BASICS!
MY DIARY
HOWEVER, IF RON HAD READ THE ONE I KEEP LOCKED HERE IN MY DESK DRAWER... HOO BOY!
BETTY'S ROOM PRIVATE
3

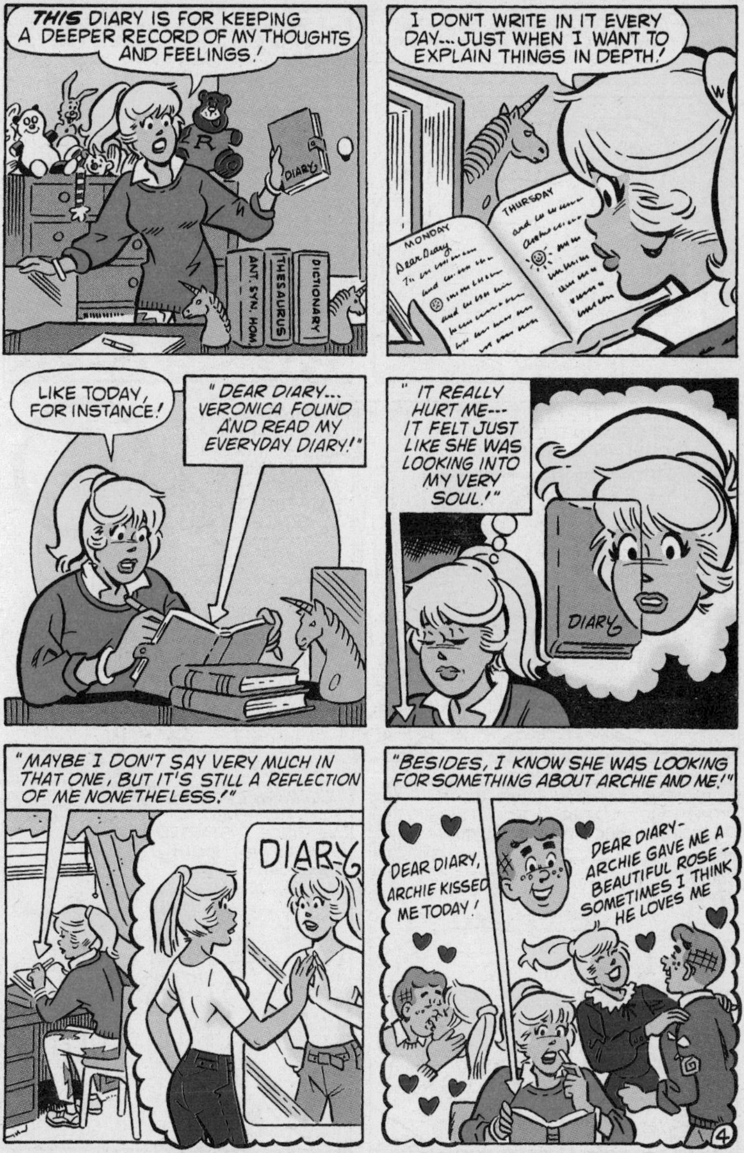
THIS DIARY IS FOR KEEPING A DEEPER RECORD OF MY THOUGHTS AND FEELINGS!
DIARY
ANT. SYN. HOM.
THESAURUS
DICTIONARY
I DON'T WRITE IN IT EVERY DAY... JUST WHEN I WANT TO EXPLAIN THINGS IN DEPTH!
MONDAY
Dear Diary
THURSDAY
LIKE TODAY, FOR INSTANCE!
"DEAR DIARY... VERONICA FOUND AND READ MY EVERYDAY DIARY!"
"IT REALLY HURT ME--- IT FELT JUST LIKE SHE WAS LOOKING INTO MY VERY SOUL!"
DIARY
"MAYBE I DON'T SAY VERY MUCH IN THAT ONE, BUT IT'S STILL A REFLECTION OF ME NONETHELESS!"
DIARY
"BESIDES, I KNOW SHE WAS LOOKING FOR SOMETHING ABOUT ARCHIE AND ME!"
DEAR DIARY, ARCHIE KISSED ME TODAY!
DEAR DIARY- ARCHIE GAVE ME A BEAUTIFUL ROSE- SOMETIMES I THINK HE LOVES ME
4

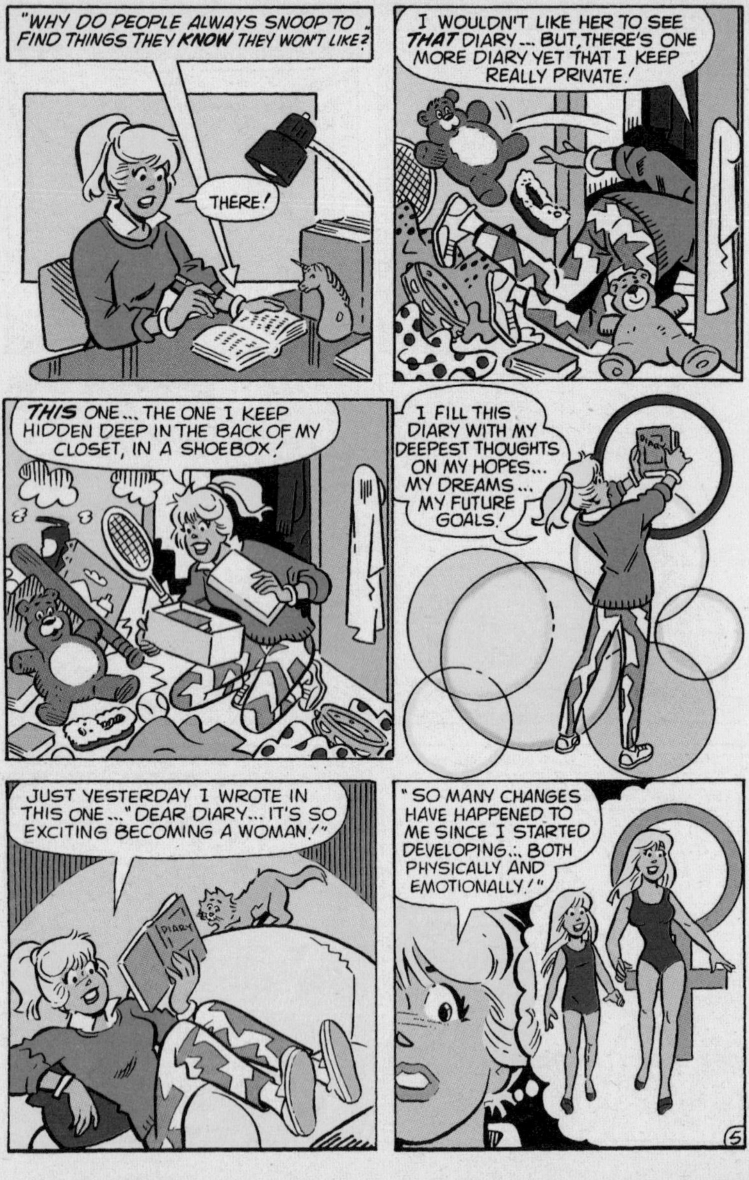
"WHY DO PEOPLE ALWAYS SNOOP TO FIND THINGS THEY KNOW THEY WON'T LIKE?"
THERE!
I WOULDN'T LIKE HER TO SEE THAT DIARY ... BUT, THERE'S ONE MORE DIARY YET THAT I KEEP REALLY PRIVATE!
THIS ONE ... THE ONE I KEEP HIDDEN DEEP IN THE BACK OF MY CLOSET, IN A SHOEBOX!
I FILL THIS DIARY WITH MY DEEPEST THOUGHTS ON MY HOPES... MY DREAMS... MY FUTURE GOALS!
JUST YESTERDAY I WROTE IN THIS ONE..."DEAR DIARY... IT'S SO EXCITING BECOMING A WOMAN!"
DIARY
"SO MANY CHANGES HAVE HAPPENED TO ME SINCE I STARTED DEVELOPING... BOTH PHYSICALLY AND EMOTIONALLY!"
5

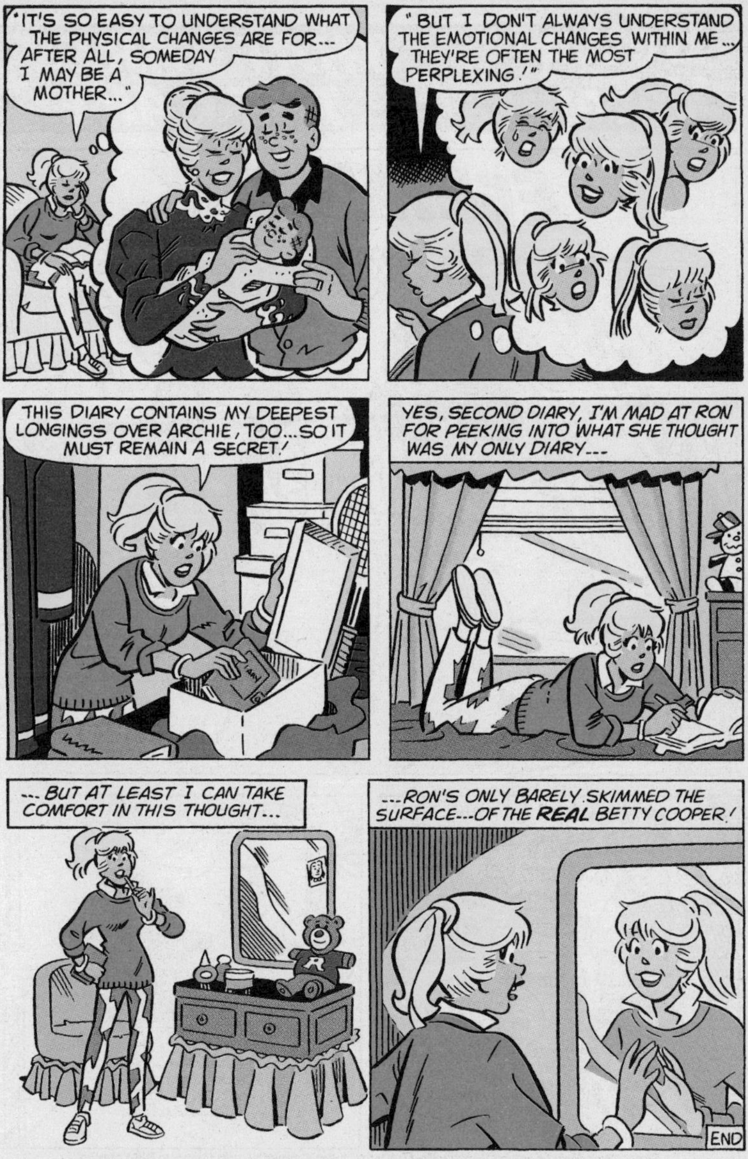
"IT'S SO EASY TO UNDERSTAND WHAT THE PHYSICAL CHANGES ARE FOR... AFTER ALL, SOMEDAY I MAY BE A MOTHER..."
"BUT I DON'T ALWAYS UNDERSTAND THE EMOTIONAL CHANGES WITHIN ME... THEY'RE OFTEN THE MOST PERPLEXING!"
THIS DIARY CONTAINS MY DEEPEST LONGINGS OVER ARCHIE, TOO... SO IT MUST REMAIN A SECRET!
YES, SECOND DIARY, I'M MAD AT RON FOR PEEKING INTO WHAT SHE THOUGHT WAS MY ONLY DIARY---
--- BUT AT LEAST I CAN TAKE COMFORT IN THIS THOUGHT...
---RON'S ONLY BARELY SKIMMED THE SURFACE---OF THE **REAL** BETTY COOPER!
END

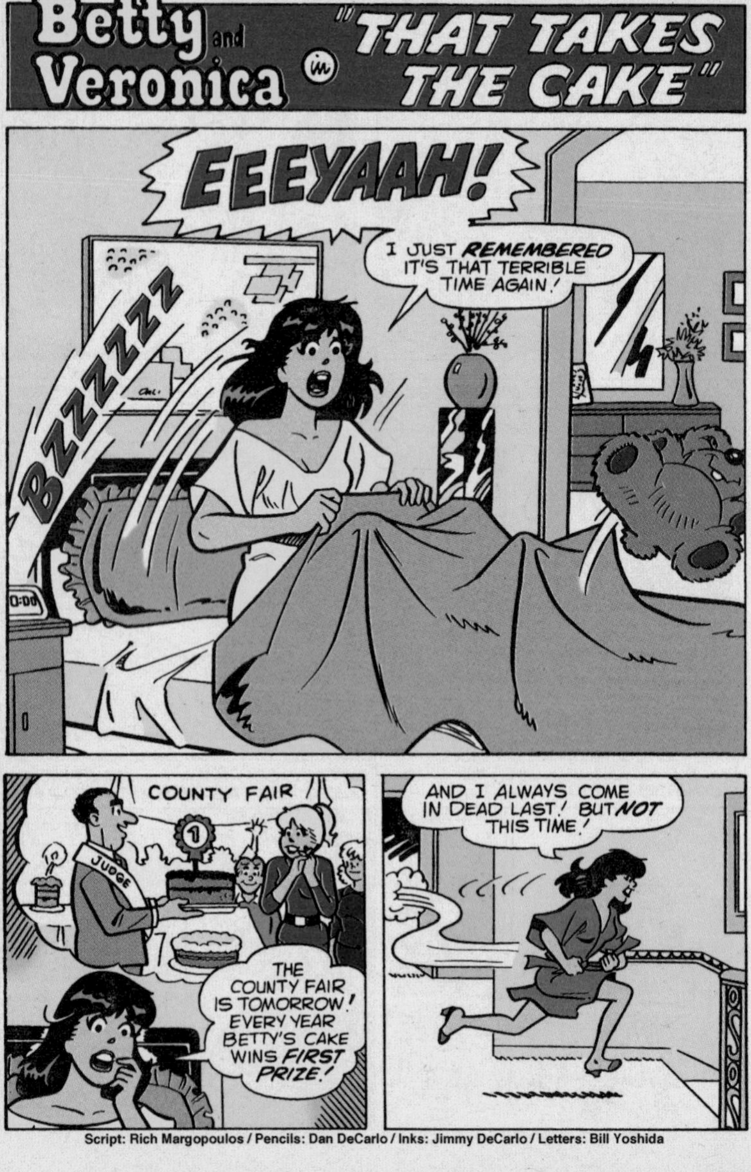
Betty and Veronica in
"THAT TAKES THE CAKE"
EEEYAAH!
BZZZZZZZ
I JUST REMEMBERED IT'S THAT TERRIBLE TIME AGAIN!
COUNTY FAIR
JUDGE
THE COUNTY FAIR IS TOMORROW! EVERY YEAR BETTY'S CAKE WINS FIRST PRIZE!
AND I ALWAYS COME IN DEAD LAST! BUT NOT THIS TIME!

Script: Rich Margopoulos / Pencils: Dan DeCarlo / Inks: Jimmy DeCarlo / Letters: Bill Yoshida

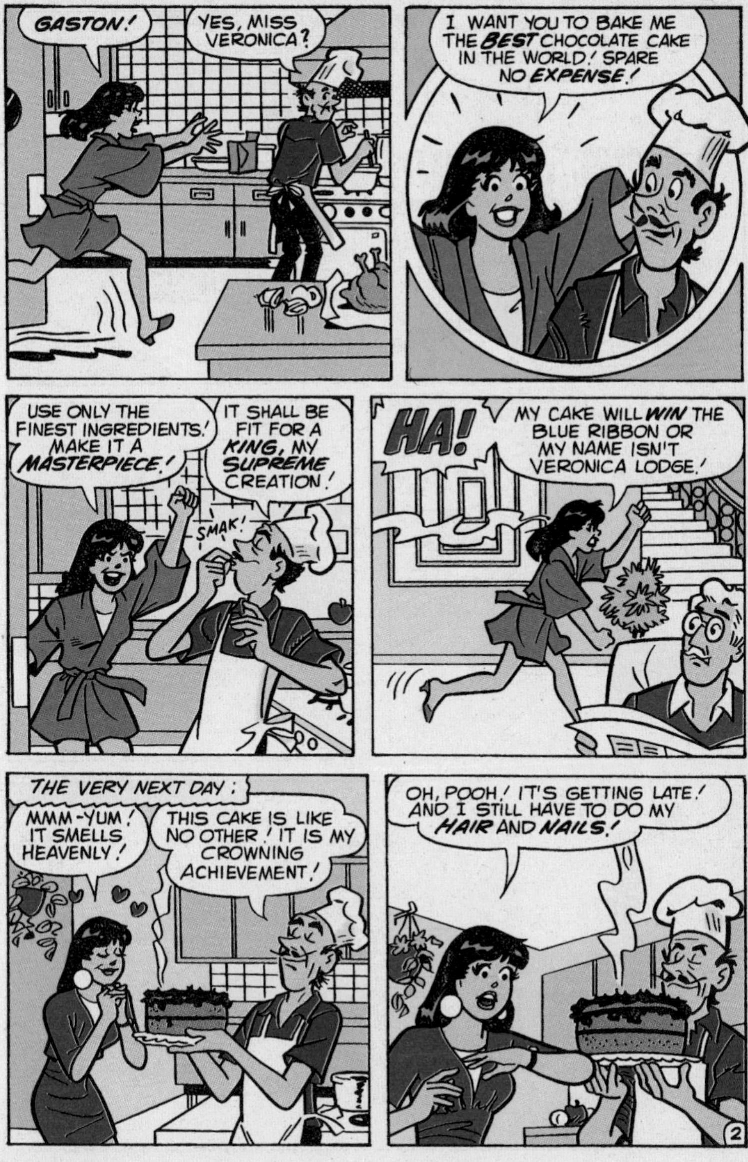
GASTON!
YES, MISS VERONICA?
I WANT YOU TO BAKE ME THE BEST CHOCOLATE CAKE IN THE WORLD! SPARE NO EXPENSE!
USE ONLY THE FINEST INGREDIENTS! MAKE IT A MASTERPIECE!
IT SHALL BE FIT FOR A KING, MY SUPREME CREATION!
SMAK!
HA!
MY CAKE WILL WIN THE BLUE RIBBON OR MY NAME ISN'T VERONICA LODGE!
THE VERY NEXT DAY:
MMM-YUM! IT SMELLS HEAVENLY!
THIS CAKE IS LIKE NO OTHER! IT IS MY CROWNING ACHIEVEMENT!
OH, POOH! IT'S GETTING LATE! AND I STILL HAVE TO DO MY HAIR AND NAILS!
2

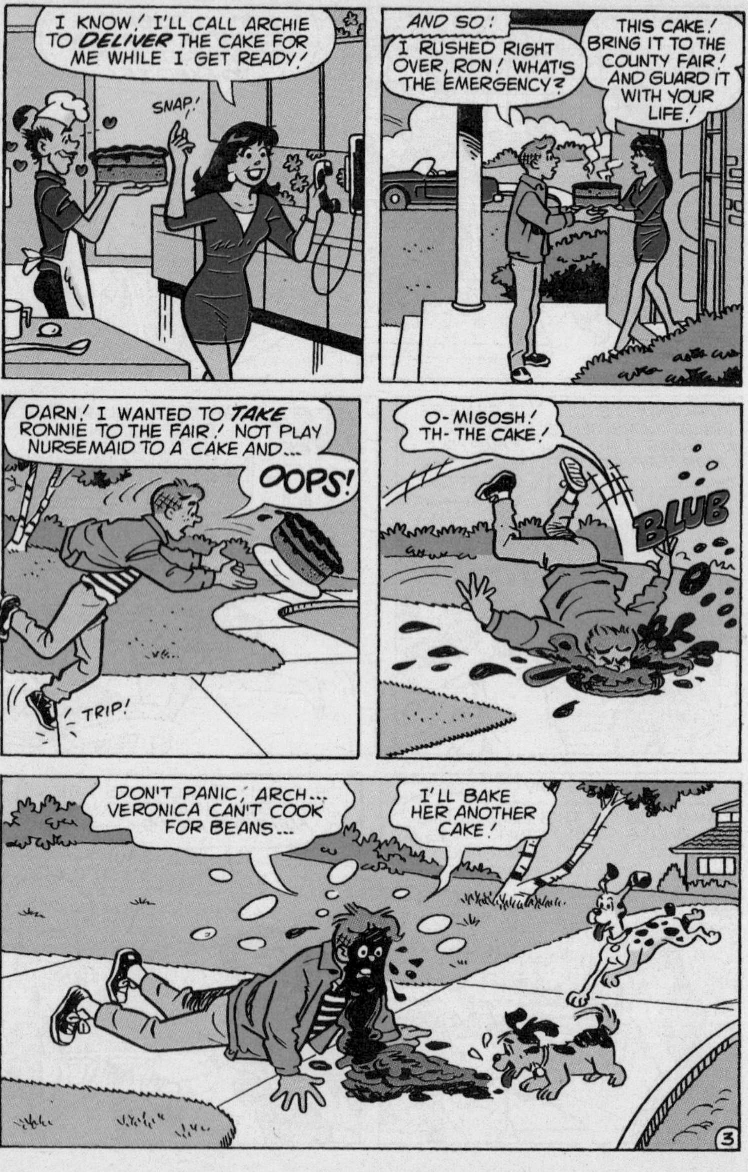

I KNOW! I'LL CALL ARCHIE TO DELIVER THE CAKE FOR ME WHILE I GET READY!
SNAP!
AND SO:
I RUSHED RIGHT OVER, RON! WHAT'S THE EMERGENCY?
THIS CAKE! BRING IT TO THE COUNTY FAIR! AND GUARD IT WITH YOUR LIFE!
DARN! I WANTED TO TAKE RONNIE TO THE FAIR! NOT PLAY NURSEMAID TO A CAKE AND...
OOPS!
TRIP!
O-MIGOSH! TH-THE CAKE!
BLUB
DON'T PANIC, ARCH... VERONICA CAN'T COOK FOR BEANS...
I'LL BAKE HER ANOTHER CAKE!
3

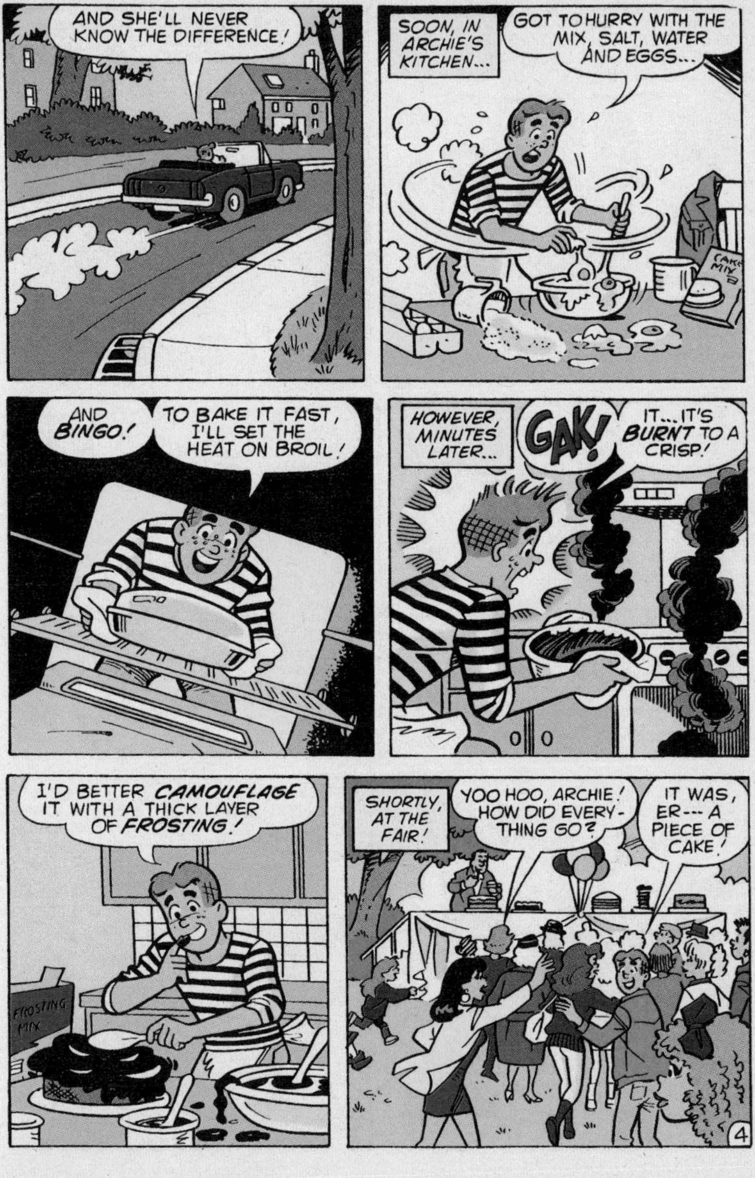
AND SHE'LL NEVER KNOW THE DIFFERENCE!
SOON, IN ARCHIE'S KITCHEN...
GOT TO HURRY WITH THE MIX, SALT, WATER AND EGGS...
CAKE MIX
AND BINGO!
TO BAKE IT FAST, I'LL SET THE HEAT ON BROIL!
HOWEVER, MINUTES LATER...
GAK!
IT...IT'S BURNT TO A CRISP!
I'D BETTER CAMOUFLAGE IT WITH A THICK LAYER OF FROSTING!
FROSTING MIX
SHORTLY, AT THE FAIR!
YOO HOO, ARCHIE! HOW DID EVERY-THING GO?
IT WAS, ER--- A PIECE OF CAKE!
4

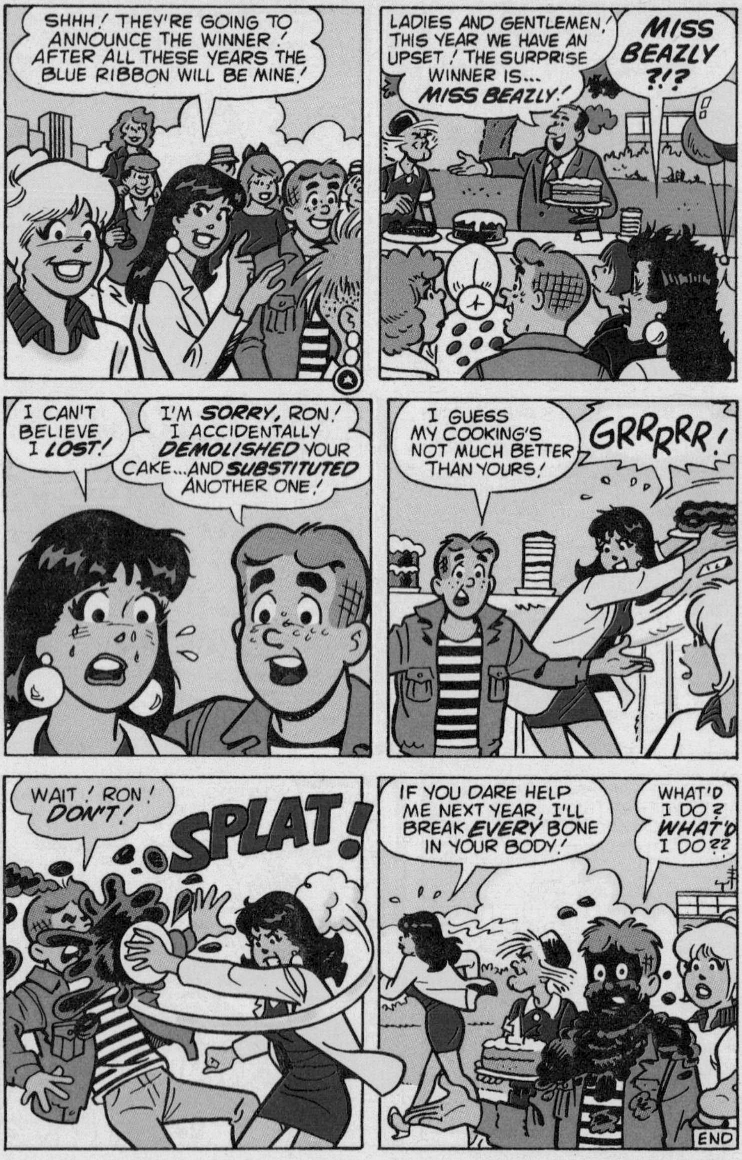

SHHH! THEY'RE GOING TO ANNOUNCE THE WINNER! AFTER ALL THESE YEARS THE BLUE RIBBON WILL BE MINE!
LADIES AND GENTLEMEN! THIS YEAR WE HAVE AN UPSET! THE SURPRISE WINNER IS... MISS BEAZLY!
MISS BEAZLY ?!?
I CAN'T BELIEVE I LOST!
I'M SORRY, RON! I ACCIDENTALLY DEMOLISHED YOUR CAKE...AND SUBSTITUTED ANOTHER ONE!
I GUESS MY COOKING'S NOT MUCH BETTER THAN YOURS!
GRRRRR!
WAIT! RON! DON'T!
SPLAT!
IF YOU DARE HELP ME NEXT YEAR, I'LL BREAK EVERY BONE IN YOUR BODY!
WHAT'D I DO? WHAT'D I DO??
END

Archie at RIVERDALE in "FREDDY the FINDER"

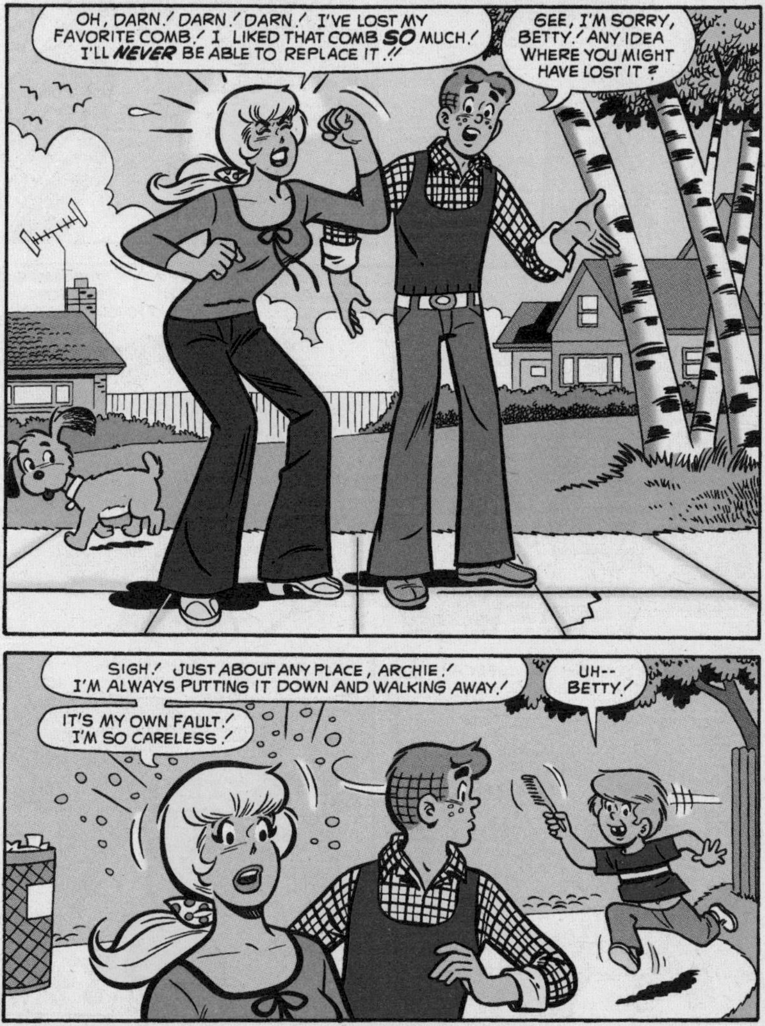
OH, DARN! DARN! DARN! I'VE LOST MY FAVORITE COMB! I LIKED THAT COMB SO MUCH! I'LL NEVER BE ABLE TO REPLACE IT!!
GEE, I'M SORRY, BETTY! ANY IDEA WHERE YOU MIGHT HAVE LOST IT?
SIGH! JUST ABOUT ANY PLACE, ARCHIE! I'M ALWAYS PUTTING IT DOWN AND WALKING AWAY!
IT'S MY OWN FAULT! I'M SO CARELESS!
UH-- BETTY!

Script: Frank Doyle / Pencils: Stan Goldberg / Inks: Jon D'Agostino / Letters: Bill Yoshida

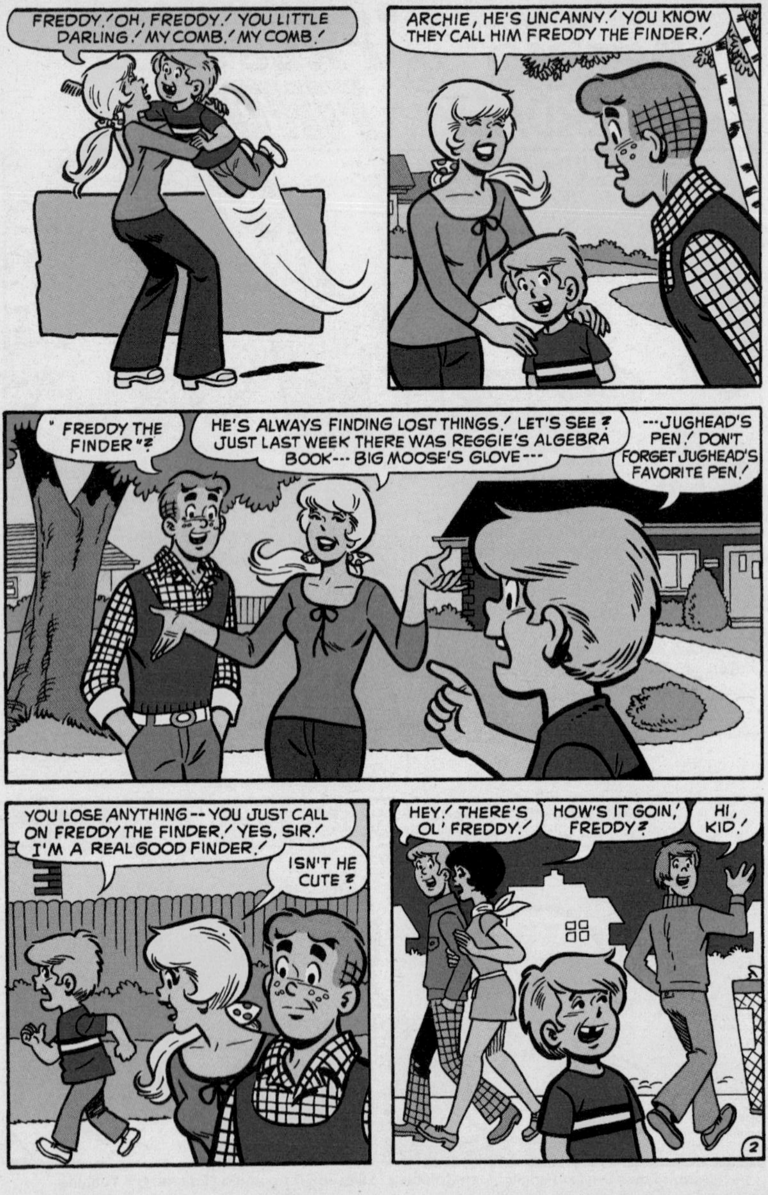
FREDDY! OH, FREDDY! YOU LITTLE DARLING! MY COMB! MY COMB!
ARCHIE, HE'S UNCANNY! YOU KNOW THEY CALL HIM FREDDY THE FINDER!
" FREDDY THE FINDER "?
HE'S ALWAYS FINDING LOST THINGS! LET'S SEE? JUST LAST WEEK THERE WAS REGGIE'S ALGEBRA BOOK--- BIG MOOSE'S GLOVE---
---JUGHEAD'S PEN! DON'T FORGET JUGHEAD'S FAVORITE PEN!
YOU LOSE ANYTHING -- YOU JUST CALL ON FREDDY THE FINDER! YES, SIR! I'M A REAL GOOD FINDER!
ISN'T HE CUTE?
HEY! THERE'S OL' FREDDY!
HOW'S IT GOIN,' FREDDY?
HI, KID!
2

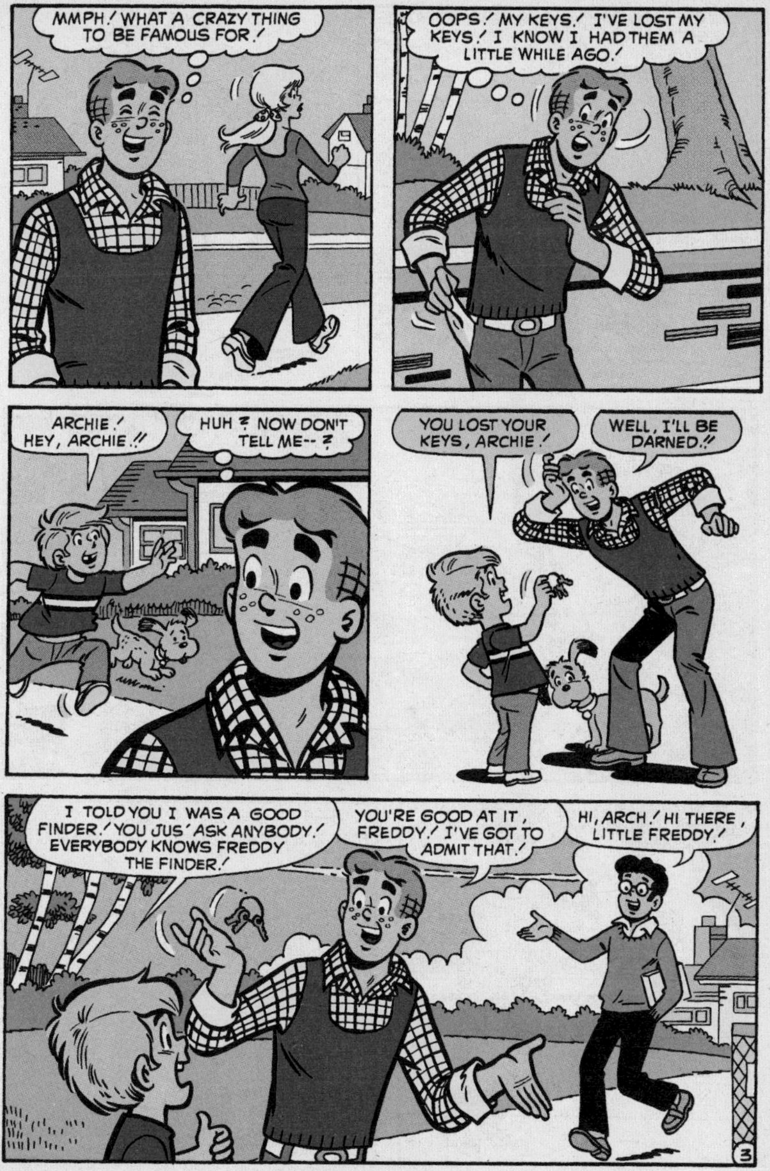

MMPH! WHAT A CRAZY THING TO BE FAMOUS FOR!
OOPS! MY KEYS! I'VE LOST MY KEYS! I KNOW I HAD THEM A LITTLE WHILE AGO!
ARCHIE! HEY, ARCHIE!!
HUH? NOW DON'T TELL ME--?
YOU LOST YOUR KEYS, ARCHIE!
WELL, I'LL BE DARNED!!
I TOLD YOU I WAS A GOOD FINDER! YOU JUS' ASK ANYBODY! EVERYBODY KNOWS FREDDY THE FINDER!
YOU'RE GOOD AT IT, FREDDY! I'VE GOT TO ADMIT THAT!
HI, ARCH! HI THERE, LITTLE FREDDY!
3

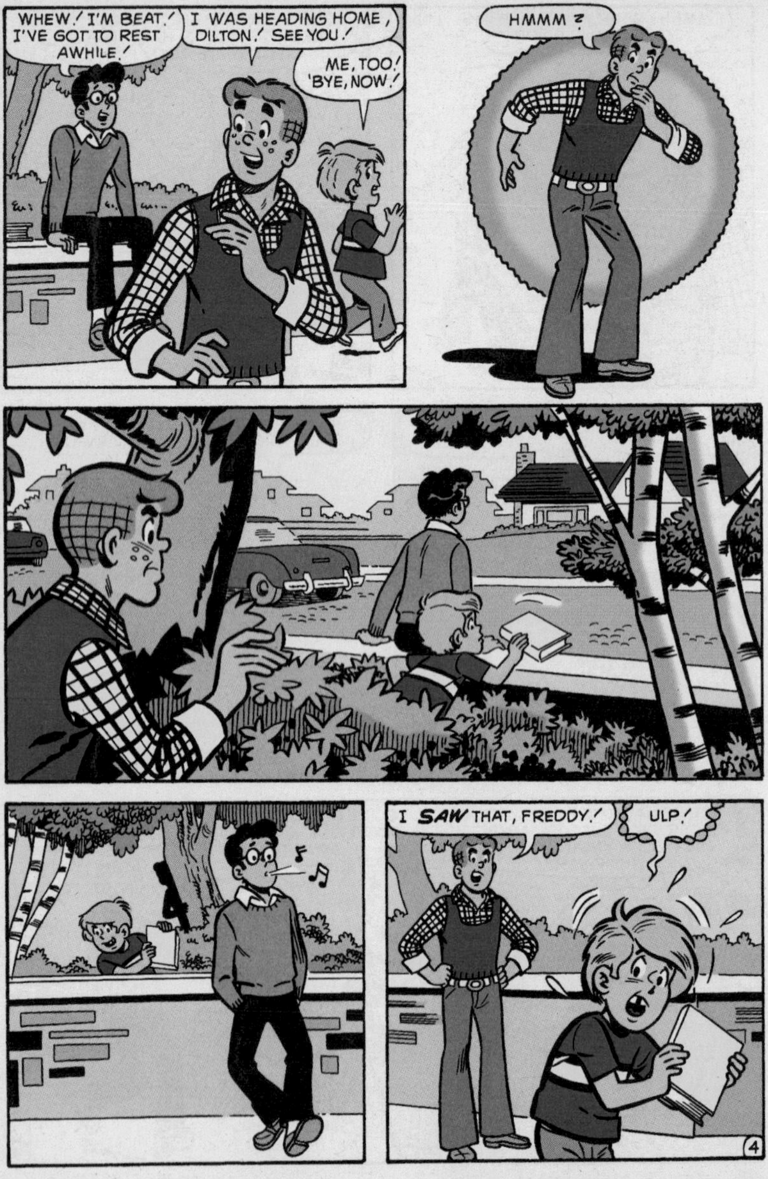

WHEW! I'M BEAT! I'VE GOT TO REST AWHILE!
I WAS HEADING HOME, DILTON! SEE YOU!
ME, TOO! 'BYE, NOW!
HMMM ?
I SAW THAT, FREDDY!
ULP!
4

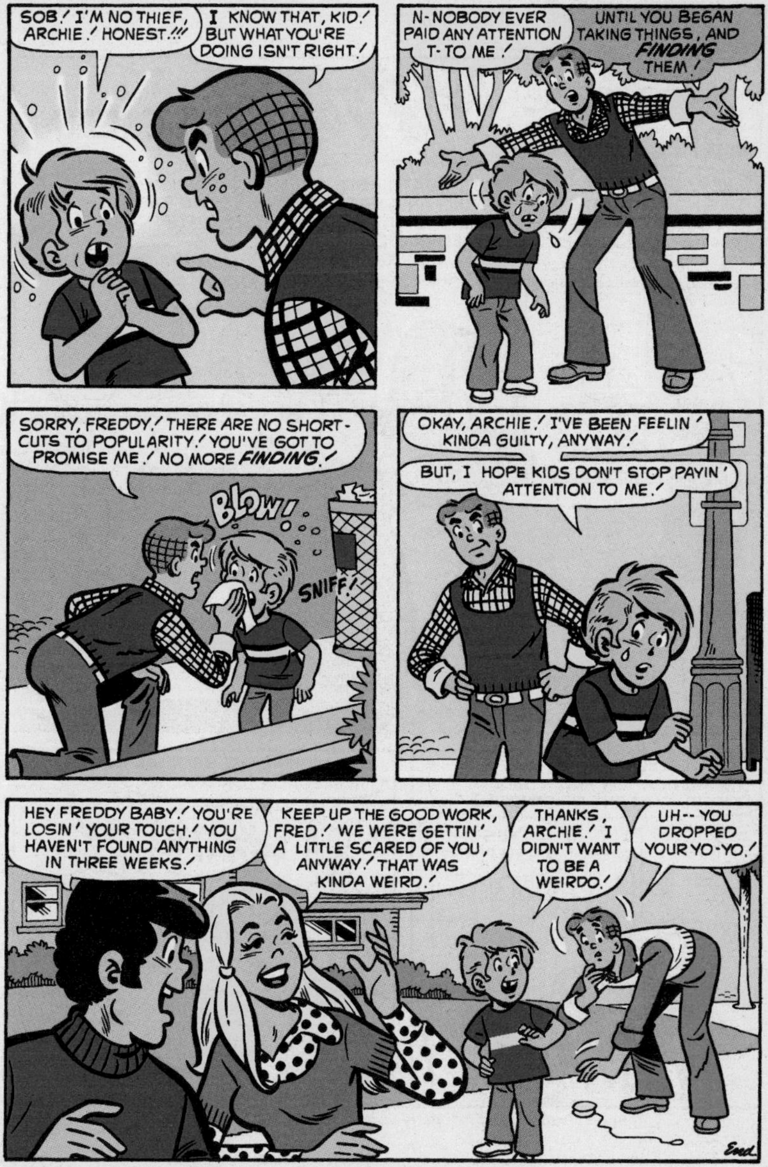

SOB! I'M NO THIEF, ARCHIE! HONEST!!!
I KNOW THAT, KID! BUT WHAT YOU'RE DOING ISN'T RIGHT!
N-NOBODY EVER PAID ANY ATTENTION T-TO ME!
UNTIL YOU BEGAN TAKING THINGS, AND FINDING THEM!
SORRY, FREDDY! THERE ARE NO SHORT-CUTS TO POPULARITY! YOU'VE GOT TO PROMISE ME! NO MORE FINDING!
BLOW!
SNIFF!
OKAY, ARCHIE! I'VE BEEN FEELIN' KINDA GUILTY, ANYWAY!
BUT, I HOPE KIDS DON'T STOP PAYIN' ATTENTION TO ME!
HEY FREDDY BABY! YOU'RE LOSIN' YOUR TOUCH! YOU HAVEN'T FOUND ANYTHING IN THREE WEEKS!
KEEP UP THE GOOD WORK, FRED! WE WERE GETTIN' A LITTLE SCARED OF YOU, ANYWAY! THAT WAS KINDA WEIRD!
THANKS, ARCHIE! I DIDN'T WANT TO BE A WEIRDO!
UH-- YOU DROPPED YOUR YO-YO!
End

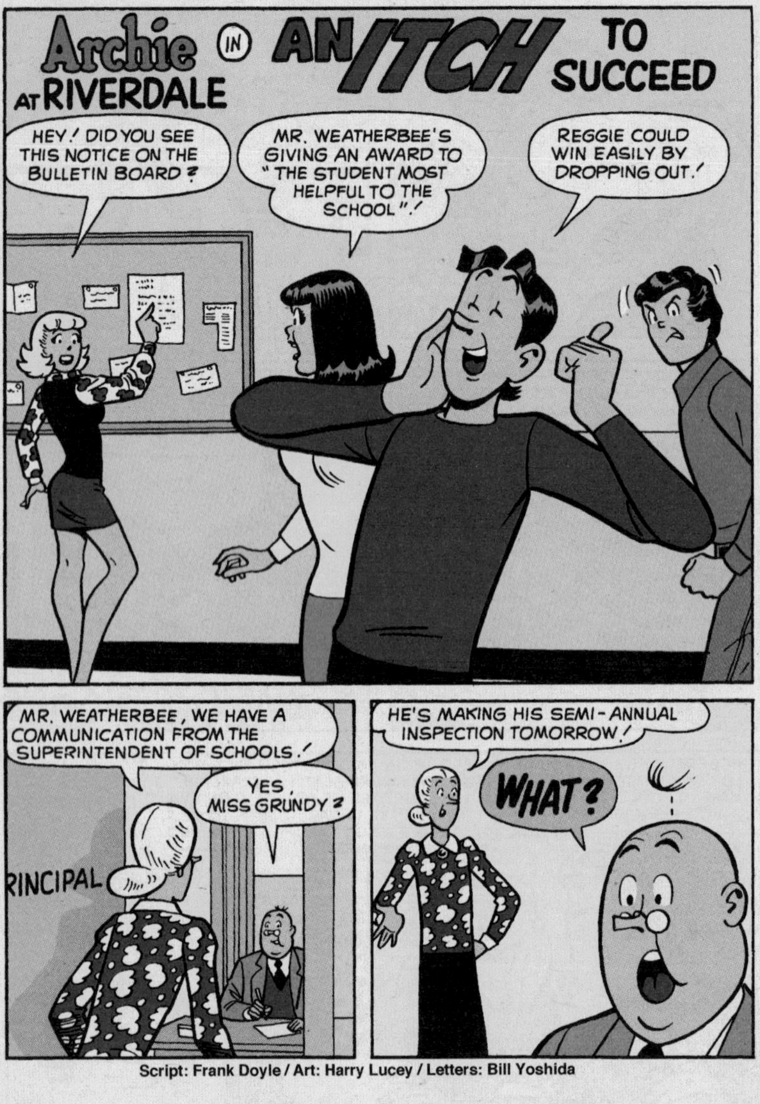
Archie AT RIVERDALE IN AN ITCH TO SUCCEED
HEY! DID YOU SEE THIS NOTICE ON THE BULLETIN BOARD?
MR. WEATHERBEE'S GIVING AN AWARD TO "THE STUDENT MOST HELPFUL TO THE SCHOOL"!
REGGIE COULD WIN EASILY BY DROPPING OUT!
MR. WEATHERBEE, WE HAVE A COMMUNICATION FROM THE SUPERINTENDENT OF SCHOOLS!
YES, MISS GRUNDY?
RINCIPAL
HE'S MAKING HIS SEMI-ANNUAL INSPECTION TOMORROW!
WHAT?

Script: Frank Doyle / Art: Harry Lucey / Letters: Bill Yoshida

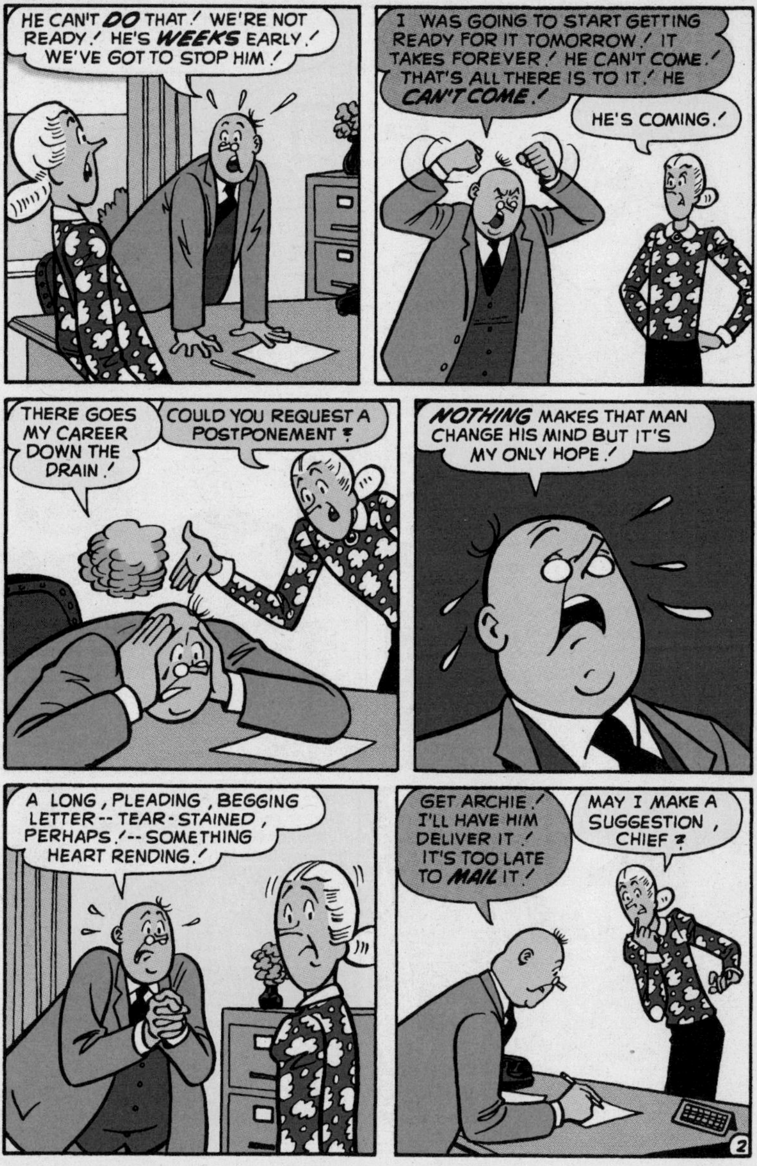

HE CAN'T DO THAT! WE'RE NOT READY! HE'S WEEKS EARLY! WE'VE GOT TO STOP HIM!
I WAS GOING TO START GETTING READY FOR IT TOMORROW! IT TAKES FOREVER! HE CAN'T COME! THAT'S ALL THERE IS TO IT! HE CAN'T COME!
HE'S COMING!
THERE GOES MY CAREER DOWN THE DRAIN!
COULD YOU REQUEST A POSTPONEMENT?
NOTHING MAKES THAT MAN CHANGE HIS MIND BUT IT'S MY ONLY HOPE!
A LONG, PLEADING, BEGGING LETTER -- TEAR-STAINED, PERHAPS! -- SOMETHING HEART RENDING!
GET ARCHIE! I'LL HAVE HIM DELIVER IT! IT'S TOO LATE TO MAIL IT!
MAY I MAKE A SUGGESTION, CHIEF?
2

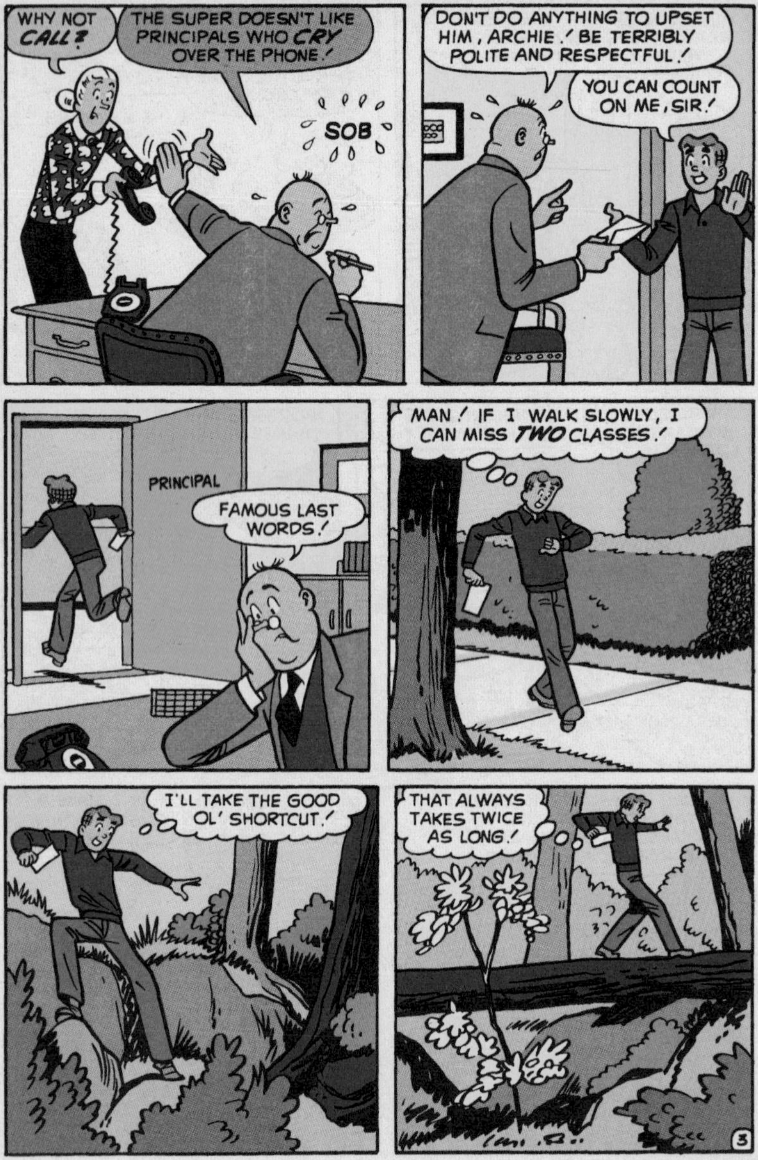
WHY NOT CALL?
THE SUPER DOESN'T LIKE PRINCIPALS WHO CRY OVER THE PHONE!
SOB
DON'T DO ANYTHING TO UPSET HIM, ARCHIE! BE TERRIBLY POLITE AND RESPECTFUL!
YOU CAN COUNT ON ME, SIR!
PRINCIPAL
FAMOUS LAST WORDS!
MAN! IF I WALK SLOWLY, I CAN MISS TWO CLASSES!
I'LL TAKE THE GOOD OL' SHORTCUT!
THAT ALWAYS TAKES TWICE AS LONG!
3

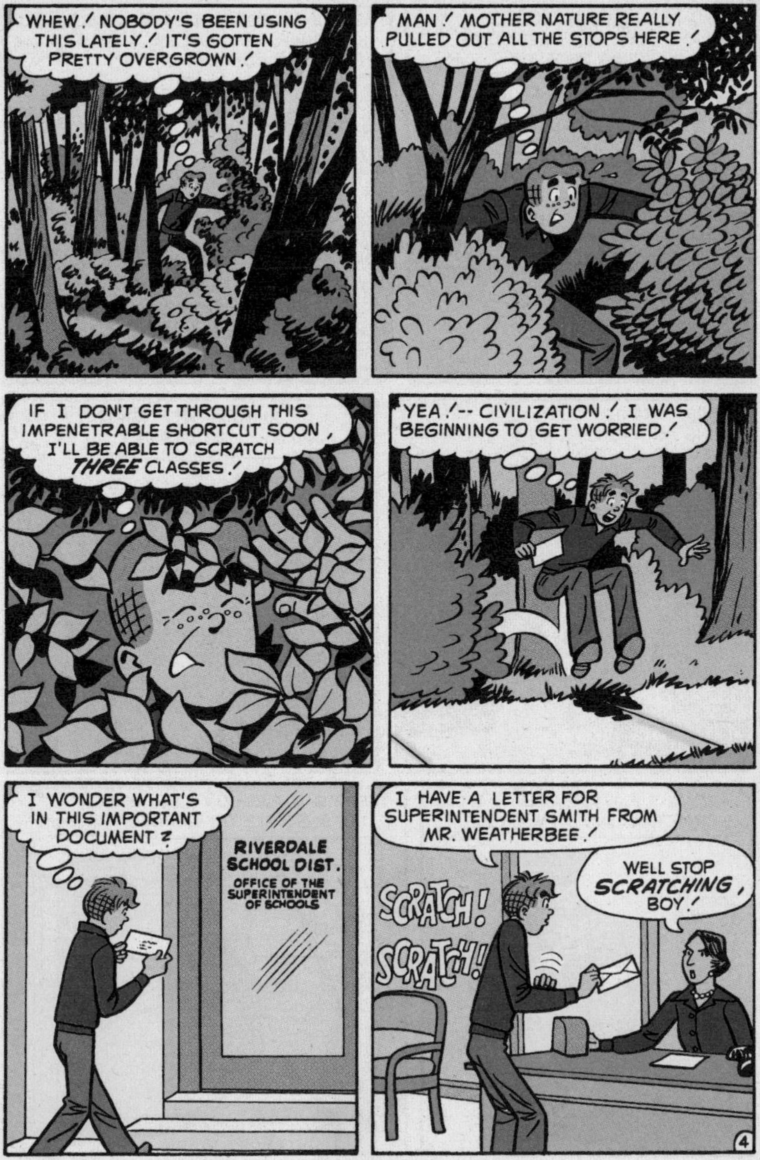
WHEW! NOBODY'S BEEN USING THIS LATELY! IT'S GOTTEN PRETTY OVERGROWN!
MAN! MOTHER NATURE REALLY PULLED OUT ALL THE STOPS HERE!
IF I DON'T GET THROUGH THIS IMPENETRABLE SHORTCUT SOON, I'LL BE ABLE TO SCRATCH THREE CLASSES!
YEA!-- CIVILIZATION! I WAS BEGINNING TO GET WORRIED!
I WONDER WHAT'S IN THIS IMPORTANT DOCUMENT?
RIVERDALE SCHOOL DIST.
OFFICE OF THE SUPERINTENDENT OF SCHOOLS
I HAVE A LETTER FOR SUPERINTENDENT SMITH FROM MR. WEATHERBEE!
SCRATCH!
SCRATCH!
WELL STOP SCRATCHING, BOY!
4

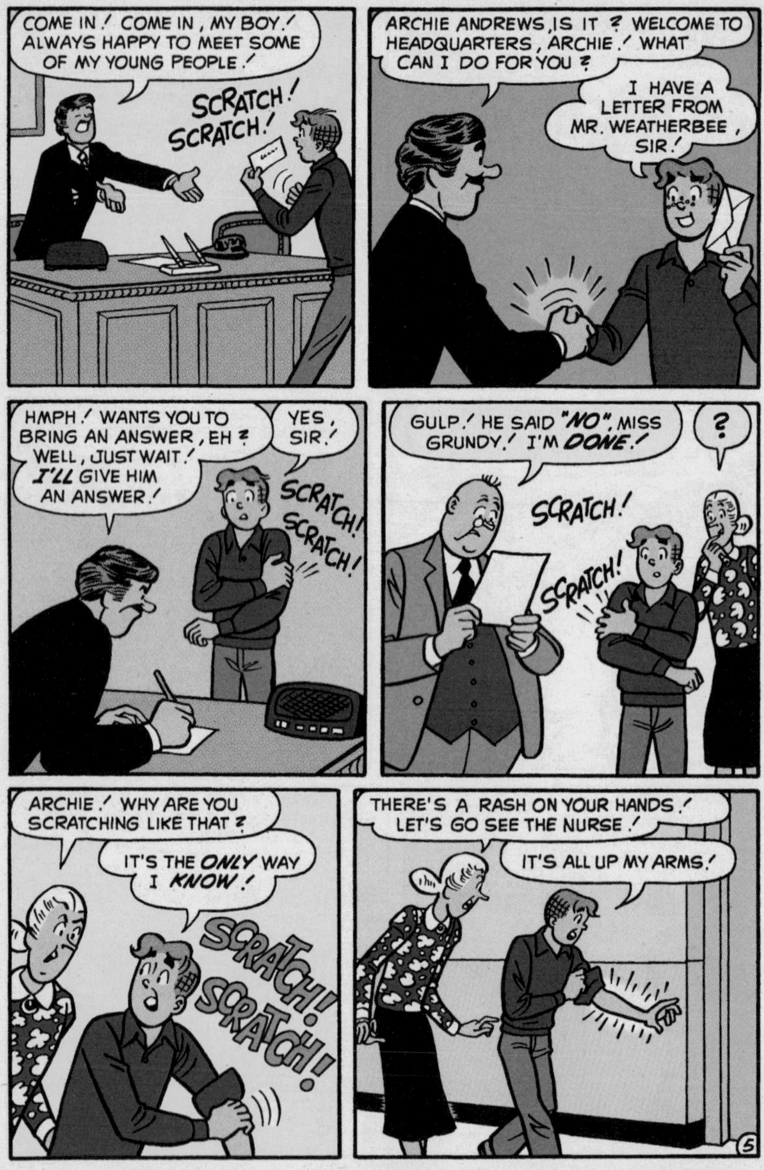
COME IN! COME IN, MY BOY! ALWAYS HAPPY TO MEET SOME OF MY YOUNG PEOPLE!
SCRATCH! SCRATCH!
ARCHIE ANDREWS, IS IT? WELCOME TO HEADQUARTERS, ARCHIE! WHAT CAN I DO FOR YOU?
I HAVE A LETTER FROM MR. WEATHERBEE, SIR!
HMPH! WANTS YOU TO BRING AN ANSWER, EH? WELL, JUST WAIT! I'LL GIVE HIM AN ANSWER!
YES, SIR!
SCRATCH! SCRATCH!
GULP! HE SAID "NO", MISS GRUNDY! I'M DONE!
?
SCRATCH!
SCRATCH!
ARCHIE! WHY ARE YOU SCRATCHING LIKE THAT?
IT'S THE ONLY WAY I KNOW!
SCRATCH! SCRATCH!
THERE'S A RASH ON YOUR HANDS! LET'S GO SEE THE NURSE!
IT'S ALL UP MY ARMS!
5

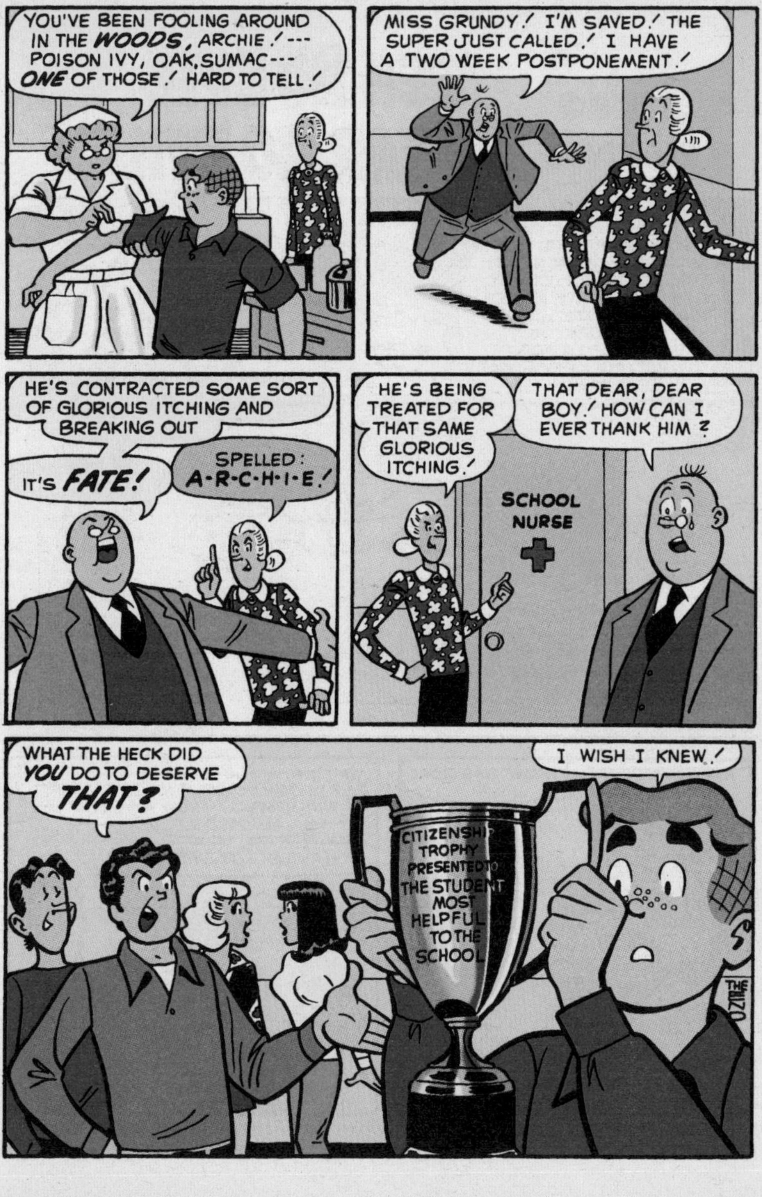

YOU'VE BEEN FOOLING AROUND IN THE WOODS, ARCHIE! --- POISON IVY, OAK, SUMAC--- ONE OF THOSE! HARD TO TELL!
MISS GRUNDY! I'M SAVED! THE SUPER JUST CALLED! I HAVE A TWO WEEK POSTPONEMENT!
HE'S CONTRACTED SOME SORT OF GLORIOUS ITCHING AND BREAKING OUT
IT'S FATE!
SPELLED: A-R-C-H-I-E!
HE'S BEING TREATED FOR THAT SAME GLORIOUS ITCHING!
THAT DEAR, DEAR BOY! HOW CAN I EVER THANK HIM?
SCHOOL NURSE
WHAT THE HECK DID YOU DO TO DESERVE THAT?
I WISH I KNEW!
CITIZENSHIP TROPHY PRESENTED TO THE STUDENT MOST HELPFUL TO THE SCHOOL
THE END

Archie at Riverdale

"SEE NO EVIL, HEAR NO EVIL" PART ONE

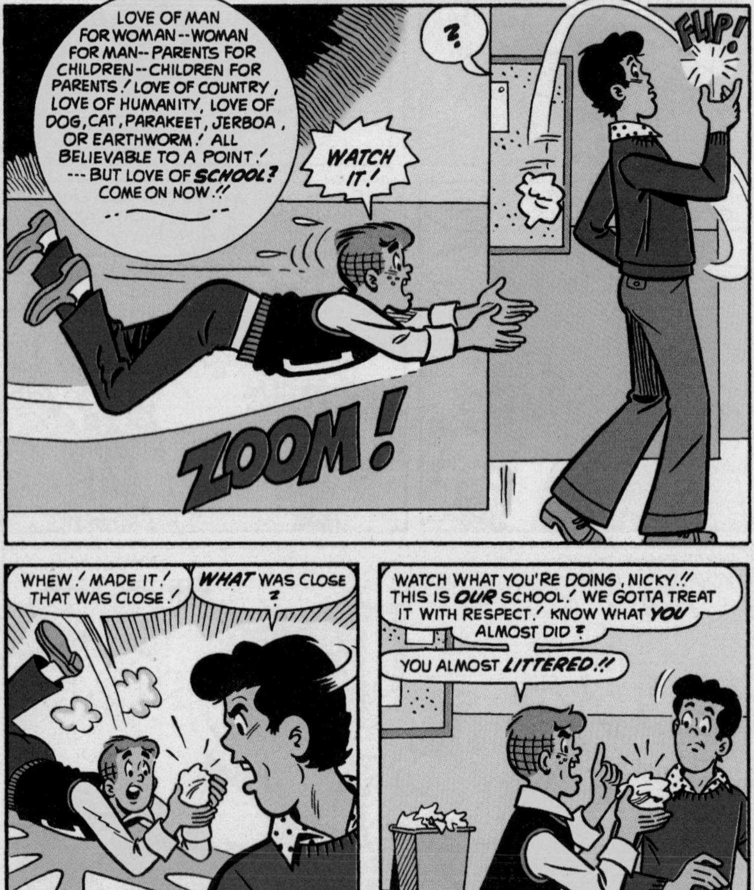
LOVE OF MAN FOR WOMAN -- WOMAN FOR MAN -- PARENTS FOR CHILDREN -- CHILDREN FOR PARENTS! LOVE OF COUNTRY, LOVE OF HUMANITY, LOVE OF DOG, CAT, PARAKEET, JERBOA, OR EARTHWORM! ALL BELIEVABLE TO A POINT! --- BUT LOVE OF SCHOOL? COME ON NOW!!
?
FLIP!
WATCH IT!
ZOOM!
WHEW! MADE IT! THAT WAS CLOSE!
WHAT WAS CLOSE?
WATCH WHAT YOU'RE DOING, NICKY!! THIS IS OUR SCHOOL! WE GOTTA TREAT IT WITH RESPECT! KNOW WHAT YOU ALMOST DID?
YOU ALMOST LITTERED!!

Script: Frank Doyle / Pencils: Stan Goldberg / Inks: Jon D'Agostino / Letters: Bill Yoshida

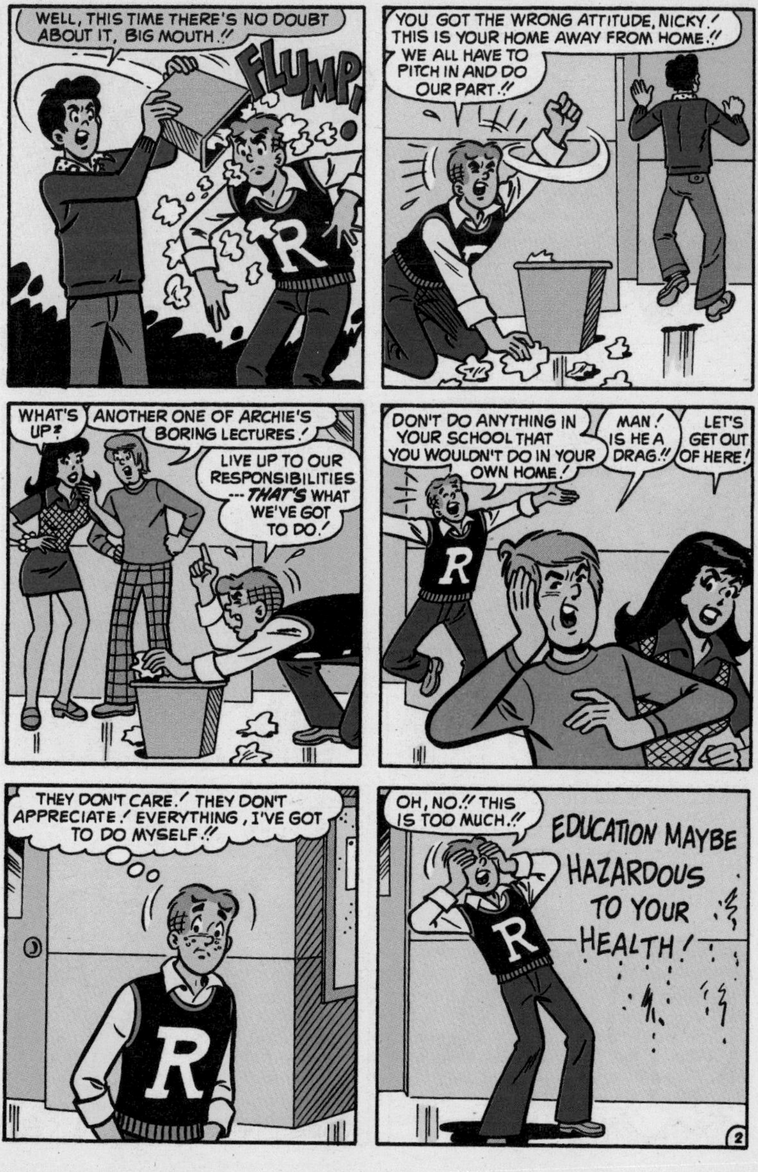
WELL, THIS TIME THERE'S NO DOUBT ABOUT IT, BIG MOUTH.!!
FLUMP!
YOU GOT THE WRONG ATTITUDE, NICKY! THIS IS YOUR HOME AWAY FROM HOME.!!
WE ALL HAVE TO PITCH IN AND DO OUR PART.!!
WHAT'S UP?
ANOTHER ONE OF ARCHIE'S BORING LECTURES.!
LIVE UP TO OUR RESPONSIBILITIES ---THAT'S WHAT WE'VE GOT TO DO.!
DON'T DO ANYTHING IN YOUR SCHOOL THAT YOU WOULDN'T DO IN YOUR OWN HOME.!
MAN! IS HE A DRAG.!!
LET'S GET OUT OF HERE!
THEY DON'T CARE.! THEY DON'T APPRECIATE.! EVERYTHING, I'VE GOT TO DO MYSELF.!!
OH, NO.!! THIS IS TOO MUCH.!!
EDUCATION MAYBE HAZARDOUS TO YOUR HEALTH!
2

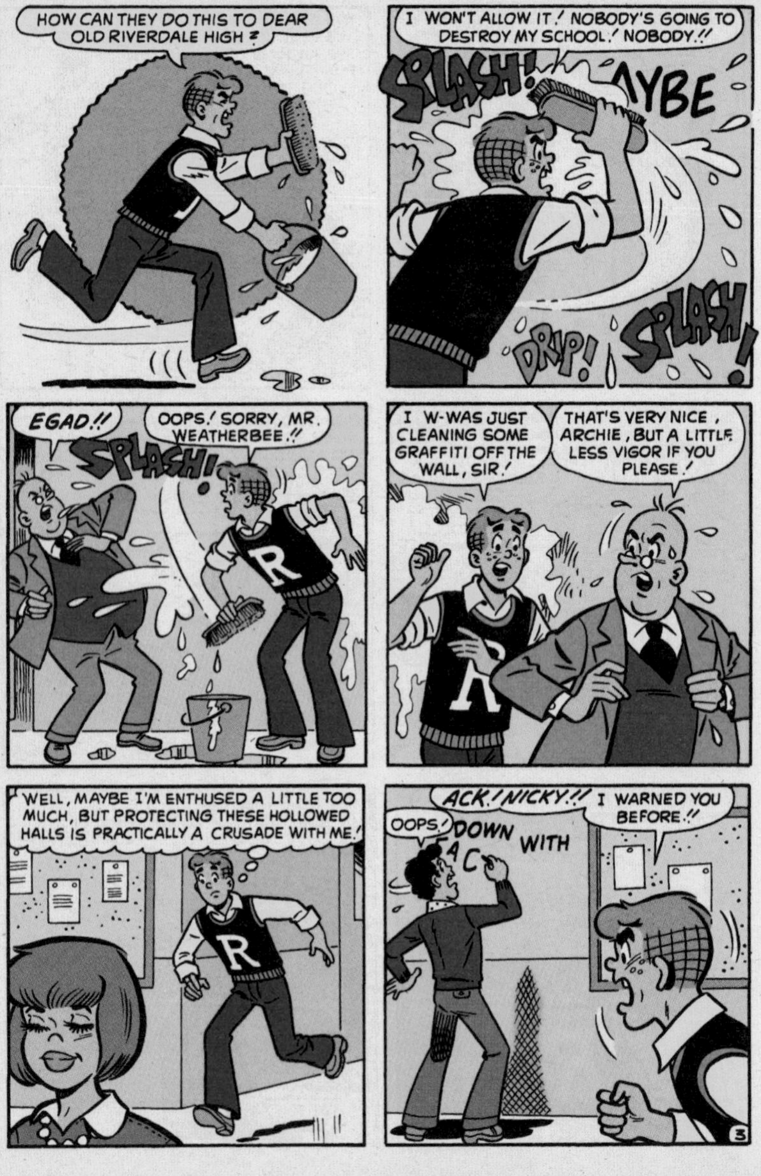

HOW CAN THEY DO THIS TO DEAR OLD RIVERDALE HIGH ?
I WON'T ALLOW IT! NOBODY'S GOING TO DESTROY MY SCHOOL! NOBODY!!
SPLASH!
YBE
DRIP!
SPLASH!
EGAD!!
OOPS! SORRY, MR. WEATHERBEE!!
SPLASH!
I W-WAS JUST CLEANING SOME GRAFFITI OFF THE WALL, SIR!
THAT'S VERY NICE, ARCHIE, BUT A LITTLE LESS VIGOR IF YOU PLEASE!
WELL, MAYBE I'M ENTHUSED A LITTLE TOO MUCH, BUT PROTECTING THESE HOLLOWED HALLS IS PRACTICALLY A CRUSADE WITH ME!
ACK! NICKY!!
I WARNED YOU BEFORE!!
OOPS!
DOWN WITH
AC

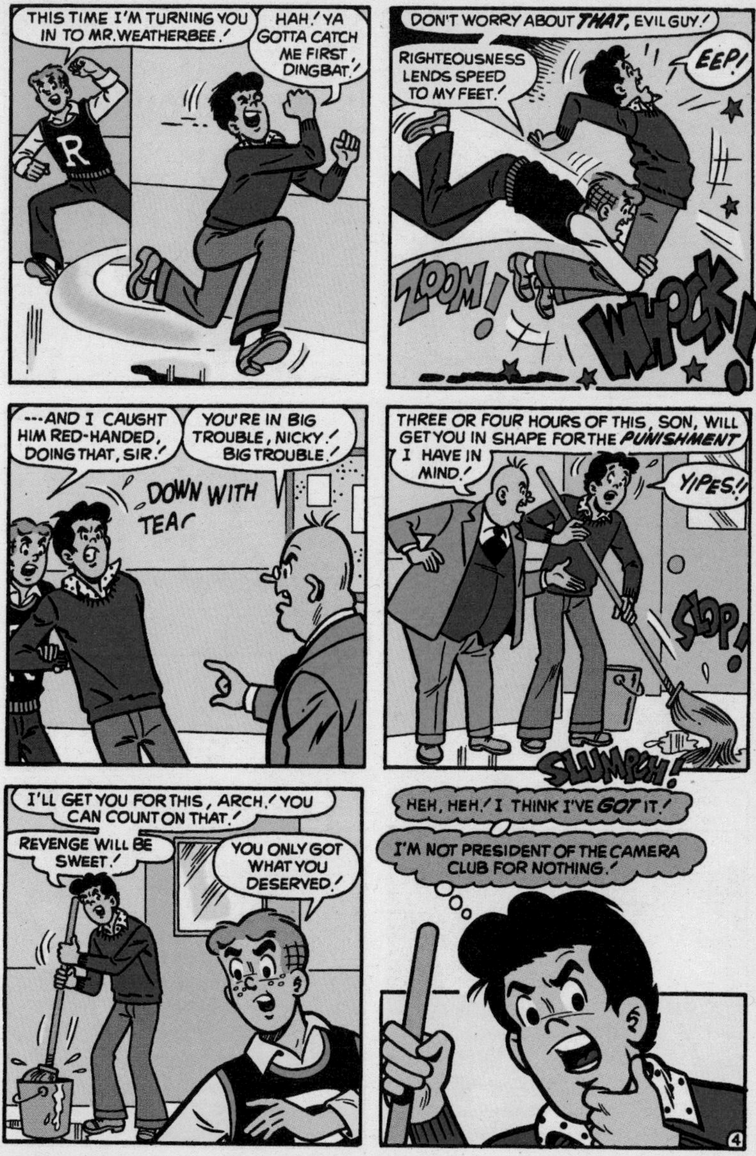
THIS TIME I'M TURNING YOU IN TO MR. WEATHERBEE!
HAH! YA GOTTA CATCH ME FIRST DINGBAT!
DON'T WORRY ABOUT THAT, EVIL GUY!
RIGHTEOUSNESS LENDS SPEED TO MY FEET!
EEP!
ZOOM!
WHOCK!
---AND I CAUGHT HIM RED-HANDED, DOING THAT, SIR!
YOU'RE IN BIG TROUBLE, NICKY! BIG TROUBLE!
DOWN WITH TEA
THREE OR FOUR HOURS OF THIS, SON, WILL GET YOU IN SHAPE FOR THE PUNISHMENT I HAVE IN MIND!
YIPES!!
SLOP!
SLUMPCH!
I'LL GET YOU FOR THIS, ARCH! YOU CAN COUNT ON THAT!
REVENGE WILL BE SWEET!
YOU ONLY GOT WHAT YOU DESERVED!
HEH, HEH! I THINK I'VE GOT IT!
I'M NOT PRESIDENT OF THE CAMERA CLUB FOR NOTHING!
4

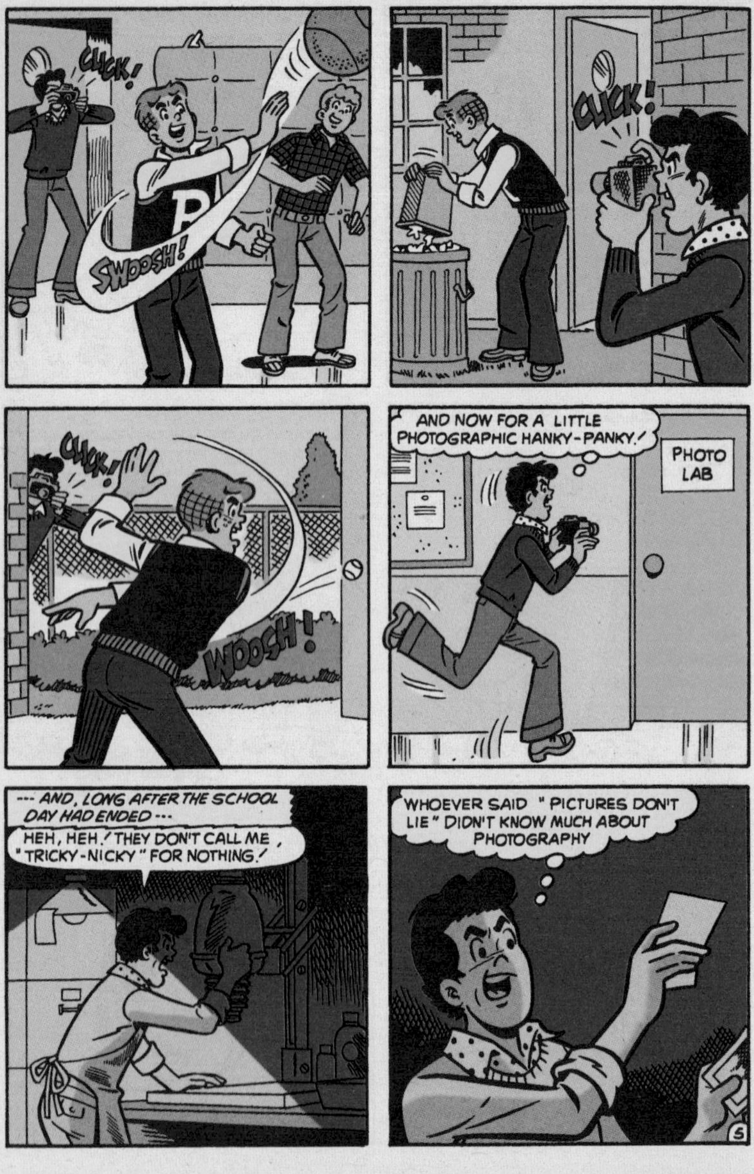
CLICK!
SWOOSH!
CLICK!
CLICK!
WOOSH!
AND NOW FOR A LITTLE PHOTOGRAPHIC HANKY-PANKY!
PHOTO LAB
--- AND, LONG AFTER THE SCHOOL DAY HAD ENDED ---
HEH, HEH! THEY DON'T CALL ME, "TRICKY-NICKY" FOR NOTHING!
WHOEVER SAID "PICTURES DON'T LIE" DIDN'T KNOW MUCH ABOUT PHOTOGRAPHY
5

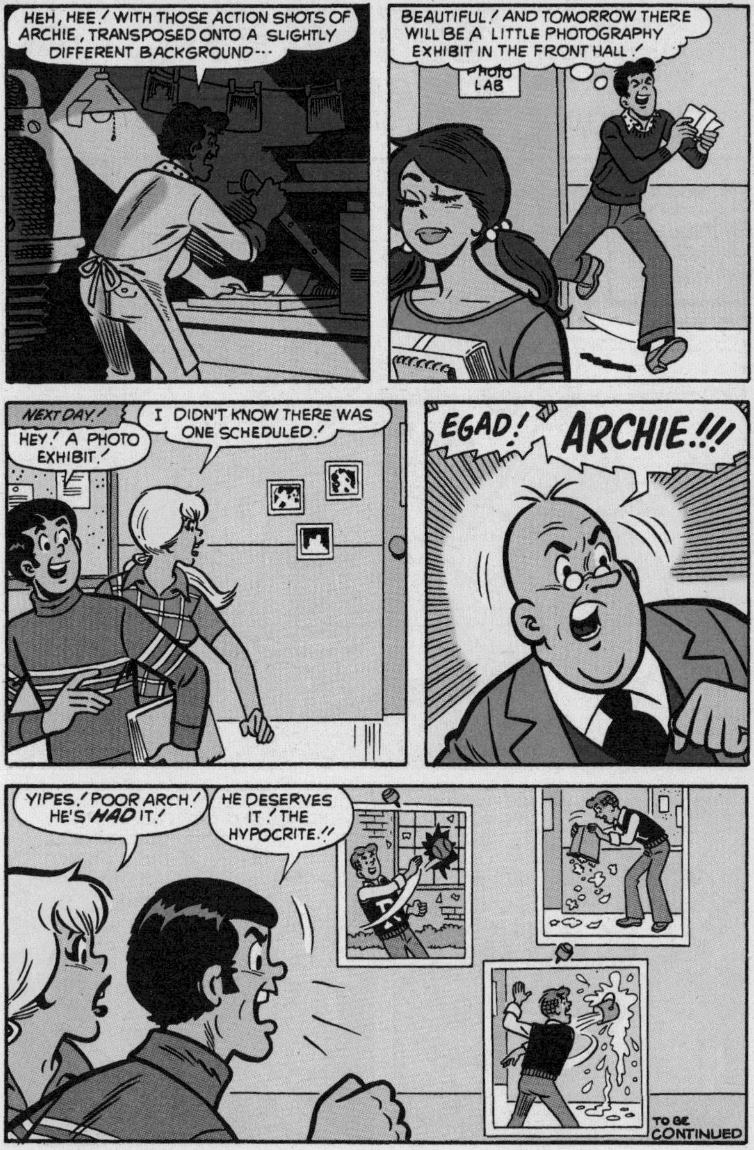
HEH, HEE! WITH THOSE ACTION SHOTS OF ARCHIE, TRANSPOSED ONTO A SLIGHTLY DIFFERENT BACKGROUND---
BEAUTIFUL! AND TOMORROW THERE WILL BE A LITTLE PHOTOGRAPHY EXHIBIT IN THE FRONT HALL!
PHOTO LAB
NEXT DAY!
HEY! A PHOTO EXHIBIT!
I DIDN'T KNOW THERE WAS ONE SCHEDULED!
EGAD! ARCHIE!!!
YIPES! POOR ARCH! HE'S HAD IT!
HE DESERVES IT! THE HYPOCRITE!!
TO BE CONTINUED

Archie AT RIVERDALE

"SEE NO EVIL, HEAR NO EVIL"

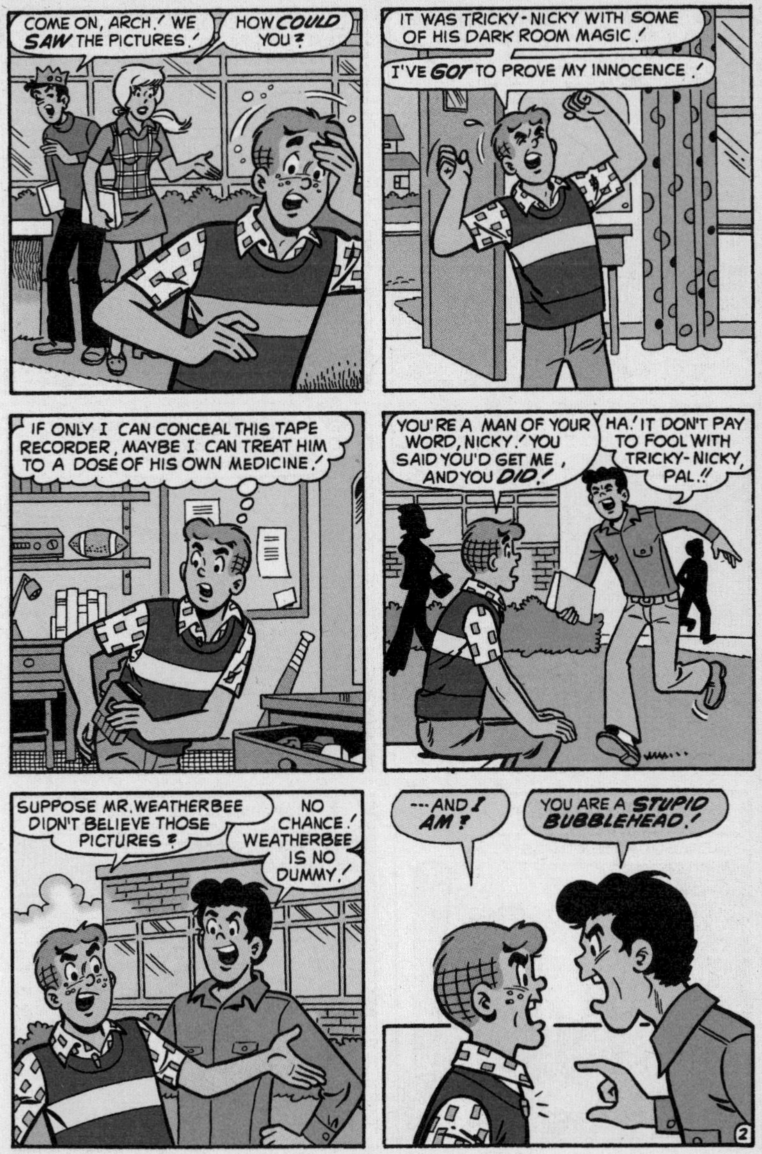

COME ON, ARCH.! WE SAW THE PICTURES.!
HOW COULD YOU ?
IT WAS TRICKY-NICKY WITH SOME OF HIS DARK ROOM MAGIC.!
I'VE GOT TO PROVE MY INNOCENCE.!
IF ONLY I CAN CONCEAL THIS TAPE RECORDER, MAYBE I CAN TREAT HIM TO A DOSE OF HIS OWN MEDICINE.!
YOU'RE A MAN OF YOUR WORD, NICKY.! YOU SAID YOU'D GET ME, AND YOU DID.!
HA.! IT DON'T PAY TO FOOL WITH TRICKY-NICKY, PAL.!!
SUPPOSE MR. WEATHERBEE DIDN'T BELIEVE THOSE PICTURES ?
NO CHANCE.! WEATHERBEE IS NO DUMMY.!
---AND I AM ?
YOU ARE A STUPID BUBBLEHEAD.!
2

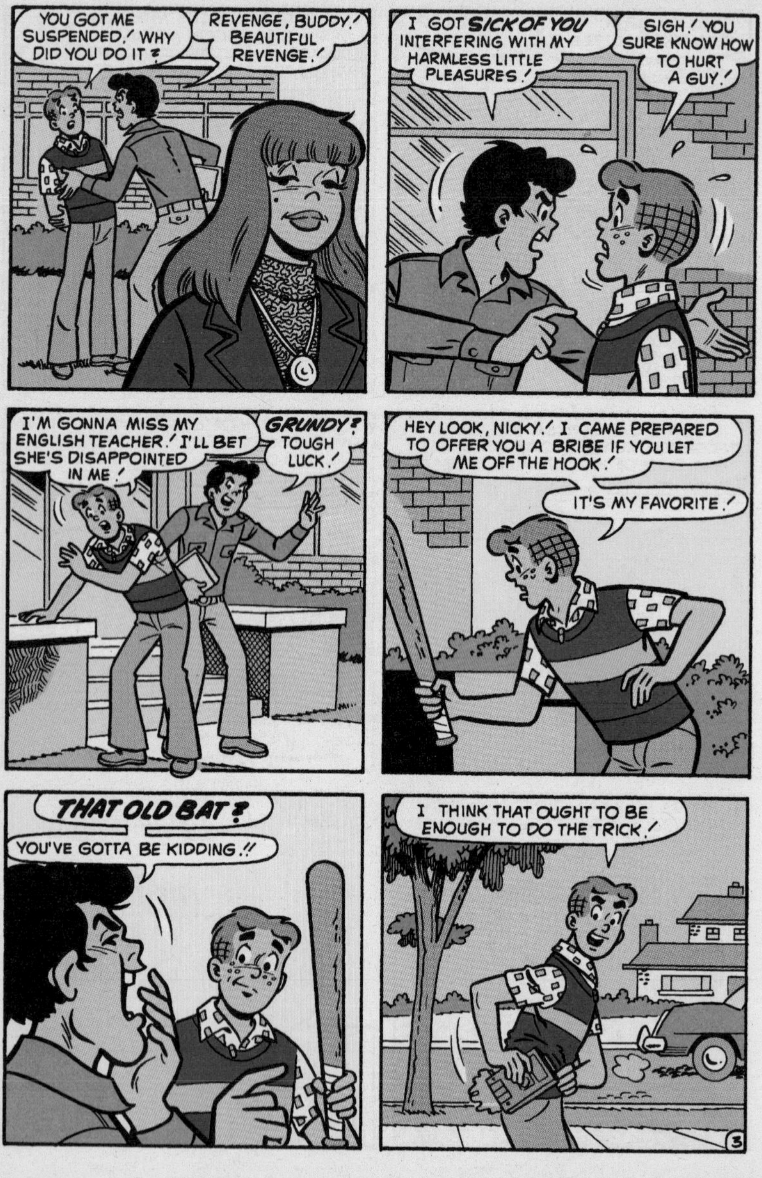
YOU GOT ME SUSPENDED! WHY DID YOU DO IT?
REVENGE, BUDDY! BEAUTIFUL REVENGE!
I GOT SICK OF YOU INTERFERING WITH MY HARMLESS LITTLE PLEASURES!
SIGH! YOU SURE KNOW HOW TO HURT A GUY!
I'M GONNA MISS MY ENGLISH TEACHER! I'LL BET SHE'S DISAPPOINTED IN ME!
GRUNDY? TOUGH LUCK!
HEY LOOK, NICKY! I CAME PREPARED TO OFFER YOU A BRIBE IF YOU LET ME OFF THE HOOK!
IT'S MY FAVORITE!
THAT OLD BAT?
YOU'VE GOTTA BE KIDDING!!
I THINK THAT OUGHT TO BE ENOUGH TO DO THE TRICK!
3

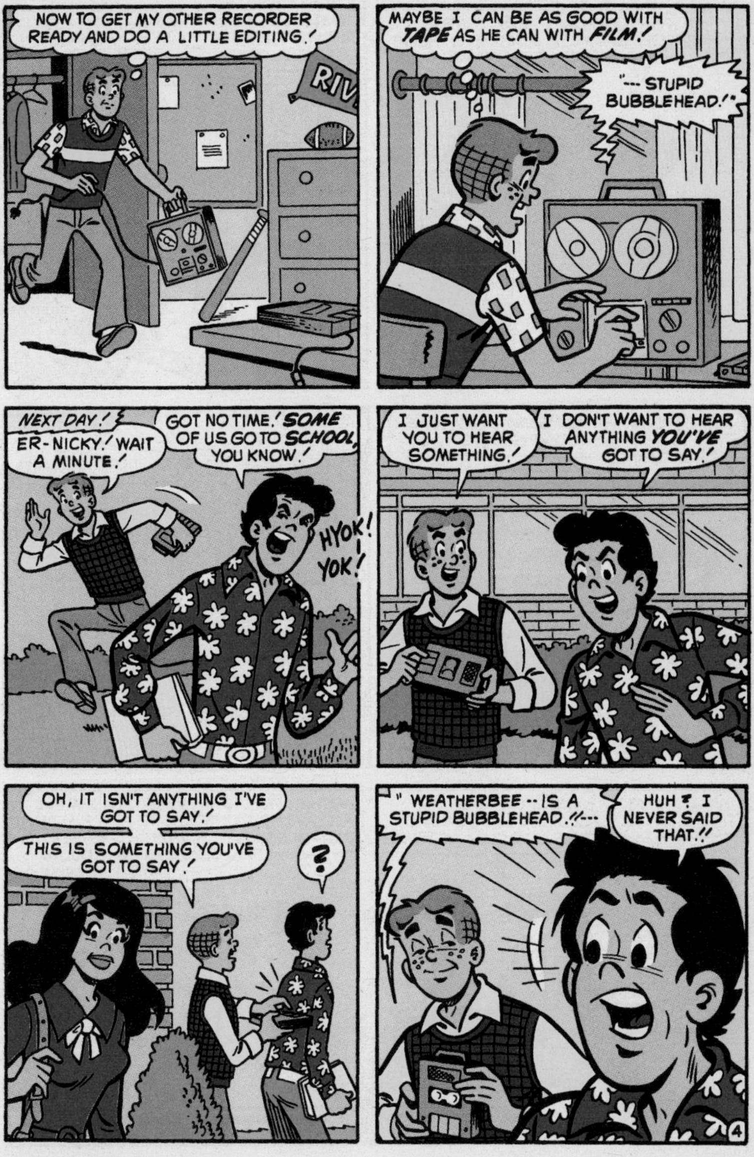
NOW TO GET MY OTHER RECORDER READY AND DO A LITTLE EDITING.!
MAYBE I CAN BE AS GOOD WITH TAPE AS HE CAN WITH FILM!
"--- STUPID BUBBLEHEAD!"
NEXT DAY!
ER-NICKY! WAIT A MINUTE!
GOT NO TIME! SOME OF US GO TO SCHOOL, YOU KNOW!
HYOK! YOK!
I JUST WANT YOU TO HEAR SOMETHING!
I DON'T WANT TO HEAR ANYTHING YOU'VE GOT TO SAY!
OH, IT ISN'T ANYTHING I'VE GOT TO SAY!
THIS IS SOMETHING YOU'VE GOT TO SAY!
?
" WEATHERBEE -- IS A STUPID BUBBLEHEAD!!---
HUH? I NEVER SAID THAT!!
4

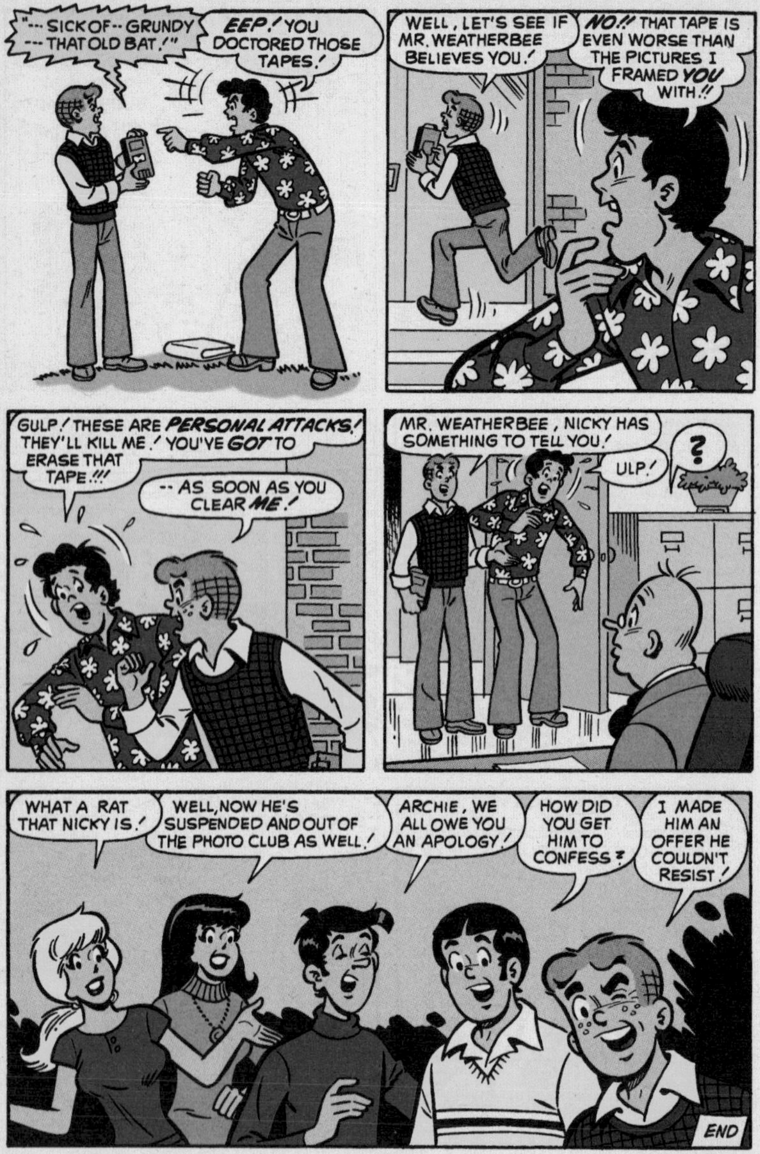
"--- SICK OF -- GRUNDY --- THAT OLD BAT!"
EEP! YOU DOCTORED THOSE TAPES!
WELL, LET'S SEE IF MR. WEATHERBEE BELIEVES YOU!
NO!! THAT TAPE IS EVEN WORSE THAN THE PICTURES I FRAMED YOU WITH!!
GULP! THESE ARE PERSONAL ATTACKS! THEY'LL KILL ME! YOU'VE GOT TO ERASE THAT TAPE!!!
-- AS SOON AS YOU CLEAR ME!
MR. WEATHERBEE, NICKY HAS SOMETHING TO TELL YOU!
ULP!
?
WHAT A RAT THAT NICKY IS!
WELL, NOW HE'S SUSPENDED AND OUT OF THE PHOTO CLUB AS WELL!
ARCHIE, WE ALL OWE YOU AN APOLOGY!
HOW DID YOU GET HIM TO CONFESS?
I MADE HIM AN OFFER HE COULDN'T RESIST!
END

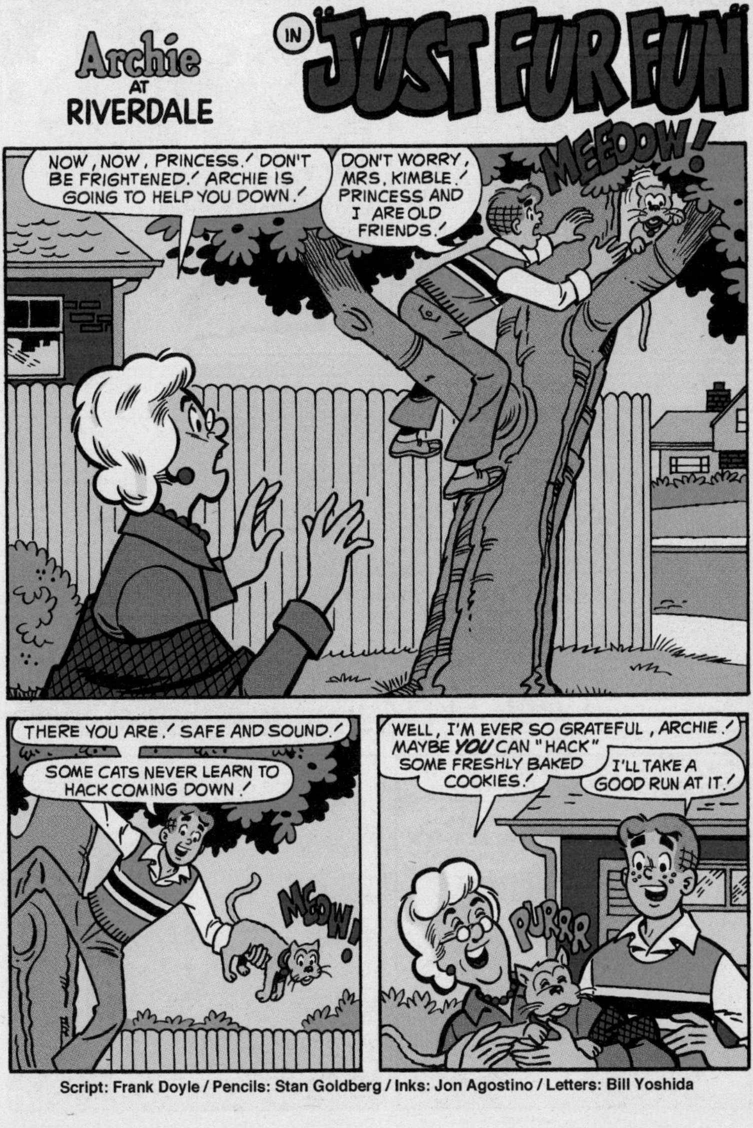
Archie AT RIVERDALE
IN "JUST FUR FUN"
NOW, NOW, PRINCESS! DON'T BE FRIGHTENED! ARCHIE IS GOING TO HELP YOU DOWN!
DON'T WORRY, MRS. KIMBLE! PRINCESS AND I ARE OLD FRIENDS!
MEEOOW!
THERE YOU ARE! SAFE AND SOUND!
SOME CATS NEVER LEARN TO HACK COMING DOWN!
MEOW!
WELL, I'M EVER SO GRATEFUL, ARCHIE! MAYBE YOU CAN "HACK" SOME FRESHLY BAKED COOKIES!
I'LL TAKE A GOOD RUN AT IT!
PURRR

Script: Frank Doyle / Pencils: Stan Goldberg / Inks: Jon Agostino / Letters: Bill Yoshida

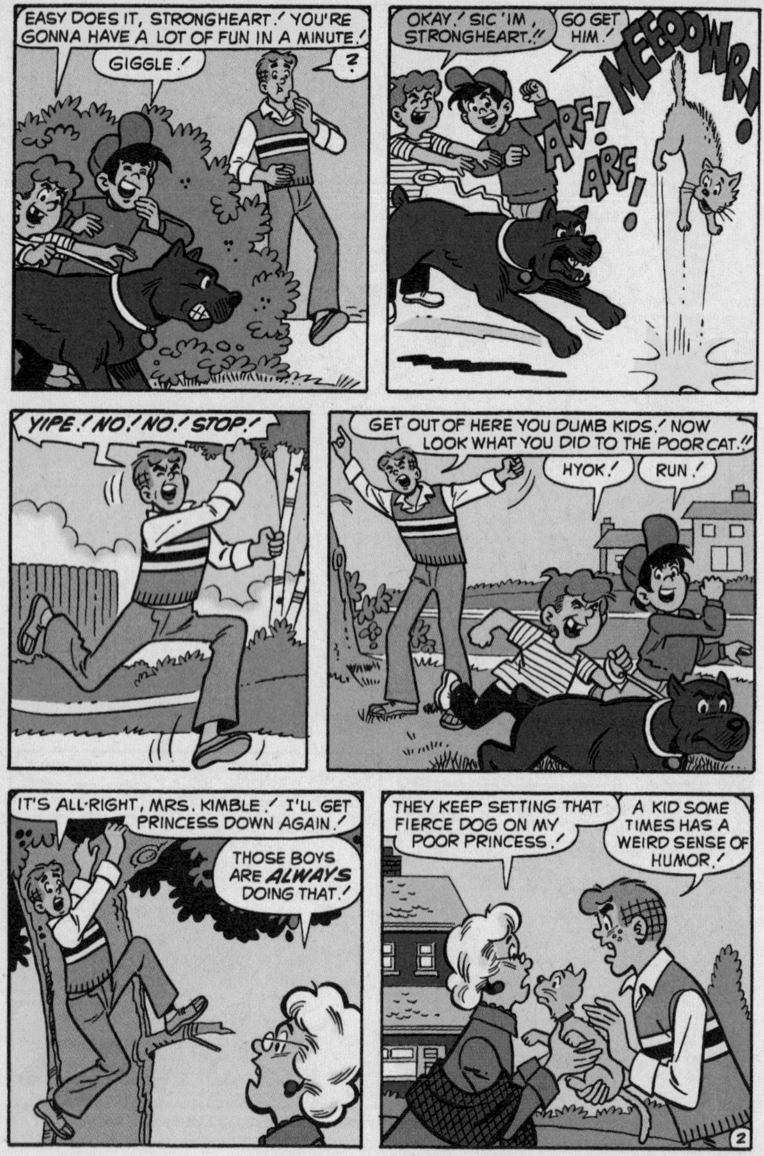
EASY DOES IT, STRONGHEART.! YOU'RE GONNA HAVE A LOT OF FUN IN A MINUTE.!
GIGGLE.!
?
OKAY.! SIC 'IM, STRONGHEART.!!
GO GET HIM.!
ARF! ARF!
MEEOOWR!
YIPE.! NO.! NO.! STOP.!
GET OUT OF HERE YOU DUMB KIDS.! NOW LOOK WHAT YOU DID TO THE POOR CAT.!!
HYOK.!
RUN.!
IT'S ALL-RIGHT, MRS. KIMBLE.! I'LL GET PRINCESS DOWN AGAIN.!
THOSE BOYS ARE ***ALWAYS*** DOING THAT.!
THEY KEEP SETTING THAT FIERCE DOG ON MY POOR PRINCESS.!
A KID SOME TIMES HAS A WEIRD SENSE OF HUMOR.!
2

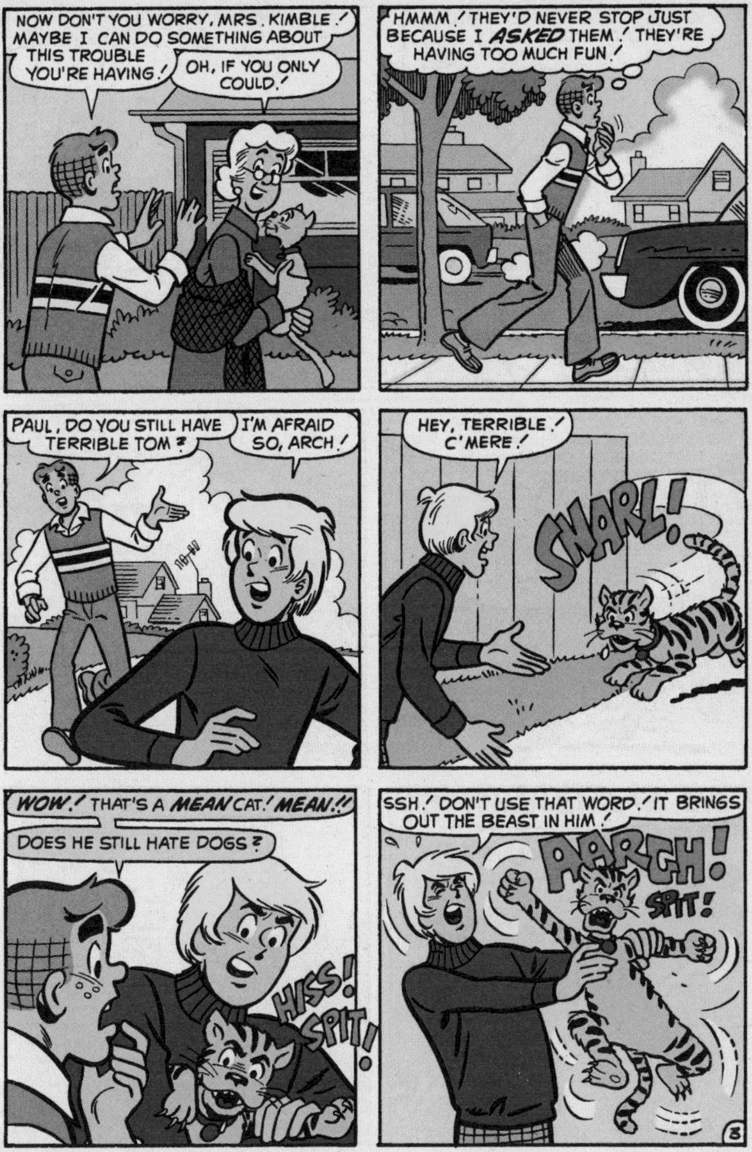
NOW DON'T YOU WORRY, MRS. KIMBLE! MAYBE I CAN DO SOMETHING ABOUT THIS TROUBLE YOU'RE HAVING!
OH, IF YOU ONLY COULD!
HMMM! THEY'D NEVER STOP JUST BECAUSE I ASKED THEM! THEY'RE HAVING TOO MUCH FUN!
PAUL, DO YOU STILL HAVE TERRIBLE TOM?
I'M AFRAID SO, ARCH!
HEY, TERRIBLE! C'MERE!
SNARL!
WOW! THAT'S A MEAN CAT! MEAN!!
DOES HE STILL HATE DOGS?
HISS! SPIT!
SSH! DON'T USE THAT WORD! IT BRINGS OUT THE BEAST IN HIM!
AARGH!
SPIT!
8

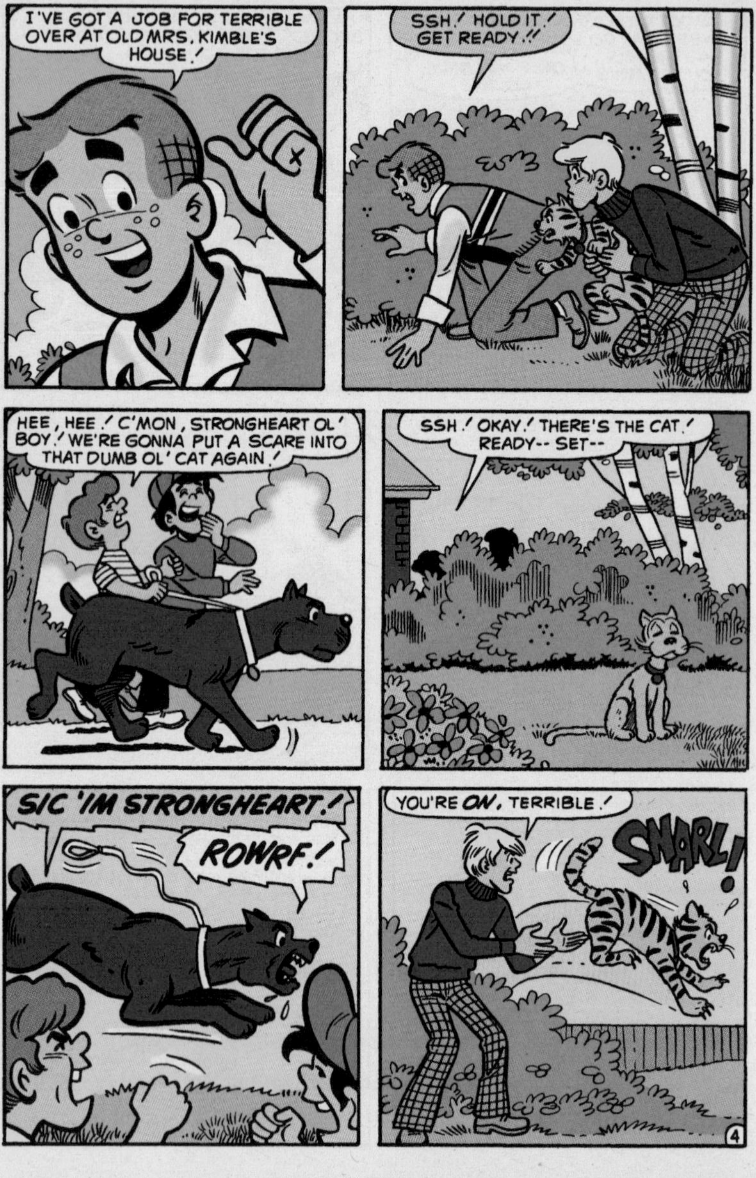
I'VE GOT A JOB FOR TERRIBLE OVER AT OLD MRS. KIMBLE'S HOUSE!
SSH! HOLD IT! GET READY!!
HEE, HEE! C'MON, STRONGHEART OL' BOY! WE'RE GONNA PUT A SCARE INTO THAT DUMB OL' CAT AGAIN!
SSH! OKAY! THERE'S THE CAT! READY-- SET--
SIC 'IM STRONGHEART!
ROWRF!
YOU'RE ON, TERRIBLE!
SNARL!
4

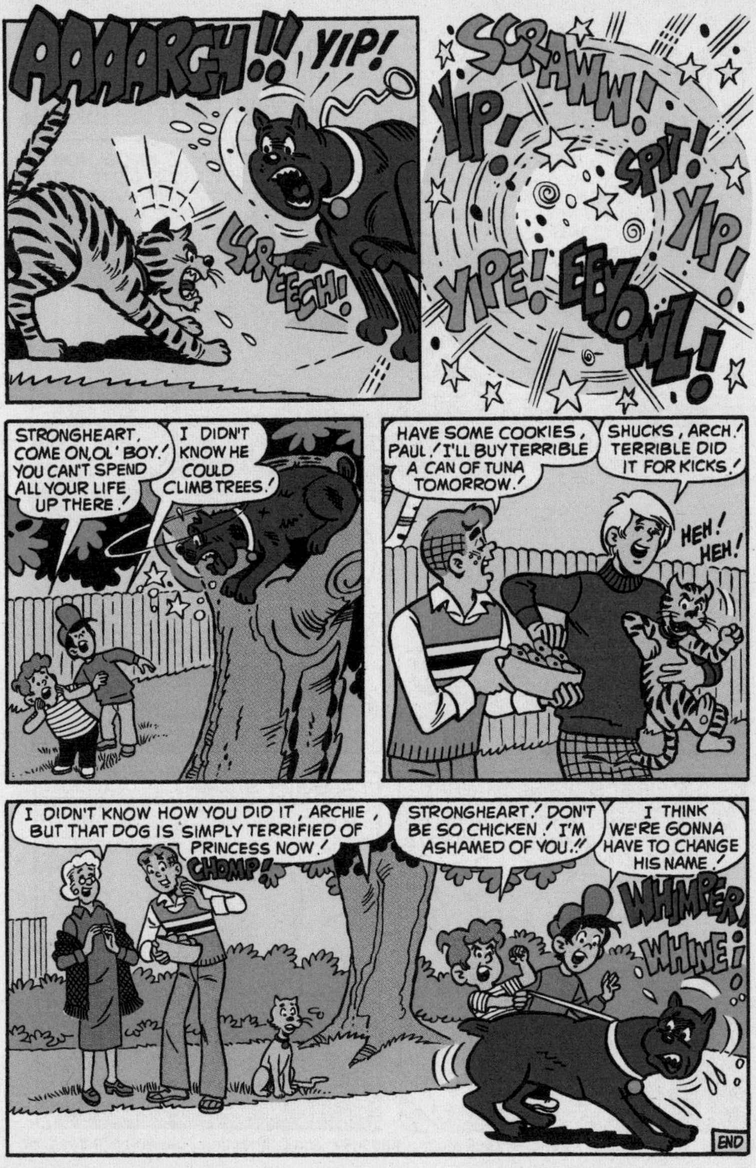
AAAARGH!!
YIP!
SKREECH!
SCRAWWW!
YIP!
SPIT!
YIP!
YIPE!
EEYOWL!
STRONGHEART, COME ON, OL' BOY! YOU CAN'T SPEND ALL YOUR LIFE UP THERE!
I DIDN'T KNOW HE COULD CLIMB TREES!
HAVE SOME COOKIES, PAUL! I'LL BUY TERRIBLE A CAN OF TUNA TOMORROW!
SHUCKS, ARCH! TERRIBLE DID IT FOR KICKS!
HEH! HEH!
I DIDN'T KNOW HOW YOU DID IT, ARCHIE, BUT THAT DOG IS SIMPLY TERRIFIED OF PRINCESS NOW!
CHOMP!
STRONGHEART! DON'T BE SO CHICKEN! I'M ASHAMED OF YOU!!
I THINK WE'RE GONNA HAVE TO CHANGE HIS NAME!
WHIMPER!
WHINE!
END

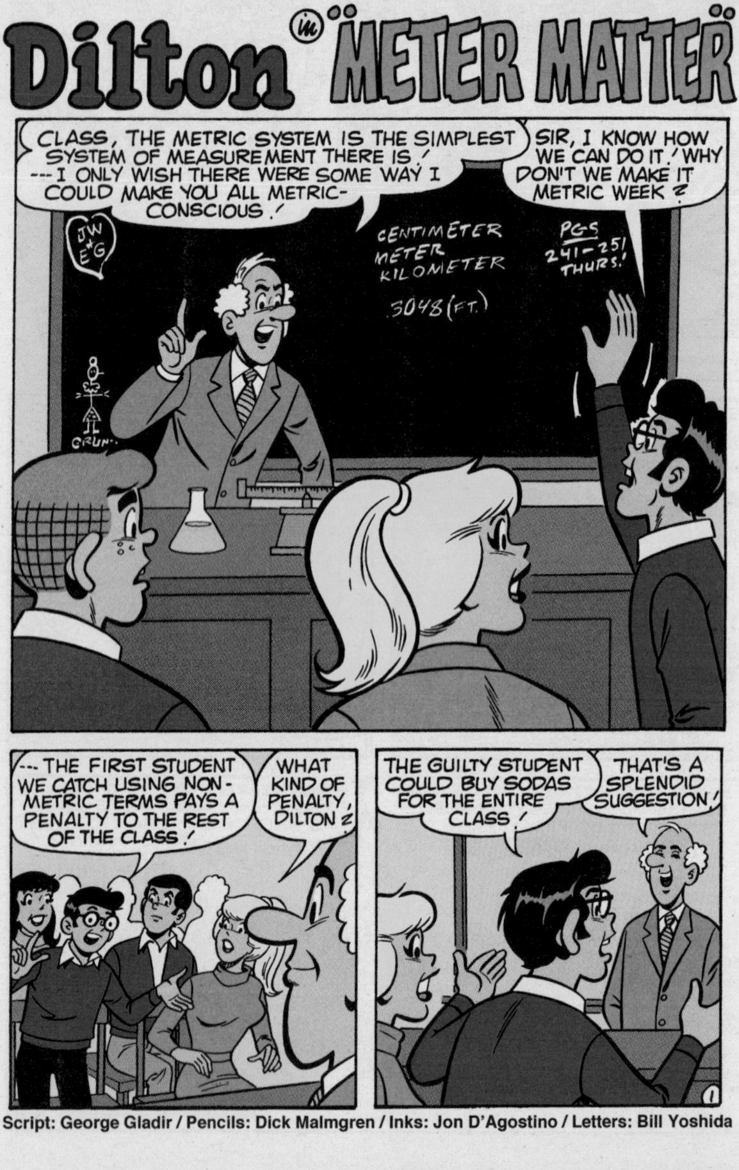
Dilton in "METER MATTER"
CLASS, THE METRIC SYSTEM IS THE SIMPLEST SYSTEM OF MEASUREMENT THERE IS! ---I ONLY WISH THERE WERE SOME WAY I COULD MAKE YOU ALL METRIC-CONSCIOUS!
SIR, I KNOW HOW WE CAN DO IT! WHY DON'T WE MAKE IT METRIC WEEK?
JW + EG
CENTIMETER
METER
KILOMETER
3048 (FT.)
PGS 241-251 THURS!
GRUN..
---THE FIRST STUDENT WE CATCH USING NON-METRIC TERMS PAYS A PENALTY TO THE REST OF THE CLASS!
WHAT KIND OF PENALTY, DILTON?
THE GUILTY STUDENT COULD BUY SODAS FOR THE ENTIRE CLASS!
THAT'S A SPLENDID SUGGESTION!
1

Script: George Gladir / Pencils: Dick Malmgren / Inks: Jon D'Agostino / Letters: Bill Yoshida

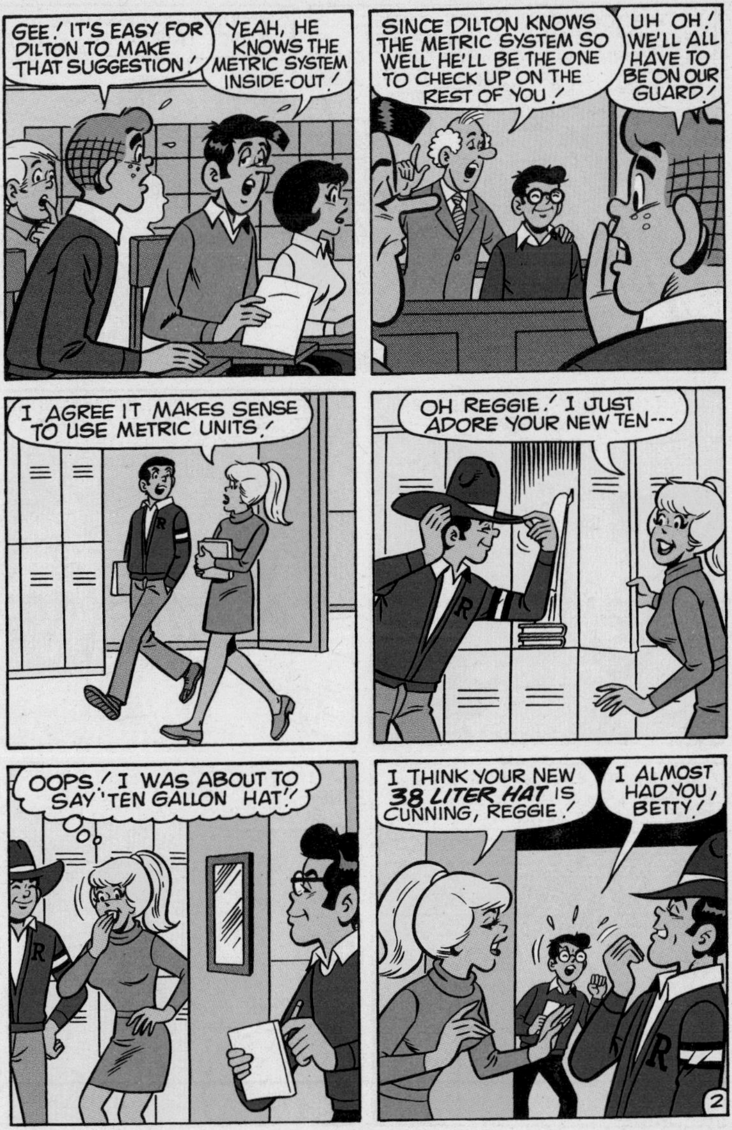
GEE! IT'S EASY FOR DILTON TO MAKE THAT SUGGESTION!
YEAH, HE KNOWS THE METRIC SYSTEM INSIDE-OUT!
SINCE DILTON KNOWS THE METRIC SYSTEM SO WELL HE'LL BE THE ONE TO CHECK UP ON THE REST OF YOU!
UH OH! WE'LL ALL HAVE TO BE ON OUR GUARD!
I AGREE IT MAKES SENSE TO USE METRIC UNITS!
OH REGGIE! I JUST ADORE YOUR NEW TEN---
OOPS! I WAS ABOUT TO SAY 'TEN GALLON HAT'!
I THINK YOUR NEW 38 LITER HAT IS CUNNING, REGGIE!
I ALMOST HAD YOU, BETTY!
2

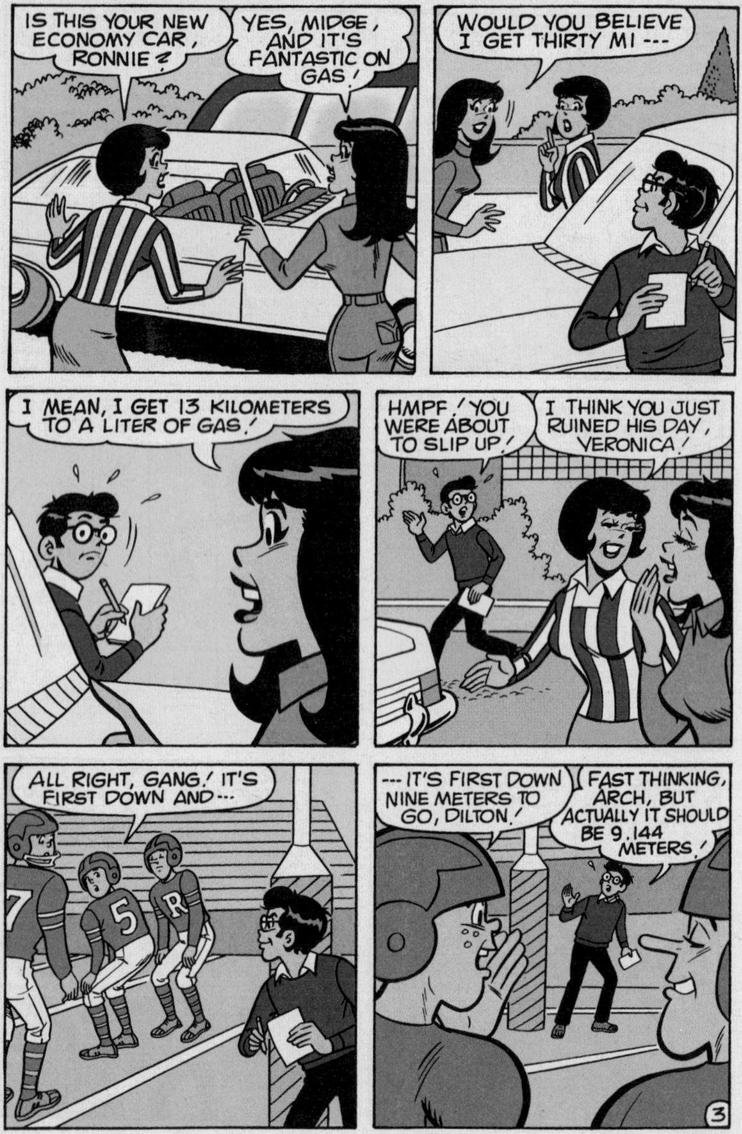
IS THIS YOUR NEW ECONOMY CAR, RONNIE?
YES, MIDGE, AND IT'S FANTASTIC ON GAS!
WOULD YOU BELIEVE I GET THIRTY MI ---
I MEAN, I GET 13 KILOMETERS TO A LITER OF GAS!
HMPF! YOU WERE ABOUT TO SLIP UP!
I THINK YOU JUST RUINED HIS DAY, VERONICA!
ALL RIGHT, GANG! IT'S FIRST DOWN AND ---
--- IT'S FIRST DOWN NINE METERS TO GO, DILTON!
FAST THINKING, ARCH, BUT ACTUALLY IT SHOULD BE 9.144 METERS!
3

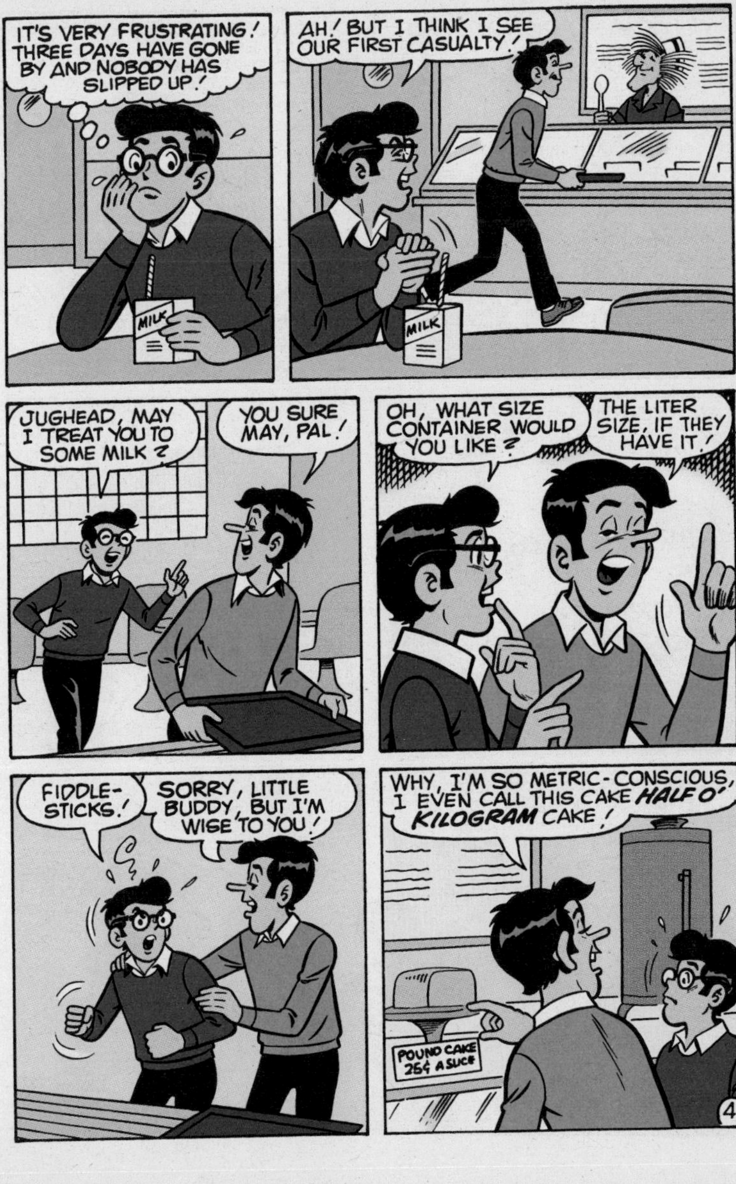

IT'S VERY FRUSTRATING! THREE DAYS HAVE GONE BY AND NOBODY HAS SLIPPED UP!
MILK
AH! BUT I THINK I SEE OUR FIRST CASUALTY!
MILK
JUGHEAD, MAY I TREAT YOU TO SOME MILK?
YOU SURE MAY, PAL!
OH, WHAT SIZE CONTAINER WOULD YOU LIKE?
THE LITER SIZE, IF THEY HAVE IT!
FIDDLE-STICKS!
SORRY, LITTLE BUDDY, BUT I'M WISE TO YOU!
WHY, I'M SO METRIC-CONSCIOUS, I EVEN CALL THIS CAKE *HALF O' KILOGRAM* CAKE!
POUND CAKE 25¢ A SLICE

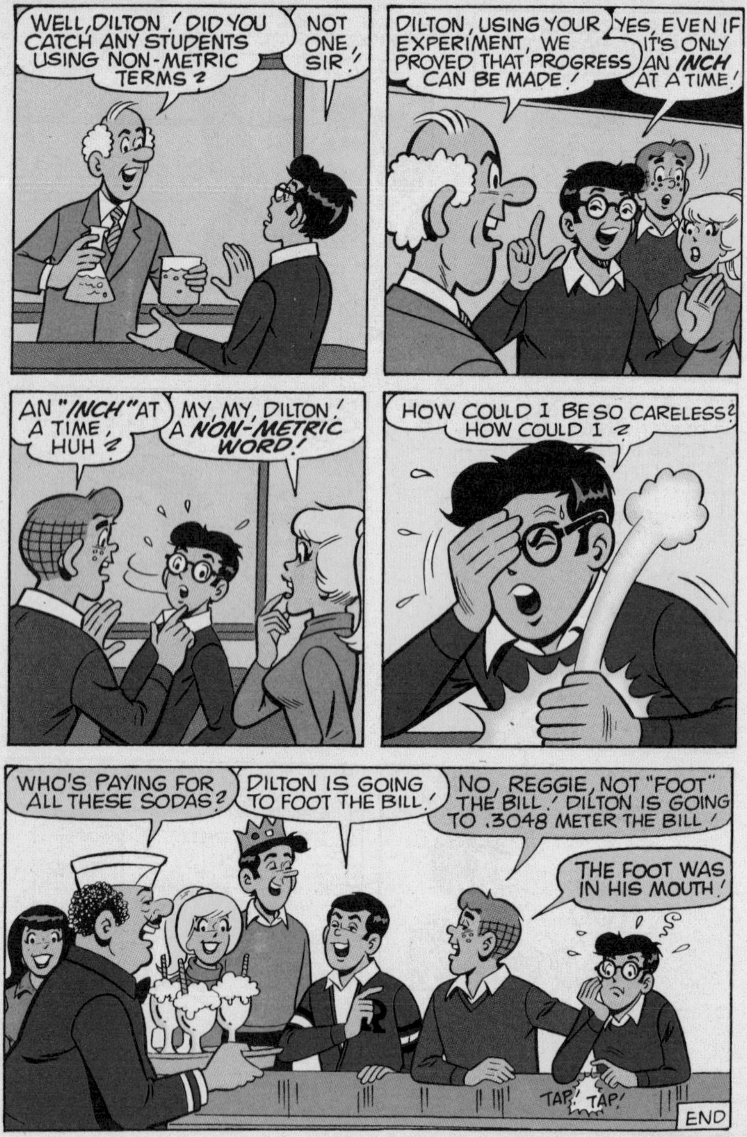
WELL, DILTON! DID YOU CATCH ANY STUDENTS USING NON-METRIC TERMS?
NOT ONE, SIR!
DILTON, USING YOUR EXPERIMENT, WE PROVED THAT PROGRESS CAN BE MADE!
YES, EVEN IF IT'S ONLY AN *INCH* AT A TIME!
AN "*INCH*" AT A TIME, HUH?
MY, MY, DILTON! A ***NON-METRIC WORD!***
HOW COULD I BE SO CARELESS? HOW COULD I?
WHO'S PAYING FOR ALL THESE SODAS?
DILTON IS GOING TO FOOT THE BILL!
NO, REGGIE, NOT "FOOT" THE BILL! DILTON IS GOING TO .3048 METER THE BILL!
THE FOOT WAS IN HIS MOUTH!
TAP! TAP!
END

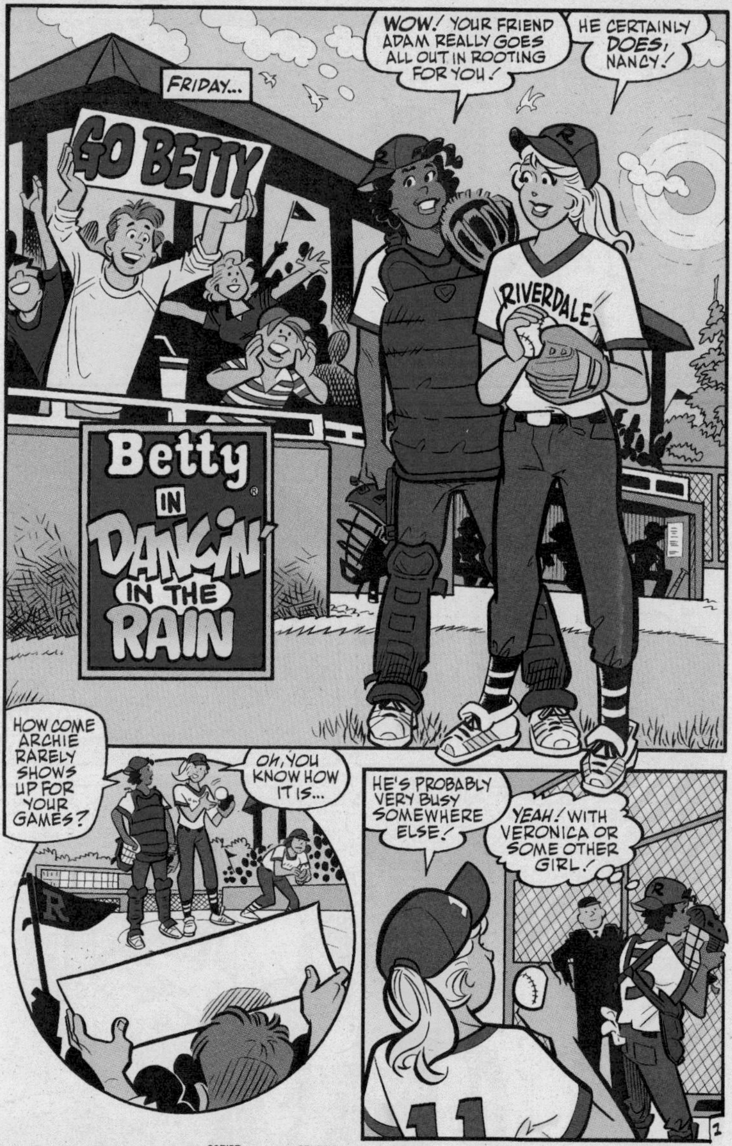
FRIDAY...
GO BETTY
WOW! YOUR FRIEND ADAM REALLY GOES ALL OUT IN ROOTING FOR YOU!
HE CERTAINLY DOES, NANCY!
Betty IN DANCIN' IN THE RAIN
RIVERDALE
HOW COME ARCHIE RARELY SHOWS UP FOR YOUR GAMES?
OH, YOU KNOW HOW IT IS...
HE'S PROBABLY VERY BUSY SOMEWHERE ELSE!
YEAH! WITH VERONICA OR SOME OTHER GIRL!
1

SCRIPT: GEORGE GLADIR PENCILS: STAN GOLDBERG INKING: RICH KOSLOWSKI LETTERING: JACK MORELLI

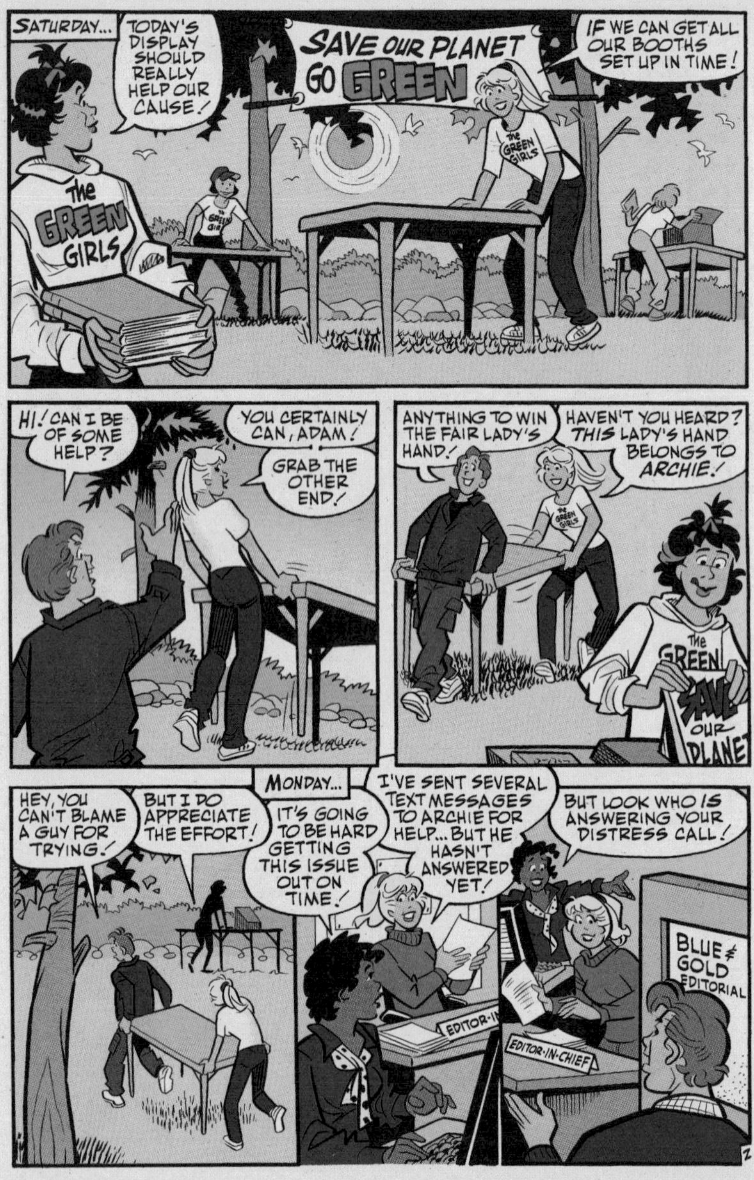

SATURDAY...
TODAY'S DISPLAY SHOULD REALLY HELP OUR CAUSE!
SAVE OUR PLANET GO GREEN
IF WE CAN GET ALL OUR BOOTHS SET UP IN TIME!
The GREEN GIRLS
HI! CAN I BE OF SOME HELP?
YOU CERTAINLY CAN, ADAM!
GRAB THE OTHER END!
ANYTHING TO WIN THE FAIR LADY'S HAND!
HAVEN'T YOU HEARD? THIS LADY'S HAND BELONGS TO ARCHIE!
SAVE OUR PLANET
HEY, YOU CAN'T BLAME A GUY FOR TRYING!
BUT I DO APPRECIATE THE EFFORT!
MONDAY...
IT'S GOING TO BE HARD GETTING THIS ISSUE OUT ON TIME!
I'VE SENT SEVERAL TEXT MESSAGES TO ARCHIE FOR HELP... BUT HE HASN'T ANSWERED YET!
BUT LOOK WHO IS ANSWERING YOUR DISTRESS CALL!
BLUE & GOLD EDITORIAL
EDITOR-IN-CHIEF
2

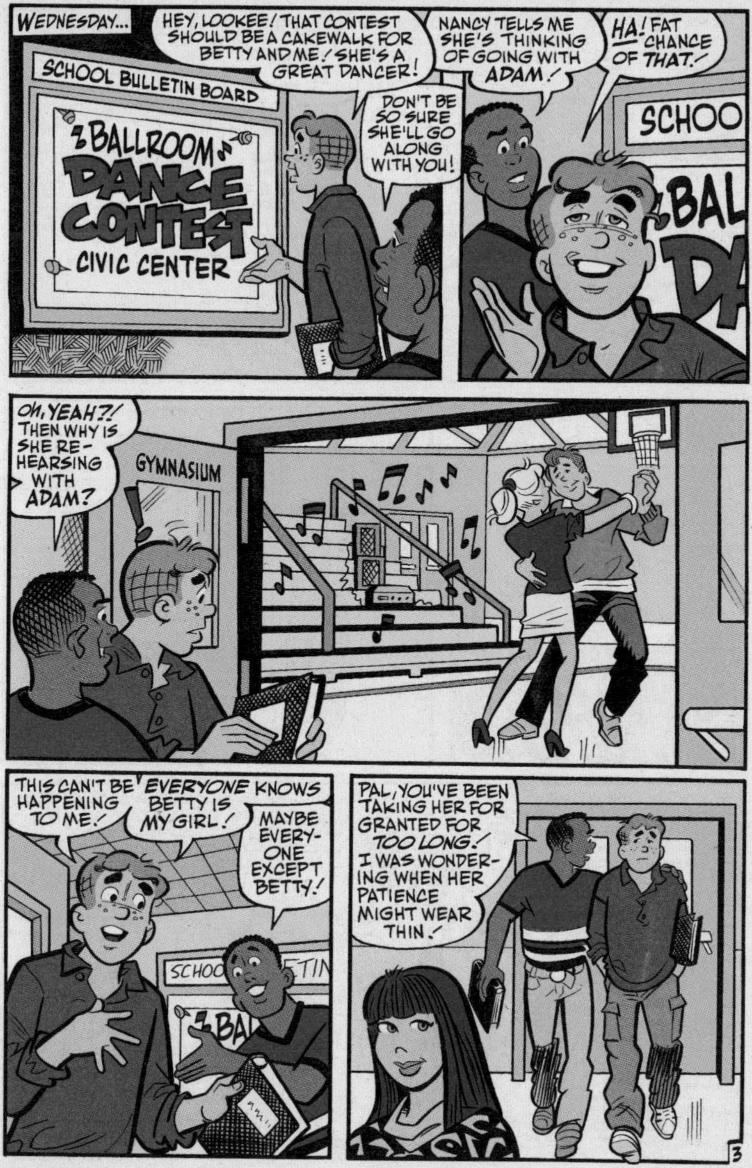

WEDNESDAY...
HEY, LOOKEE! THAT CONTEST SHOULD BE A CAKEWALK FOR BETTY AND ME! SHE'S A GREAT DANCER!
SCHOOL BULLETIN BOARD
BALLROOM DANCE CONTEST CIVIC CENTER
DON'T BE SO SURE SHE'LL GO ALONG WITH YOU!
NANCY TELLS ME SHE'S THINKING OF GOING WITH ADAM!
HA! FAT CHANCE OF THAT!
SCHOO
OH, YEAH?! THEN WHY IS SHE RE-HEARSING WITH ADAM?
GYMNASIUM
THIS CAN'T BE HAPPENING TO ME!
EVERYONE KNOWS BETTY IS MY GIRL!
MAYBE EVERY-ONE EXCEPT BETTY!
PAL, YOU'VE BEEN TAKING HER FOR GRANTED FOR TOO LONG! I WAS WONDER-ING WHEN HER PATIENCE MIGHT WEAR THIN!
3

FRIDAY... SCHOOL CAFETERIA

ARCHIE, DID YOU HEAR THE LATEST?

ADAM INJURED HIS LEG AT BASEBALL PRACTICE YESTERDAY!

THAT MEANS BETTY'S WITHOUT A PARTNER FOR THE CONTEST!

BETTY, IF YOU'RE LOOKING FOR A NEW DANCE PARTNER, LOOK NO FURTHER.!

BUT I AM LOOKING FURTHER. SEVERAL BOYS HAVE ALREADY ASKED ME!

...SO I'M CHOOSING THE BEST DANCER FROM THE GROUP!

THE BEST DANCER? NOT *ME*?!

JUG! YOU'VE GOT TO HELP ME!

...EVERYONE KNOWS YOUR DANCE-TEACHER AUNT REALLY TAUGHT YOU HOW TO DANCE WHEN YOU WERE YOUNG!

STUDY HALL

SO?

SO...YOU CAN HELP ME BEAT OUT THE COMPETITION TO BE BETTY'S PARTNER.!

QUIET PLEASE!

YEAH, BUT *I'M* ALSO ENTERING THE CONTEST WITH *GOOGIE GROGAN*! I'VE DECIDED I CAN'T AFFORD TO PASS ON THE CONTEST'S *SUPER BUFFET*!

STUDY HALL

4

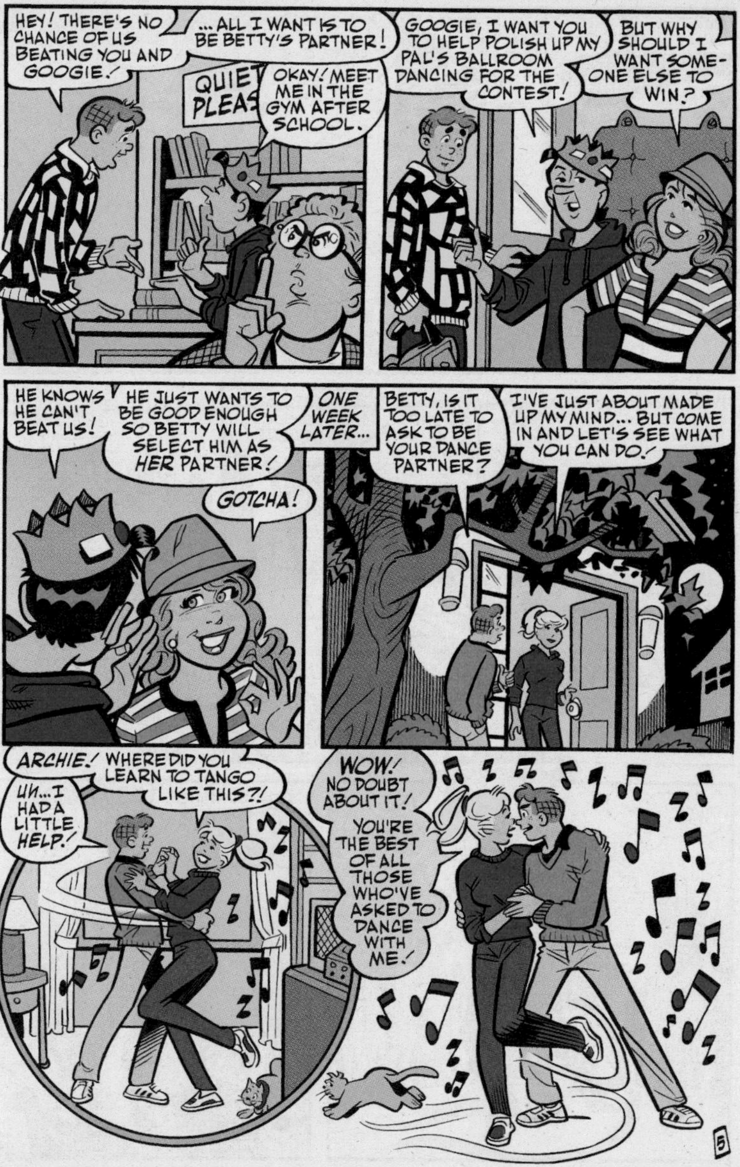
HEY! THERE'S NO CHANCE OF US BEATING YOU AND GOOGIE.!
...ALL I WANT IS TO BE BETTY'S PARTNER!
QUIET PLEAS
OKAY! MEET ME IN THE GYM AFTER SCHOOL.
GOOGIE, I WANT YOU TO HELP POLISH UP MY PAL'S BALLROOM DANCING FOR THE CONTEST!
BUT WHY SHOULD I WANT SOME-ONE ELSE TO WIN?
HE KNOWS HE CAN'T BEAT US!
HE JUST WANTS TO BE GOOD ENOUGH SO BETTY WILL SELECT HIM AS HER PARTNER!
GOTCHA!
ONE WEEK LATER...
BETTY, IS IT TOO LATE TO ASK TO BE YOUR DANCE PARTNER?
I'VE JUST ABOUT MADE UP MY MIND... BUT COME IN AND LET'S SEE WHAT YOU CAN DO.!
ARCHIE! WHERE DID YOU LEARN TO TANGO LIKE THIS?!
UH...I HAD A LITTLE HELP.!
WOW! NO DOUBT ABOUT IT! YOU'RE THE BEST OF ALL THOSE WHO'VE ASKED TO DANCE WITH ME.!
5

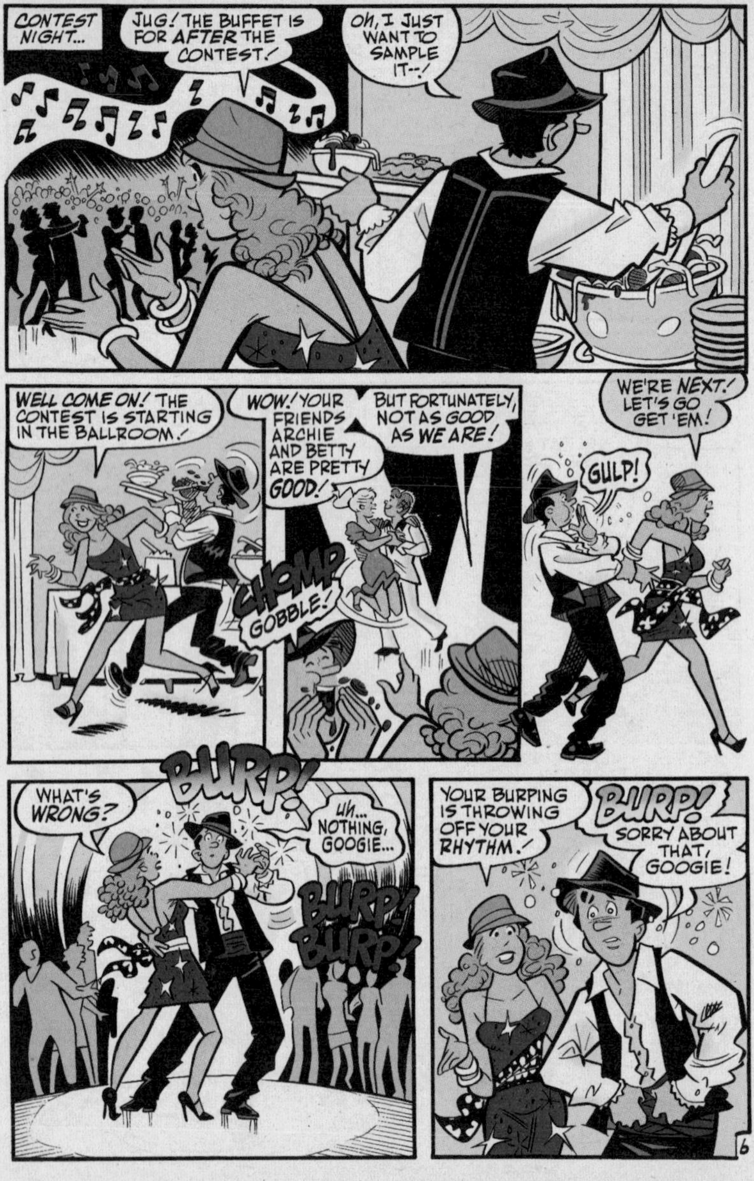

CONTEST NIGHT...
JUG! THE BUFFET IS FOR AFTER THE CONTEST!
OH, I JUST WANT TO SAMPLE IT--!
WELL COME ON! THE CONTEST IS STARTING IN THE BALLROOM!
WOW! YOUR FRIENDS ARCHIE AND BETTY ARE PRETTY GOOD!
BUT FORTUNATELY, NOT AS GOOD AS WE ARE!
CHOMP
GOBBLE!
WE'RE NEXT! LET'S GO GET 'EM!
GULP!
BURP!
WHAT'S WRONG?
UH... NOTHING, GOOGIE...
BURP! BURP!
YOUR BURPING IS THROWING OFF YOUR RHYTHM!
BURP!
SORRY ABOUT THAT, GOOGIE!

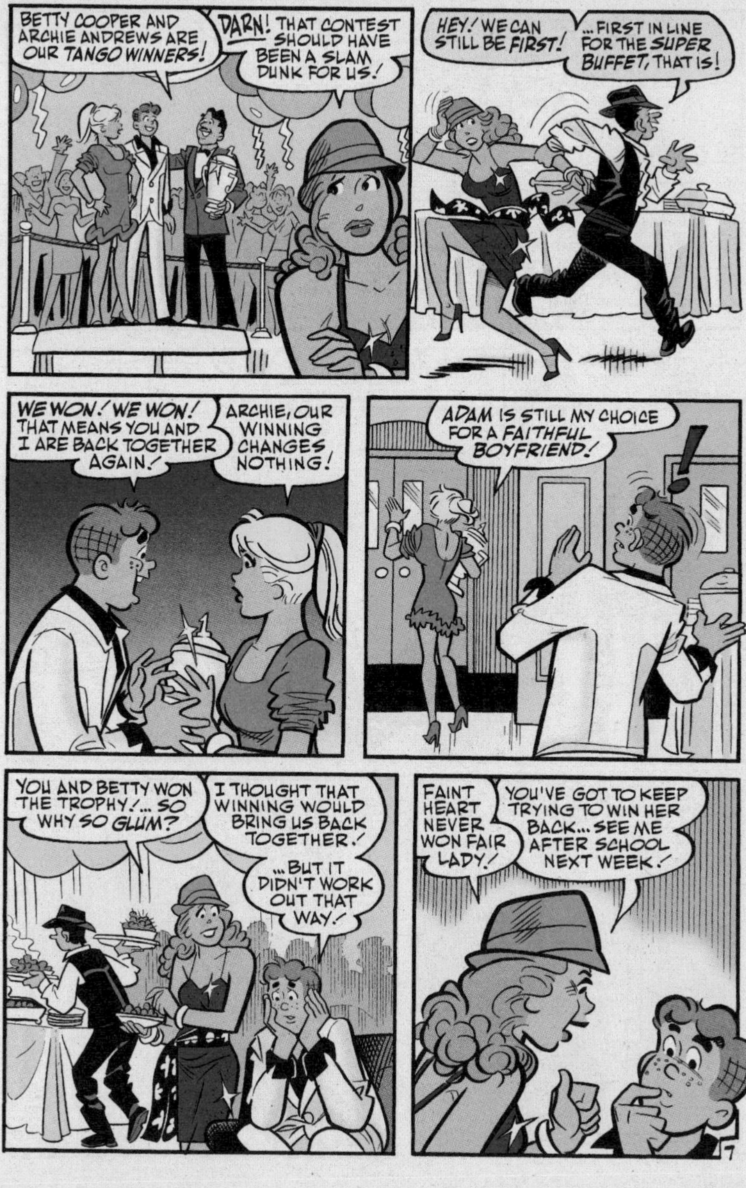

BETTY COOPER AND ARCHIE ANDREWS ARE OUR TANGO WINNERS!
DARN! THAT CONTEST SHOULD HAVE BEEN A SLAM DUNK FOR US!
HEY! WE CAN STILL BE FIRST!
...FIRST IN LINE FOR THE SUPER BUFFET, THAT IS!
WE WON! WE WON! THAT MEANS YOU AND I ARE BACK TOGETHER AGAIN!
ARCHIE, OUR WINNING CHANGES NOTHING!
ADAM IS STILL MY CHOICE FOR A FAITHFUL BOYFRIEND!
!
YOU AND BETTY WON THE TROPHY!... SO WHY SO GLUM?
I THOUGHT THAT WINNING WOULD BRING US BACK TOGETHER!
...BUT IT DIDN'T WORK OUT THAT WAY!
FAINT HEART NEVER WON FAIR LADY!
YOU'VE GOT TO KEEP TRYING TO WIN HER BACK... SEE ME AFTER SCHOOL NEXT WEEK!

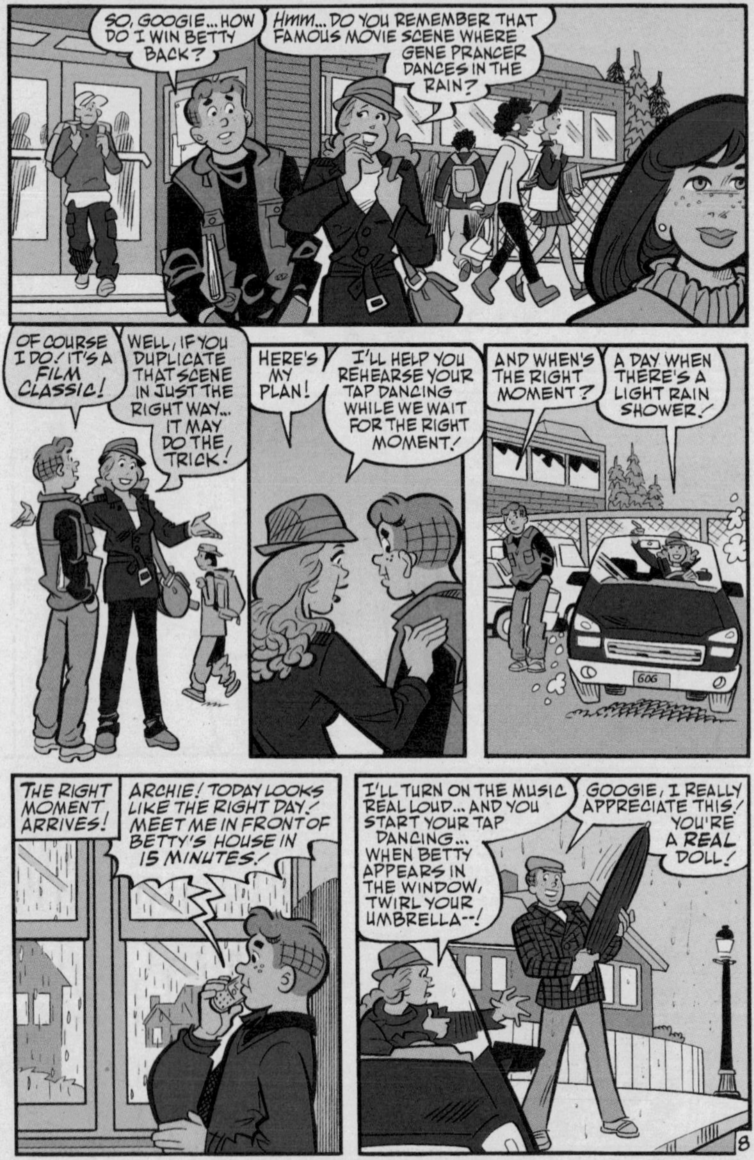

SO, GOOGIE... HOW DO I WIN BETTY BACK?
HMM... DO YOU REMEMBER THAT FAMOUS MOVIE SCENE WHERE GENE PRANCER DANCES IN THE RAIN?
OF COURSE I DO! IT'S A FILM CLASSIC!
WELL, IF YOU DUPLICATE THAT SCENE IN JUST THE RIGHT WAY... IT MAY DO THE TRICK!
HERE'S MY PLAN!
I'LL HELP YOU REHEARSE YOUR TAP DANCING WHILE WE WAIT FOR THE RIGHT MOMENT!
AND WHEN'S THE RIGHT MOMENT?
A DAY WHEN THERE'S A LIGHT RAIN SHOWER!
GOG
THE RIGHT MOMENT ARRIVES!
ARCHIE! TODAY LOOKS LIKE THE RIGHT DAY! MEET ME IN FRONT OF BETTY'S HOUSE IN 15 MINUTES!
I'LL TURN ON THE MUSIC REAL LOUD... AND YOU START YOUR TAP DANCING... WHEN BETTY APPEARS IN THE WINDOW, TWIRL YOUR UMBRELLA--!
GOOGIE, I REALLY APPRECIATE THIS! YOU'RE A REAL DOLL!

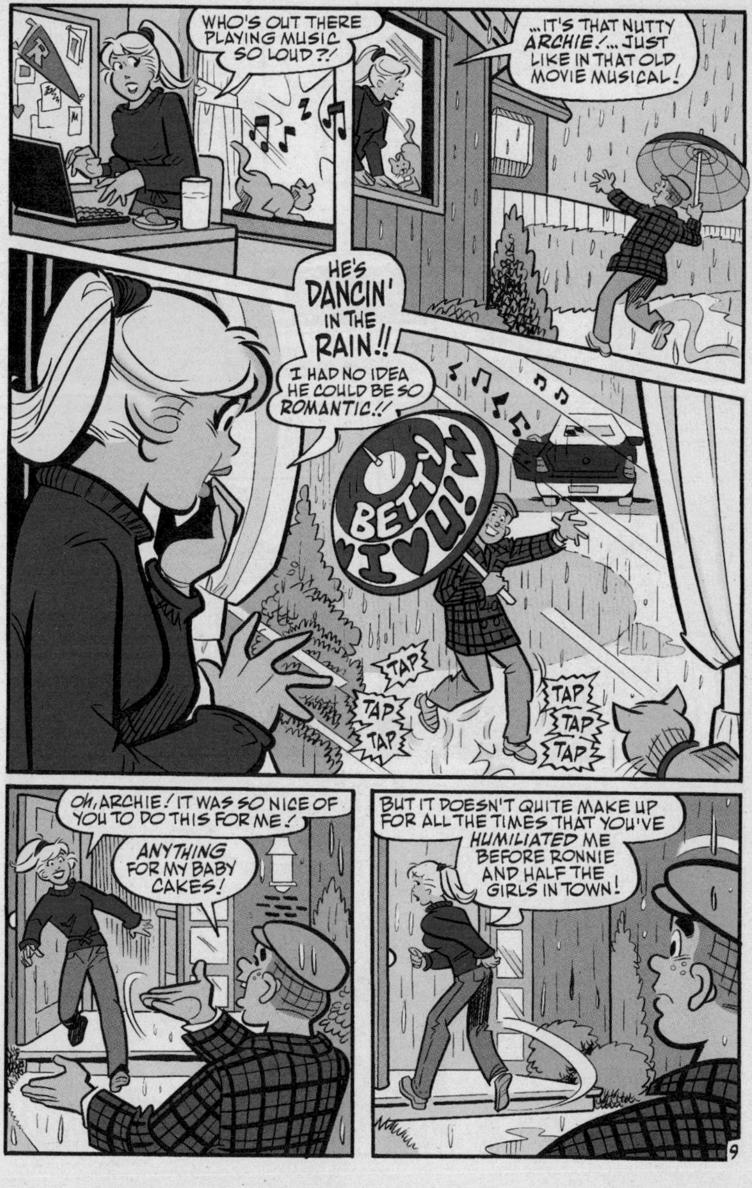
WHO'S OUT THERE PLAYING MUSIC SO LOUD?!
...IT'S THAT NUTTY ARCHIE!... JUST LIKE IN THAT OLD MOVIE MUSICAL!
HE'S DANCIN' IN THE RAIN!!
I HAD NO IDEA HE COULD BE SO ROMANTIC!!
OH, BETTY! I ♥ U!
TAP
TAP
TAP
TAP
TAP
TAP
OH, ARCHIE! IT WAS SO NICE OF YOU TO DO THIS FOR ME!
ANYTHING FOR MY BABY CAKES!
BUT IT DOESN'T QUITE MAKE UP FOR ALL THE TIMES THAT YOU'VE HUMILIATED ME BEFORE RONNIE AND HALF THE GIRLS IN TOWN!

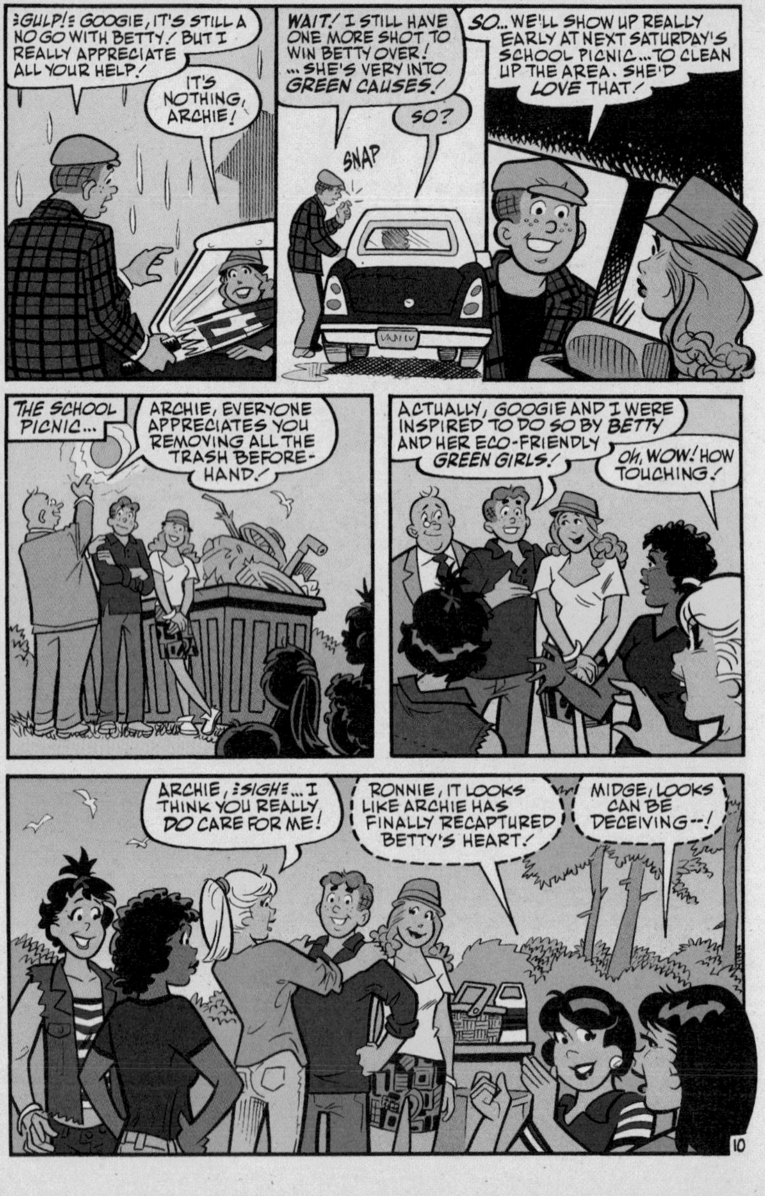

:GULP!: GOOGIE, IT'S STILL A NO GO WITH BETTY! BUT I REALLY APPRECIATE ALL YOUR HELP!
IT'S NOTHING, ARCHIE!
WAIT! I STILL HAVE ONE MORE SHOT TO WIN BETTY OVER! ...SHE'S VERY INTO GREEN CAUSES!
SO?
SNAP
SO... WE'LL SHOW UP REALLY EARLY AT NEXT SATURDAY'S SCHOOL PICNIC... TO CLEAN UP THE AREA. SHE'D LOVE THAT!
THE SCHOOL PICNIC...
ARCHIE, EVERYONE APPRECIATES YOU REMOVING ALL THE TRASH BEFORE-HAND!
ACTUALLY, GOOGIE AND I WERE INSPIRED TO DO SO BY BETTY AND HER ECO-FRIENDLY GREEN GIRLS!
OH, WOW! HOW TOUCHING!
ARCHIE, :SIGH: ...I THINK YOU REALLY DO CARE FOR ME!
RONNIE, IT LOOKS LIKE ARCHIE HAS FINALLY RECAPTURED BETTY'S HEART!
MIDGE, LOOKS CAN BE DECEIVING--!

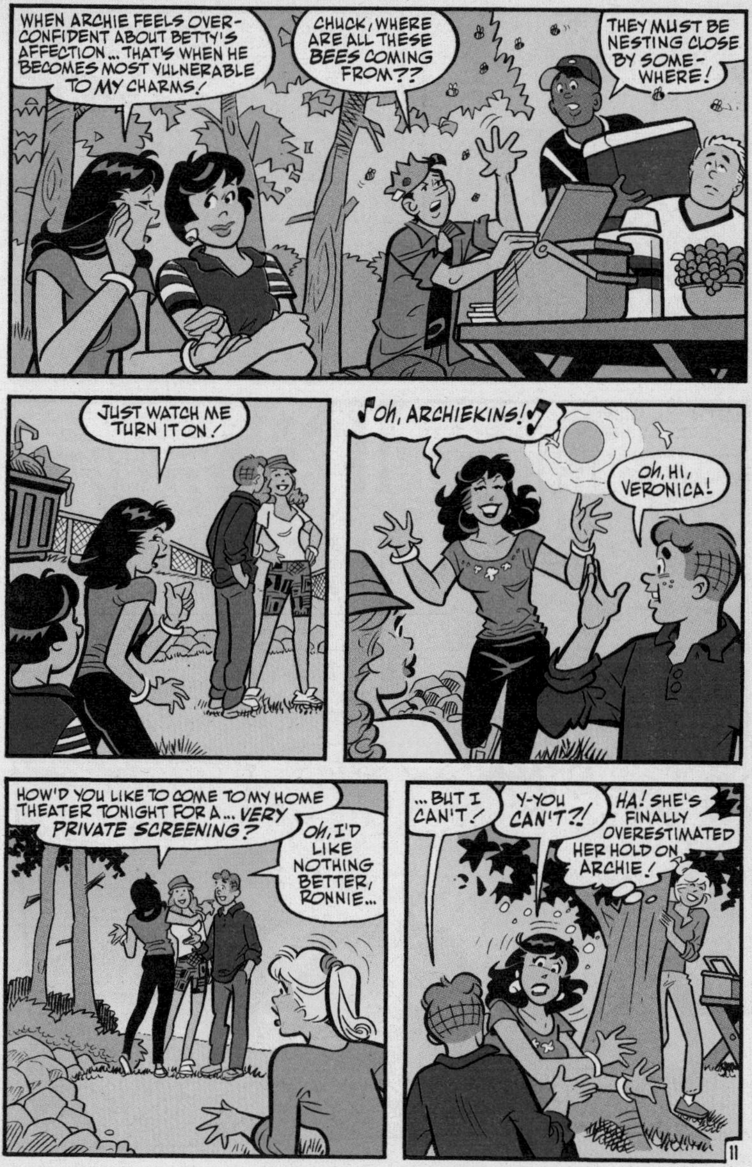
WHEN ARCHIE FEELS OVER-CONFIDENT ABOUT BETTY'S AFFECTION ... THAT'S WHEN HE BECOMES MOST VULNERABLE TO MY CHARMS!
CHUCK, WHERE ARE ALL THESE BEES COMING FROM??
THEY MUST BE NESTING CLOSE BY SOME-WHERE!
JUST WATCH ME TURN IT ON!
Oh, ARCHIEKINS!
Oh, HI, VERONICA!
HOW'D YOU LIKE TO COME TO MY HOME THEATER TONIGHT FOR A ... VERY PRIVATE SCREENING?
Oh, I'D LIKE NOTHING BETTER, RONNIE...
... BUT I CAN'T!
Y-YOU CAN'T?!
HA! SHE'S FINALLY OVERESTIMATED HER HOLD ON ARCHIE!

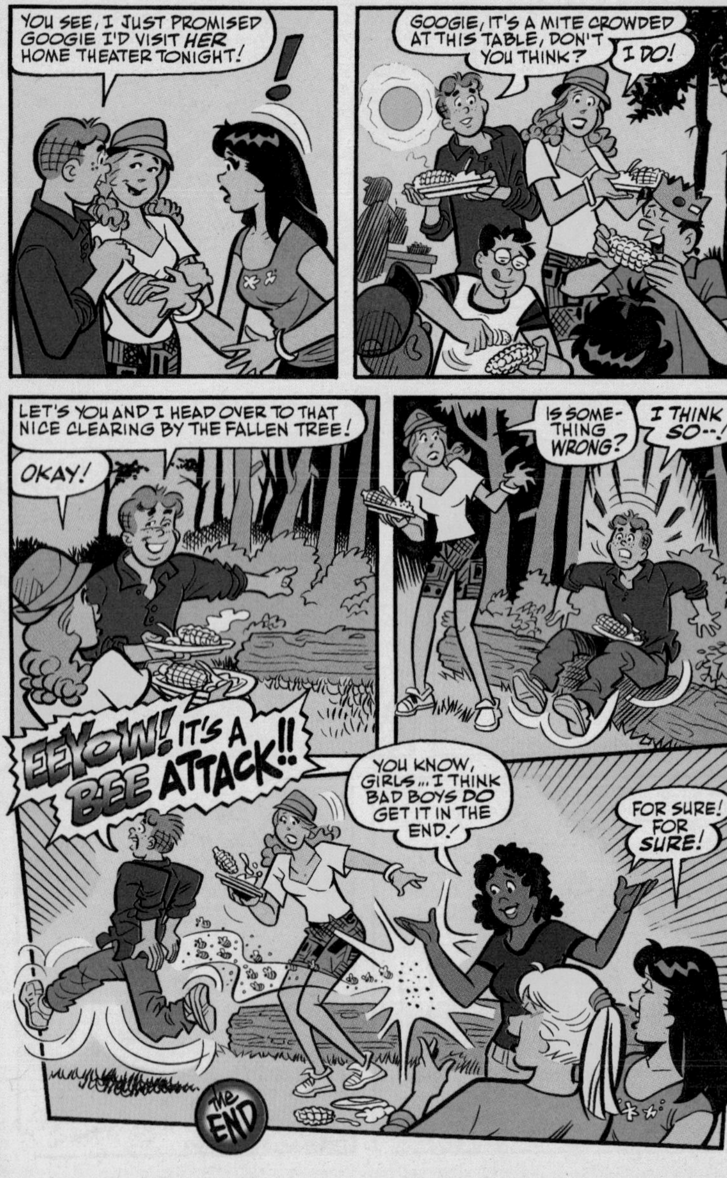
YOU SEE, I JUST PROMISED GOOGIE I'D VISIT HER HOME THEATER TONIGHT!
!
GOOGIE, IT'S A MITE CROWDED AT THIS TABLE, DON'T YOU THINK?
I DO!
LET'S YOU AND I HEAD OVER TO THAT NICE CLEARING BY THE FALLEN TREE!
OKAY!
IS SOME-THING WRONG?
I THINK SO--!
EEYOW! IT'S A BEE ATTACK!!
YOU KNOW, GIRLS... I THINK BAD BOYS DO GET IT IN THE END!
FOR SURE! FOR SURE!
the END

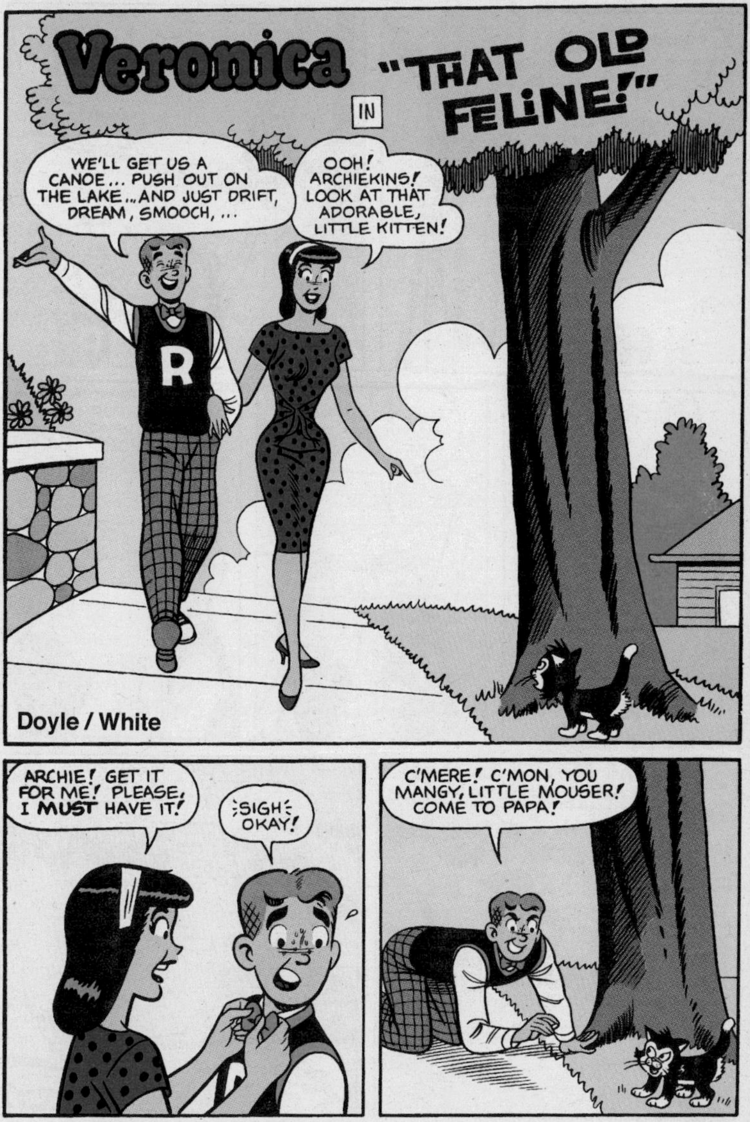
Veronica
IN
"THAT OLD FELINE!"
WE'LL GET US A CANOE... PUSH OUT ON THE LAKE...AND JUST DRIFT, DREAM, SMOOCH, ...
OOH! ARCHIEKINS! LOOK AT THAT ADORABLE, LITTLE KITTEN!
Doyle / White
ARCHIE! GET IT FOR ME! PLEASE, I MUST HAVE IT!
SIGH OKAY!
C'MERE! C'MON, YOU MANGY, LITTLE MOUSER! COME TO PAPA!

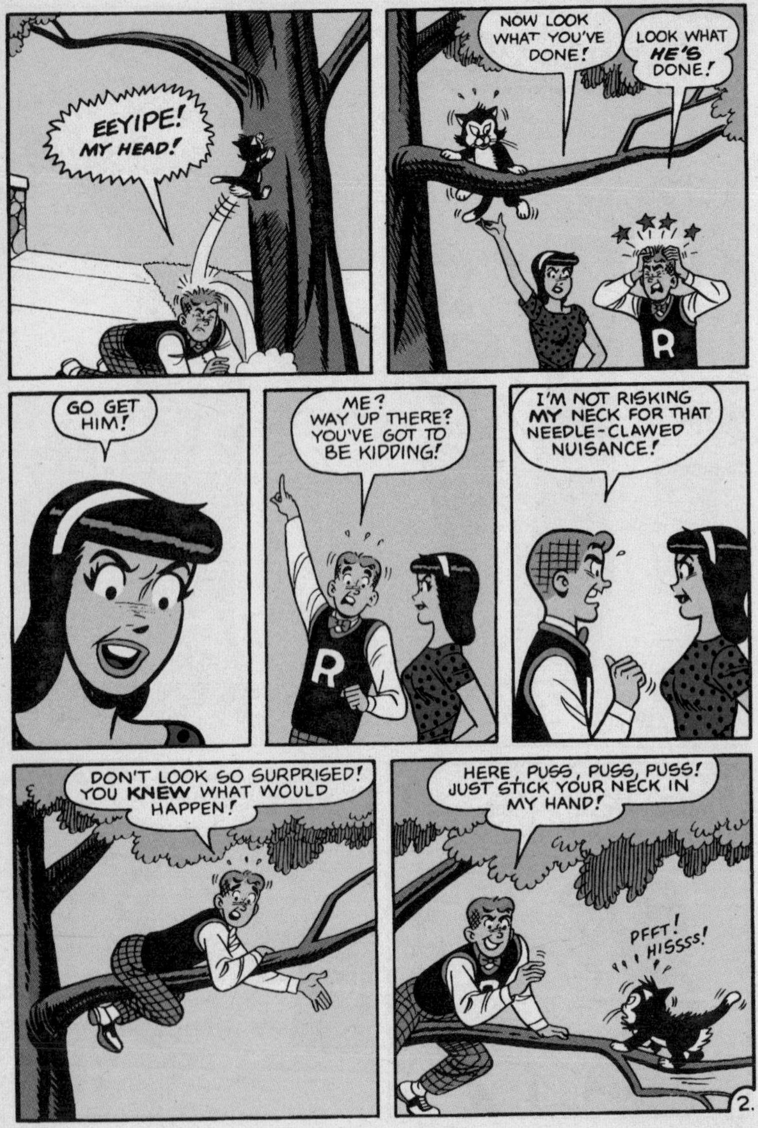
EEYIPE! MY HEAD!
NOW LOOK WHAT YOU'VE DONE!
LOOK WHAT HE'S DONE!
GO GET HIM!
ME? WAY UP THERE? YOU'VE GOT TO BE KIDDING!
I'M NOT RISKING MY NECK FOR THAT NEEDLE-CLAWED NUISANCE!
DON'T LOOK SO SURPRISED! YOU KNEW WHAT WOULD HAPPEN!
HERE, PUSS, PUSS, PUSS! JUST STICK YOUR NECK IN MY HAND!
PFFT! HISSSS!
R
R
R
2.

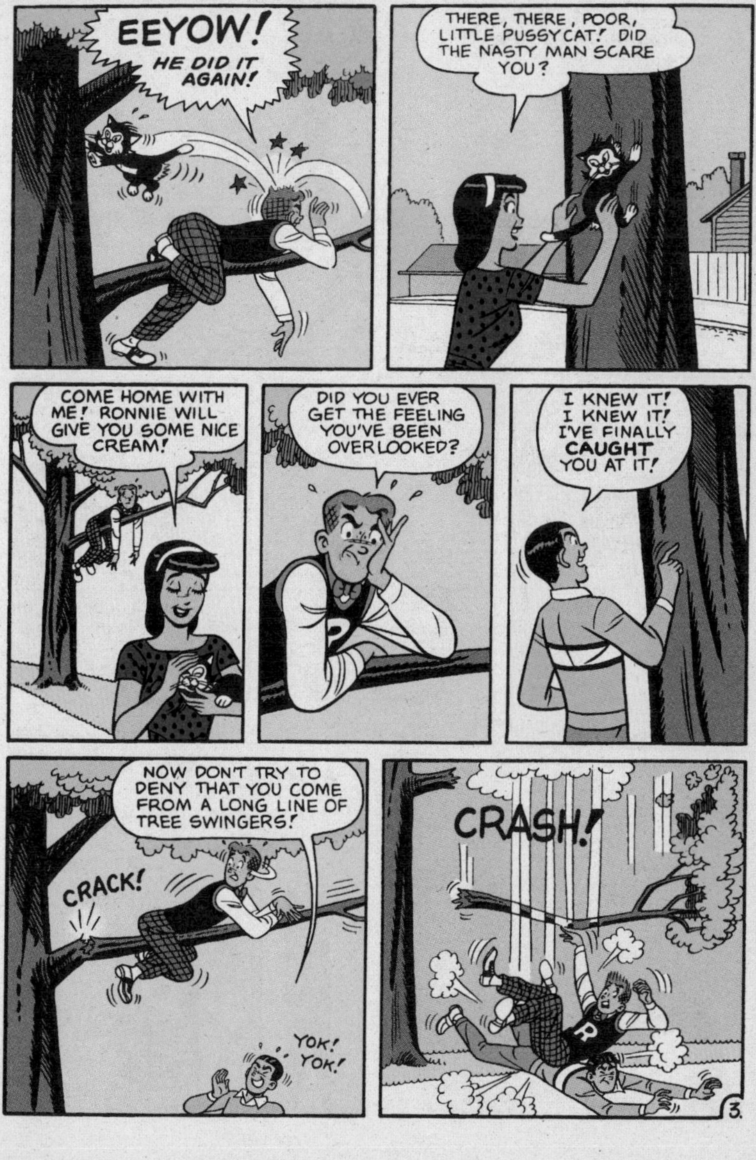
EEYOW!
HE DID IT AGAIN!
THERE, THERE, POOR, LITTLE PUSSYCAT! DID THE NASTY MAN SCARE YOU?
COME HOME WITH ME! RONNIE WILL GIVE YOU SOME NICE CREAM!
DID YOU EVER GET THE FEELING YOU'VE BEEN OVERLOOKED?
I KNEW IT! I KNEW IT! I'VE FINALLY CAUGHT YOU AT IT!
NOW DON'T TRY TO DENY THAT YOU COME FROM A LONG LINE OF TREE SWINGERS!
CRACK!
YOK! YOK!
CRASH!

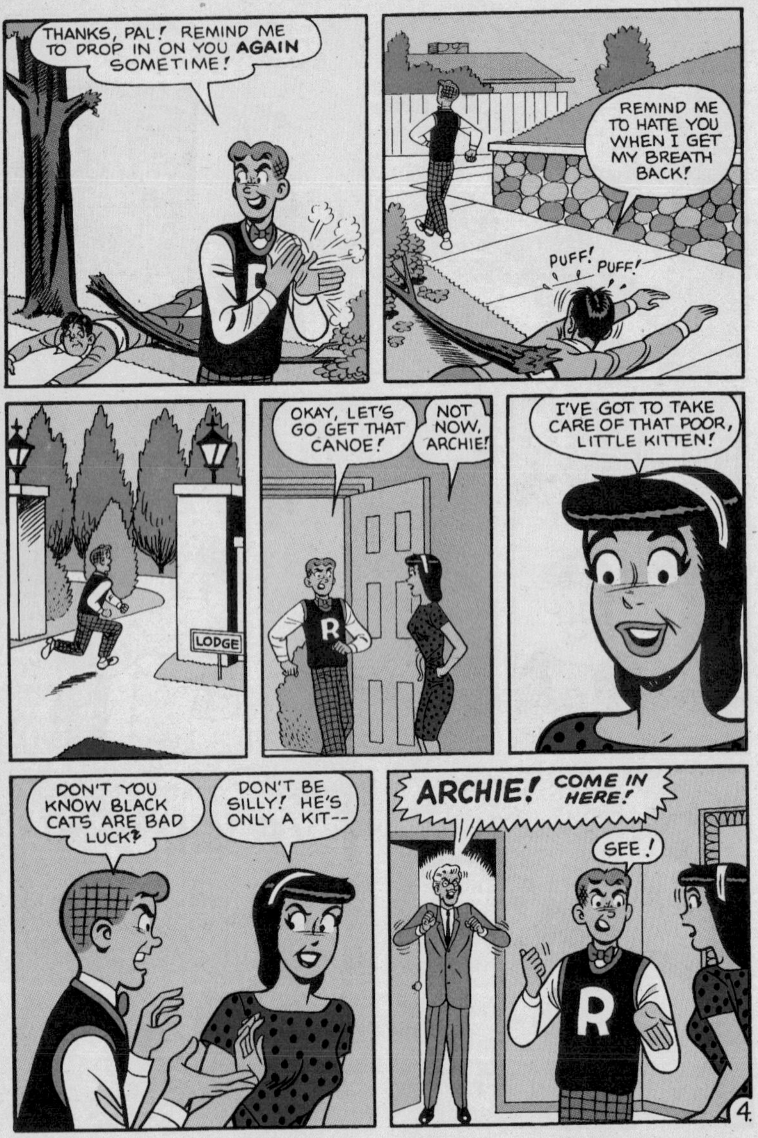
THANKS, PAL! REMIND ME TO DROP IN ON YOU AGAIN SOMETIME!
REMIND ME TO HATE YOU WHEN I GET MY BREATH BACK!
PUFF! PUFF!
LODGE
OKAY, LET'S GO GET THAT CANOE!
NOT NOW, ARCHIE!
I'VE GOT TO TAKE CARE OF THAT POOR, LITTLE KITTEN!
DON'T YOU KNOW BLACK CATS ARE BAD LUCK?
DON'T BE SILLY! HE'S ONLY A KIT--
ARCHIE! COME IN HERE!
SEE!
4.

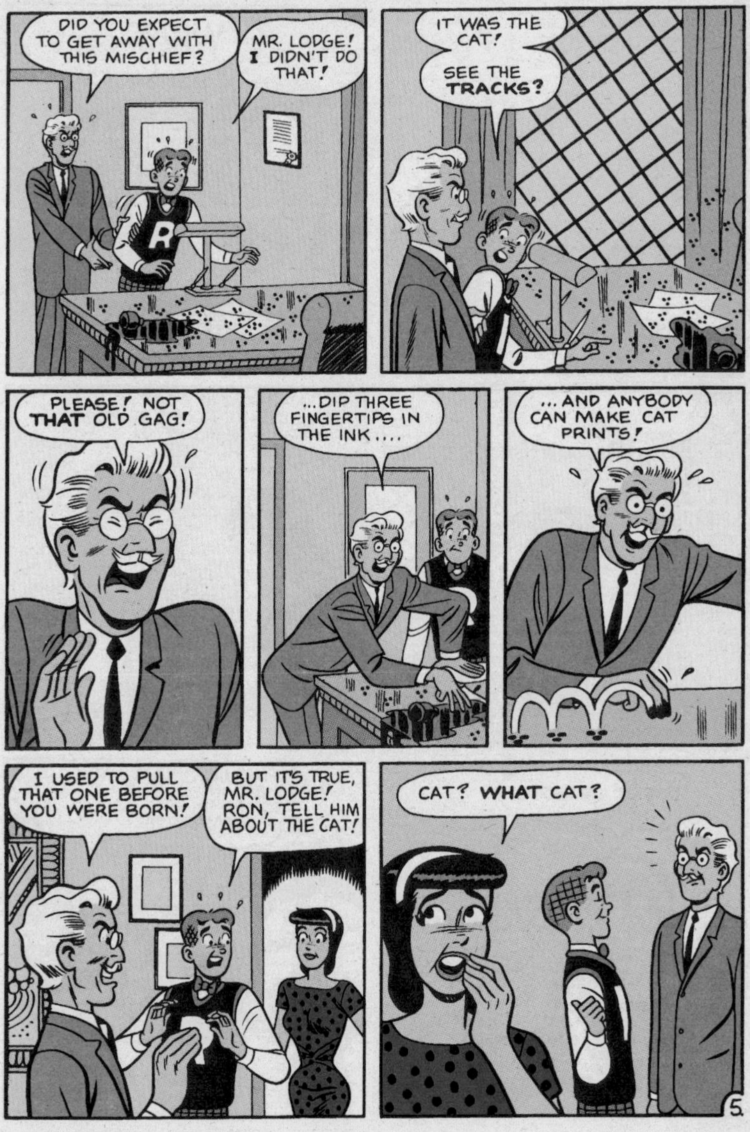
DID YOU EXPECT TO GET AWAY WITH THIS MISCHIEF?
MR. LODGE! I DIDN'T DO THAT!
IT WAS THE CAT!
SEE THE TRACKS?
PLEASE! NOT THAT OLD GAG!
...DIP THREE FINGERTIPS IN THE INK....
...AND ANYBODY CAN MAKE CAT PRINTS!
I USED TO PULL THAT ONE BEFORE YOU WERE BORN!
BUT IT'S TRUE, MR. LODGE! RON, TELL HIM ABOUT THE CAT!
CAT? WHAT CAT?
5

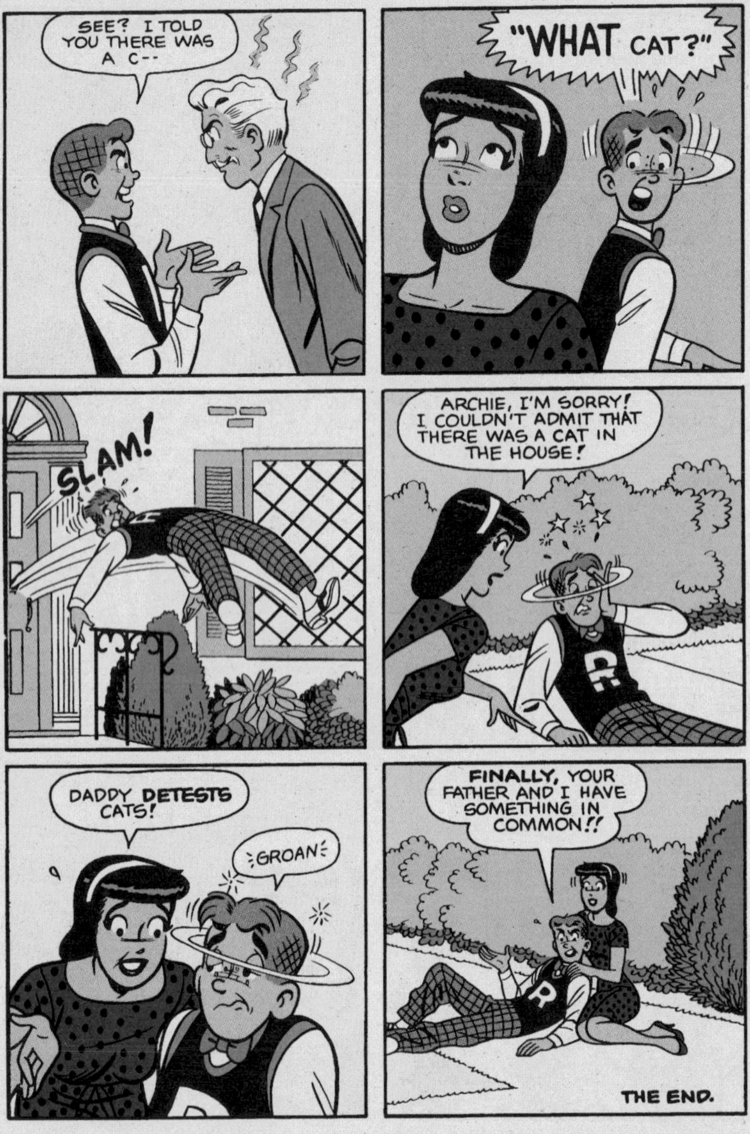
SEE? I TOLD YOU THERE WAS A C--
"WHAT CAT?"
SLAM!
ARCHIE, I'M SORRY! I COULDN'T ADMIT THAT THERE WAS A CAT IN THE HOUSE!
DADDY DETESTS CATS!
GROAN
FINALLY, YOUR FATHER AND I HAVE SOMETHING IN COMMON!!
THE END.

Betty and Veronica in "The UNKINDEST CUT"

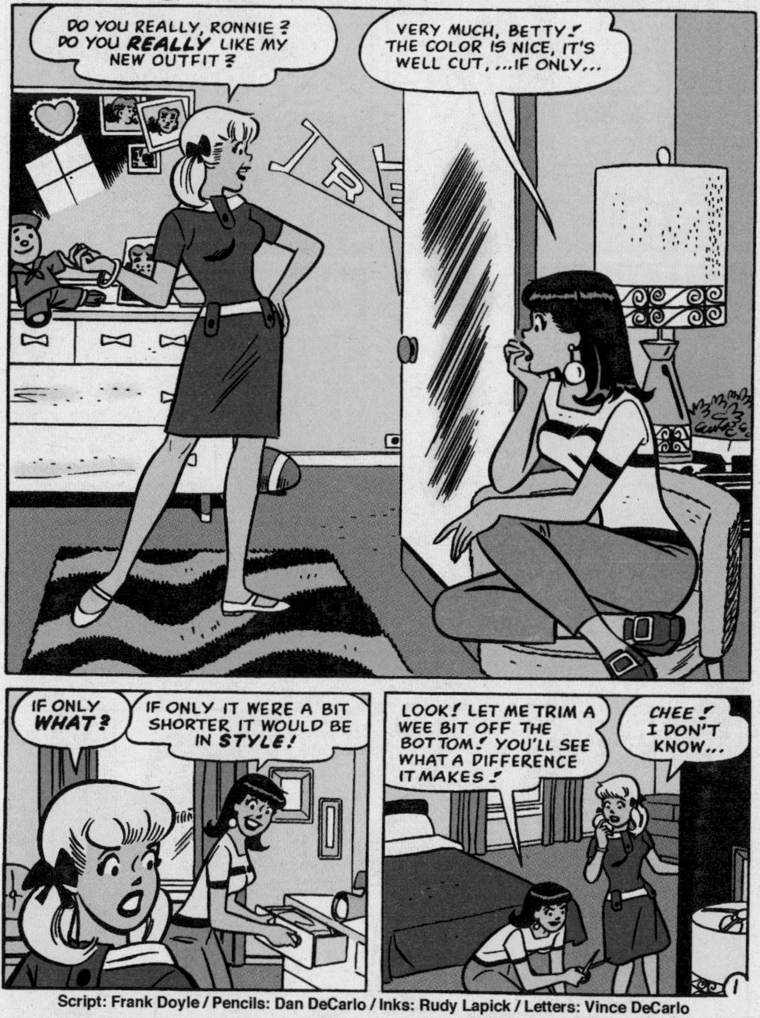
DO YOU REALLY, RONNIE? DO YOU REALLY LIKE MY NEW OUTFIT?
VERY MUCH, BETTY! THE COLOR IS NICE, IT'S WELL CUT, ...IF ONLY...
IF ONLY WHAT?
IF ONLY IT WERE A BIT SHORTER IT WOULD BE IN STYLE!
LOOK! LET ME TRIM A WEE BIT OFF THE BOTTOM! YOU'LL SEE WHAT A DIFFERENCE IT MAKES!
CHEE! I DON'T KNOW...
1

Script: Frank Doyle / Pencils: Dan DeCarlo / Inks: Rudy Lapick / Letters: Vince DeCarlo

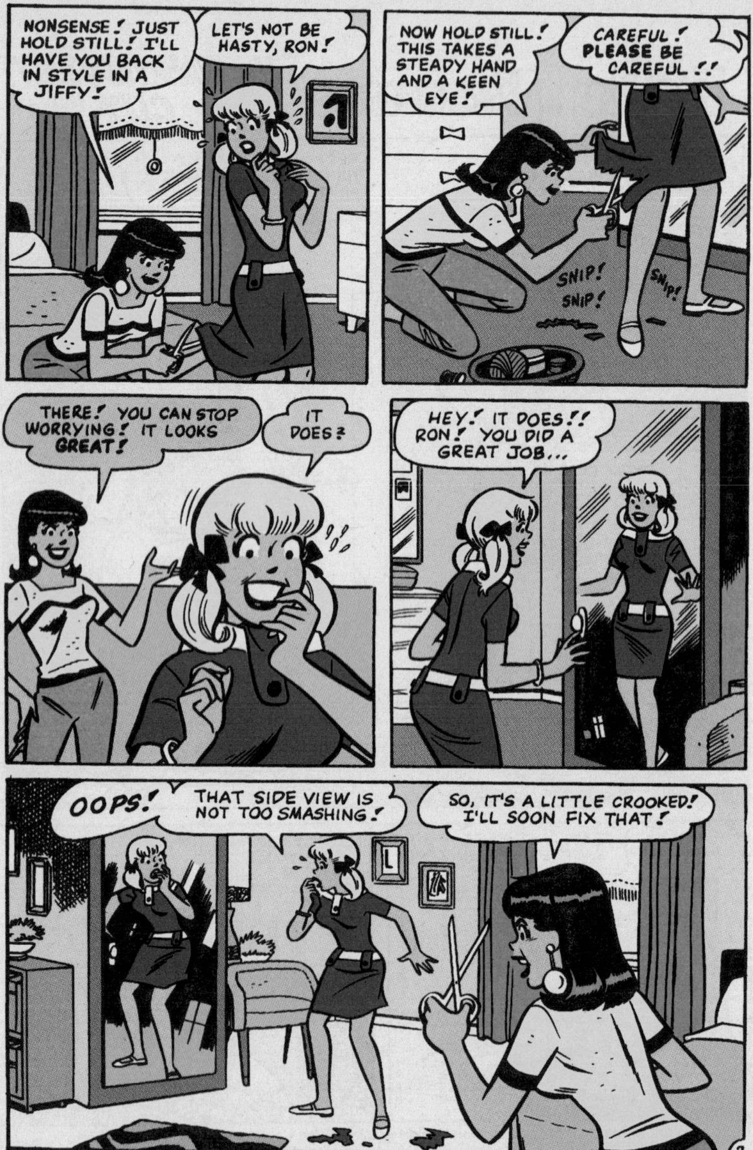
NONSENSE! JUST HOLD STILL! I'LL HAVE YOU BACK IN STYLE IN A JIFFY!
LET'S NOT BE HASTY, RON!
NOW HOLD STILL! THIS TAKES A STEADY HAND AND A KEEN EYE!
CAREFUL! PLEASE BE CAREFUL!!
SNIP! SNIP!
SNIP!
THERE! YOU CAN STOP WORRYING! IT LOOKS GREAT!
IT DOES?
HEY! IT DOES!! RON! YOU DID A GREAT JOB...
OOPS!
THAT SIDE VIEW IS NOT TOO SMASHING!
SO, IT'S A LITTLE CROOKED! I'LL SOON FIX THAT!

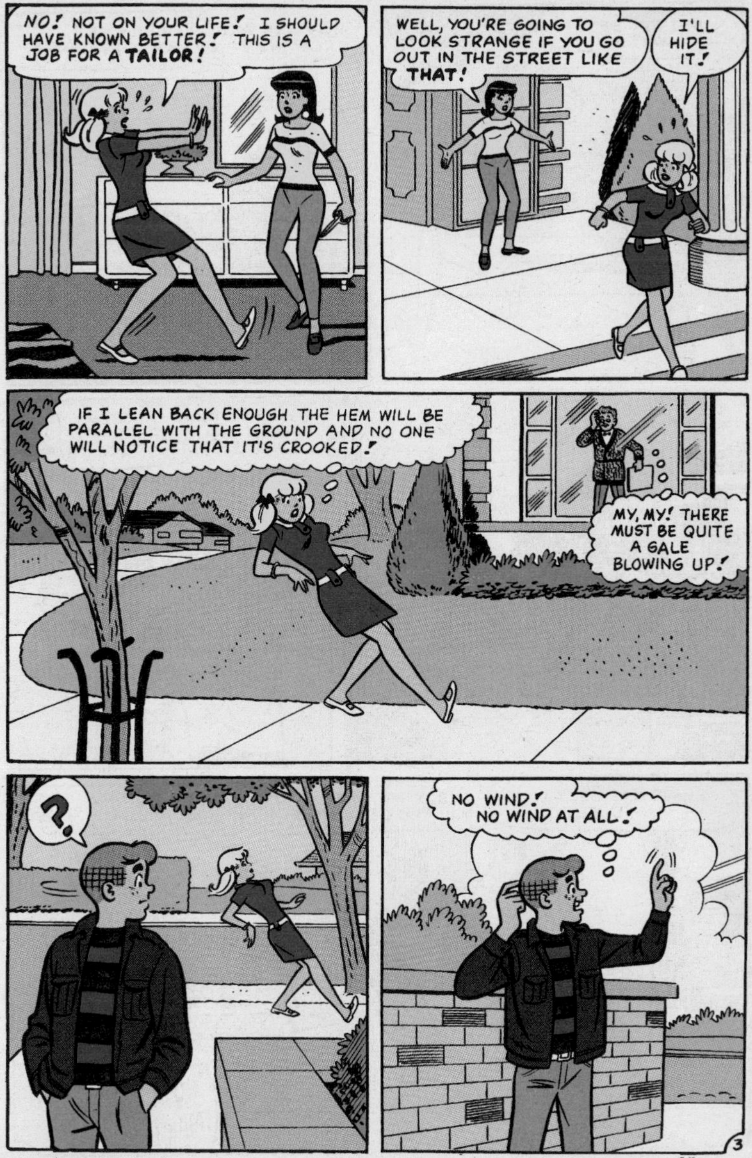
NO! NOT ON YOUR LIFE! I SHOULD HAVE KNOWN BETTER! THIS IS A JOB FOR A **TAILOR**!
WELL, YOU'RE GOING TO LOOK STRANGE IF YOU GO OUT IN THE STREET LIKE **THAT**!
I'LL HIDE IT!
IF I LEAN BACK ENOUGH THE HEM WILL BE PARALLEL WITH THE GROUND AND NO ONE WILL NOTICE THAT IT'S CROOKED!
MY, MY! THERE MUST BE QUITE A GALE BLOWING UP!
?
NO WIND! NO WIND AT ALL!

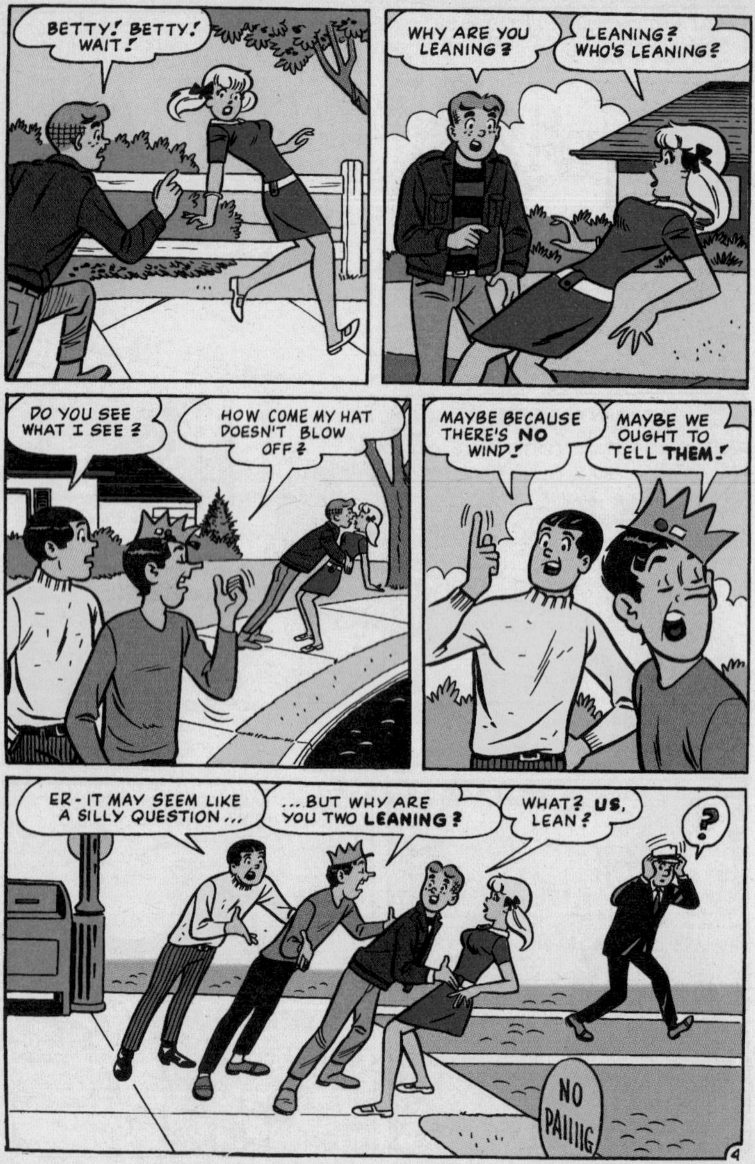
BETTY! BETTY! WAIT!
WHY ARE YOU LEANING?
LEANING? WHO'S LEANING?
DO YOU SEE WHAT I SEE?
HOW COME MY HAT DOESN'T BLOW OFF?
MAYBE BECAUSE THERE'S NO WIND!
MAYBE WE OUGHT TO TELL THEM!
ER - IT MAY SEEM LIKE A SILLY QUESTION ...
... BUT WHY ARE YOU TWO LEANING?
WHAT? US, LEAN?
?
NO PA[illegible]G
4

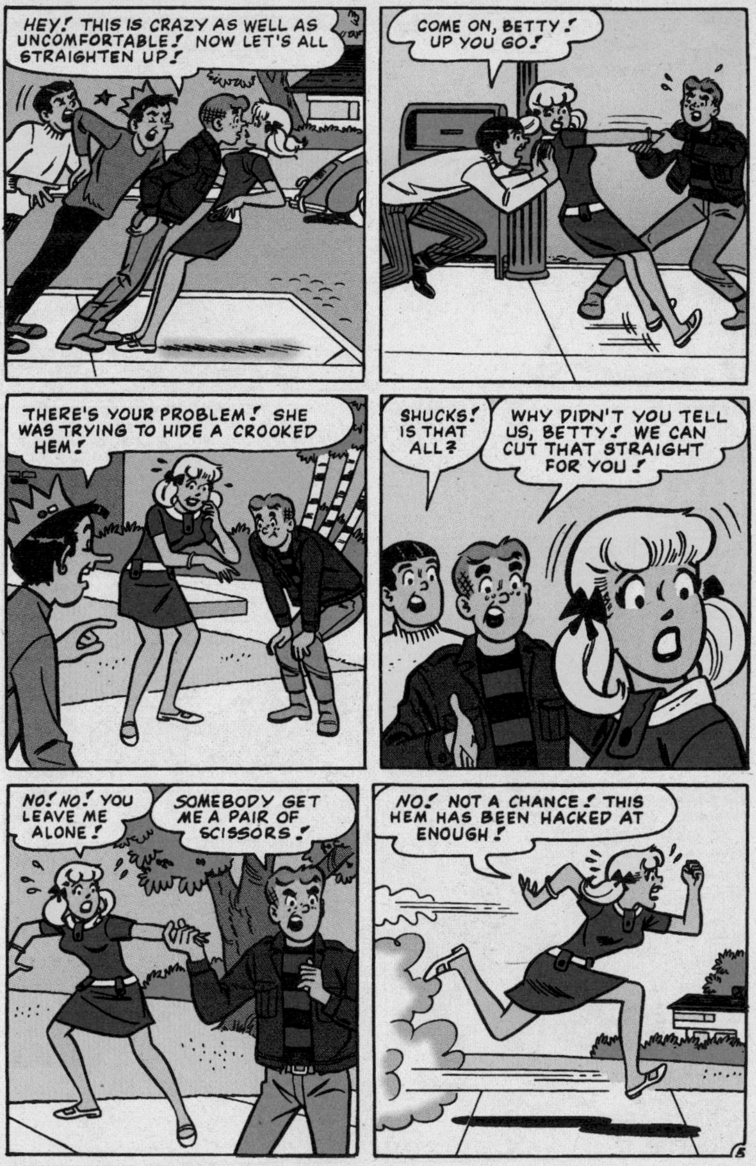
HEY! THIS IS CRAZY AS WELL AS UNCOMFORTABLE! NOW LET'S ALL STRAIGHTEN UP!
COME ON, BETTY! UP YOU GO!
THERE'S YOUR PROBLEM! SHE WAS TRYING TO HIDE A CROOKED HEM!
SHUCKS! IS THAT ALL?
WHY DIDN'T YOU TELL US, BETTY! WE CAN CUT THAT STRAIGHT FOR YOU!
NO! NO! YOU LEAVE ME ALONE!
SOMEBODY GET ME A PAIR OF SCISSORS!
NO! NOT A CHANCE! THIS HEM HAS BEEN HACKED AT ENOUGH!
5

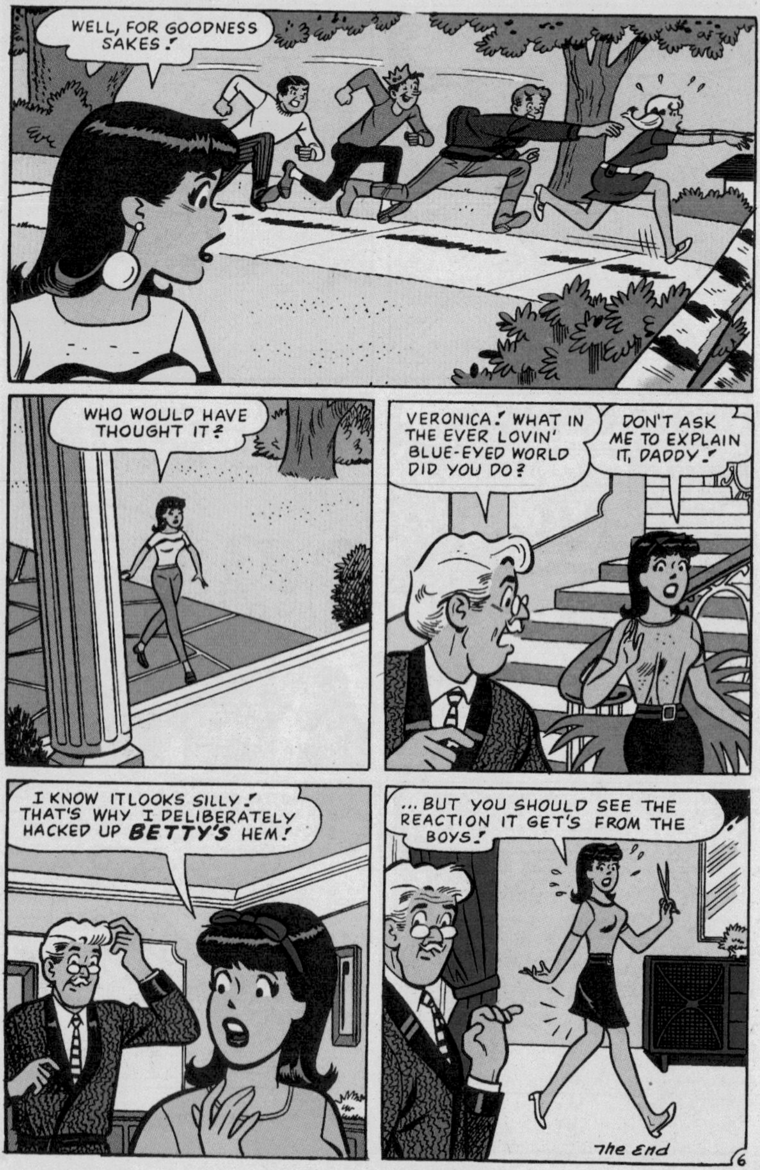

WELL, FOR GOODNESS SAKES!
WHO WOULD HAVE THOUGHT IT?
VERONICA! WHAT IN THE EVER LOVIN' BLUE-EYED WORLD DID YOU DO?
DON'T ASK ME TO EXPLAIN IT, DADDY!
I KNOW ITLOOKS SILLY! THAT'S WHY I DELIBERATELY HACKED UP BETTY'S HEM!
... BUT YOU SHOULD SEE THE REACTION IT GET'S FROM THE BOYS!
The End

Betty and Veronica in THE PLAY IS THE THING

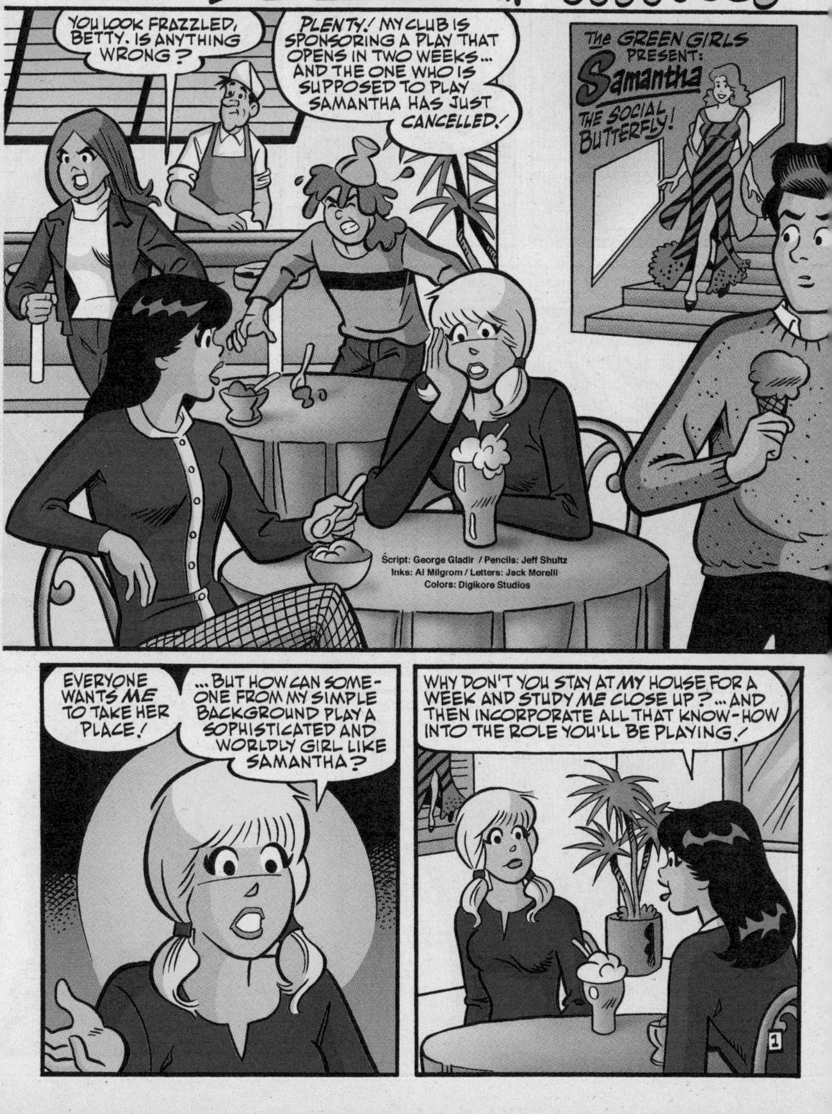

YOU LOOK FRAZZLED, BETTY. IS ANYTHING WRONG?
PLENTY! MY CLUB IS SPONSORING A PLAY THAT OPENS IN TWO WEEKS... AND THE ONE WHO IS SUPPOSED TO PLAY SAMANTHA HAS JUST CANCELLED!
The GREEN GIRLS PRESENT: Samantha THE SOCIAL BUTTERFLY!
Script: George Gladir / Pencils: Jeff Shultz
Inks: Al Milgrom / Letters: Jack Morelli
Colors: Digikore Studios
EVERYONE WANTS ME TO TAKE HER PLACE!
...BUT HOW CAN SOMEONE FROM MY SIMPLE BACKGROUND PLAY A SOPHISTICATED AND WORLDLY GIRL LIKE SAMANTHA?
WHY DON'T YOU STAY AT MY HOUSE FOR A WEEK AND STUDY ME CLOSE UP? ...AND THEN INCORPORATE ALL THAT KNOW-HOW INTO THE ROLE YOU'LL BE PLAYING!
1

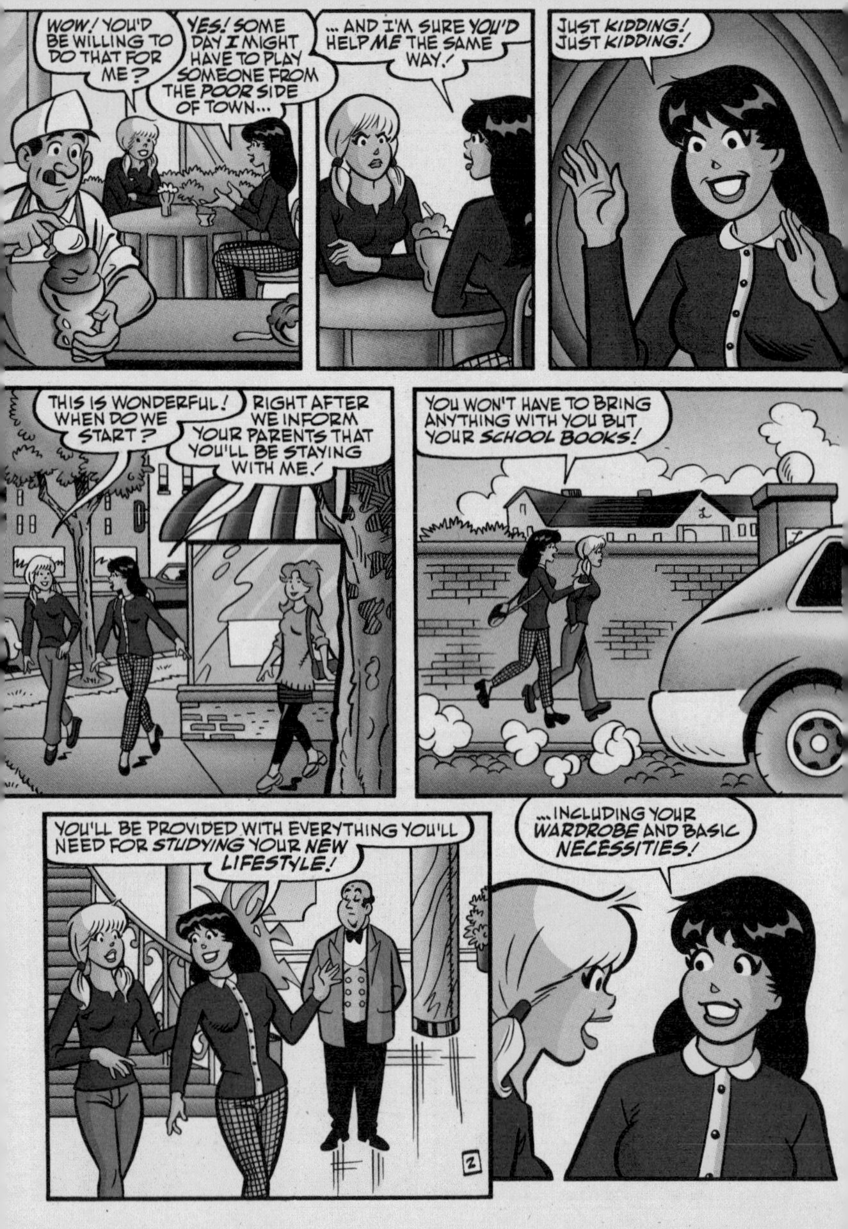
WOW! YOU'D BE WILLING TO DO THAT FOR ME?
YES! SOME DAY I MIGHT HAVE TO PLAY SOMEONE FROM THE POOR SIDE OF TOWN...
... AND I'M SURE YOU'D HELP ME THE SAME WAY!
JUST KIDDING! JUST KIDDING!
THIS IS WONDERFUL! WHEN DO WE START?
RIGHT AFTER WE INFORM YOUR PARENTS THAT YOU'LL BE STAYING WITH ME!
YOU WON'T HAVE TO BRING ANYTHING WITH YOU BUT YOUR SCHOOL BOOKS!
YOU'LL BE PROVIDED WITH EVERYTHING YOU'LL NEED FOR STUDYING YOUR NEW LIFESTYLE!
2
...INCLUDING YOUR WARDROBE AND BASIC NECESSITIES!

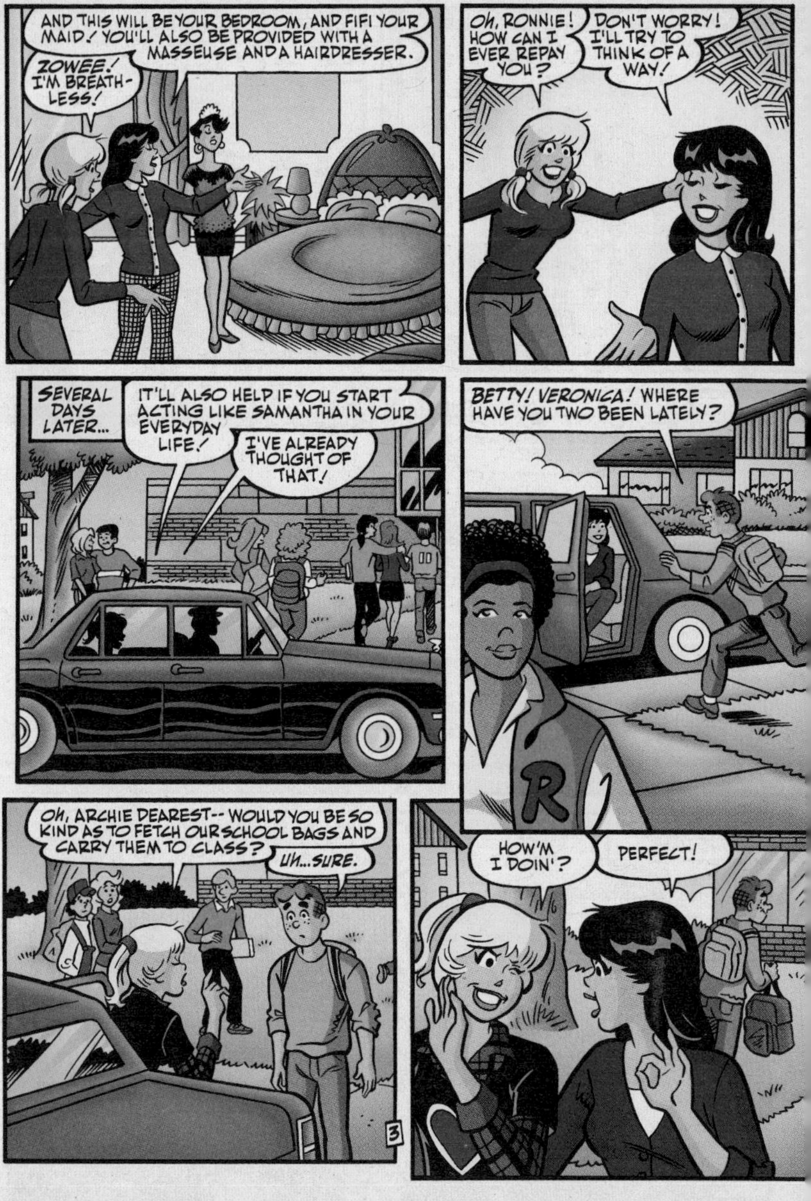
AND THIS WILL BE YOUR BEDROOM, AND FIFI YOUR MAID! YOU'LL ALSO BE PROVIDED WITH A MASSEUSE AND A HAIRDRESSER.
ZOWEE! I'M BREATHLESS!
OH, RONNIE! HOW CAN I EVER REPAY YOU?
DON'T WORRY! I'LL TRY TO THINK OF A WAY!
SEVERAL DAYS LATER...
IT'LL ALSO HELP IF YOU START ACTING LIKE SAMANTHA IN YOUR EVERYDAY LIFE!
I'VE ALREADY THOUGHT OF THAT!
BETTY! VERONICA! WHERE HAVE YOU TWO BEEN LATELY?
OH, ARCHIE DEAREST-- WOULD YOU BE SO KIND AS TO FETCH OUR SCHOOL BAGS AND CARRY THEM TO CLASS?
UH...SURE.
3
HOW'M I DOIN'?
PERFECT!

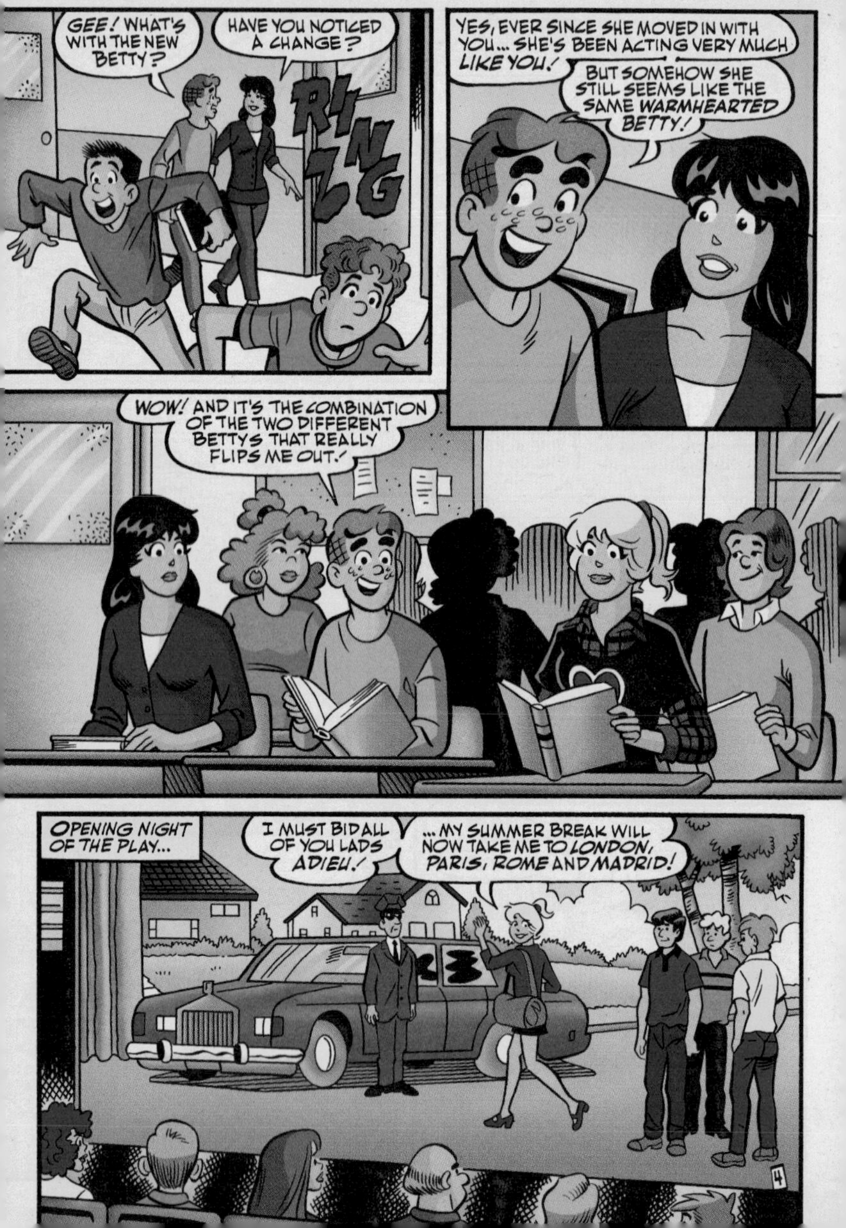
GEE! WHAT'S WITH THE NEW BETTY?
HAVE YOU NOTICED A CHANGE?
RING
YES, EVER SINCE SHE MOVED IN WITH YOU... SHE'S BEEN ACTING VERY MUCH LIKE YOU!
BUT SOMEHOW SHE STILL SEEMS LIKE THE SAME WARMHEARTED BETTY!
WOW! AND IT'S THE COMBINATION OF THE TWO DIFFERENT BETTYS THAT REALLY FLIPS ME OUT!
OPENING NIGHT OF THE PLAY...
I MUST BID ALL OF YOU LADS ADIEU!
...MY SUMMER BREAK WILL NOW TAKE ME TO LONDON, PARIS, ROME AND MADRID!
4

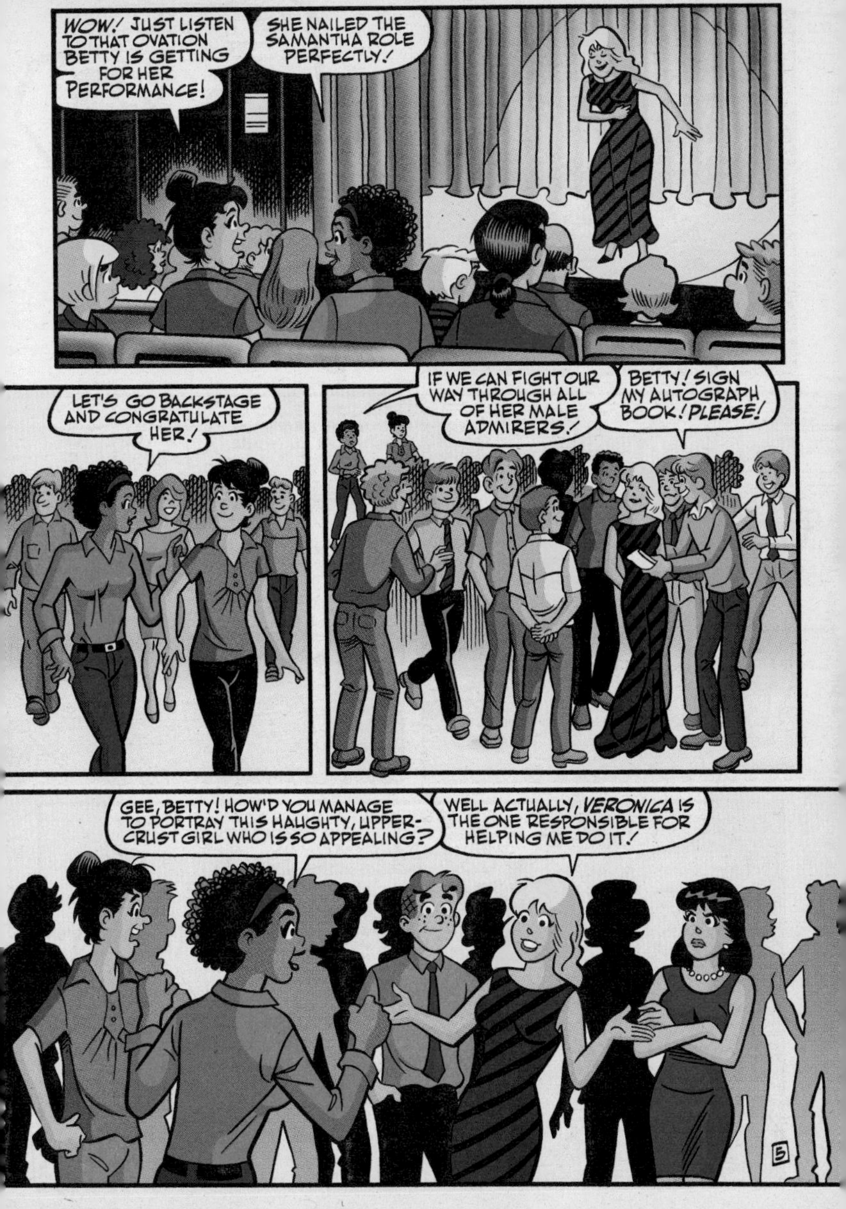
WOW! JUST LISTEN TO THAT OVATION BETTY IS GETTING FOR HER PERFORMANCE!
SHE NAILED THE SAMANTHA ROLE PERFECTLY!
LET'S GO BACKSTAGE AND CONGRATULATE HER!
IF WE CAN FIGHT OUR WAY THROUGH ALL OF HER MALE ADMIRERS!
BETTY! SIGN MY AUTOGRAPH BOOK! PLEASE!
GEE, BETTY! HOW'D YOU MANAGE TO PORTRAY THIS HAUGHTY, UPPER-CRUST GIRL WHO IS SO APPEALING?
WELL ACTUALLY, VERONICA IS THE ONE RESPONSIBLE FOR HELPING ME DO IT!
5

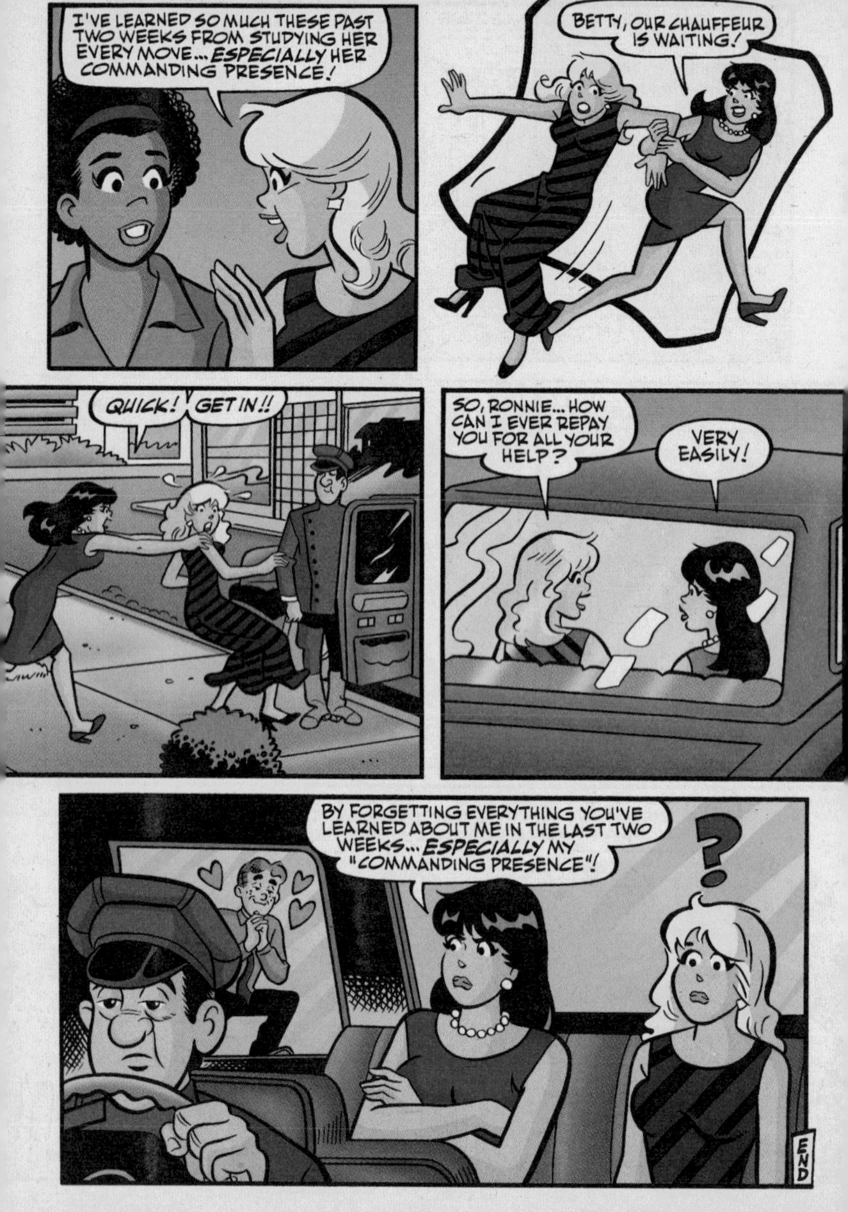

I'VE LEARNED SO MUCH THESE PAST TWO WEEKS FROM STUDYING HER EVERY MOVE... *ESPECIALLY* HER COMMANDING PRESENCE!
BETTY, OUR CHAUFFEUR IS WAITING!
QUICK!
GET IN!!
SO, RONNIE... HOW CAN I EVER REPAY YOU FOR ALL YOUR HELP?
VERY EASILY!
BY FORGETTING EVERYTHING YOU'VE LEARNED ABOUT ME IN THE LAST TWO WEEKS... *ESPECIALLY* MY "COMMANDING PRESENCE"!
?
END

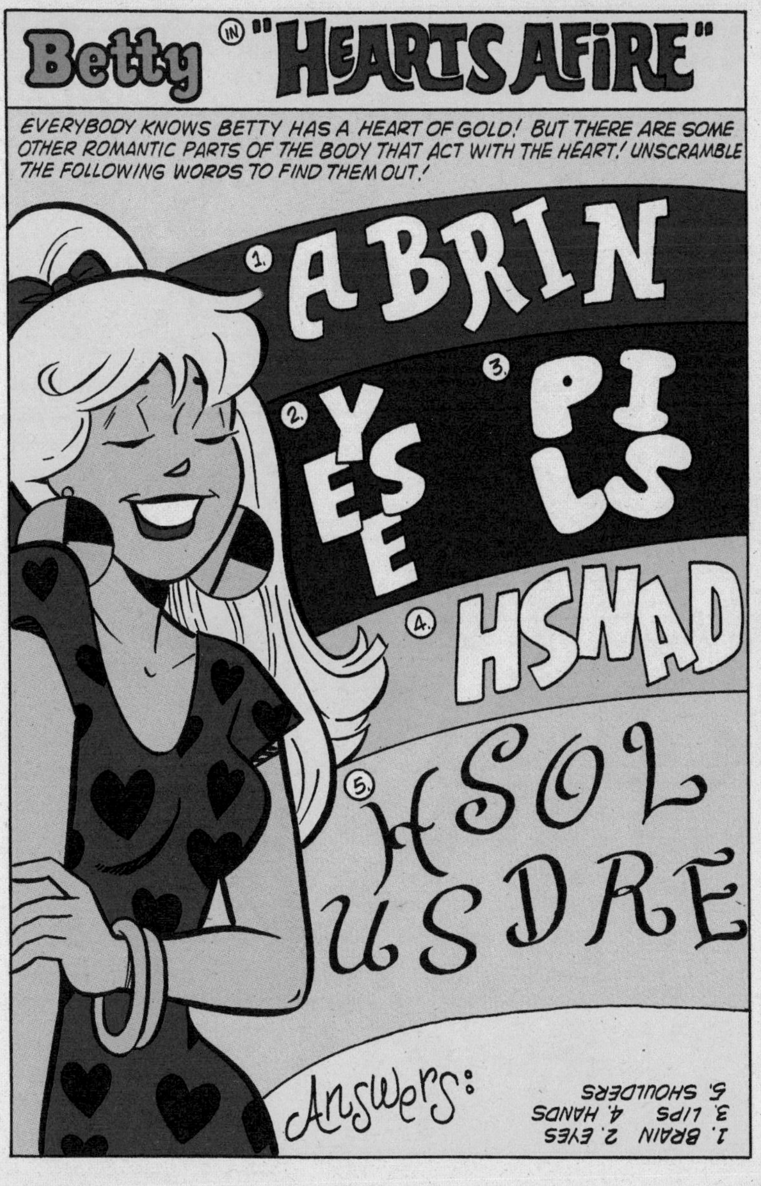

Betty IN "HEARTS AFIRE"
EVERYBODY KNOWS BETTY HAS A HEART OF GOLD! BUT THERE ARE SOME OTHER ROMANTIC PARTS OF THE BODY THAT ACT WITH THE HEART! UNSCRAMBLE THE FOLLOWING WORDS TO FIND THEM OUT!
1. ABRIN
2. YESE
3. PILS
4. HSNAD
5. HSOL USDRE
Answers:
1. BRAIN 2. EYES
3. LIPS 4. HANDS
5. SHOULDERS

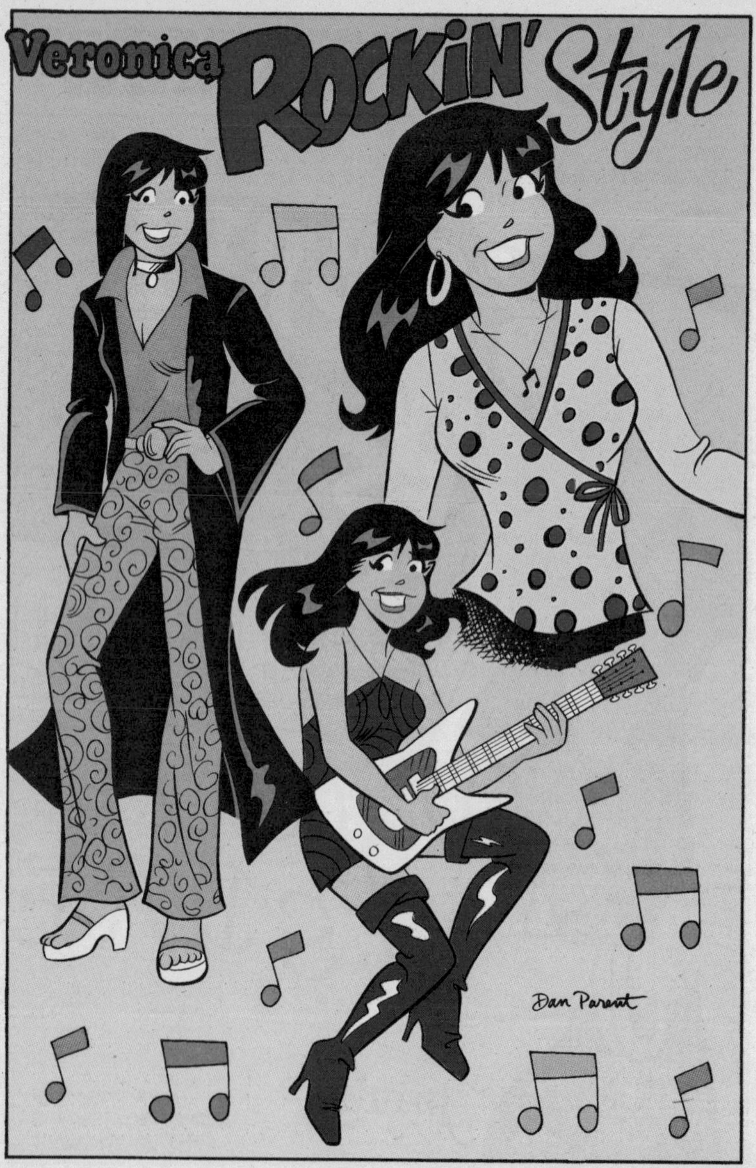
Veronica
ROCKIN' Style
Dan Parent

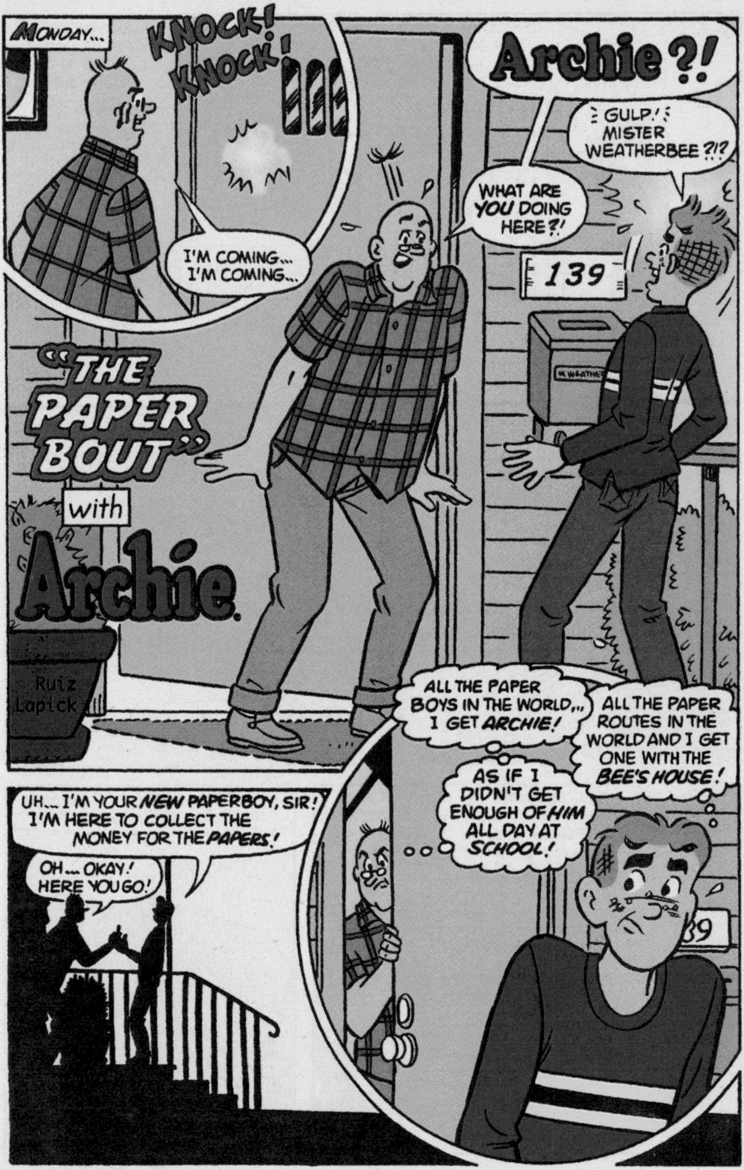
MONDAY...
KNOCK! KNOCK!
I'M COMING... I'M COMING...
"THE PAPER BOUT"
with
Archie
Ruiz
Lapick
Archie?!
WHAT ARE YOU DOING HERE?!
GULP! MISTER WEATHERBEE?!?
139
UH... I'M YOUR NEW PAPERBOY, SIR! I'M HERE TO COLLECT THE MONEY FOR THE PAPERS!
OH... OKAY! HERE YOU GO!
ALL THE PAPER BOYS IN THE WORLD,.. I GET ARCHIE!
AS IF I DIDN'T GET ENOUGH OF HIM ALL DAY AT SCHOOL!
ALL THE PAPER ROUTES IN THE WORLD AND I GET ONE WITH THE BEE'S HOUSE!

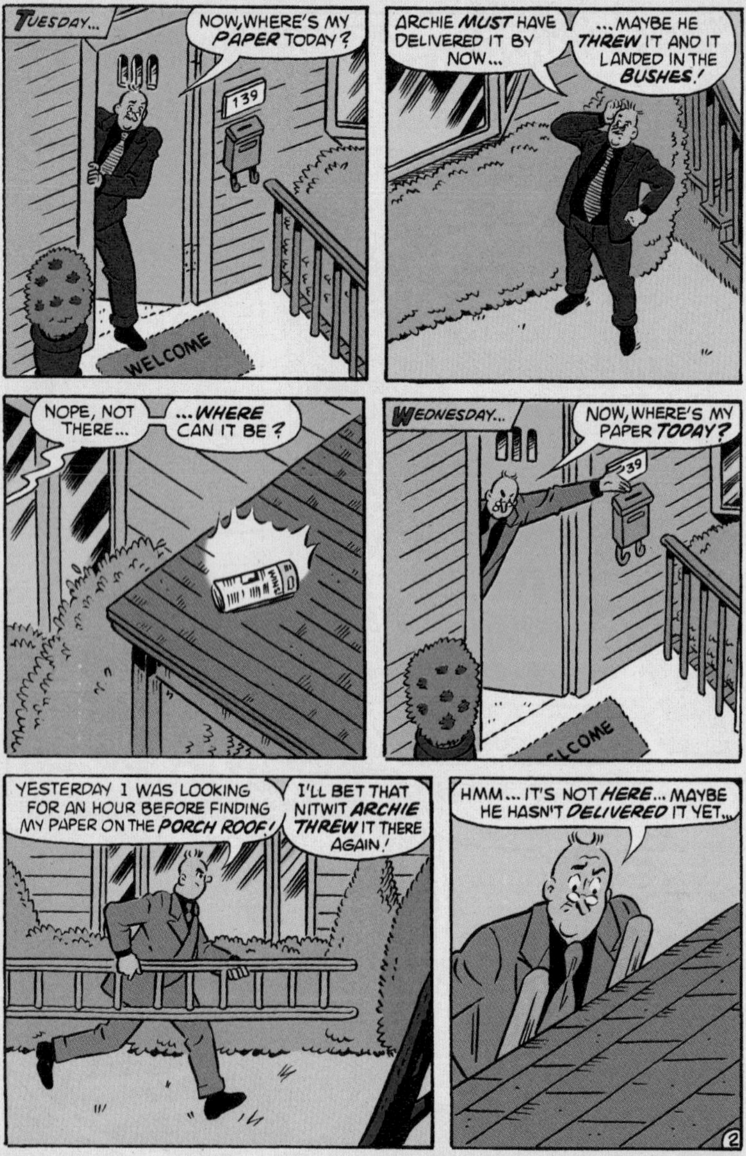
TUESDAY...
NOW, WHERE'S MY PAPER TODAY?
139
WELCOME
ARCHIE MUST HAVE DELIVERED IT BY NOW...
...MAYBE HE THREW IT AND IT LANDED IN THE BUSHES!
NOPE, NOT THERE...
...WHERE CAN IT BE?
WEDNESDAY...
NOW, WHERE'S MY PAPER TODAY?
39
LCOME
YESTERDAY I WAS LOOKING FOR AN HOUR BEFORE FINDING MY PAPER ON THE PORCH ROOF!
I'LL BET THAT NITWIT ARCHIE THREW IT THERE AGAIN!
HMM... IT'S NOT HERE... MAYBE HE HASN'T DELIVERED IT YET...
2

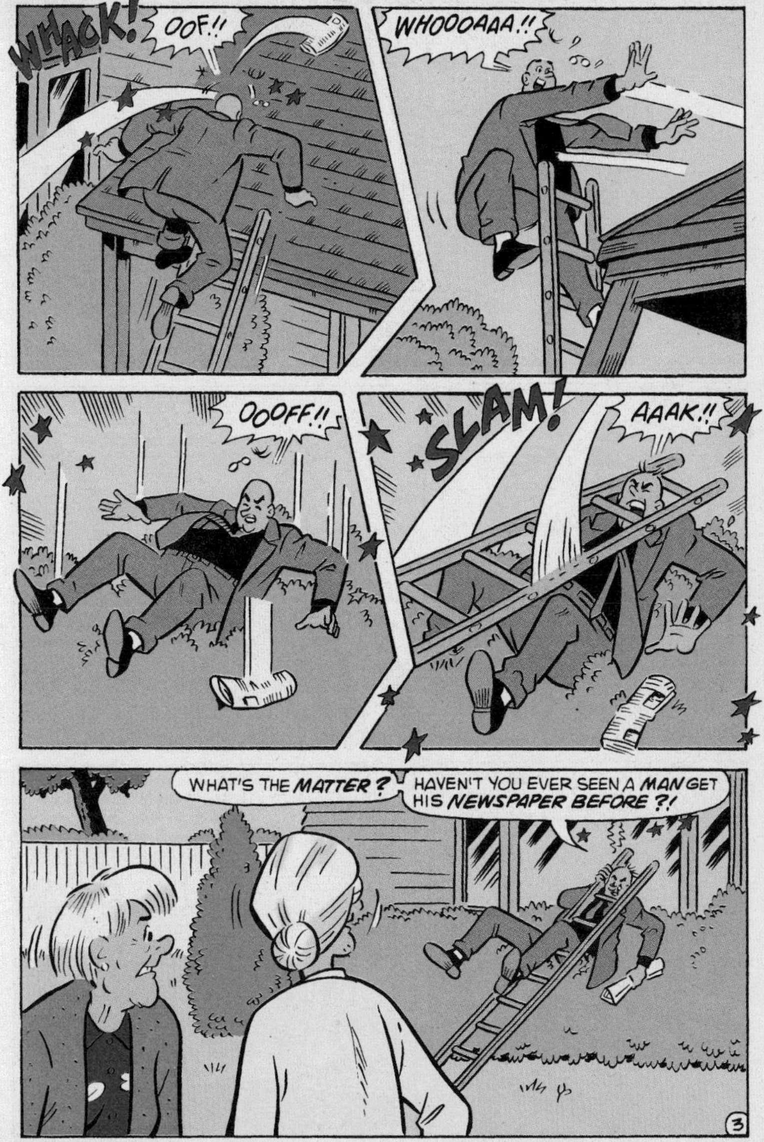
WHACK!
OOF!!
WHOOOAAA!!
OOOFF!!
SLAM!
AAAK!!
WHAT'S THE MATTER?
HAVEN'T YOU EVER SEEN A MAN GET HIS NEWSPAPER BEFORE?!
3

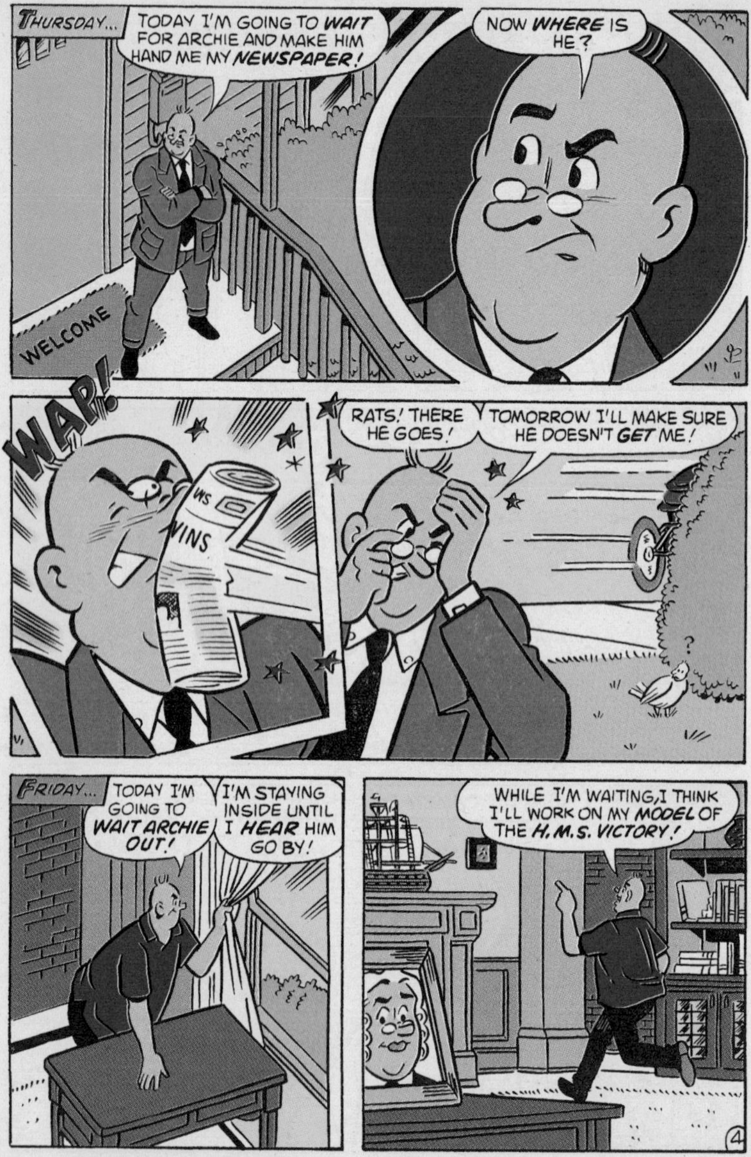
THURSDAY...
TODAY I'M GOING TO WAIT FOR ARCHIE AND MAKE HIM HAND ME MY NEWSPAPER!
WELCOME
NOW WHERE IS HE?
WAP!
RATS! THERE HE GOES!
TOMORROW I'LL MAKE SURE HE DOESN'T GET ME!
?
FRIDAY...
TODAY I'M GOING TO WAIT ARCHIE OUT!
I'M STAYING INSIDE UNTIL I HEAR HIM GO BY!
WHILE I'M WAITING, I THINK I'LL WORK ON MY MODEL OF THE H.M.S. VICTORY!
4

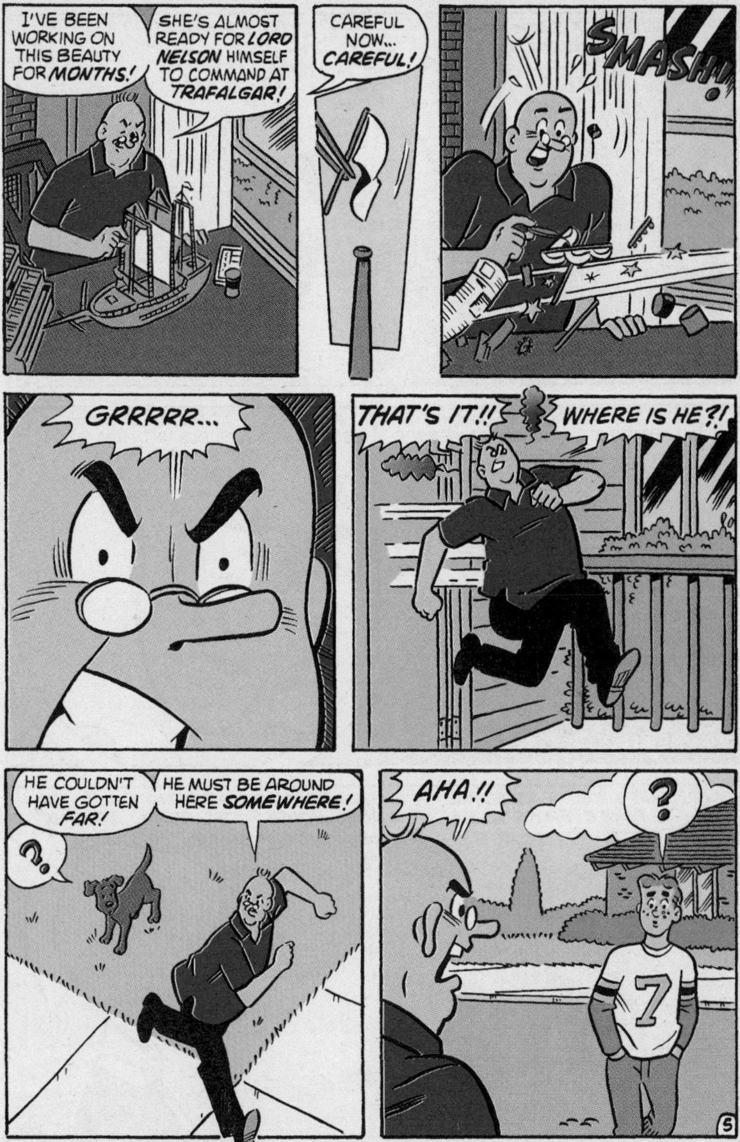
I'VE BEEN WORKING ON THIS BEAUTY FOR MONTHS!
SHE'S ALMOST READY FOR LORD NELSON HIMSELF TO COMMAND AT TRAFALGAR!
CAREFUL NOW... CAREFUL!
SMASH!!
GRRRRR...
THAT'S IT!!
WHERE IS HE?!
HE COULDN'T HAVE GOTTEN FAR!
HE MUST BE AROUND HERE SOMEWHERE!
?
AHA!!
?
7
5

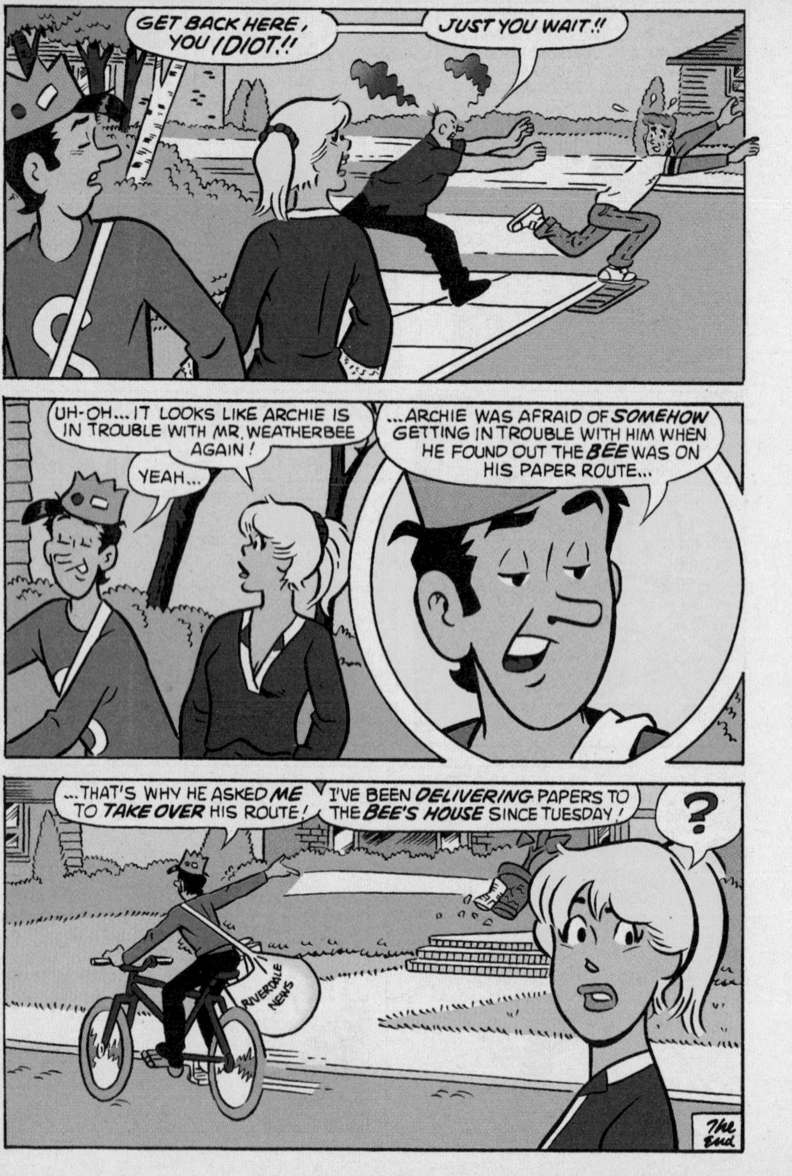
GET BACK HERE, YOU IDIOT!!
JUST YOU WAIT!!
UH-OH... IT LOOKS LIKE ARCHIE IS IN TROUBLE WITH MR. WEATHERBEE AGAIN!
YEAH...
...ARCHIE WAS AFRAID OF SOMEHOW GETTING IN TROUBLE WITH HIM WHEN HE FOUND OUT THE BEE WAS ON HIS PAPER ROUTE...
...THAT'S WHY HE ASKED ME TO TAKE OVER HIS ROUTE!
I'VE BEEN DELIVERING PAPERS TO THE BEE'S HOUSE SINCE TUESDAY!
?
RIVERDALE NEWS
The End

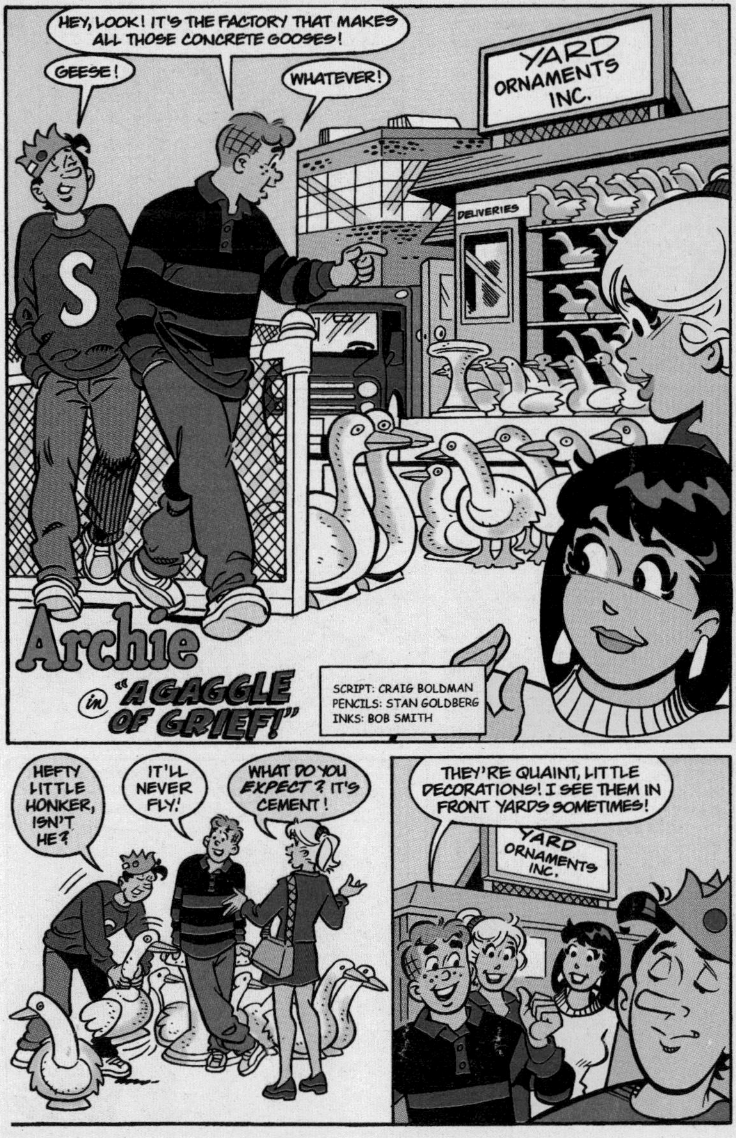
HEY, LOOK! IT'S THE FACTORY THAT MAKES ALL THOSE CONCRETE GOOSES!
GEESE!
WHATEVER!
YARD ORNAMENTS INC.
DELIVERIES
Archie
in "A GAGGLE OF GRIEF!"
SCRIPT: CRAIG BOLDMAN
PENCILS: STAN GOLDBERG
INKS: BOB SMITH
HEFTY LITTLE HONKER, ISN'T HE?
IT'LL NEVER FLY!
WHAT DO YOU EXPECT? IT'S CEMENT!
THEY'RE QUAINT, LITTLE DECORATIONS! I SEE THEM IN FRONT YARDS SOMETIMES!
YARD ORNAMENTS INC.

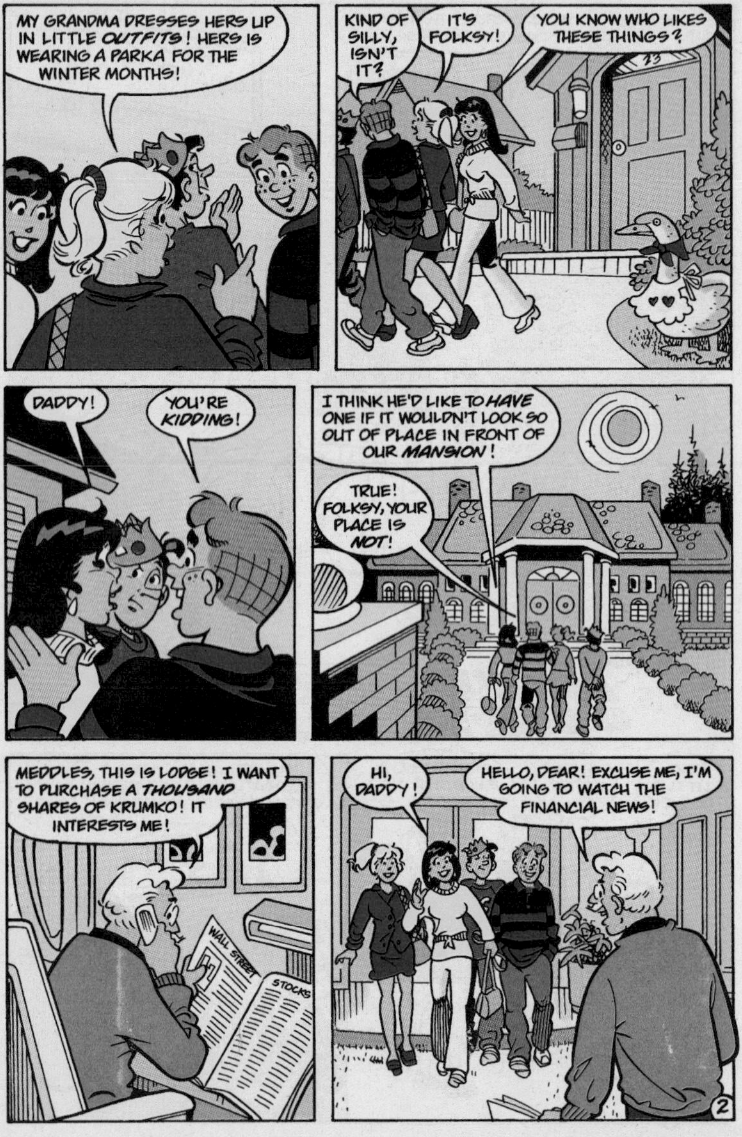
MY GRANDMA DRESSES HERS UP IN LITTLE OUTFITS! HERS IS WEARING A PARKA FOR THE WINTER MONTHS!
KIND OF SILLY, ISN'T IT?
IT'S FOLKSY!
YOU KNOW WHO LIKES THESE THINGS?
DADDY!
YOU'RE KIDDING!
I THINK HE'D LIKE TO HAVE ONE IF IT WOULDN'T LOOK SO OUT OF PLACE IN FRONT OF OUR MANSION!
TRUE! FOLKSY, YOUR PLACE IS NOT!
MEDDLES, THIS IS LODGE! I WANT TO PURCHASE A THOUSAND SHARES OF KRUMKO! IT INTERESTS ME!
WALL STREET
STOCKS
HI, DADDY!
HELLO, DEAR! EXCUSE ME, I'M GOING TO WATCH THE FINANCIAL NEWS!
2

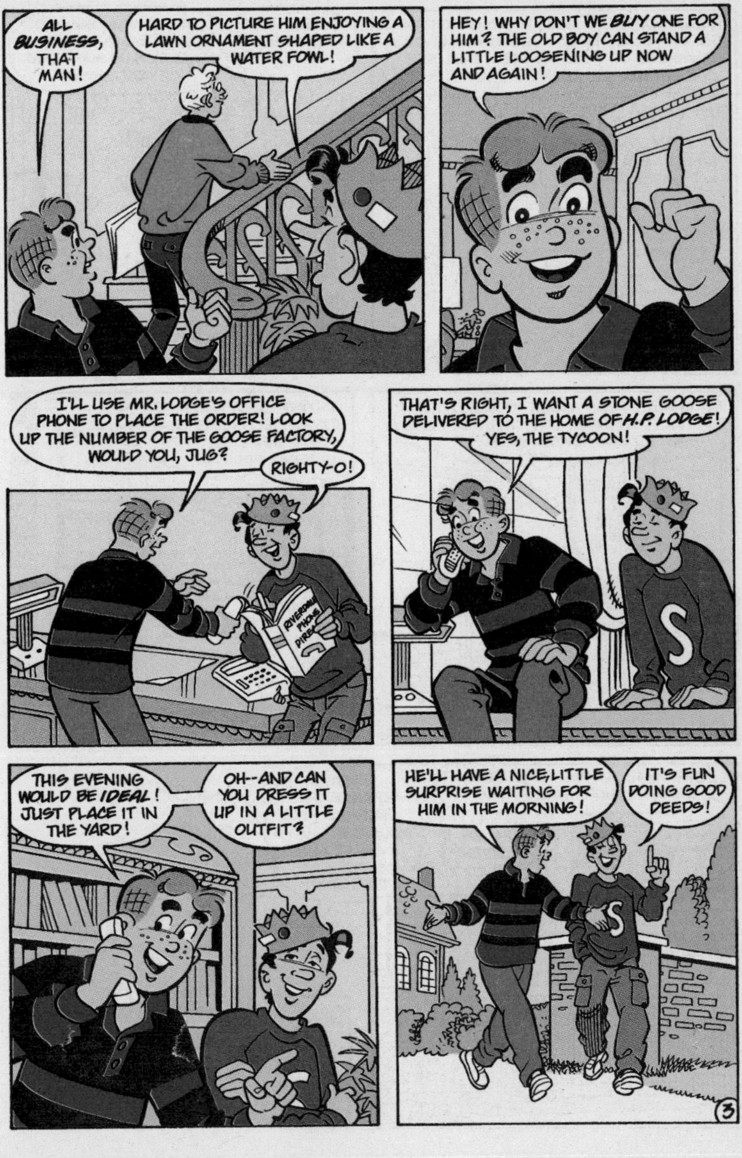
ALL BUSINESS, THAT MAN!
HARD TO PICTURE HIM ENJOYING A LAWN ORNAMENT SHAPED LIKE A WATER FOWL!
HEY! WHY DON'T WE BUY ONE FOR HIM? THE OLD BOY CAN STAND A LITTLE LOOSENING UP NOW AND AGAIN!
I'LL USE MR. LODGE'S OFFICE PHONE TO PLACE THE ORDER! LOOK UP THE NUMBER OF THE GOOSE FACTORY, WOULD YOU, JUG?
RIGHTY-O!
THAT'S RIGHT, I WANT A STONE GOOSE DELIVERED TO THE HOME OF H.P. LODGE! YES, THE TYCOON!
THIS EVENING WOULD BE IDEAL! JUST PLACE IT IN THE YARD!
OH--AND CAN YOU DRESS IT UP IN A LITTLE OUTFIT?
HE'LL HAVE A NICE, LITTLE SURPRISE WAITING FOR HIM IN THE MORNING!
IT'S FUN DOING GOOD DEEDS!
3

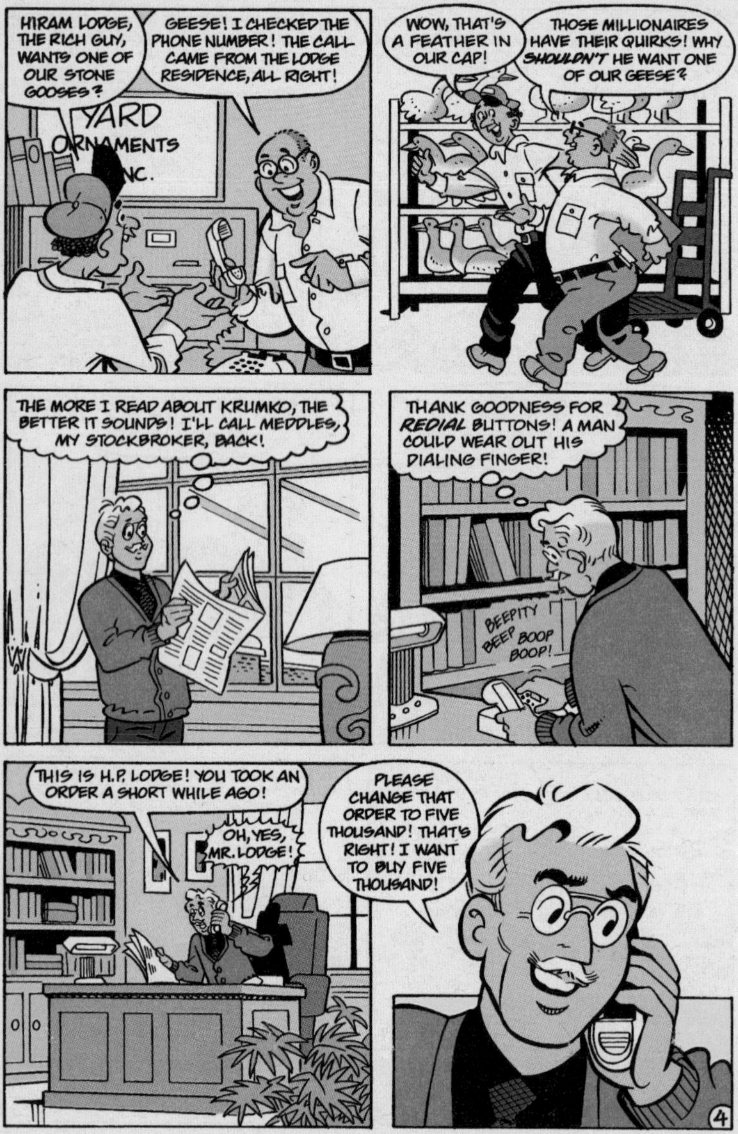
HIRAM LODGE, THE RICH GUY, WANTS ONE OF OUR STONE GOOSES?
GEESE! I CHECKED THE PHONE NUMBER! THE CALL CAME FROM THE LODGE RESIDENCE, ALL RIGHT!
YARD ORNAMENTS INC.
WOW, THAT'S A FEATHER IN OUR CAP!
THOSE MILLIONAIRES HAVE THEIR QUIRKS! WHY SHOULDN'T HE WANT ONE OF OUR GEESE?
THE MORE I READ ABOUT KRUMKO, THE BETTER IT SOUNDS! I'LL CALL MEDDLES, MY STOCKBROKER, BACK!
THANK GOODNESS FOR REDIAL BUTTONS! A MAN COULD WEAR OUT HIS DIALING FINGER!
BEEPITY BEEP BOOP BOOP!
THIS IS H.P. LODGE! YOU TOOK AN ORDER A SHORT WHILE AGO!
OH, YES, MR. LODGE!
PLEASE CHANGE THAT ORDER TO FIVE THOUSAND! THAT'S RIGHT! I WANT TO BUY FIVE THOUSAND!
4

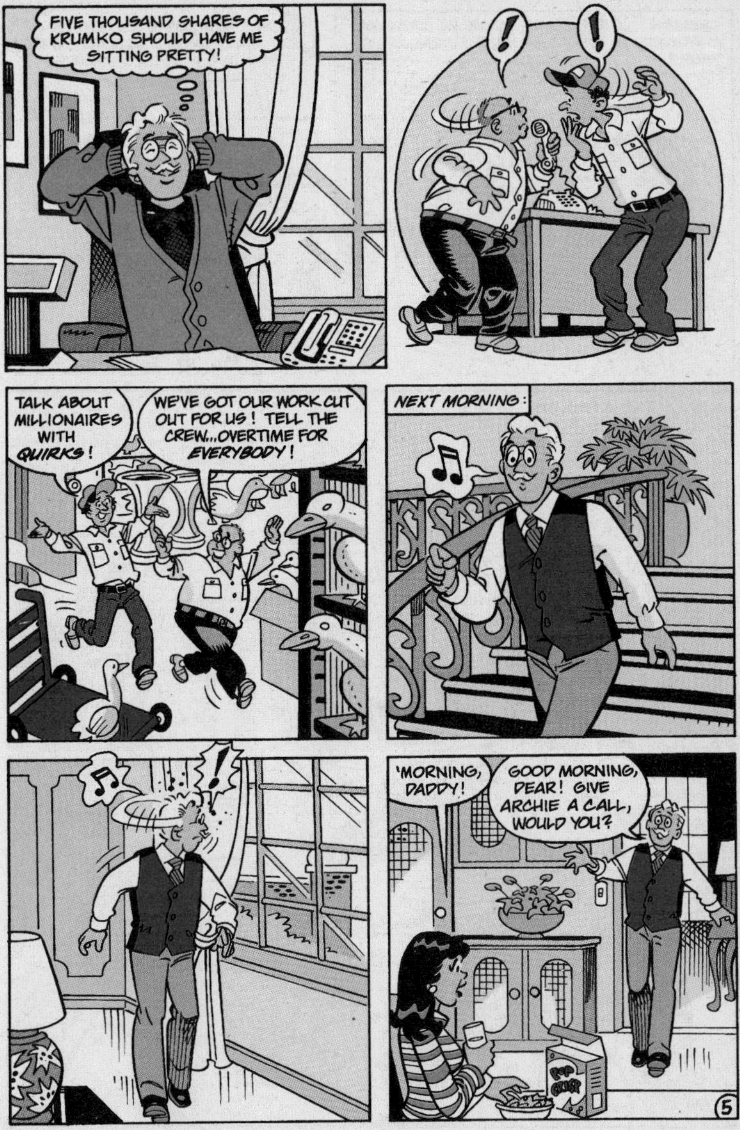
FIVE THOUSAND SHARES OF KRUMKO SHOULD HAVE ME SITTING PRETTY!
!
!
TALK ABOUT MILLIONAIRES WITH QUIRKS!
WE'VE GOT OUR WORK CUT OUT FOR US! TELL THE CREW...OVERTIME FOR EVERYBODY!
NEXT MORNING:
!
'MORNING, DADDY!
GOOD MORNING, DEAR! GIVE ARCHIE A CALL, WOULD YOU?
POP CRISP
5

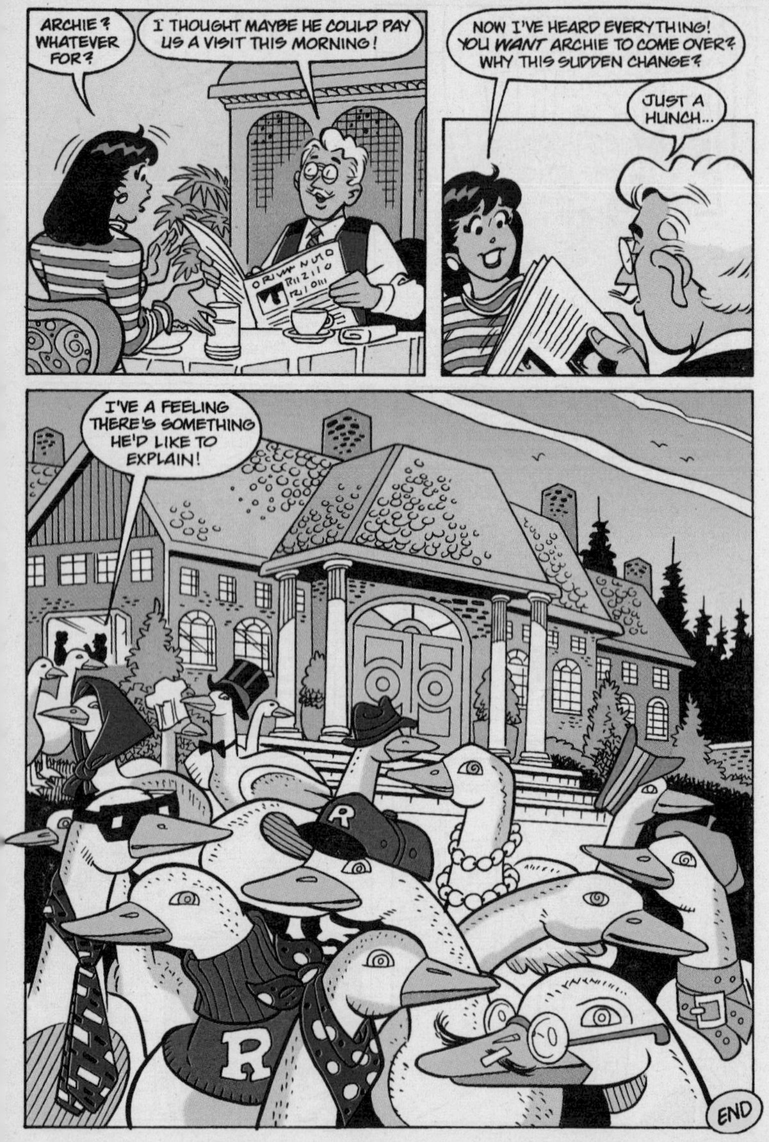
ARCHIE? WHATEVER FOR?
I THOUGHT MAYBE HE COULD PAY US A VISIT THIS MORNING!
NOW I'VE HEARD EVERYTHING! YOU WANT ARCHIE TO COME OVER? WHY THIS SUDDEN CHANGE?
JUST A HUNCH...
I'VE A FEELING THERE'S SOMETHING HE'D LIKE TO EXPLAIN!
END

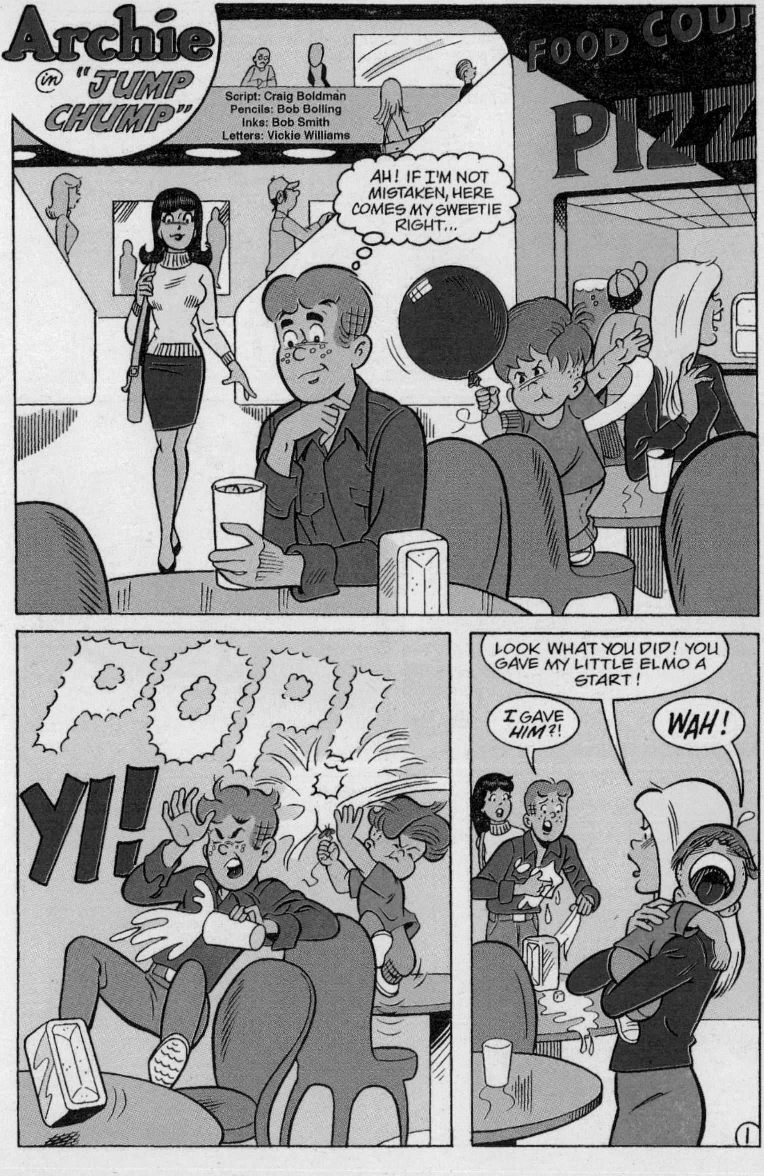
Archie
in "JUMP CHUMP"
Script: Craig Boldman
Pencils: Bob Bolling
Inks: Bob Smith
Letters: Vickie Williams
FOOD COU
PIZZ
AH! IF I'M NOT MISTAKEN, HERE COMES MY SWEETIE RIGHT...
POP!
YI!
LOOK WHAT YOU DID! YOU GAVE MY LITTLE ELMO A START!
I GAVE HIM?!
WAH!
1

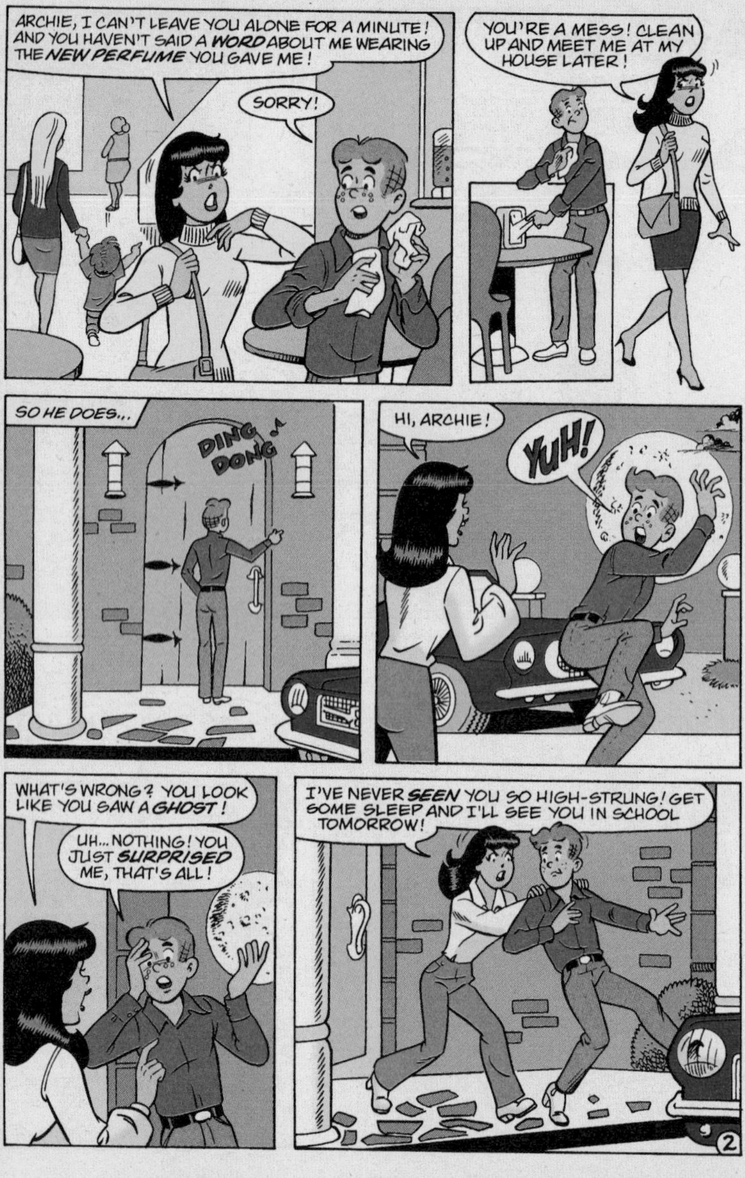
ARCHIE, I CAN'T LEAVE YOU ALONE FOR A MINUTE! AND YOU HAVEN'T SAID A WORD ABOUT ME WEARING THE NEW PERFUME YOU GAVE ME!
SORRY!
YOU'RE A MESS! CLEAN UP AND MEET ME AT MY HOUSE LATER!
SO HE DOES...
DING DONG
HI, ARCHIE!
YUH!
WHAT'S WRONG? YOU LOOK LIKE YOU SAW A GHOST!
UH...NOTHING! YOU JUST SURPRISED ME, THAT'S ALL!
I'VE NEVER SEEN YOU SO HIGH-STRUNG! GET SOME SLEEP AND I'LL SEE YOU IN SCHOOL TOMORROW!
2

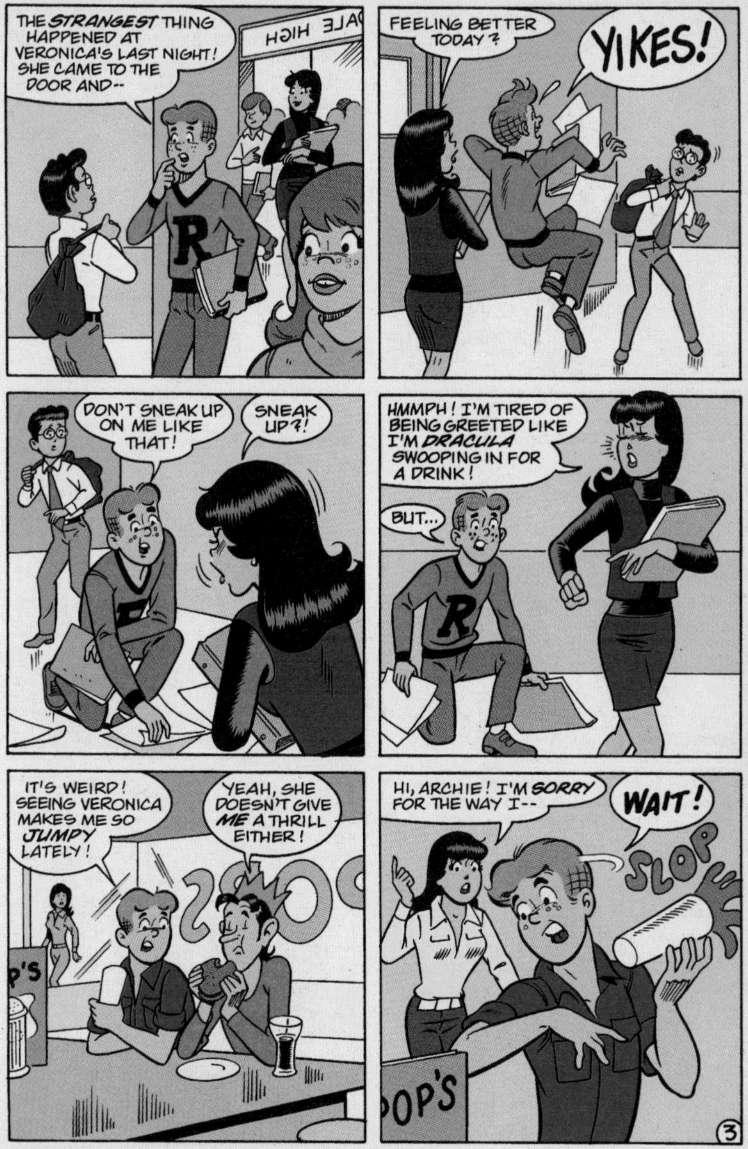
THE STRANGEST THING HAPPENED AT VERONICA'S LAST NIGHT! SHE CAME TO THE DOOR AND--
FEELING BETTER TODAY?
YIKES!
DON'T SNEAK UP ON ME LIKE THAT!
SNEAK UP?!
HMMPH! I'M TIRED OF BEING GREETED LIKE I'M DRACULA SWOOPING IN FOR A DRINK!
BUT...
IT'S WEIRD! SEEING VERONICA MAKES ME SO JUMPY LATELY!
YEAH, SHE DOESN'T GIVE ME A THRILL EITHER!
POP'S
HI, ARCHIE! I'M SORRY FOR THE WAY I--
WAIT!
SLOP
POP'S
3

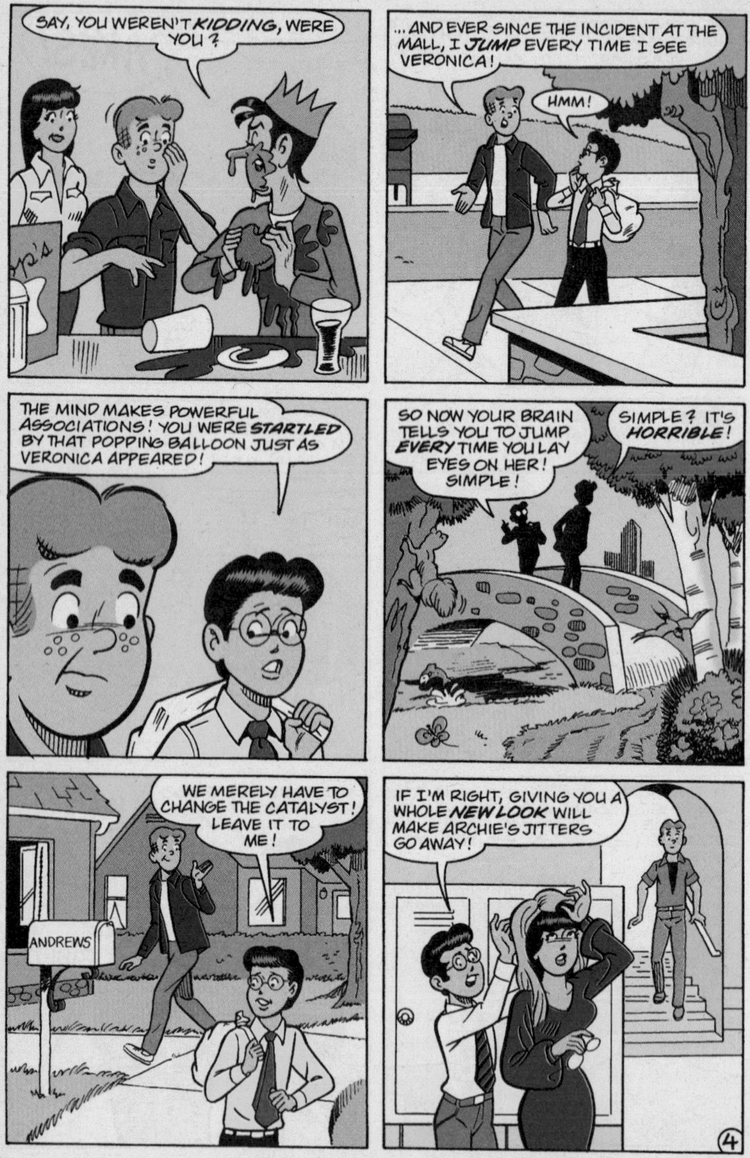
SAY, YOU WEREN'T KIDDING, WERE YOU ?
...AND EVER SINCE THE INCIDENT AT THE MALL, I JUMP EVERY TIME I SEE VERONICA !
HMM !
THE MIND MAKES POWERFUL ASSOCIATIONS ! YOU WERE STARTLED BY THAT POPPING BALLOON JUST AS VERONICA APPEARED !
SO NOW YOUR BRAIN TELLS YOU TO JUMP EVERY TIME YOU LAY EYES ON HER ! SIMPLE !
SIMPLE ? IT'S HORRIBLE !
WE MERELY HAVE TO CHANGE THE CATALYST ! LEAVE IT TO ME !
ANDREWS
IF I'M RIGHT, GIVING YOU A WHOLE NEW LOOK WILL MAKE ARCHIE'S JITTERS GO AWAY !
4

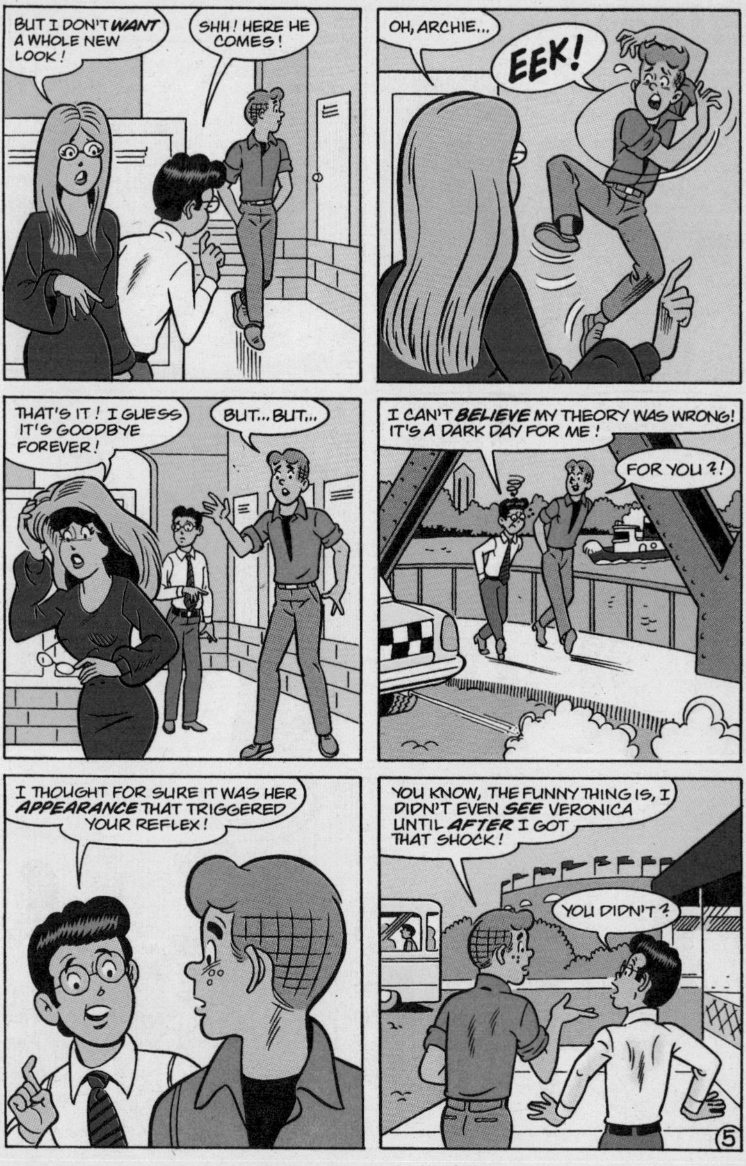
BUT I DON'T WANT A WHOLE NEW LOOK!
SHH! HERE HE COMES!
OH, ARCHIE...
EEK!
THAT'S IT! I GUESS IT'S GOODBYE FOREVER!
BUT... BUT...
I CAN'T BELIEVE MY THEORY WAS WRONG! IT'S A DARK DAY FOR ME!
FOR YOU?!
I THOUGHT FOR SURE IT WAS HER APPEARANCE THAT TRIGGERED YOUR REFLEX!
YOU KNOW, THE FUNNY THING IS, I DIDN'T EVEN SEE VERONICA UNTIL AFTER I GOT THAT SHOCK!
YOU DIDN'T?
5

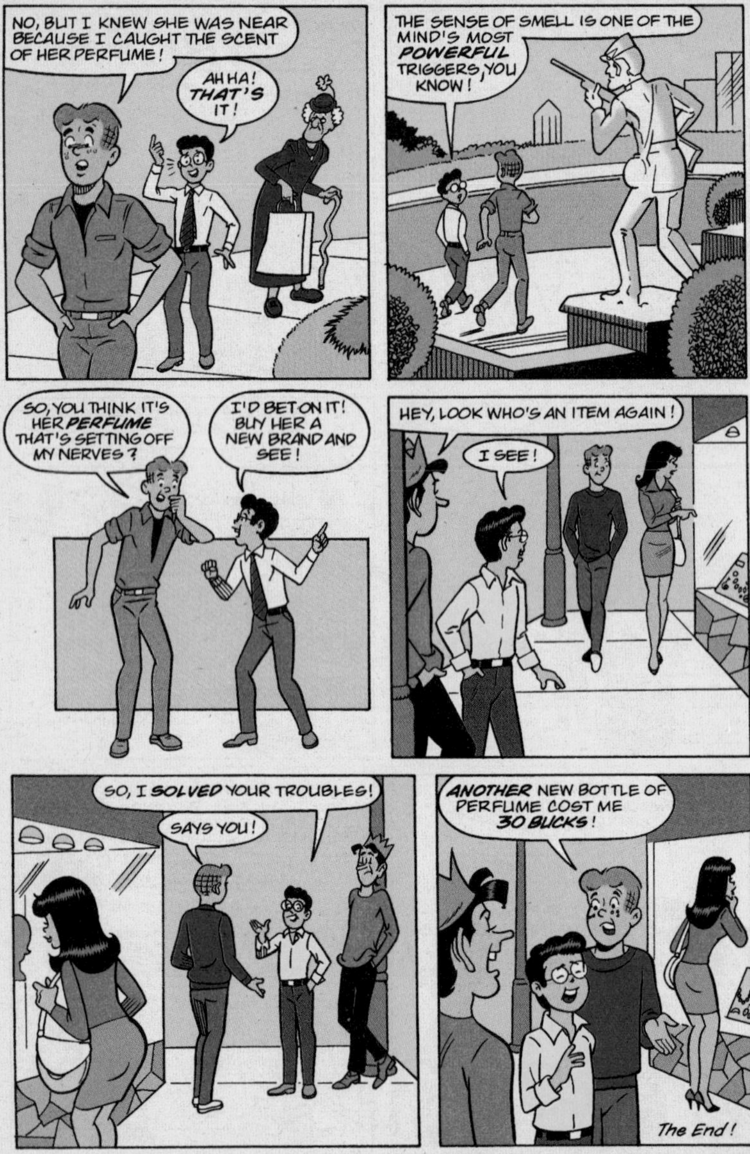
NO, BUT I KNEW SHE WAS NEAR BECAUSE I CAUGHT THE SCENT OF HER PERFUME!
AH HA! THAT'S IT!
THE SENSE OF SMELL IS ONE OF THE MIND'S MOST POWERFUL TRIGGERS, YOU KNOW!
SO, YOU THINK IT'S HER PERFUME THAT'S SETTING OFF MY NERVES?
I'D BET ON IT! BUY HER A NEW BRAND AND SEE!
HEY, LOOK WHO'S AN ITEM AGAIN!
I SEE!
SO, I SOLVED YOUR TROUBLES!
SAYS YOU!
ANOTHER NEW BOTTLE OF PERFUME COST ME 30 BUCKS!
The End!

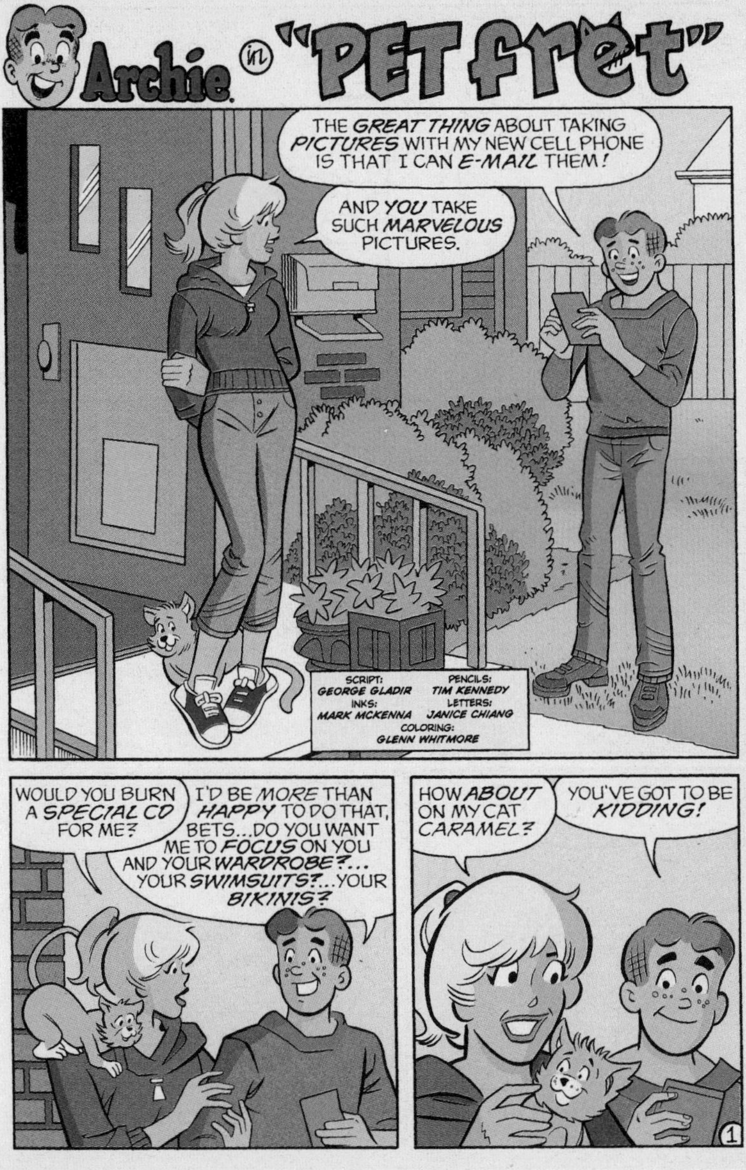
Archie in "PET fret"
THE GREAT THING ABOUT TAKING PICTURES WITH MY NEW CELL PHONE IS THAT I CAN E-MAIL THEM!
AND YOU TAKE SUCH MARVELOUS PICTURES.
SCRIPT: GEORGE GLADIR PENCILS: TIM KENNEDY INKS: MARK MCKENNA LETTERS: JANICE CHIANG COLORING: GLENN WHITMORE
WOULD YOU BURN A SPECIAL CD FOR ME?
I'D BE MORE THAN HAPPY TO DO THAT, BETS...DO YOU WANT ME TO FOCUS ON YOU AND YOUR WARDROBE?... YOUR SWIMSUITS?...YOUR BIKINIS?
HOW ABOUT ON MY CAT CARAMEL?
YOU'VE GOT TO BE KIDDING!
1

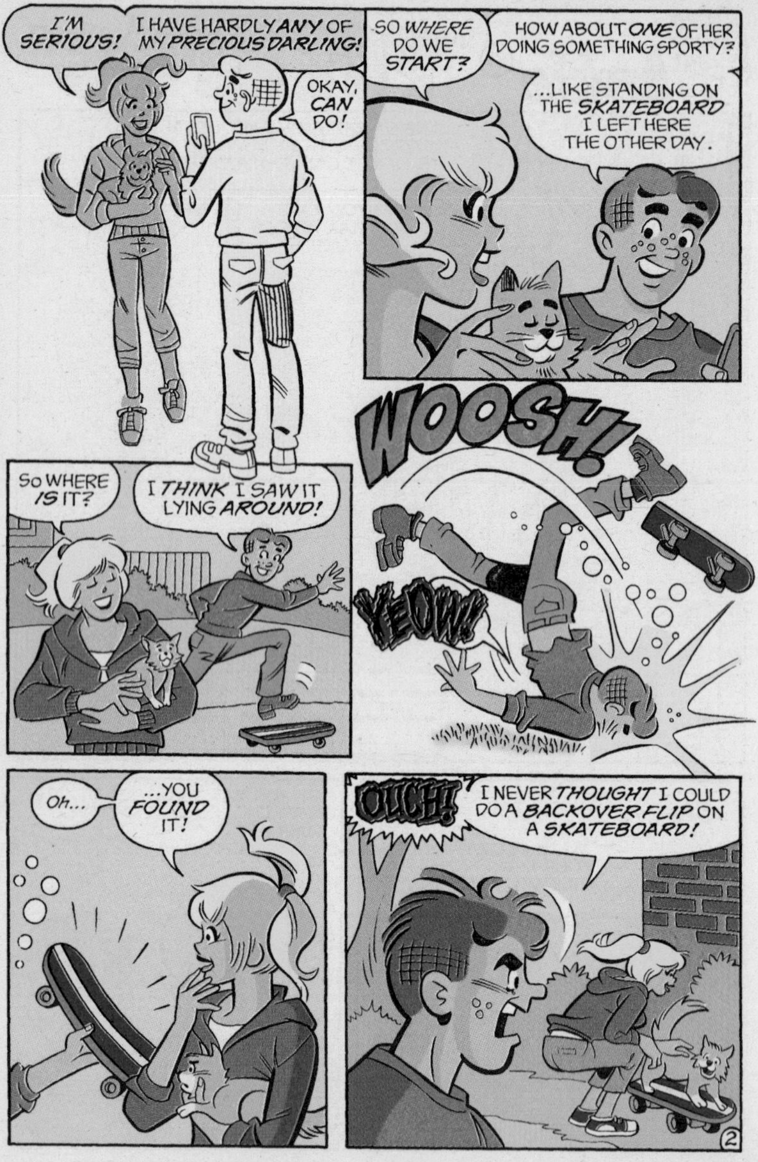
I'M SERIOUS!
I HAVE HARDLY ANY OF MY PRECIOUS DARLING!
OKAY, CAN DO!
SO WHERE DO WE START?
HOW ABOUT ONE OF HER DOING SOMETHING SPORTY?
...LIKE STANDING ON THE SKATEBOARD I LEFT HERE THE OTHER DAY.
So WHERE IS IT?
I THINK I SAW IT LYING AROUND!
WOOSH!
YEOW!
Oh...
...YOU FOUND IT!
OUCH!
I NEVER THOUGHT I COULD DO A BACKOVER FLIP ON A SKATEBOARD!
2

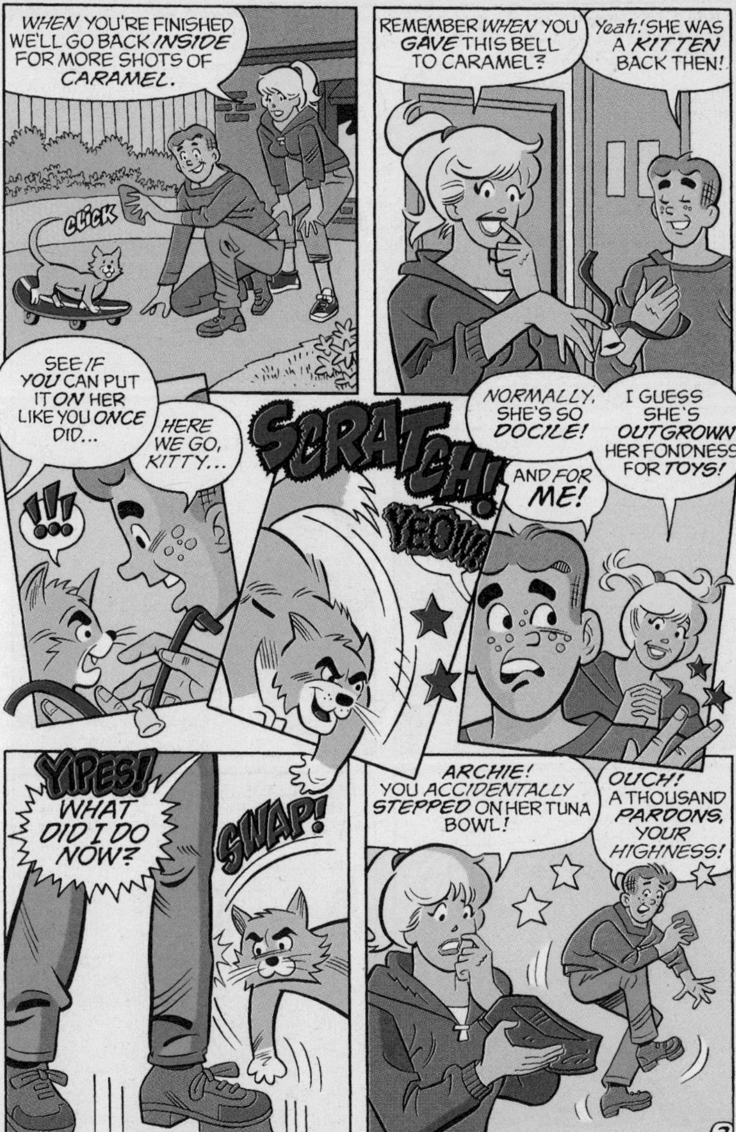
WHEN YOU'RE FINISHED WE'LL GO BACK INSIDE FOR MORE SHOTS OF CARAMEL.
CLICK
REMEMBER WHEN YOU GAVE THIS BELL TO CARAMEL?
Yeah! SHE WAS A KITTEN BACK THEN!
SEE IF YOU CAN PUT IT ON HER LIKE YOU ONCE DID...
HERE WE GO, KITTY...
!!!
SCRATCH!
YEOW!
NORMALLY, SHE'S SO DOCILE!
AND FOR ME!
I GUESS SHE'S OUTGROWN HER FONDNESS FOR TOYS!
YIPES! WHAT DID I DO NOW?
SWAP!
ARCHIE! YOU ACCIDENTALLY STEPPED ON HER TUNA BOWL!
OUCH! A THOUSAND PARDONS, YOUR HIGHNESS!
3

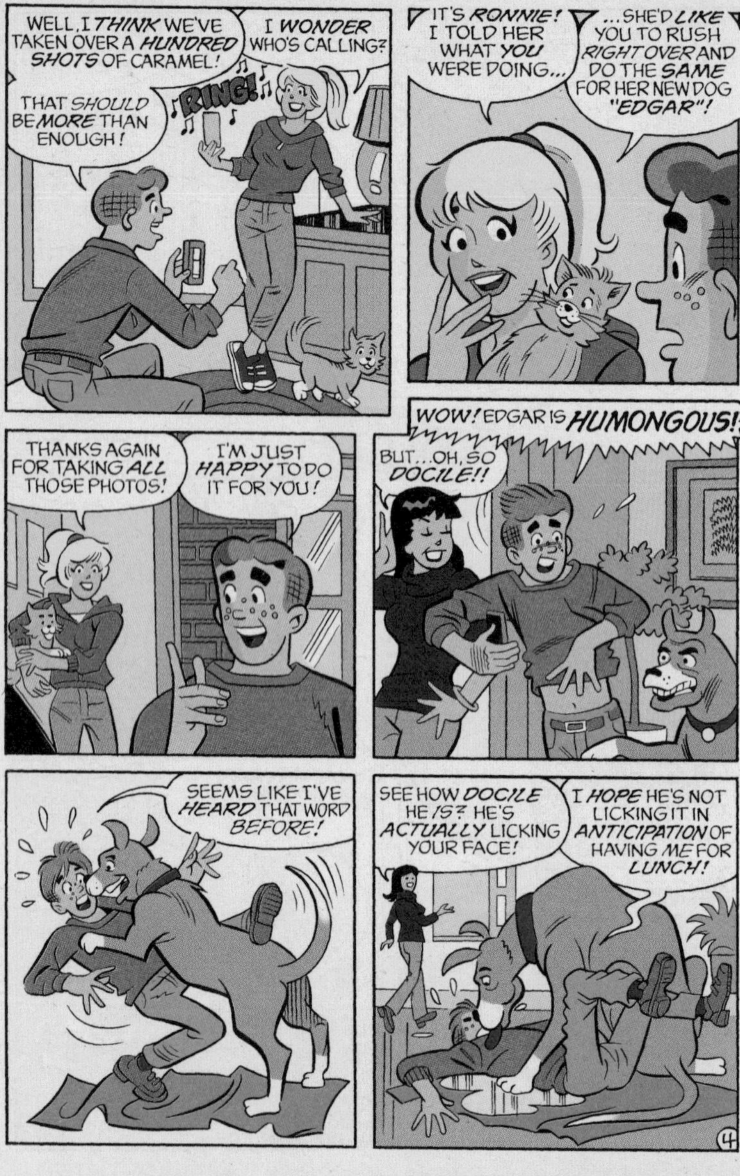
WELL, I THINK WE'VE TAKEN OVER A HUNDRED SHOTS OF CARAMEL!
THAT SHOULD BE MORE THAN ENOUGH!
I WONDER WHO'S CALLING?
RING!
IT'S RONNIE! I TOLD HER WHAT YOU WERE DOING...
...SHE'D LIKE YOU TO RUSH RIGHT OVER AND DO THE SAME FOR HER NEW DOG "EDGAR"!
THANKS AGAIN FOR TAKING ALL THOSE PHOTOS!
I'M JUST HAPPY TO DO IT FOR YOU!
WOW! EDGAR IS HUMONGOUS!
BUT...OH, SO DOCILE!!
SEEMS LIKE I'VE HEARD THAT WORD BEFORE!
SEE HOW DOCILE HE IS? HE'S ACTUALLY LICKING YOUR FACE!
I HOPE HE'S NOT LICKING IT IN ANTICIPATION OF HAVING ME FOR LUNCH!
4

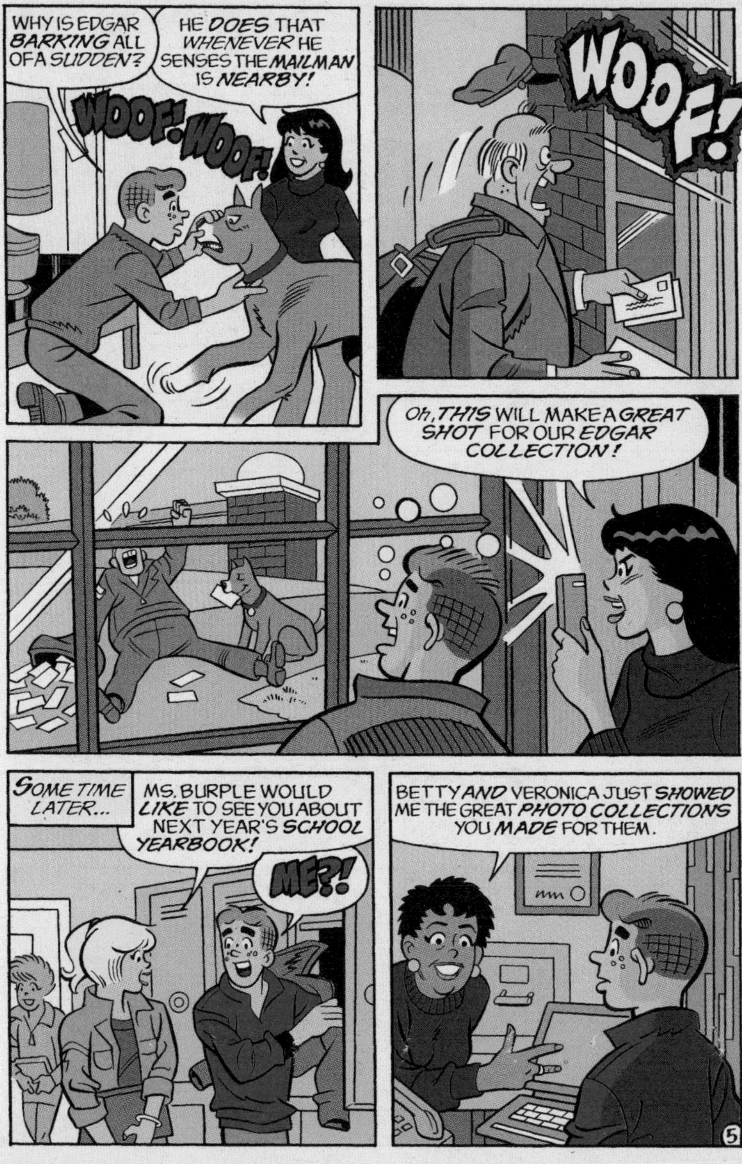

WHY IS EDGAR BARKING ALL OF A SUDDEN?
HE DOES THAT WHENEVER HE SENSES THE MAILMAN IS NEARBY!
WOOF! WOOF!
WOOF!
Oh, THIS WILL MAKE A GREAT SHOT FOR OUR EDGAR COLLECTION!
SOME TIME LATER...
MS. BURPLE WOULD LIKE TO SEE YOU ABOUT NEXT YEAR'S SCHOOL YEARBOOK!
ME?!
BETTY AND VERONICA JUST SHOWED ME THE GREAT PHOTO COLLECTIONS YOU MADE FOR THEM.

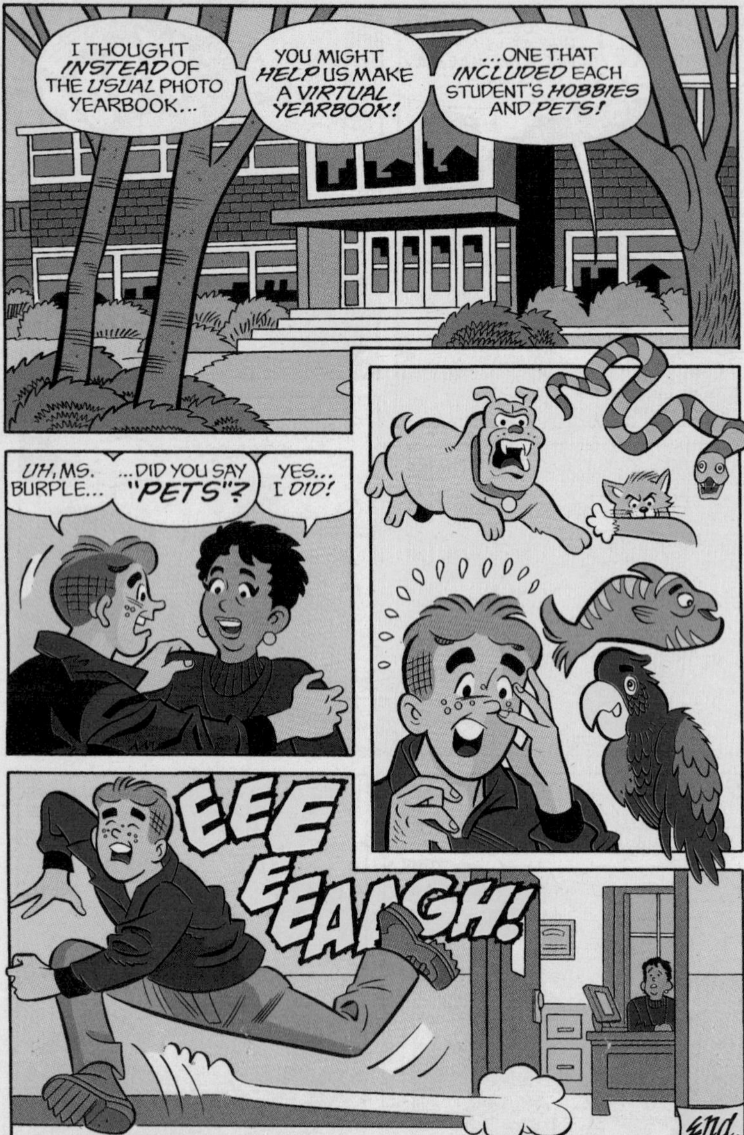
I THOUGHT INSTEAD OF THE USUAL PHOTO YEARBOOK...
YOU MIGHT HELP US MAKE A VIRTUAL YEARBOOK!
...ONE THAT INCLUDED EACH STUDENT'S HOBBIES AND PETS!
UH, MS. BURPLE...
...DID YOU SAY "PETS"?
YES... I DID!
EEEEEEAAGH!
End.

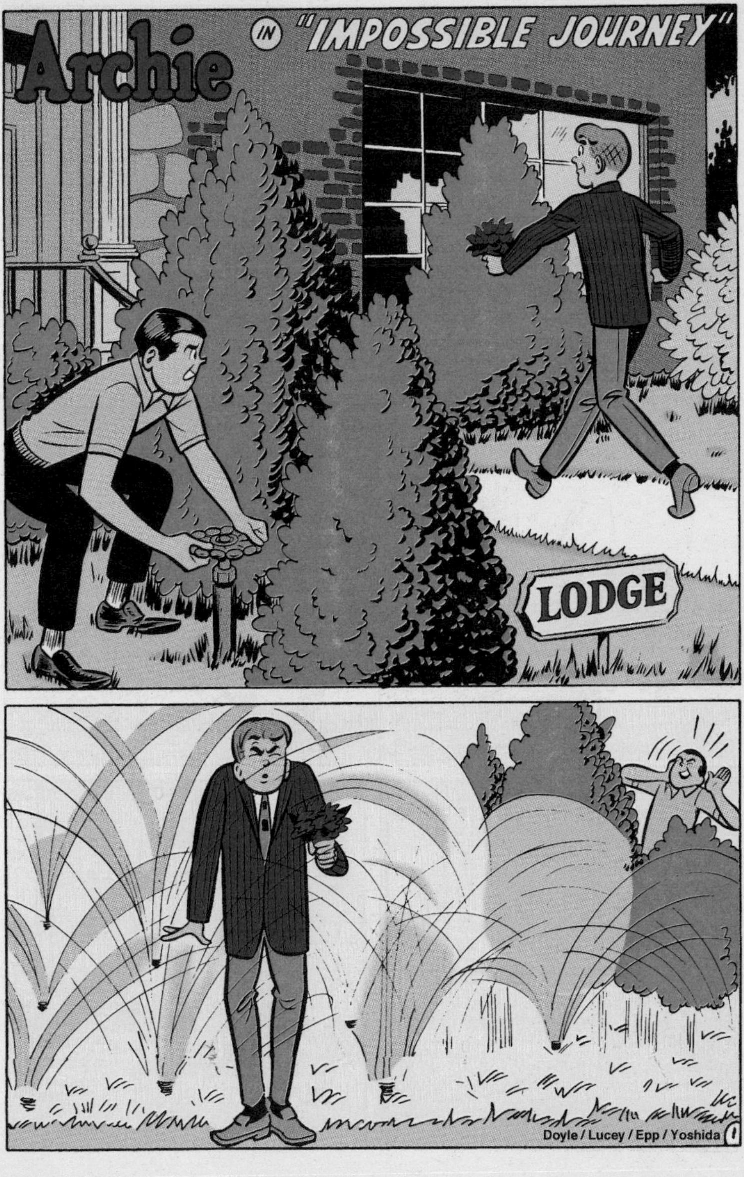
Archie
IN "IMPOSSIBLE JOURNEY"
LODGE
Doyle / Lucey / Epp / Yoshida

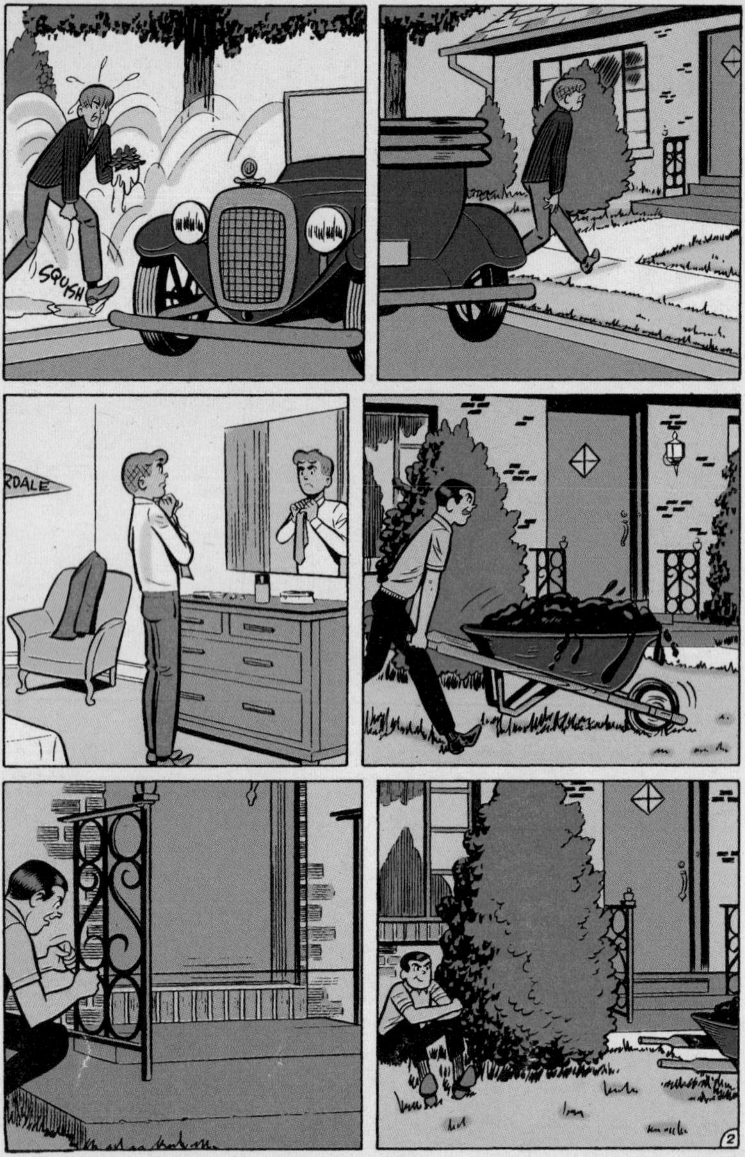
SQUISH
2

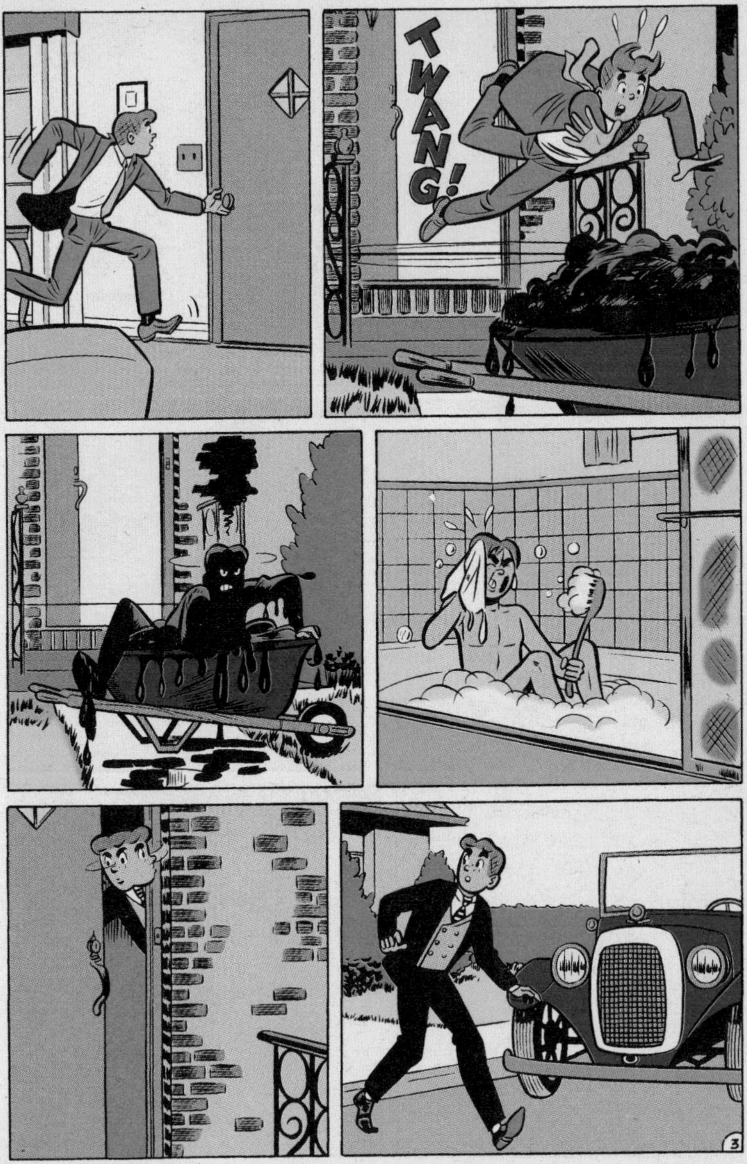
TWANG!
3

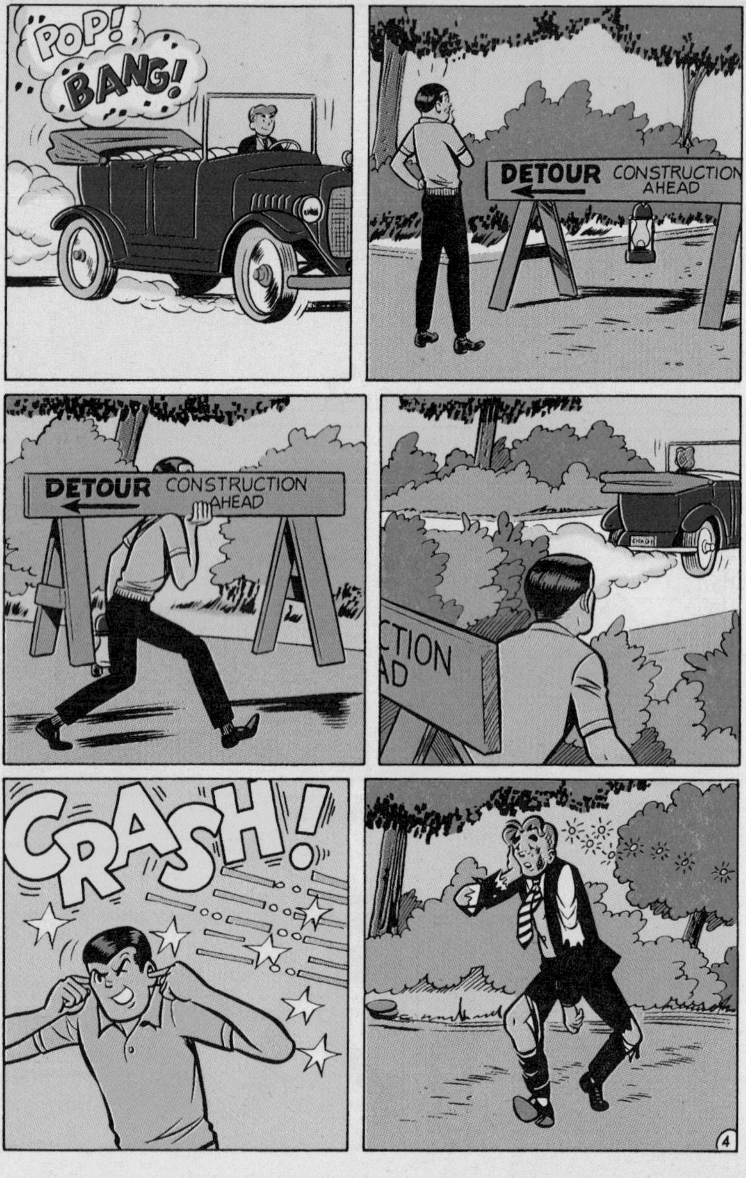
POP!
BANG!
DETOUR CONSTRUCTION AHEAD
DETOUR CONSTRUCTION AHEAD
CTION
AD
CRASH!
4

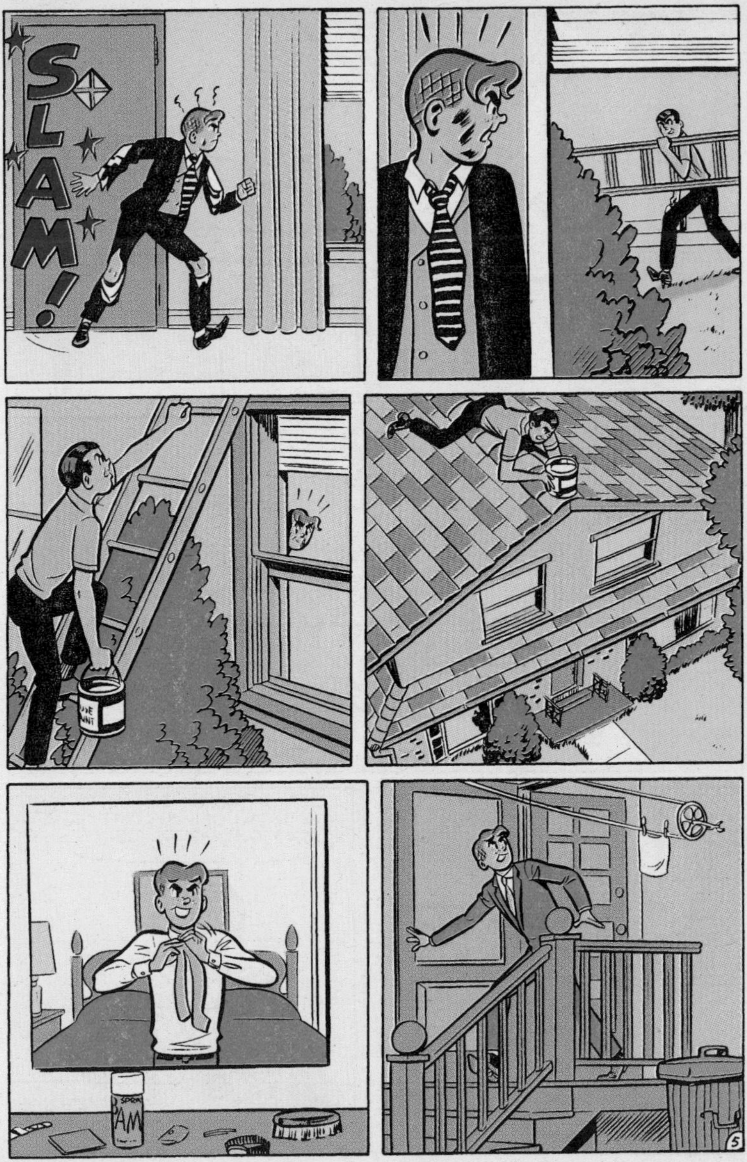
SLAM!

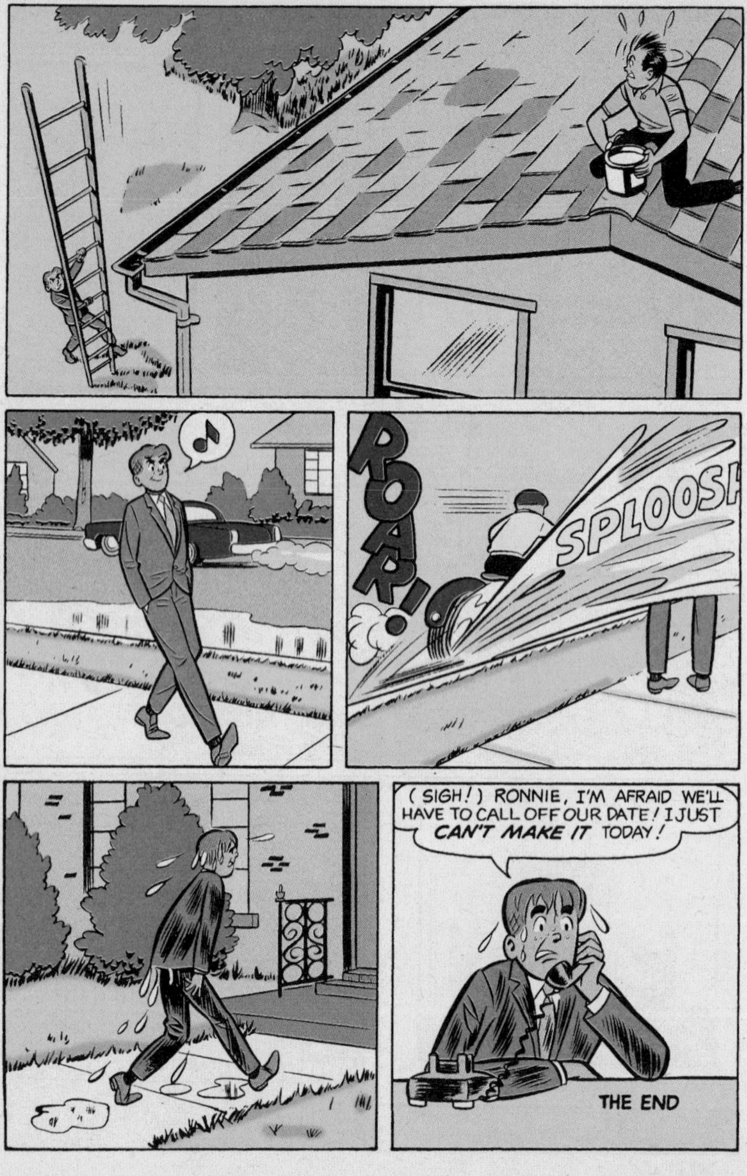
ROAR!
SPLOOSH
(SIGH!) RONNIE, I'M AFRAID WE'LL HAVE TO CALL OFF OUR DATE! I JUST CAN'T MAKE IT TODAY!
THE END

PROFESSOR FLUTESNOOT JUST GAVE ME THIS CARD! IT TELLS WHAT WILL HAPPEN IF I CONTINUE TO FOOL AROUND IN CLASS!!

CROSS OUT THE F's, J's, and Y's TO READ WHAT IT SAYS!!

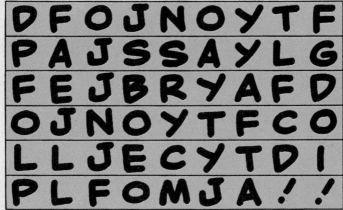

D F O J N O Y T F
P A J S S A Y L G
F E J B R Y A F D
O J N O Y T F C O
L L J E C Y T D I
P L F O M J A ! !

ANSWER: "DO NOT PASS ALGEBRA ... DO NOT COLLECT DIPLOMA!!"

Archie CLASS CLOWN!

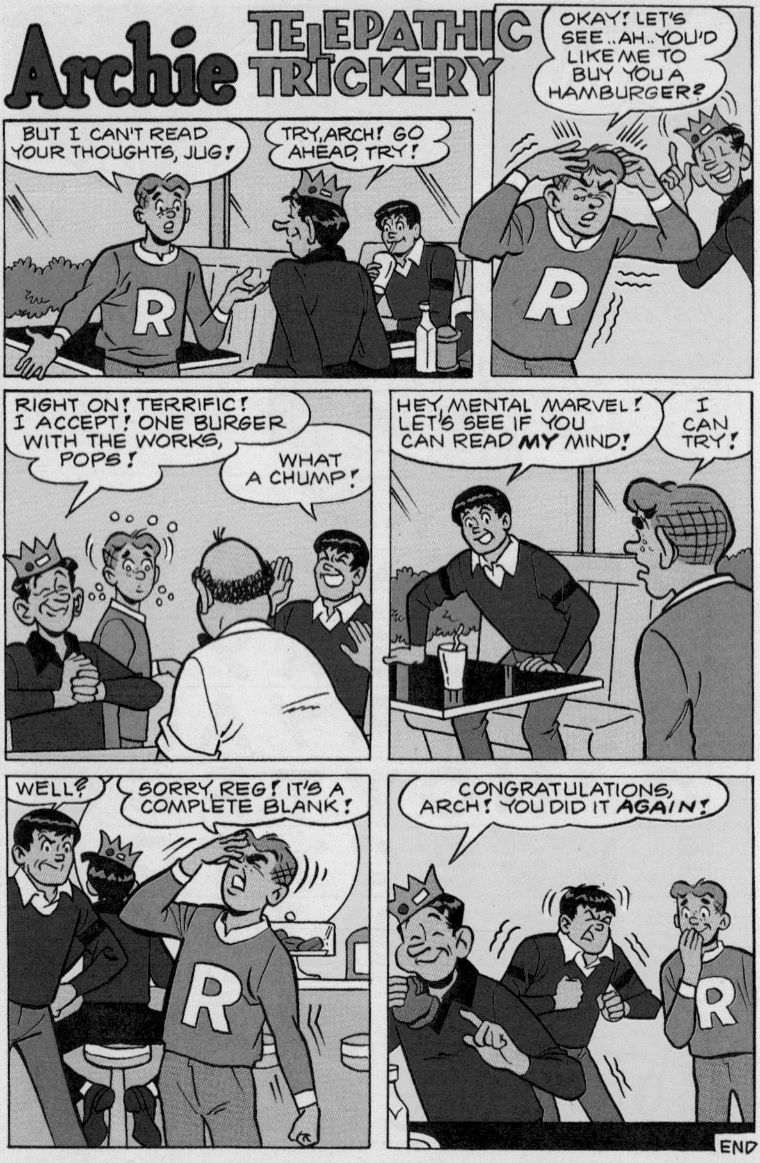
Archie
TELEPATHIC TRICKERY
BUT I CAN'T READ YOUR THOUGHTS, JUG!
TRY, ARCH! GO AHEAD, TRY!
OKAY! LET'S SEE..AH..YOU'D LIKE ME TO BUY YOU A HAMBURGER?
RIGHT ON! TERRIFIC! I ACCEPT! ONE BURGER WITH THE WORKS, POPS!
WHAT A CHUMP!
HEY, MENTAL MARVEL! LET'S SEE IF YOU CAN READ MY MIND!
I CAN TRY!
WELL?
SORRY, REG! IT'S A COMPLETE BLANK!
CONGRATULATIONS, ARCH! YOU DID IT AGAIN!
END

Betty and **Veronica**

PHEW!

HI, BETTY! WHAT'S WRONG? YOU LOOK LIKE YOU JUST RAN A MARATHON WEARING CEMENT SNEAKERS!

Pellowski / DeCarlo / Flood / Yoshida

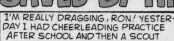

"SAVED BY THE BELL" DING DING

I'M REALLY DRAGGING, RON! YESTERDAY I HAD CHEERLEADING PRACTICE AFTER SCHOOL AND THEN A SCOUT LEADER'S MEETING AT NIGHT!

WHEN I WENT HOME I HAD A TON OF MATH HOMEWORK AND AN ESSAY TO FINISH!

BUMMER!

HOMEROOM 182 NEWS

1

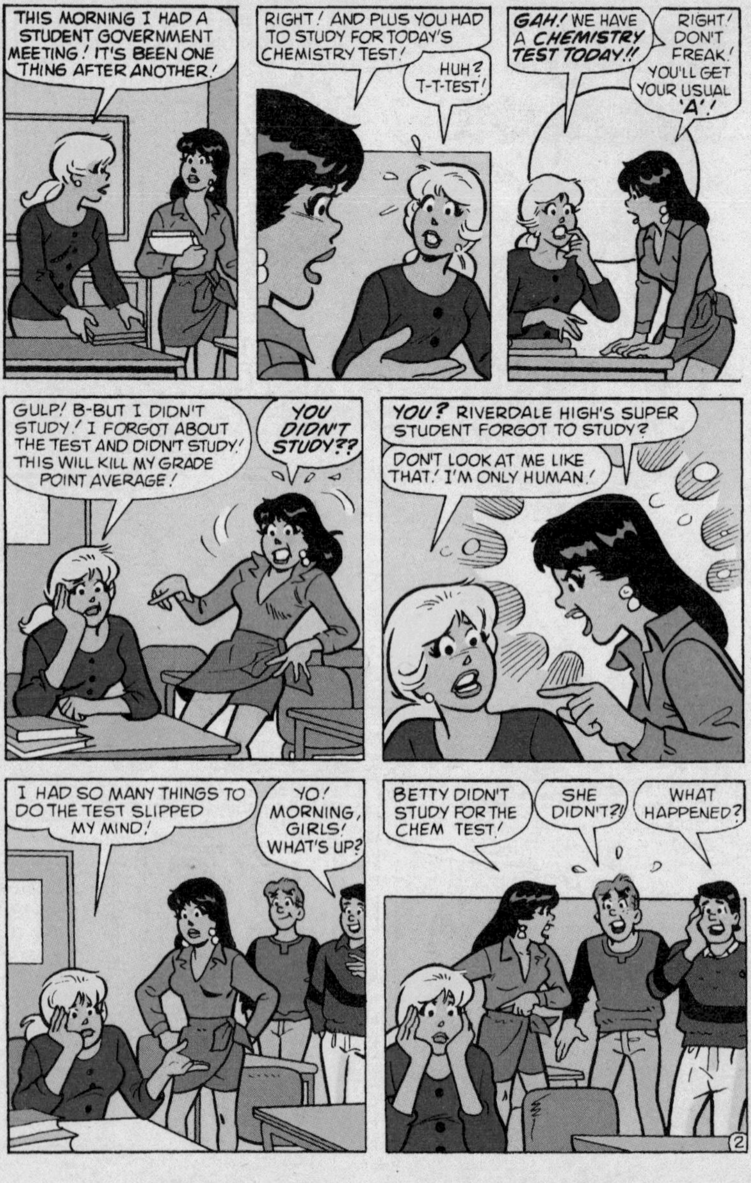
THIS MORNING I HAD A STUDENT GOVERNMENT MEETING! IT'S BEEN ONE THING AFTER ANOTHER!
RIGHT! AND PLUS YOU HAD TO STUDY FOR TODAY'S CHEMISTRY TEST!
HUH? T-T-TEST!
GAH! WE HAVE A CHEMISTRY TEST TODAY!!
RIGHT! DON'T FREAK! YOU'LL GET YOUR USUAL 'A'!
GULP! B-BUT I DIDN'T STUDY! I FORGOT ABOUT THE TEST AND DIDN'T STUDY! THIS WILL KILL MY GRADE POINT AVERAGE!
YOU DIDN'T STUDY??
YOU? RIVERDALE HIGH'S SUPER STUDENT FORGOT TO STUDY?
DON'T LOOK AT ME LIKE THAT! I'M ONLY HUMAN!
I HAD SO MANY THINGS TO DO THE TEST SLIPPED MY MIND!
YO! MORNING, GIRLS! WHAT'S UP?
BETTY DIDN'T STUDY FOR THE CHEM TEST!
SHE DIDN'T?!
WHAT HAPPENED?
2

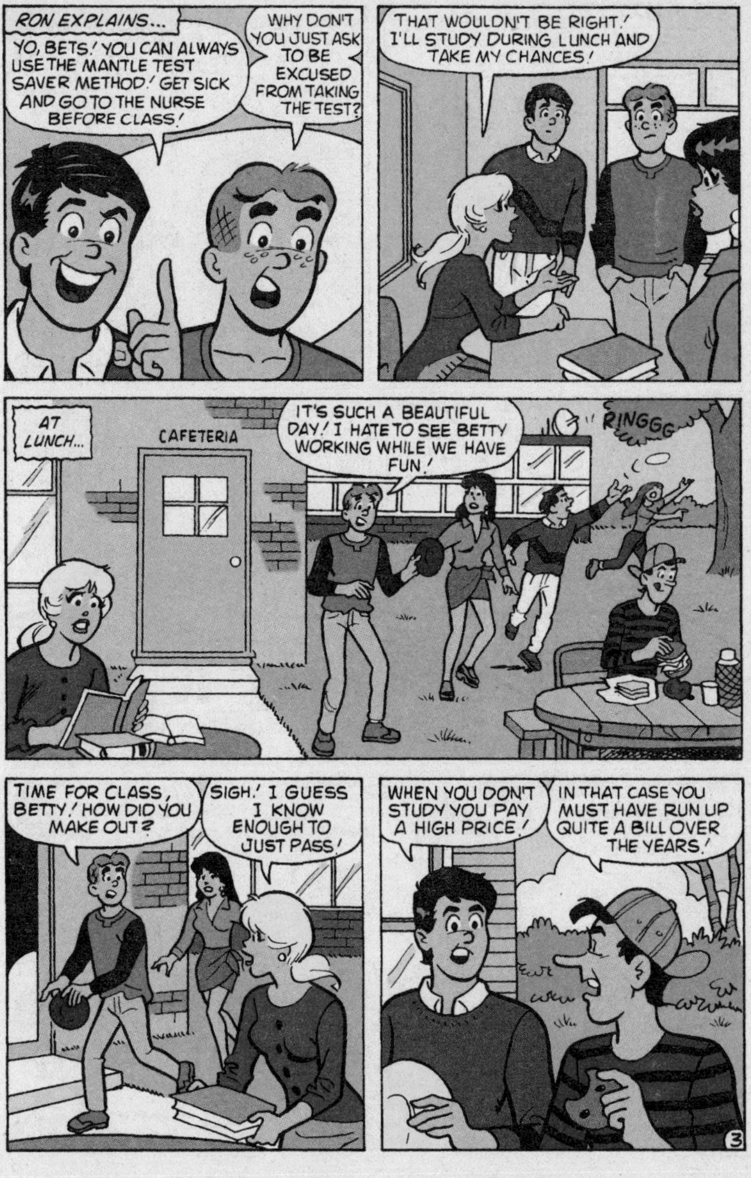
RON EXPLAINS...
YO, BETS! YOU CAN ALWAYS USE THE MANTLE TEST SAVER METHOD! GET SICK AND GO TO THE NURSE BEFORE CLASS!
WHY DON'T YOU JUST ASK TO BE EXCUSED FROM TAKING THE TEST?
THAT WOULDN'T BE RIGHT! I'LL STUDY DURING LUNCH AND TAKE MY CHANCES!
AT LUNCH...
CAFETERIA
IT'S SUCH A BEAUTIFUL DAY! I HATE TO SEE BETTY WORKING WHILE WE HAVE FUN!
RINGGG
TIME FOR CLASS, BETTY! HOW DID YOU MAKE OUT?
SIGH! I GUESS I KNOW ENOUGH TO JUST PASS!
WHEN YOU DON'T STUDY YOU PAY A HIGH PRICE!
IN THAT CASE YOU MUST HAVE RUN UP QUITE A BILL OVER THE YEARS!
3

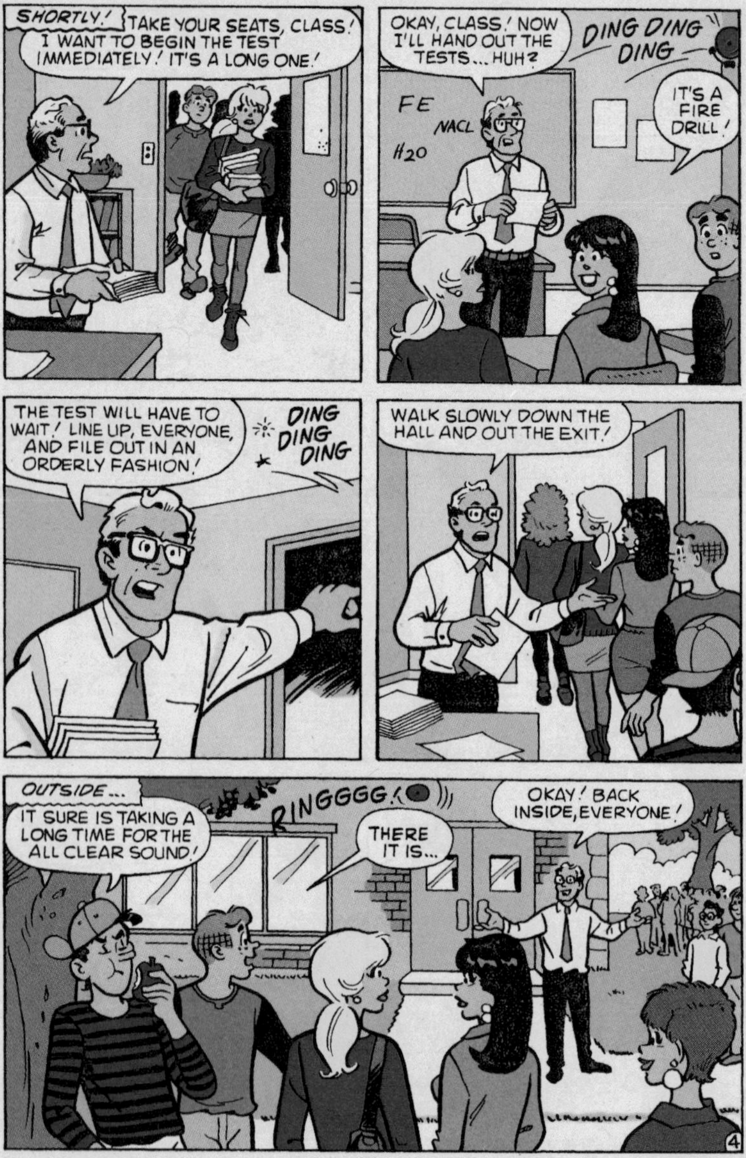
SHORTLY!
TAKE YOUR SEATS, CLASS! I WANT TO BEGIN THE TEST IMMEDIATELY! IT'S A LONG ONE!
OKAY, CLASS! NOW I'LL HAND OUT THE TESTS... HUH?
DING DING DING
FE
NACL
H20
IT'S A FIRE DRILL!
THE TEST WILL HAVE TO WAIT! LINE UP, EVERYONE, AND FILE OUT IN AN ORDERLY FASHION!
DING DING DING
WALK SLOWLY DOWN THE HALL AND OUT THE EXIT!
OUTSIDE...
IT SURE IS TAKING A LONG TIME FOR THE ALL CLEAR SOUND!
RINGGGG!
THERE IT IS...
OKAY! BACK INSIDE, EVERYONE!
4

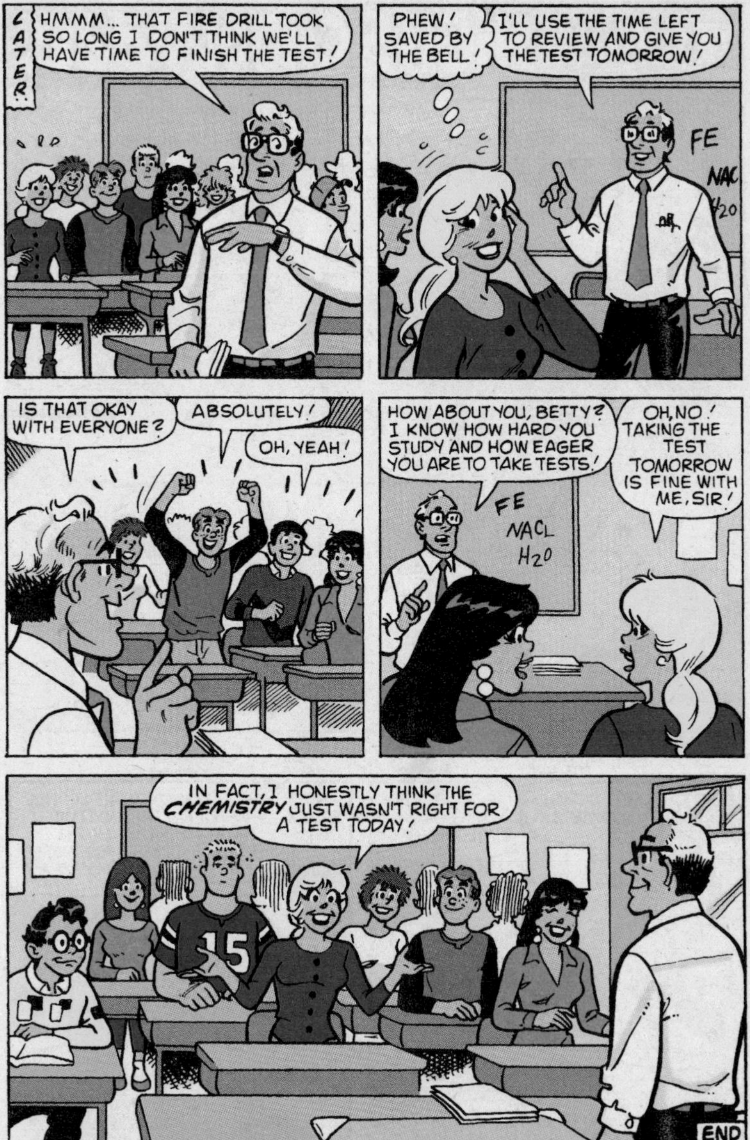
LATER:
HMMM... THAT FIRE DRILL TOOK SO LONG I DON'T THINK WE'LL HAVE TIME TO FINISH THE TEST!
PHEW! SAVED BY THE BELL!
I'LL USE THE TIME LEFT TO REVIEW AND GIVE YOU THE TEST TOMORROW!
FE
NAC
H20
IS THAT OKAY WITH EVERYONE?
ABSOLUTELY!
OH, YEAH!
HOW ABOUT YOU, BETTY? I KNOW HOW HARD YOU STUDY AND HOW EAGER YOU ARE TO TAKE TESTS!
FE
NACL
H20
OH, NO! TAKING THE TEST TOMORROW IS FINE WITH ME, SIR!
IN FACT, I HONESTLY THINK THE CHEMISTRY JUST WASN'T RIGHT FOR A TEST TODAY!
15
END

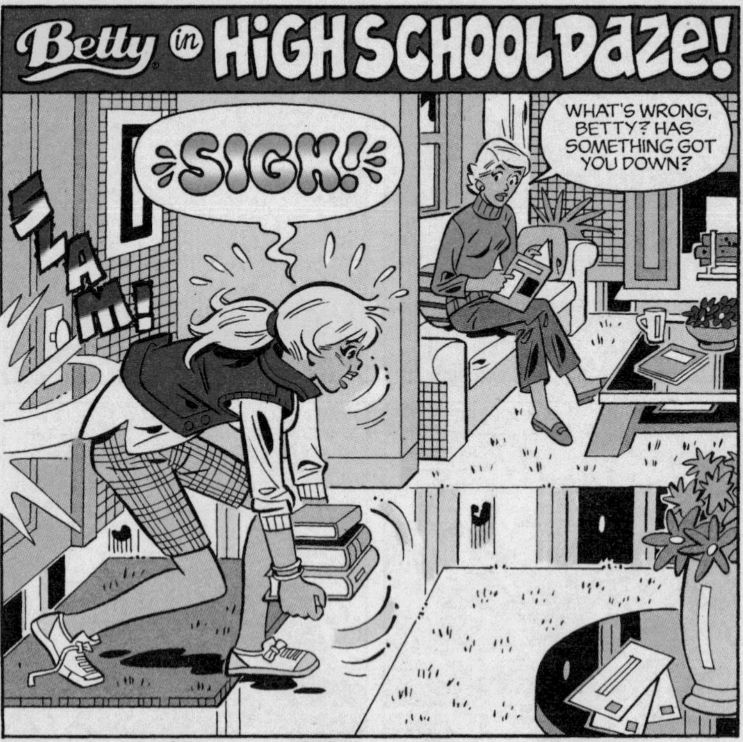
Betty in HIGH SCHOOL DAZE!
SLAM!
SIGH!
WHAT'S WRONG, BETTY? HAS SOMETHING GOT YOU DOWN?

Script: MIKE PELLOWSKI
Pencils: PAT KENNEDY
Inks: KEN SELIG
Letters: JANICE CHIANG

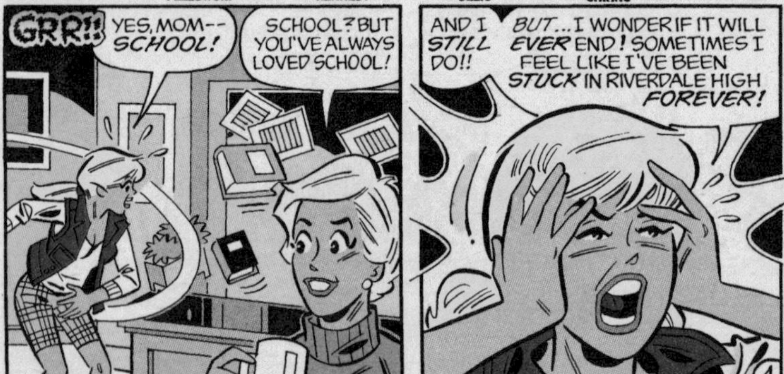
GRR!!
YES, MOM-- *SCHOOL!*
SCHOOL? BUT YOU'VE ALWAYS LOVED SCHOOL!
AND I *STILL* DO!!
BUT... I WONDER IF IT WILL *EVER* END! SOMETIMES I FEEL LIKE I'VE BEEN *STUCK* IN RIVERDALE HIGH *FOREVER!*
1

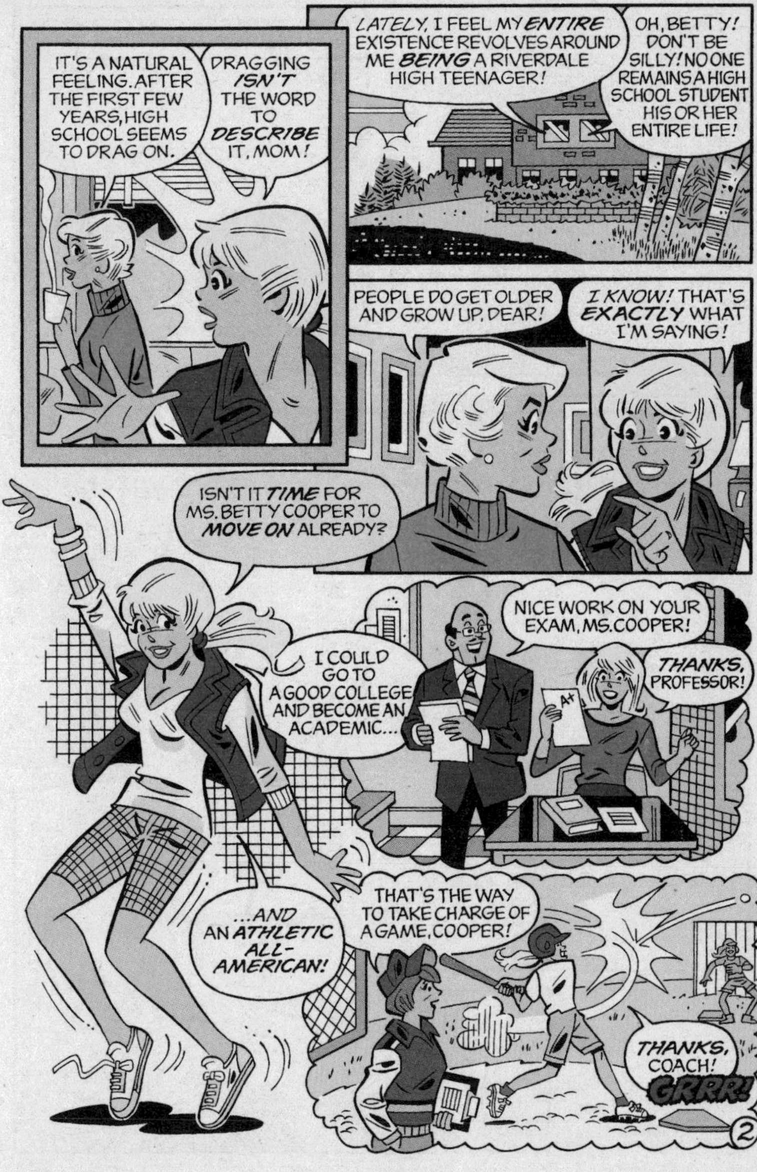
IT'S A NATURAL FEELING. AFTER THE FIRST FEW YEARS, HIGH SCHOOL SEEMS TO DRAG ON.
DRAGGING ISN'T THE WORD TO DESCRIBE IT, MOM!
LATELY, I FEEL MY ENTIRE EXISTENCE REVOLVES AROUND ME BEING A RIVERDALE HIGH TEENAGER!
OH, BETTY! DON'T BE SILLY! NO ONE REMAINS A HIGH SCHOOL STUDENT HIS OR HER ENTIRE LIFE!
PEOPLE DO GET OLDER AND GROW UP, DEAR!
I KNOW! THAT'S EXACTLY WHAT I'M SAYING!
ISN'T IT TIME FOR MS. BETTY COOPER TO MOVE ON ALREADY?
I COULD GO TO A GOOD COLLEGE AND BECOME AN ACADEMIC...
NICE WORK ON YOUR EXAM, MS. COOPER!
A+
THANKS, PROFESSOR!
...AND AN ATHLETIC ALL-AMERICAN!
THAT'S THE WAY TO TAKE CHARGE OF A GAME, COOPER!
THANKS, COACH!
GRRR!
2

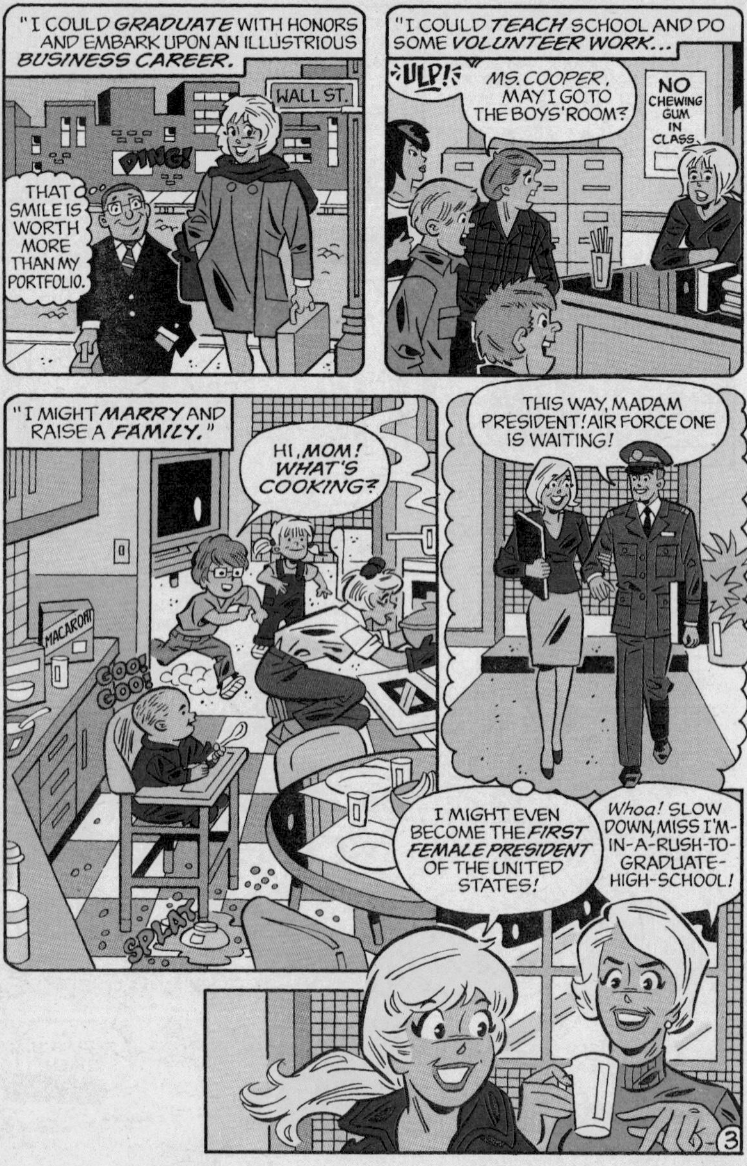
"I COULD GRADUATE WITH HONORS AND EMBARK UPON AN ILLUSTRIOUS BUSINESS CAREER.
WALL ST.
DING!
THAT SMILE IS WORTH MORE THAN MY PORTFOLIO.
"I COULD TEACH SCHOOL AND DO SOME VOLUNTEER WORK...
ULP!
MS. COOPER, MAY I GO TO THE BOYS' ROOM?
NO CHEWING GUM IN CLASS.
"I MIGHT MARRY AND RAISE A FAMILY."
HI, MOM! WHAT'S COOKING?
MACARONI
GOO! GOO!
SPLAT
THIS WAY, MADAM PRESIDENT! AIR FORCE ONE IS WAITING!
I MIGHT EVEN BECOME THE FIRST FEMALE PRESIDENT OF THE UNITED STATES!
Whoa! SLOW DOWN, MISS I'M-IN-A-RUSH-TO-GRADUATE-HIGH-SCHOOL!

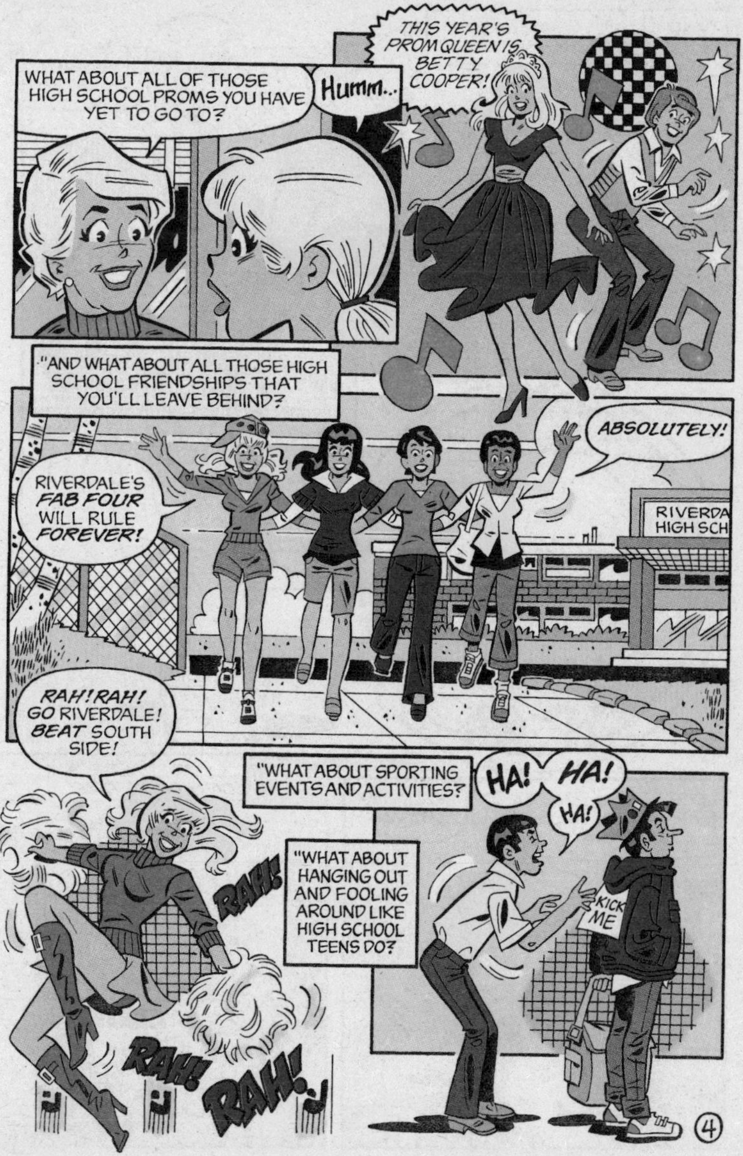
WHAT ABOUT ALL OF THOSE HIGH SCHOOL PROMS YOU HAVE YET TO GO TO?
Humm...
THIS YEAR'S PROM QUEEN IS BETTY COOPER!
"AND WHAT ABOUT ALL THOSE HIGH SCHOOL FRIENDSHIPS THAT YOU'LL LEAVE BEHIND?
RIVERDALE'S FAB FOUR WILL RULE FOREVER!
ABSOLUTELY!
RIVERDA
HIGH SCH
RAH! RAH! GO RIVERDALE! BEAT SOUTH SIDE!
"WHAT ABOUT SPORTING EVENTS AND ACTIVITIES?
RAH!
RAH!
RAH!
HA!
HA!
HA!
"WHAT ABOUT HANGING OUT AND FOOLING AROUND LIKE HIGH SCHOOL TEENS DO?
KICK ME

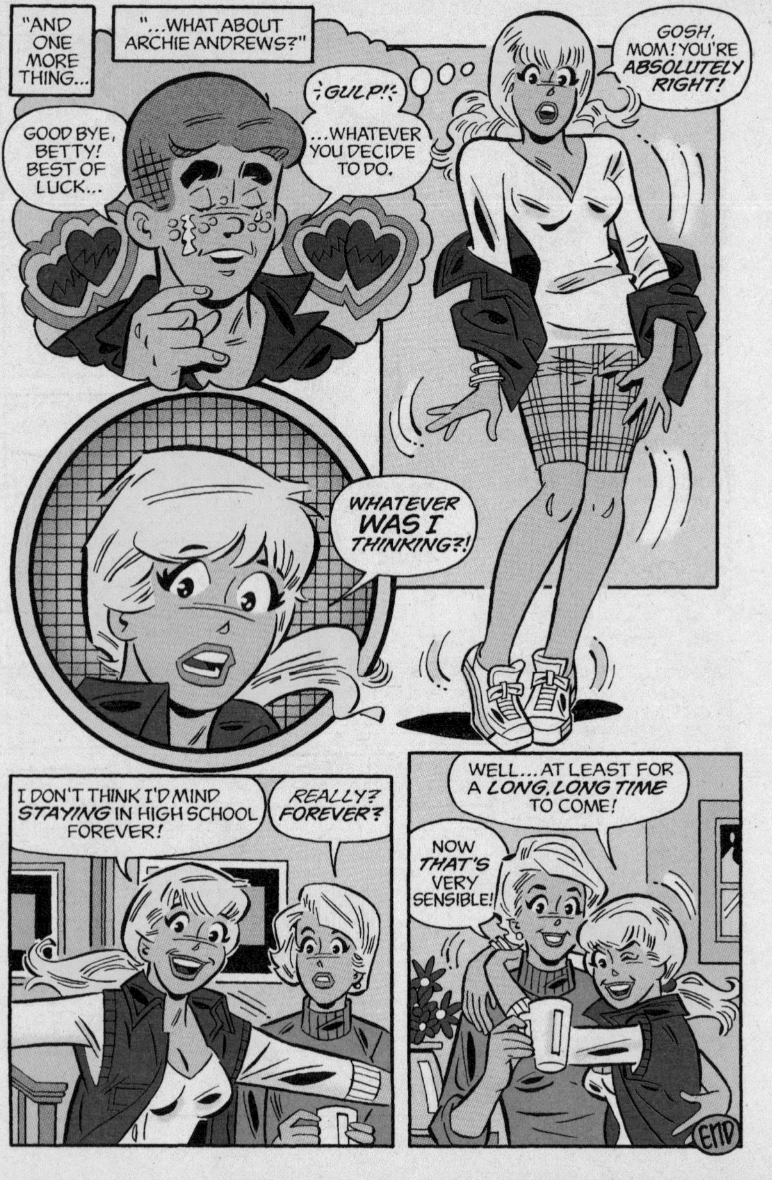

"AND ONE MORE THING...
"...WHAT ABOUT ARCHIE ANDREWS?"
GOOD BYE, BETTY! BEST OF LUCK...
GULP!
...WHATEVER YOU DECIDE TO DO.
GOSH, MOM! YOU'RE ABSOLUTELY RIGHT!
WHATEVER WAS I THINKING?!
I DON'T THINK I'D MIND STAYING IN HIGH SCHOOL FOREVER!
REALLY? FOREVER?
WELL... AT LEAST FOR A LONG, LONG TIME TO COME!
NOW THAT'S VERY SENSIBLE!
END

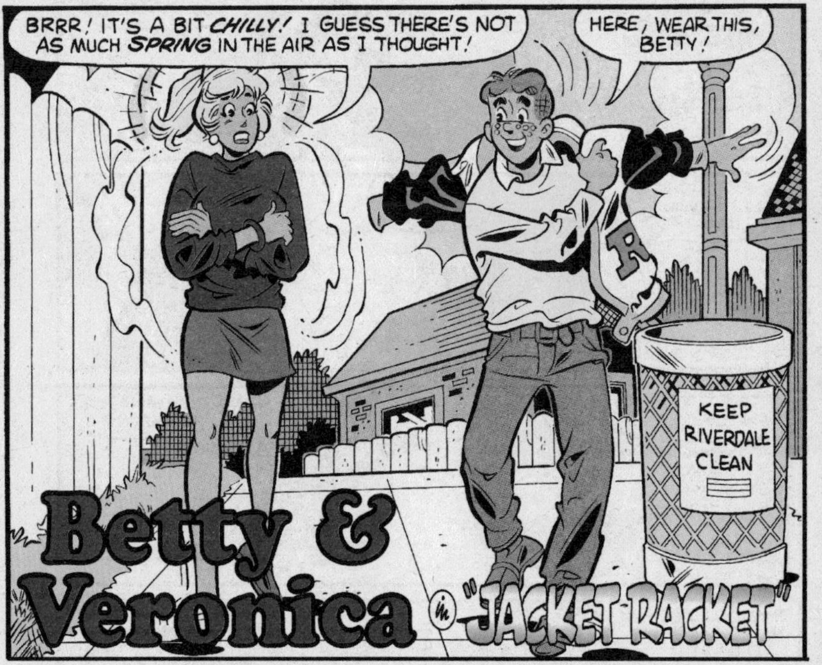
BRRR! IT'S A BIT CHILLY! I GUESS THERE'S NOT AS MUCH SPRING IN THE AIR AS I THOUGHT!
HERE, WEAR THIS, BETTY!
KEEP RIVERDALE CLEAN
Betty & Veronica in "JACKET RACKET"

SCRIPT: BILL GOLLIHER PENCILS: TIM KENNEDY INKS: KEN SELIG LETTERS: BILL YOSHIDA

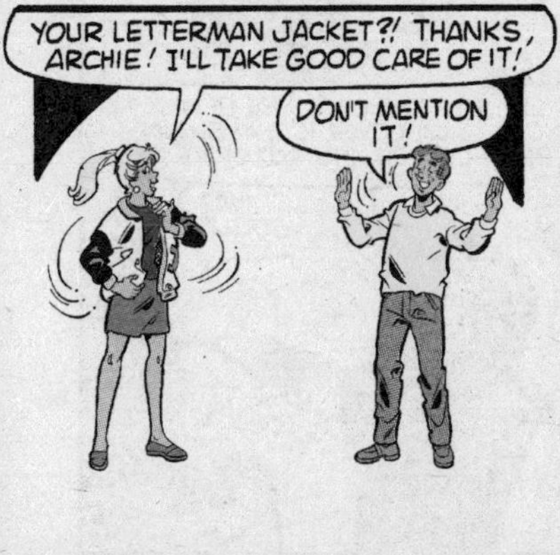
YOUR LETTERMAN JACKET?! THANKS, ARCHIE! I'LL TAKE GOOD CARE OF IT!
DON'T MENTION IT!

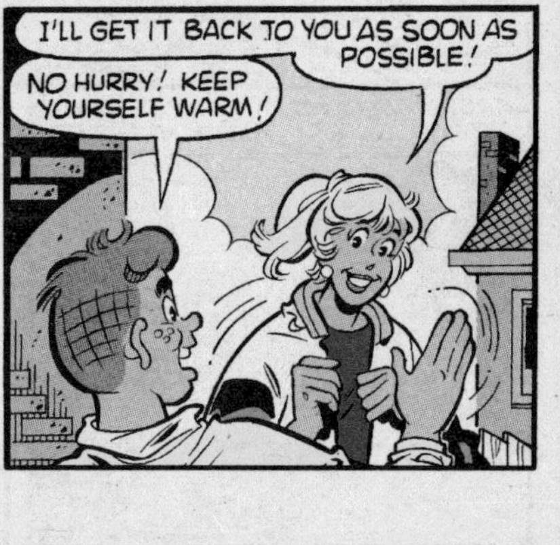
I'LL GET IT BACK TO YOU AS SOON AS POSSIBLE!
NO HURRY! KEEP YOURSELF WARM!

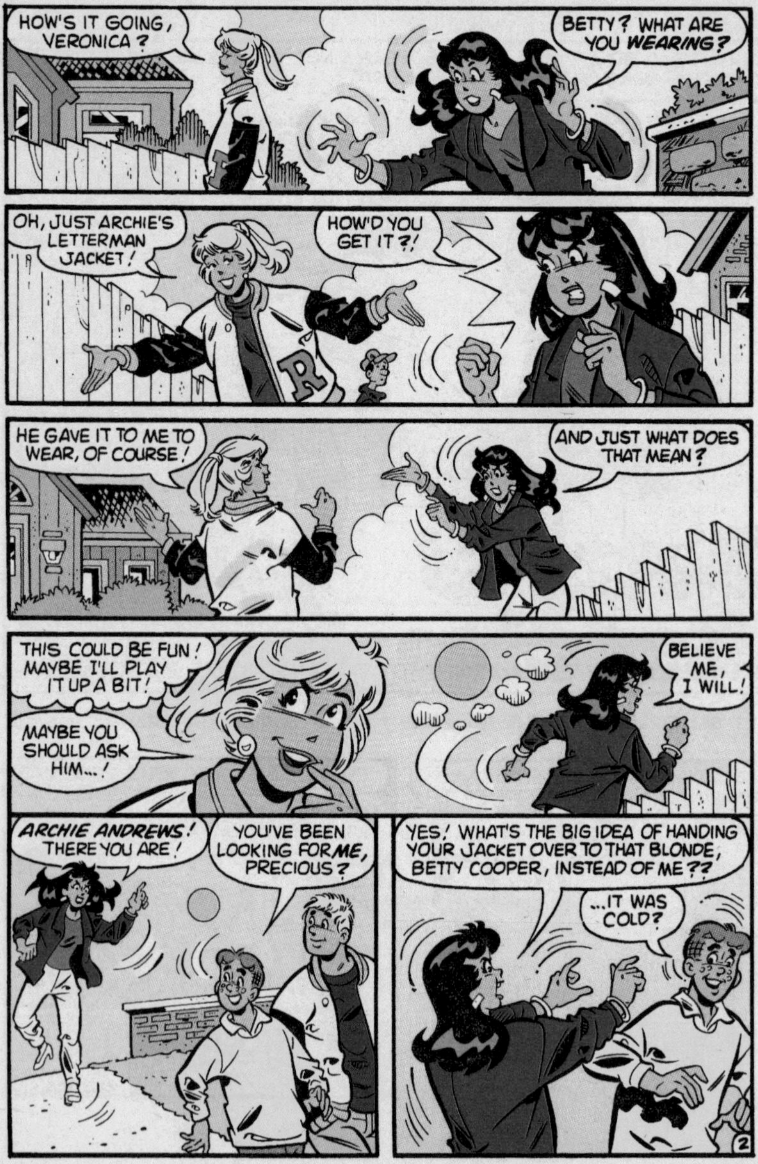

HOW'S IT GOING, VERONICA ?
BETTY? WHAT ARE YOU WEARING?
OH, JUST ARCHIE'S LETTERMAN JACKET!
HOW'D YOU GET IT ?!
HE GAVE IT TO ME TO WEAR, OF COURSE!
AND JUST WHAT DOES THAT MEAN ?
THIS COULD BE FUN! MAYBE I'LL PLAY IT UP A BIT!
MAYBE YOU SHOULD ASK HIM...!
BELIEVE ME, I WILL!
ARCHIE ANDREWS! THERE YOU ARE!
YOU'VE BEEN LOOKING FOR ME, PRECIOUS?
YES! WHAT'S THE BIG IDEA OF HANDING YOUR JACKET OVER TO THAT BLONDE, BETTY COOPER, INSTEAD OF ME??
...IT WAS COLD?
2

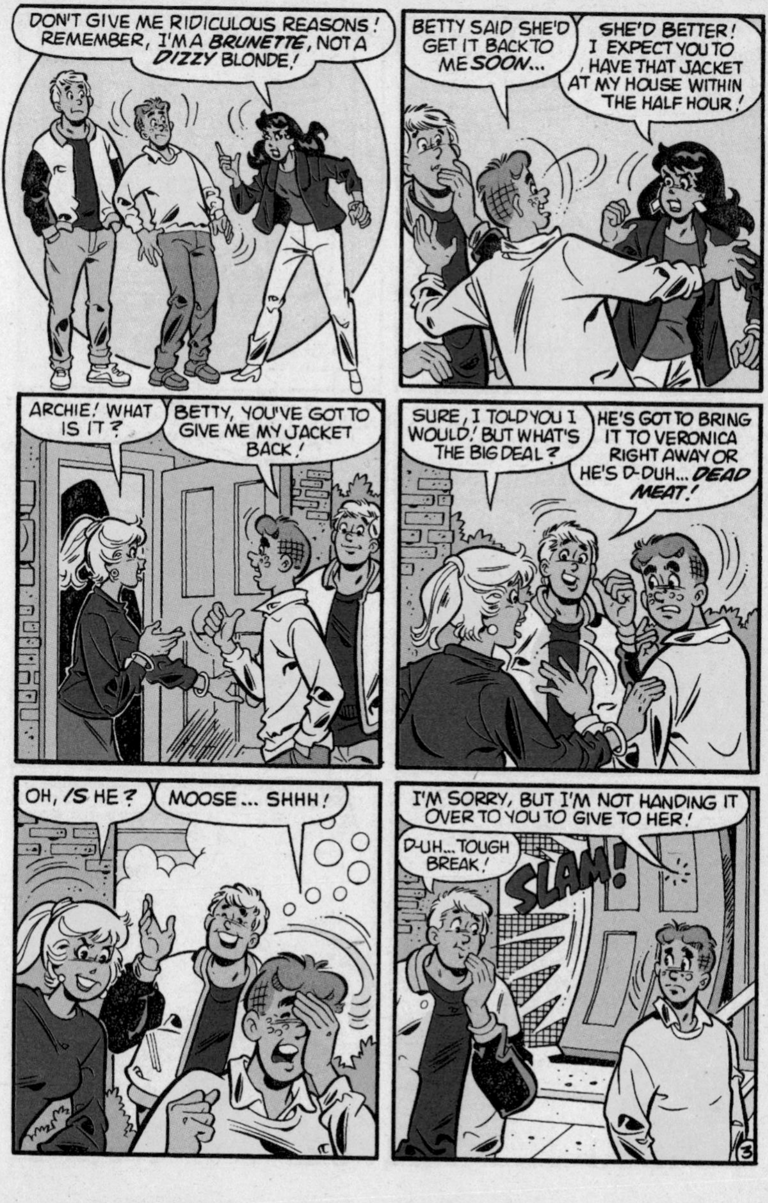

DON'T GIVE ME RIDICULOUS REASONS! REMEMBER, I'M A BRUNETTE, NOT A DIZZY BLONDE!
BETTY SAID SHE'D GET IT BACK TO ME SOON...
SHE'D BETTER! I EXPECT YOU TO HAVE THAT JACKET AT MY HOUSE WITHIN THE HALF HOUR!
ARCHIE! WHAT IS IT?
BETTY, YOU'VE GOT TO GIVE ME MY JACKET BACK!
SURE, I TOLD YOU I WOULD! BUT WHAT'S THE BIG DEAL?
HE'S GOT TO BRING IT TO VERONICA RIGHT AWAY OR HE'S D-DUH... DEAD MEAT!
OH, IS HE?
MOOSE... SHHH!
I'M SORRY, BUT I'M NOT HANDING IT OVER TO YOU TO GIVE TO HER!
D-UH... TOUGH BREAK!
SLAM!
3

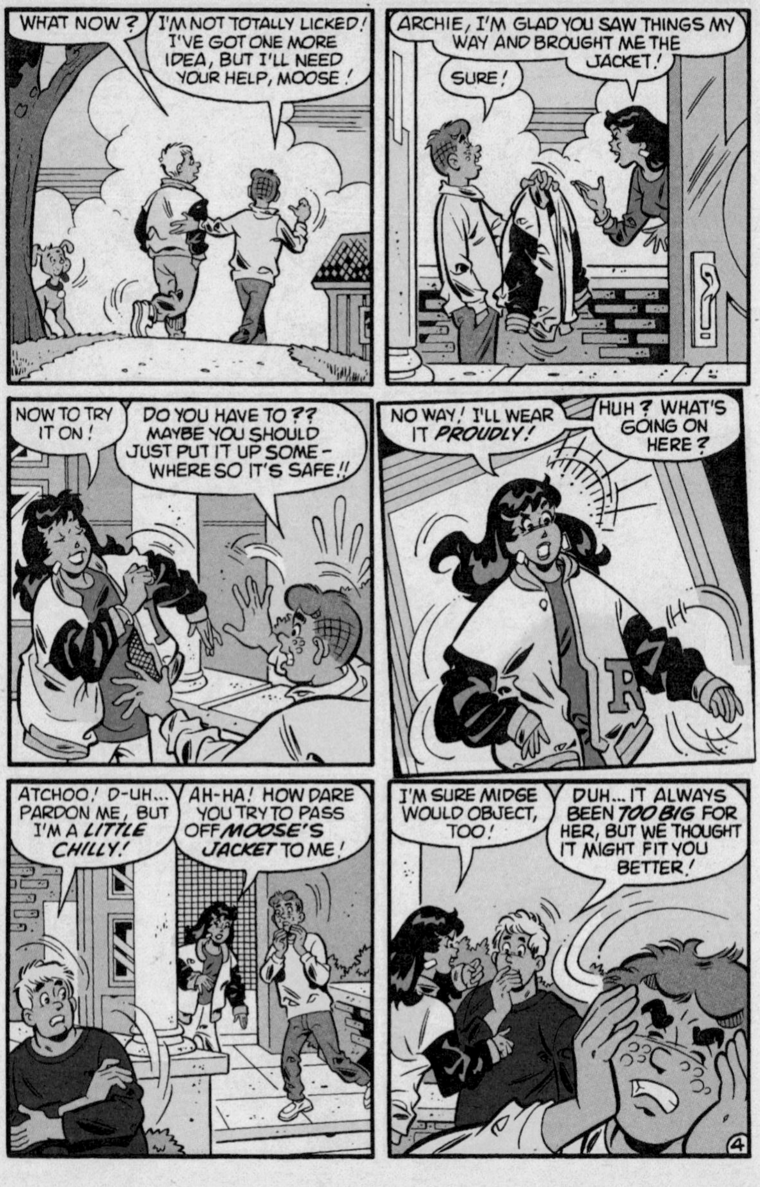
WHAT NOW?
I'M NOT TOTALLY LICKED! I'VE GOT ONE MORE IDEA, BUT I'LL NEED YOUR HELP, MOOSE!
ARCHIE, I'M GLAD YOU SAW THINGS MY WAY AND BROUGHT ME THE JACKET!
SURE!
NOW TO TRY IT ON!
DO YOU HAVE TO?? MAYBE YOU SHOULD JUST PUT IT UP SOME-WHERE SO IT'S SAFE!!
NO WAY! I'LL WEAR IT PROUDLY!
HUH? WHAT'S GOING ON HERE?
ATCHOO! D-UH... PARDON ME, BUT I'M A LITTLE CHILLY!
AH-HA! HOW DARE YOU TRY TO PASS OFF MOOSE'S JACKET TO ME!
I'M SURE MIDGE WOULD OBJECT, TOO!
DUH... IT ALWAYS BEEN TOO BIG FOR HER, BUT WE THOUGHT IT MIGHT FIT YOU BETTER!
4

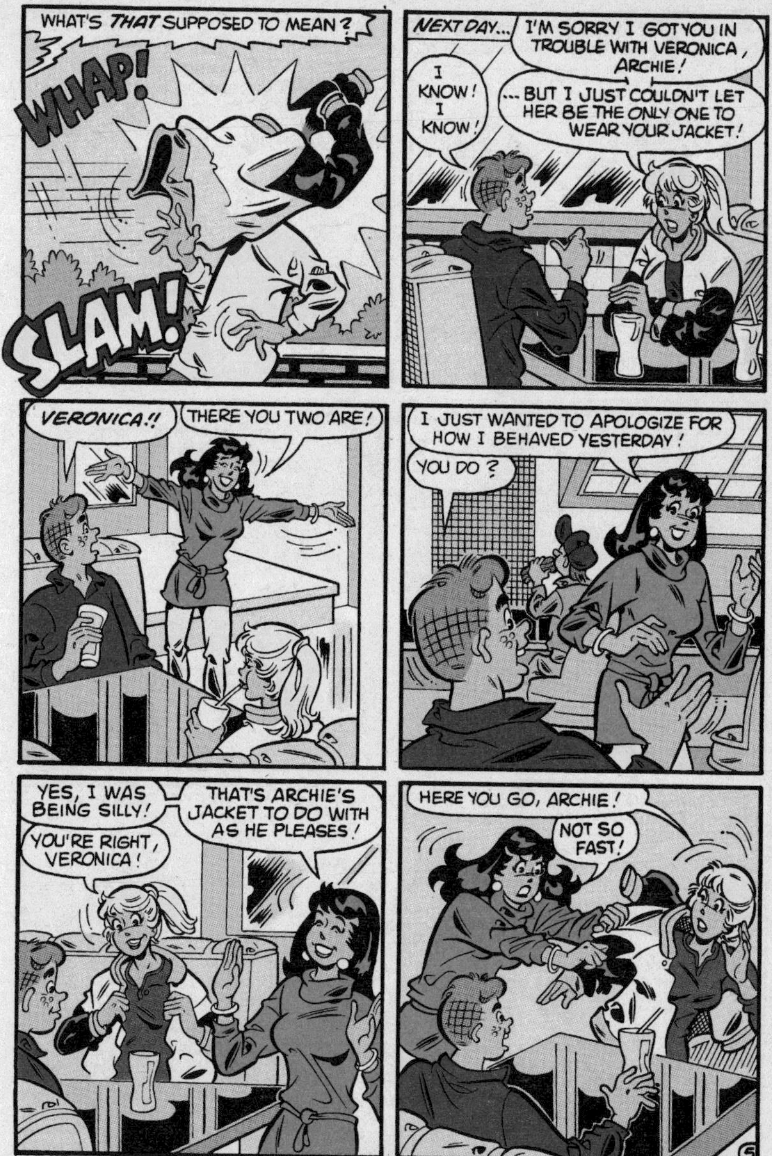
WHAT'S THAT SUPPOSED TO MEAN?
WHAP!
SLAM!
NEXT DAY...
I'M SORRY I GOT YOU IN TROUBLE WITH VERONICA, ARCHIE!
I KNOW! I KNOW!
... BUT I JUST COULDN'T LET HER BE THE ONLY ONE TO WEAR YOUR JACKET!
VERONICA!!
THERE YOU TWO ARE!
I JUST WANTED TO APOLOGIZE FOR HOW I BEHAVED YESTERDAY!
YOU DO?
YES, I WAS BEING SILLY!
THAT'S ARCHIE'S JACKET TO DO WITH AS HE PLEASES!
YOU'RE RIGHT, VERONICA!
HERE YOU GO, ARCHIE!
NOT SO FAST!
5

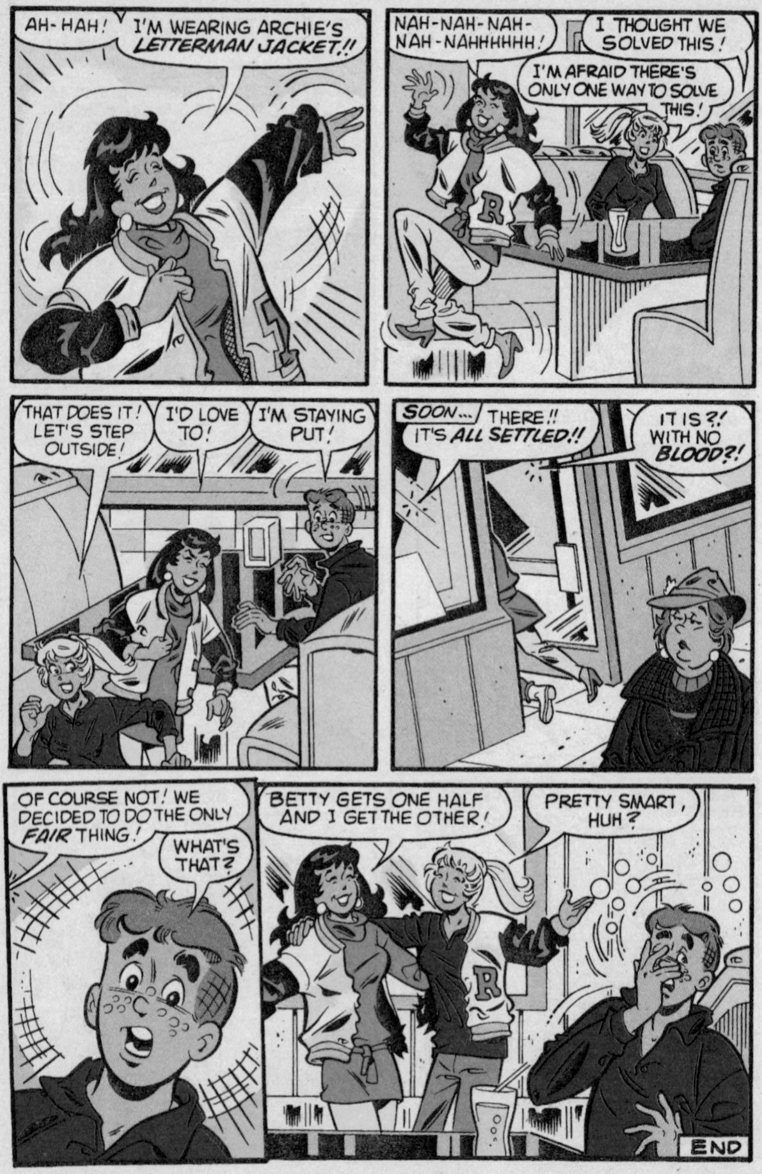
AH-HAH!
I'M WEARING ARCHIE'S *LETTERMAN JACKET*!!
NAH-NAH-NAH-NAH-NAHHHHHH!
I THOUGHT WE SOLVED THIS!
I'M AFRAID THERE'S ONLY ONE WAY TO SOLVE THIS!
THAT DOES IT! LET'S STEP OUTSIDE!
I'D LOVE TO!
I'M STAYING PUT!
SOON...
THERE!! IT'S *ALL SETTLED!!*
IT IS?! WITH NO *BLOOD?!*
OF COURSE NOT! WE DECIDED TO DO THE ONLY *FAIR* THING!
WHAT'S THAT?
BETTY GETS ONE HALF AND I GET THE OTHER!
PRETTY SMART, HUH?
END

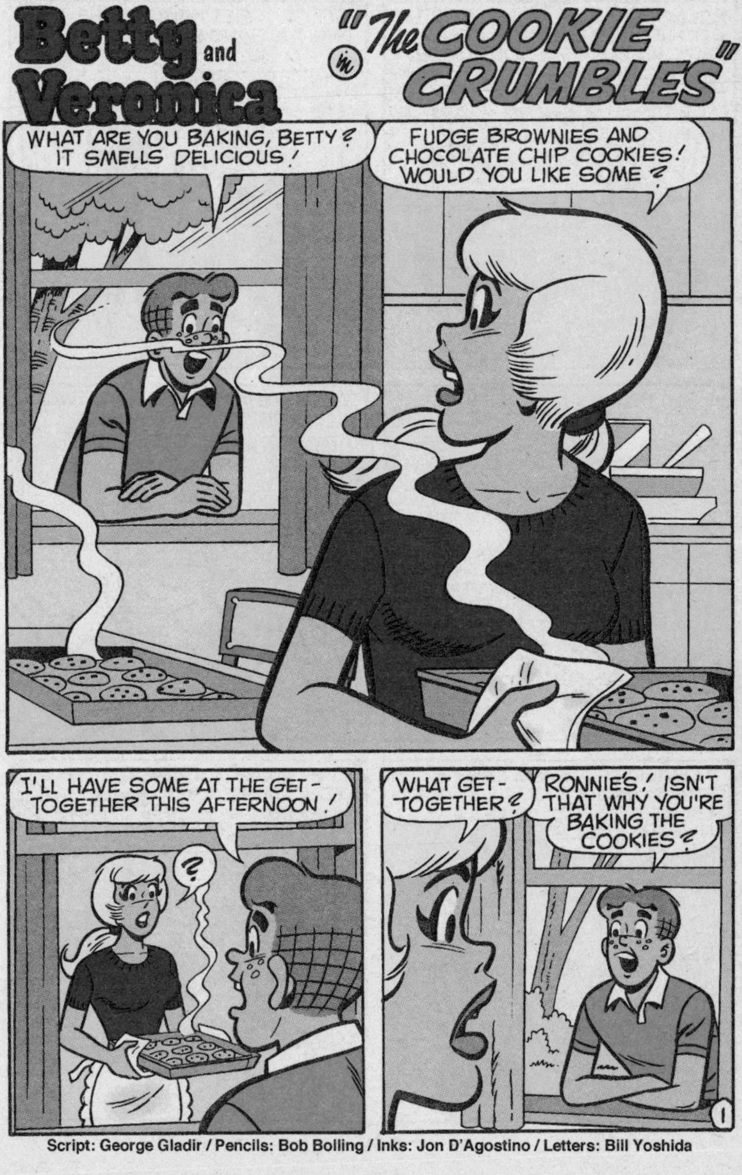
Betty and Veronica
in "The COOKIE CRUMBLES"
WHAT ARE YOU BAKING, BETTY? IT SMELLS DELICIOUS!
FUDGE BROWNIES AND CHOCOLATE CHIP COOKIES! WOULD YOU LIKE SOME?
I'LL HAVE SOME AT THE GET-TOGETHER THIS AFTERNOON!
?
WHAT GET-TOGETHER?
RONNIE'S! ISN'T THAT WHY YOU'RE BAKING THE COOKIES?
1

Script: George Gladir / Pencils: Bob Bolling / Inks: Jon D'Agostino / Letters: Bill Yoshida

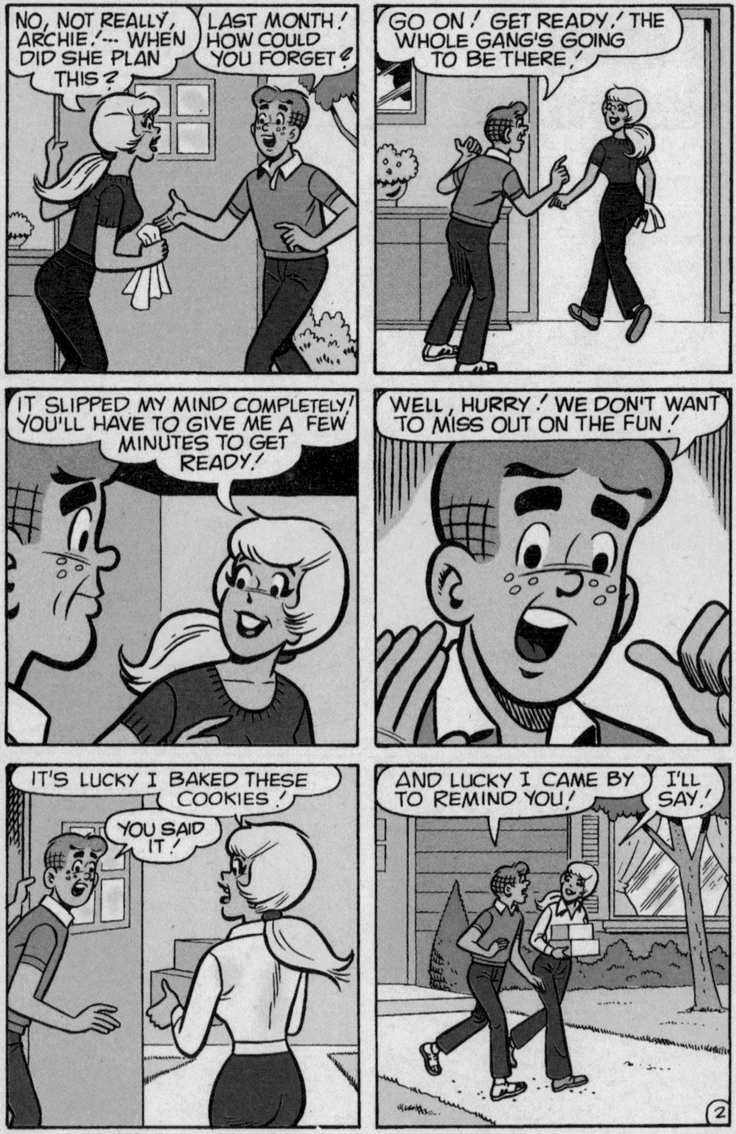
NO, NOT REALLY, ARCHIE!--- WHEN DID SHE PLAN THIS?
LAST MONTH! HOW COULD YOU FORGET?
GO ON! GET READY! THE WHOLE GANG'S GOING TO BE THERE!
IT SLIPPED MY MIND COMPLETELY! YOU'LL HAVE TO GIVE ME A FEW MINUTES TO GET READY!
WELL, HURRY! WE DON'T WANT TO MISS OUT ON THE FUN!
IT'S LUCKY I BAKED THESE COOKIES!
YOU SAID IT!
AND LUCKY I CAME BY TO REMIND YOU!
I'LL SAY!
2

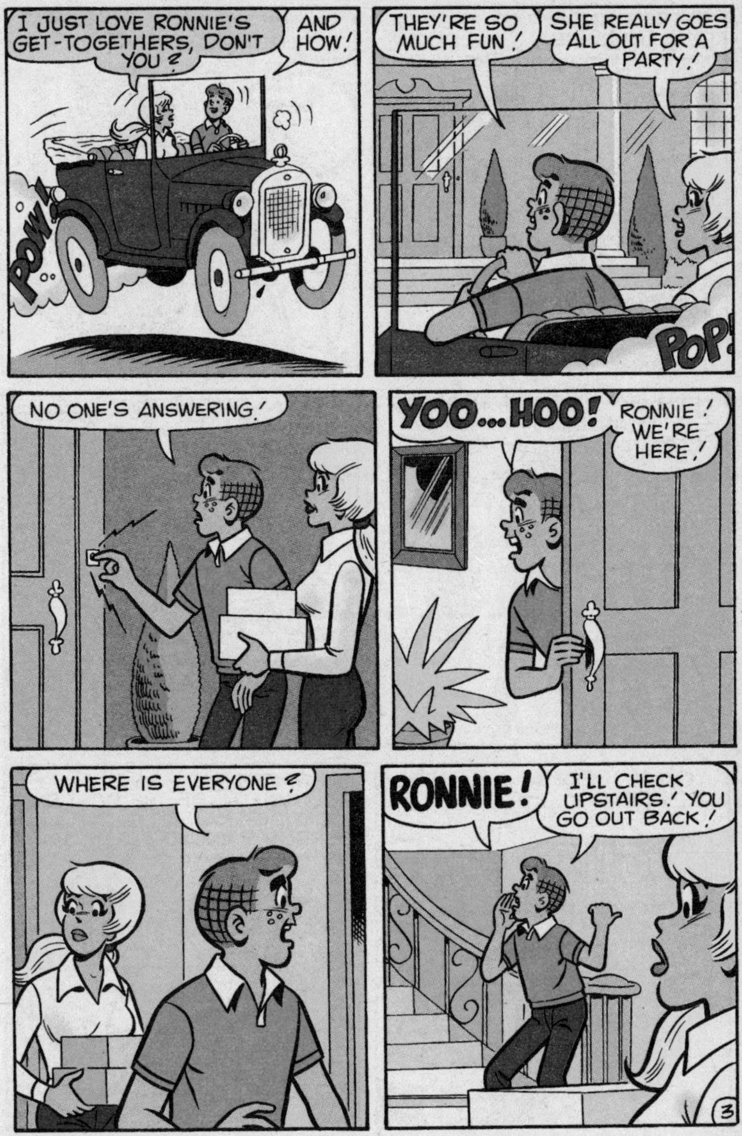
I JUST LOVE RONNIE'S GET-TOGETHERS, DON'T YOU?
AND HOW!
POW!
THEY'RE SO MUCH FUN!
SHE REALLY GOES ALL OUT FOR A PARTY!
POP!
NO ONE'S ANSWERING!
YOO...HOO!
RONNIE! WE'RE HERE!
WHERE IS EVERYONE?
RONNIE!
I'LL CHECK UPSTAIRS! YOU GO OUT BACK!
3

THERE'S NOT A SOUL UP THERE!
THERE'S NO ONE IN THE WHOLE HOUSE!
WHERE THE HECK COULD THEY BE?
?
LET'S GO TO POP TATE'S AND SEE IF ANYBODY'S THERE!
BOY! THAT BURNS ME UP!
LOOK! THERE'S RONNIE!
WHAT ARE YOU DOING HERE? YOU HAVE TO BE THE MOST RUDE, INCONSIDERATE PERSON I KNOW!
?
4

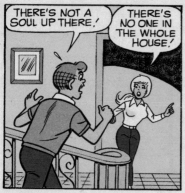

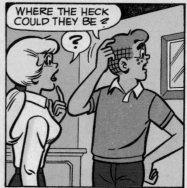

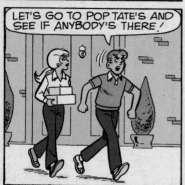

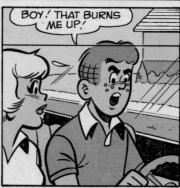

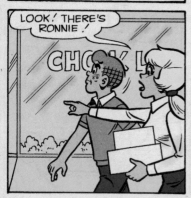

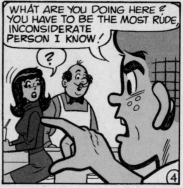

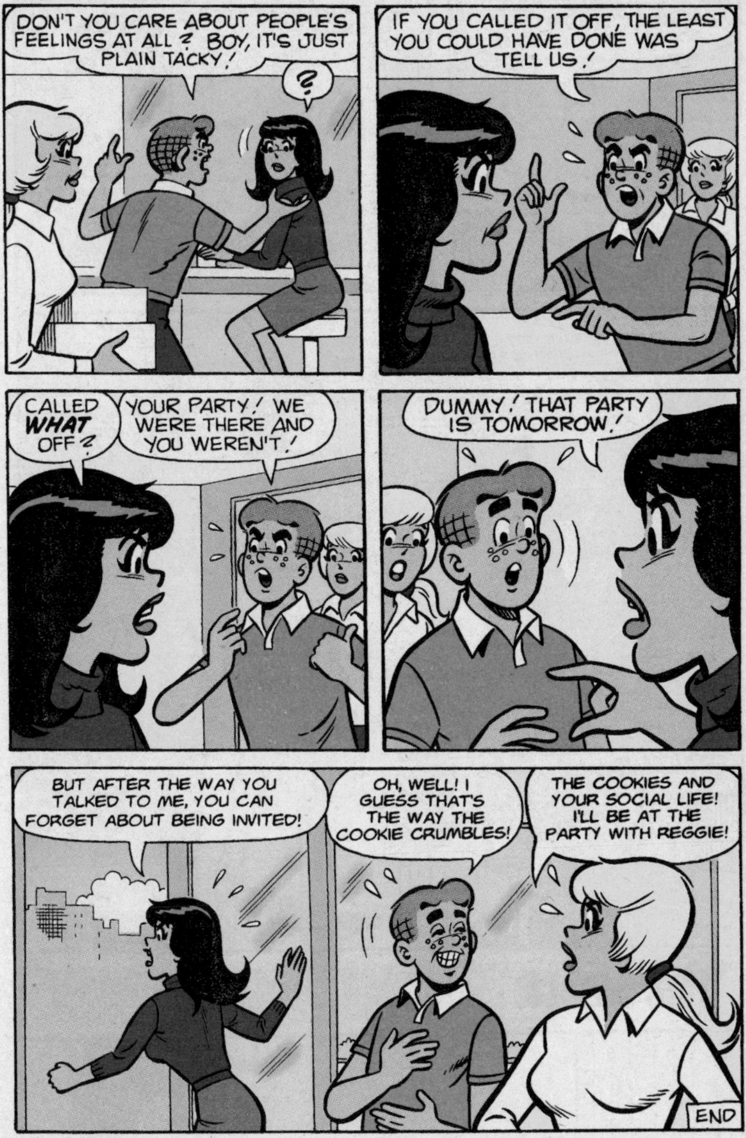
DON'T YOU CARE ABOUT PEOPLE'S FEELINGS AT ALL? BOY, IT'S JUST PLAIN TACKY!
?
IF YOU CALLED IT OFF, THE LEAST YOU COULD HAVE DONE WAS TELL US!
CALLED **WHAT** OFF?
YOUR PARTY! WE WERE THERE AND YOU WEREN'T!
DUMMY! THAT PARTY IS TOMORROW!
BUT AFTER THE WAY YOU TALKED TO ME, YOU CAN FORGET ABOUT BEING INVITED!
OH, WELL! I GUESS THAT'S THE WAY THE COOKIE CRUMBLES!
THE COOKIES AND YOUR SOCIAL LIFE! I'LL BE AT THE PARTY WITH REGGIE!
END

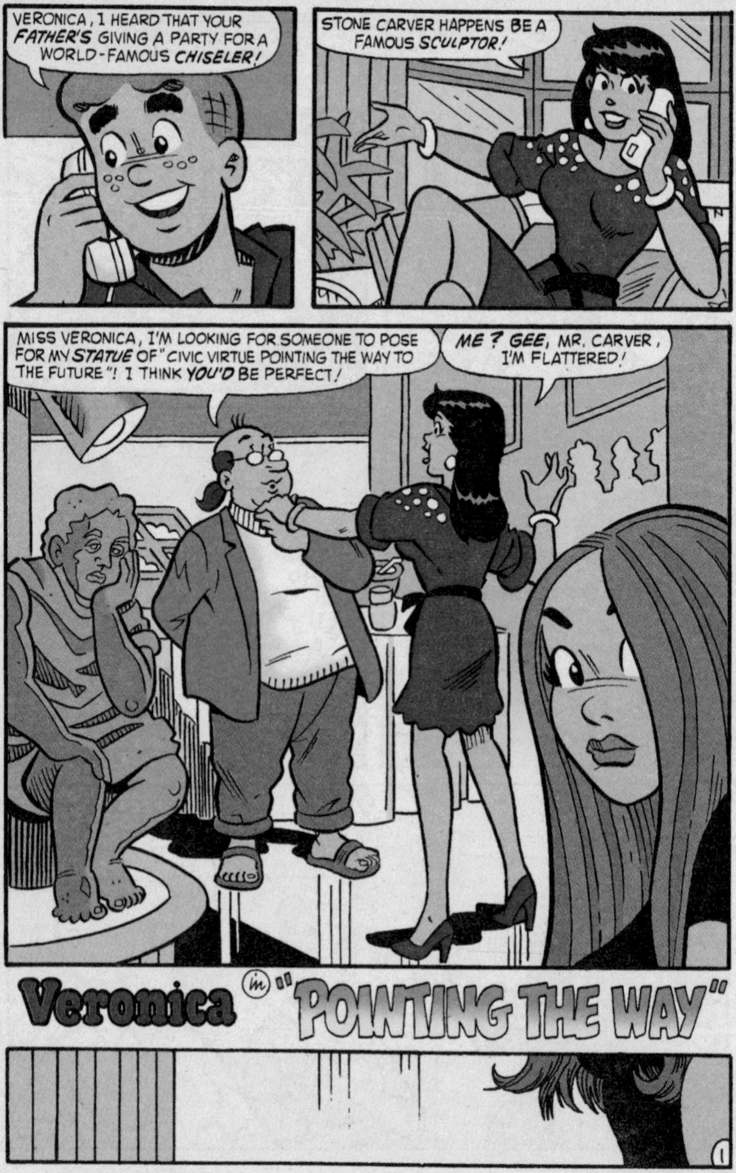
VERONICA, I HEARD THAT YOUR FATHER'S GIVING A PARTY FOR A WORLD-FAMOUS CHISELER!
STONE CARVER HAPPENS BE A FAMOUS SCULPTOR!
MISS VERONICA, I'M LOOKING FOR SOMEONE TO POSE FOR MY STATUE OF "CIVIC VIRTUE POINTING THE WAY TO THE FUTURE"! I THINK YOU'D BE PERFECT!
ME? GEE, MR. CARVER, I'M FLATTERED!
Veronica in "POINTING THE WAY"
1

Script: Hal Smith / Pencils: Tim Kennedy / Inks: Rudy Lapick / Letters: Bill Yoshida

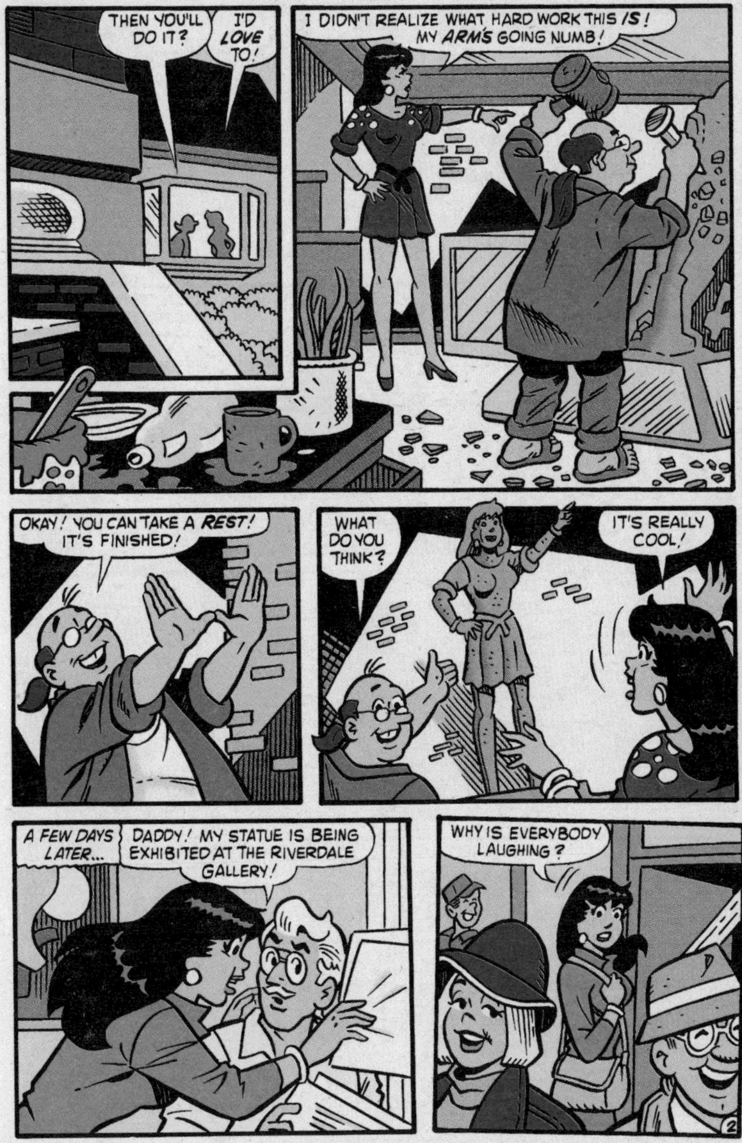
THEN YOU'LL DO IT?
I'D LOVE TO!
I DIDN'T REALIZE WHAT HARD WORK THIS IS! MY ARM'S GOING NUMB!
OKAY! YOU CAN TAKE A REST! IT'S FINISHED!
WHAT DO YOU THINK?
IT'S REALLY COOL!
A FEW DAYS LATER...
DADDY! MY STATUE IS BEING EXHIBITED AT THE RIVERDALE GALLERY!
WHY IS EVERYBODY LAUGHING?
2

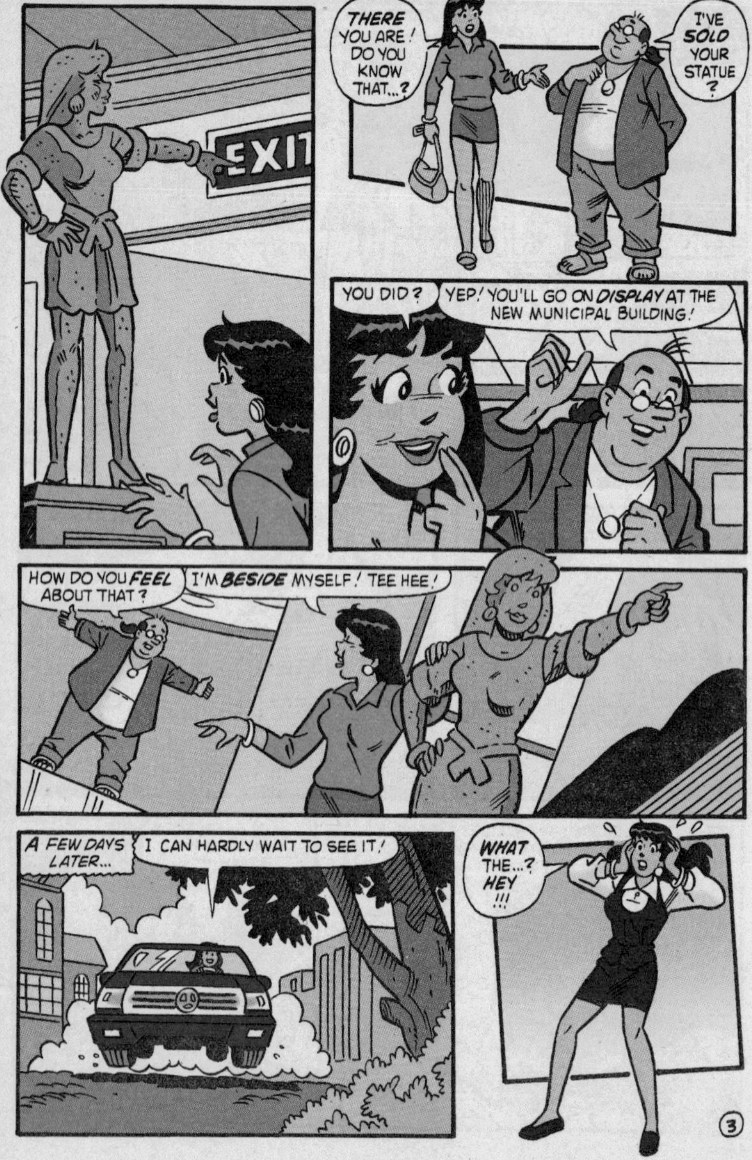
EXIT
THERE YOU ARE! DO YOU KNOW THAT...?
I'VE SOLD YOUR STATUE?
YOU DID?
YEP! YOU'LL GO ON DISPLAY AT THE NEW MUNICIPAL BUILDING!
HOW DO YOU FEEL ABOUT THAT?
I'M BESIDE MYSELF! TEE HEE!
A FEW DAYS LATER...
I CAN HARDLY WAIT TO SEE IT!
WHAT THE...? HEY !!!

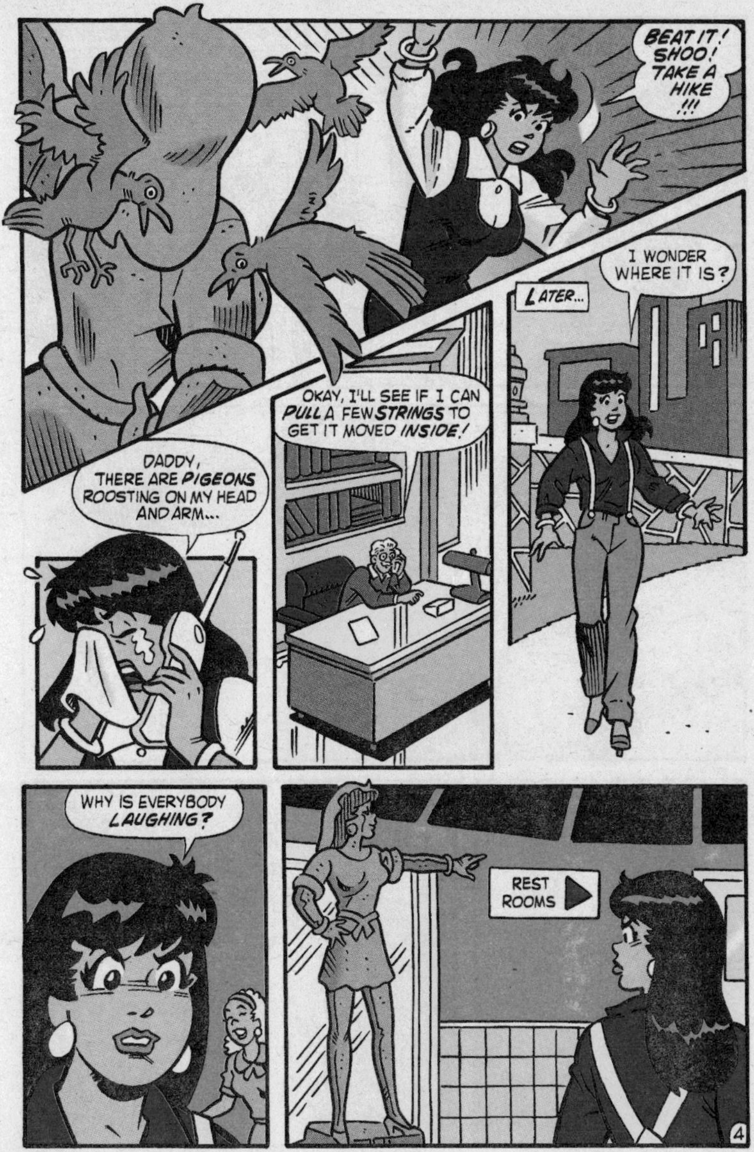
BEAT IT! SHOO! TAKE A HIKE !!!
DADDY, THERE ARE PIGEONS ROOSTING ON MY HEAD AND ARM...
OKAY, I'LL SEE IF I CAN PULL A FEW STRINGS TO GET IT MOVED INSIDE!
LATER...
I WONDER WHERE IT IS?
WHY IS EVERYBODY LAUGHING?
REST ROOMS
4

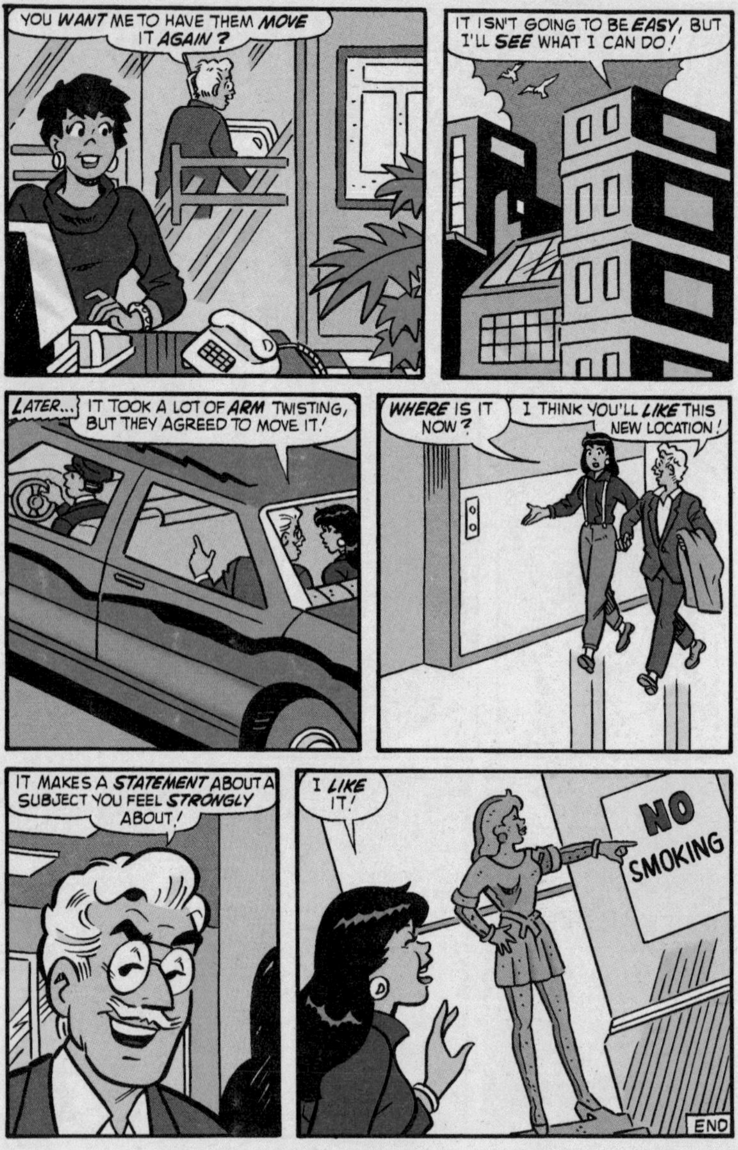
YOU WANT ME TO HAVE THEM MOVE IT AGAIN?
IT ISN'T GOING TO BE EASY, BUT I'LL SEE WHAT I CAN DO!
LATER...
IT TOOK A LOT OF ARM TWISTING, BUT THEY AGREED TO MOVE IT!
WHERE IS IT NOW?
I THINK YOU'LL LIKE THIS NEW LOCATION!
IT MAKES A STATEMENT ABOUT A SUBJECT YOU FEEL STRONGLY ABOUT!
I LIKE IT!
NO SMOKING
END

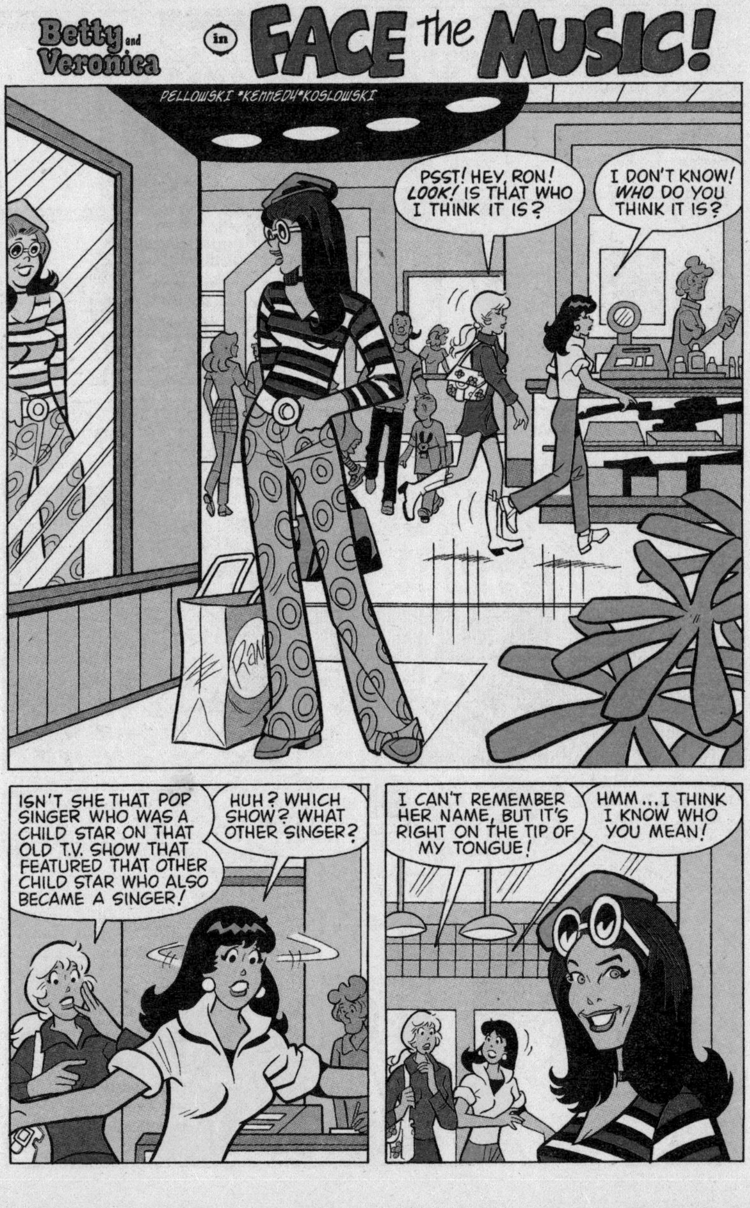
Betty and Veronica in FACE the MUSIC!
PELLOWSKI *KENNEDY*KOSLOWSKI
PSST! HEY, RON! LOOK! IS THAT WHO I THINK IT IS?
I DON'T KNOW! WHO DO YOU THINK IT IS?
ISN'T SHE THAT POP SINGER WHO WAS A CHILD STAR ON THAT OLD T.V. SHOW THAT FEATURED THAT OTHER CHILD STAR WHO ALSO BECAME A SINGER!
HUH? WHICH SHOW? WHAT OTHER SINGER?
I CAN'T REMEMBER HER NAME, BUT IT'S RIGHT ON THE TIP OF MY TONGUE!
HMM... I THINK I KNOW WHO YOU MEAN!

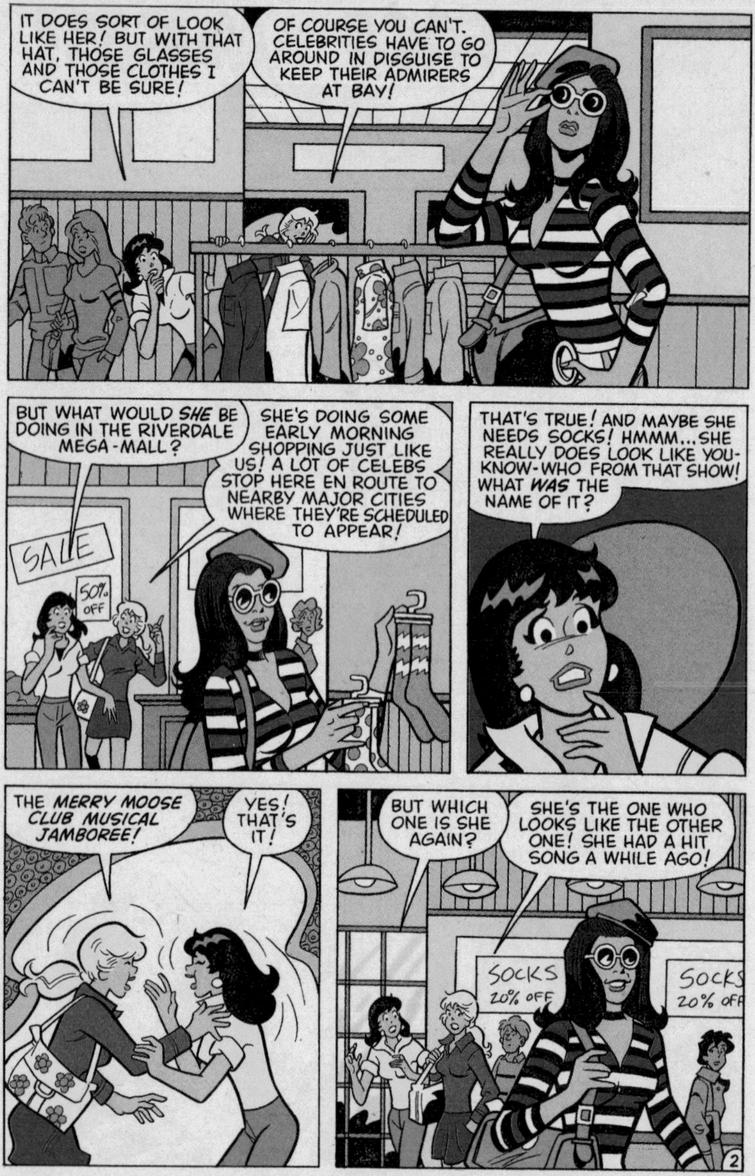

IT DOES SORT OF LOOK LIKE HER! BUT WITH THAT HAT, THOSE GLASSES AND THOSE CLOTHES I CAN'T BE SURE!
OF COURSE YOU CAN'T. CELEBRITIES HAVE TO GO AROUND IN DISGUISE TO KEEP THEIR ADMIRERS AT BAY!
BUT WHAT WOULD SHE BE DOING IN THE RIVERDALE MEGA-MALL?
SHE'S DOING SOME EARLY MORNING SHOPPING JUST LIKE US! A LOT OF CELEBS STOP HERE EN ROUTE TO NEARBY MAJOR CITIES WHERE THEY'RE SCHEDULED TO APPEAR!
SALE
50% OFF
THAT'S TRUE! AND MAYBE SHE NEEDS SOCKS! HMMM...SHE REALLY DOES LOOK LIKE YOU-KNOW-WHO FROM THAT SHOW! WHAT WAS THE NAME OF IT?
THE MERRY MOOSE CLUB MUSICAL JAMBOREE!
YES! THAT'S IT!
BUT WHICH ONE IS SHE AGAIN?
SHE'S THE ONE WHO LOOKS LIKE THE OTHER ONE! SHE HAD A HIT SONG A WHILE AGO!
SOCKS 20% OFF
SOCKS 20% OFF
2

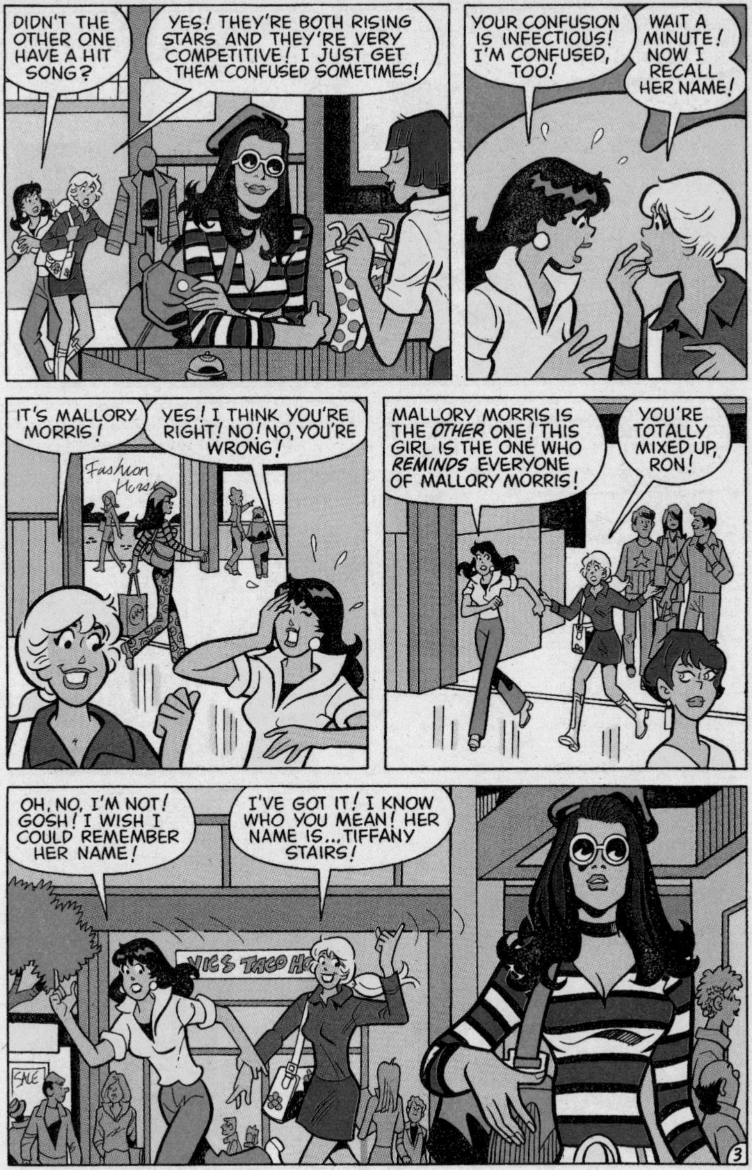

DIDN'T THE OTHER ONE HAVE A HIT SONG?
YES! THEY'RE BOTH RISING STARS AND THEY'RE VERY COMPETITIVE! I JUST GET THEM CONFUSED SOMETIMES!
YOUR CONFUSION IS INFECTIOUS! I'M CONFUSED, TOO!
WAIT A MINUTE! NOW I RECALL HER NAME!
IT'S MALLORY MORRIS!
YES! I THINK YOU'RE RIGHT! NO! NO, YOU'RE WRONG!
MALLORY MORRIS IS THE *OTHER* ONE! THIS GIRL IS THE ONE WHO *REMINDS* EVERYONE OF MALLORY MORRIS!
YOU'RE TOTALLY MIXED UP, RON!
OH, NO, I'M NOT! GOSH! I WISH I COULD REMEMBER HER NAME!
I'VE GOT IT! I KNOW WHO YOU MEAN! HER NAME IS... TIFFANY STAIRS!
VIC'S TACO H
SALE
3

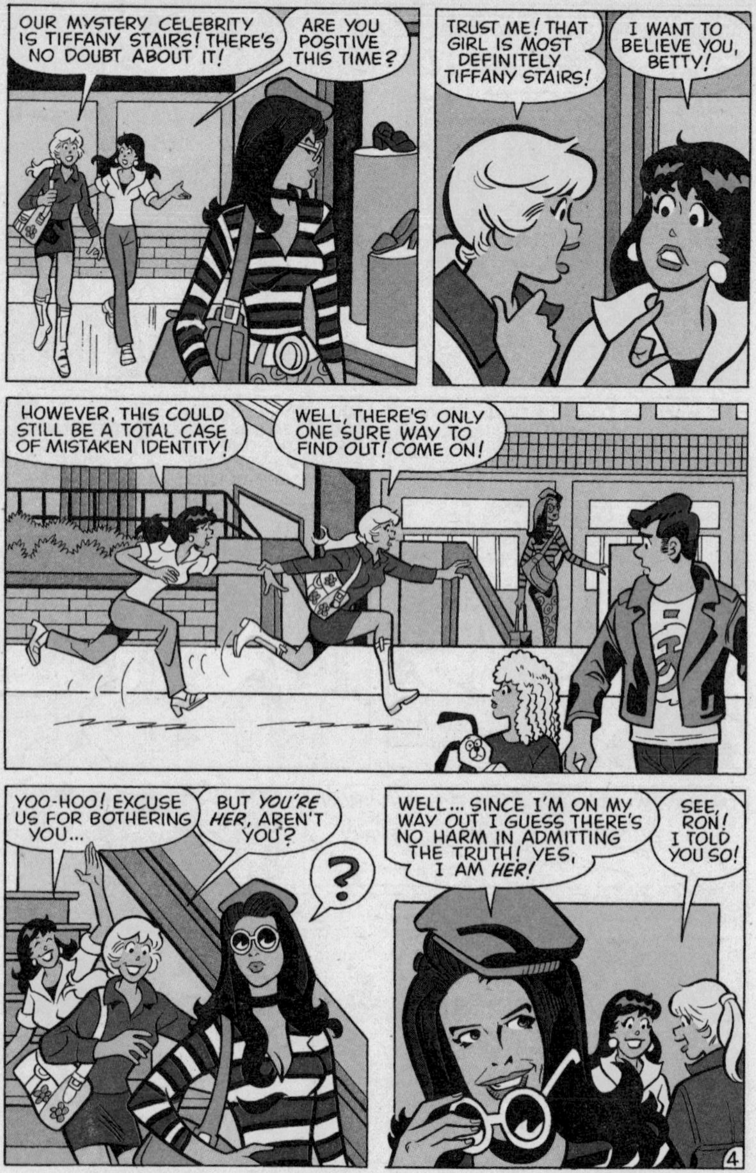

OUR MYSTERY CELEBRITY IS TIFFANY STAIRS! THERE'S NO DOUBT ABOUT IT!
ARE YOU POSITIVE THIS TIME?
TRUST ME! THAT GIRL IS MOST DEFINITELY TIFFANY STAIRS!
I WANT TO BELIEVE YOU, BETTY!
HOWEVER, THIS COULD STILL BE A TOTAL CASE OF MISTAKEN IDENTITY!
WELL, THERE'S ONLY ONE SURE WAY TO FIND OUT! COME ON!
YOO-HOO! EXCUSE US FOR BOTHERING YOU...
BUT *YOU'RE HER*, AREN'T YOU?
?
WELL... SINCE I'M ON MY WAY OUT I GUESS THERE'S NO HARM IN ADMITTING THE TRUTH! YES, I AM *HER*!
SEE, RON! I TOLD YOU SO!

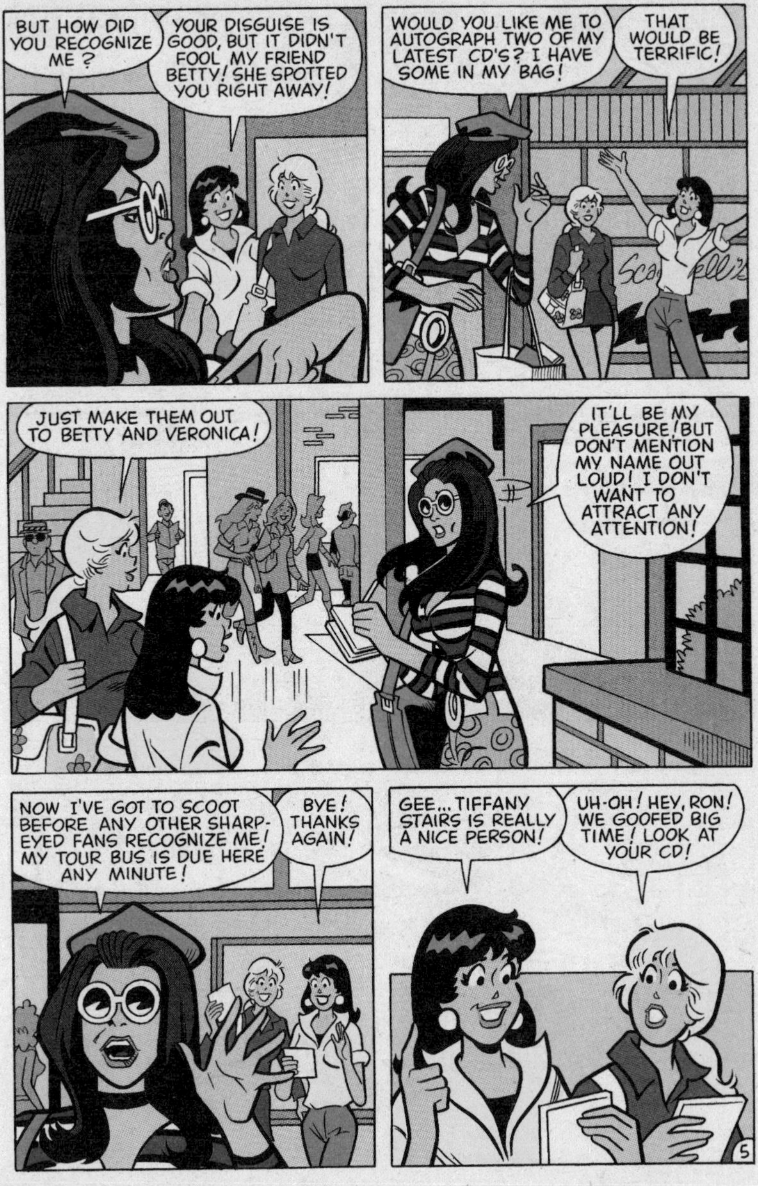
BUT HOW DID YOU RECOGNIZE ME ?
YOUR DISGUISE IS GOOD, BUT IT DIDN'T FOOL MY FRIEND BETTY! SHE SPOTTED YOU RIGHT AWAY!
WOULD YOU LIKE ME TO AUTOGRAPH TWO OF MY LATEST CD'S? I HAVE SOME IN MY BAG!
THAT WOULD BE TERRIFIC!
JUST MAKE THEM OUT TO BETTY AND VERONICA!
IT'LL BE MY PLEASURE! BUT DON'T MENTION MY NAME OUT LOUD! I DON'T WANT TO ATTRACT ANY ATTENTION!
NOW I'VE GOT TO SCOOT BEFORE ANY OTHER SHARP-EYED FANS RECOGNIZE ME! MY TOUR BUS IS DUE HERE ANY MINUTE!
BYE! THANKS AGAIN!
GEE... TIFFANY STAIRS IS REALLY A NICE PERSON!
UH-OH! HEY, RON! WE GOOFED BIG TIME! LOOK AT YOUR CD!
5

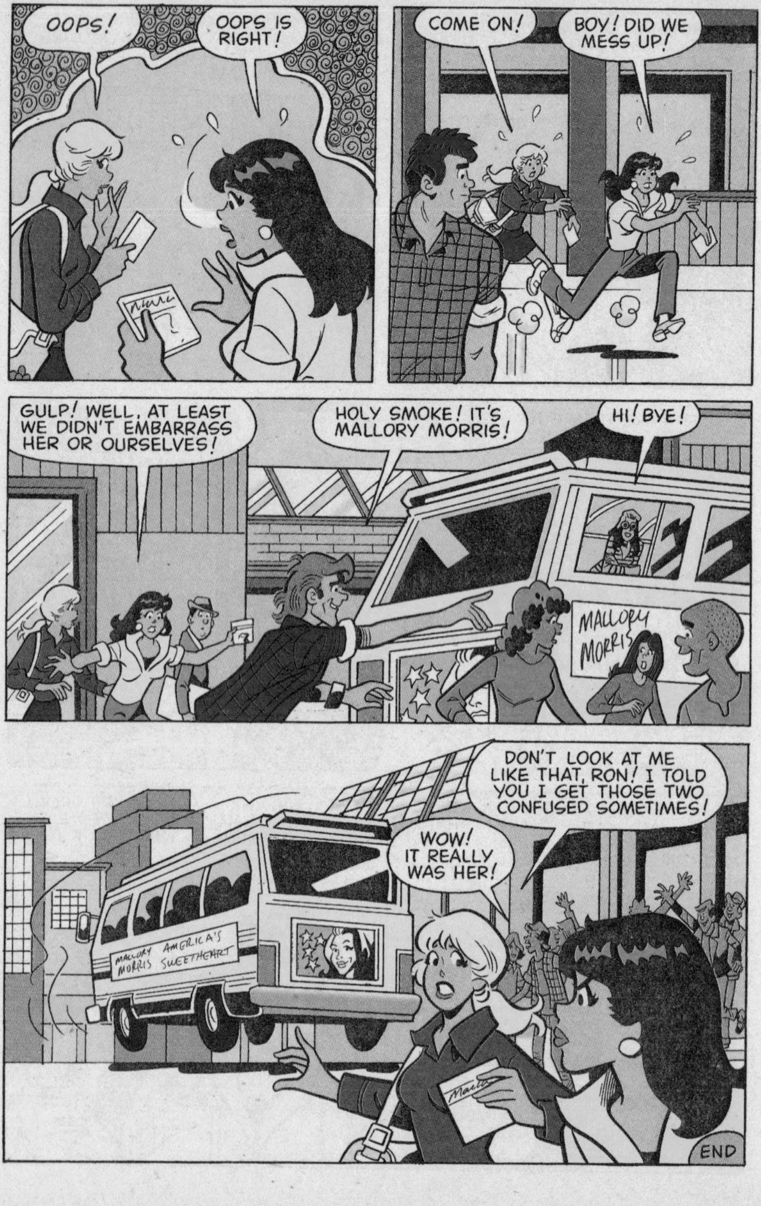
OOPS!
OOPS IS RIGHT!
COME ON!
BOY! DID WE MESS UP!
GULP! WELL, AT LEAST WE DIDN'T EMBARRASS HER OR OURSELVES!
HOLY SMOKE! IT'S MALLORY MORRIS!
HI! BYE!
MALLORY MORRIS
DON'T LOOK AT ME LIKE THAT, RON! I TOLD YOU I GET THOSE TWO CONFUSED SOMETIMES!
WOW! IT REALLY WAS HER!
MALLORY MORRIS AMERICA'S SWEETHEART
END

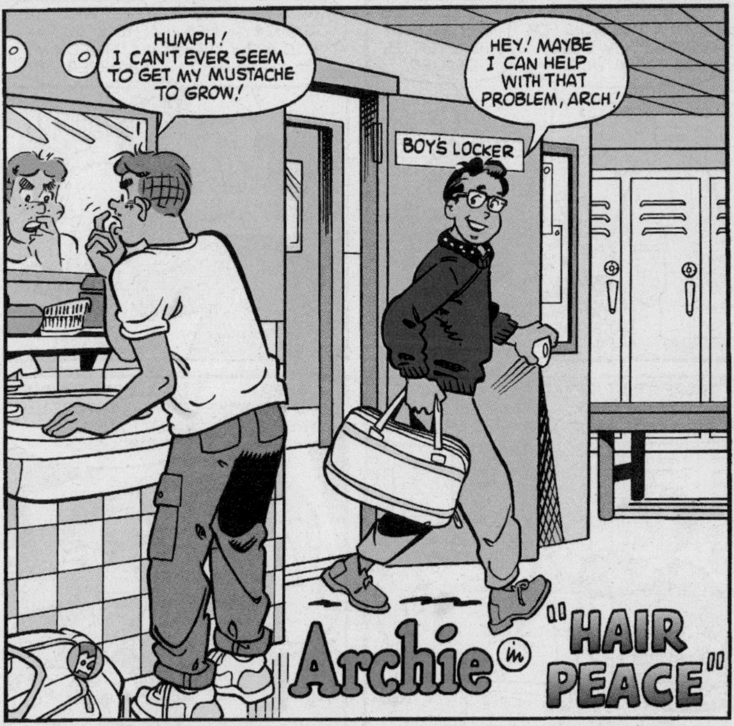
HUMPH! I CAN'T EVER SEEM TO GET MY MUSTACHE TO GROW!
HEY! MAYBE I CAN HELP WITH THAT PROBLEM, ARCH!
BOY'S LOCKER
Archie in "HAIR PEACE"

Script: Mike Pellowski / Pencils: Stan Goldberg / Inks: Bob Smith / Letters: Bill Yoshida

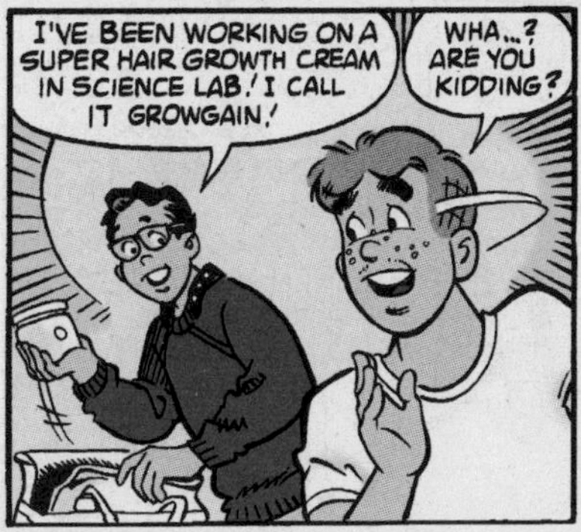
I'VE BEEN WORKING ON A SUPER HAIR GROWTH CREAM IN SCIENCE LAB! I CALL IT GROWGAIN!
WHA...? ARE YOU KIDDING?

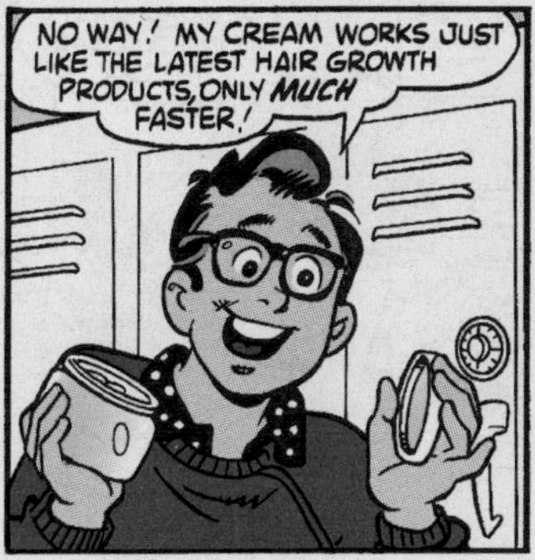
NO WAY! MY CREAM WORKS JUST LIKE THE LATEST HAIR GROWTH PRODUCTS, ONLY MUCH FASTER!

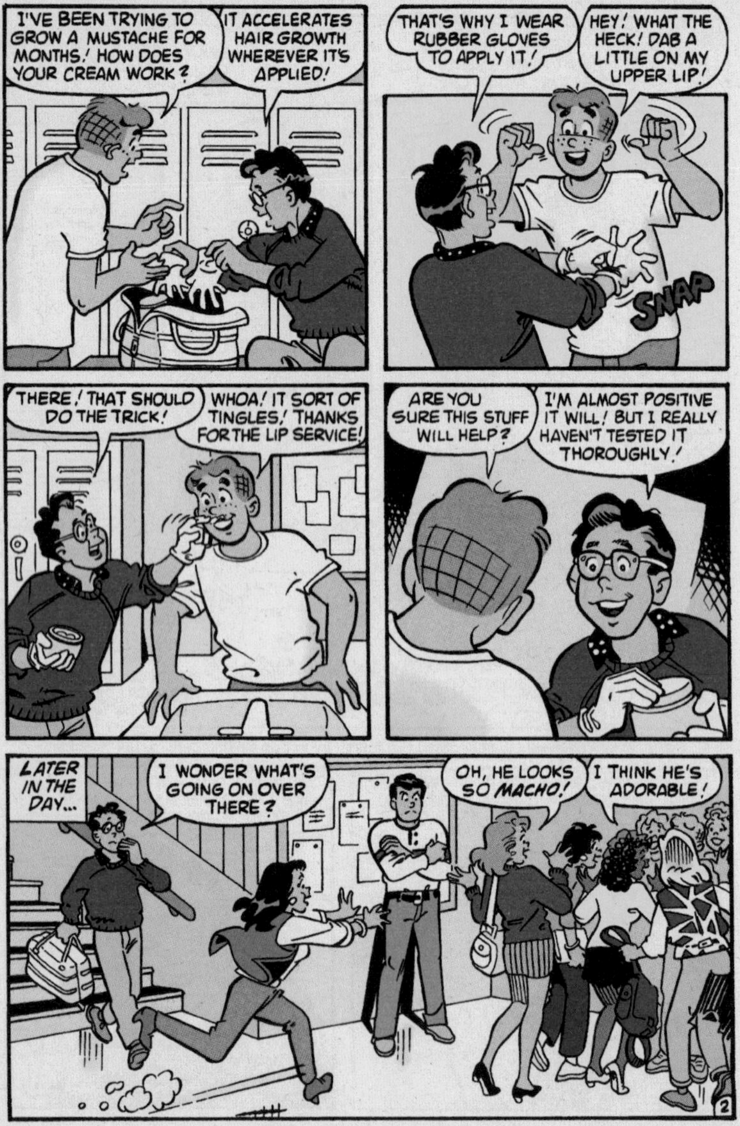
I'VE BEEN TRYING TO GROW A MUSTACHE FOR MONTHS! HOW DOES YOUR CREAM WORK?
IT ACCELERATES HAIR GROWTH WHEREVER IT'S APPLIED!
THAT'S WHY I WEAR RUBBER GLOVES TO APPLY IT!
HEY! WHAT THE HECK! DAB A LITTLE ON MY UPPER LIP!
SNAP
THERE! THAT SHOULD DO THE TRICK!
WHOA! IT SORT OF TINGLES! THANKS FOR THE LIP SERVICE!
ARE YOU SURE THIS STUFF WILL HELP?
I'M ALMOST POSITIVE IT WILL! BUT I REALLY HAVEN'T TESTED IT THOROUGHLY!
LATER IN THE DAY...
I WONDER WHAT'S GOING ON OVER THERE?
OH, HE LOOKS SO MACHO!
I THINK HE'S ADORABLE!
2

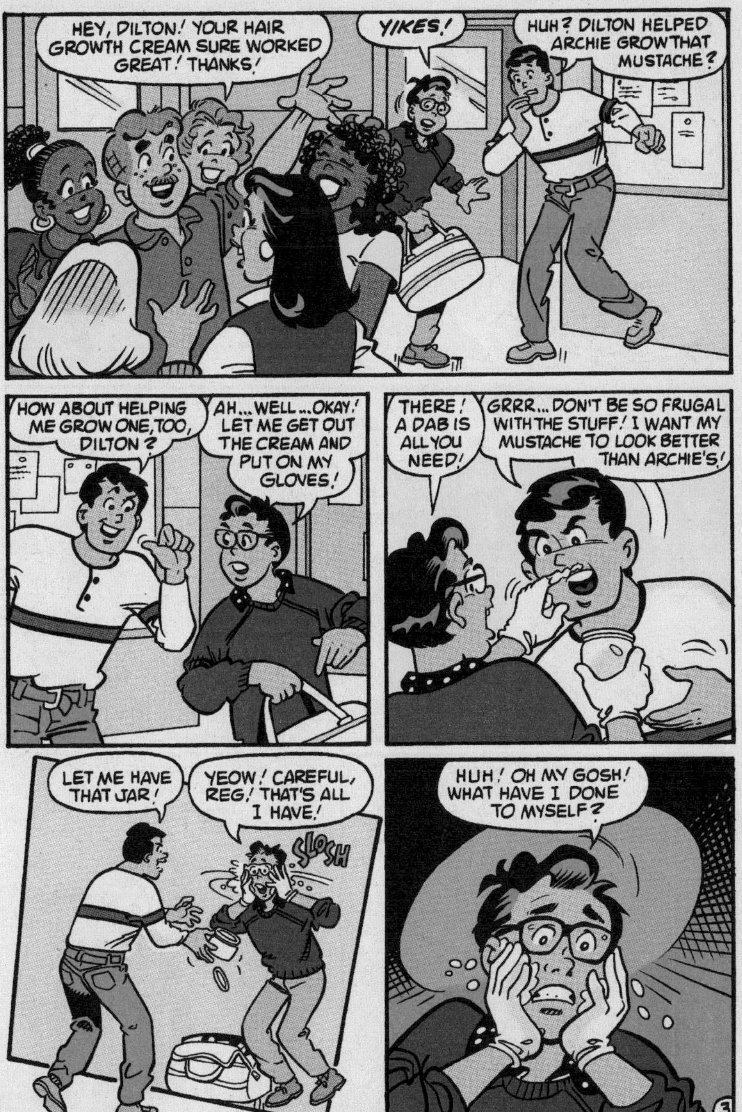
HEY, DILTON! YOUR HAIR GROWTH CREAM SURE WORKED GREAT! THANKS!
YIKES!
HUH? DILTON HELPED ARCHIE GROW THAT MUSTACHE?
HOW ABOUT HELPING ME GROW ONE, TOO, DILTON?
AH... WELL... OKAY! LET ME GET OUT THE CREAM AND PUT ON MY GLOVES!
THERE! A DAB IS ALL YOU NEED!
GRRR... DON'T BE SO FRUGAL WITH THE STUFF! I WANT MY MUSTACHE TO LOOK BETTER THAN ARCHIE'S!
LET ME HAVE THAT JAR!
YEOW! CAREFUL, REG! THAT'S ALL I HAVE!
SLOSH
HUH! OH MY GOSH! WHAT HAVE I DONE TO MYSELF?
3

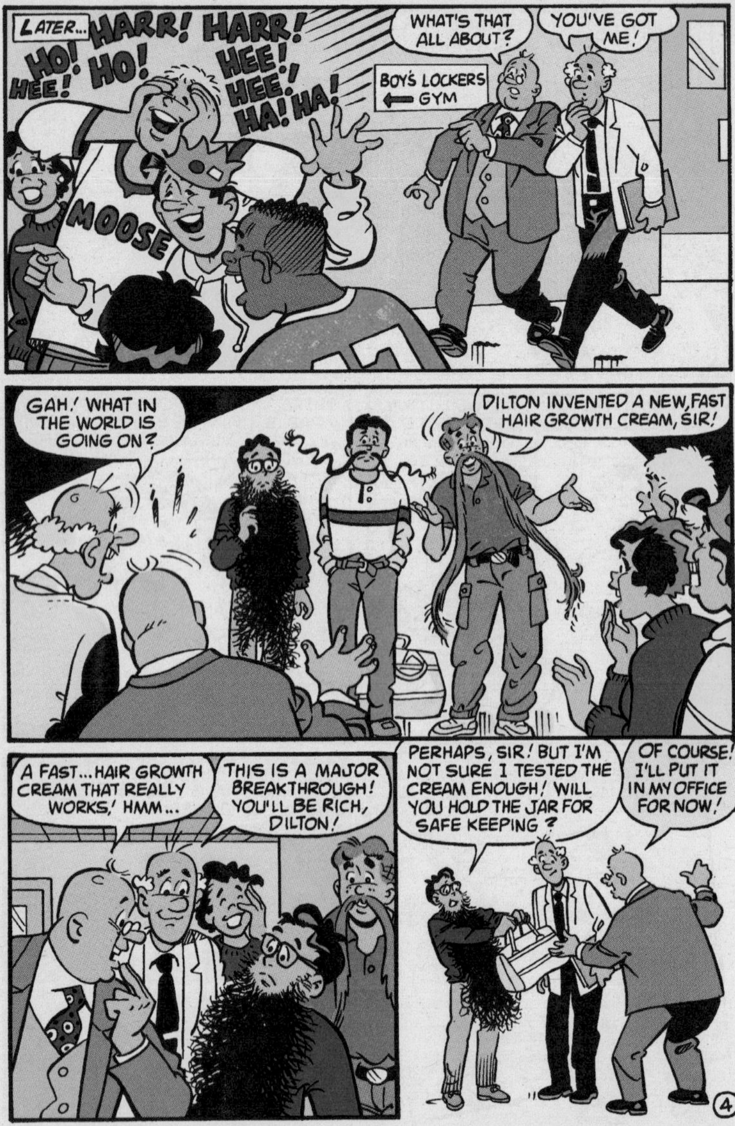

LATER...
HARR! HARR!
HO! HEE! HO!
HEE! HEE! HA! HA!
WHAT'S THAT ALL ABOUT?
YOU'VE GOT ME!
BOY'S LOCKERS
GYM
MOOSE
GAH! WHAT IN THE WORLD IS GOING ON?
DILTON INVENTED A NEW, FAST HAIR GROWTH CREAM, SIR!
A FAST... HAIR GROWTH CREAM THAT REALLY WORKS! HMM...
THIS IS A MAJOR BREAKTHROUGH! YOU'LL BE RICH, DILTON!
PERHAPS, SIR! BUT I'M NOT SURE I TESTED THE CREAM ENOUGH! WILL YOU HOLD THE JAR FOR SAFE KEEPING?
OF COURSE! I'LL PUT IT IN MY OFFICE FOR NOW!
4

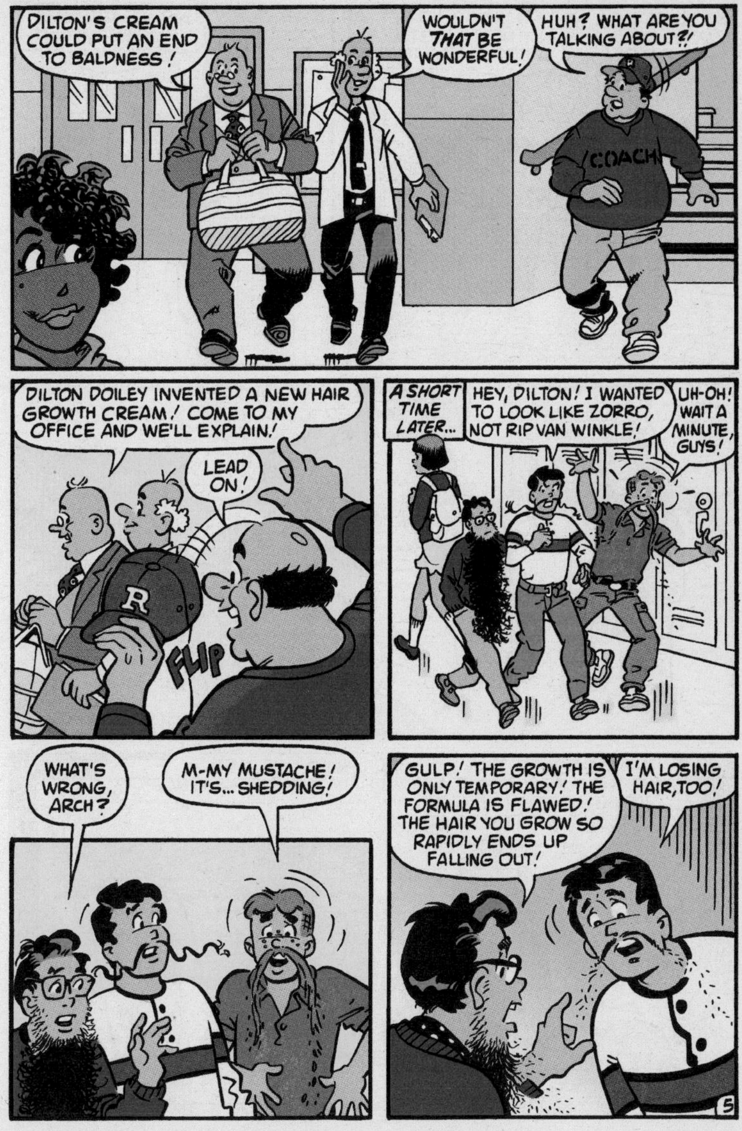
DILTON'S CREAM COULD PUT AN END TO BALDNESS!
WOULDN'T *THAT* BE WONDERFUL!
HUH? WHAT ARE YOU TALKING ABOUT?!
COACH
DILTON DOILEY INVENTED A NEW HAIR GROWTH CREAM! COME TO MY OFFICE AND WE'LL EXPLAIN!
LEAD ON!
FLIP
A SHORT TIME LATER...
HEY, DILTON! I WANTED TO LOOK LIKE ZORRO, NOT RIP VAN WINKLE!
UH-OH! WAIT A MINUTE, GUYS!
WHAT'S WRONG, ARCH?
M-MY MUSTACHE! IT'S... SHEDDING!
GULP! THE GROWTH IS ONLY TEMPORARY! THE FORMULA IS FLAWED! THE HAIR YOU GROW SO RAPIDLY ENDS UP FALLING OUT!
I'M LOSING HAIR, TOO!
5

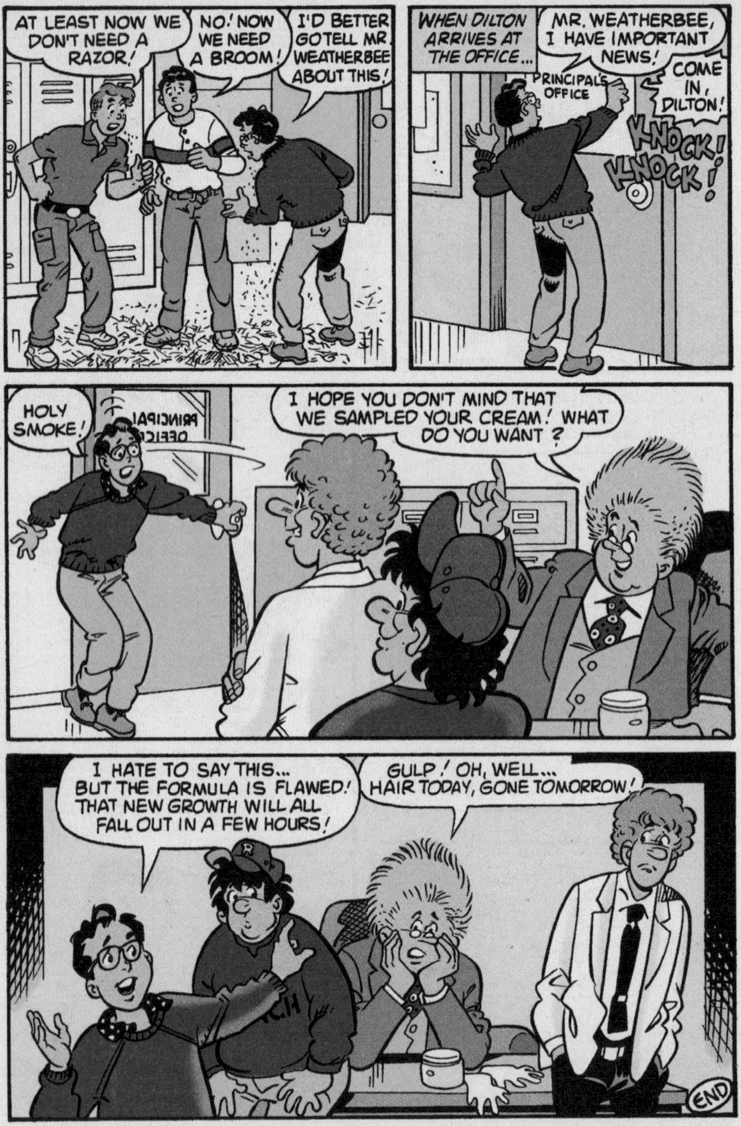
AT LEAST NOW WE DON'T NEED A RAZOR!
NO! NOW WE NEED A BROOM!
I'D BETTER GO TELL MR. WEATHERBEE ABOUT THIS!
WHEN DILTON ARRIVES AT THE OFFICE...
MR. WEATHERBEE, I HAVE IMPORTANT NEWS!
PRINCIPAL'S OFFICE
COME IN, DILTON!
KNOCK! KNOCK!
HOLY SMOKE!
I HOPE YOU DON'T MIND THAT WE SAMPLED YOUR CREAM! WHAT DO YOU WANT?
I HATE TO SAY THIS... BUT THE FORMULA IS FLAWED! THAT NEW GROWTH WILL ALL FALL OUT IN A FEW HOURS!
GULP! OH, WELL... HAIR TODAY, GONE TOMORROW!
END

Reggie in The WINNER

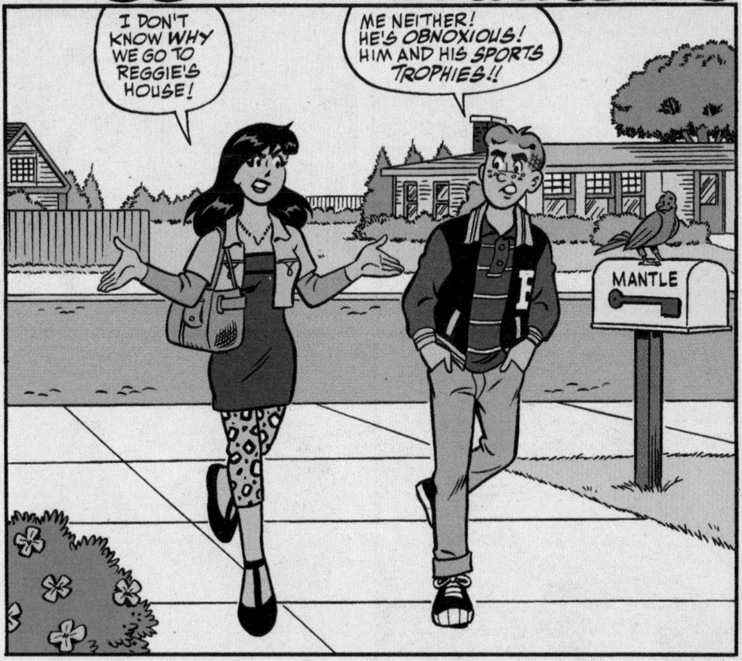
I DON'T KNOW WHY WE GO TO REGGIE'S HOUSE!
ME NEITHER! HE'S OBNOXIOUS! HIM AND HIS SPORTS TROPHIES!!
MANTLE

SCRIPT: CRAIG BOLDMAN PENCILS: FERNANDO RUIZ INKS: JON D'AGOSTINO
LETTERS: JACK MORELLI

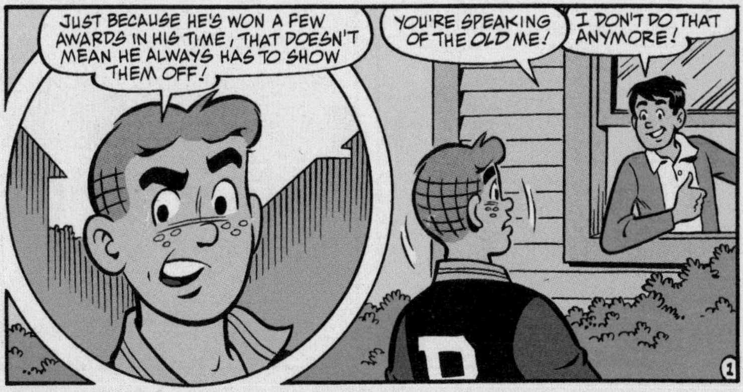
JUST BECAUSE HE'S WON A FEW AWARDS IN HIS TIME, THAT DOESN'T MEAN HE ALWAYS HAS TO SHOW THEM OFF!
YOU'RE SPEAKING OF THE OLD ME!
I DON'T DO THAT ANYMORE!

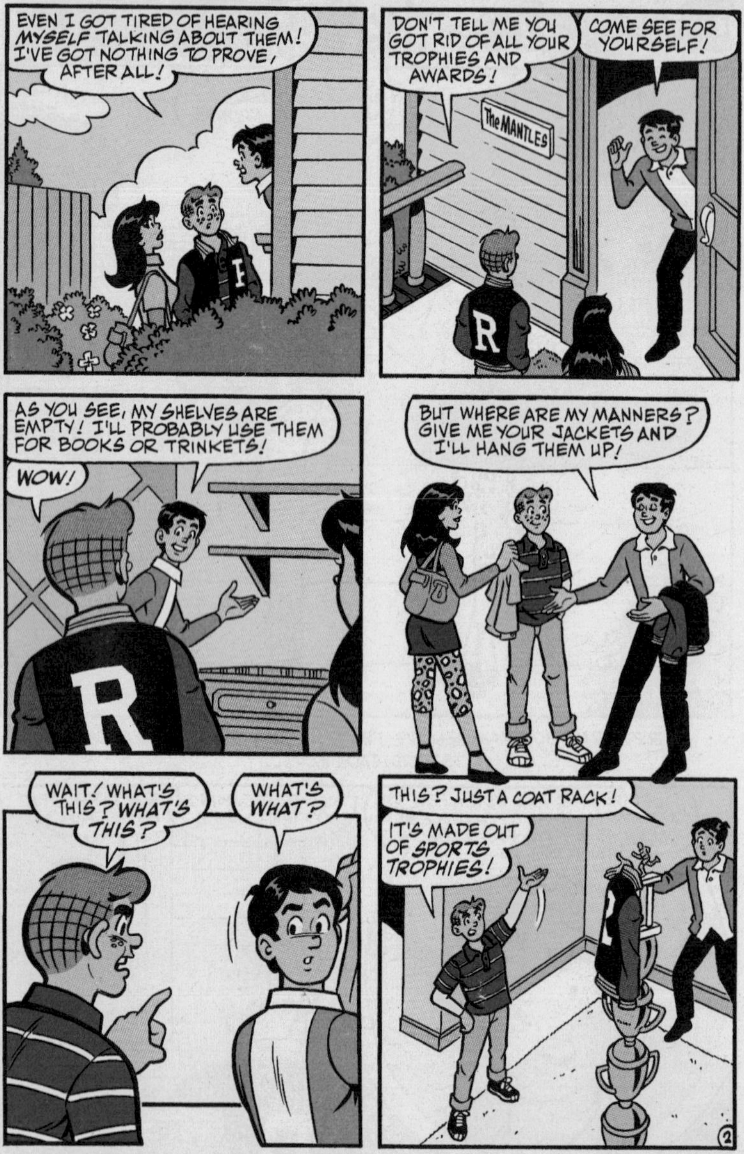
EVEN I GOT TIRED OF HEARING MYSELF TALKING ABOUT THEM! I'VE GOT NOTHING TO PROVE, AFTER ALL!
DON'T TELL ME YOU GOT RID OF ALL YOUR TROPHIES AND AWARDS!
COME SEE FOR YOURSELF!
The MANTLES
AS YOU SEE, MY SHELVES ARE EMPTY! I'LL PROBABLY USE THEM FOR BOOKS OR TRINKETS!
WOW!
BUT WHERE ARE MY MANNERS? GIVE ME YOUR JACKETS AND I'LL HANG THEM UP!
WAIT! WHAT'S THIS? WHAT'S THIS?
WHAT'S WHAT?
THIS? JUST A COAT RACK!
IT'S MADE OUT OF SPORTS TROPHIES!
2

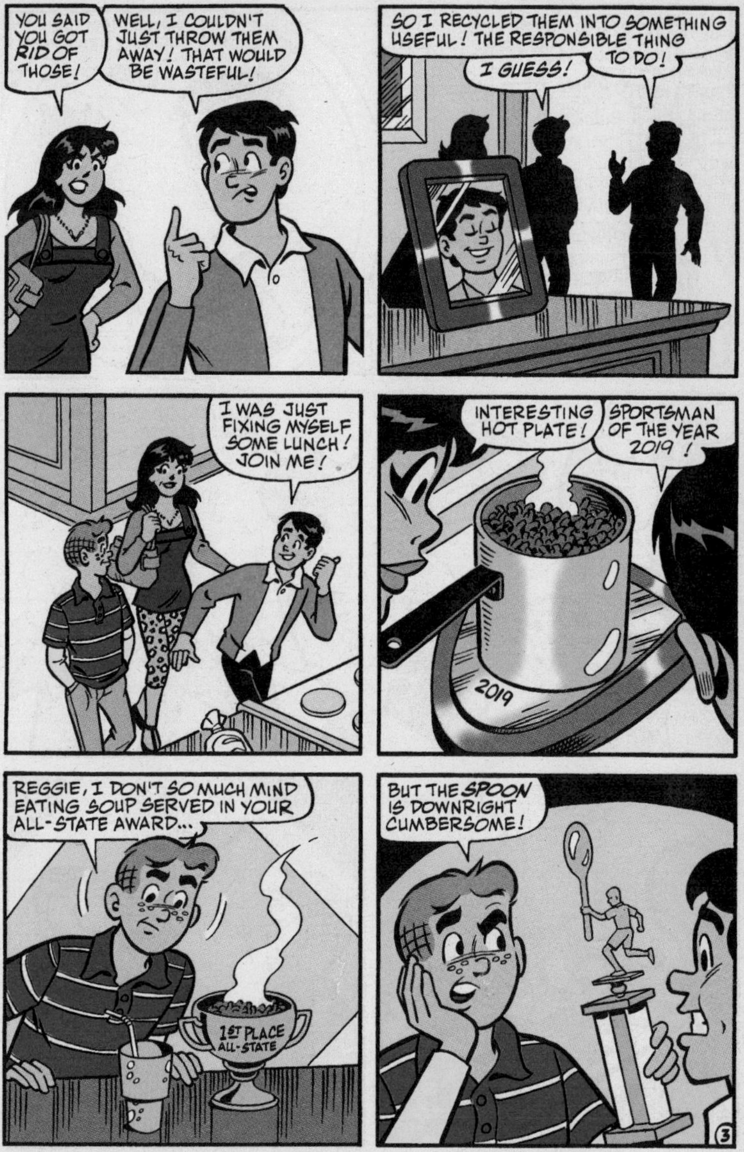
YOU SAID YOU GOT RID OF THOSE!
WELL, I COULDN'T JUST THROW THEM AWAY! THAT WOULD BE WASTEFUL!
SO I RECYCLED THEM INTO SOMETHING USEFUL! THE RESPONSIBLE THING TO DO!
I GUESS!
I WAS JUST FIXING MYSELF SOME LUNCH! JOIN ME!
INTERESTING HOT PLATE!
SPORTSMAN OF THE YEAR 2019!
2019
REGGIE, I DON'T SO MUCH MIND EATING SOUP SERVED IN YOUR ALL-STATE AWARD...
1ST PLACE ALL-STATE
BUT THE SPOON IS DOWNRIGHT CUMBERSOME!
3

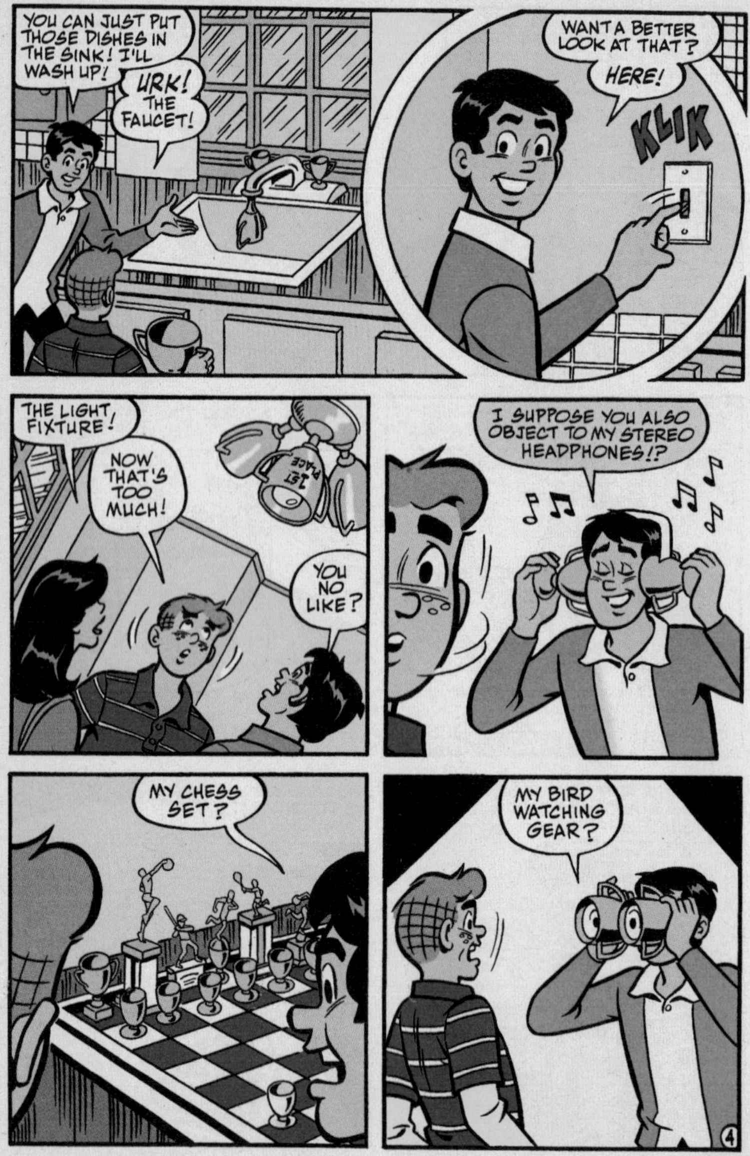

YOU CAN JUST PUT THOSE DISHES IN THE SINK! I'LL WASH UP!
URK! THE FAUCET!
WANT A BETTER LOOK AT THAT?
HERE!
KLIK
THE LIGHT FIXTURE!
NOW THAT'S TOO MUCH!
1ST PLACE
YOU NO LIKE?
I SUPPOSE YOU ALSO OBJECT TO MY STEREO HEADPHONES!?
MY CHESS SET?
MY BIRD WATCHING GEAR?
4

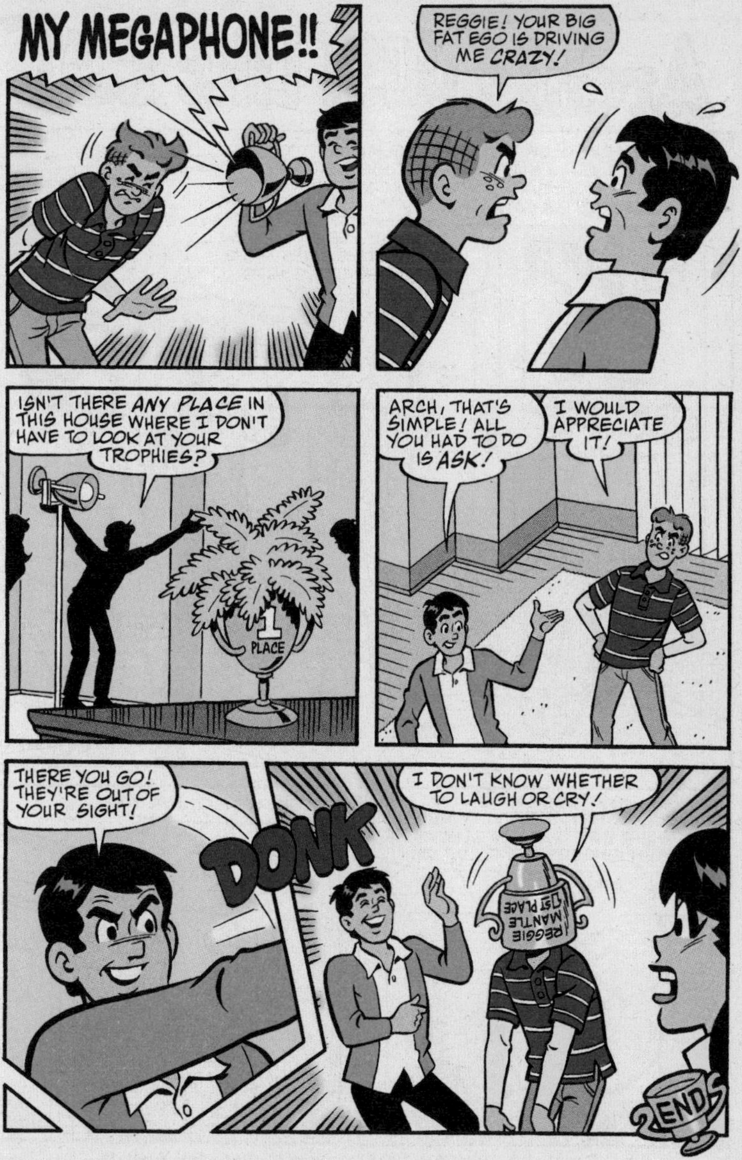
MY MEGAPHONE!!
REGGIE! YOUR BIG FAT EGO IS DRIVING ME CRAZY!
ISN'T THERE ANY PLACE IN THIS HOUSE WHERE I DON'T HAVE TO LOOK AT YOUR TROPHIES?
1 PLACE
ARCH, THAT'S SIMPLE! ALL YOU HAD TO DO IS ASK!
I WOULD APPRECIATE IT!
THERE YOU GO! THEY'RE OUT OF YOUR SIGHT!
DONK
I DON'T KNOW WHETHER TO LAUGH OR CRY!
REGGIE MANTLE 1ST PLACE
END

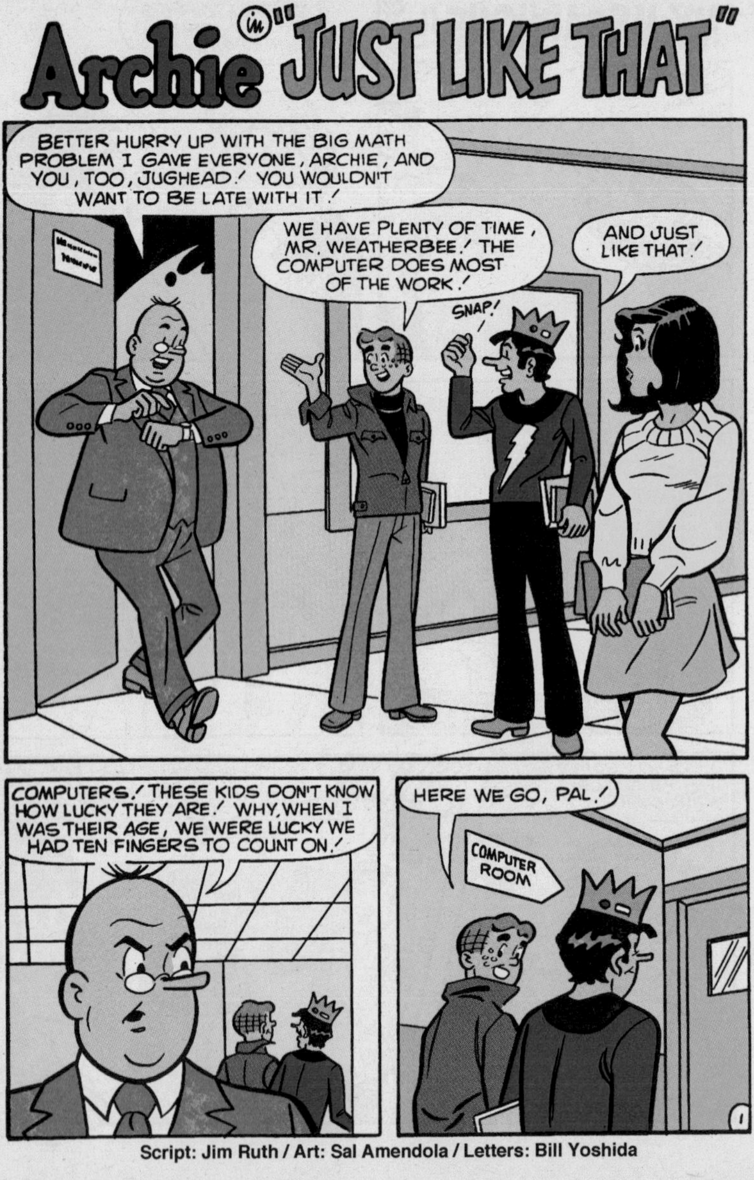
Archie in "JUST LIKE THAT"
BETTER HURRY UP WITH THE BIG MATH PROBLEM I GAVE EVERYONE, ARCHIE, AND YOU, TOO, JUGHEAD! YOU WOULDN'T WANT TO BE LATE WITH IT!
WE HAVE PLENTY OF TIME, MR. WEATHERBEE! THE COMPUTER DOES MOST OF THE WORK!
AND JUST LIKE THAT!
SNAP!
COMPUTERS! THESE KIDS DON'T KNOW HOW LUCKY THEY ARE! WHY, WHEN I WAS THEIR AGE, WE WERE LUCKY WE HAD TEN FINGERS TO COUNT ON!
HERE WE GO, PAL!
COMPUTER ROOM
1

Script: Jim Ruth / Art: Sal Amendola / Letters: Bill Yoshida

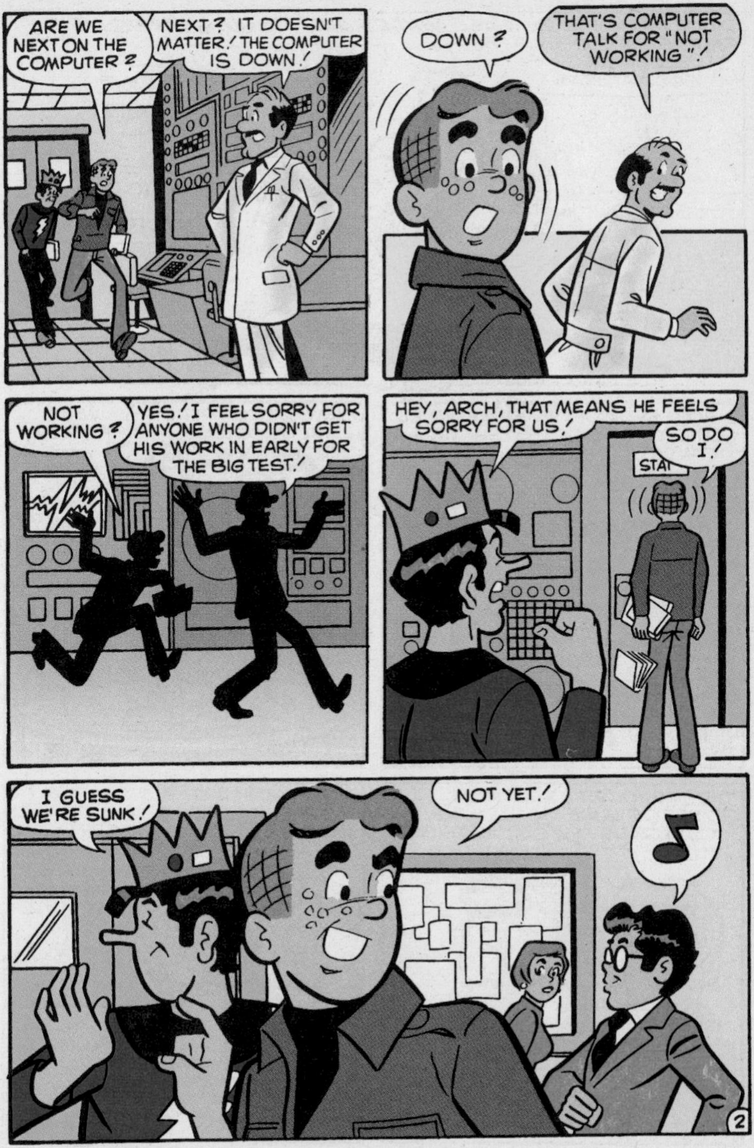
ARE WE NEXT ON THE COMPUTER?
NEXT? IT DOESN'T MATTER! THE COMPUTER IS DOWN!
DOWN?
THAT'S COMPUTER TALK FOR "NOT WORKING"!
NOT WORKING?
YES! I FEEL SORRY FOR ANYONE WHO DIDN'T GET HIS WORK IN EARLY FOR THE BIG TEST!
HEY, ARCH, THAT MEANS HE FEELS SORRY FOR US!
SO DO I!
I GUESS WE'RE SUNK!
NOT YET!
2

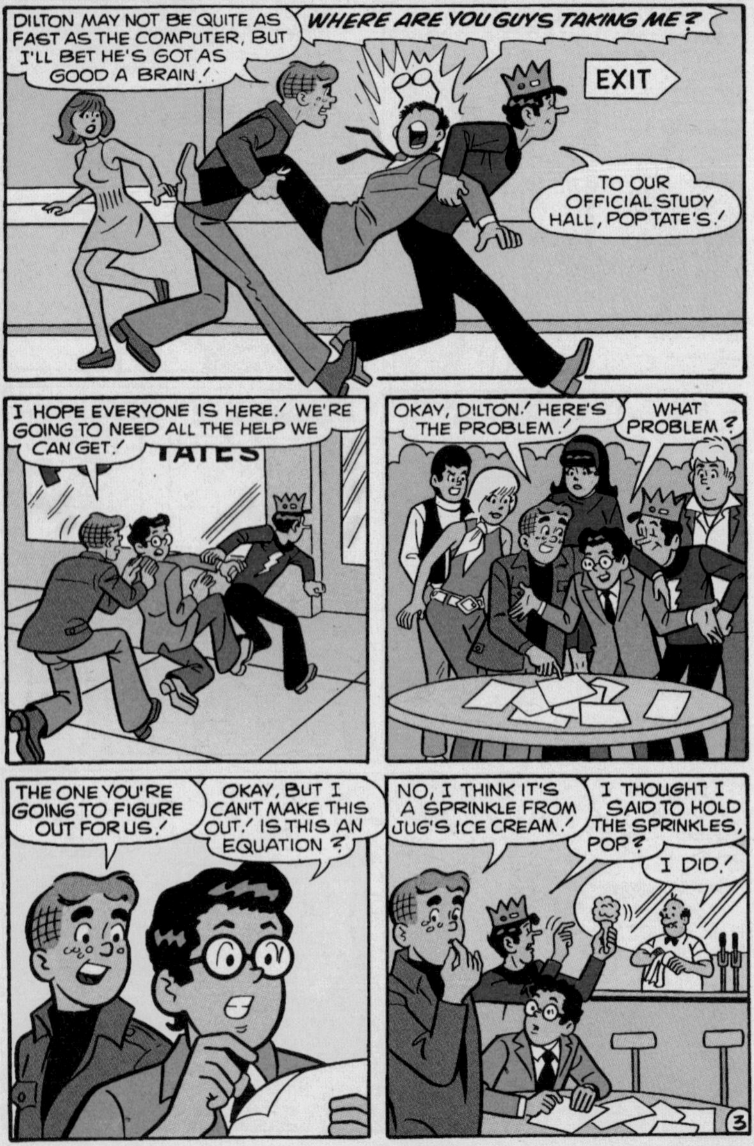
DILTON MAY NOT BE QUITE AS FAST AS THE COMPUTER, BUT I'LL BET HE'S GOT AS GOOD A BRAIN!
WHERE ARE YOU GUYS TAKING ME?
EXIT
TO OUR OFFICIAL STUDY HALL, POP TATE'S!
I HOPE EVERYONE IS HERE! WE'RE GOING TO NEED ALL THE HELP WE CAN GET!
OKAY, DILTON! HERE'S THE PROBLEM!
WHAT PROBLEM?
THE ONE YOU'RE GOING TO FIGURE OUT FOR US!
OKAY, BUT I CAN'T MAKE THIS OUT! IS THIS AN EQUATION?
NO, I THINK IT'S A SPRINKLE FROM JUG'S ICE CREAM!
I THOUGHT I SAID TO HOLD THE SPRINKLES, POP?
I DID!
3

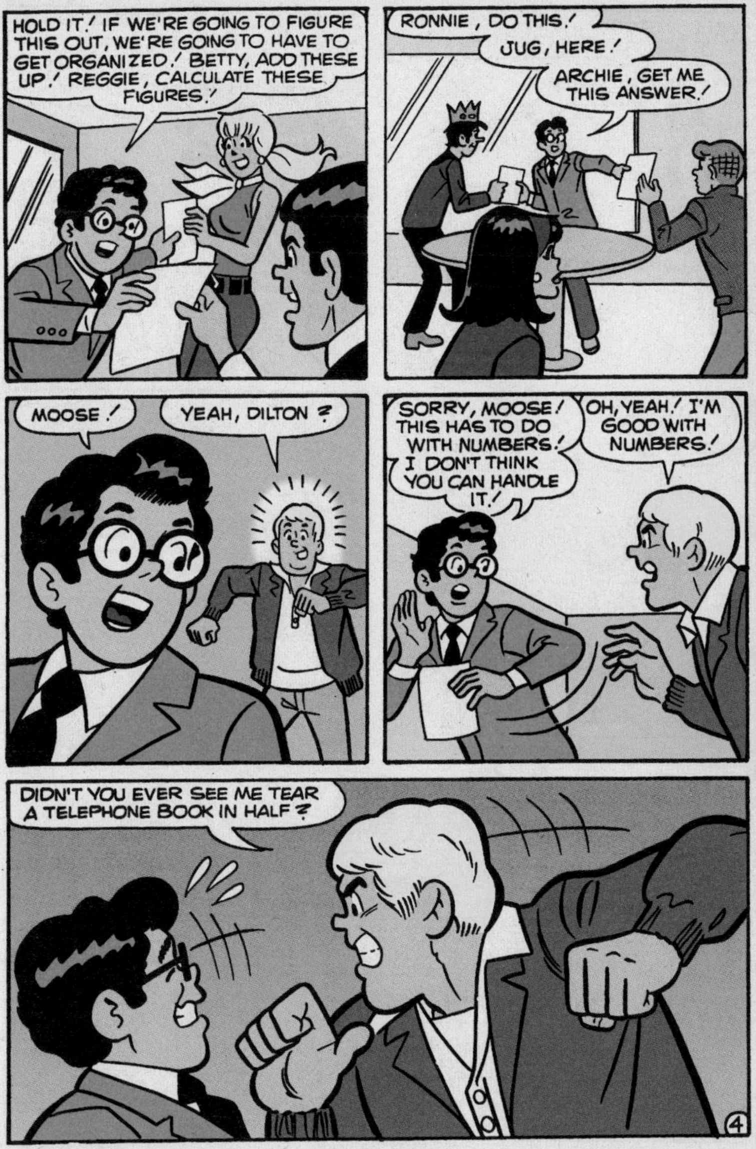
HOLD IT! IF WE'RE GOING TO FIGURE THIS OUT, WE'RE GOING TO HAVE TO GET ORGANIZED! BETTY, ADD THESE UP! REGGIE, CALCULATE THESE FIGURES!
RONNIE, DO THIS!
JUG, HERE!
ARCHIE, GET ME THIS ANSWER!
MOOSE!
YEAH, DILTON ?
SORRY, MOOSE! THIS HAS TO DO WITH NUMBERS! I DON'T THINK YOU CAN HANDLE IT!
OH, YEAH! I'M GOOD WITH NUMBERS!
DIDN'T YOU EVER SEE ME TEAR A TELEPHONE BOOK IN HALF ?
4

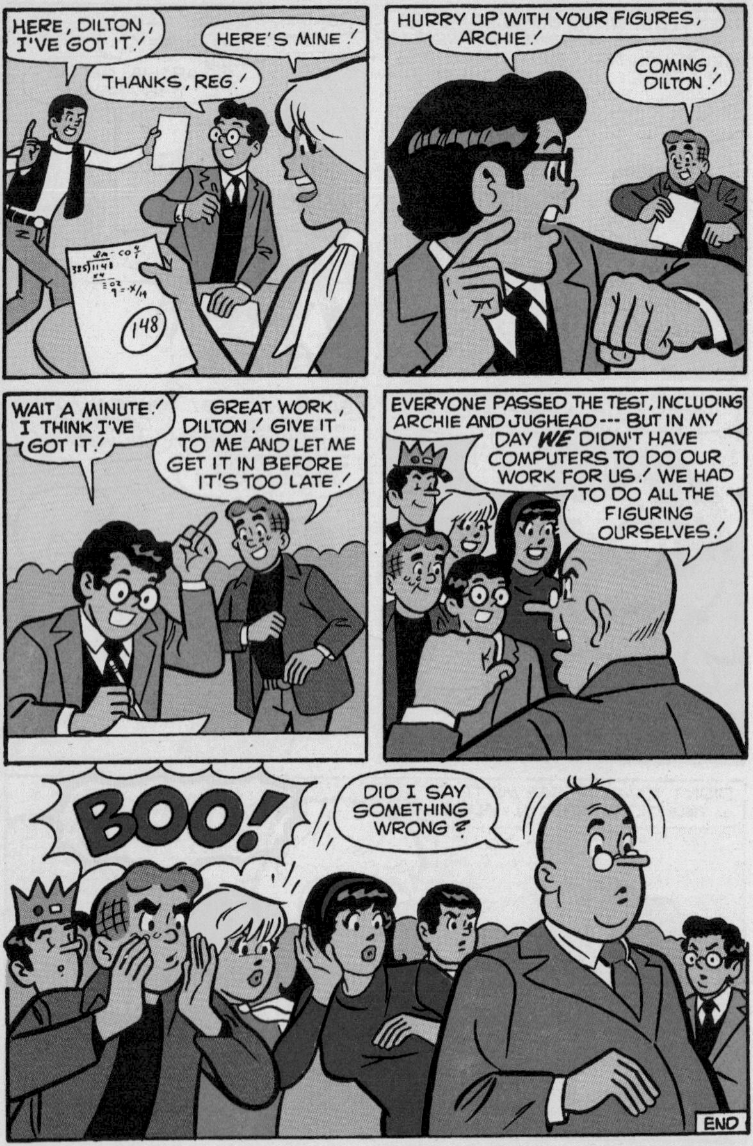
HERE, DILTON, I'VE GOT IT!
THANKS, REG!
HERE'S MINE!
148
HURRY UP WITH YOUR FIGURES, ARCHIE!
COMING, DILTON!
WAIT A MINUTE! I THINK I'VE GOT IT!
GREAT WORK, DILTON! GIVE IT TO ME AND LET ME GET IT IN BEFORE IT'S TOO LATE!
EVERYONE PASSED THE TEST, INCLUDING ARCHIE AND JUGHEAD --- BUT IN MY DAY WE DIDN'T HAVE COMPUTERS TO DO OUR WORK FOR US! WE HAD TO DO ALL THE FIGURING OURSELVES!
BOO!
DID I SAY SOMETHING WRONG?
END

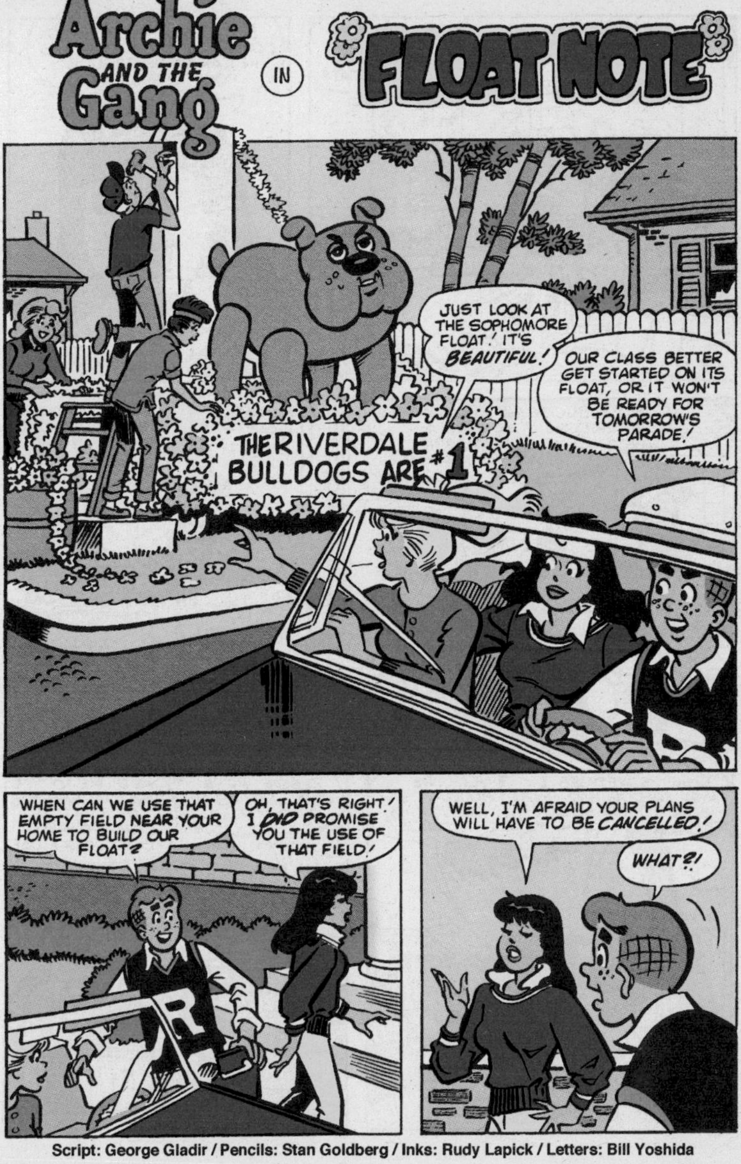
Archie AND THE Gang IN "FLOAT NOTE"
JUST LOOK AT THE SOPHOMORE FLOAT! IT'S BEAUTIFUL!
OUR CLASS BETTER GET STARTED ON ITS FLOAT, OR IT WON'T BE READY FOR TOMORROW'S PARADE!
THE RIVERDALE BULLDOGS ARE #1
WHEN CAN WE USE THAT EMPTY FIELD NEAR YOUR HOME TO BUILD OUR FLOAT?
OH, THAT'S RIGHT! I DID PROMISE YOU THE USE OF THAT FIELD!
WELL, I'M AFRAID YOUR PLANS WILL HAVE TO BE CANCELLED!
WHAT?!

Script: George Gladir / Pencils: Stan Goldberg / Inks: Rudy Lapick / Letters: Bill Yoshida

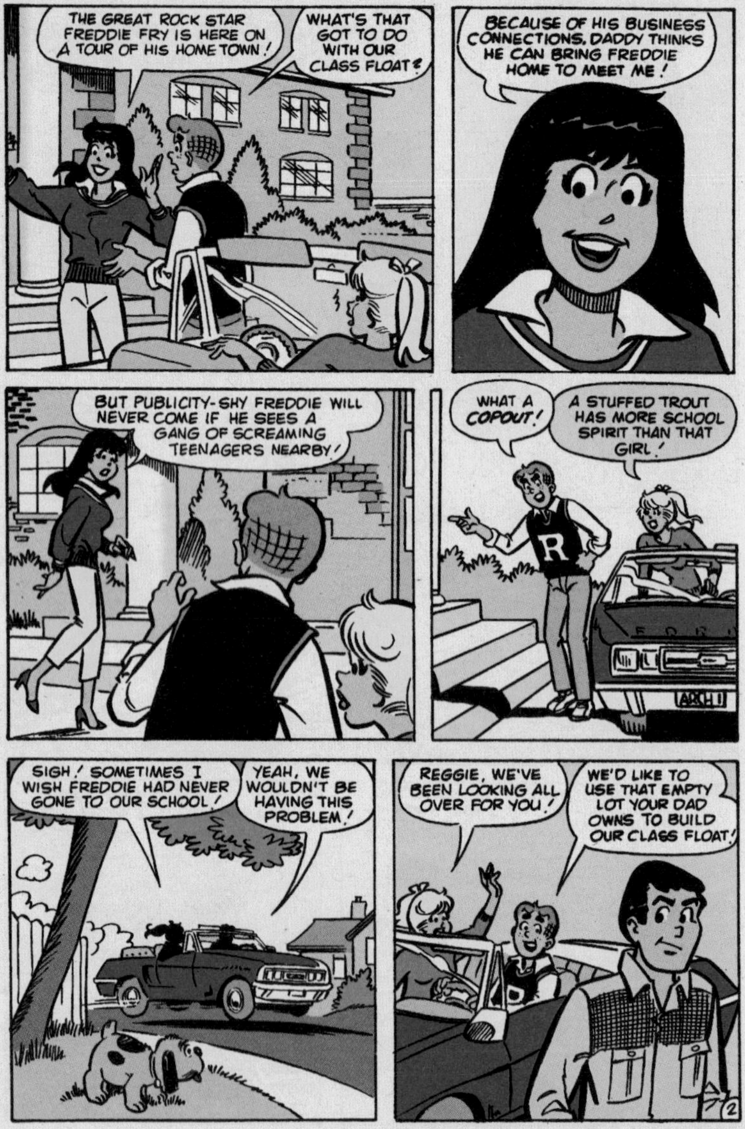
THE GREAT ROCK STAR FREDDIE FRY IS HERE ON A TOUR OF HIS HOME TOWN!
WHAT'S THAT GOT TO DO WITH OUR CLASS FLOAT?
BECAUSE OF HIS BUSINESS CONNECTIONS, DADDY THINKS HE CAN BRING FREDDIE HOME TO MEET ME!
BUT PUBLICITY-SHY FREDDIE WILL NEVER COME IF HE SEES A GANG OF SCREAMING TEENAGERS NEARBY!
WHAT A COPOUT!
A STUFFED TROUT HAS MORE SCHOOL SPIRIT THAN THAT GIRL!
R
ARCH I
SIGH! SOMETIMES I WISH FREDDIE HAD NEVER GONE TO OUR SCHOOL!
YEAH, WE WOULDN'T BE HAVING THIS PROBLEM!
REGGIE, WE'VE BEEN LOOKING ALL OVER FOR YOU!
WE'D LIKE TO USE THAT EMPTY LOT YOUR DAD OWNS TO BUILD OUR CLASS FLOAT!
2

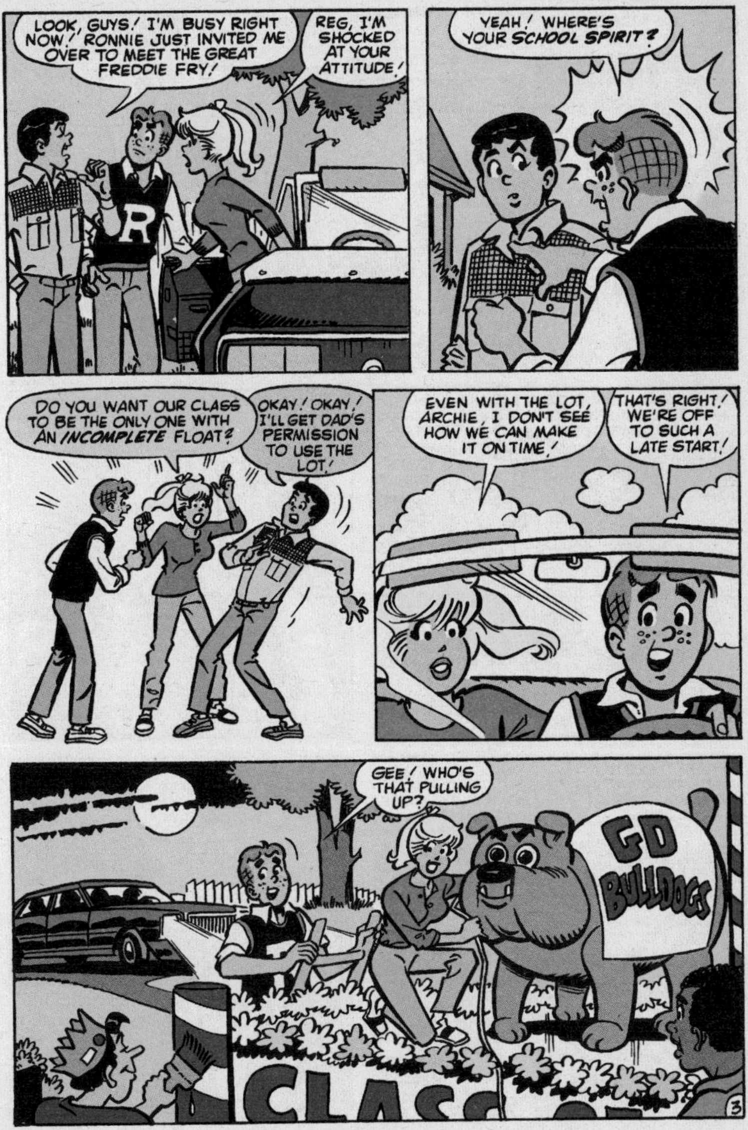
LOOK, GUYS! I'M BUSY RIGHT NOW! RONNIE JUST INVITED ME OVER TO MEET THE GREAT FREDDIE FRY!
REG, I'M SHOCKED AT YOUR ATTITUDE!
YEAH! WHERE'S YOUR SCHOOL SPIRIT?
DO YOU WANT OUR CLASS TO BE THE ONLY ONE WITH AN INCOMPLETE FLOAT?
OKAY! OKAY! I'LL GET DAD'S PERMISSION TO USE THE LOT!
EVEN WITH THE LOT, ARCHIE, I DON'T SEE HOW WE CAN MAKE IT ON TIME!
THAT'S RIGHT! WE'RE OFF TO SUCH A LATE START!
GEE! WHO'S THAT PULLING UP?
GD
BULLDOGS
CLASS
3

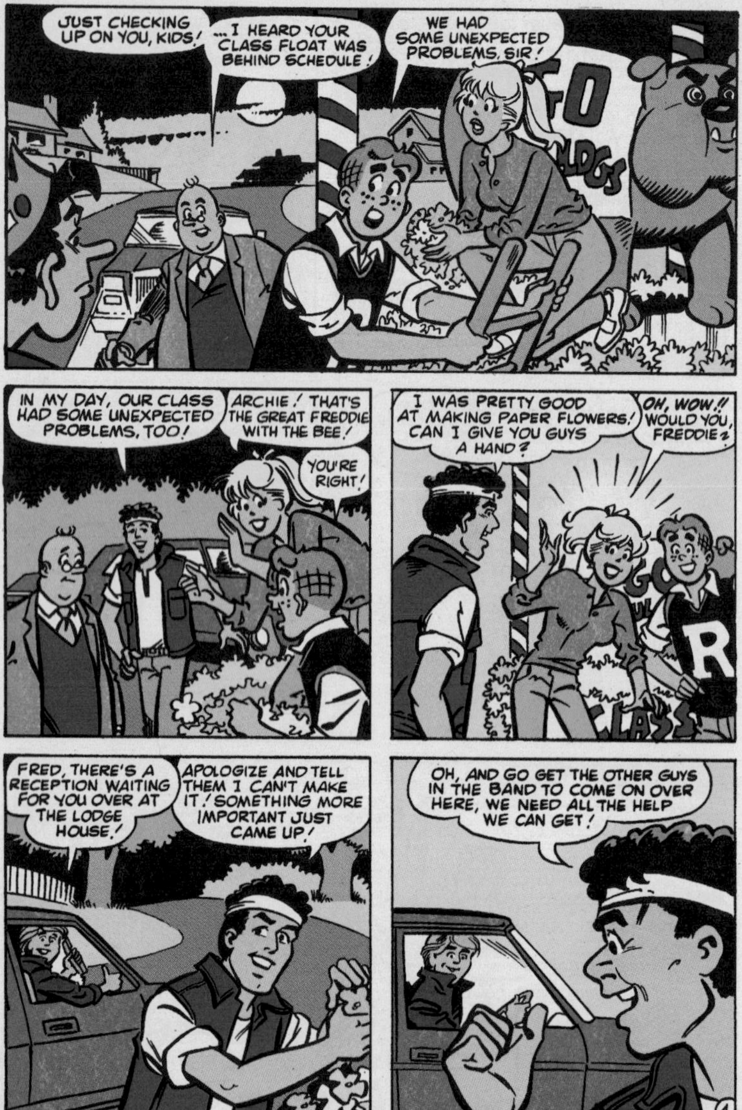

JUST CHECKING UP ON YOU, KIDS!
...I HEARD YOUR CLASS FLOAT WAS BEHIND SCHEDULE!
WE HAD SOME UNEXPECTED PROBLEMS, SIR!
IN MY DAY, OUR CLASS HAD SOME UNEXPECTED PROBLEMS, TOO!
ARCHIE! THAT'S THE GREAT FREDDIE WITH THE BEE!
YOU'RE RIGHT!
I WAS PRETTY GOOD AT MAKING PAPER FLOWERS! CAN I GIVE YOU GUYS A HAND?
OH, WOW!! WOULD YOU, FREDDIE?
FRED, THERE'S A RECEPTION WAITING FOR YOU OVER AT THE LODGE HOUSE!
APOLOGIZE AND TELL THEM I CAN'T MAKE IT! SOMETHING MORE IMPORTANT JUST CAME UP!
OH, AND GO GET THE OTHER GUYS IN THE BAND TO COME ON OVER HERE, WE NEED ALL THE HELP WE CAN GET!
4

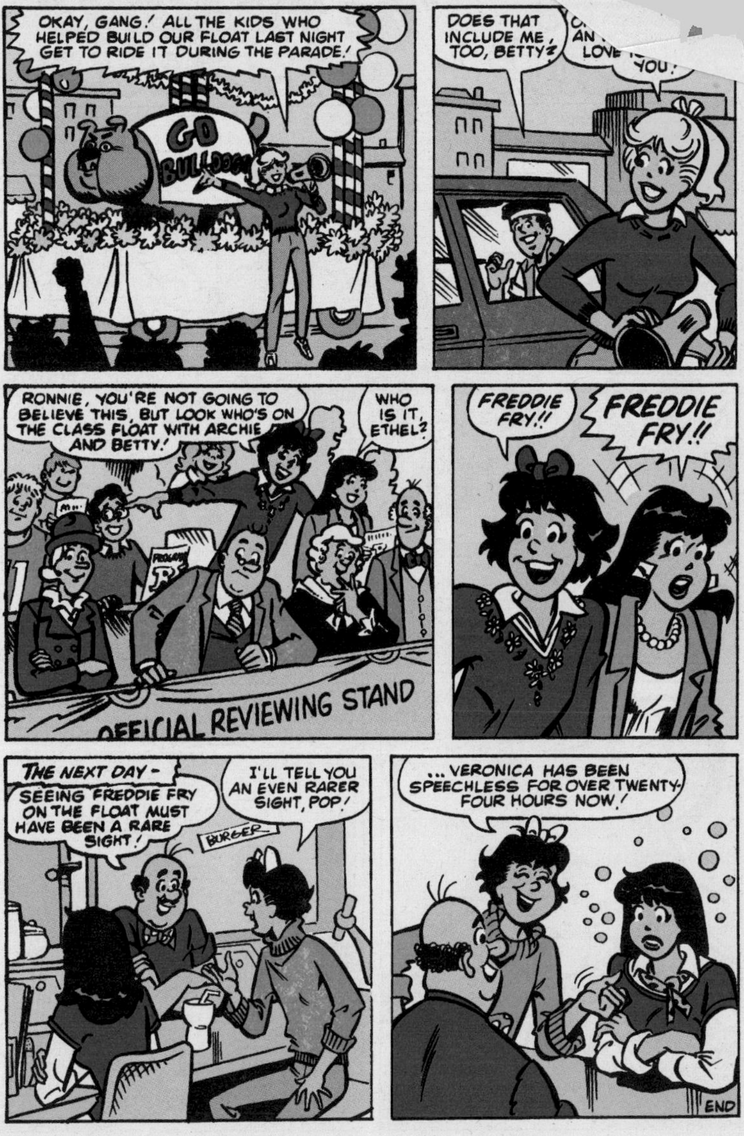
OKAY, GANG! ALL THE KIDS WHO HELPED BUILD OUR FLOAT LAST NIGHT GET TO RIDE IT DURING THE PARADE!
GO BULLDOGS
DOES THAT INCLUDE ME, TOO, BETTY?
RONNIE, YOU'RE NOT GOING TO BELIEVE THIS, BUT LOOK WHO'S ON THE CLASS FLOAT WITH ARCHIE AND BETTY!
WHO IS IT, ETHEL?
OFFICIAL REVIEWING STAND
FREDDIE FRY!!
FREDDIE FRY!!
THE NEXT DAY -
SEEING FREDDIE FRY ON THE FLOAT MUST HAVE BEEN A RARE SIGHT!
I'LL TELL YOU AN EVEN RARER SIGHT, POP!
BURGER
...VERONICA HAS BEEN SPEECHLESS FOR OVER TWENTY-FOUR HOURS NOW!
END

Archie in "The Trouble with Girls"

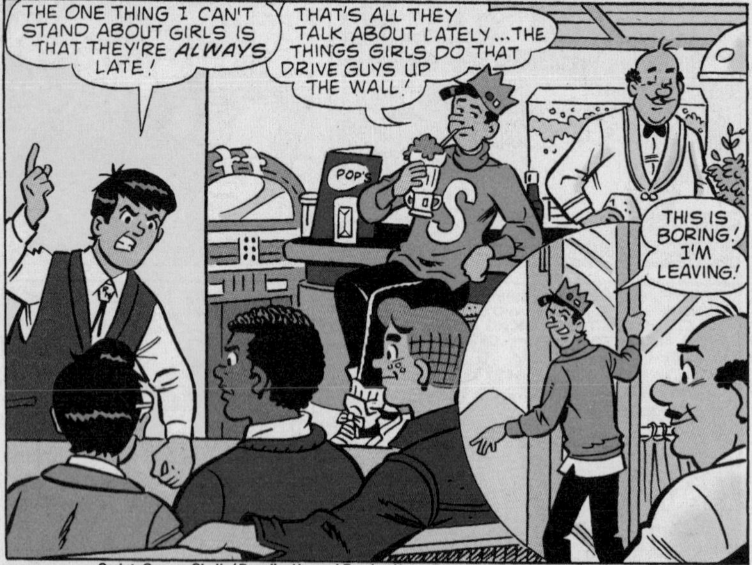
THE ONE THING I CAN'T STAND ABOUT GIRLS IS THAT THEY'RE *ALWAYS* LATE!
THAT'S ALL THEY TALK ABOUT LATELY ... THE THINGS GIRLS DO THAT DRIVE GUYS UP THE WALL!
POP'S
THIS IS BORING! I'M LEAVING!

Script: George Gladir / Pencils: Howard Bender / Inks: Rudy Lapick / Letters: Bill Yoshida

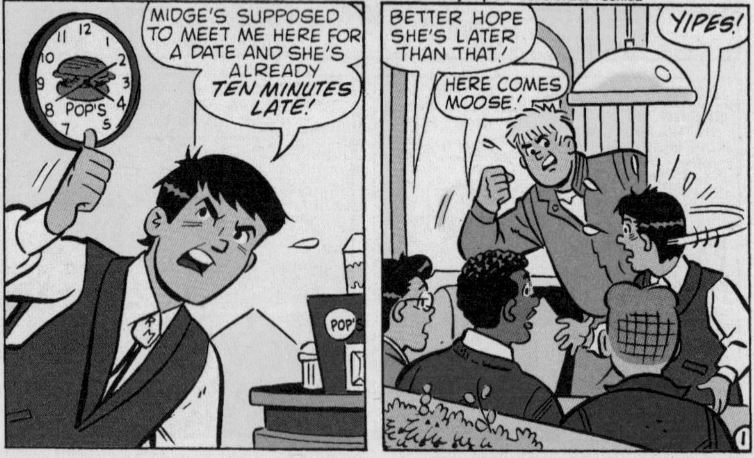
POP'S
MIDGE'S SUPPOSED TO MEET ME HERE FOR A DATE AND SHE'S ALREADY *TEN MINUTES LATE!*
POP'S
BETTER HOPE SHE'S LATER THAN THAT!
HERE COMES MOOSE!
YIPES!

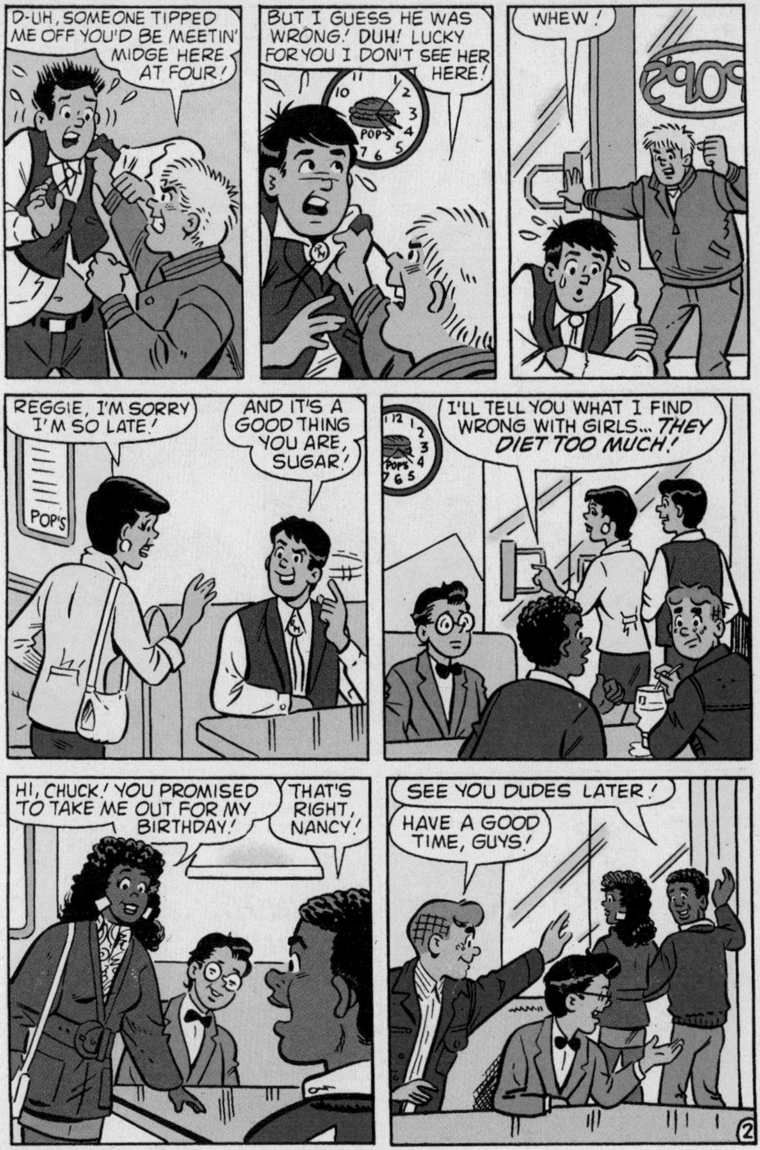
D-UH, SOMEONE TIPPED ME OFF YOU'D BE MEETIN' MIDGE HERE AT FOUR!
BUT I GUESS HE WAS WRONG! DUH! LUCKY FOR YOU I DON'T SEE HER HERE!
WHEW!
POP'S
REGGIE, I'M SORRY I'M SO LATE!
AND IT'S A GOOD THING YOU ARE, SUGAR!
POP'S
I'LL TELL YOU WHAT I FIND WRONG WITH GIRLS... *THEY DIET TOO MUCH!*
HI, CHUCK! YOU PROMISED TO TAKE ME OUT FOR MY BIRTHDAY!
THAT'S RIGHT, NANCY!
SEE YOU DUDES LATER!
HAVE A GOOD TIME, GUYS!

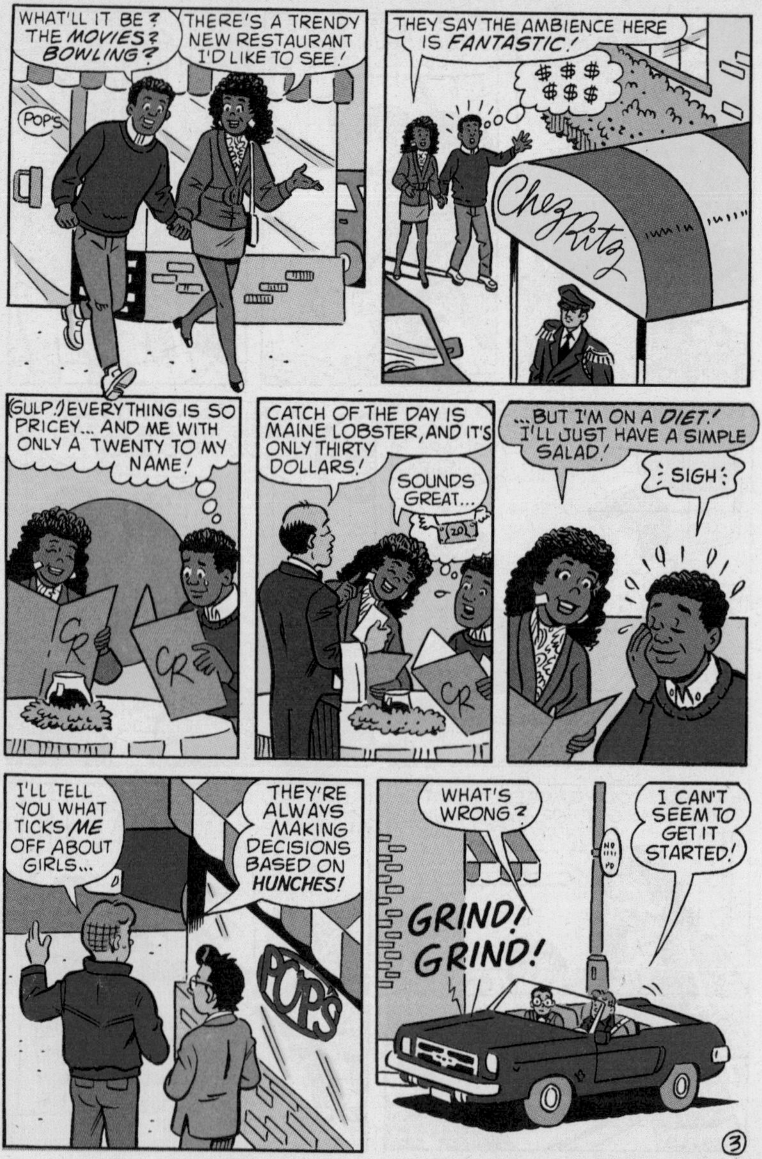

WHAT'LL IT BE? THE *MOVIES*? *BOWLING*?
THERE'S A TRENDY NEW RESTAURANT I'D LIKE TO SEE!
POP'S
THEY SAY THE AMBIENCE HERE IS *FANTASTIC*!
$ $ $ $ $ $
Chez Ritz
(GULP!) EVERYTHING IS SO PRICEY... AND ME WITH ONLY A TWENTY TO MY NAME!
CR
CATCH OF THE DAY IS MAINE LOBSTER, AND IT'S ONLY THIRTY DOLLARS!
SOUNDS GREAT...
20
...BUT I'M ON A *DIET*! I'LL JUST HAVE A SIMPLE SALAD!
SIGH
I'LL TELL YOU WHAT TICKS *ME* OFF ABOUT GIRLS...
THEY'RE ALWAYS MAKING DECISIONS BASED ON **HUNCHES**!
POP'S
WHAT'S WRONG?
GRIND! GRIND!
I CAN'T SEEM TO GET IT STARTED!

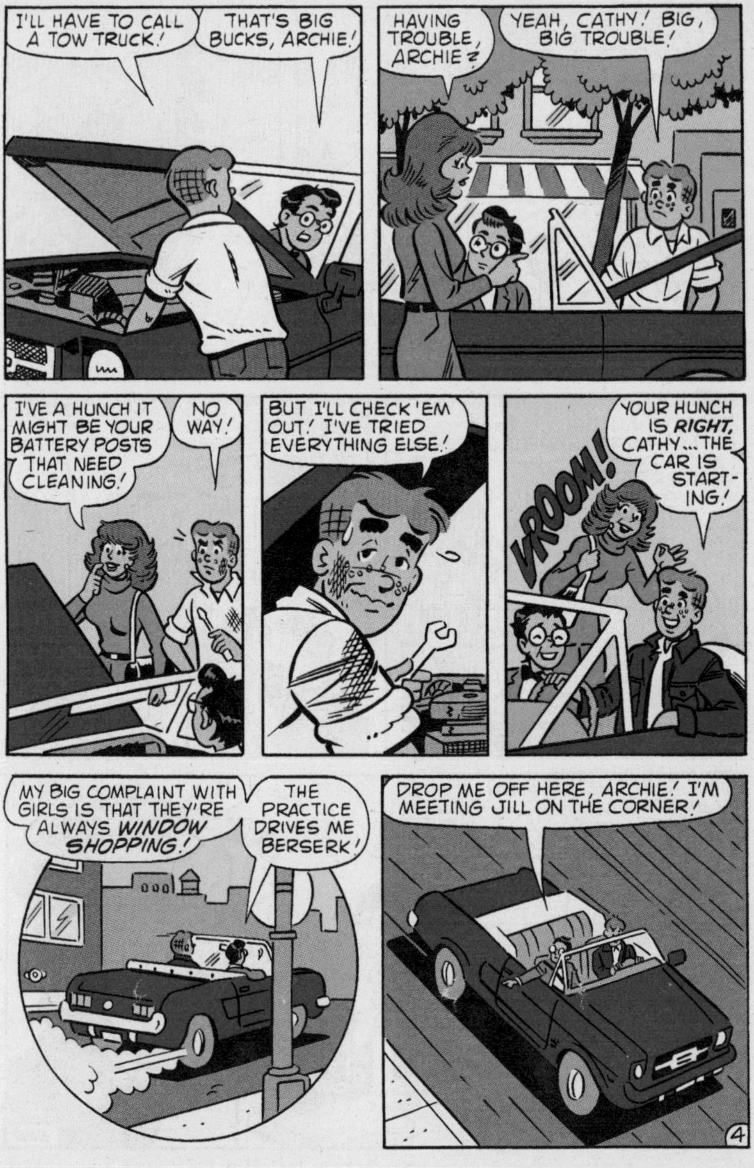
I'LL HAVE TO CALL A TOW TRUCK!
THAT'S BIG BUCKS, ARCHIE!
HAVING TROUBLE, ARCHIE?
YEAH, CATHY! BIG, BIG TROUBLE!
I'VE A HUNCH IT MIGHT BE YOUR BATTERY POSTS THAT NEED CLEANING!
NO WAY!
BUT I'LL CHECK 'EM OUT! I'VE TRIED EVERYTHING ELSE!
VROOM!
YOUR HUNCH IS RIGHT, CATHY... THE CAR IS STARTING!
MY BIG COMPLAINT WITH GIRLS IS THAT THEY'RE ALWAYS WINDOW SHOPPING!
THE PRACTICE DRIVES ME BERSERK!
DROP ME OFF HERE, ARCHIE! I'M MEETING JILL ON THE CORNER!
4

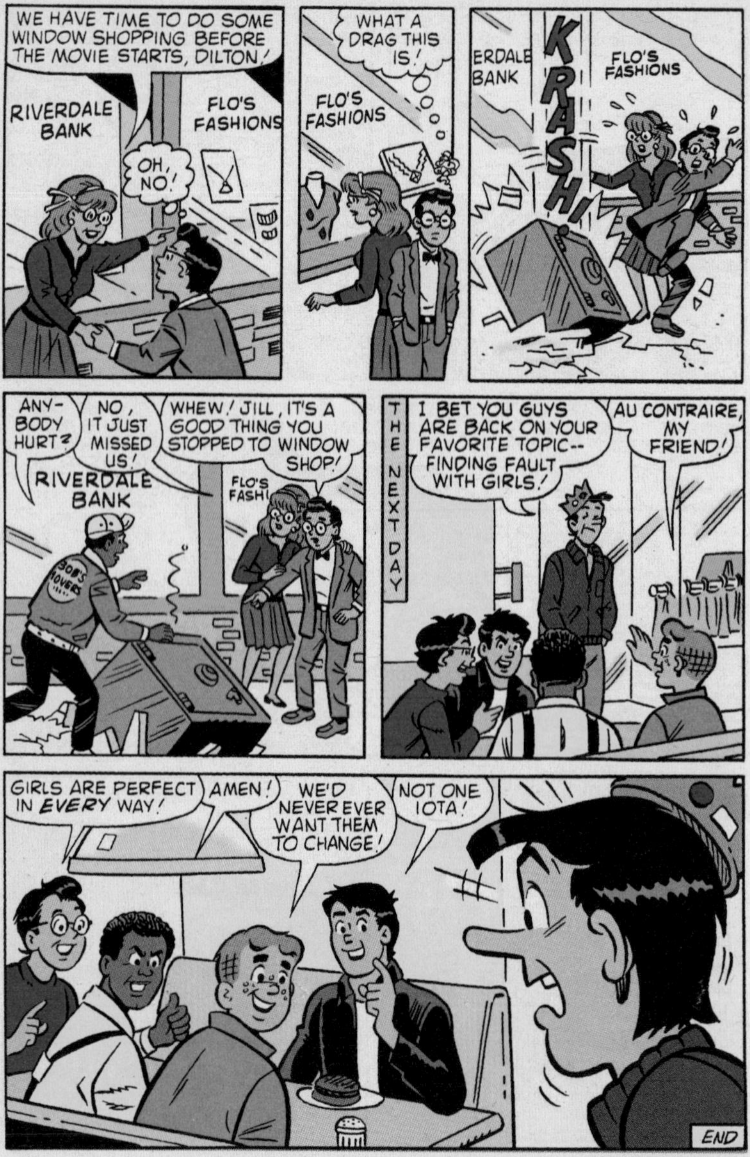
WE HAVE TIME TO DO SOME WINDOW SHOPPING BEFORE THE MOVIE STARTS, DILTON!
RIVERDALE BANK
FLO'S FASHIONS
OH, NO!
WHAT A DRAG THIS IS!
FLO'S FASHIONS
ERDALE BANK
FLO'S FASHIONS
KRASH!
ANY-BODY HURT?
NO, IT JUST MISSED US!
WHEW! JILL, IT'S A GOOD THING YOU STOPPED TO WINDOW SHOP!
RIVERDALE BANK
FLO'S FASH
BOB'S MOVERS
THE NEXT DAY
I BET YOU GUYS ARE BACK ON YOUR FAVORITE TOPIC-- FINDING FAULT WITH GIRLS!
AU CONTRAIRE, MY FRIEND!
GIRLS ARE PERFECT IN *EVERY* WAY!
AMEN!
WE'D NEVER EVER WANT THEM TO CHANGE!
NOT ONE IOTA!
END

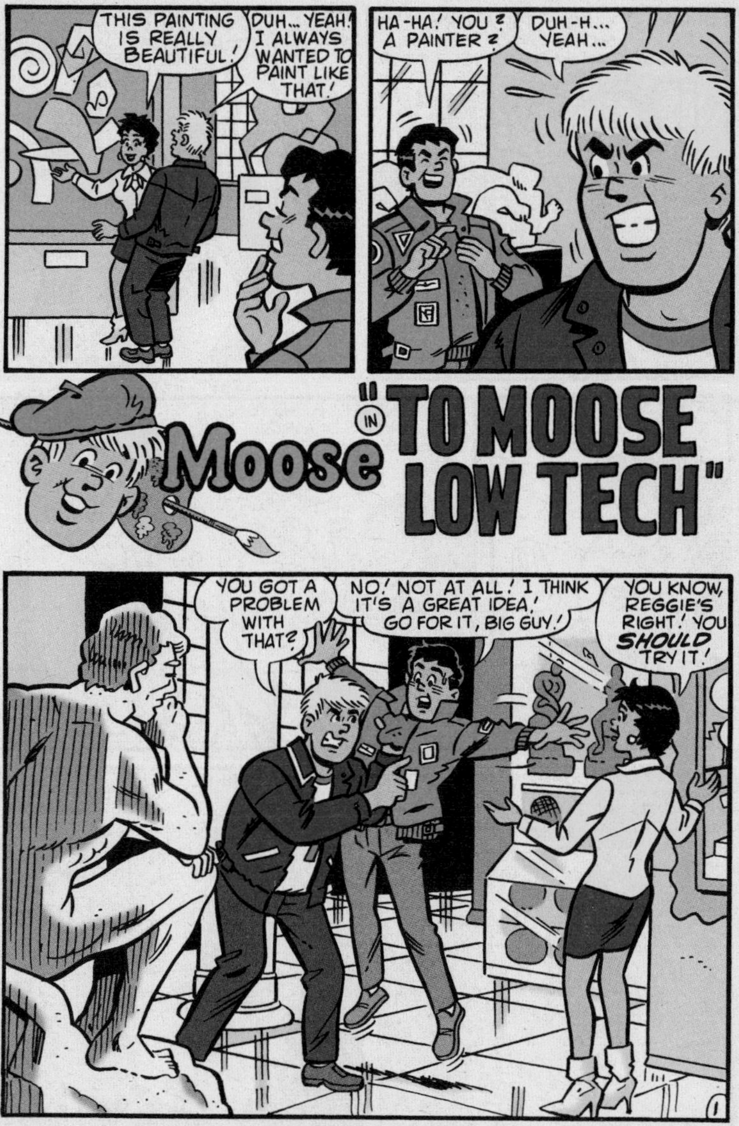
THIS PAINTING IS REALLY BEAUTIFUL!
DUH... YEAH! I ALWAYS WANTED TO PAINT LIKE THAT!
HA-HA! YOU? A PAINTER?
DUH-H... YEAH...
Moose
IN
"TO MOOSE LOW TECH"
YOU GOT A PROBLEM WITH THAT?
NO! NOT AT ALL! I THINK IT'S A GREAT IDEA! GO FOR IT, BIG GUY!
YOU KNOW, REGGIE'S RIGHT! YOU SHOULD TRY IT!
1

Script: Hal Smith / Pencils: Howard Bender / Inks: Rudy Lapick / Letters: Bill Yoshida

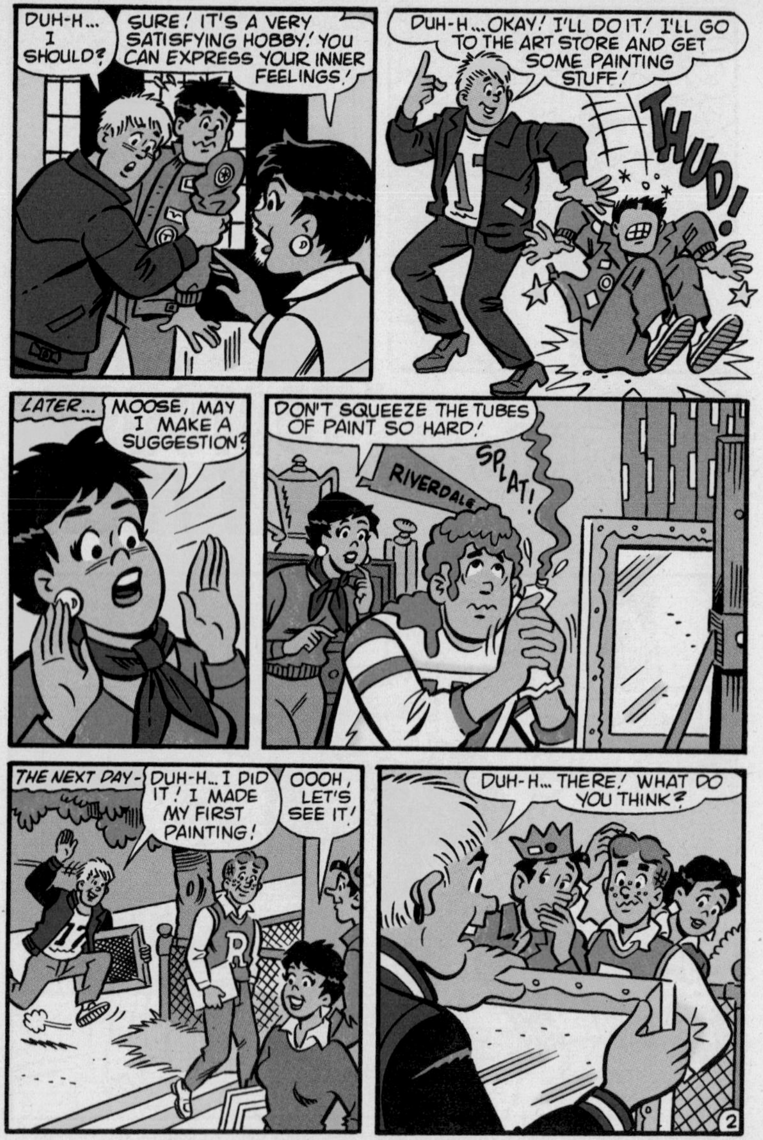
DUH-H... I SHOULD?
SURE! IT'S A VERY SATISFYING HOBBY! YOU CAN EXPRESS YOUR INNER FEELINGS!
DUH-H...OKAY! I'LL DO IT! I'LL GO TO THE ART STORE AND GET SOME PAINTING STUFF!
THUD!
LATER...
MOOSE, MAY I MAKE A SUGGESTION?
DON'T SQUEEZE THE TUBES OF PAINT SO HARD!
RIVERDALE
SPLAT!
THE NEXT DAY-
DUH-H... I DID IT! I MADE MY FIRST PAINTING!
OOOH, LET'S SEE IT!
DUH-H... THERE! WHAT DO YOU THINK?
R
17
2

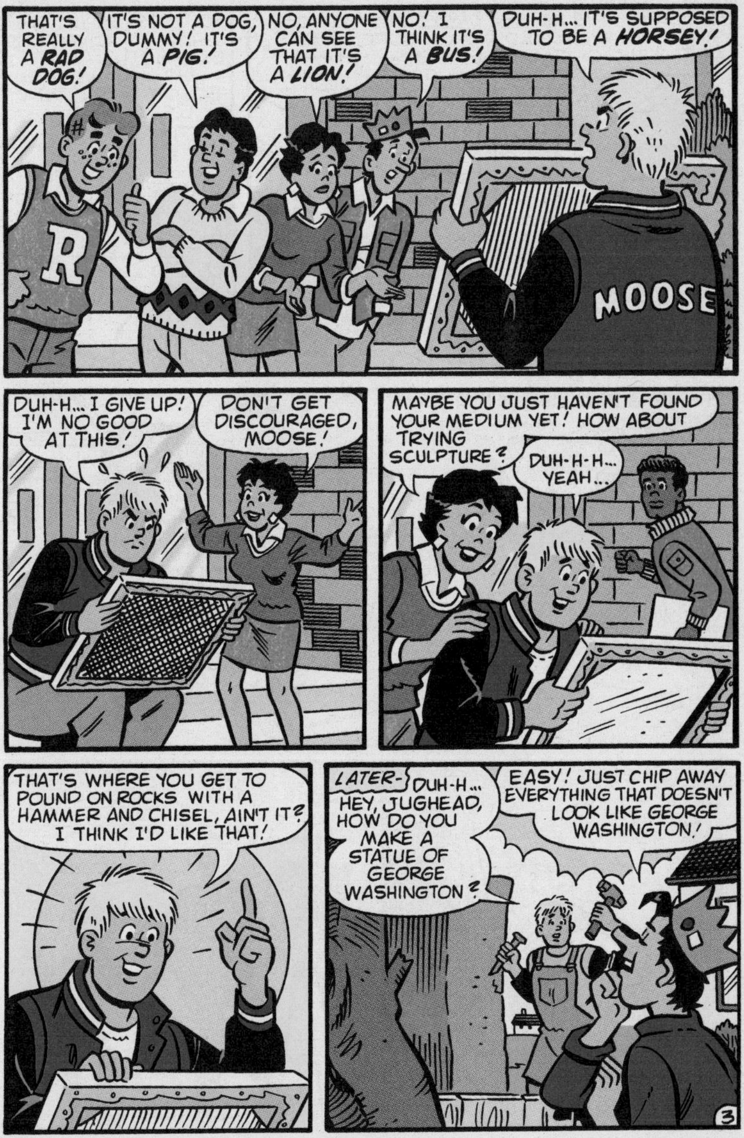

THAT'S REALLY A RAD DOG!
IT'S NOT A DOG, DUMMY! IT'S A PIG!
NO, ANYONE CAN SEE THAT IT'S A LION!
NO! I THINK IT'S A BUS!
DUH-H... IT'S SUPPOSED TO BE A HORSEY!
MOOSE
DUH-H... I GIVE UP! I'M NO GOOD AT THIS!
DON'T GET DISCOURAGED, MOOSE!
MAYBE YOU JUST HAVEN'T FOUND YOUR MEDIUM YET! HOW ABOUT TRYING SCULPTURE?
DUH-H-H... YEAH...
THAT'S WHERE YOU GET TO POUND ON ROCKS WITH A HAMMER AND CHISEL, AIN'T IT? I THINK I'D LIKE THAT!
LATER-
DUH-H... HEY, JUGHEAD, HOW DO YOU MAKE A STATUE OF GEORGE WASHINGTON?
EASY! JUST CHIP AWAY EVERYTHING THAT DOESN'T LOOK LIKE GEORGE WASHINGTON!
3

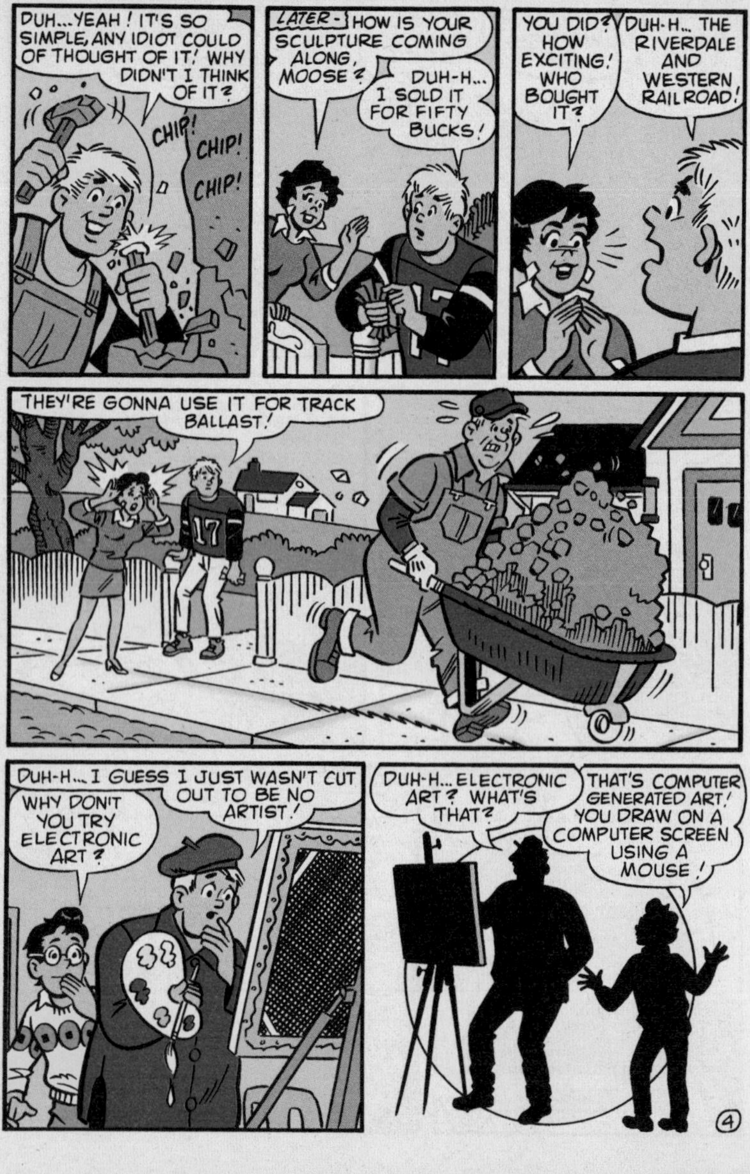
DUH...YEAH! IT'S SO SIMPLE, ANY IDIOT COULD OF THOUGHT OF IT! WHY DIDN'T I THINK OF IT?
CHIP! CHIP! CHIP!
LATER-
HOW IS YOUR SCULPTURE COMING ALONG, MOOSE?
DUH-H... I SOLD IT FOR FIFTY BUCKS!
YOU DID? HOW EXCITING! WHO BOUGHT IT?
DUH-H... THE RIVERDALE AND WESTERN RAILROAD!
THEY'RE GONNA USE IT FOR TRACK BALLAST!
DUH-H... I GUESS I JUST WASN'T CUT OUT TO BE NO ARTIST!
WHY DON'T YOU TRY ELECTRONIC ART?
DUH-H... ELECTRONIC ART? WHAT'S THAT?
THAT'S COMPUTER GENERATED ART! YOU DRAW ON A COMPUTER SCREEN USING A MOUSE!
4

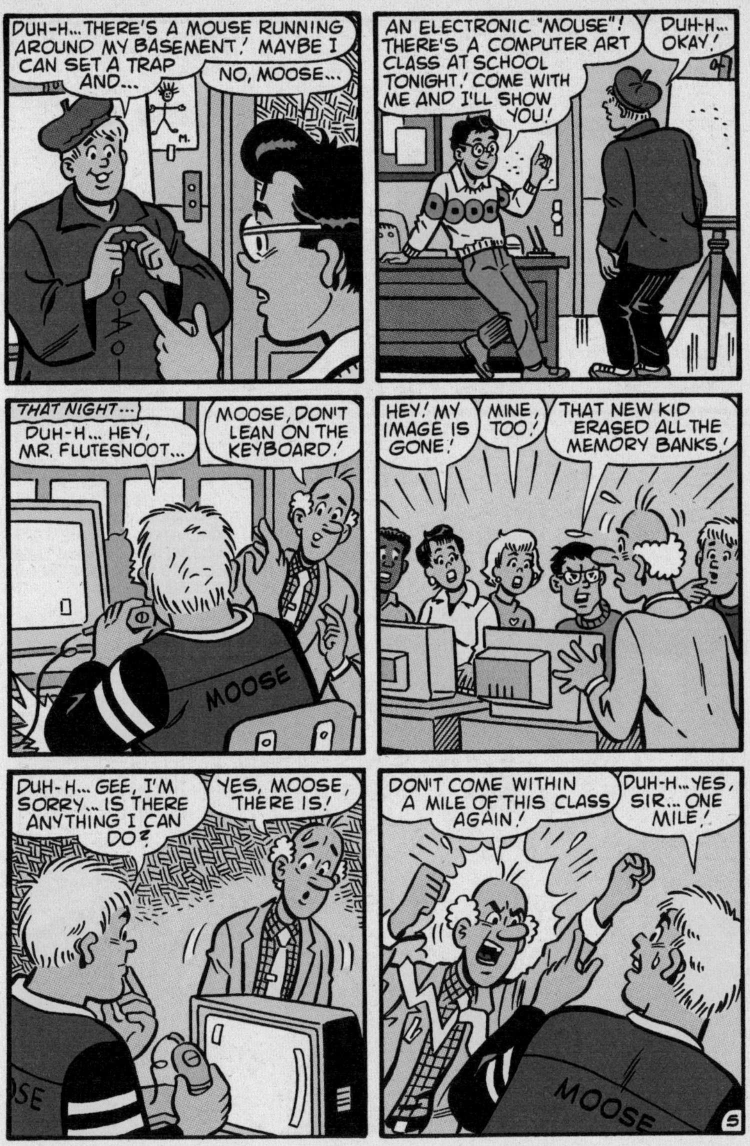

DUH-H... THERE'S A MOUSE RUNNING AROUND MY BASEMENT! MAYBE I CAN SET A TRAP AND...
NO, MOOSE...
AN ELECTRONIC "MOUSE"! THERE'S A COMPUTER ART CLASS AT SCHOOL TONIGHT! COME WITH ME AND I'LL SHOW YOU!
DUH-H... OKAY!
THAT NIGHT...
DUH-H... HEY, MR. FLUTESNOOT...
MOOSE, DON'T LEAN ON THE KEYBOARD!
MOOSE
HEY! MY IMAGE IS GONE!
MINE, TOO!
THAT NEW KID ERASED ALL THE MEMORY BANKS!
DUH-H... GEE, I'M SORRY... IS THERE ANYTHING I CAN DO?
YES, MOOSE, THERE IS!
DON'T COME WITHIN A MILE OF THIS CLASS AGAIN!
DUH-H... YES, SIR... ONE MILE!
MOOSE
5

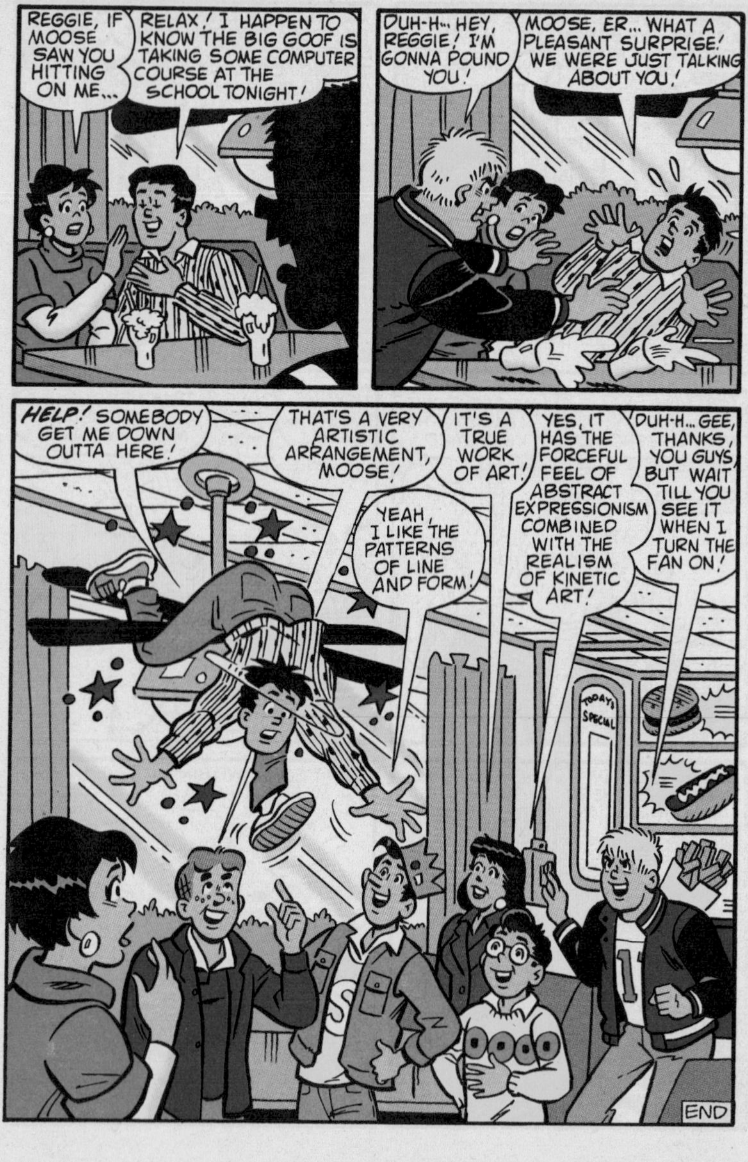
REGGIE, IF MOOSE SAW YOU HITTING ON ME...
RELAX! I HAPPEN TO KNOW THE BIG GOOF IS TAKING SOME COMPUTER COURSE AT THE SCHOOL TONIGHT!
DUH-H... HEY, REGGIE! I'M GONNA POUND YOU!
MOOSE, ER... WHAT A PLEASANT SURPRISE! WE WERE JUST TALKING ABOUT YOU!
HELP! SOMEBODY GET ME DOWN OUTTA HERE!
THAT'S A VERY ARTISTIC ARRANGEMENT, MOOSE!
YEAH, I LIKE THE PATTERNS OF LINE AND FORM!
IT'S A TRUE WORK OF ART!
YES, IT HAS THE FORCEFUL FEEL OF ABSTRACT EXPRESSIONISM COMBINED WITH THE REALISM OF KINETIC ART!
DUH-H... GEE, THANKS, YOU GUYS BUT WAIT TILL YOU SEE IT WHEN I TURN THE FAN ON!
TODAY'S SPECIAL
END

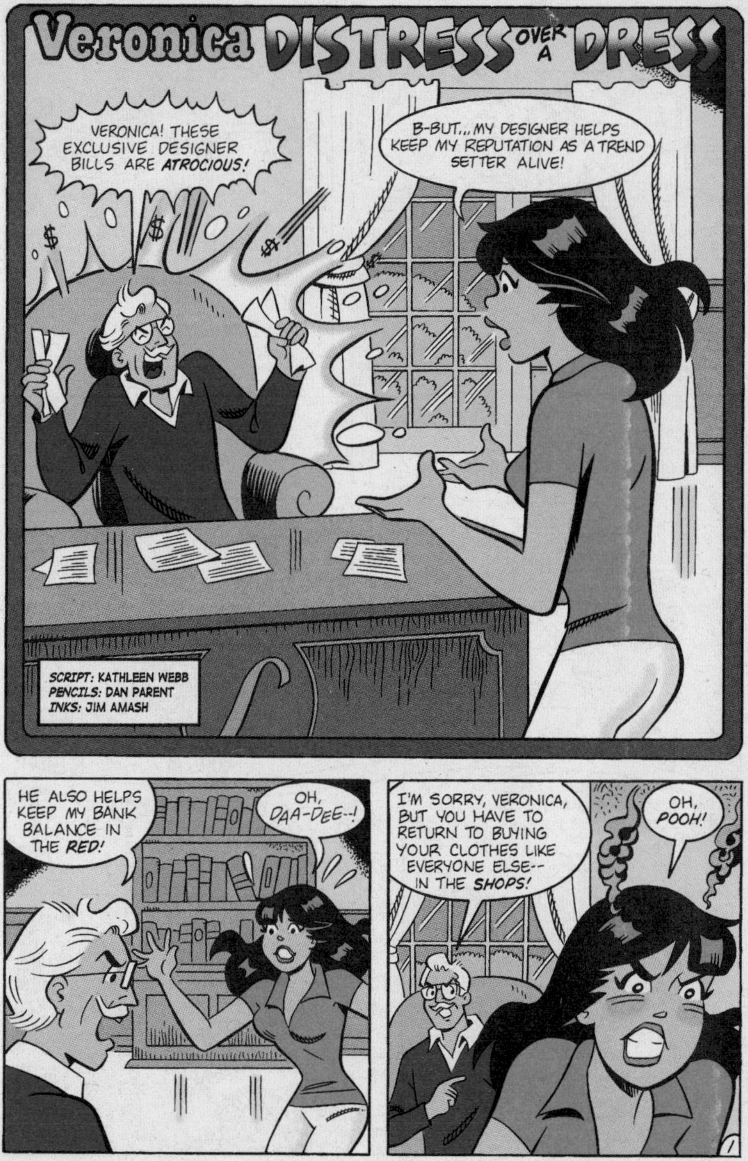
Veronica
DISTRESS OVER A DRESS
VERONICA! THESE EXCLUSIVE DESIGNER BILLS ARE *ATROCIOUS!*
B-BUT... MY DESIGNER HELPS KEEP MY REPUTATION AS A TREND SETTER ALIVE!
SCRIPT: KATHLEEN WEBB
PENCILS: DAN PARENT
INKS: JIM AMASH
HE ALSO HELPS KEEP MY BANK BALANCE IN THE *RED!*
OH, *DAA-DEE--!*
I'M SORRY, VERONICA, BUT YOU HAVE TO RETURN TO BUYING YOUR CLOTHES LIKE EVERYONE ELSE-- IN THE *SHOPS!*
OH, *POOH!*
1

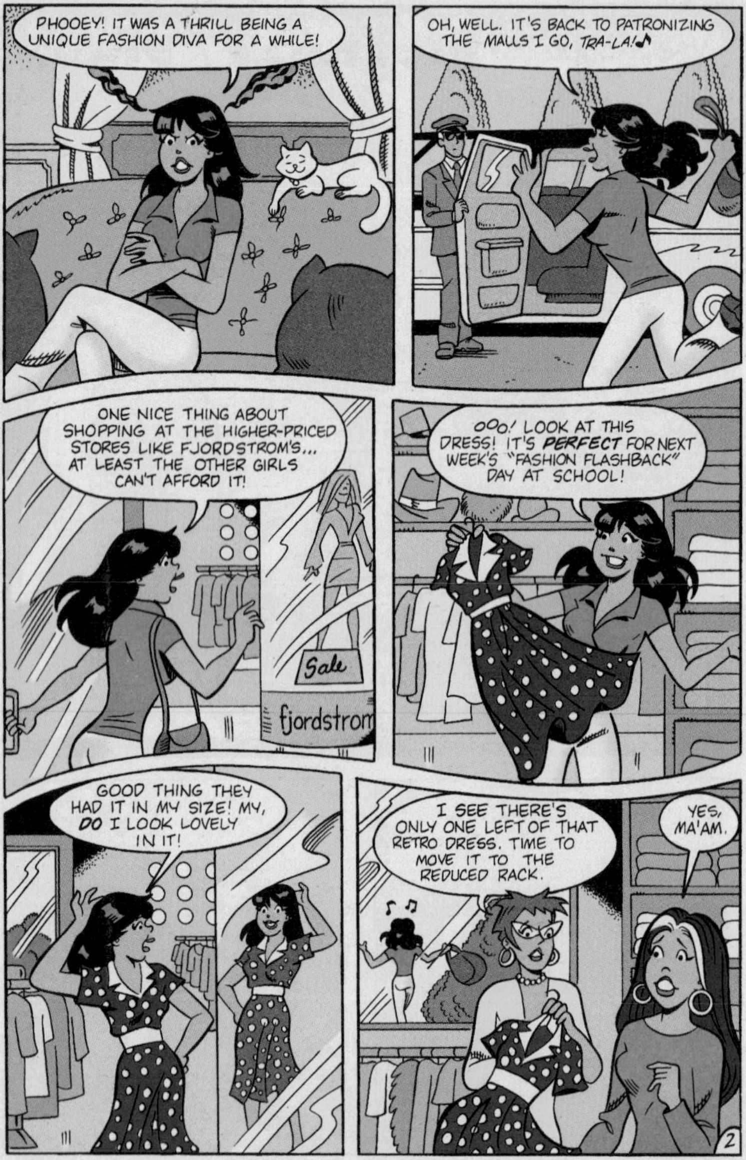
PHOOEY! IT WAS A THRILL BEING A UNIQUE FASHION DIVA FOR A WHILE!
OH, WELL. IT'S BACK TO PATRONIZING THE MALLS I GO, TRA-LA!♪
ONE NICE THING ABOUT SHOPPING AT THE HIGHER-PRICED STORES LIKE FJORDSTROM'S... AT LEAST THE OTHER GIRLS CAN'T AFFORD IT!
Sale
fjordstrom
OOO! LOOK AT THIS DRESS! IT'S PERFECT FOR NEXT WEEK'S "FASHION FLASHBACK" DAY AT SCHOOL!
GOOD THING THEY HAD IT IN MY SIZE! MY, DO I LOOK LOVELY IN IT!
I SEE THERE'S ONLY ONE LEFT OF THAT RETRO DRESS. TIME TO MOVE IT TO THE REDUCED RACK.
YES, MA'AM.
2

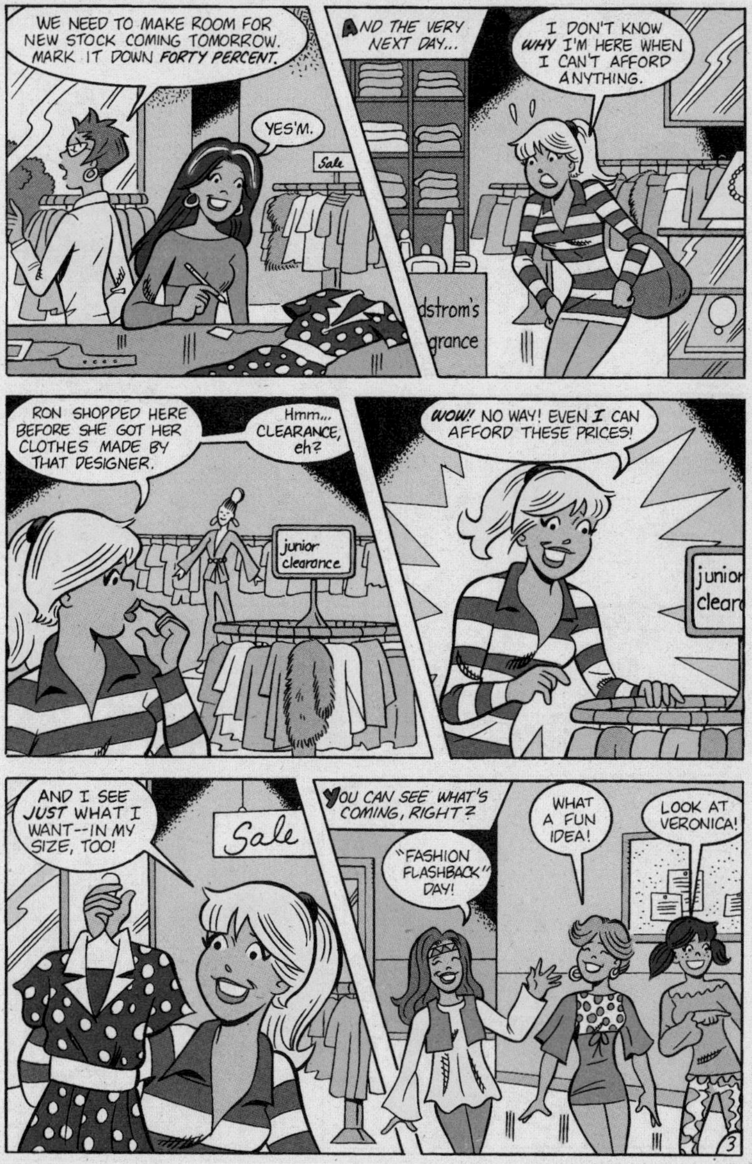

WE NEED TO MAKE ROOM FOR NEW STOCK COMING TOMORROW. MARK IT DOWN FORTY PERCENT.
YES'M.
Sale
AND THE VERY NEXT DAY...
I DON'T KNOW WHY I'M HERE WHEN I CAN'T AFFORD ANYTHING.
dstrom's
grance
RON SHOPPED HERE BEFORE SHE GOT HER CLOTHES MADE BY THAT DESIGNER.
Hmm... CLEARANCE, eh?
junior clearance
WOW! NO WAY! EVEN I CAN AFFORD THESE PRICES!
junior
cleara
AND I SEE JUST WHAT I WANT--IN MY SIZE, TOO!
Sale
YOU CAN SEE WHAT'S COMING, RIGHT?
"FASHION FLASHBACK" DAY!
WHAT A FUN IDEA!
LOOK AT VERONICA!
3

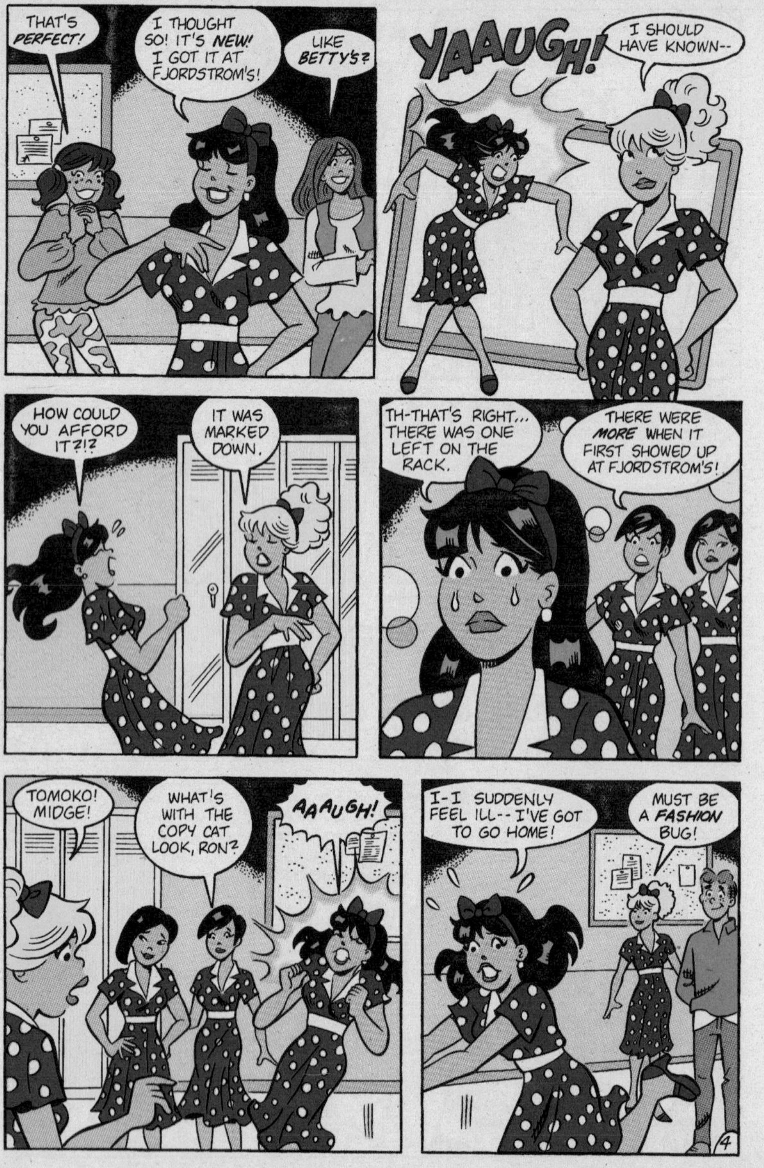
THAT'S PERFECT!
I THOUGHT SO! IT'S NEW! I GOT IT AT FJORDSTROM'S!
LIKE BETTY'S?
YAAAUGH!
I SHOULD HAVE KNOWN--
HOW COULD YOU AFFORD IT?!?
IT WAS MARKED DOWN.
TH-THAT'S RIGHT... THERE WAS ONE LEFT ON THE RACK.
THERE WERE MORE WHEN IT FIRST SHOWED UP AT FJORDSTROM'S!
TOMOKO! MIDGE!
WHAT'S WITH THE COPY CAT LOOK, RON?
AAAUGH!
I-I SUDDENLY FEEL ILL-- I'VE GOT TO GO HOME!
MUST BE A FASHION BUG!
4

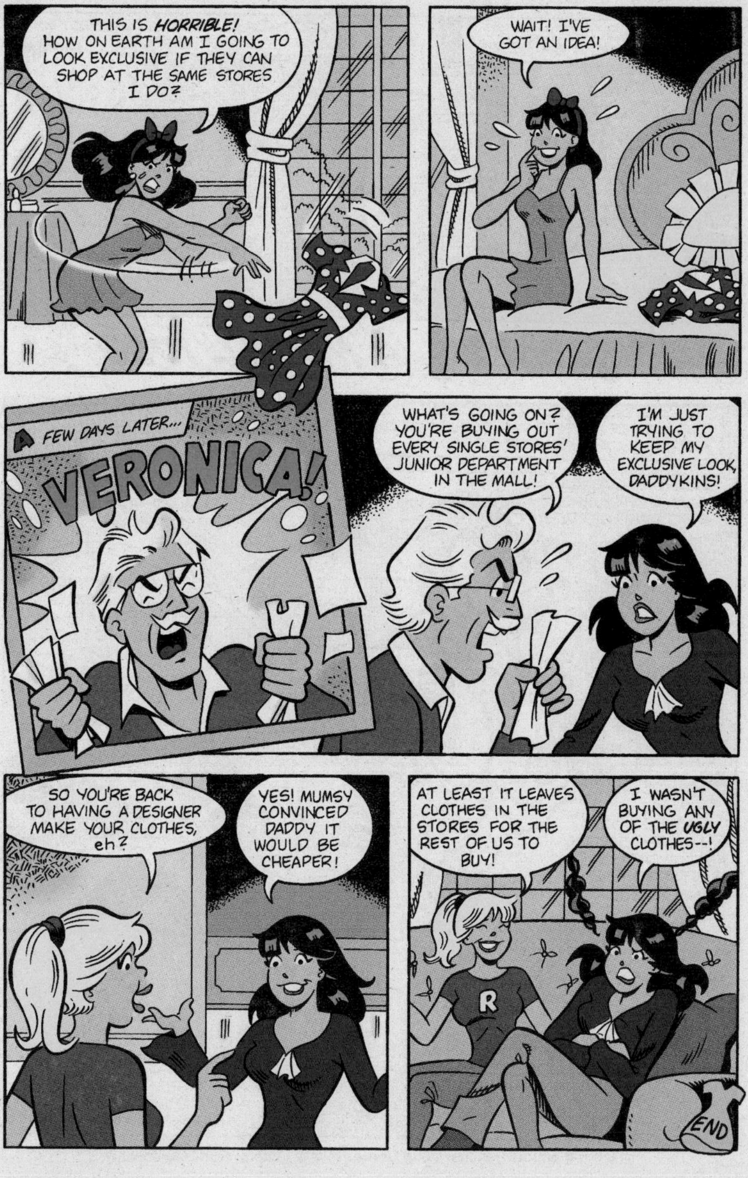
THIS IS HORRIBLE! HOW ON EARTH AM I GOING TO LOOK EXCLUSIVE IF THEY CAN SHOP AT THE SAME STORES I DO?
WAIT! I'VE GOT AN IDEA!
A FEW DAYS LATER...
VERONICA!
WHAT'S GOING ON? YOU'RE BUYING OUT EVERY SINGLE STORES' JUNIOR DEPARTMENT IN THE MALL!
I'M JUST TRYING TO KEEP MY EXCLUSIVE LOOK, DADDYKINS!
SO YOU'RE BACK TO HAVING A DESIGNER MAKE YOUR CLOTHES, eh?
YES! MUMSY CONVINCED DADDY IT WOULD BE CHEAPER!
AT LEAST IT LEAVES CLOTHES IN THE STORES FOR THE REST OF US TO BUY!
I WASN'T BUYING ANY OF THE UGLY CLOTHES--!
R
END

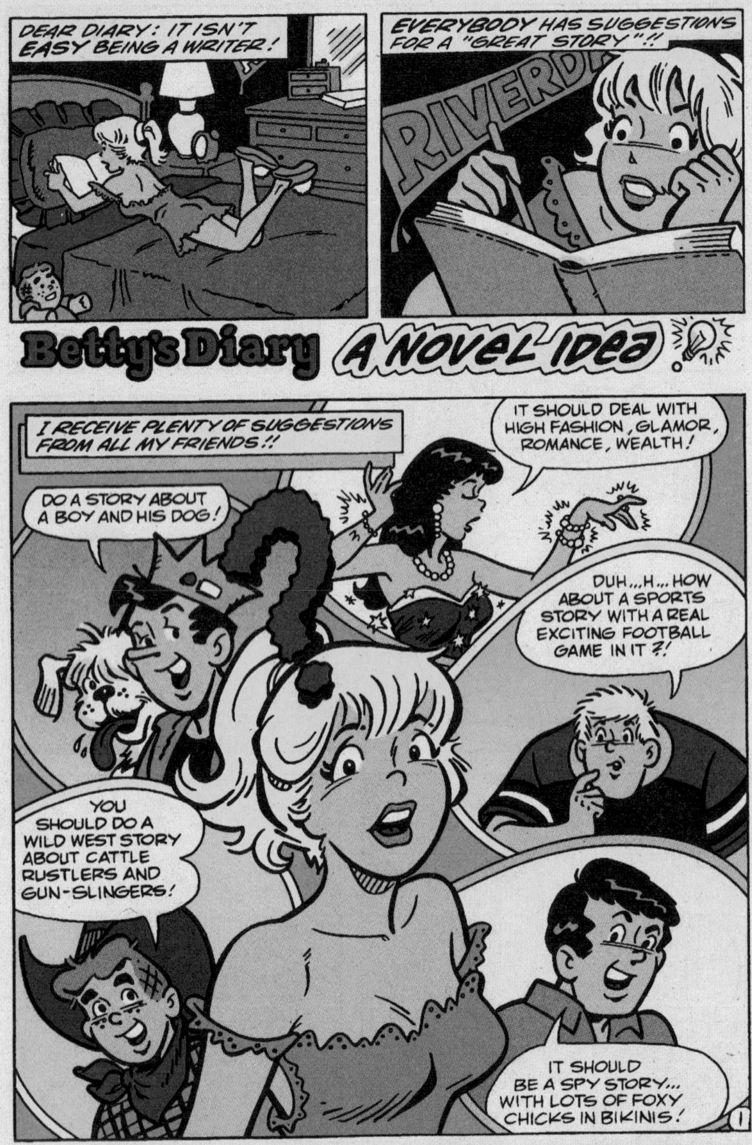
DEAR DIARY: IT ISN'T EASY BEING A WRITER!
EVERYBODY HAS SUGGESTIONS FOR A "GREAT STORY"!!
RIVERD
Betty's Diary
A NOVEL IDEA
I RECEIVE PLENTY OF SUGGESTIONS FROM ALL MY FRIENDS!!
IT SHOULD DEAL WITH HIGH FASHION, GLAMOR, ROMANCE, WEALTH!
DO A STORY ABOUT A BOY AND HIS DOG!
DUH...H... HOW ABOUT A SPORTS STORY WITH A REAL EXCITING FOOTBALL GAME IN IT ?!
YOU SHOULD DO A WILD WEST STORY ABOUT CATTLE RUSTLERS AND GUN-SLINGERS!
IT SHOULD BE A SPY STORY... WITH LOTS OF FOXY CHICKS IN BIKINIS!
1

Script: Hal Smith / Pencils: Doug Crane / Inks & Letters: Rod Ollerenshaw

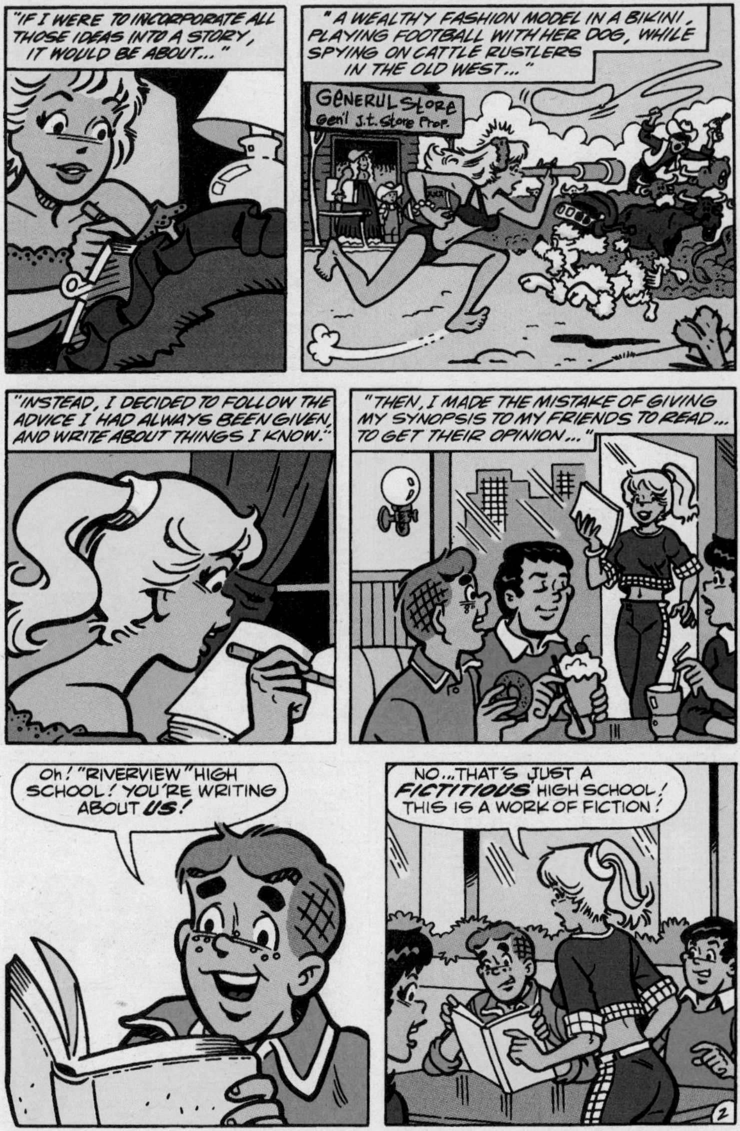
"IF I WERE TO INCORPORATE ALL THOSE IDEAS INTO A STORY, IT WOULD BE ABOUT..."
"A WEALTHY FASHION MODEL IN A BIKINI, PLAYING FOOTBALL WITH HER DOG, WHILE SPYING ON CATTLE RUSTLERS IN THE OLD WEST..."
GENERUL STORE
Gen'l J.t. Store Prop.
"INSTEAD, I DECIDED TO FOLLOW THE ADVICE I HAD ALWAYS BEEN GIVEN, AND WRITE ABOUT THINGS I KNOW."
"THEN, I MADE THE MISTAKE OF GIVING MY SYNOPSIS TO MY FRIENDS TO READ... TO GET THEIR OPINION..."
Oh! "RIVERVIEW" HIGH SCHOOL! YOU'RE WRITING ABOUT US!
NO...THAT'S JUST A FICTITIOUS HIGH SCHOOL! THIS IS A WORK OF FICTION!
2

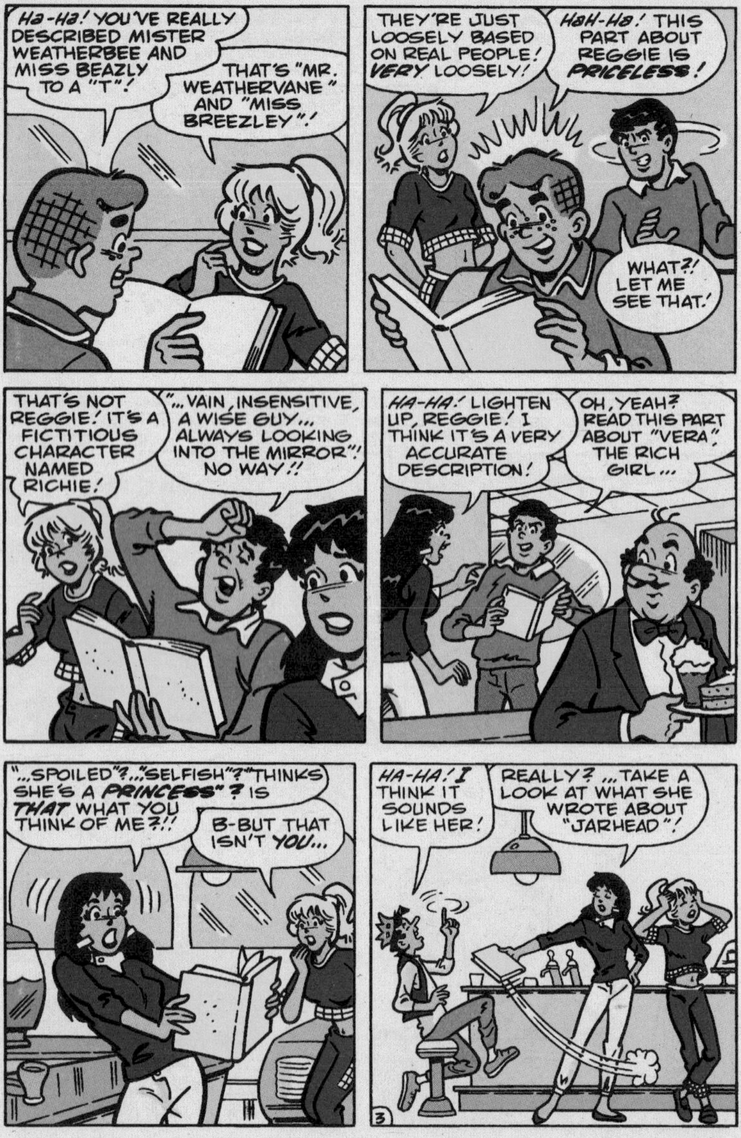
HA-HA! YOU'VE REALLY DESCRIBED MISTER WEATHERBEE AND MISS BEAZLY TO A "T"!
THAT'S "MR. WEATHERVANE" AND "MISS BREEZLEY"!
THEY'RE JUST LOOSELY BASED ON REAL PEOPLE! VERY LOOSELY!
HAH-HA! THIS PART ABOUT REGGIE IS PRICELESS!
WHAT?! LET ME SEE THAT!
THAT'S NOT REGGIE! IT'S A FICTITIOUS CHARACTER NAMED RICHIE!
"...VAIN, INSENSITIVE, A WISE GUY... ALWAYS LOOKING INTO THE MIRROR"!! NO WAY!!
HA-HA! LIGHTEN UP, REGGIE! I THINK IT'S A VERY ACCURATE DESCRIPTION!
OH, YEAH? READ THIS PART ABOUT "VERA", THE RICH GIRL...
"...SPOILED"?..."SELFISH"?"THINKS SHE'S A PRINCESS"? IS THAT WHAT YOU THINK OF ME?!!
B-BUT THAT ISN'T YOU...
HA-HA! I THINK IT SOUNDS LIKE HER!
REALLY? ...TAKE A LOOK AT WHAT SHE WROTE ABOUT "JARHEAD"!
3

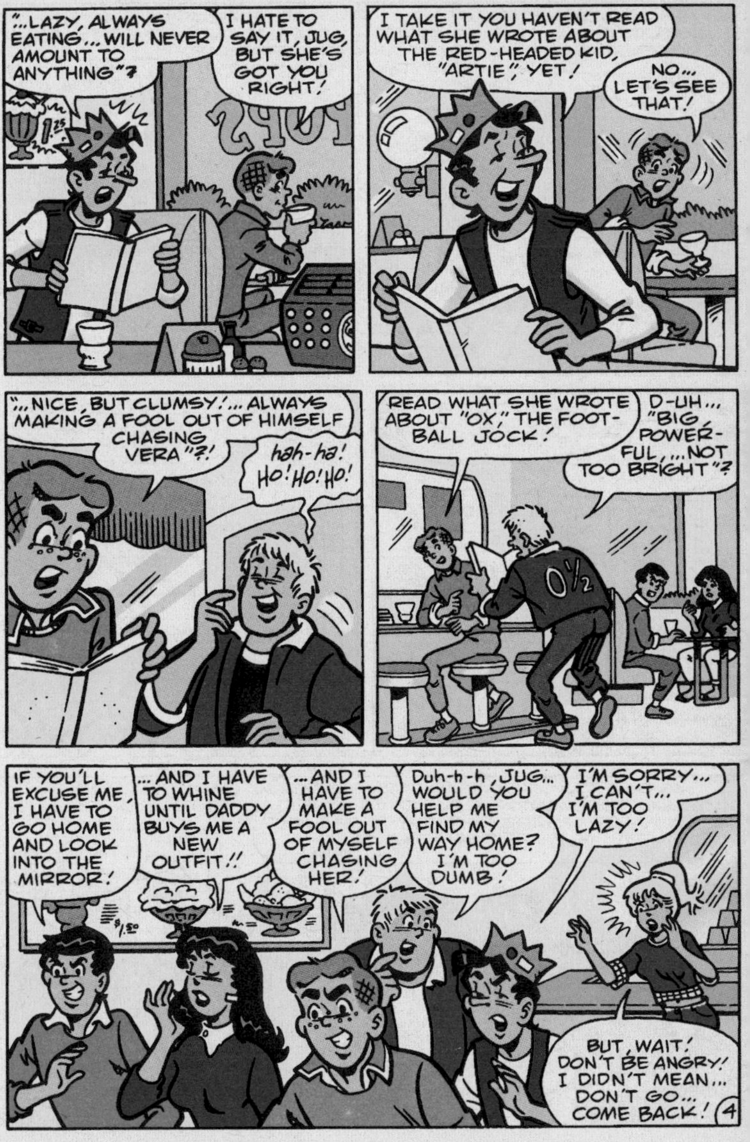
"...LAZY, ALWAYS EATING... WILL NEVER AMOUNT TO ANYTHING"?
I HATE TO SAY IT, JUG, BUT SHE'S GOT YOU RIGHT!
I TAKE IT YOU HAVEN'T READ WHAT SHE WROTE ABOUT THE RED-HEADED KID, "ARTIE", YET!
NO... LET'S SEE THAT!
"...NICE, BUT CLUMSY!... ALWAYS MAKING A FOOL OUT OF HIMSELF CHASING VERA"?!
hah-ha! HO! HO! HO!
READ WHAT SHE WROTE ABOUT "OX," THE FOOT-BALL JOCK!
D-UH... "BIG, POWER-FUL, ...NOT TOO BRIGHT"?
IF YOU'LL EXCUSE ME, I HAVE TO GO HOME AND LOOK INTO THE MIRROR!
...AND I HAVE TO WHINE UNTIL DADDY BUYS ME A NEW OUTFIT!!
...AND I HAVE TO MAKE A FOOL OUT OF MYSELF CHASING HER!
Duh-h-h, JUG... WOULD YOU HELP ME FIND MY WAY HOME? I'M TOO DUMB!
I'M SORRY... I CAN'T... I'M TOO LAZY!
BUT, WAIT! DON'T BE ANGRY! I DIDN'T MEAN... DON'T GO... COME BACK!
4

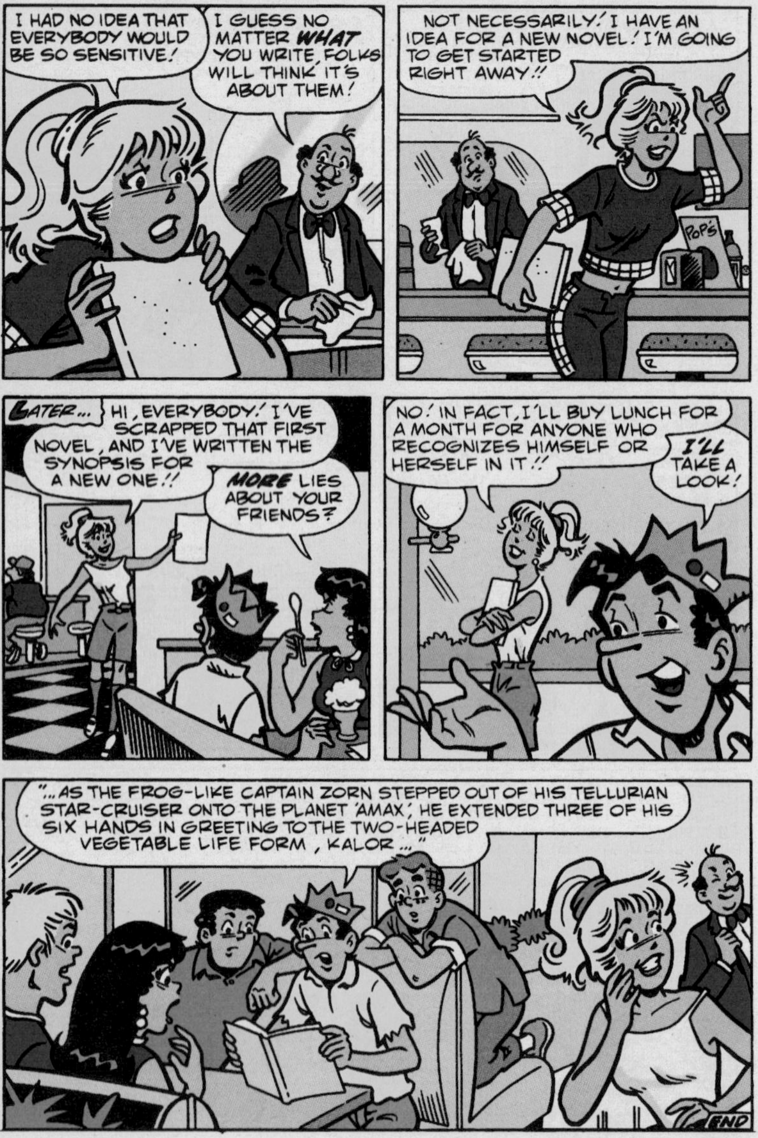
I HAD NO IDEA THAT EVERYBODY WOULD BE SO SENSITIVE!
I GUESS NO MATTER WHAT YOU WRITE, FOLKS WILL THINK IT'S ABOUT THEM!
NOT NECESSARILY! I HAVE AN IDEA FOR A NEW NOVEL! I'M GOING TO GET STARTED RIGHT AWAY!!
POP'S
LATER...
HI, EVERYBODY! I'VE SCRAPPED THAT FIRST NOVEL, AND I'VE WRITTEN THE SYNOPSIS FOR A NEW ONE!!
MORE LIES ABOUT YOUR FRIENDS?
NO! IN FACT, I'LL BUY LUNCH FOR A MONTH FOR ANYONE WHO RECOGNIZES HIMSELF OR HERSELF IN IT!!
I'LL TAKE A LOOK!
"...AS THE FROG-LIKE CAPTAIN ZORN STEPPED OUT OF HIS TELLURIAN STAR-CRUISER ONTO THE PLANET 'AMAX,' HE EXTENDED THREE OF HIS SIX HANDS IN GREETING TO THE TWO-HEADED VEGETABLE LIFE FORM, KALOR..."
END

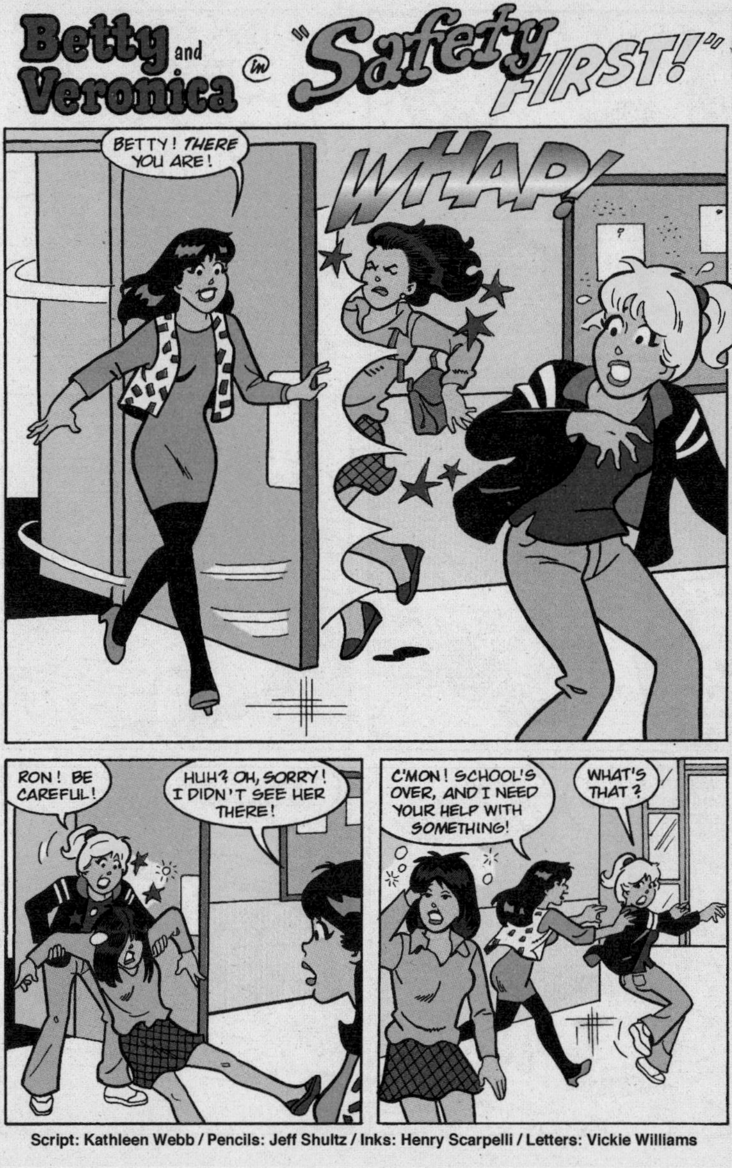
Betty and Veronica in "Safety FIRST!"
BETTY! THERE YOU ARE!
WHAP!
RON! BE CAREFUL!
HUH? OH, SORRY! I DIDN'T SEE HER THERE!
C'MON! SCHOOL'S OVER, AND I NEED YOUR HELP WITH SOMETHING!
WHAT'S THAT?

Script: Kathleen Webb / Pencils: Jeff Shultz / Inks: Henry Scarpelli / Letters: Vickie Williams

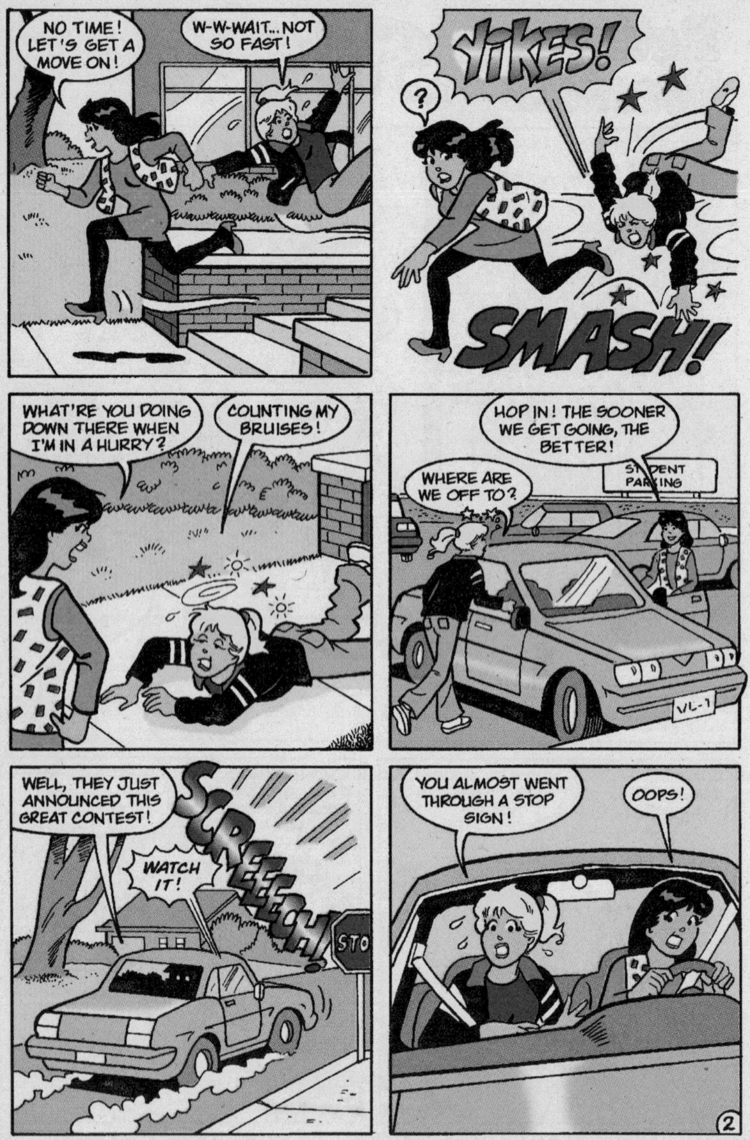
NO TIME! LET'S GET A MOVE ON!
W-W-WAIT... NOT SO FAST!
YIKES!
?
SMASH!
WHAT'RE YOU DOING DOWN THERE WHEN I'M IN A HURRY?
COUNTING MY BRUISES!
HOP IN! THE SOONER WE GET GOING, THE BETTER!
WHERE ARE WE OFF TO?
STUDENT PARKING
VL-1
WELL, THEY JUST ANNOUNCED THIS GREAT CONTEST!
SCREEECH!
WATCH IT!
STO
YOU ALMOST WENT THROUGH A STOP SIGN!
OOPS!
2

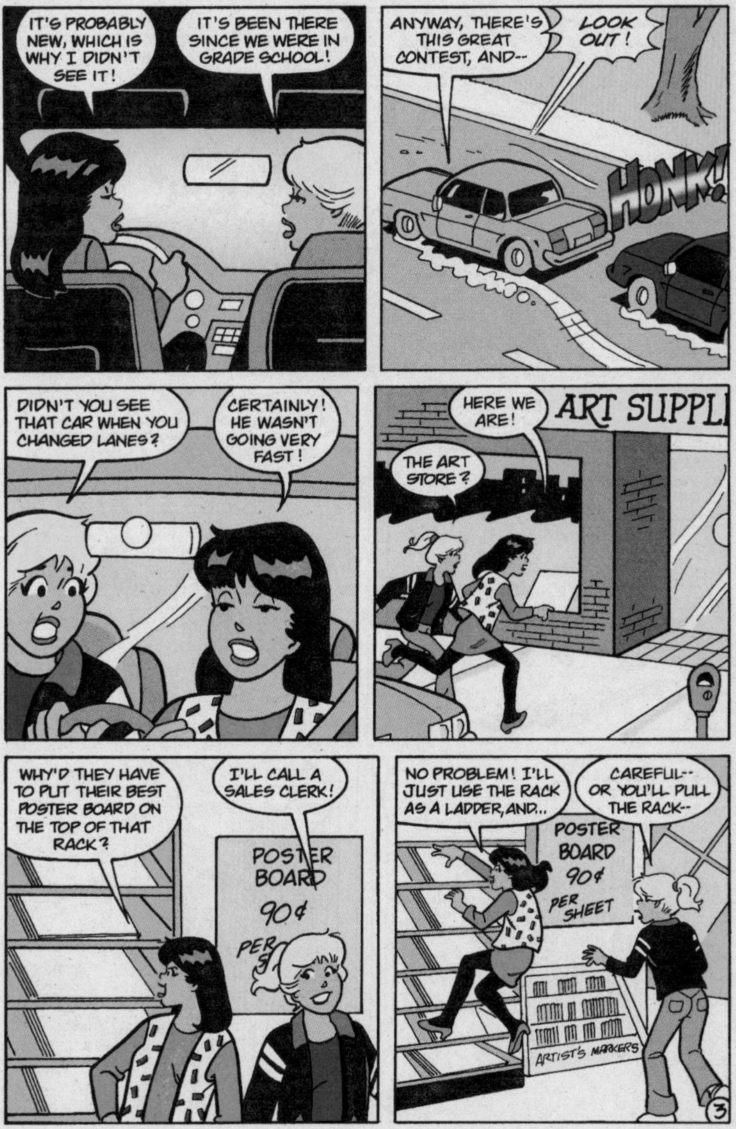

IT'S PROBABLY NEW, WHICH IS WHY I DIDN'T SEE IT!
IT'S BEEN THERE SINCE WE WERE IN GRADE SCHOOL!
ANYWAY, THERE'S THIS GREAT CONTEST, AND--
LOOK OUT!
HONK!
DIDN'T YOU SEE THAT CAR WHEN YOU CHANGED LANES?
CERTAINLY! HE WASN'T GOING VERY FAST!
HERE WE ARE!
ART SUPPL
THE ART STORE?
WHY'D THEY HAVE TO PUT THEIR BEST POSTER BOARD ON THE TOP OF THAT RACK?
I'LL CALL A SALES CLERK!
POSTER BOARD 90¢
NO PROBLEM! I'LL JUST USE THE RACK AS A LADDER, AND...
CAREFUL-- OR YOU'LL PULL THE RACK--
POSTER BOARD 90¢ PER SHEET
ARTIST'S MARKERS

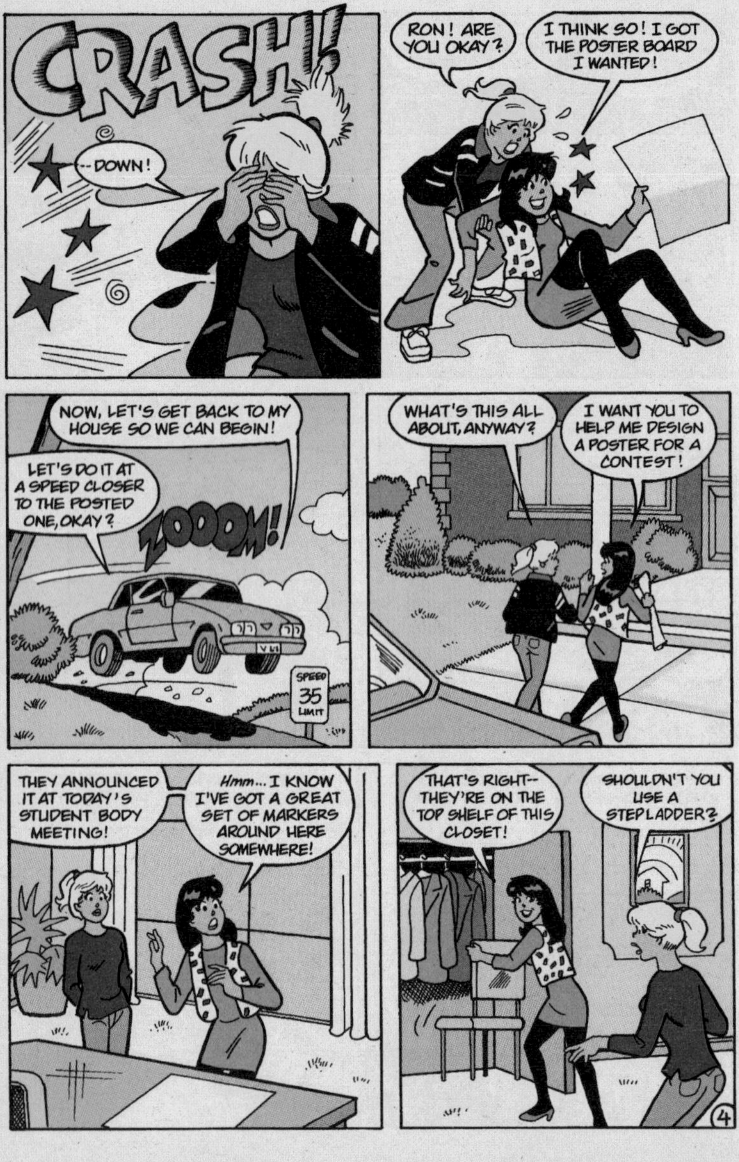
CRASH!
--DOWN!
RON! ARE YOU OKAY?
I THINK SO! I GOT THE POSTER BOARD I WANTED!
NOW, LET'S GET BACK TO MY HOUSE SO WE CAN BEGIN!
LET'S DO IT AT A SPEED CLOSER TO THE POSTED ONE, OKAY?
ZOOOM!
SPEED 35 LIMIT
WHAT'S THIS ALL ABOUT, ANYWAY?
I WANT YOU TO HELP ME DESIGN A POSTER FOR A CONTEST!
THEY ANNOUNCED IT AT TODAY'S STUDENT BODY MEETING!
Hmm... I KNOW I'VE GOT A GREAT SET OF MARKERS AROUND HERE SOMEWHERE!
THAT'S RIGHT-- THEY'RE ON THE TOP SHELF OF THIS CLOSET!
SHOULDN'T YOU USE A STEPLADDER?
4

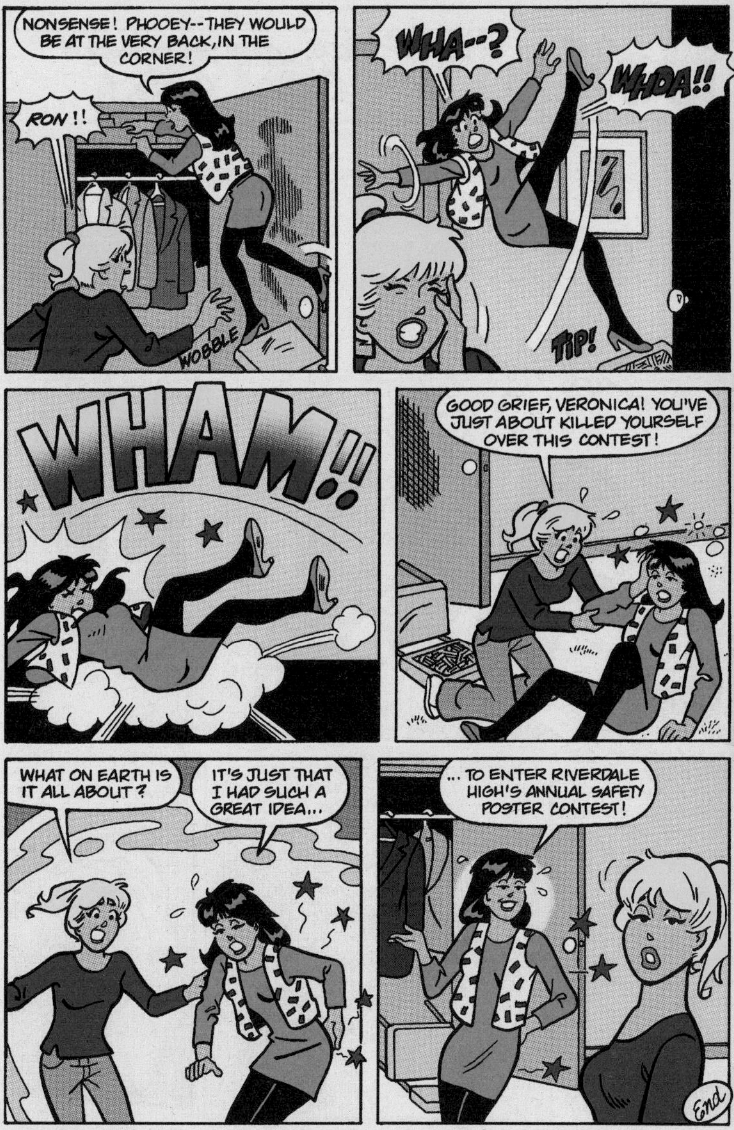
NONSENSE! PHOOEY--THEY WOULD BE AT THE VERY BACK, IN THE CORNER!
RON!!
WOBBLE
WHA--?
WHOA!!
TIP!
WHAM!!
GOOD GRIEF, VERONICA! YOU'VE JUST ABOUT KILLED YOURSELF OVER THIS CONTEST!
WHAT ON EARTH IS IT ALL ABOUT?
IT'S JUST THAT I HAD SUCH A GREAT IDEA...
... TO ENTER RIVERDALE HIGH'S ANNUAL SAFETY POSTER CONTEST!
End

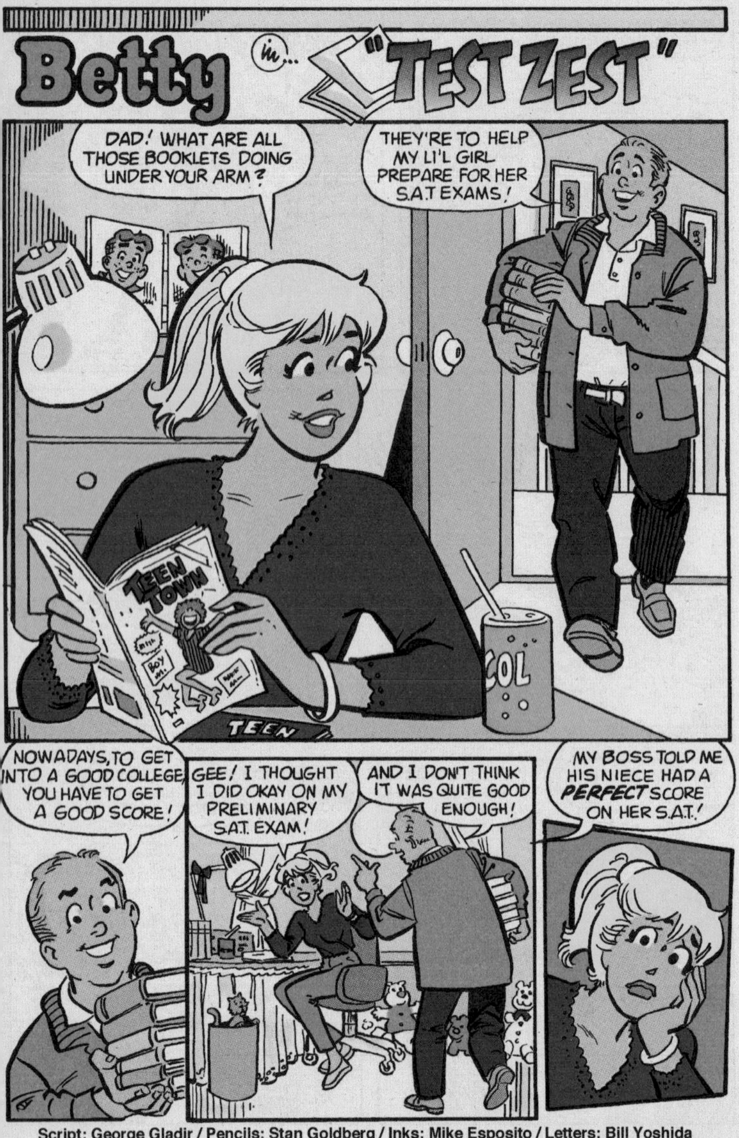
Betty in... "TEST ZEST"
DAD! WHAT ARE ALL THOSE BOOKLETS DOING UNDER YOUR ARM?
THEY'RE TO HELP MY LI'L GIRL PREPARE FOR HER S.A.T EXAMS!
TEEN TOWN
COL
TEEN
NOWADAYS, TO GET INTO A GOOD COLLEGE, YOU HAVE TO GET A GOOD SCORE!
GEE! I THOUGHT I DID OKAY ON MY PRELIMINARY S.A.T. EXAM!
AND I DON'T THINK IT WAS QUITE GOOD ENOUGH!
MY BOSS TOLD ME HIS NIECE HAD A PERFECT SCORE ON HER S.A.T.!

Script: George Gladir / Pencils: Stan Goldberg / Inks: Mike Esposito / Letters: Bill Yoshida

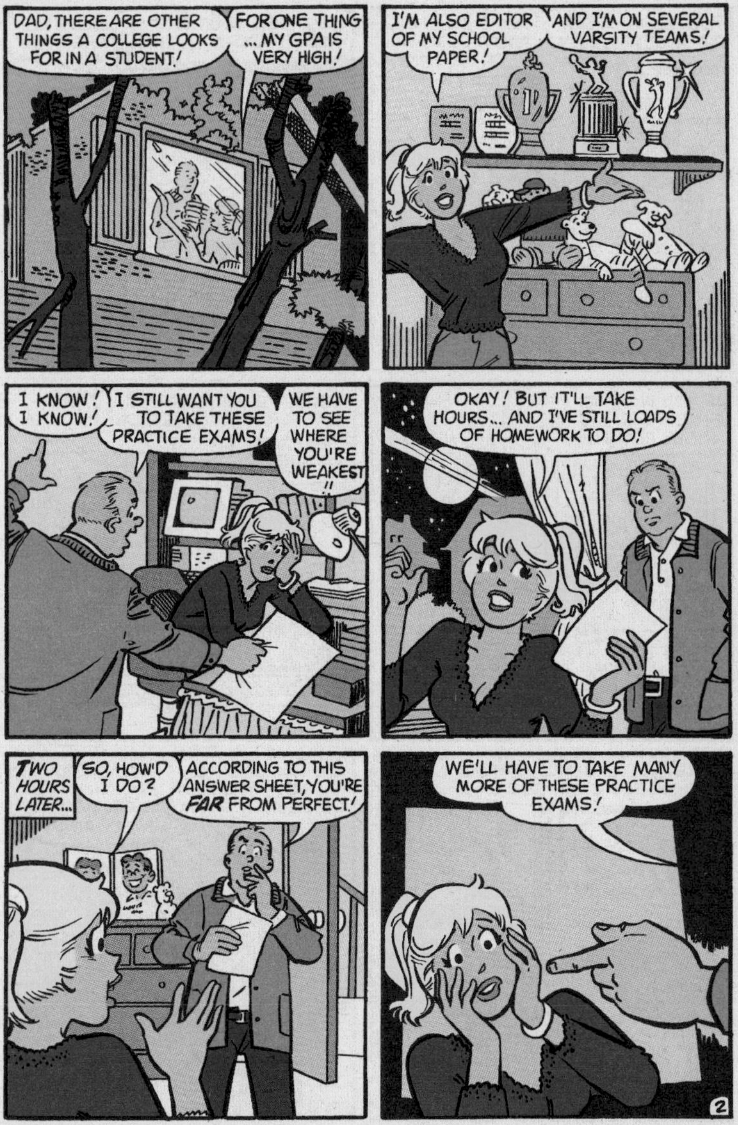

DAD, THERE ARE OTHER THINGS A COLLEGE LOOKS FOR IN A STUDENT!
FOR ONE THING ... MY GPA IS VERY HIGH!
I'M ALSO EDITOR OF MY SCHOOL PAPER!
AND I'M ON SEVERAL VARSITY TEAMS!
I KNOW! I KNOW!
I STILL WANT YOU TO TAKE THESE PRACTICE EXAMS!
WE HAVE TO SEE WHERE YOU'RE WEAKEST!!
OKAY! BUT IT'LL TAKE HOURS... AND I'VE STILL LOADS OF HOMEWORK TO DO!
TWO HOURS LATER...
SO, HOW'D I DO?
ACCORDING TO THIS ANSWER SHEET, YOU'RE FAR FROM PERFECT!
WE'LL HAVE TO TAKE MANY MORE OF THESE PRACTICE EXAMS!
2

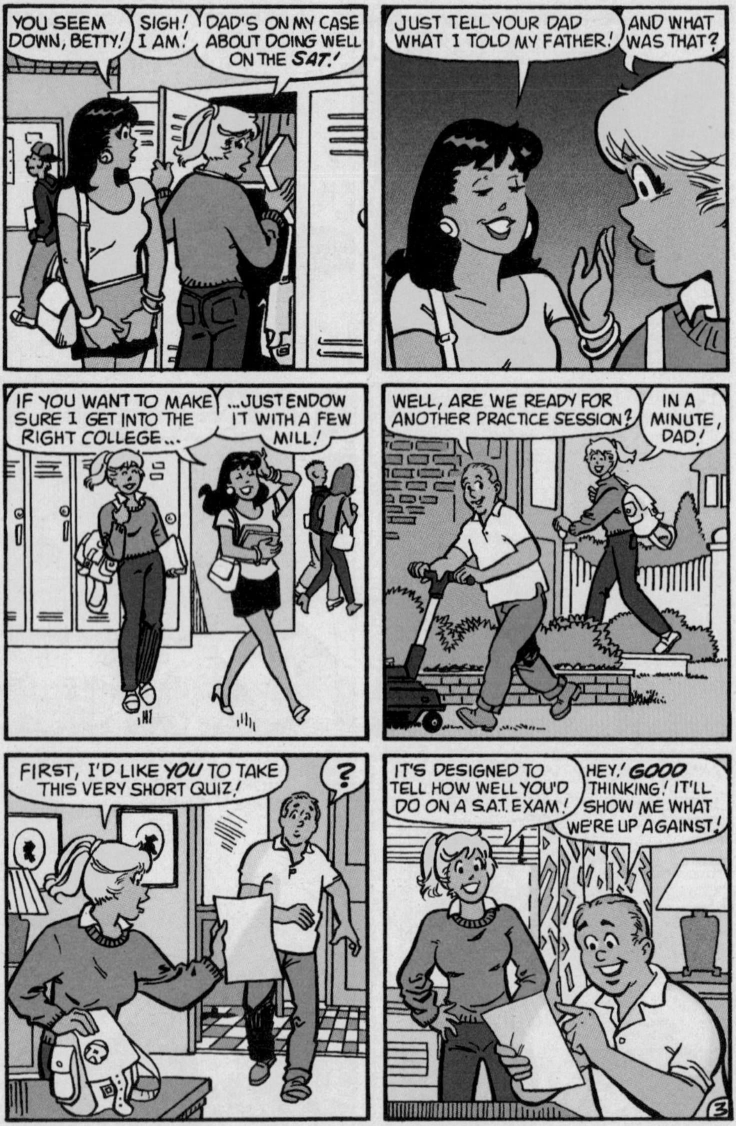

YOU SEEM DOWN, BETTY!
SIGH! I AM!
DAD'S ON MY CASE ABOUT DOING WELL ON THE SAT!
JUST TELL YOUR DAD WHAT I TOLD MY FATHER!
AND WHAT WAS THAT?
IF YOU WANT TO MAKE SURE I GET INTO THE RIGHT COLLEGE...
...JUST ENDOW IT WITH A FEW MILL!
WELL, ARE WE READY FOR ANOTHER PRACTICE SESSION?
IN A MINUTE, DAD!
FIRST, I'D LIKE YOU TO TAKE THIS VERY SHORT QUIZ!
?
IT'S DESIGNED TO TELL HOW WELL YOU'D DO ON A S.A.T. EXAM!
HEY! GOOD THINKING! IT'LL SHOW ME WHAT WE'RE UP AGAINST!
3

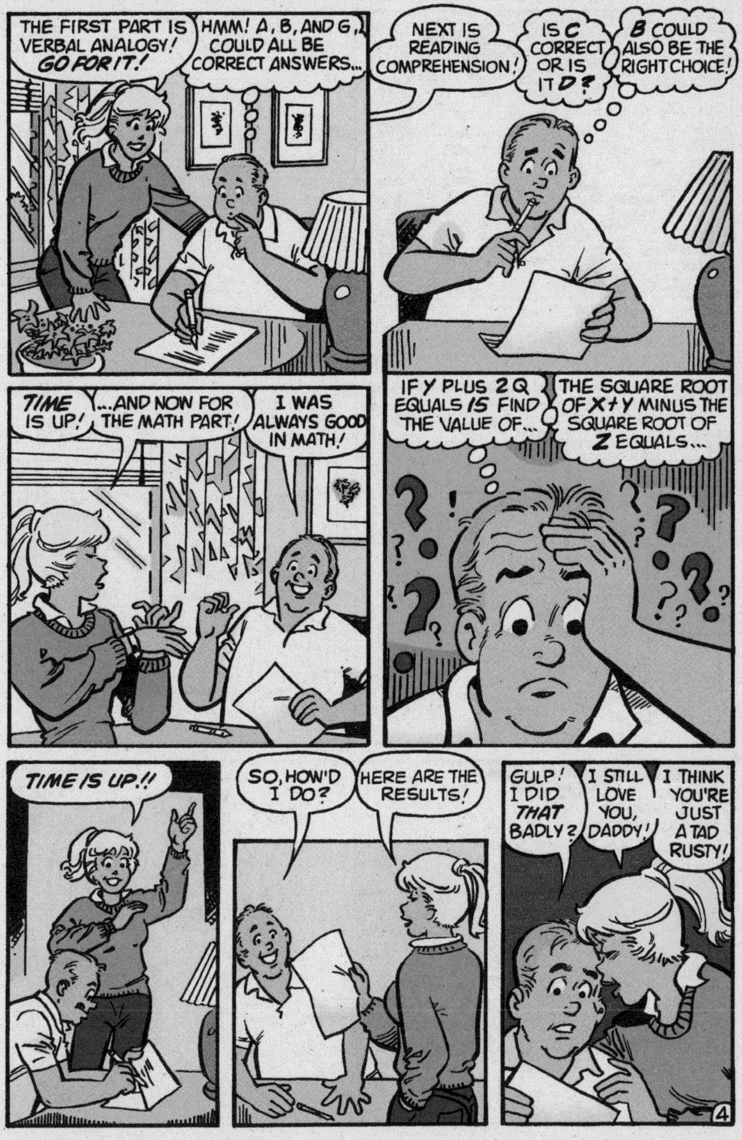
THE FIRST PART IS VERBAL ANALOGY! GO FOR IT!
HMM! A, B, AND G, COULD ALL BE CORRECT ANSWERS...
NEXT IS READING COMPREHENSION!
IS C CORRECT OR IS IT D?
B COULD ALSO BE THE RIGHT CHOICE!
TIME IS UP!
...AND NOW FOR THE MATH PART!
I WAS ALWAYS GOOD IN MATH!
IF Y PLUS 2Q EQUALS 15 FIND THE VALUE OF...
THE SQUARE ROOT OF X+Y MINUS THE SQUARE ROOT OF Z EQUALS...
TIME IS UP!!
SO, HOW'D I DO?
HERE ARE THE RESULTS!
GULP! I DID THAT BADLY?
I STILL LOVE YOU, DADDY!
I THINK YOU'RE JUST A TAD RUSTY!
4

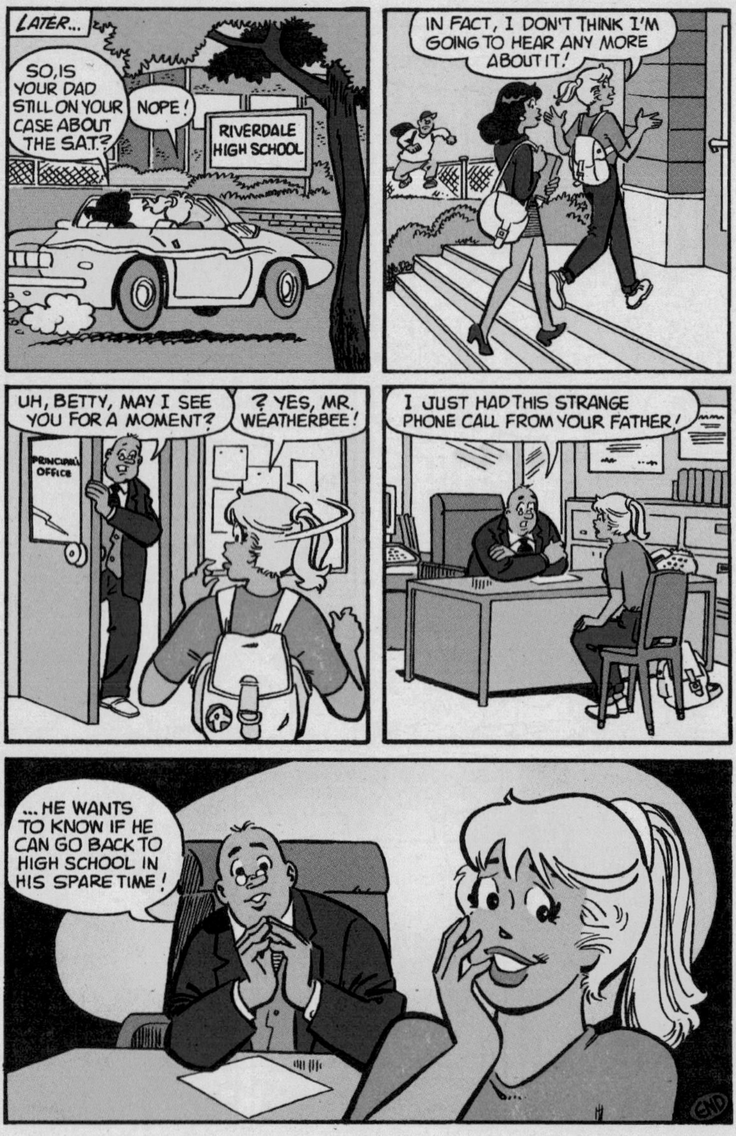
LATER...
SO, IS YOUR DAD STILL ON YOUR CASE ABOUT THE S.A.T.?
NOPE!
RIVERDALE HIGH SCHOOL
IN FACT, I DON'T THINK I'M GOING TO HEAR ANY MORE ABOUT IT!
UH, BETTY, MAY I SEE YOU FOR A MOMENT?
? YES, MR. WEATHERBEE!
PRINCIPAL'S OFFICE
I JUST HAD THIS STRANGE PHONE CALL FROM YOUR FATHER!
...HE WANTS TO KNOW IF HE CAN GO BACK TO HIGH SCHOOL IN HIS SPARE TIME!
END

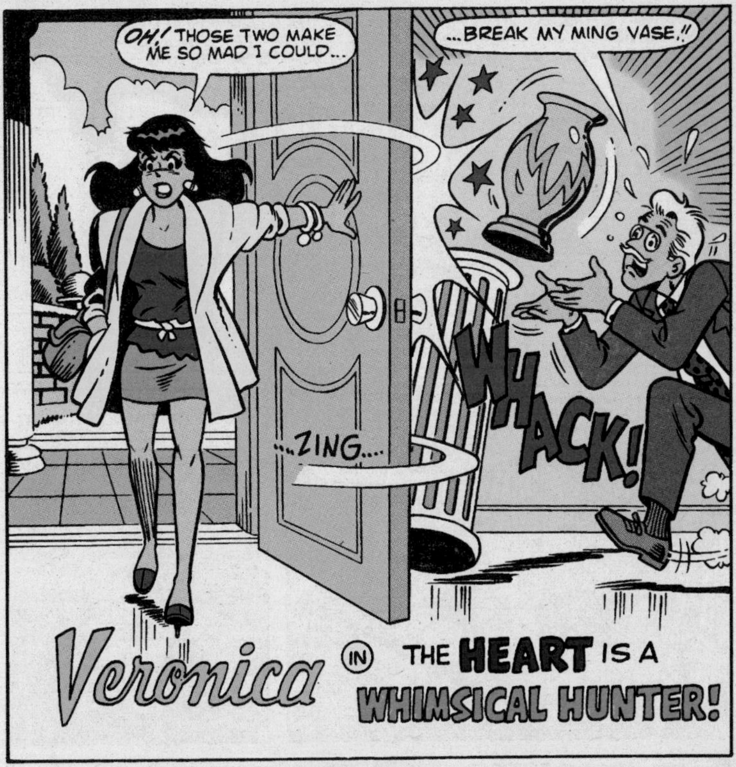
OH! THOSE TWO MAKE ME SO MAD I COULD...
...BREAK MY MING VASE!!
...ZING....
WHACK!
Veronica IN THE HEART IS A WHIMSICAL HUNTER!

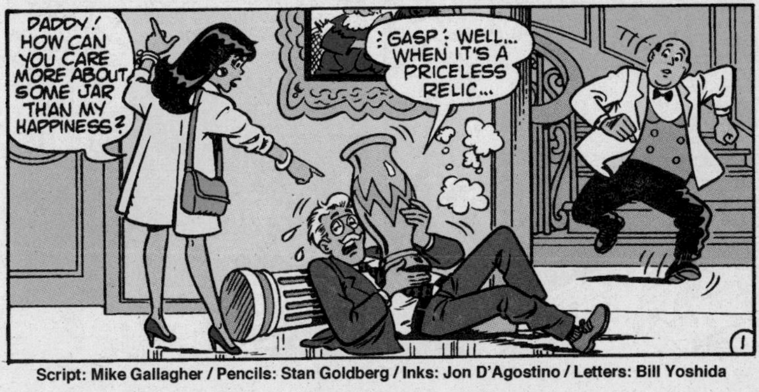
DADDY! HOW CAN YOU CARE MORE ABOUT SOME JAR THAN MY HAPPINESS?
GASP! WELL... WHEN IT'S A PRICELESS RELIC...
1

Script: Mike Gallagher / Pencils: Stan Goldberg / Inks: Jon D'Agostino / Letters: Bill Yoshida

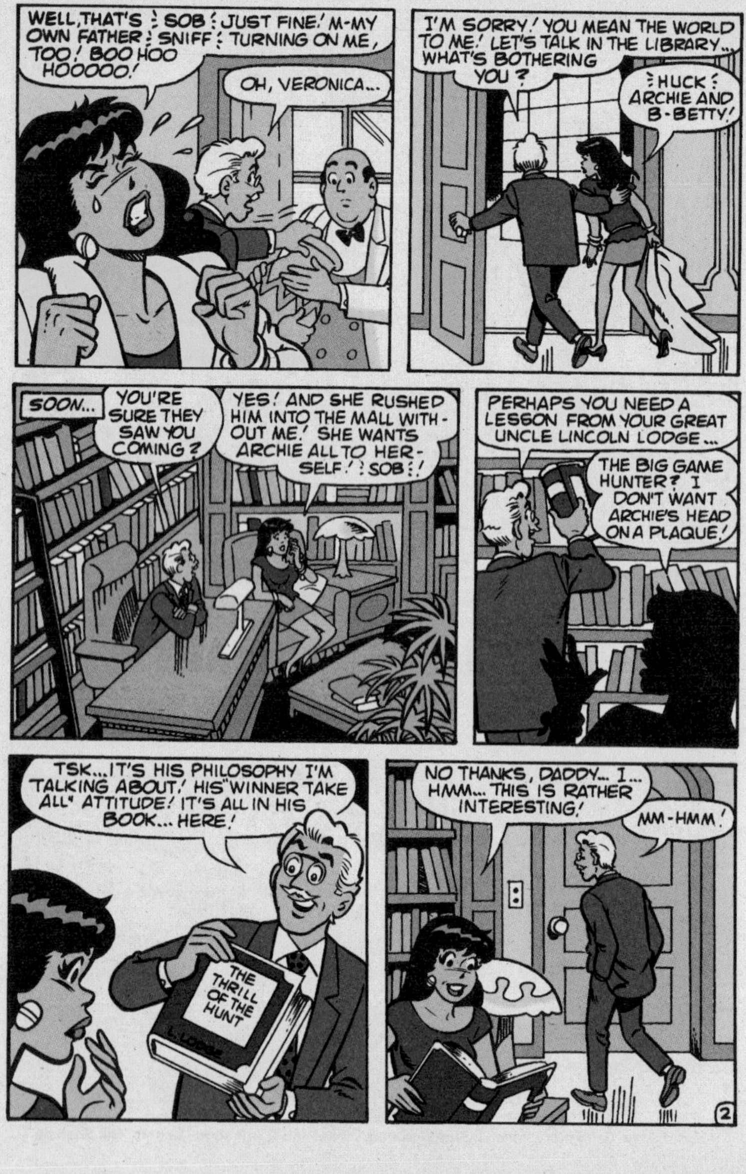
WELL, THAT'S ⁝SOB⁝ JUST FINE! M-MY OWN FATHER ⁝SNIFF⁝ TURNING ON ME, TOO! BOO HOO HOOOOO!
OH, VERONICA...
I'M SORRY! YOU MEAN THE WORLD TO ME! LET'S TALK IN THE LIBRARY... WHAT'S BOTHERING YOU?
⁝HUCK⁝ ARCHIE AND B-BETTY!
SOON...
YOU'RE SURE THEY SAW YOU COMING?
YES! AND SHE RUSHED HIM INTO THE MALL WITH-OUT ME! SHE WANTS ARCHIE ALL TO HER-SELF! ⁝SOB⁝!
PERHAPS YOU NEED A LESSON FROM YOUR GREAT UNCLE LINCOLN LODGE...
THE BIG GAME HUNTER? I DON'T WANT ARCHIE'S HEAD ON A PLAQUE!
TSK... IT'S HIS PHILOSOPHY I'M TALKING ABOUT! HIS "WINNER TAKE ALL" ATTITUDE! IT'S ALL IN HIS BOOK... HERE!
THE THRILL OF THE HUNT
L. LODGE
NO THANKS, DADDY... I... HMM... THIS IS RATHER INTERESTING!
MM-HMM!
2

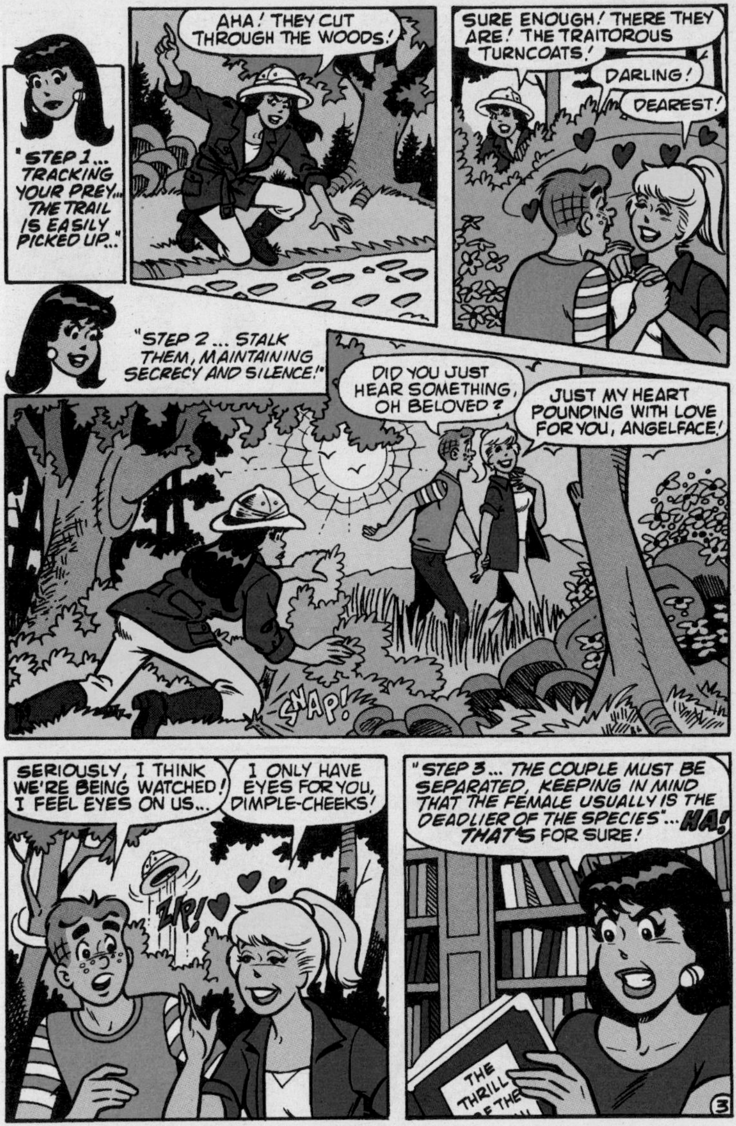
"STEP 1... TRACKING YOUR PREY... THE TRAIL IS EASILY PICKED UP..."
AHA! THEY CUT THROUGH THE WOODS!
SURE ENOUGH! THERE THEY ARE! THE TRAITOROUS TURNCOATS!
DARLING!
DEAREST!
"STEP 2 ... STALK THEM, MAINTAINING SECRECY AND SILENCE!"
DID YOU JUST HEAR SOMETHING, OH BELOVED?
JUST MY HEART POUNDING WITH LOVE FOR YOU, ANGELFACE!
SNAP!
SERIOUSLY, I THINK WE'RE BEING WATCHED! I FEEL EYES ON US...
I ONLY HAVE EYES FOR YOU, DIMPLE-CHEEKS!
ZIP!
"STEP 3 ... THE COUPLE MUST BE SEPARATED, KEEPING IN MIND THAT THE FEMALE USUALLY IS THE DEADLIER OF THE SPECIES"... HA! THAT'S FOR SURE!
3

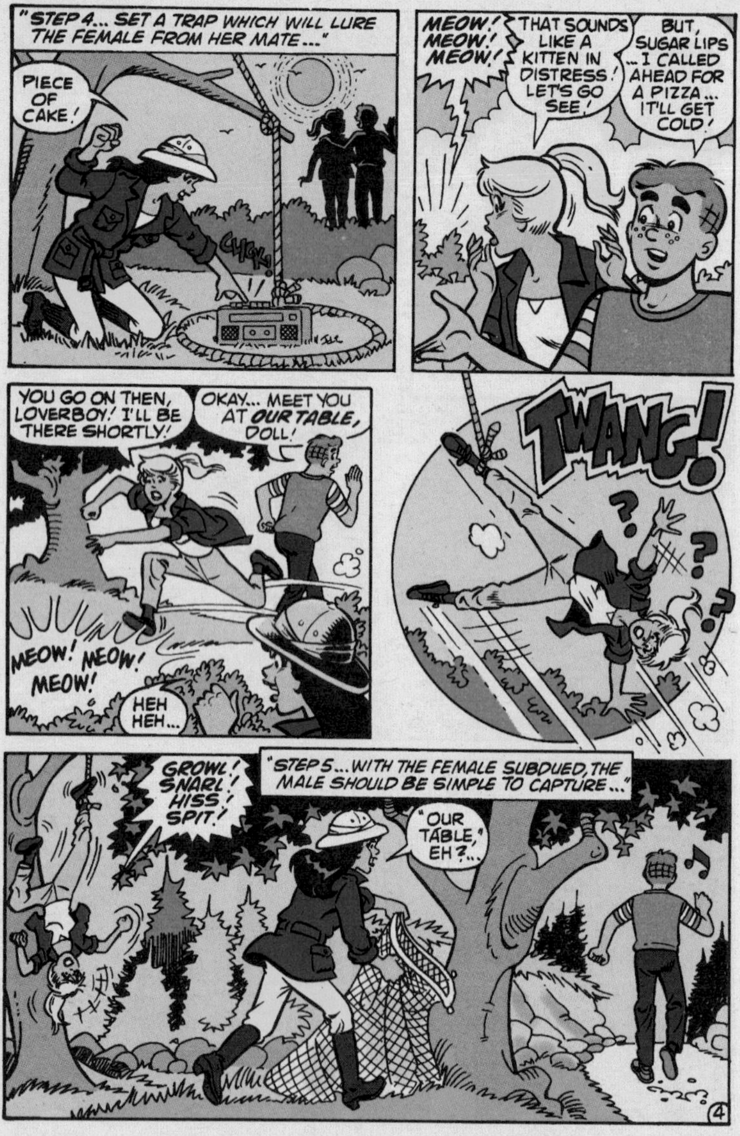
"STEP 4... SET A TRAP WHICH WILL LURE THE FEMALE FROM HER MATE..."
PIECE OF CAKE!
MEOW! MEOW! MEOW!
THAT SOUNDS LIKE A KITTEN IN DISTRESS! LET'S GO SEE!
BUT, SUGAR LIPS ...I CALLED AHEAD FOR A PIZZA... IT'LL GET COLD!
YOU GO ON THEN, LOVERBOY! I'LL BE THERE SHORTLY!
OKAY... MEET YOU AT OUR TABLE, DOLL!
MEOW! MEOW! MEOW!
HEH HEH...
TWANG!
"STEP 5... WITH THE FEMALE SUBDUED, THE MALE SHOULD BE SIMPLE TO CAPTURE..."
GROWL! SNARL! HISS! SPIT!
"OUR TABLE," EH?...
4

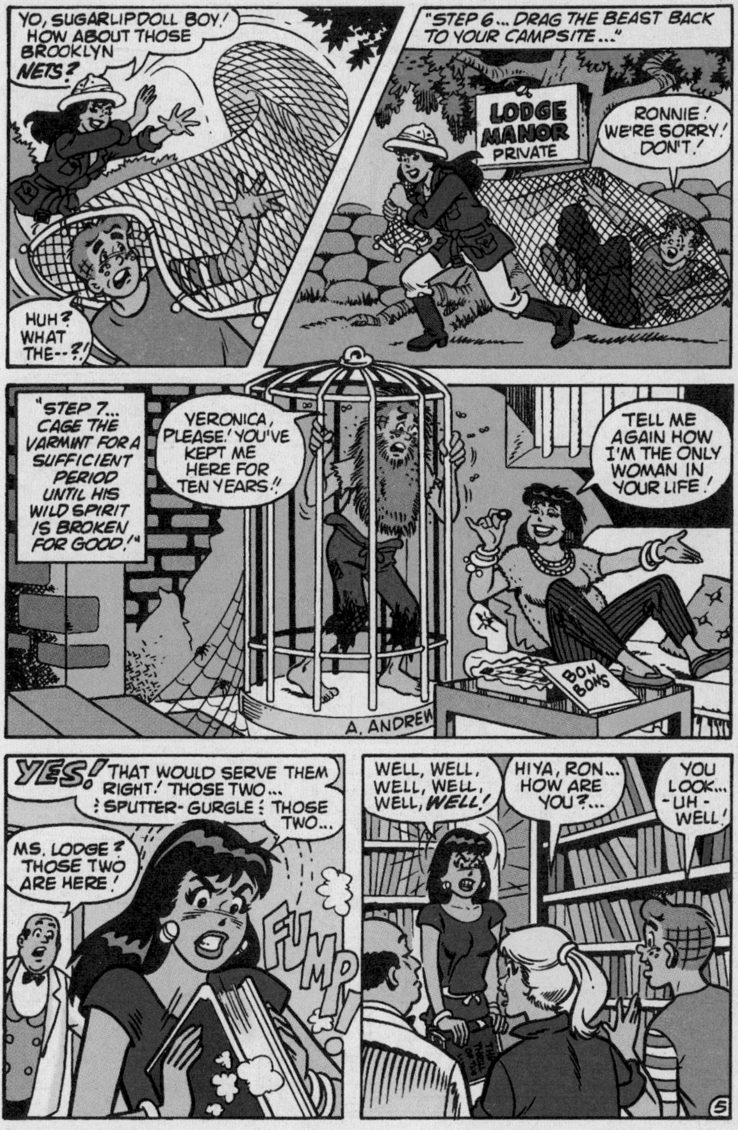
YO, SUGARLIPDOLL BOY! HOW ABOUT THOSE BROOKLYN NETS?
HUH? WHAT THE--?!
"STEP 6... DRAG THE BEAST BACK TO YOUR CAMPSITE..."
LODGE MANOR PRIVATE
RONNIE! WE'RE SORRY! DON'T!
"STEP 7... CAGE THE VARMINT FOR A SUFFICIENT PERIOD UNTIL HIS WILD SPIRIT IS BROKEN FOR GOOD!"
VERONICA, PLEASE! YOU'VE KEPT ME HERE FOR TEN YEARS!!
TELL ME AGAIN HOW I'M THE ONLY WOMAN IN YOUR LIFE!
BON BONS
A. ANDREW
YES! THAT WOULD SERVE THEM RIGHT! THOSE TWO... ⁝ SPUTTER-GURGLE ⁝ THOSE TWO...
MS. LODGE? THOSE TWO ARE HERE!
FUMP
WELL, WELL, WELL, WELL, WELL, WELL!
HIYA, RON... HOW ARE YOU?...
YOU LOOK... -UH- WELL!

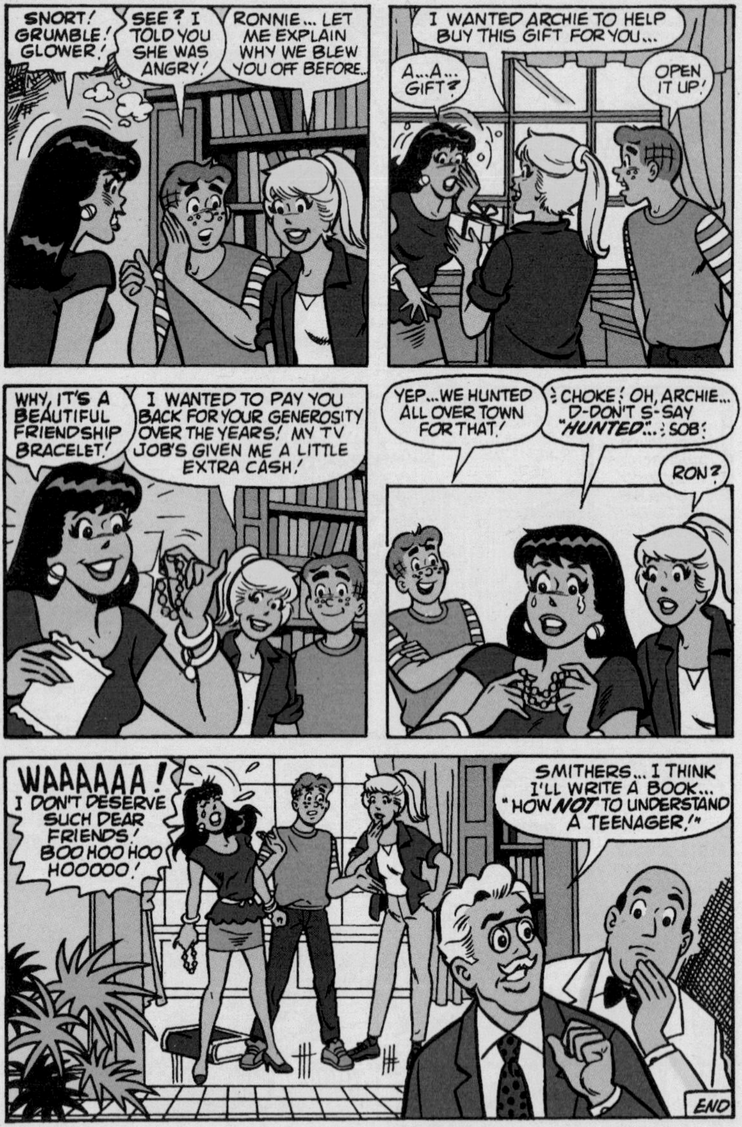
SNORT! GRUMBLE! GLOWER!
SEE? I TOLD YOU SHE WAS ANGRY!
RONNIE... LET ME EXPLAIN WHY WE BLEW YOU OFF BEFORE...
I WANTED ARCHIE TO HELP BUY THIS GIFT FOR YOU...
A...A... GIFT?
OPEN IT UP!
WHY, IT'S A BEAUTIFUL FRIENDSHIP BRACELET!
I WANTED TO PAY YOU BACK FOR YOUR GENEROSITY OVER THE YEARS! MY TV JOB'S GIVEN ME A LITTLE EXTRA CASH!
YEP...WE HUNTED ALL OVER TOWN FOR THAT!
CHOKE! OH, ARCHIE... D-DON'T S-SAY "HUNTED"... SOB!
RON?
WAAAAAA! I DON'T DESERVE SUCH DEAR FRIENDS! BOO HOO HOO HOOOOO!
SMITHERS... I THINK I'LL WRITE A BOOK... "HOW NOT TO UNDERSTAND A TEENAGER!"
END

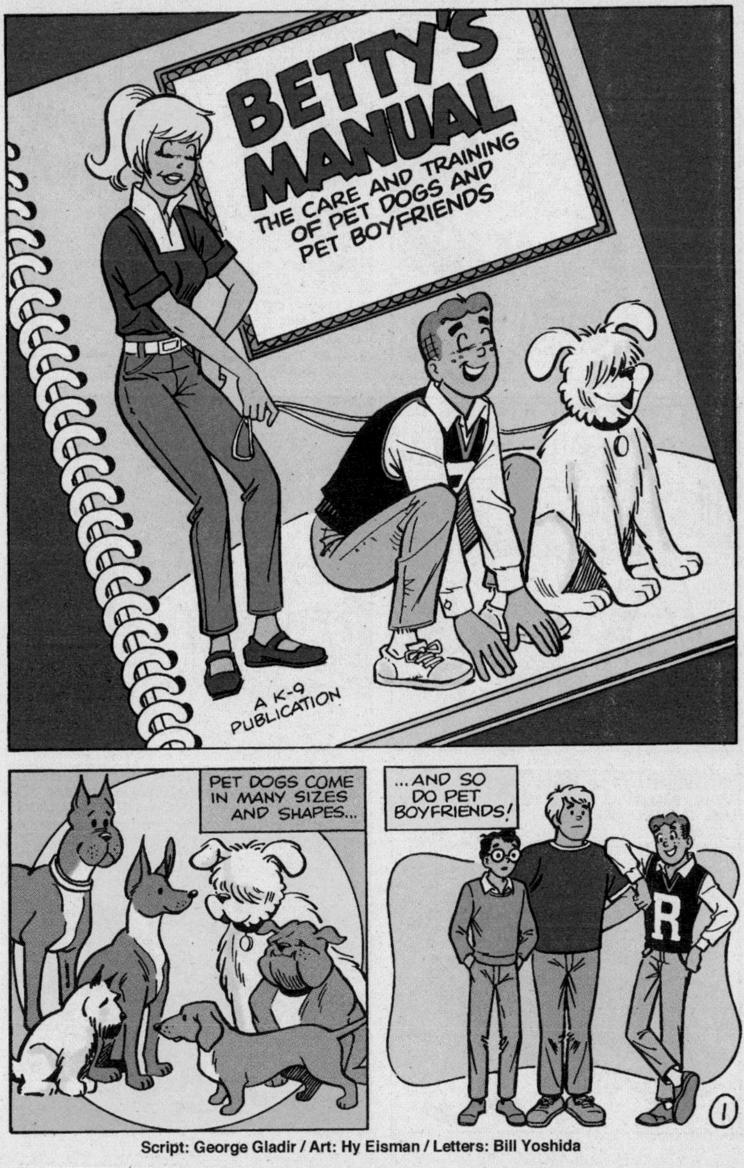

BETTY'S MANUAL
THE CARE AND TRAINING OF PET DOGS AND PET BOYFRIENDS
A K-9 PUBLICATION
PET DOGS COME IN MANY SIZES AND SHAPES...
...AND SO DO PET BOYFRIENDS!
1

Script: George Gladir / Art: Hy Eisman / Letters: Bill Yoshida

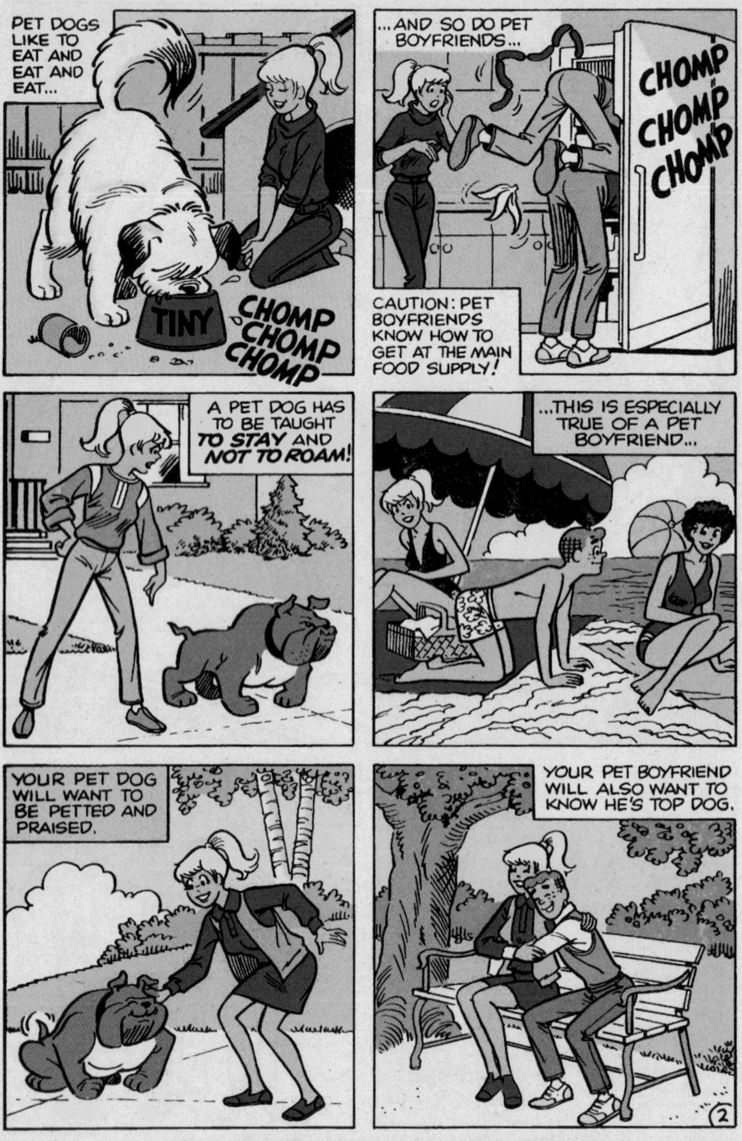
PET DOGS LIKE TO EAT AND EAT AND EAT...
TINY
CHOMP CHOMP CHOMP
...AND SO DO PET BOYFRIENDS...
CHOMP CHOMP CHOMP
CAUTION: PET BOYFRIENDS KNOW HOW TO GET AT THE MAIN FOOD SUPPLY!
A PET DOG HAS TO BE TAUGHT TO STAY AND NOT TO ROAM!
...THIS IS ESPECIALLY TRUE OF A PET BOYFRIEND...
YOUR PET DOG WILL WANT TO BE PETTED AND PRAISED.
YOUR PET BOYFRIEND WILL ALSO WANT TO KNOW HE'S TOP DOG.
2

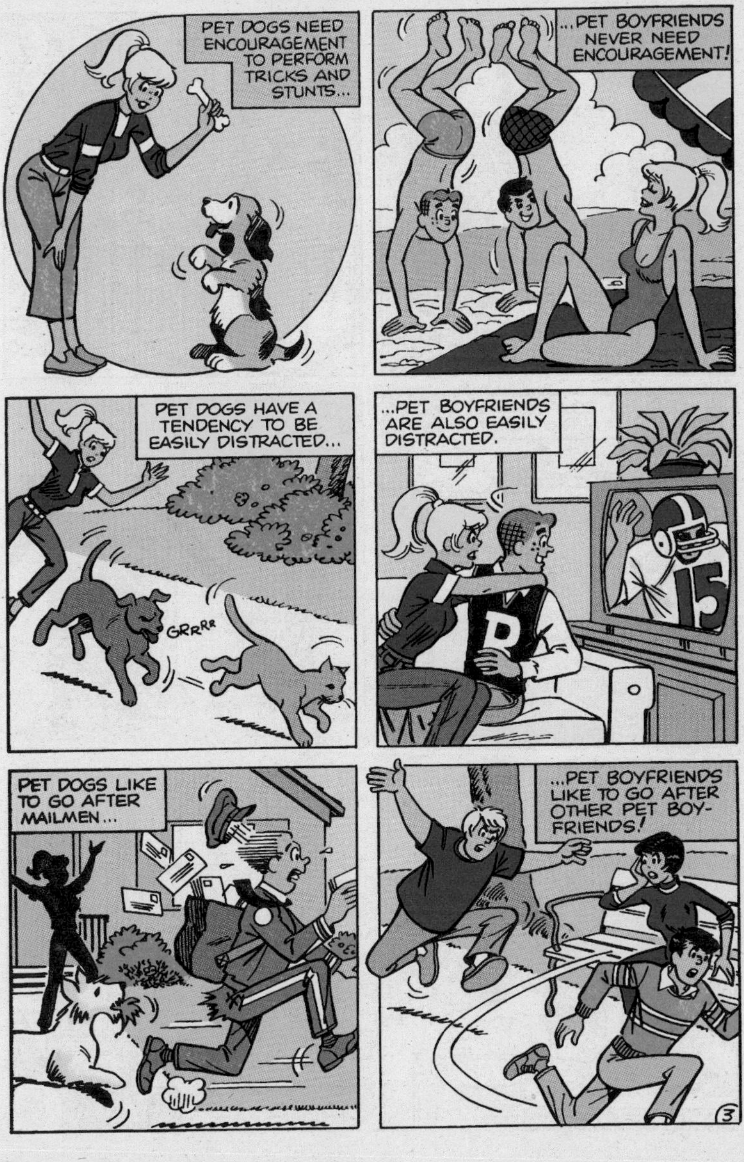
PET DOGS NEED ENCOURAGEMENT TO PERFORM TRICKS AND STUNTS...
...PET BOYFRIENDS NEVER NEED ENCOURAGEMENT!
PET DOGS HAVE A TENDENCY TO BE EASILY DISTRACTED...
GRRRR
...PET BOYFRIENDS ARE ALSO EASILY DISTRACTED.
15
PET DOGS LIKE TO GO AFTER MAILMEN...
...PET BOYFRIENDS LIKE TO GO AFTER OTHER PET BOY-FRIENDS!
3

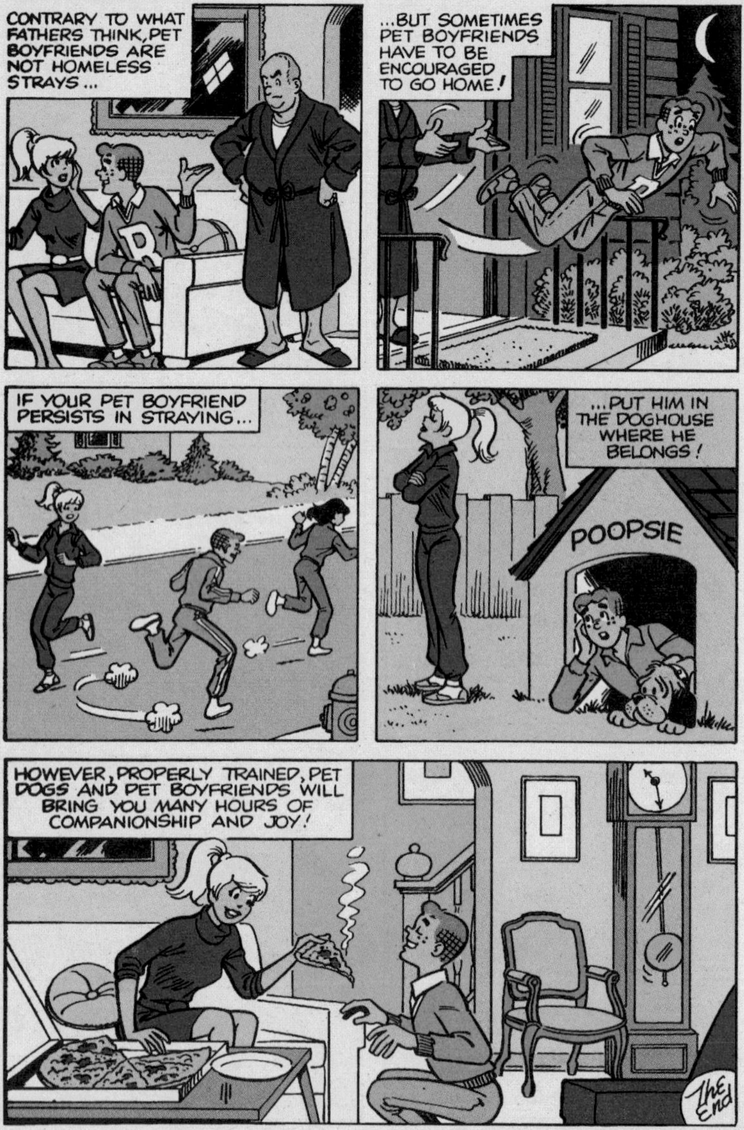
CONTRARY TO WHAT FATHERS THINK, PET BOYFRIENDS ARE NOT HOMELESS STRAYS...
...BUT SOMETIMES PET BOYFRIENDS HAVE TO BE ENCOURAGED TO GO HOME!
IF YOUR PET BOYFRIEND PERSISTS IN STRAYING...
...PUT HIM IN THE DOGHOUSE WHERE HE BELONGS!
POOPSIE
HOWEVER, PROPERLY TRAINED, PET DOGS AND PET BOYFRIENDS WILL BRING YOU MANY HOURS OF COMPANIONSHIP AND JOY!
The End

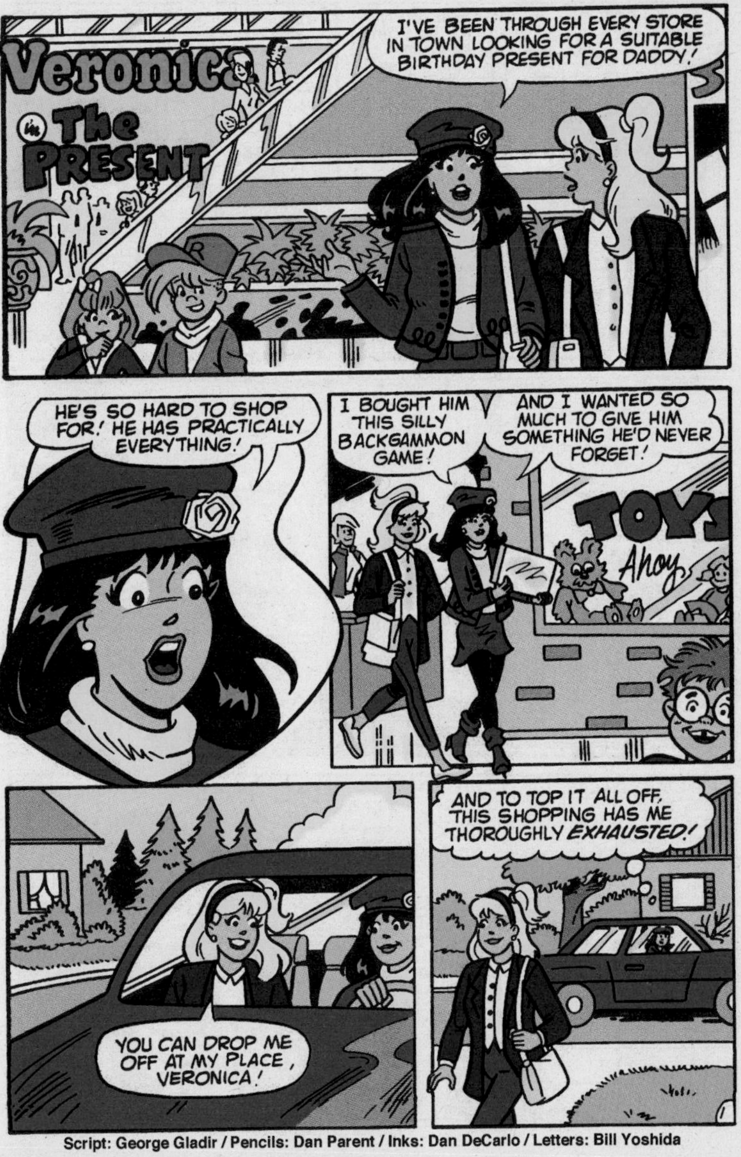
Veronica
in The PRESENT
I'VE BEEN THROUGH EVERY STORE IN TOWN LOOKING FOR A SUITABLE BIRTHDAY PRESENT FOR DADDY!
HE'S SO HARD TO SHOP FOR! HE HAS PRACTICALLY EVERYTHING!
I BOUGHT HIM THIS SILLY BACKGAMMON GAME!
AND I WANTED SO MUCH TO GIVE HIM SOMETHING HE'D NEVER FORGET!
TOYS
Ahoy
YOU CAN DROP ME OFF AT MY PLACE, VERONICA!
AND TO TOP IT ALL OFF, THIS SHOPPING HAS ME THOROUGHLY EXHAUSTED!
1

Script: George Gladir / Pencils: Dan Parent / Inks: Dan DeCarlo / Letters: Bill Yoshida

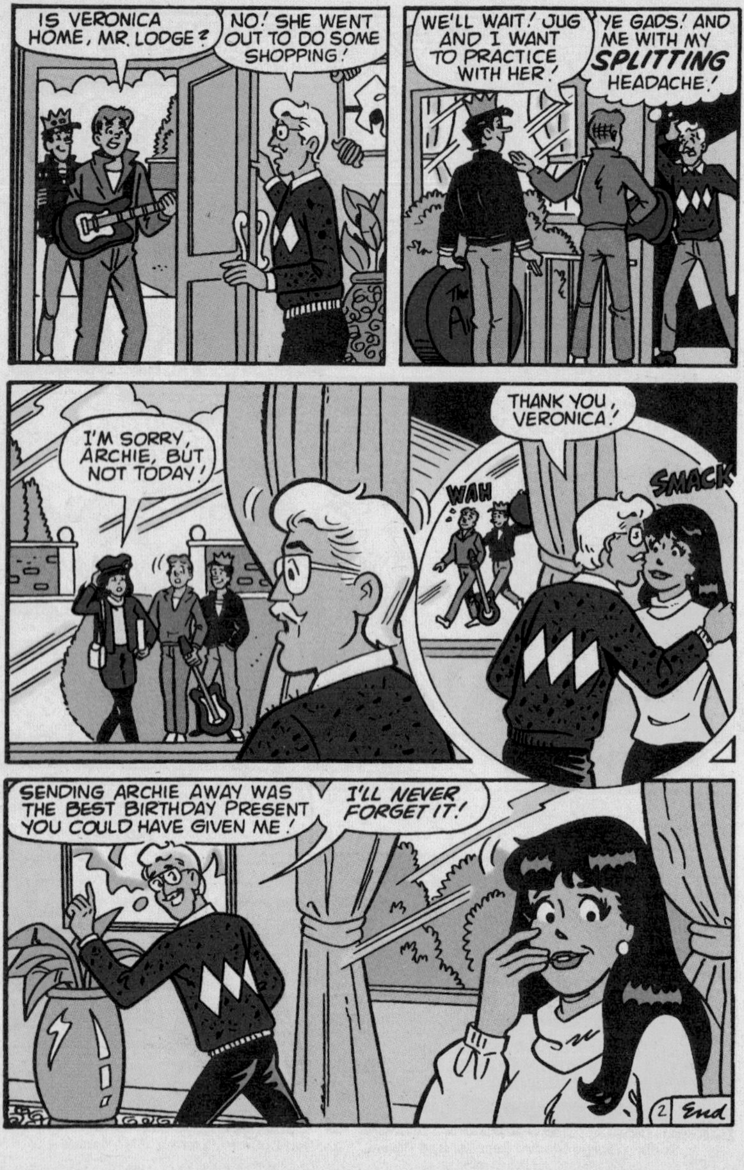
IS VERONICA HOME, MR. LODGE?
NO! SHE WENT OUT TO DO SOME SHOPPING!
WE'LL WAIT! JUG AND I WANT TO PRACTICE WITH HER!
YE GADS! AND ME WITH MY SPLITTING HEADACHE!
I'M SORRY, ARCHIE, BUT NOT TODAY!
THANK YOU, VERONICA!
WAH
SMACK
SENDING ARCHIE AWAY WAS THE BEST BIRTHDAY PRESENT YOU COULD HAVE GIVEN ME!
I'LL NEVER FORGET IT!
2
End

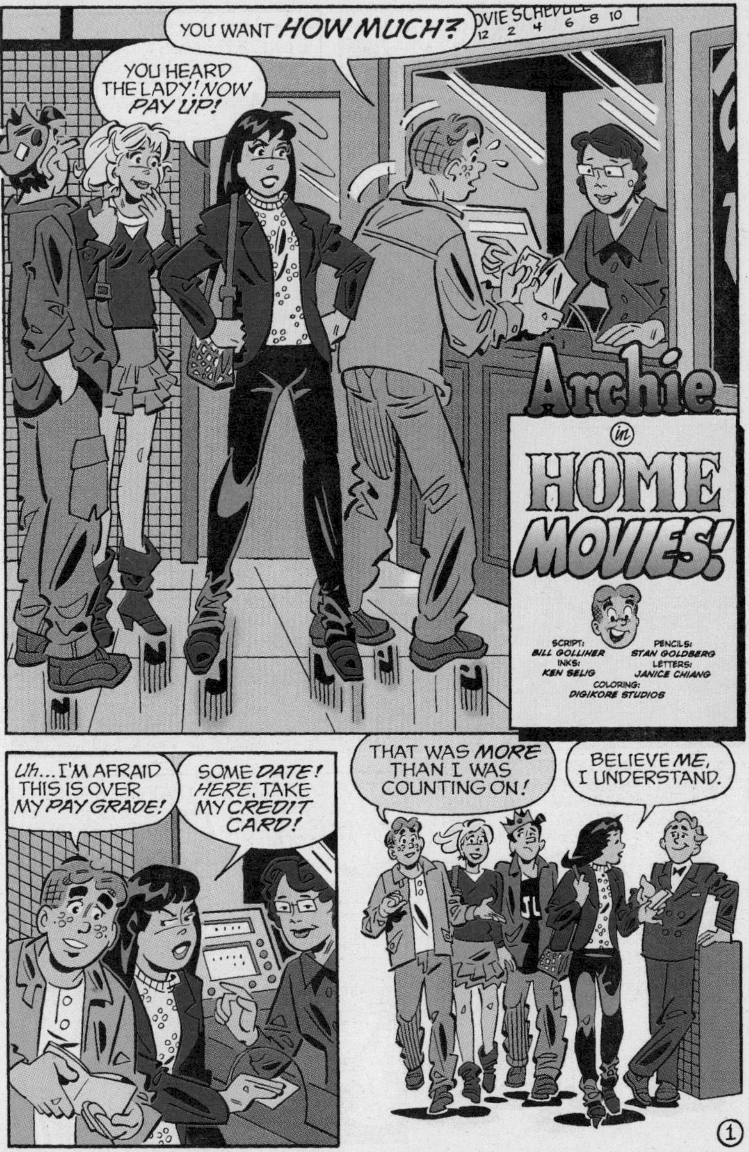
YOU WANT HOW MUCH?
OVIE SCHEDULE 10 12 2 4 6 8 10
YOU HEARD THE LADY! NOW PAY UP!
Archie
in
HOME MOVIES!
SCRIPT: BILL GOLLIHER
PENCILS: STAN GOLDBERG
INKS: KEN SELIG
LETTERS: JANICE CHIANG
COLORING: DIGIKORE STUDIOS
Uh... I'M AFRAID THIS IS OVER MY PAY GRADE!
SOME DATE! HERE, TAKE MY CREDIT CARD!
THAT WAS MORE THAN I WAS COUNTING ON!
BELIEVE ME, I UNDERSTAND.

LET'S SEE! HOW ABOUT SOME SNACKS?

ER... I THINK I CAN GO *HALVES* ON A BOX OF *JELLYBEANS!*

¡HMMPH! I'LL *GET* THE FOOD, TOO!

SORRY, IT'S JUST THAT TIMES ARE A *LITTLE TOUGH!*

SOME PEOPLE DON'T REALIZE THAT!!

AFTERWARDS...

THANKS, VERONICA FOR A *WONDERFUL* EVENING.

DON'T MENTION IT! EVEN *IF I* DID *COVER* EVERYTHING!

COMING SOON *REVENGE OF THE SWAMP THING* STAR SKY

CINEMA 10

THERE MUST BE SOME *THEATER* I CAN *AFFORD.*

WHY OF COURSE THERE IS! I'VE *GOT IT!*

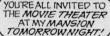

YOU'RE ALL INVITED TO THE *MOVIE THEATER* AT MY *MANSION TOMORROW NIGHT!*

THAT SOUNDS LIKE FUN!

IT WILL BE OUR VERY OWN *BUDGET-MINDED MOVIE NIGHT!*

THAT SOUNDS LIKE THE BEST KIND! SEE YA TOMORROW!

2

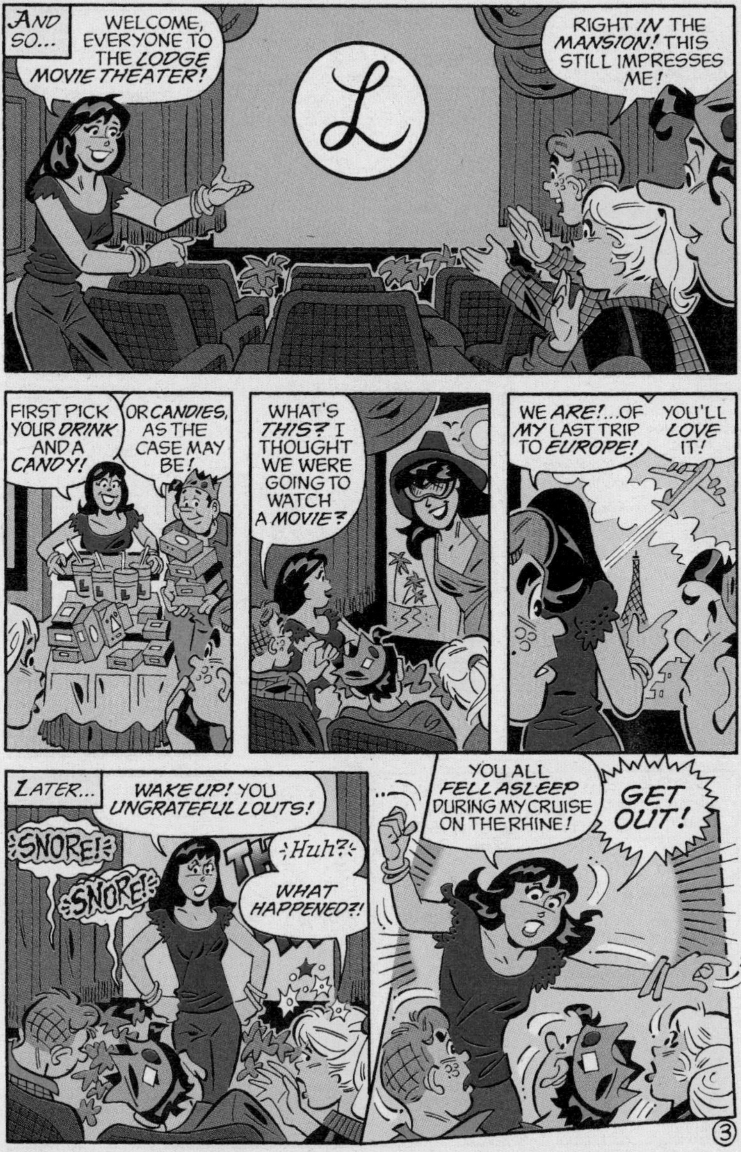
AND SO...
WELCOME, EVERYONE TO THE LODGE MOVIE THEATER!
RIGHT IN THE MANSION! THIS STILL IMPRESSES ME!
FIRST PICK YOUR DRINK AND A CANDY!
OR CANDIES, AS THE CASE MAY BE!
WHAT'S THIS? I THOUGHT WE WERE GOING TO WATCH A MOVIE?
WE ARE!...OF MY LAST TRIP TO EUROPE!
YOU'LL LOVE IT!
LATER...
WAKE UP! YOU UNGRATEFUL LOUTS!
SNORE!
SNORE!
Huh?
WHAT HAPPENED?!
YOU ALL FELL ASLEEP DURING MY CRUISE ON THE RHINE!
GET OUT!

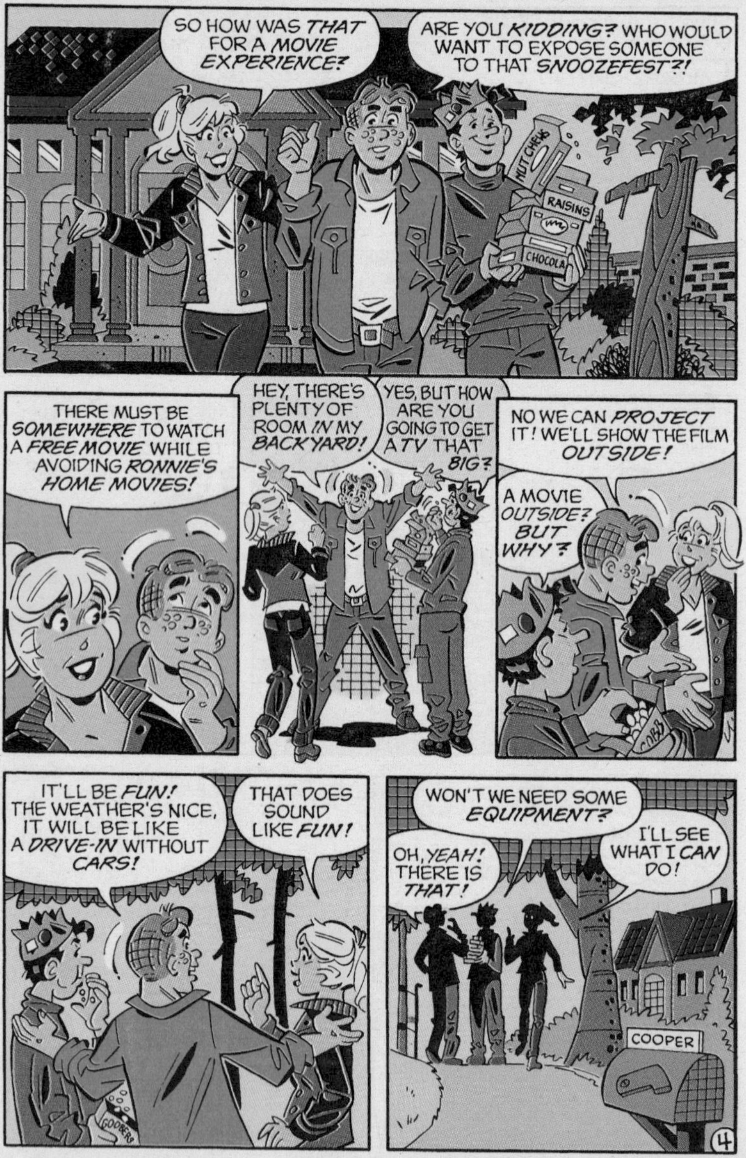

SO HOW WAS *THAT* FOR A *MOVIE EXPERIENCE?*
ARE YOU *KIDDING?* WHO WOULD WANT TO EXPOSE SOMEONE TO THAT *SNOOZEFEST?!*
NUT CHEWS
RAISINS
CHOCOLA
THERE MUST BE *SOMEWHERE* TO WATCH A *FREE MOVIE* WHILE AVOIDING *RONNIE'S HOME MOVIES!*
HEY, THERE'S PLENTY OF ROOM *IN* MY *BACKYARD!*
YES, BUT HOW ARE YOU GOING TO GET A *TV* THAT *BIG?*
NO WE CAN *PROJECT* IT! WE'LL SHOW THE FILM *OUTSIDE!*
A MOVIE *OUTSIDE? BUT WHY?*
COBBS
IT'LL BE *FUN!* THE WEATHER'S NICE, IT WILL BE LIKE A *DRIVE-IN* WITHOUT *CARS!*
THAT DOES SOUND LIKE *FUN!*
GOOBERS
WON'T WE NEED SOME *EQUIPMENT?*
OH, *YEAH!* THERE IS *THAT!*
I'LL SEE WHAT I *CAN* DO!
COOPER
4

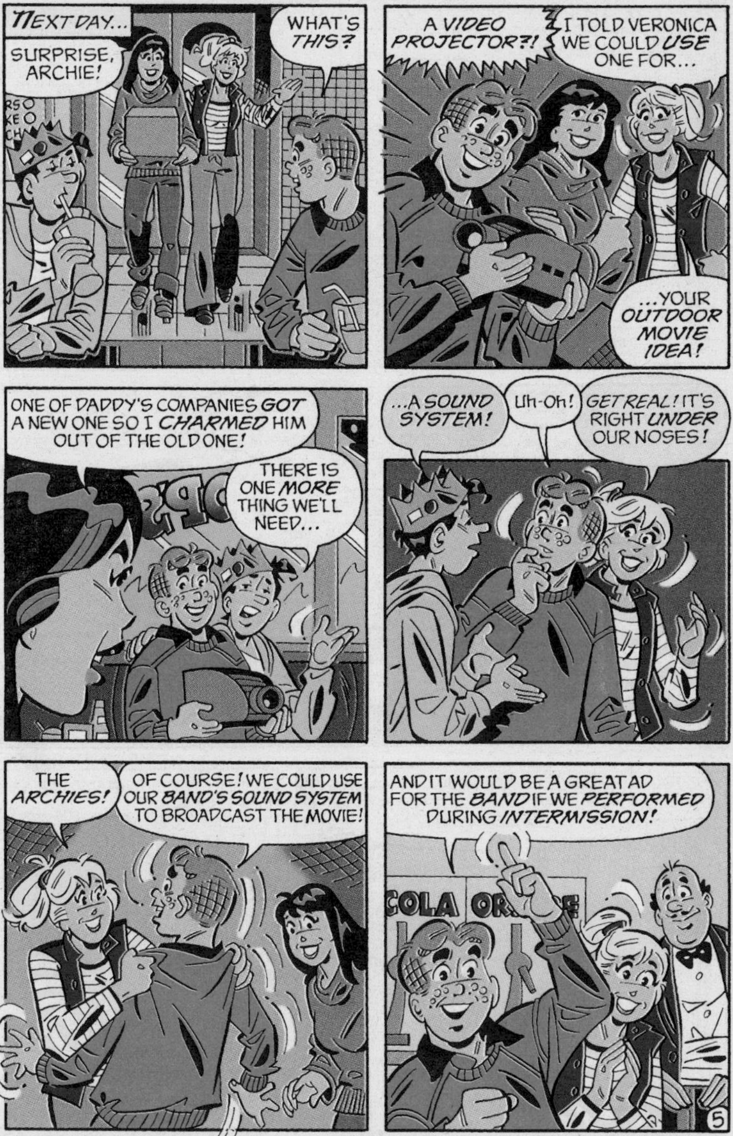
NEXT DAY...
SURPRISE, ARCHIE!
WHAT'S THIS?
A VIDEO PROJECTOR?!
I TOLD VERONICA WE COULD USE ONE FOR...
...YOUR OUTDOOR MOVIE IDEA!
ONE OF DADDY'S COMPANIES GOT A NEW ONE SO I CHARMED HIM OUT OF THE OLD ONE!
THERE IS ONE MORE THING WE'LL NEED...
...A SOUND SYSTEM!
Uh-Oh!
GET REAL! IT'S RIGHT UNDER OUR NOSES!
THE ARCHIES!
OF COURSE! WE COULD USE OUR BAND'S SOUND SYSTEM TO BROADCAST THE MOVIE!
AND IT WOULD BE A GREAT AD FOR THE BAND IF WE PERFORMED DURING INTERMISSION!
COLA
5

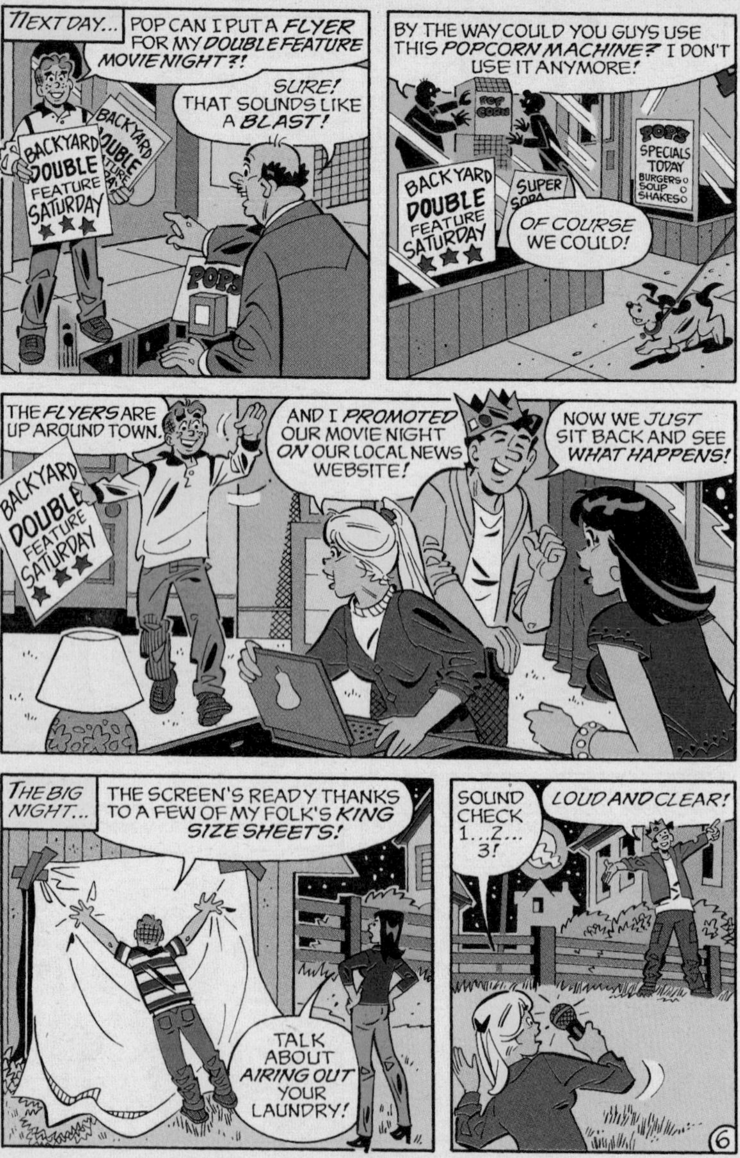
NEXT DAY...
POP CAN I PUT A FLYER FOR MY DOUBLE FEATURE MOVIE NIGHT?!
SURE! THAT SOUNDS LIKE A BLAST!
BACKYARD DOUBLE FEATURE SATURDAY
POP'S
BY THE WAY COULD YOU GUYS USE THIS POPCORN MACHINE? I DON'T USE IT ANYMORE!
POP CORN
POP'S SPECIALS TODAY BURGERS SOUP SHAKES
BACK YARD DOUBLE FEATURE SATURDAY
OF COURSE WE COULD!
THE FLYERS ARE UP AROUND TOWN.
AND I PROMOTED OUR MOVIE NIGHT ON OUR LOCAL NEWS WEBSITE!
NOW WE JUST SIT BACK AND SEE WHAT HAPPENS!
BACKYARD DOUBLE FEATURE SATURDAY
THE BIG NIGHT...
THE SCREEN'S READY THANKS TO A FEW OF MY FOLK'S KING SIZE SHEETS!
TALK ABOUT AIRING OUT YOUR LAUNDRY!
SOUND CHECK 1...2... 3!
LOUD AND CLEAR!
6

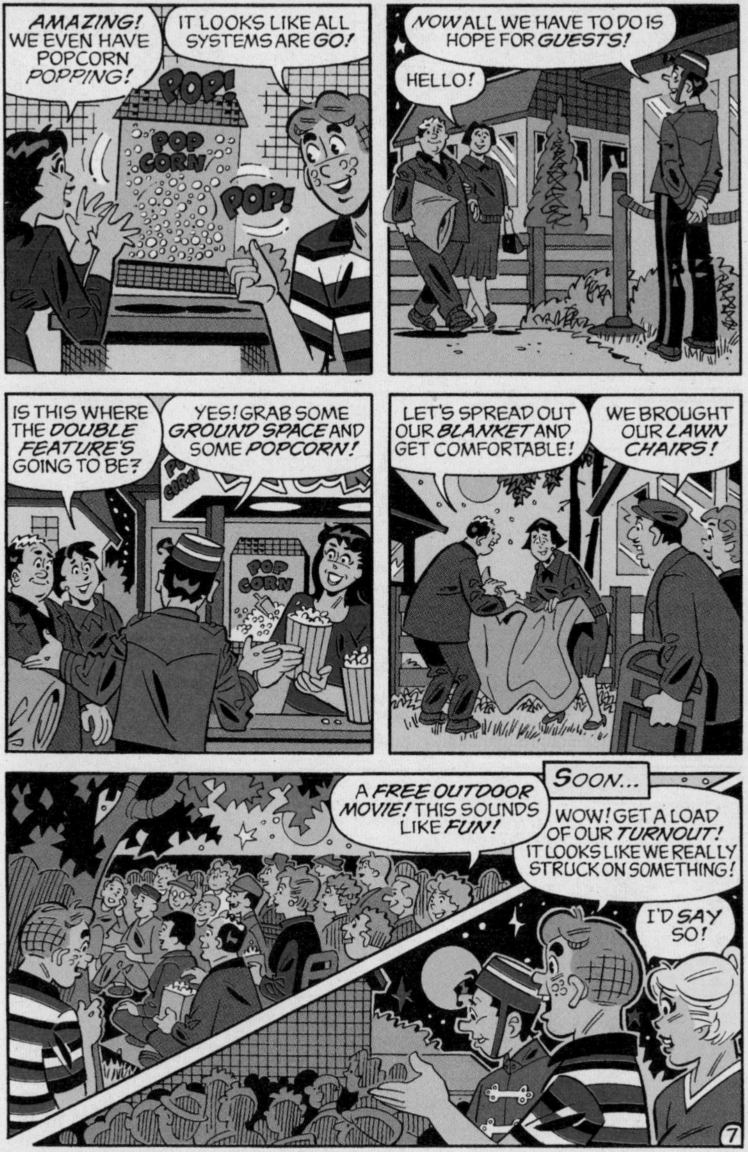
AMAZING! WE EVEN HAVE POPCORN POPPING!
IT LOOKS LIKE ALL SYSTEMS ARE GO!
POP!
POP CORN
POP!
NOW ALL WE HAVE TO DO IS HOPE FOR GUESTS!
HELLO!
IS THIS WHERE THE DOUBLE FEATURE'S GOING TO BE?
YES! GRAB SOME GROUND SPACE AND SOME POPCORN!
POP CORN
LET'S SPREAD OUT OUR BLANKET AND GET COMFORTABLE!
WE BROUGHT OUR LAWN CHAIRS!
SOON...
A FREE OUTDOOR MOVIE! THIS SOUNDS LIKE FUN!
WOW! GET A LOAD OF OUR TURNOUT! IT LOOKS LIKE WE REALLY STRUCK ON SOMETHING!
I'D SAY SO!

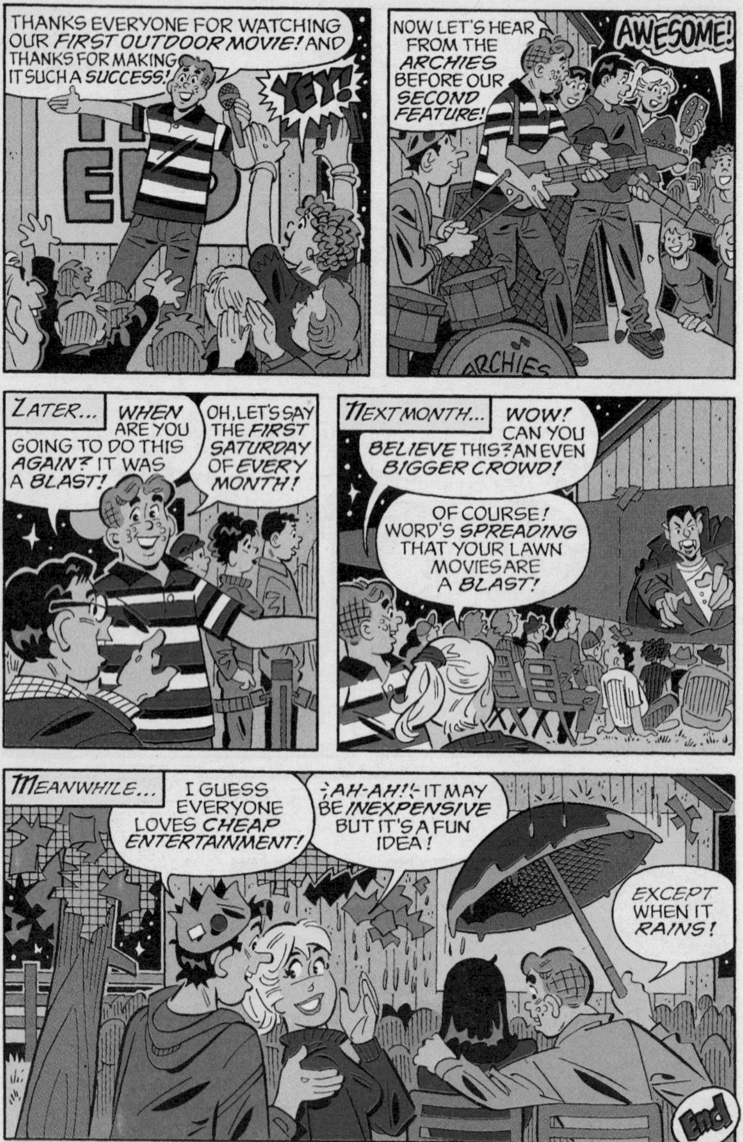
THANKS EVERYONE FOR WATCHING OUR FIRST OUTDOOR MOVIE! AND THANKS FOR MAKING IT SUCH A SUCCESS!
YEY!
NOW LET'S HEAR FROM THE ARCHIES BEFORE OUR SECOND FEATURE!
AWESOME!
ARCHIES
LATER...
WHEN ARE YOU GOING TO DO THIS AGAIN? IT WAS A BLAST!
OH, LET'S SAY THE FIRST SATURDAY OF EVERY MONTH!
NEXT MONTH...
WOW! CAN YOU BELIEVE THIS? AN EVEN BIGGER CROWD!
OF COURSE! WORD'S SPREADING THAT YOUR LAWN MOVIES ARE A BLAST!
MEANWHILE...
I GUESS EVERYONE LOVES CHEAP ENTERTAINMENT!
AH-AH! IT MAY BE INEXPENSIVE BUT IT'S A FUN IDEA!
EXCEPT WHEN IT RAINS!
End

Archie in "Getting Belted"

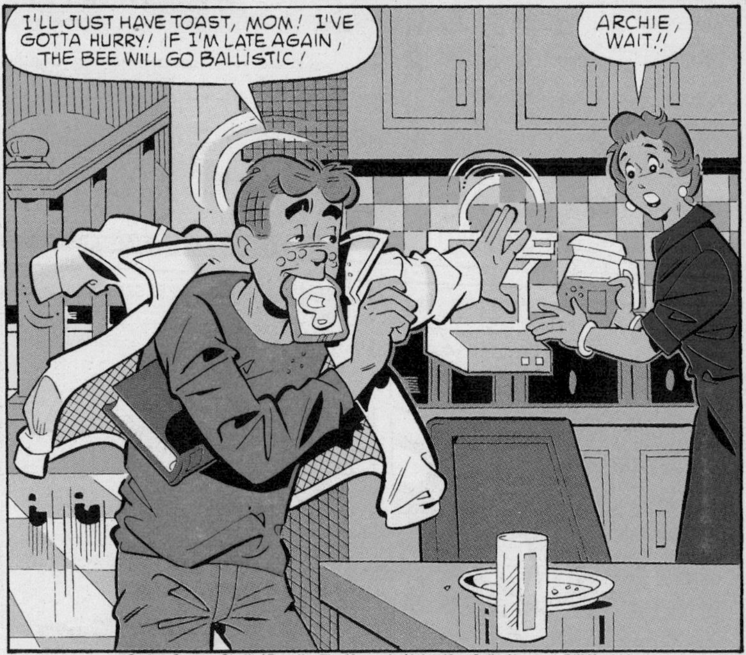
I'LL JUST HAVE TOAST, MOM! I'VE GOTTA HURRY! IF I'M LATE AGAIN, THE BEE WILL GO BALLISTIC!
ARCHIE, WAIT!!

Script: George Gladir / Pencils: Tim Kennedy / Inks: Ken Selig / Letters: Bill Yoshida

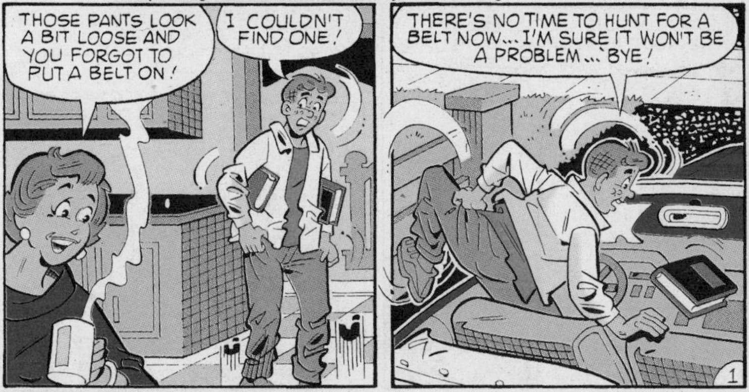
THOSE PANTS LOOK A BIT LOOSE AND YOU FORGOT TO PUT A BELT ON!
I COULDN'T FIND ONE!
THERE'S NO TIME TO HUNT FOR A BELT NOW... I'M SURE IT WON'T BE A PROBLEM...`BYE!

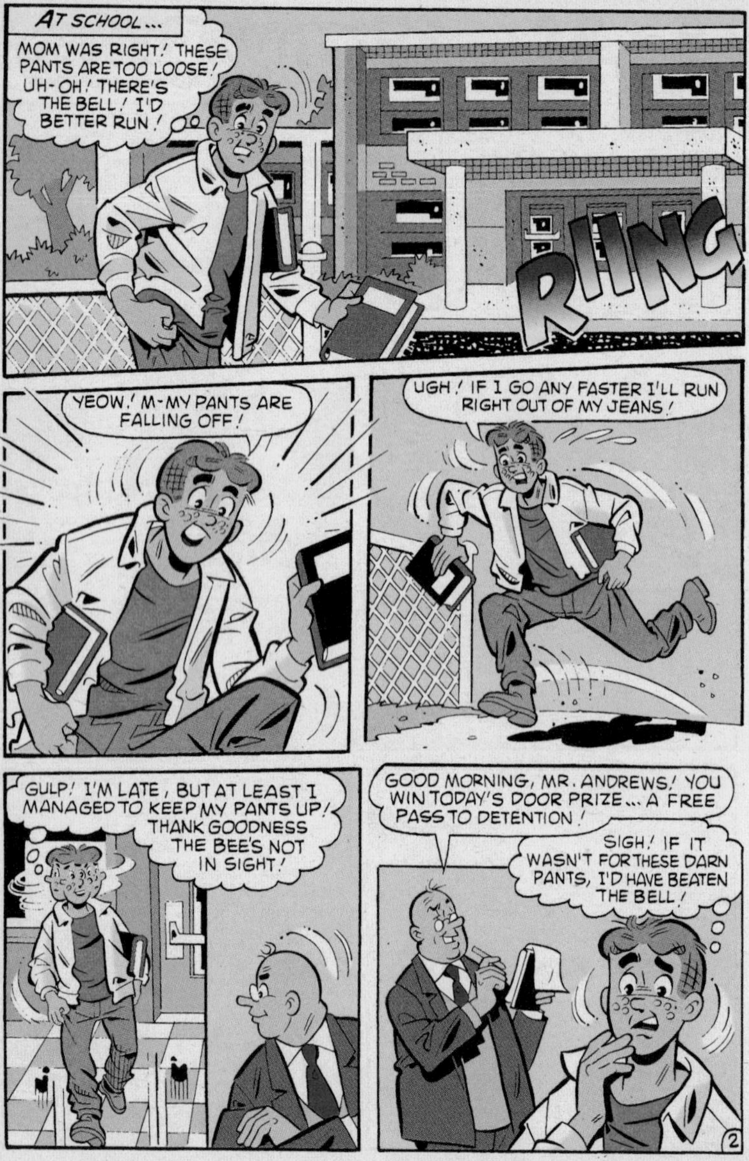
AT SCHOOL...
MOM WAS RIGHT! THESE PANTS ARE TOO LOOSE! UH-OH! THERE'S THE BELL! I'D BETTER RUN!
RIIING
YEOW! M-MY PANTS ARE FALLING OFF!
UGH! IF I GO ANY FASTER I'LL RUN RIGHT OUT OF MY JEANS!
GULP! I'M LATE, BUT AT LEAST I MANAGED TO KEEP MY PANTS UP! THANK GOODNESS THE BEE'S NOT IN SIGHT!
GOOD MORNING, MR. ANDREWS! YOU WIN TODAY'S DOOR PRIZE... A FREE PASS TO DETENTION!
SIGH! IF IT WASN'T FOR THESE DARN PANTS, I'D HAVE BEATEN THE BELL!
2

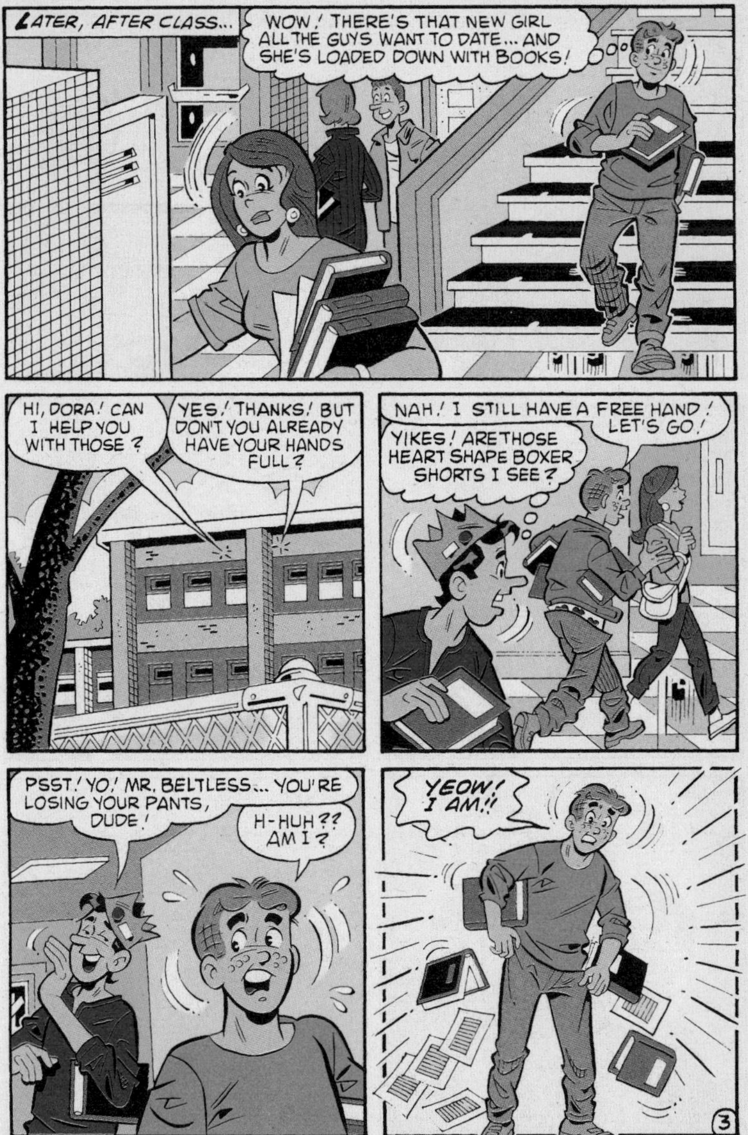
LATER, AFTER CLASS...
WOW! THERE'S THAT NEW GIRL ALL THE GUYS WANT TO DATE... AND SHE'S LOADED DOWN WITH BOOKS!
HI, DORA! CAN I HELP YOU WITH THOSE?
YES! THANKS! BUT DON'T YOU ALREADY HAVE YOUR HANDS FULL?
NAH! I STILL HAVE A FREE HAND! LET'S GO!
YIKES! ARE THOSE HEART SHAPE BOXER SHORTS I SEE?
PSST! YO! MR. BELTLESS... YOU'RE LOSING YOUR PANTS, DUDE!
H-HUH?? AM I?
YEOW! I AM!!
3

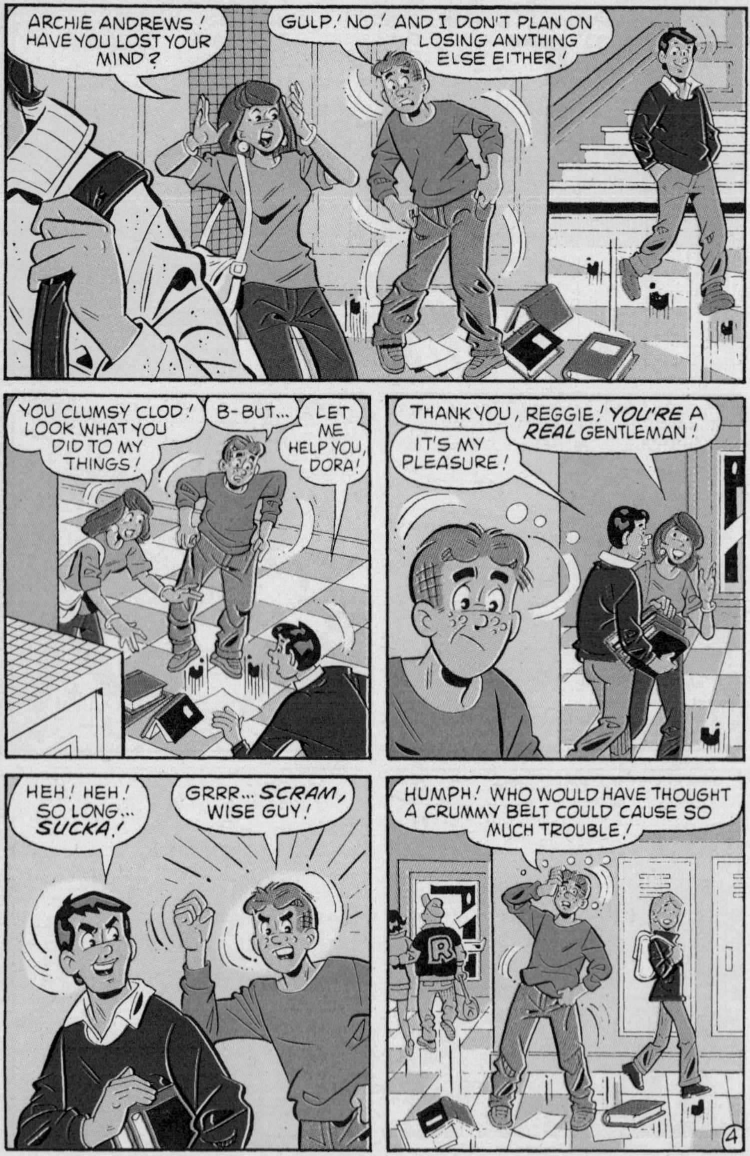

ARCHIE ANDREWS! HAVE YOU LOST YOUR MIND?
GULP! NO! AND I DON'T PLAN ON LOSING ANYTHING ELSE EITHER!
YOU CLUMSY CLOD! LOOK WHAT YOU DID TO MY THINGS!
B-BUT...
LET ME HELP YOU, DORA!
THANK YOU, REGGIE! *YOU'RE* A *REAL* GENTLEMAN!
IT'S MY PLEASURE!
HEH! HEH! SO LONG... *SUCKA!*
GRRR... *SCRAM*, WISE GUY!
HUMPH! WHO WOULD HAVE THOUGHT A CRUMMY BELT COULD CAUSE SO MUCH TROUBLE!
R
4

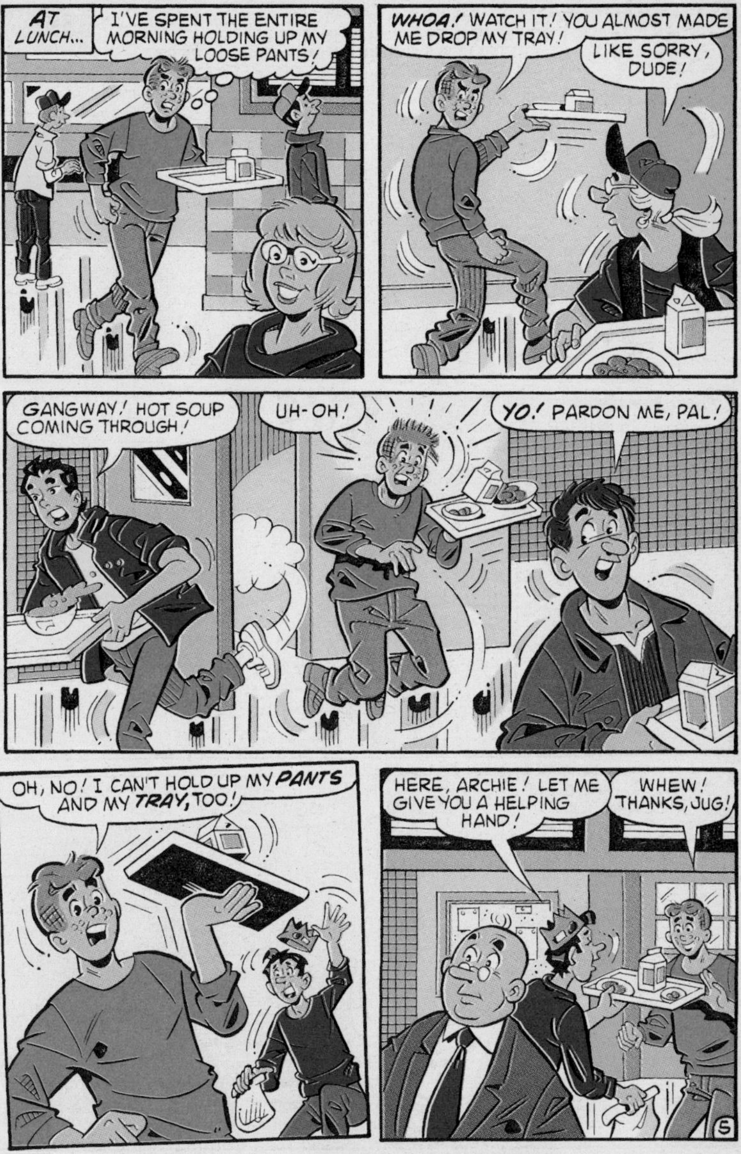

AT LUNCH...
I'VE SPENT THE ENTIRE MORNING HOLDING UP MY LOOSE PANTS!
WHOA! WATCH IT! YOU ALMOST MADE ME DROP MY TRAY!
LIKE SORRY, DUDE!
GANGWAY! HOT SOUP COMING THROUGH!
UH-OH!
YO! PARDON ME, PAL!
OH, NO! I CAN'T HOLD UP MY PANTS AND MY TRAY, TOO!
HERE, ARCHIE! LET ME GIVE YOU A HELPING HAND!
WHEW! THANKS, JUG!
5

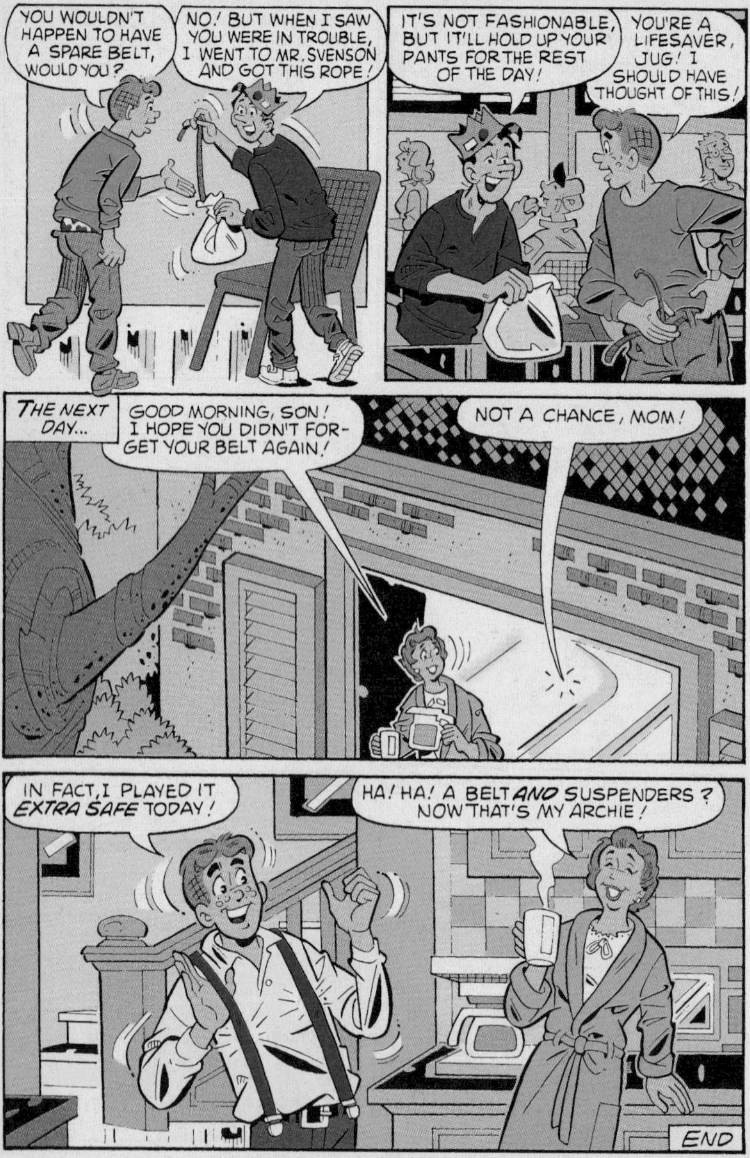

YOU WOULDN'T HAPPEN TO HAVE A SPARE BELT, WOULD YOU?
NO! BUT WHEN I SAW YOU WERE IN TROUBLE, I WENT TO MR. SVENSON AND GOT THIS ROPE!
IT'S NOT FASHIONABLE, BUT IT'LL HOLD UP YOUR PANTS FOR THE REST OF THE DAY!
YOU'RE A LIFESAVER, JUG! I SHOULD HAVE THOUGHT OF THIS!
THE NEXT DAY...
GOOD MORNING, SON! I HOPE YOU DIDN'T FORGET YOUR BELT AGAIN!
NOT A CHANCE, MOM!
IN FACT, I PLAYED IT EXTRA SAFE TODAY!
HA! HA! A BELT AND SUSPENDERS? NOW THAT'S MY ARCHIE!
END

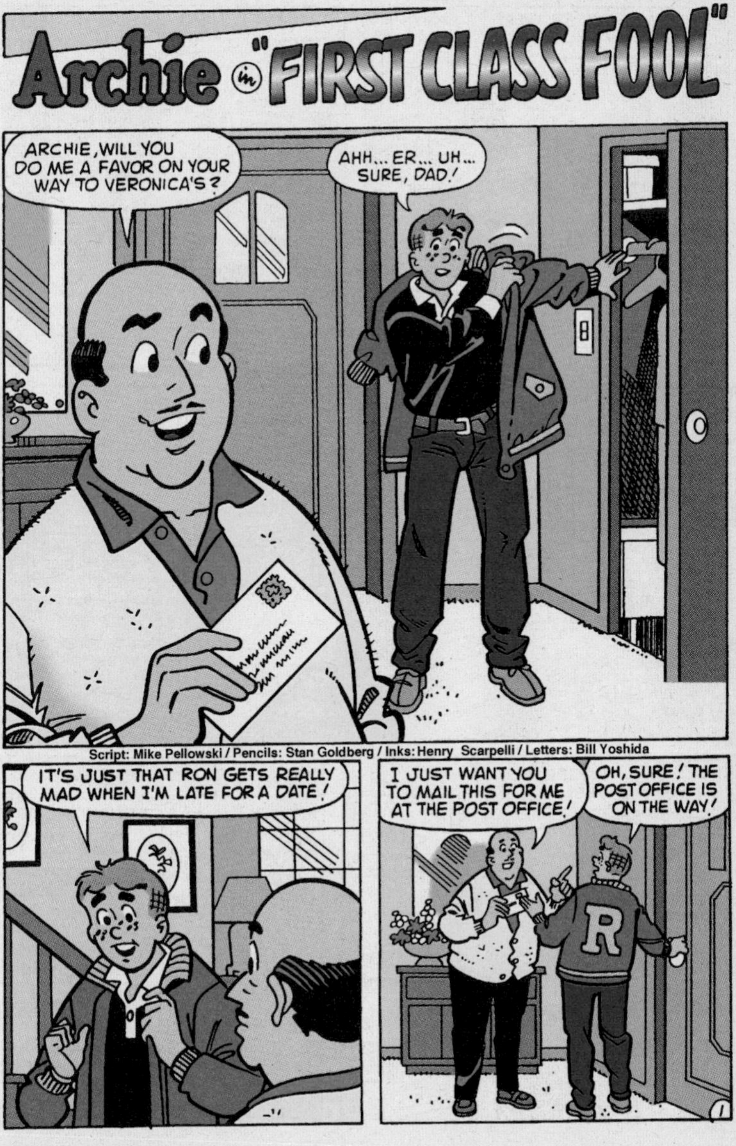
Archie in "FIRST CLASS FOOL"
ARCHIE, WILL YOU DO ME A FAVOR ON YOUR WAY TO VERONICA'S?
AHH... ER... UH... SURE, DAD!
Script: Mike Pellowski / Pencils: Stan Goldberg / Inks: Henry Scarpelli / Letters: Bill Yoshida
IT'S JUST THAT RON GETS REALLY MAD WHEN I'M LATE FOR A DATE!
I JUST WANT YOU TO MAIL THIS FOR ME AT THE POST OFFICE!
OH, SURE! THE POST OFFICE IS ON THE WAY!
R
1

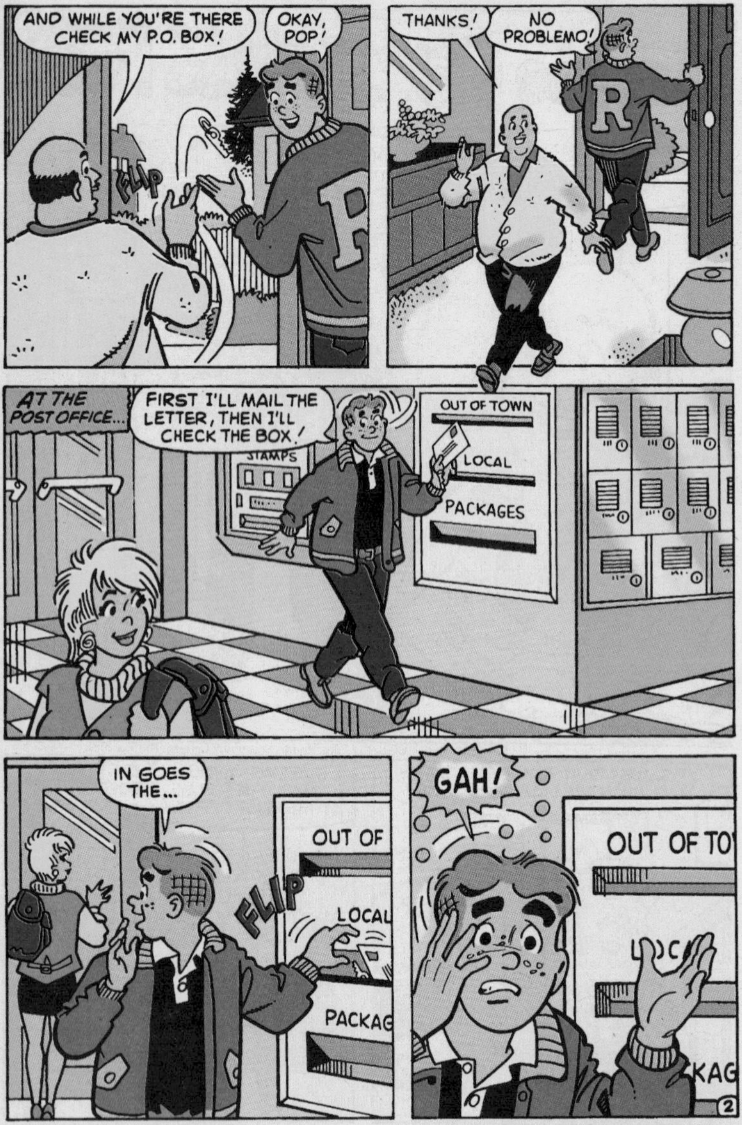
AND WHILE YOU'RE THERE CHECK MY P.O. BOX!
OKAY, POP!
FLIP
THANKS!
NO PROBLEMO!
AT THE POST OFFICE...
FIRST I'LL MAIL THE LETTER, THEN I'LL CHECK THE BOX!
STAMPS
OUT OF TOWN
LOCAL
PACKAGES
IN GOES THE...
FLIP
OUT OF
LOCAL
PACKAG
GAH!
OUT OF TO
KAG
2

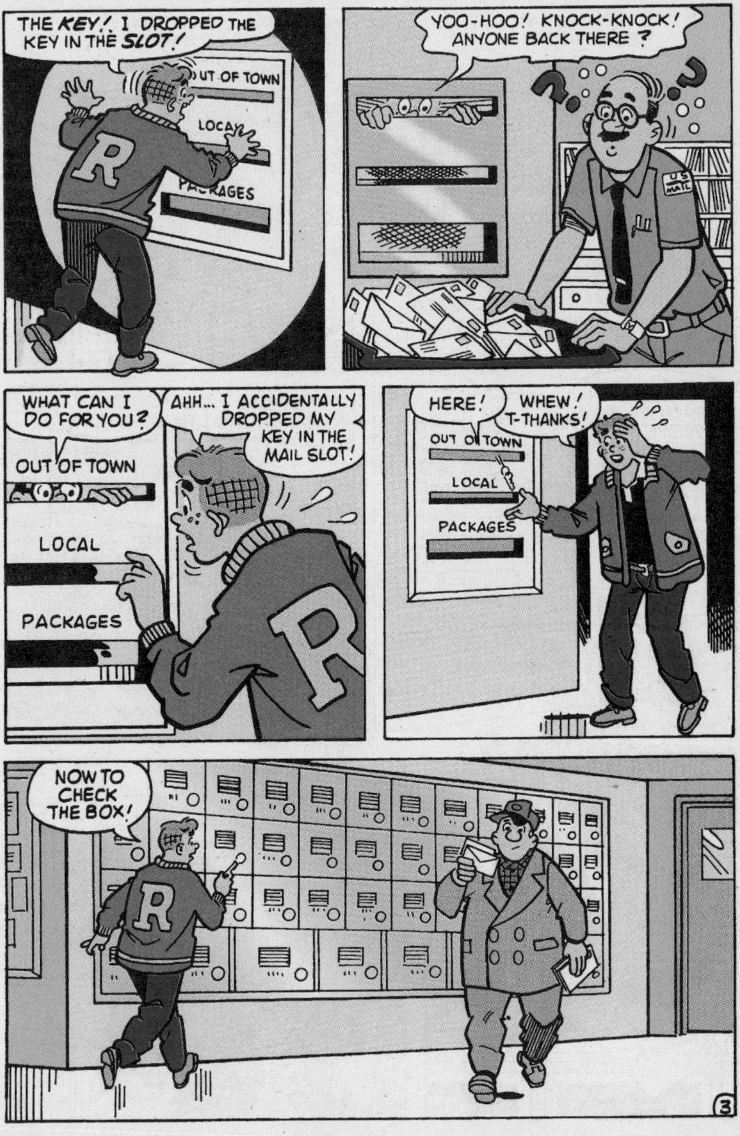
THE KEY! I DROPPED THE KEY IN THE SLOT!
OUT OF TOWN
LOCAL
PACKAGES
YOO-HOO! KNOCK-KNOCK! ANYONE BACK THERE?
US MAIL
WHAT CAN I DO FOR YOU?
AHH... I ACCIDENTALLY DROPPED MY KEY IN THE MAIL SLOT!
OUT OF TOWN
LOCAL
PACKAGES
HERE!
WHEW! T-THANKS!
OUT OF TOWN
LOCAL
PACKAGES
NOW TO CHECK THE BOX!

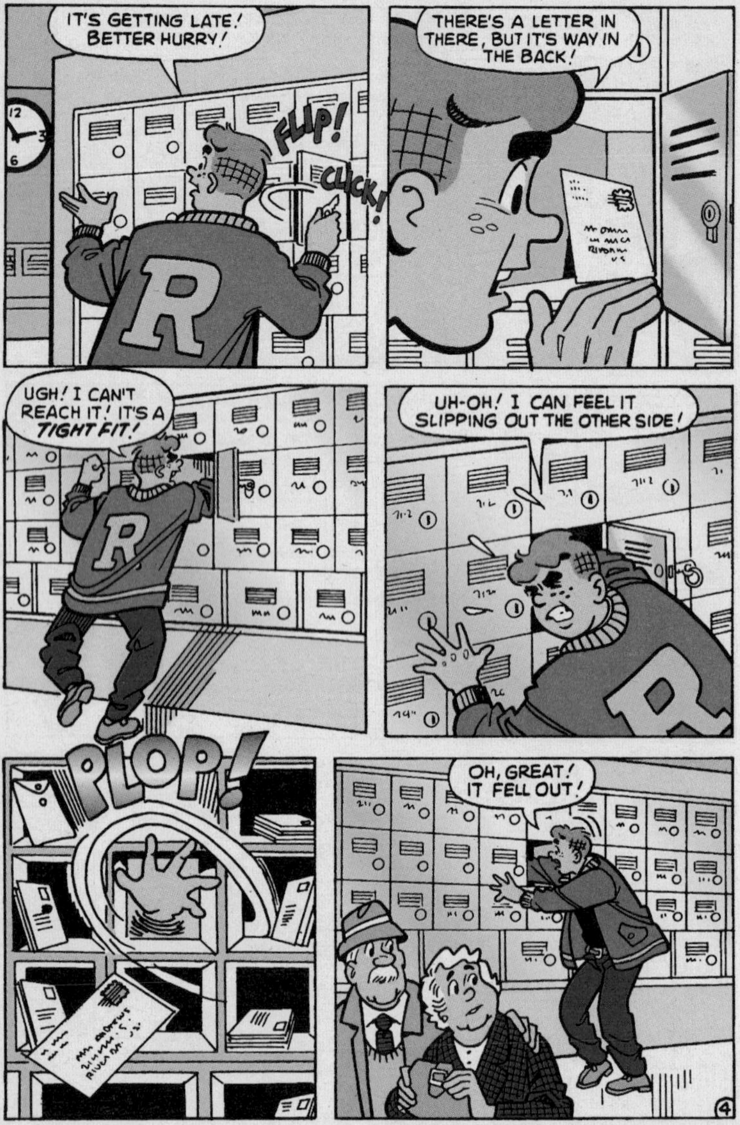

IT'S GETTING LATE! BETTER HURRY!
FLIP!
CLICK!
THERE'S A LETTER IN THERE, BUT IT'S WAY IN THE BACK!
UGH! I CAN'T REACH IT! IT'S A TIGHT FIT!
UH-OH! I CAN FEEL IT SLIPPING OUT THE OTHER SIDE!
PLOP!
OH, GREAT! IT FELL OUT!
4

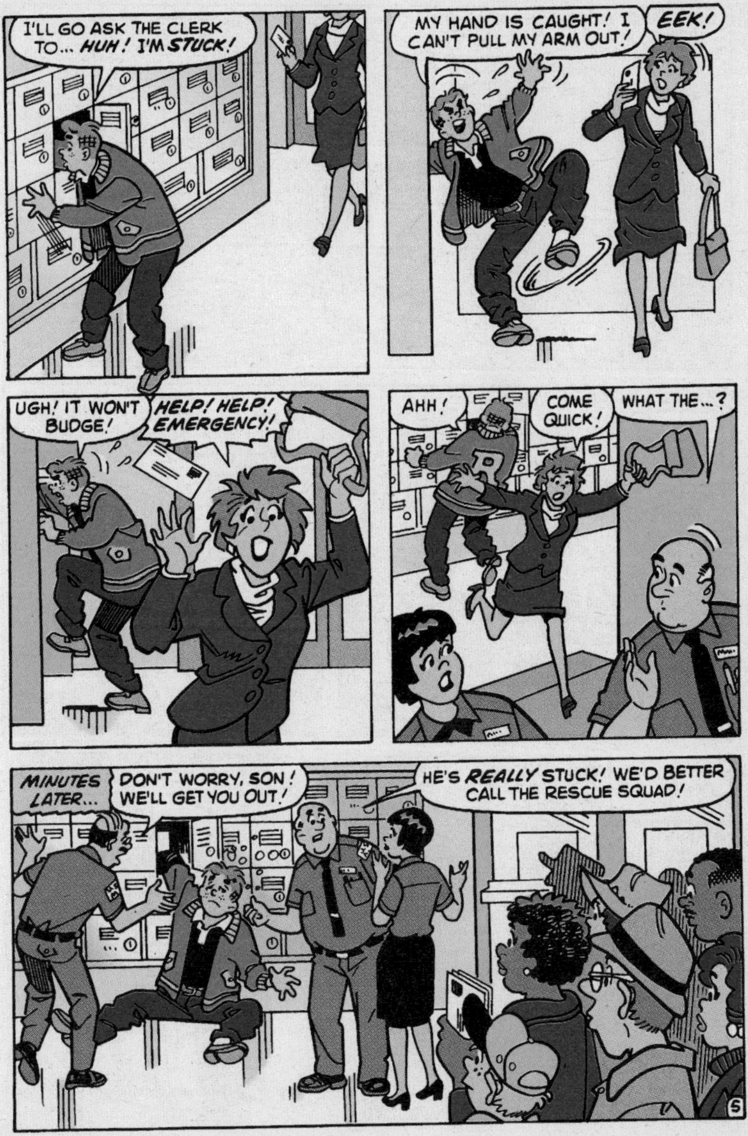

I'LL GO ASK THE CLERK TO... HUH! I'M STUCK!
MY HAND IS CAUGHT! I CAN'T PULL MY ARM OUT!
EEK!
UGH! IT WON'T BUDGE!
HELP! HELP! EMERGENCY!
AHH!
COME QUICK!
WHAT THE...?
MINUTES LATER...
DON'T WORRY, SON! WE'LL GET YOU OUT!
HE'S REALLY STUCK! WE'D BETTER CALL THE RESCUE SQUAD!
5

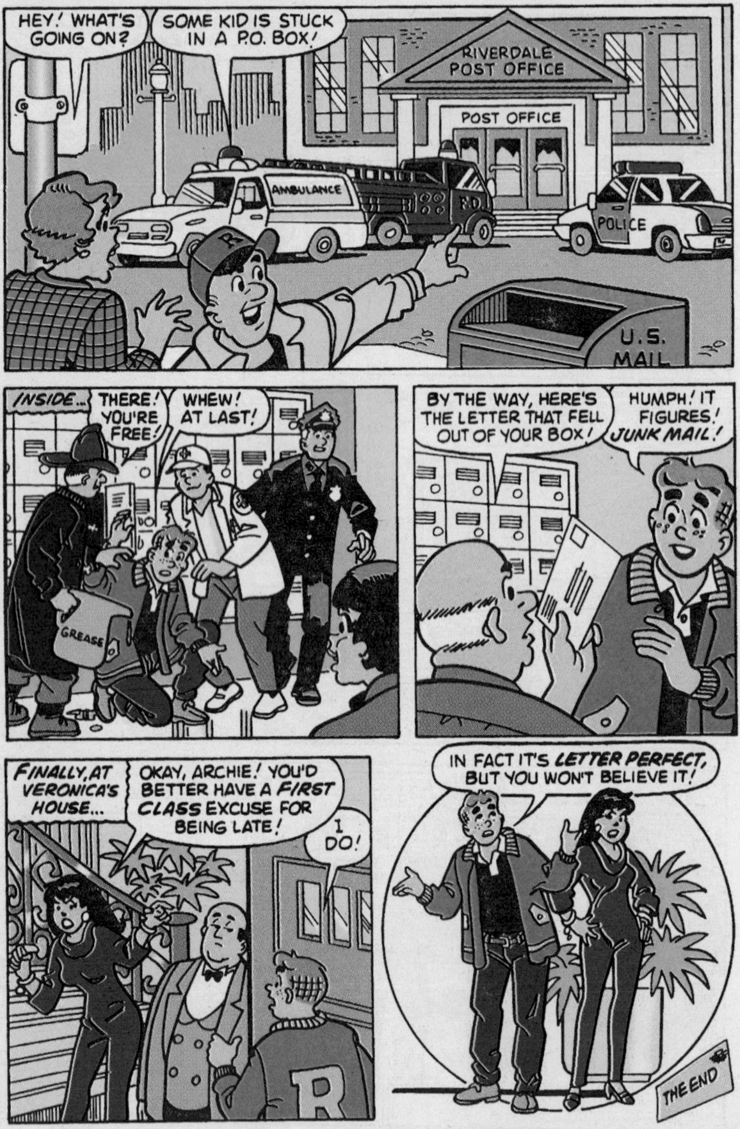
HEY! WHAT'S GOING ON?
SOME KID IS STUCK IN A P.O. BOX!
RIVERDALE POST OFFICE
POST OFFICE
AMBULANCE
F.D.
POLICE
U.S. MAIL
INSIDE...
THERE! YOU'RE FREE!
WHEW! AT LAST!
GREASE
BY THE WAY, HERE'S THE LETTER THAT FELL OUT OF YOUR BOX!
HUMPH! IT FIGURES! JUNK MAIL!
FINALLY, AT VERONICA'S HOUSE...
OKAY, ARCHIE! YOU'D BETTER HAVE A FIRST CLASS EXCUSE FOR BEING LATE!
I DO!
IN FACT IT'S LETTER PERFECT, BUT YOU WON'T BELIEVE IT!
THE END

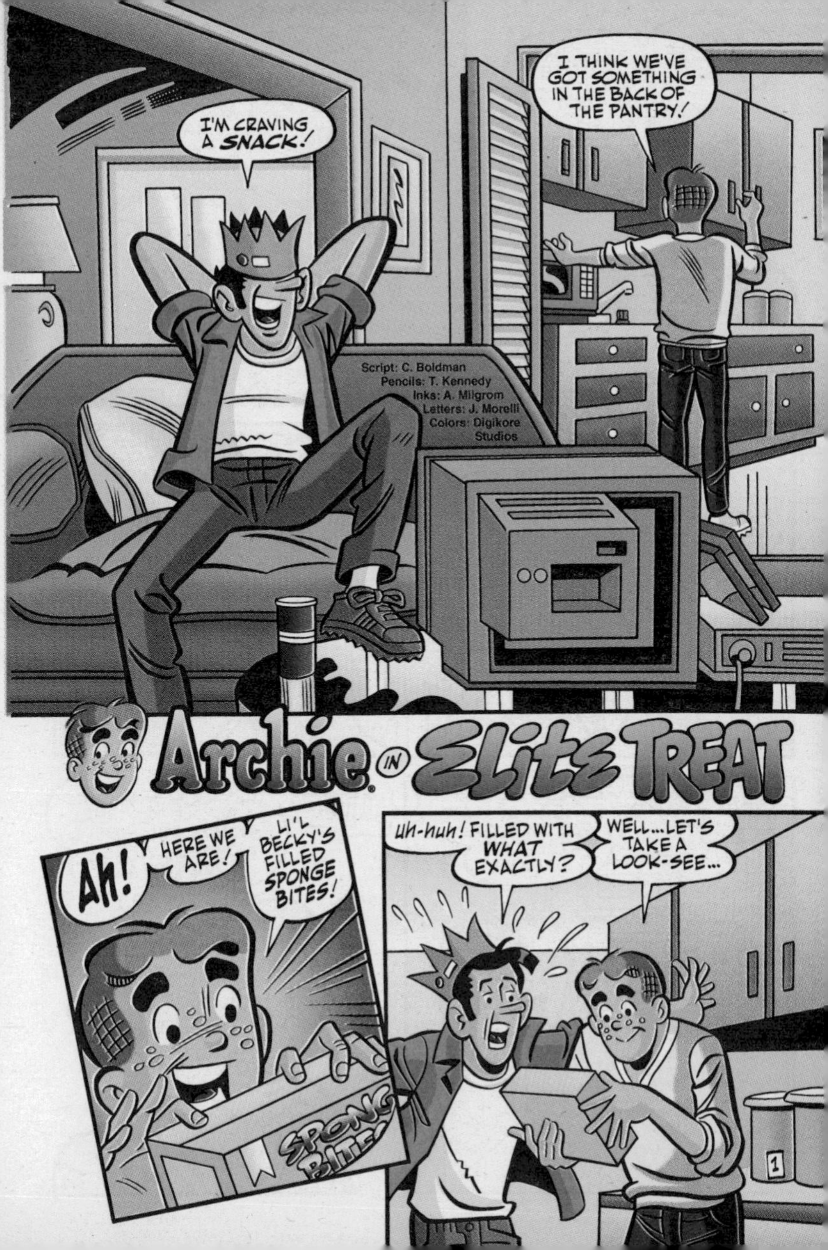
I'M CRAVING A SNACK!
I THINK WE'VE GOT SOMETHING IN THE BACK OF THE PANTRY!
Script: C. Boldman
Pencils: T. Kennedy
Inks: A. Milgrom
Letters: J. Morelli
Colors: Digikore Studios
Archie in Elite TREAT
Ah!
HERE WE ARE!
LI'L BECKY'S FILLED SPONGE BITES!
Uh-huh! FILLED WITH WHAT EXACTLY?
WELL...LET'S TAKE A LOOK-SEE...
1

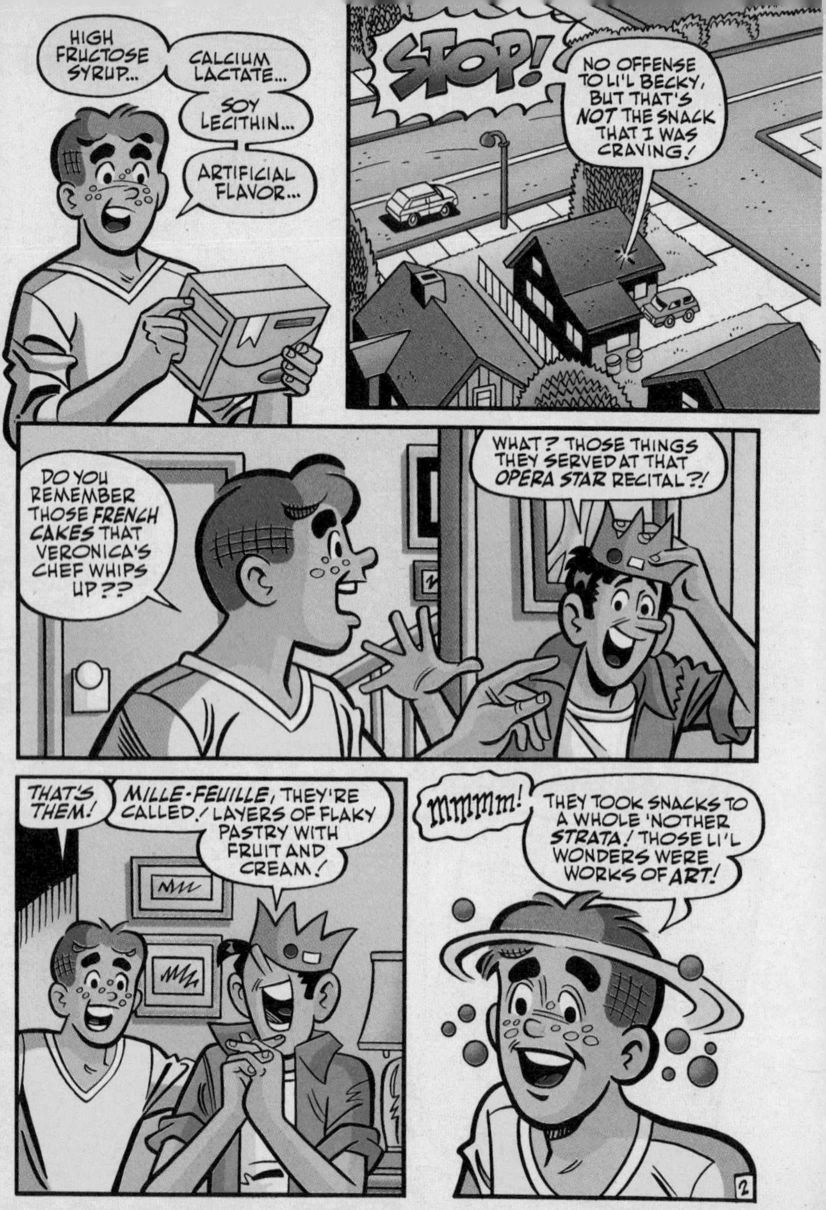
HIGH FRUCTOSE SYRUP...
CALCIUM LACTATE...
SOY LECITHIN...
ARTIFICIAL FLAVOR...
STOP!
NO OFFENSE TO LI'L BECKY, BUT THAT'S NOT THE SNACK THAT I WAS CRAVING!
DO YOU REMEMBER THOSE FRENCH CAKES THAT VERONICA'S CHEF WHIPS UP??
WHAT? THOSE THINGS THEY SERVED AT THAT OPERA STAR RECITAL?!
THAT'S THEM!
MILLE-FEUILLE, THEY'RE CALLED! LAYERS OF FLAKY PASTRY WITH FRUIT AND CREAM!
MMMMM!
THEY TOOK SNACKS TO A WHOLE 'NOTHER STRATA! THOSE LI'L WONDERS WERE WORKS OF ART!
2

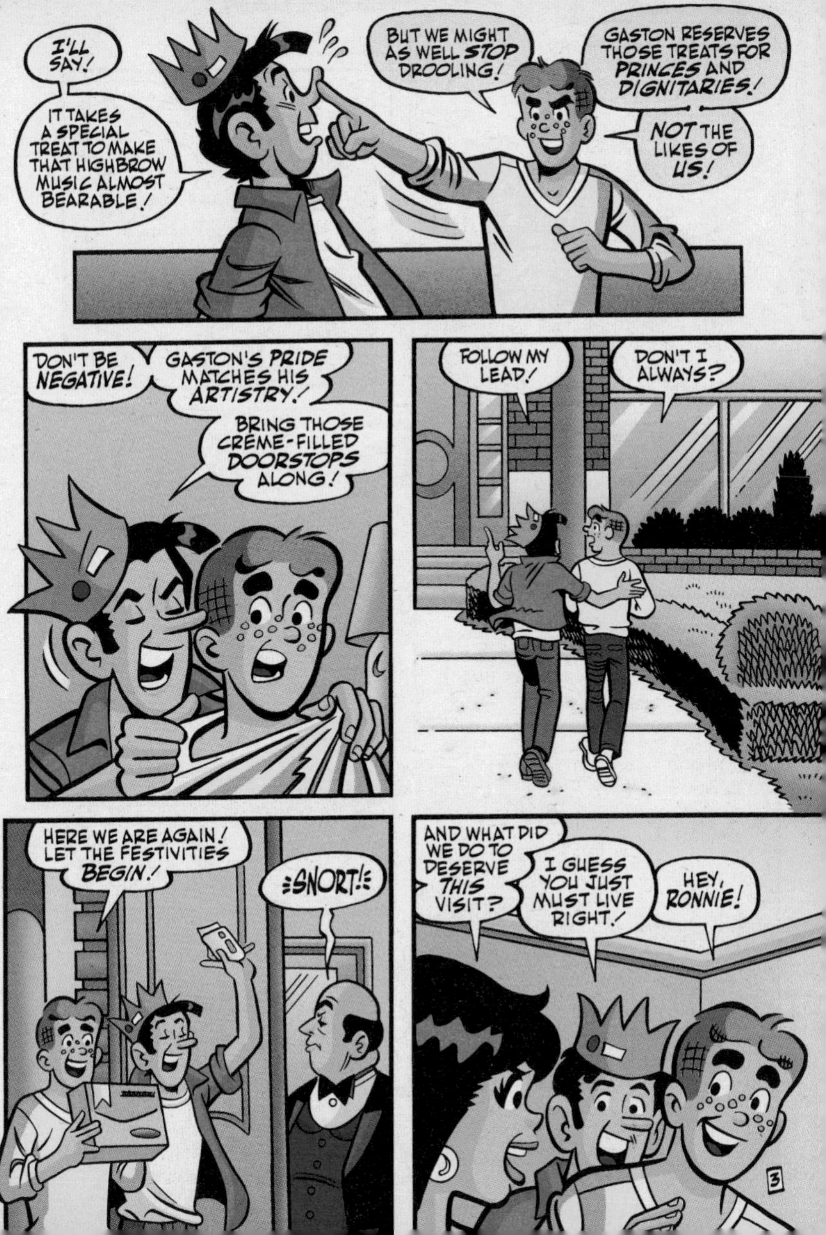
I'LL SAY!
IT TAKES A SPECIAL TREAT TO MAKE THAT HIGHBROW MUSIC ALMOST BEARABLE!
BUT WE MIGHT AS WELL STOP DROOLING!
GASTON RESERVES THOSE TREATS FOR PRINCES AND DIGNITARIES!
NOT THE LIKES OF US!
DON'T BE NEGATIVE!
GASTON'S PRIDE MATCHES HIS ARTISTRY!
BRING THOSE CREME-FILLED DOORSTOPS ALONG!
FOLLOW MY LEAD!
DON'T I ALWAYS?
HERE WE ARE AGAIN! LET THE FESTIVITIES BEGIN!
SNORT!
AND WHAT DID WE DO TO DESERVE THIS VISIT?
I GUESS YOU JUST MUST LIVE RIGHT!
HEY, RONNIE!
3

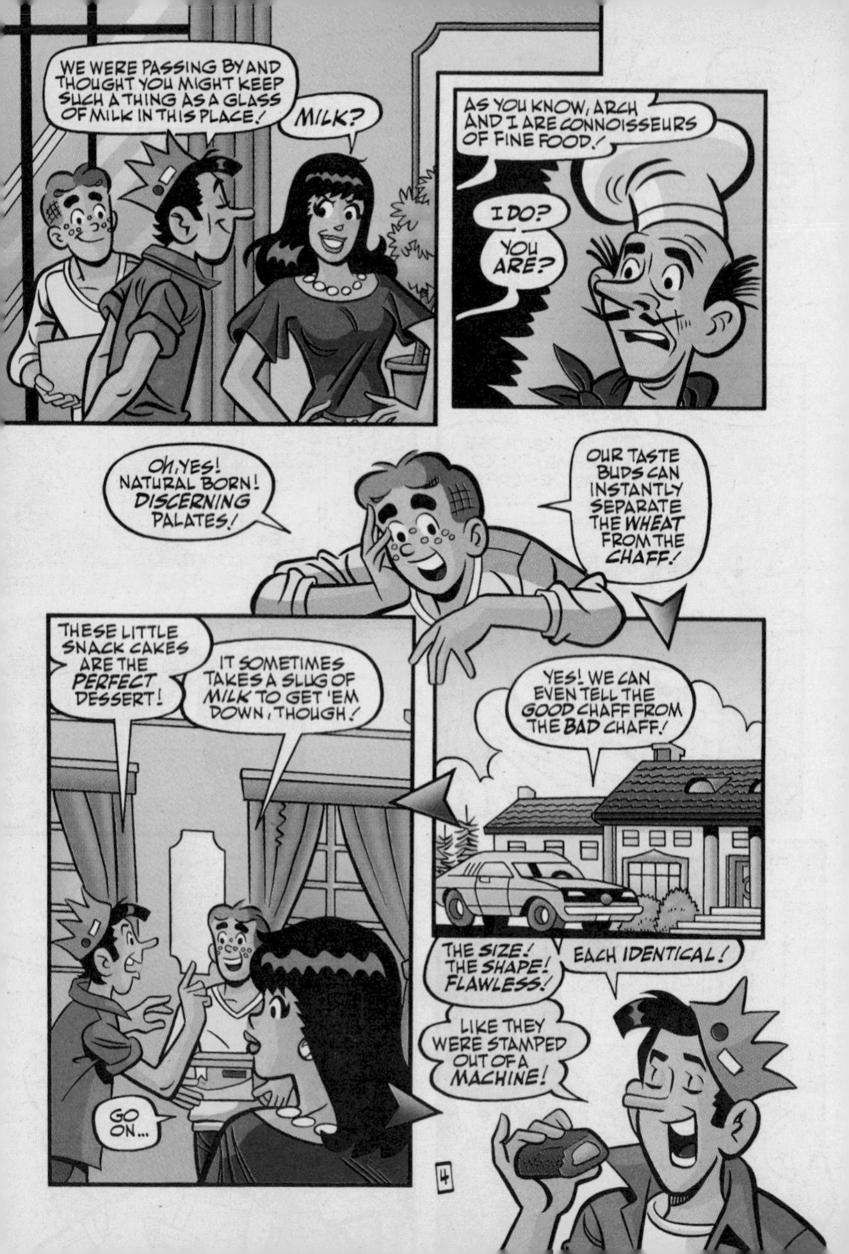
WE WERE PASSING BY AND THOUGHT YOU MIGHT KEEP SUCH A THING AS A GLASS OF MILK IN THIS PLACE!
MILK?
AS YOU KNOW, ARCH AND I ARE CONNOISSEURS OF FINE FOOD!
I DO?
YOU ARE?
OH, YES! NATURAL BORN! DISCERNING PALATES!
OUR TASTE BUDS CAN INSTANTLY SEPARATE THE WHEAT FROM THE CHAFF!
YES! WE CAN EVEN TELL THE GOOD CHAFF FROM THE BAD CHAFF!
THESE LITTLE SNACK CAKES ARE THE PERFECT DESSERT!
IT SOMETIMES TAKES A SLUG OF MILK TO GET 'EM DOWN, THOUGH!
GO ON...
THE SIZE! THE SHAPE! FLAWLESS!
EACH IDENTICAL!
LIKE THEY WERE STAMPED OUT OF A MACHINE!
4

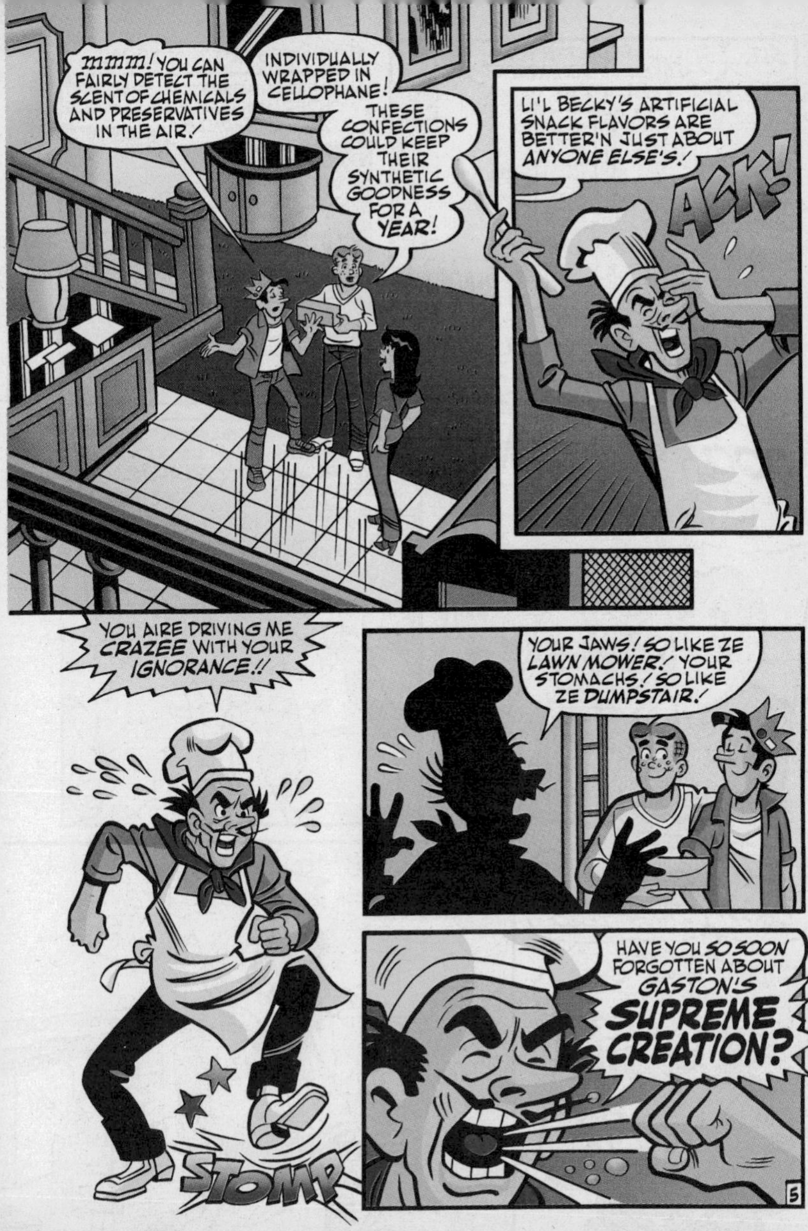

MMMM! YOU CAN FAIRLY DETECT THE SCENT OF CHEMICALS AND PRESERVATIVES IN THE AIR!
INDIVIDUALLY WRAPPED IN CELLOPHANE!
THESE CONFECTIONS COULD KEEP THEIR SYNTHETIC GOODNESS FOR A YEAR!
LI'L BECKY'S ARTIFICIAL SNACK FLAVORS ARE BETTER'N JUST ABOUT ANYONE ELSE'S!
ACK!
YOU AIRE DRIVING ME CRAZEE WITH YOUR IGNORANCE!!
STOMP
YOUR JAWS! SO LIKE ZE LAWN MOWER! YOUR STOMACHS! SO LIKE ZE DUMPSTAIR!
HAVE YOU SO SOON FORGOTTEN ABOUT GASTON'S SUPREME CREATION?
5

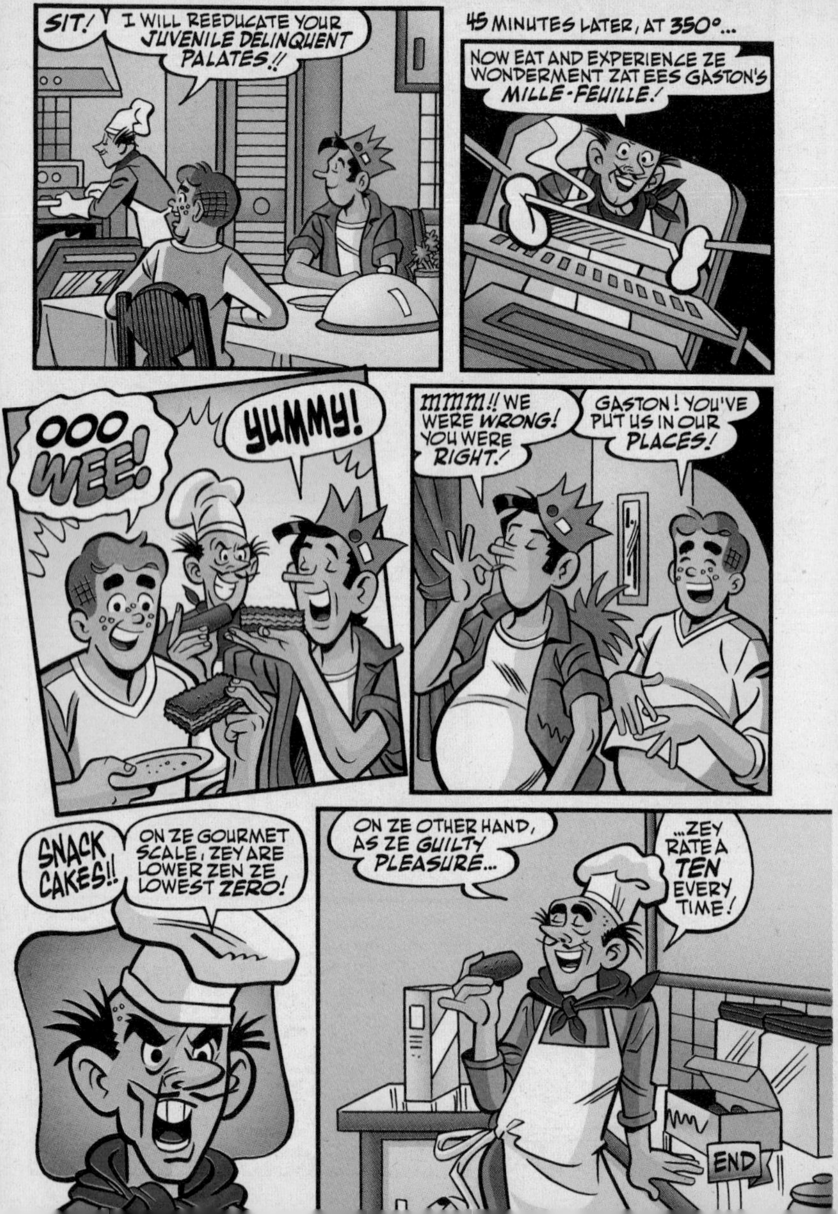
SIT!
I WILL REEDUCATE YOUR JUVENILE DELINQUENT PALATES!!
45 MINUTES LATER, AT 350°...
NOW EAT AND EXPERIENCE ZE WONDERMENT ZAT EES GASTON'S MILLE-FEUILLE!
OOO WEE!
YUMMY!
MMMM!! WE WERE WRONG! YOU WERE RIGHT!
GASTON! YOU'VE PUT US IN OUR PLACES!
SNACK CAKES!!
ON ZE GOURMET SCALE, ZEY ARE LOWER ZEN ZE LOWEST ZERO!
ON ZE OTHER HAND, AS ZE GUILTY PLEASURE...
...ZEY RATE A TEN EVERY TIME!
END

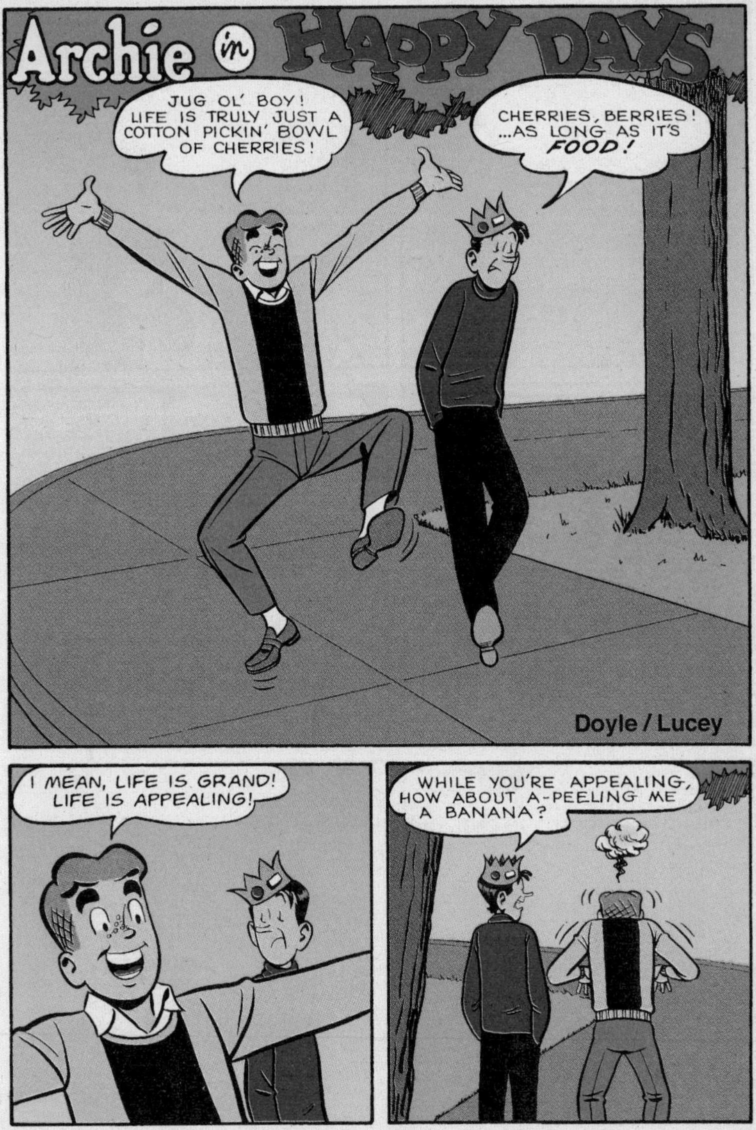
Archie in HAPPY DAYS
JUG OL' BOY! LIFE IS TRULY JUST A COTTON PICKIN' BOWL OF CHERRIES!
CHERRIES, BERRIES! ...AS LONG AS IT'S FOOD!
Doyle / Lucey
I MEAN, LIFE IS GRAND! LIFE IS APPEALING!
WHILE YOU'RE APPEALING, HOW ABOUT A-PEELING ME A BANANA?

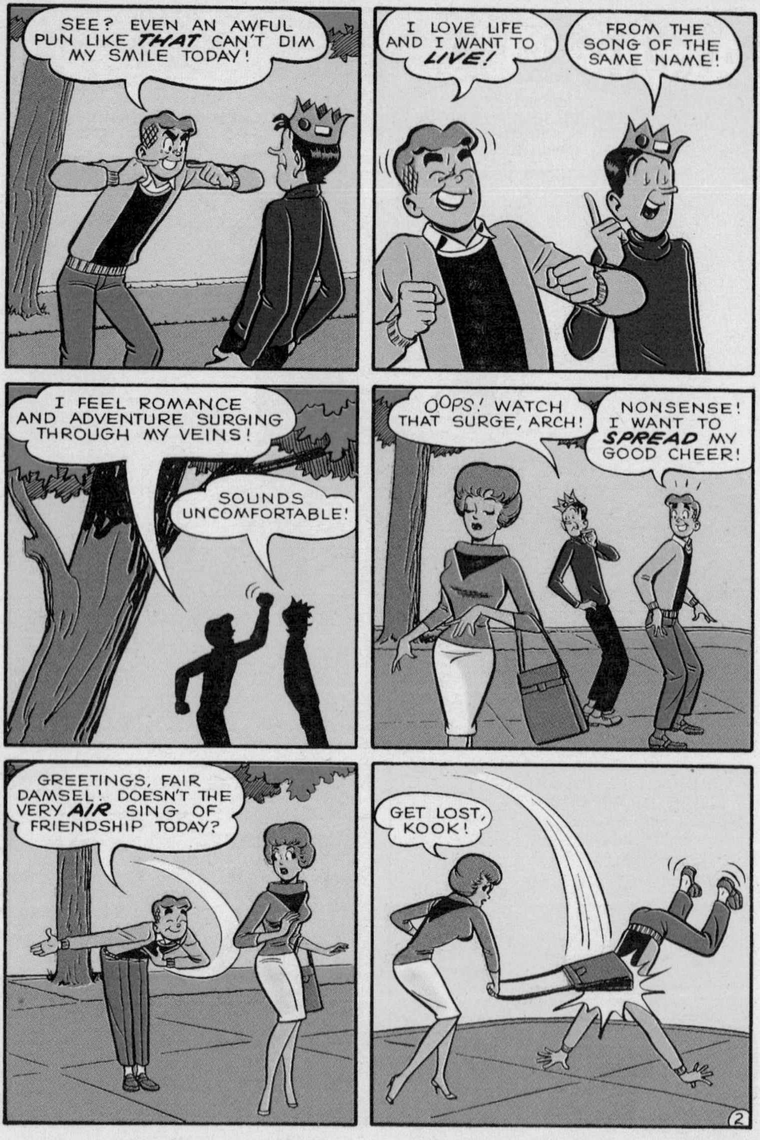
SEE? EVEN AN AWFUL PUN LIKE THAT CAN'T DIM MY SMILE TODAY!
I LOVE LIFE AND I WANT TO LIVE!
FROM THE SONG OF THE SAME NAME!
I FEEL ROMANCE AND ADVENTURE SURGING THROUGH MY VEINS!
SOUNDS UNCOMFORTABLE!
OOPS! WATCH THAT SURGE, ARCH!
NONSENSE! I WANT TO SPREAD MY GOOD CHEER!
GREETINGS, FAIR DAMSEL! DOESN'T THE VERY AIR SING OF FRIENDSHIP TODAY?
GET LOST, KOOK!
2

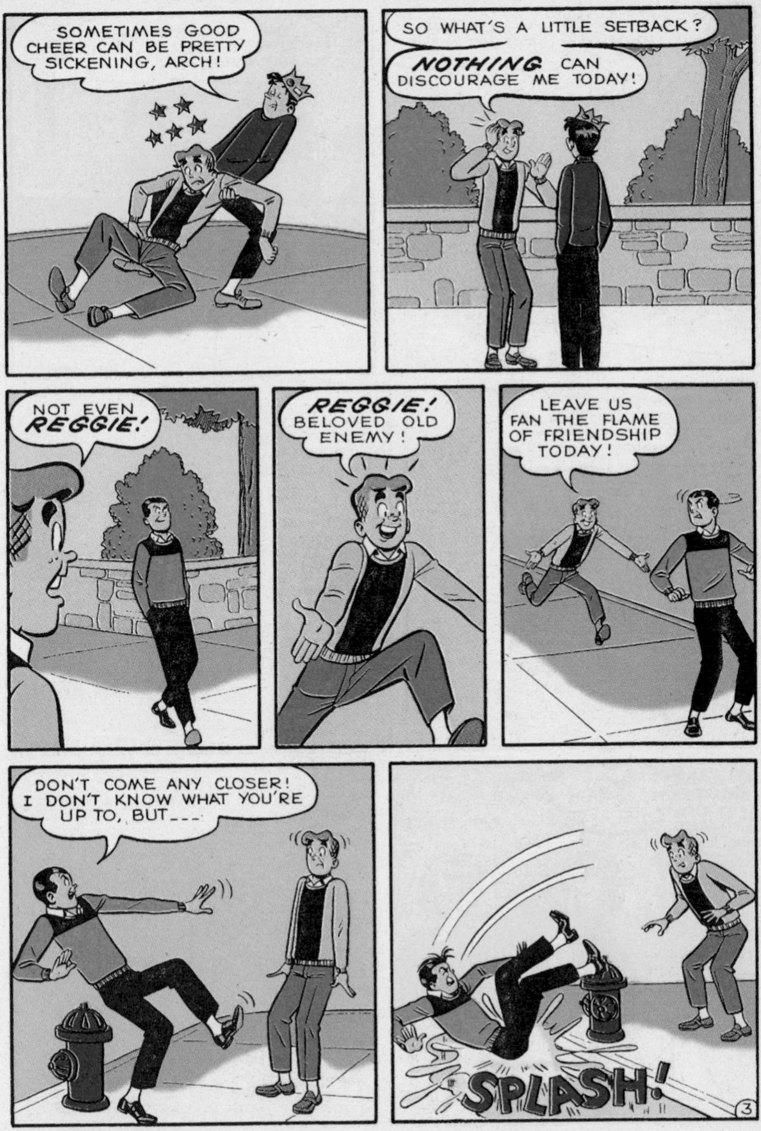
SOMETIMES GOOD CHEER CAN BE PRETTY SICKENING, ARCH!
SO WHAT'S A LITTLE SETBACK?
NOTHING CAN DISCOURAGE ME TODAY!
NOT EVEN REGGIE!
REGGIE! BELOVED OLD ENEMY!
LEAVE US FAN THE FLAME OF FRIENDSHIP TODAY!
DON'T COME ANY CLOSER! I DON'T KNOW WHAT YOU'RE UP TO, BUT---
SPLASH!
3

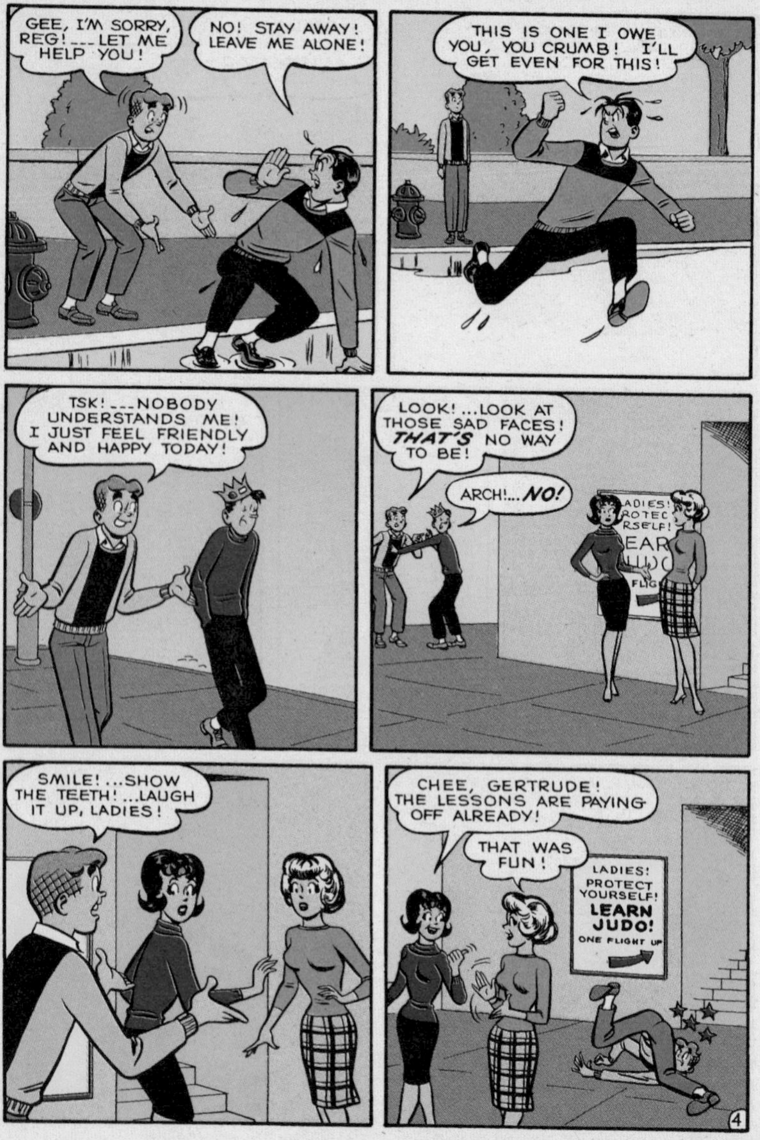
GEE, I'M SORRY, REG!---LET ME HELP YOU!
NO! STAY AWAY! LEAVE ME ALONE!
THIS IS ONE I OWE YOU, YOU CRUMB! I'LL GET EVEN FOR THIS!
TSK!---NOBODY UNDERSTANDS ME! I JUST FEEL FRIENDLY AND HAPPY TODAY!
LOOK! ...LOOK AT THOSE SAD FACES! *THAT'S* NO WAY TO BE!
ARCH!... *NO!*
SMILE! ...SHOW THE TEETH! ...LAUGH IT UP, LADIES!
CHEE, GERTRUDE! THE LESSONS ARE PAYING OFF ALREADY!
THAT WAS FUN!
LADIES! PROTECT YOURSELF! LEARN JUDO! ONE FLIGHT UP
4

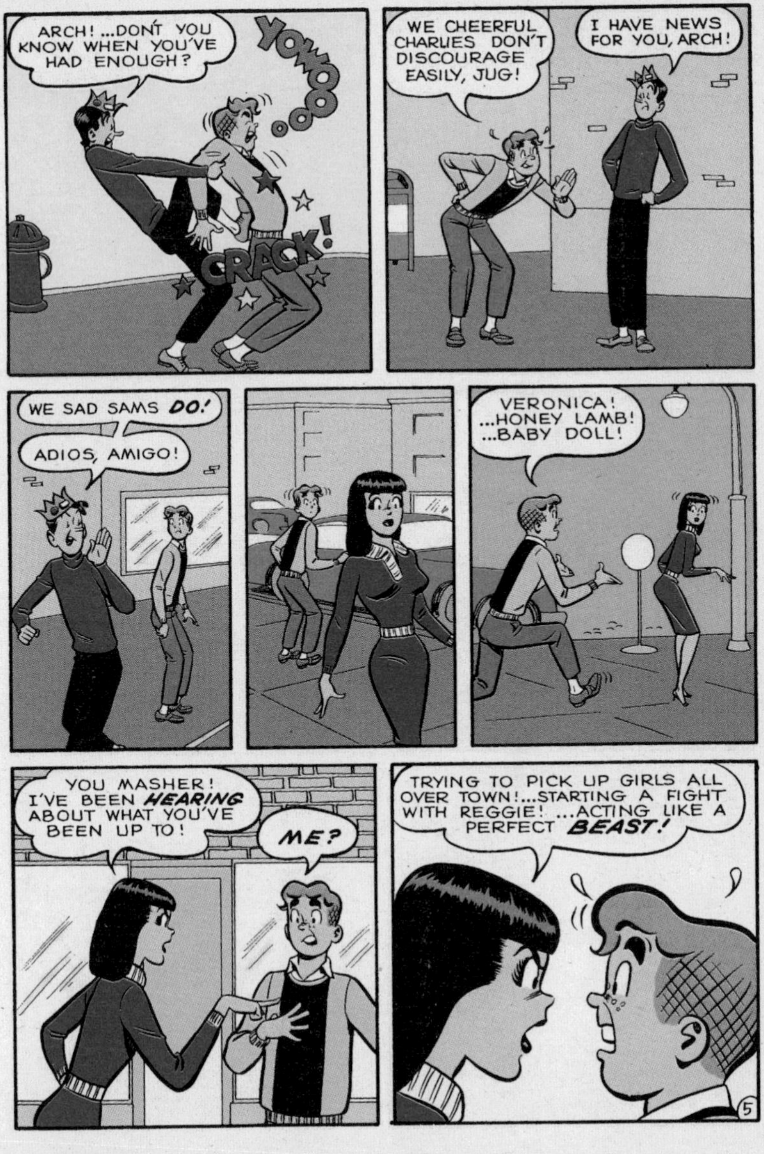
ARCH! ...DON'T YOU KNOW WHEN YOU'VE HAD ENOUGH?
YOWOOOOO
CRACK!
WE CHEERFUL CHARLIES DON'T DISCOURAGE EASILY, JUG!
I HAVE NEWS FOR YOU, ARCH!
WE SAD SAMS *DO!*
ADIOS, AMIGO!
VERONICA! ...HONEY LAMB! ...BABY DOLL!
YOU MASHER! I'VE BEEN ***HEARING*** ABOUT WHAT YOU'VE BEEN UP TO!
ME?
TRYING TO PICK UP GIRLS ALL OVER TOWN!...STARTING A FIGHT WITH REGGIE! ...ACTING LIKE A PERFECT ***BEAST!***
5

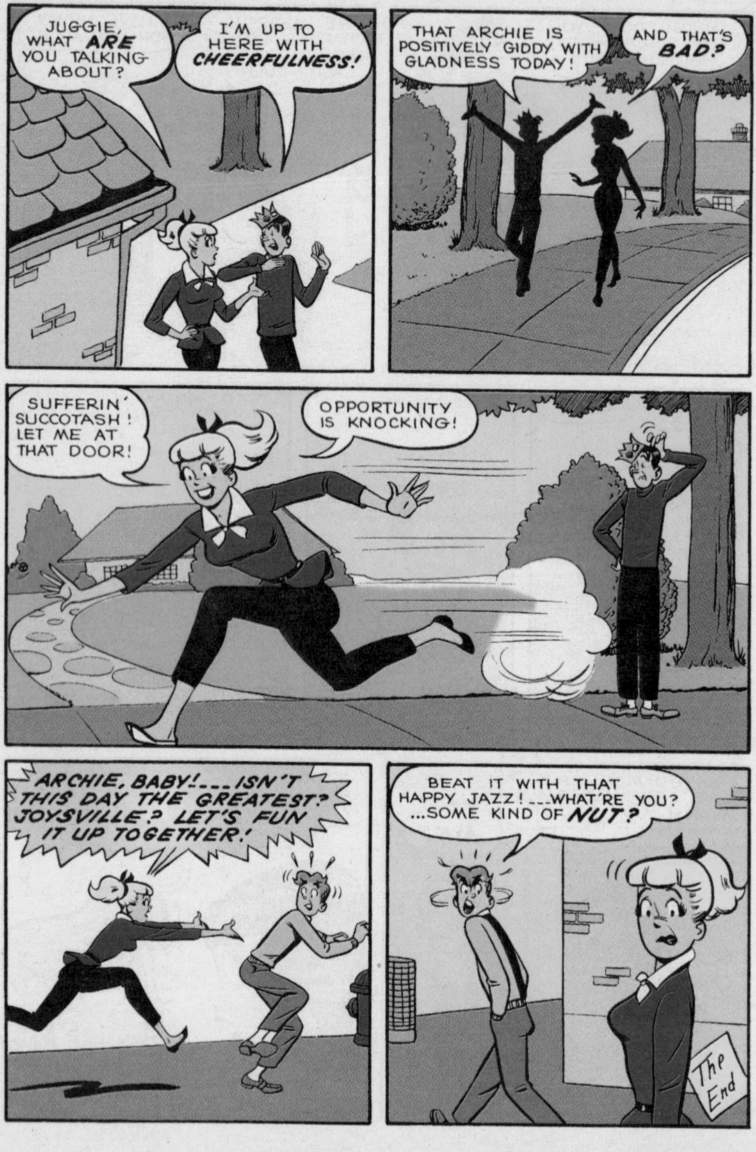
JUGGIE, WHAT ARE YOU TALKING ABOUT?
I'M UP TO HERE WITH CHEERFULNESS!
THAT ARCHIE IS POSITIVELY GIDDY WITH GLADNESS TODAY!
AND THAT'S BAD?
SUFFERIN' SUCCOTASH! LET ME AT THAT DOOR!
OPPORTUNITY IS KNOCKING!
ARCHIE, BABY!...ISN'T THIS DAY THE GREATEST? JOYSVILLE? LET'S FUN IT UP TOGETHER!
BEAT IT WITH THAT HAPPY JAZZ!...WHAT'RE YOU? ...SOME KIND OF NUT?
The End

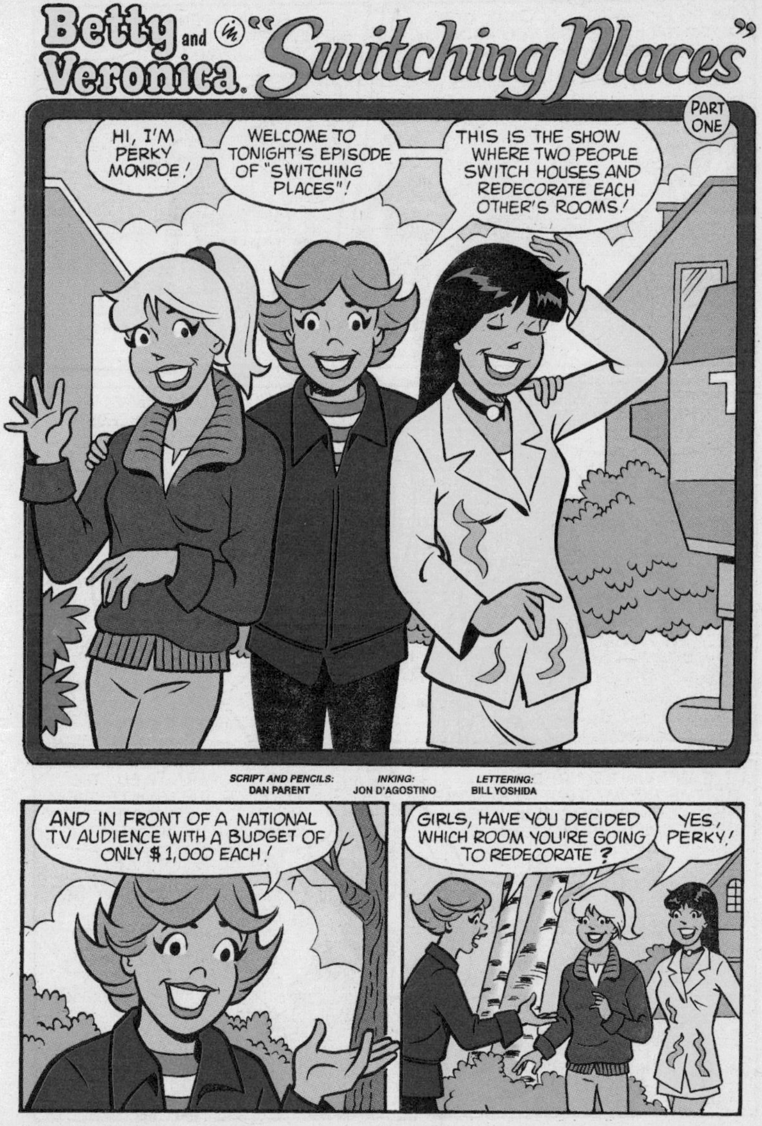
Betty and Veronica in "Switching Places"
PART ONE
HI, I'M PERKY MONROE!
WELCOME TO TONIGHT'S EPISODE OF "SWITCHING PLACES"!
THIS IS THE SHOW WHERE TWO PEOPLE SWITCH HOUSES AND REDECORATE EACH OTHER'S ROOMS!
SCRIPT AND PENCILS: DAN PARENT
INKING: JON D'AGOSTINO
LETTERING: BILL YOSHIDA
AND IN FRONT OF A NATIONAL TV AUDIENCE WITH A BUDGET OF ONLY $1,000 EACH!
GIRLS, HAVE YOU DECIDED WHICH ROOM YOU'RE GOING TO REDECORATE?
YES, PERKY!

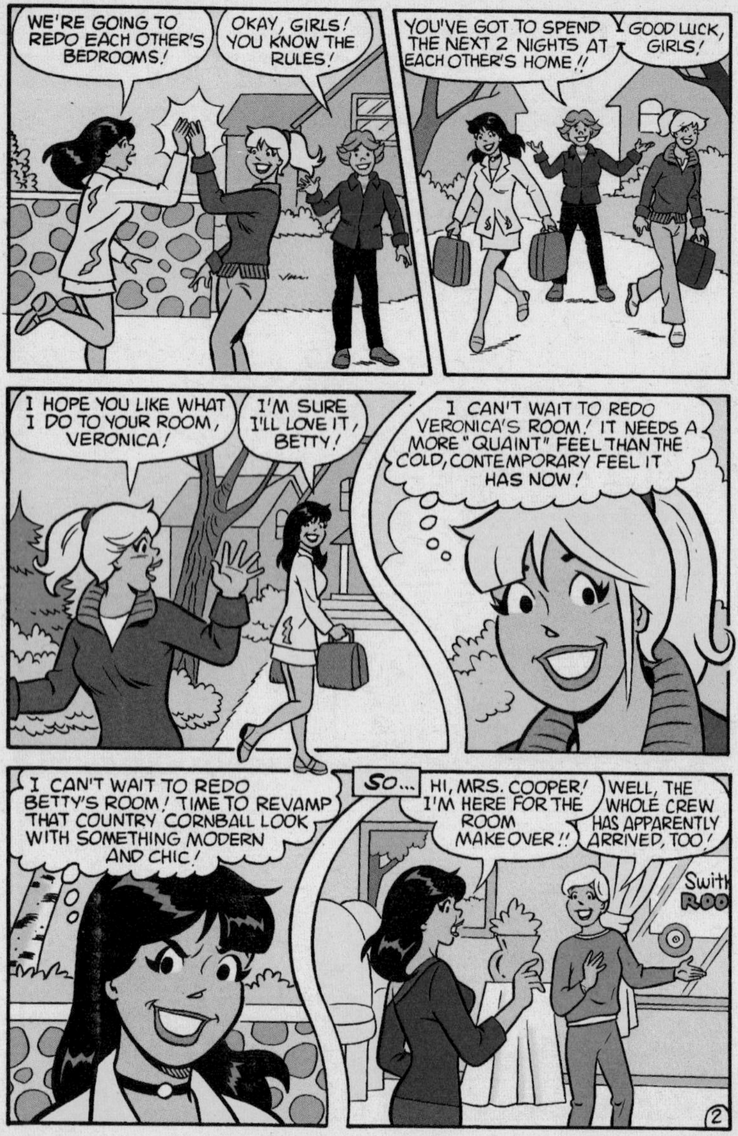
WE'RE GOING TO REDO EACH OTHER'S BEDROOMS!
OKAY, GIRLS! YOU KNOW THE RULES!
YOU'VE GOT TO SPEND THE NEXT 2 NIGHTS AT EACH OTHER'S HOME!!
GOOD LUCK, GIRLS!
I HOPE YOU LIKE WHAT I DO TO YOUR ROOM, VERONICA!
I'M SURE I'LL LOVE IT, BETTY!
I CAN'T WAIT TO REDO VERONICA'S ROOM! IT NEEDS A MORE "QUAINT" FEEL THAN THE COLD, CONTEMPORARY FEEL IT HAS NOW!
I CAN'T WAIT TO REDO BETTY'S ROOM! TIME TO REVAMP THAT COUNTRY CORNBALL LOOK WITH SOMETHING MODERN AND CHIC!
SO...
HI, MRS. COOPER! I'M HERE FOR THE ROOM MAKEOVER!!
WELL, THE WHOLE CREW HAS APPARENTLY ARRIVED, TOO!
2

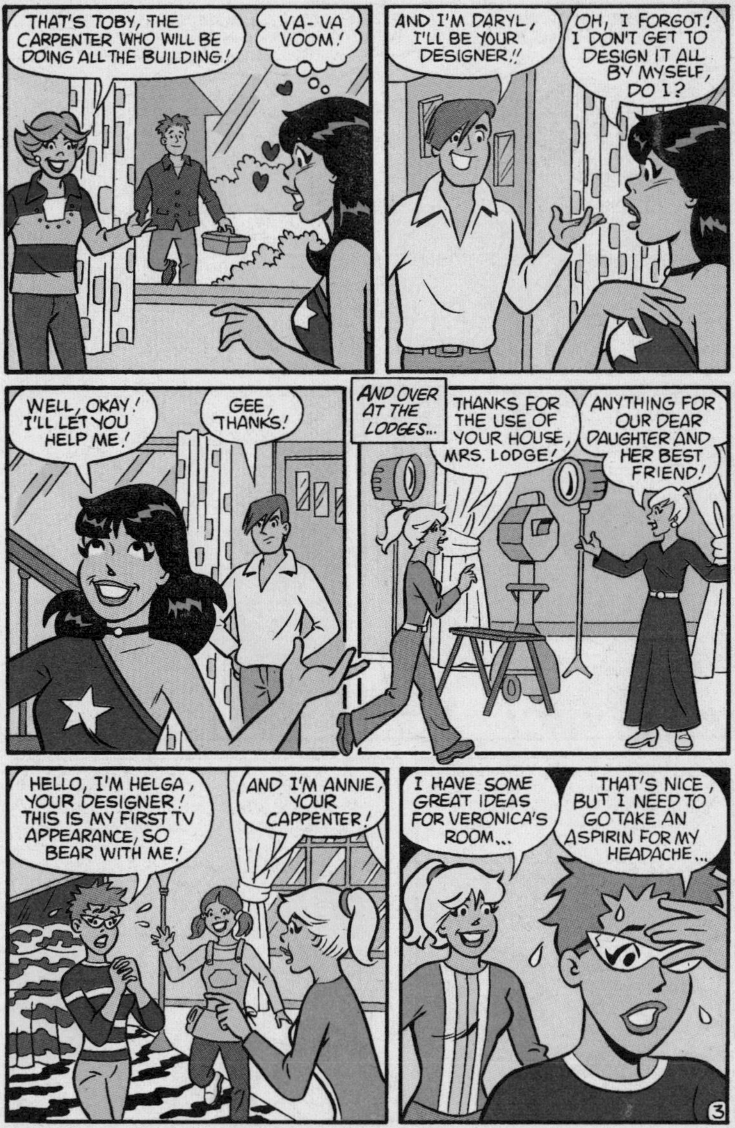
THAT'S TOBY, THE CARPENTER WHO WILL BE DOING ALL THE BUILDING!
VA-VA VOOM!
AND I'M DARYL, I'LL BE YOUR DESIGNER!!
OH, I FORGOT! I DON'T GET TO DESIGN IT ALL BY MYSELF, DO I?
WELL, OKAY! I'LL LET YOU HELP ME!
GEE, THANKS!
AND OVER AT THE LODGES...
THANKS FOR THE USE OF YOUR HOUSE, MRS. LODGE!
ANYTHING FOR OUR DEAR DAUGHTER AND HER BEST FRIEND!
HELLO, I'M HELGA, YOUR DESIGNER! THIS IS MY FIRST TV APPEARANCE, SO BEAR WITH ME!
AND I'M ANNIE, YOUR CARPENTER!
I HAVE SOME GREAT IDEAS FOR VERONICA'S ROOM...
THAT'S NICE, BUT I NEED TO GO TAKE AN ASPIRIN FOR MY HEADACHE...
3

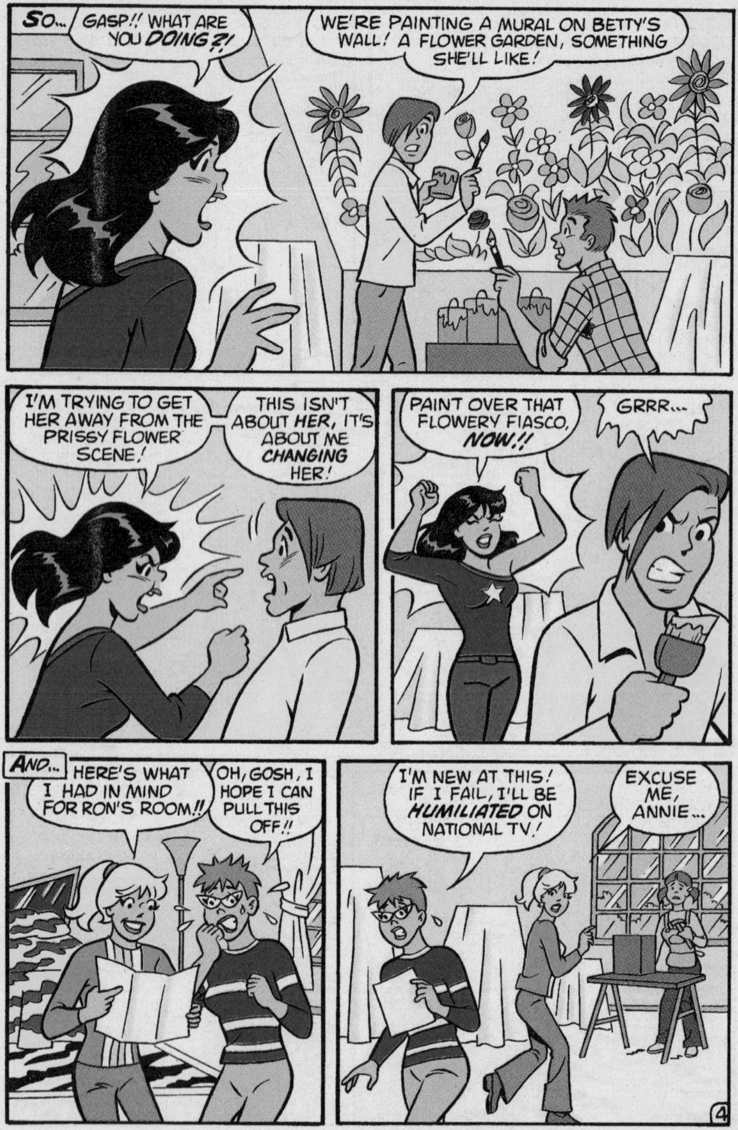

SO...
GASP!! WHAT ARE YOU DOING?!
WE'RE PAINTING A MURAL ON BETTY'S WALL! A FLOWER GARDEN, SOMETHING SHE'LL LIKE!
I'M TRYING TO GET HER AWAY FROM THE PRISSY FLOWER SCENE!
THIS ISN'T ABOUT HER, IT'S ABOUT ME CHANGING HER!
PAINT OVER THAT FLOWERY FIASCO, NOW!!
GRRR...
AND...
HERE'S WHAT I HAD IN MIND FOR RON'S ROOM!!
OH, GOSH, I HOPE I CAN PULL THIS OFF!!
I'M NEW AT THIS! IF I FAIL, I'LL BE HUMILIATED ON NATIONAL TV!
EXCUSE ME, ANNIE...

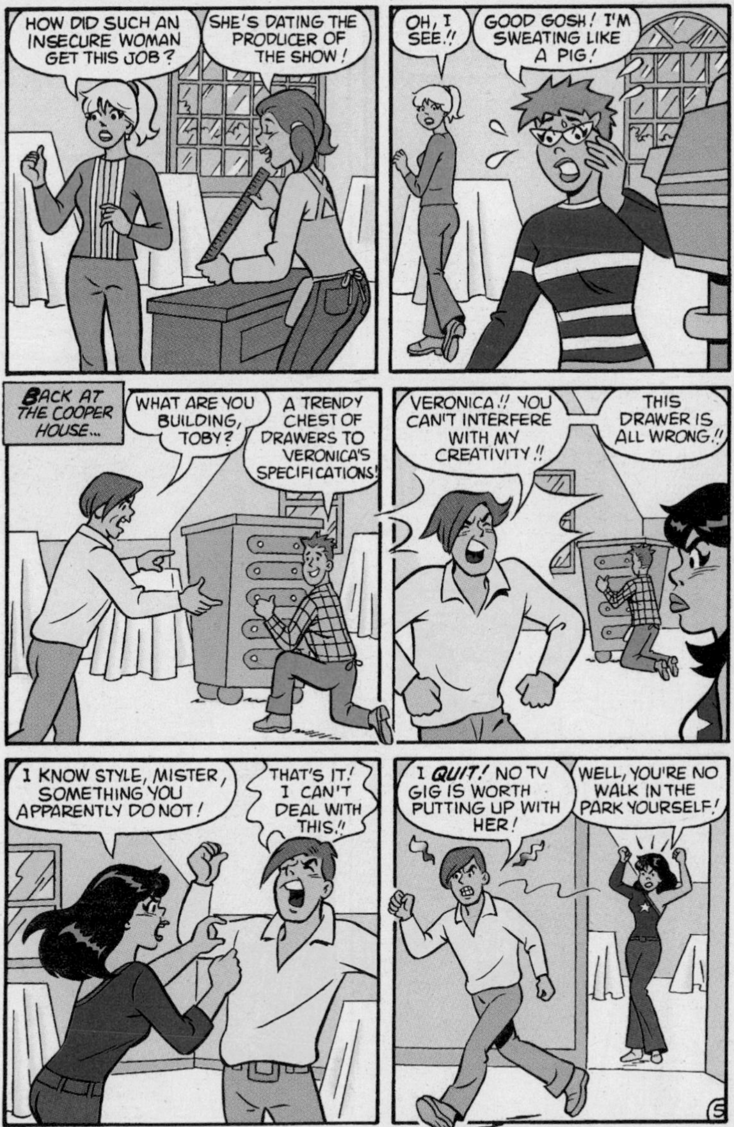

HOW DID SUCH AN INSECURE WOMAN GET THIS JOB?
SHE'S DATING THE PRODUCER OF THE SHOW!
OH, I SEE.!!
GOOD GOSH! I'M SWEATING LIKE A PIG!
BACK AT THE COOPER HOUSE...
WHAT ARE YOU BUILDING, TOBY?
A TRENDY CHEST OF DRAWERS TO VERONICA'S SPECIFICATIONS!
VERONICA!! YOU CAN'T INTERFERE WITH MY CREATIVITY!!
THIS DRAWER IS ALL WRONG!!
I KNOW STYLE, MISTER, SOMETHING YOU APPARENTLY DO NOT!
THAT'S IT! I CAN'T DEAL WITH THIS!!
I QUIT! NO TV GIG IS WORTH PUTTING UP WITH HER!
WELL, YOU'RE NO WALK IN THE PARK YOURSELF!
5

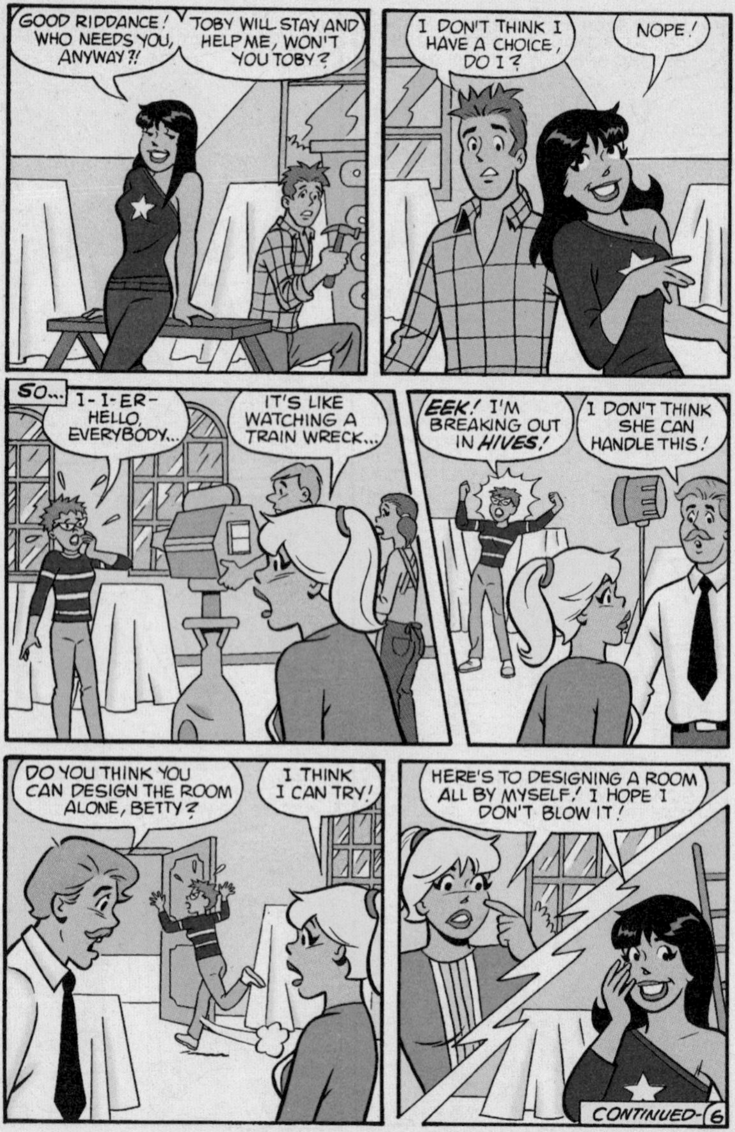
GOOD RIDDANCE! WHO NEEDS YOU, ANYWAY?!
TOBY WILL STAY AND HELP ME, WON'T YOU TOBY?
I DON'T THINK I HAVE A CHOICE, DO I?
NOPE!
SO...
I-I-ER- HELLO, EVERYBODY...
IT'S LIKE WATCHING A TRAIN WRECK...
EEK! I'M BREAKING OUT IN HIVES!
I DON'T THINK SHE CAN HANDLE THIS!
DO YOU THINK YOU CAN DESIGN THE ROOM ALONE, BETTY?
I THINK I CAN TRY!
HERE'S TO DESIGNING A ROOM ALL BY MYSELF! I HOPE I DON'T BLOW IT!
CONTINUED- 6

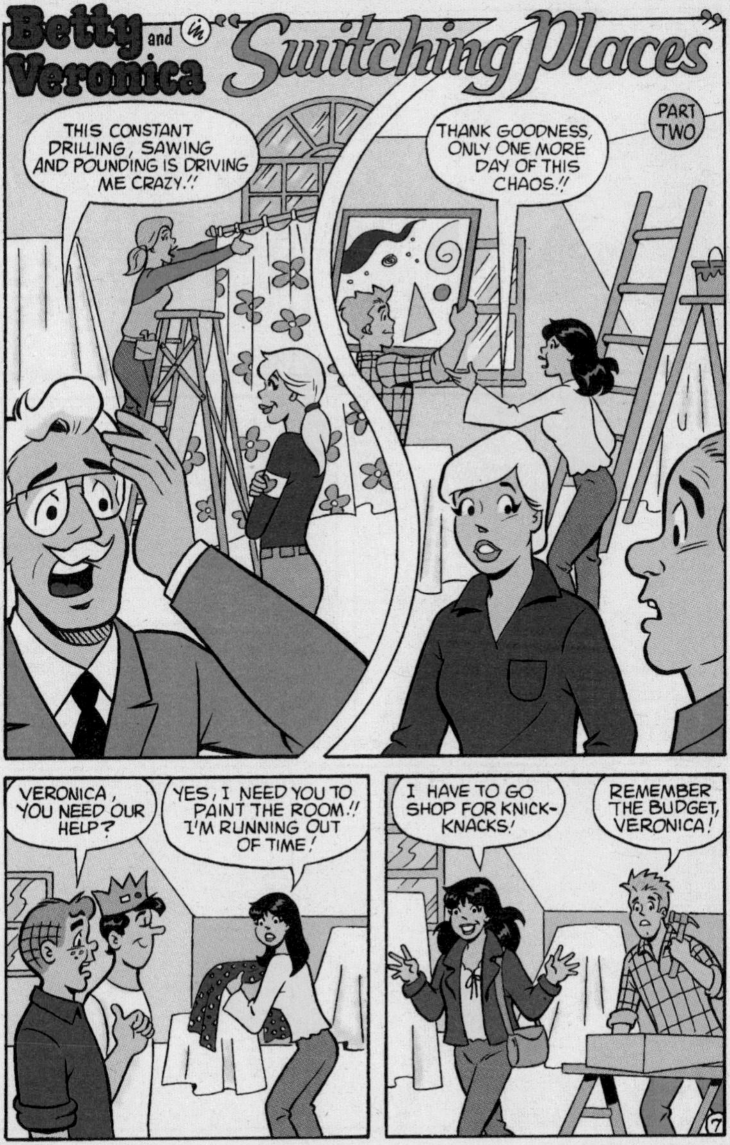
Betty and Veronica in "Switching Places"
PART TWO
THIS CONSTANT DRILLING, SAWING AND POUNDING IS DRIVING ME CRAZY!!
THANK GOODNESS, ONLY ONE MORE DAY OF THIS CHAOS!!
VERONICA, YOU NEED OUR HELP?
YES, I NEED YOU TO PAINT THE ROOM!! I'M RUNNING OUT OF TIME!
I HAVE TO GO SHOP FOR KNICK-KNACKS!
REMEMBER THE BUDGET, VERONICA!
7

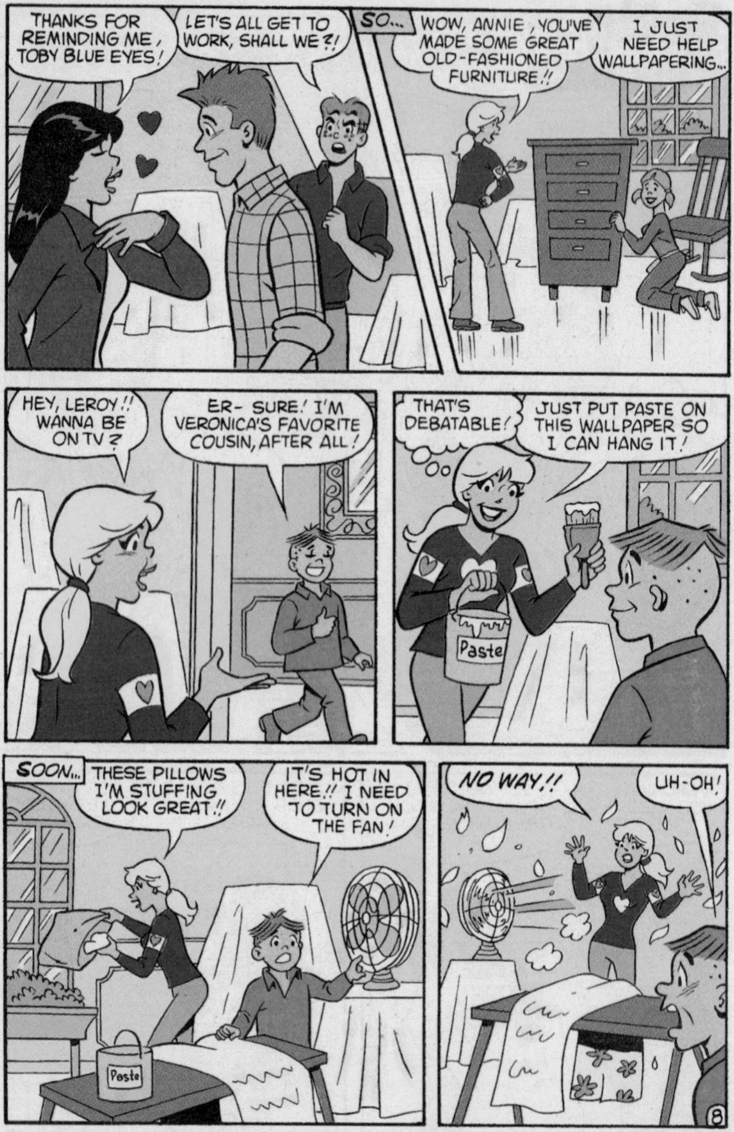
THANKS FOR REMINDING ME, TOBY BLUE EYES!
LET'S ALL GET TO WORK, SHALL WE?!
SO...
WOW, ANNIE, YOU'VE MADE SOME GREAT OLD-FASHIONED FURNITURE!!
I JUST NEED HELP WALLPAPERING...
HEY, LEROY!! WANNA BE ON TV?
ER- SURE! I'M VERONICA'S FAVORITE COUSIN, AFTER ALL!
THAT'S DEBATABLE!
JUST PUT PASTE ON THIS WALLPAPER SO I CAN HANG IT!
Paste
SOON...
THESE PILLOWS I'M STUFFING LOOK GREAT!!
IT'S HOT IN HERE!! I NEED TO TURN ON THE FAN!
Paste
NO WAY!!
UH-OH!
8

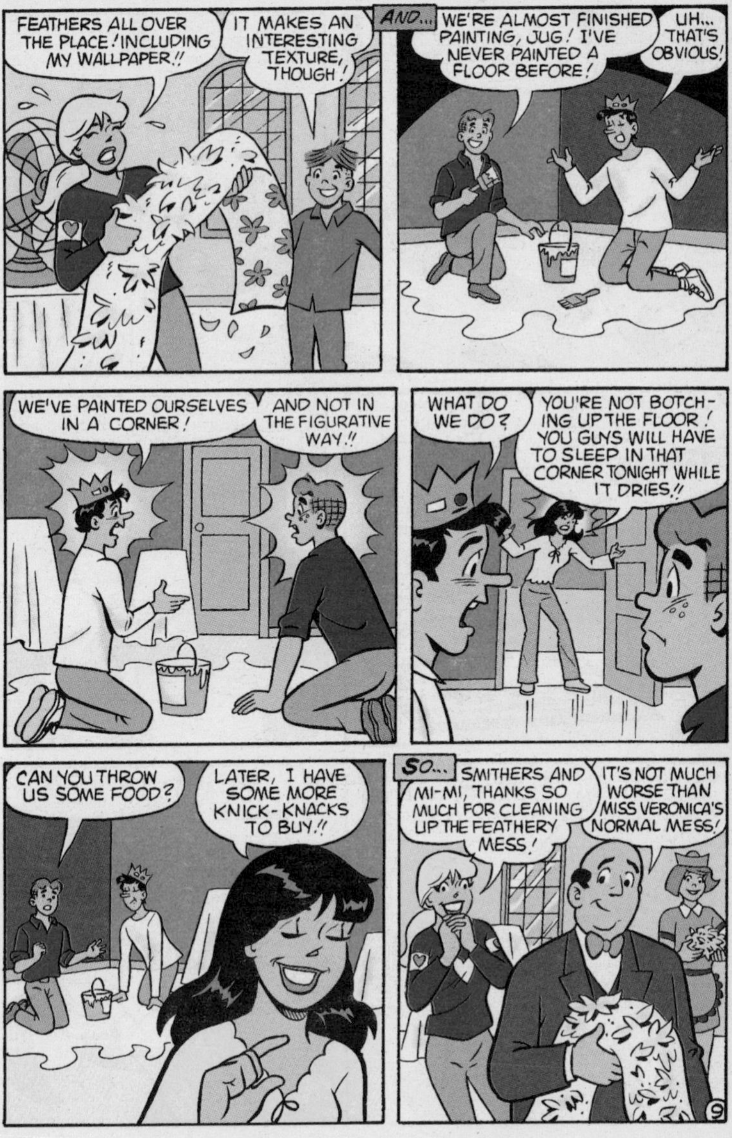

FEATHERS ALL OVER THE PLACE! INCLUDING MY WALLPAPER!!
IT MAKES AN INTERESTING TEXTURE, THOUGH!
AND...
WE'RE ALMOST FINISHED PAINTING, JUG! I'VE NEVER PAINTED A FLOOR BEFORE!
UH... THAT'S OBVIOUS!
WE'VE PAINTED OURSELVES IN A CORNER!
AND NOT IN THE FIGURATIVE WAY!!
WHAT DO WE DO?
YOU'RE NOT BOTCHING UP THE FLOOR! YOU GUYS WILL HAVE TO SLEEP IN THAT CORNER TONIGHT WHILE IT DRIES!!
CAN YOU THROW US SOME FOOD?
LATER, I HAVE SOME MORE KNICK-KNACKS TO BUY!!
SO...
SMITHERS AND MI-MI, THANKS SO MUCH FOR CLEANING UP THE FEATHERY MESS!
IT'S NOT MUCH WORSE THAN MISS VERONICA'S NORMAL MESS!
9

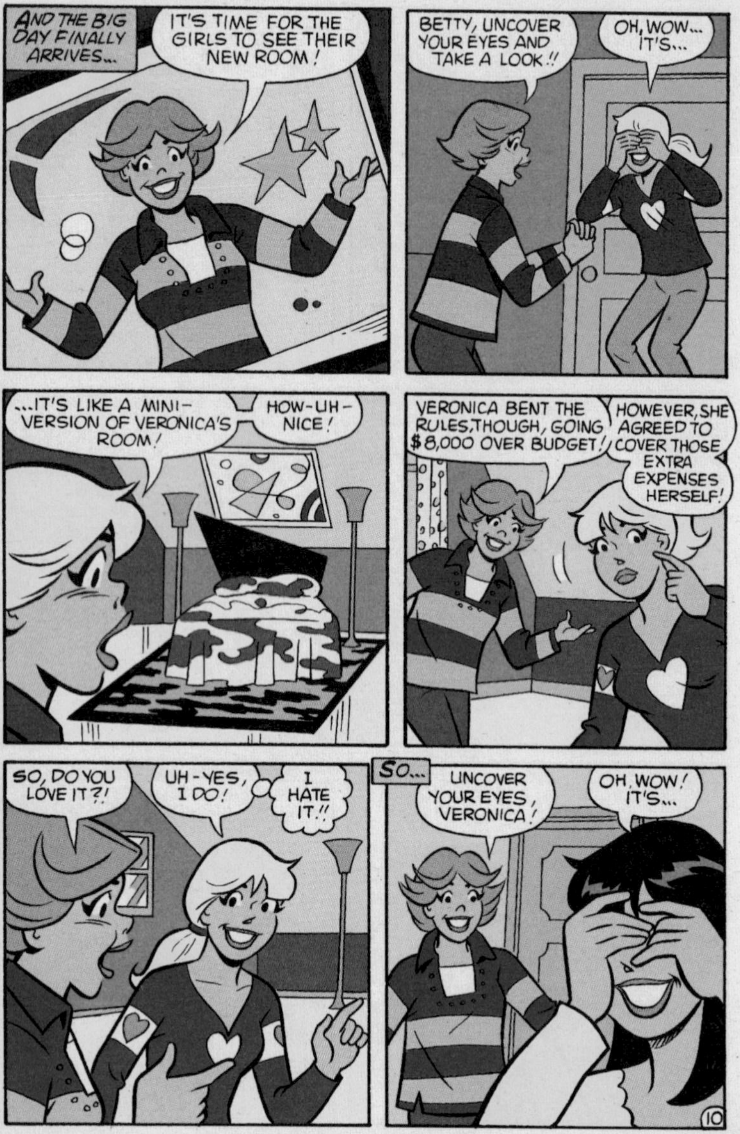
AND THE BIG DAY FINALLY ARRIVES...
IT'S TIME FOR THE GIRLS TO SEE THEIR NEW ROOM!
BETTY, UNCOVER YOUR EYES AND TAKE A LOOK!!
OH, WOW... IT'S...
...IT'S LIKE A MINI-VERSION OF VERONICA'S ROOM!
HOW-UH-NICE!
VERONICA BENT THE RULES, THOUGH, GOING $8,000 OVER BUDGET!
HOWEVER, SHE AGREED TO COVER THOSE EXTRA EXPENSES HERSELF!
SO, DO YOU LOVE IT?!
UH-YES, I DO!
I HATE IT!!
SO...
UNCOVER YOUR EYES, VERONICA!
OH, WOW! IT'S...
10

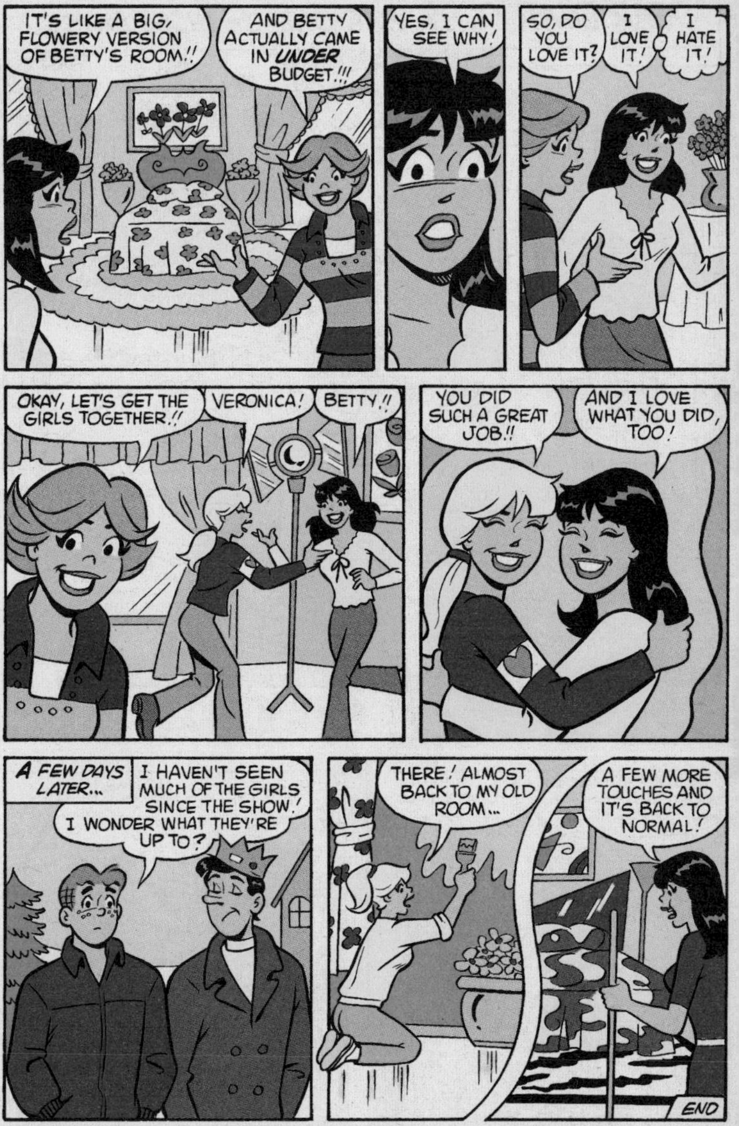
IT'S LIKE A BIG, FLOWERY VERSION OF BETTY'S ROOM!!
AND BETTY ACTUALLY CAME IN *UNDER* BUDGET!!!
YES, I CAN SEE WHY!
SO, DO YOU LOVE IT?
I LOVE IT!
I HATE IT!
OKAY, LET'S GET THE GIRLS TOGETHER!!
VERONICA!
BETTY!!
YOU DID SUCH A GREAT JOB!!
AND I LOVE WHAT YOU DID, TOO!
A FEW DAYS LATER...
I HAVEN'T SEEN MUCH OF THE GIRLS SINCE THE SHOW! I WONDER WHAT THEY'RE UP TO?
THERE! ALMOST BACK TO MY OLD ROOM...
A FEW MORE TOUCHES AND IT'S BACK TO NORMAL!
END

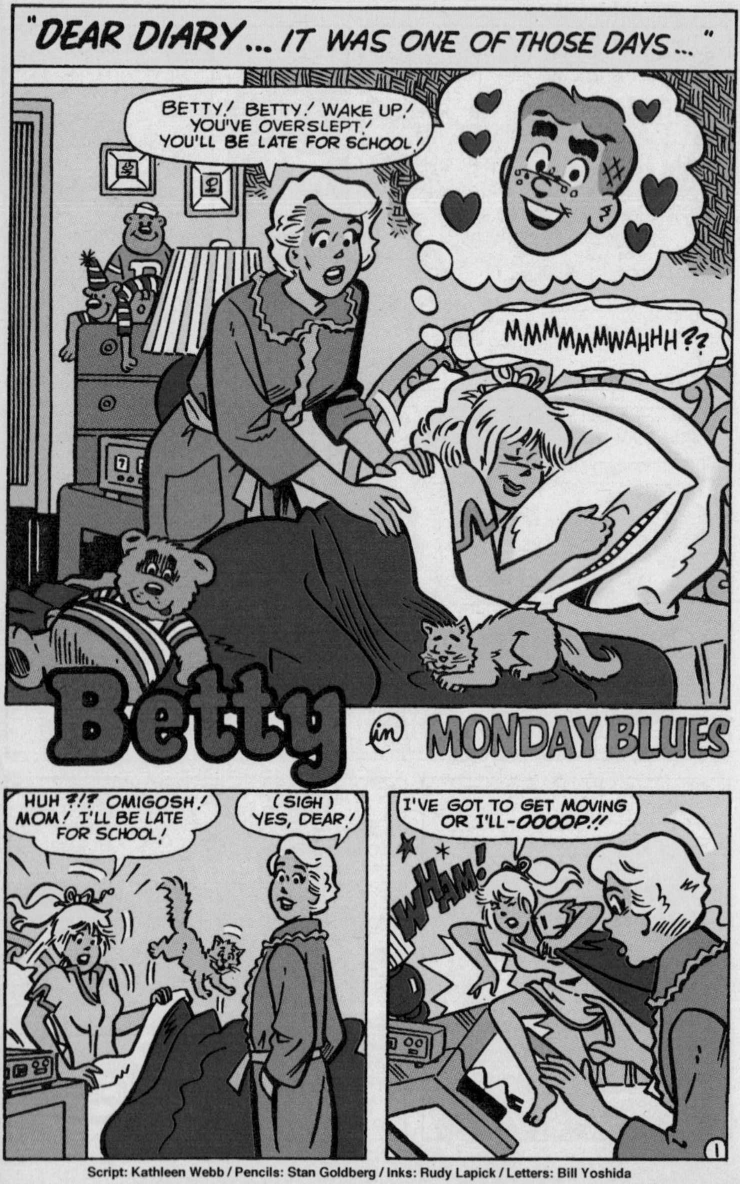
"DEAR DIARY... IT WAS ONE OF THOSE DAYS..."
BETTY! BETTY! WAKE UP! YOU'VE OVERSLEPT! YOU'LL BE LATE FOR SCHOOL!
MMMMMMMWAHHH??
Betty in MONDAY BLUES
HUH ?!? OMIGOSH! MOM! I'LL BE LATE FOR SCHOOL!
(SIGH) YES, DEAR!
I'VE GOT TO GET MOVING OR I'LL-OOOOP!!
WHAM!
1

Script: Kathleen Webb / Pencils: Stan Goldberg / Inks: Rudy Lapick / Letters: Bill Yoshida

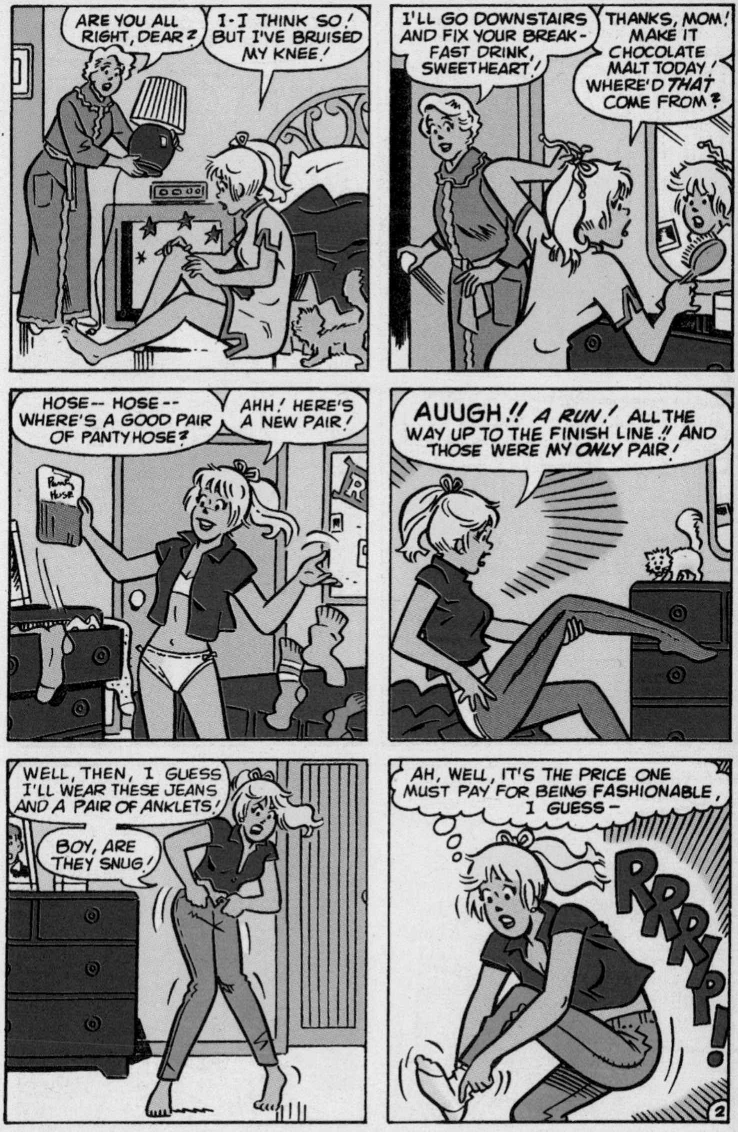
ARE YOU ALL RIGHT, DEAR?
I-I THINK SO! BUT I'VE BRUISED MY KNEE!
I'LL GO DOWNSTAIRS AND FIX YOUR BREAK-FAST DRINK, SWEETHEART!
THANKS, MOM! MAKE IT CHOCOLATE MALT TODAY! WHERE'D *THAT* COME FROM?
HOSE-- HOSE-- WHERE'S A GOOD PAIR OF PANTYHOSE?
AHH! HERE'S A NEW PAIR!
AUUGH!! *A RUN!* ALL THE WAY UP TO THE FINISH LINE!! AND THOSE WERE MY *ONLY* PAIR!
WELL, THEN, I GUESS I'LL WEAR THESE JEANS AND A PAIR OF ANKLETS!
BOY, ARE THEY SNUG!
AH, WELL, IT'S THE PRICE ONE MUST PAY FOR BEING FASHIONABLE, I GUESS-
RRRIPP!
2

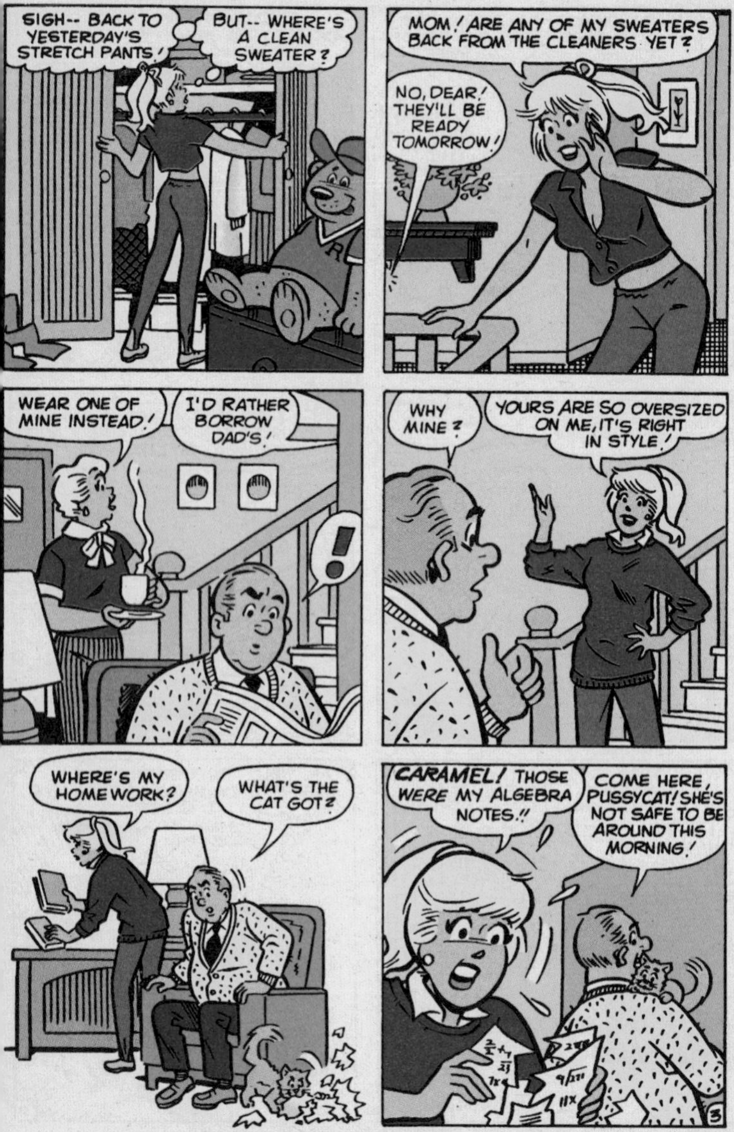
SIGH-- BACK TO YESTERDAY'S STRETCH PANTS!
BUT-- WHERE'S A CLEAN SWEATER?
MOM! ARE ANY OF MY SWEATERS BACK FROM THE CLEANERS YET?
NO, DEAR! THEY'LL BE READY TOMORROW!
WEAR ONE OF MINE INSTEAD!
I'D RATHER BORROW DAD'S!
!
WHY MINE?
YOURS ARE SO OVERSIZED ON ME, IT'S RIGHT IN STYLE!
WHERE'S MY HOMEWORK?
WHAT'S THE CAT GOT?
CARAMEL! THOSE WERE MY ALGEBRA NOTES!!
COME HERE, PUSSYCAT! SHE'S NOT SAFE TO BE AROUND THIS MORNING!
3

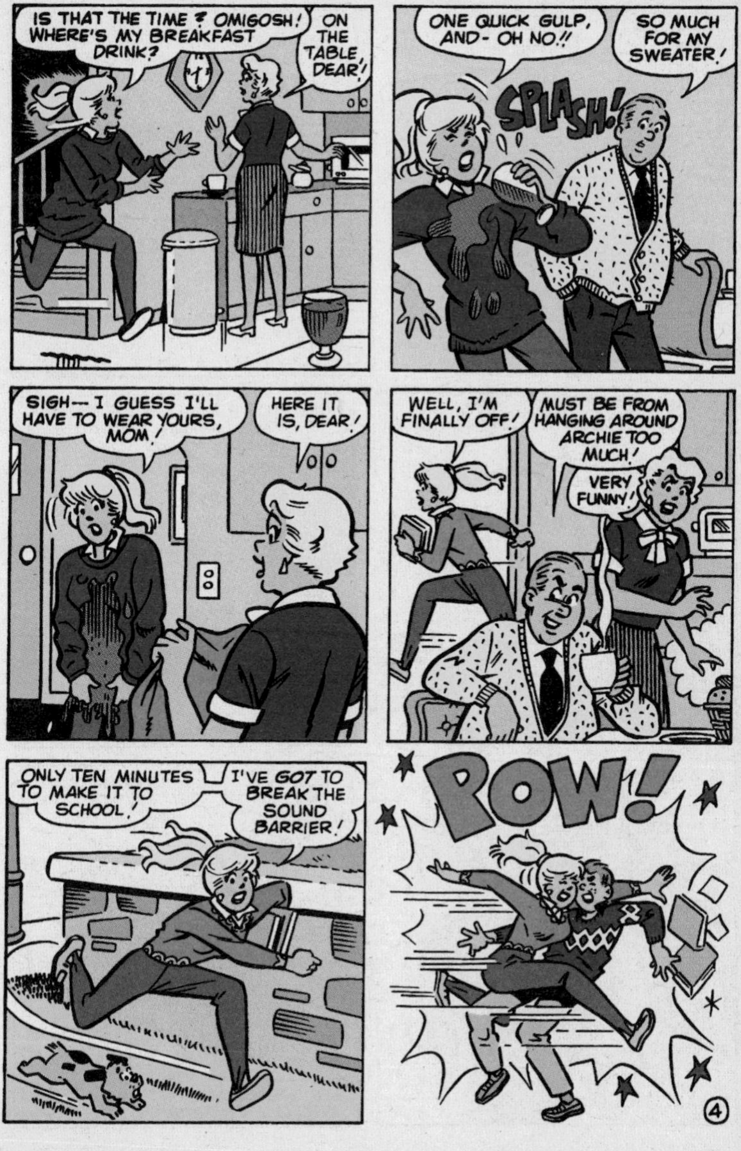
IS THAT THE TIME? OMIGOSH! WHERE'S MY BREAKFAST DRINK?
ON THE TABLE, DEAR!
ONE QUICK GULP, AND- OH NO!!
SPLASH!
SO MUCH FOR MY SWEATER!
SIGH--- I GUESS I'LL HAVE TO WEAR YOURS, MOM!
HERE IT IS, DEAR!
WELL, I'M FINALLY OFF!
MUST BE FROM HANGING AROUND ARCHIE TOO MUCH!
VERY FUNNY!
ONLY TEN MINUTES TO MAKE IT TO SCHOOL!
I'VE GOT TO BREAK THE SOUND BARRIER!
POW!

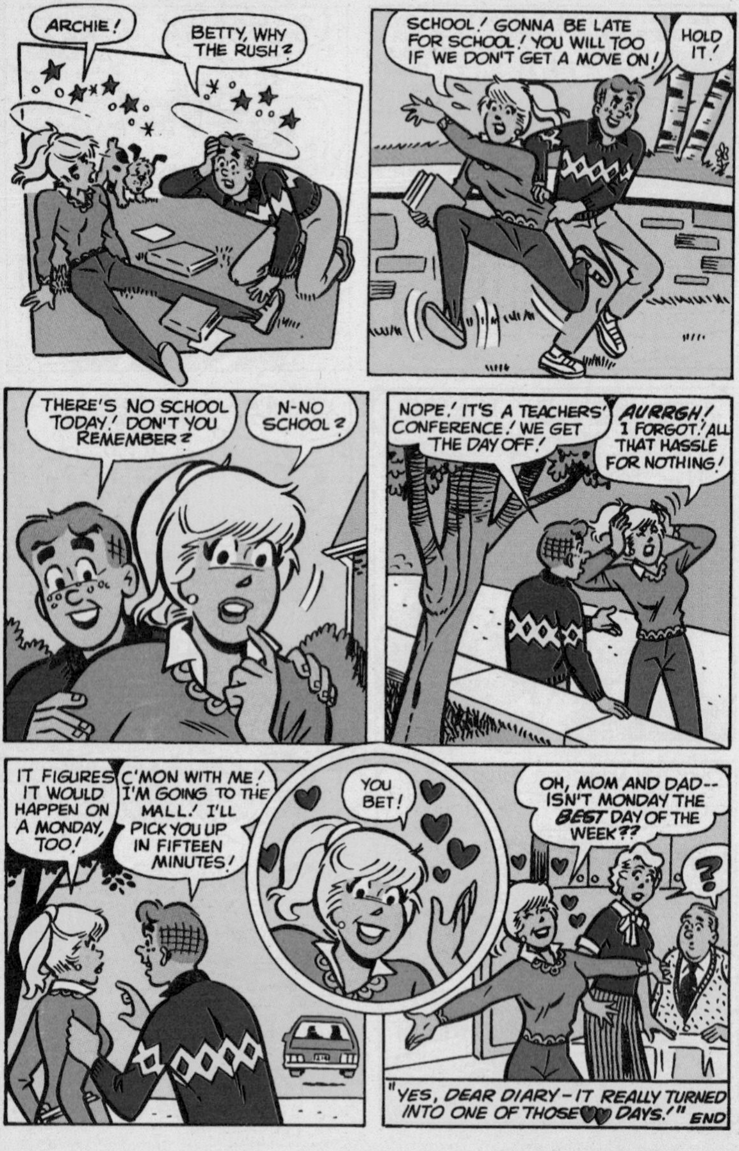

ARCHIE!
BETTY, WHY THE RUSH?
SCHOOL! GONNA BE LATE FOR SCHOOL! YOU WILL TOO IF WE DON'T GET A MOVE ON!
HOLD IT!
THERE'S NO SCHOOL TODAY! DON'T YOU REMEMBER?
N-NO SCHOOL?
NOPE! IT'S A TEACHERS' CONFERENCE! WE GET THE DAY OFF!
AURRGH! I FORGOT! ALL THAT HASSLE FOR NOTHING!
IT FIGURES IT WOULD HAPPEN ON A MONDAY, TOO!
C'MON WITH ME! I'M GOING TO THE MALL! I'LL PICK YOU UP IN FIFTEEN MINUTES!
YOU BET!
OH, MOM AND DAD-- ISN'T MONDAY THE BEST DAY OF THE WEEK??
?
"YES, DEAR DIARY – IT REALLY TURNED INTO ONE OF THOSE ♥♥ DAYS!"
END

Betty and Veronica in "STOP the INSANITY"

Veronica: YOU'VE SEEN ONE MALL, YOU'VE SEEN 'EM ALL, I ALWAYS SAY!

Betty: SIGH! YOU'RE RIGHT! THERE IS AN INHERENT SAMENESS BUILT INTO THEM!

Script:
K. Webb
Pencils:
T. Kennedy
Inks:
R. Lapick

Betty: NEVER THOUGHT I COULD GET BORED HERE...BUT I FEEL A FEW YAWNS COMING ON...

Veronica: LET'S LIVEN THINGS UP A BIT THEN...

Betty: ER...WHAT EXACTLY DO YOU MEAN BY "LIVEN"?

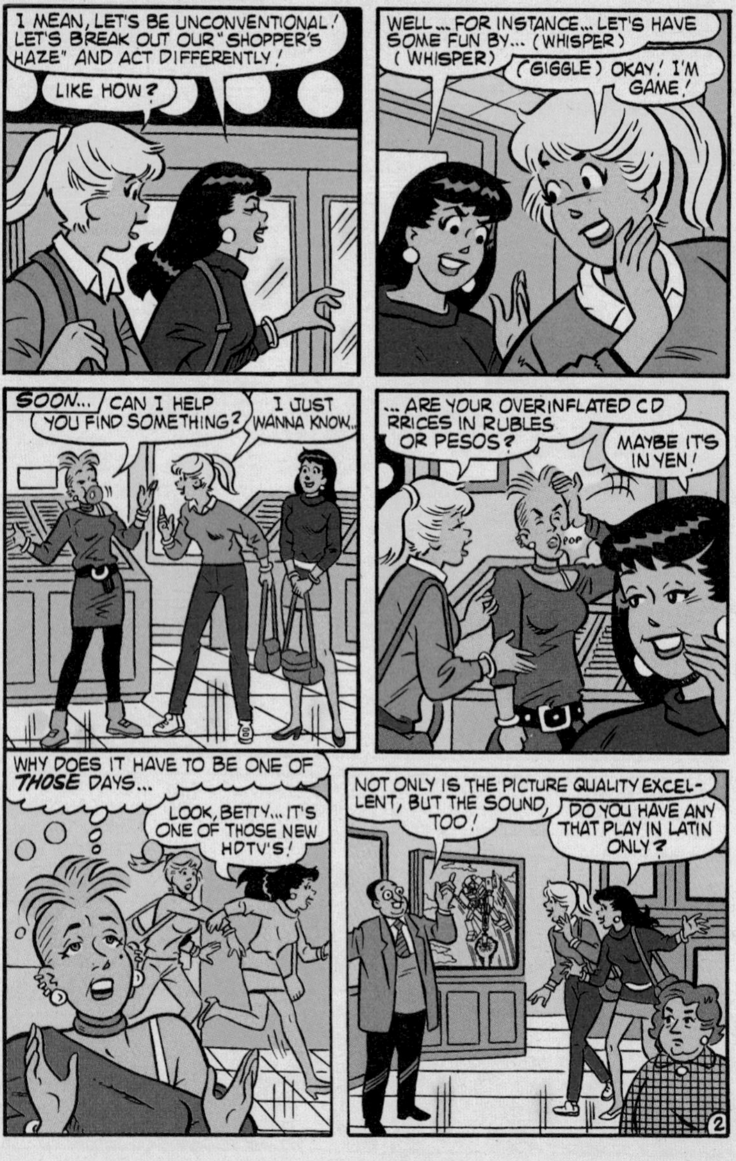
I MEAN, LET'S BE UNCONVENTIONAL! LET'S BREAK OUT OUR "SHOPPER'S HAZE" AND ACT DIFFERENTLY!
LIKE HOW?
WELL... FOR INSTANCE... LET'S HAVE SOME FUN BY... (WHISPER) (WHISPER)
(GIGGLE) OKAY! I'M GAME!
SOON...
CAN I HELP YOU FIND SOMETHING?
I JUST WANNA KNOW...
... ARE YOUR OVERINFLATED CD RRICES IN RUBLES OR PESOS?
MAYBE IT'S IN YEN!
POP
WHY DOES IT HAVE TO BE ONE OF THOSE DAYS...
LOOK, BETTY... IT'S ONE OF THOSE NEW HDTV'S!
NOT ONLY IS THE PICTURE QUALITY EXCEL-LENT, BUT THE SOUND, TOO!
DO YOU HAVE ANY THAT PLAY IN LATIN ONLY?
2

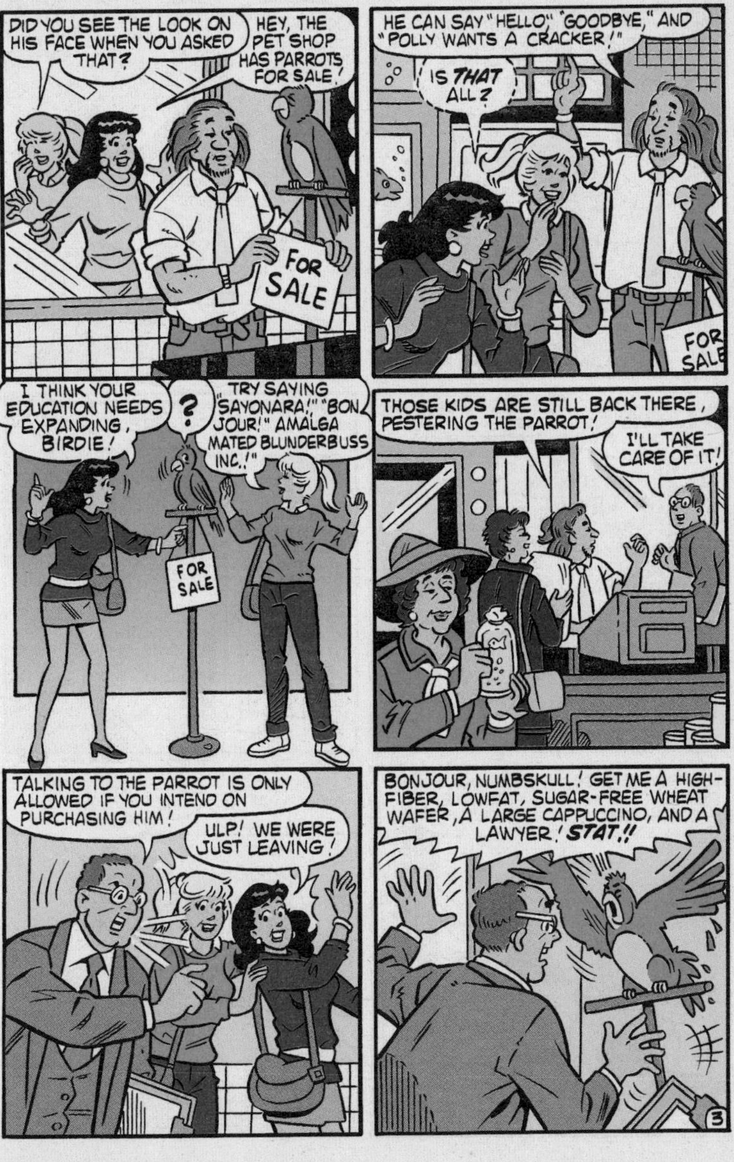

DID YOU SEE THE LOOK ON HIS FACE WHEN YOU ASKED THAT?
HEY, THE PET SHOP HAS PARROTS FOR SALE!
FOR SALE
HE CAN SAY "HELLO," "GOODBYE," AND "POLLY WANTS A CRACKER!"
IS THAT ALL?
FOR SALE
I THINK YOUR EDUCATION NEEDS EXPANDING, BIRDIE!
?
TRY SAYING "SAYONARA!," "BONJOUR!," "AMALGAMATED BLUNDERBUSS INC.!"
FOR SALE
THOSE KIDS ARE STILL BACK THERE, PESTERING THE PARROT!
I'LL TAKE CARE OF IT!
TALKING TO THE PARROT IS ONLY ALLOWED IF YOU INTEND ON PURCHASING HIM!
ULP! WE WERE JUST LEAVING!
BONJOUR, NUMBSKULL! GET ME A HIGH-FIBER, LOWFAT, SUGAR-FREE WHEAT WAFER, A LARGE CAPPUCCINO, AND A LAWYER! STAT!!
3

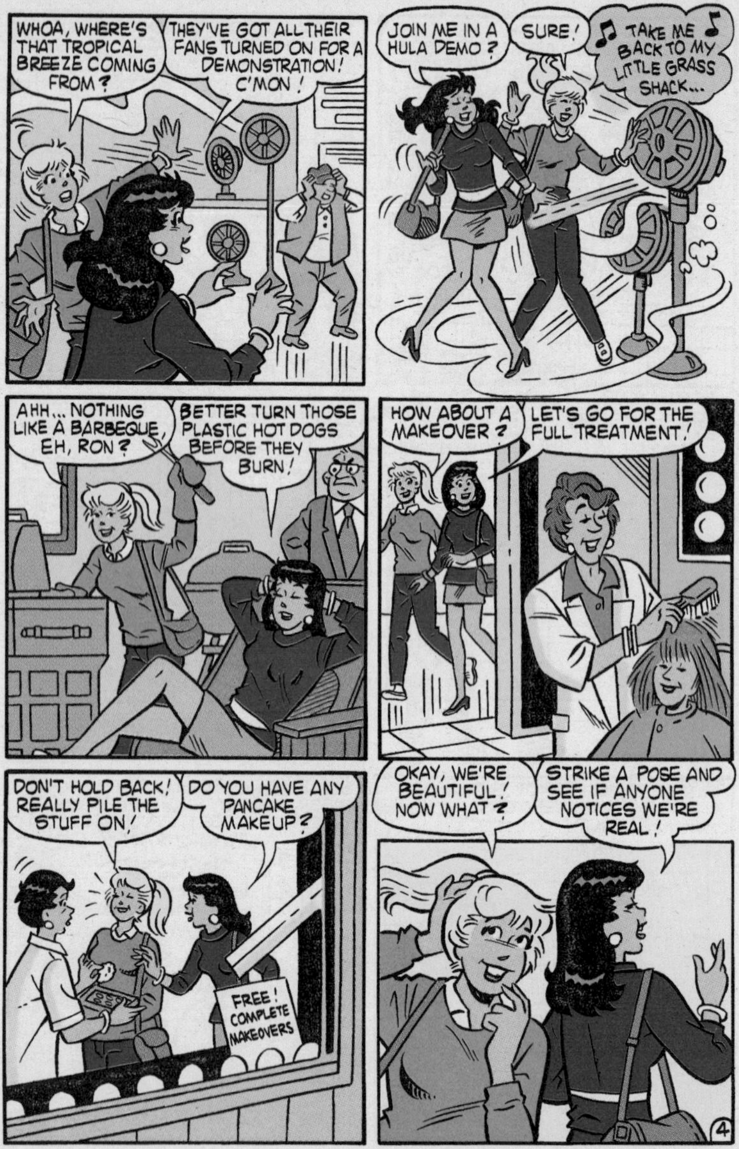
WHOA, WHERE'S THAT TROPICAL BREEZE COMING FROM?
THEY'VE GOT ALL THEIR FANS TURNED ON FOR A DEMONSTRATION! C'MON!
JOIN ME IN A HULA DEMO?
SURE!
TAKE ME BACK TO MY LITTLE GRASS SHACK...
AHH... NOTHING LIKE A BARBEQUE, EH, RON?
BETTER TURN THOSE PLASTIC HOT DOGS BEFORE THEY BURN!
HOW ABOUT A MAKEOVER?
LET'S GO FOR THE FULL TREATMENT!
DON'T HOLD BACK! REALLY PILE THE STUFF ON!
DO YOU HAVE ANY PANCAKE MAKEUP?
FREE! COMPLETE MAKEOVERS
OKAY, WE'RE BEAUTIFUL! NOW WHAT?
STRIKE A POSE AND SEE IF ANYONE NOTICES WE'RE REAL!
4

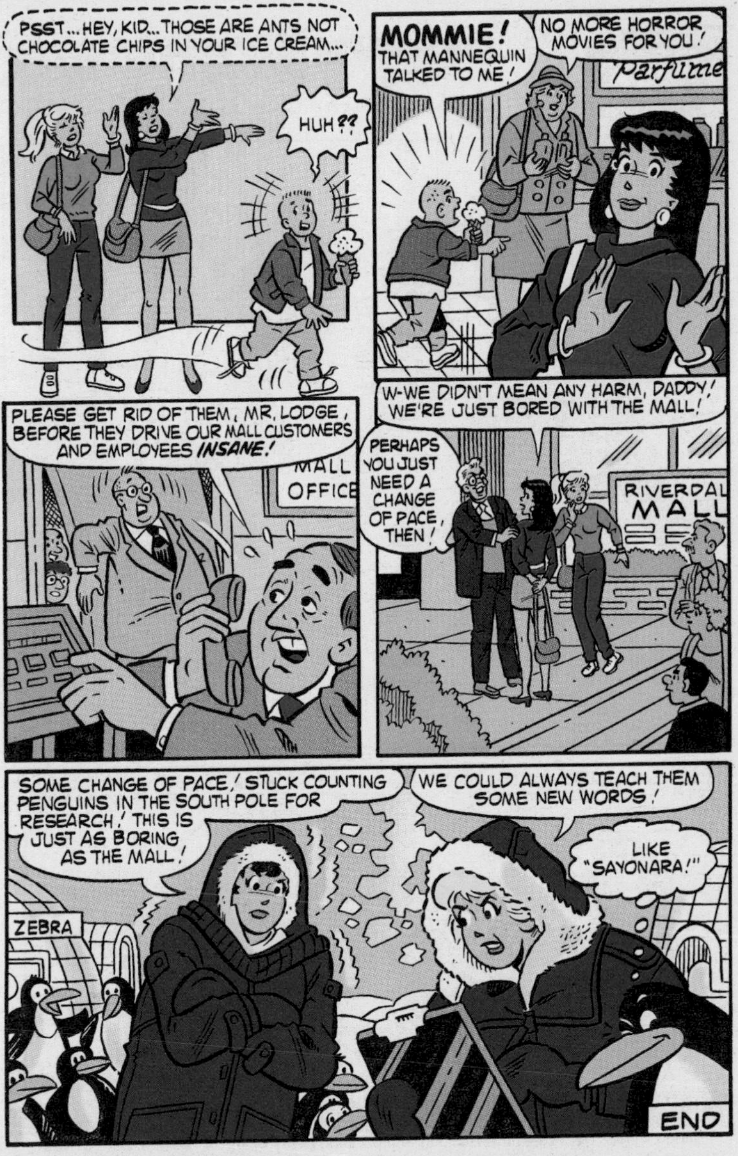
PSST... HEY, KID... THOSE ARE ANTS NOT CHOCOLATE CHIPS IN YOUR ICE CREAM...
HUH??
MOMMIE! THAT MANNEQUIN TALKED TO ME!
NO MORE HORROR MOVIES FOR YOU!
Parfume
PLEASE GET RID OF THEM, MR. LODGE, BEFORE THEY DRIVE OUR MALL CUSTOMERS AND EMPLOYEES INSANE!
MALL OFFICE
W-WE DIDN'T MEAN ANY HARM, DADDY! WE'RE JUST BORED WITH THE MALL!
PERHAPS YOU JUST NEED A CHANGE OF PACE, THEN!
RIVERDAL MALL
SOME CHANGE OF PACE! STUCK COUNTING PENGUINS IN THE SOUTH POLE FOR RESEARCH! THIS IS JUST AS BORING AS THE MALL!
WE COULD ALWAYS TEACH THEM SOME NEW WORDS!
LIKE "SAYONARA!"
ZEBRA
END

Betty and Veronica in "Stormy Weatherbee"

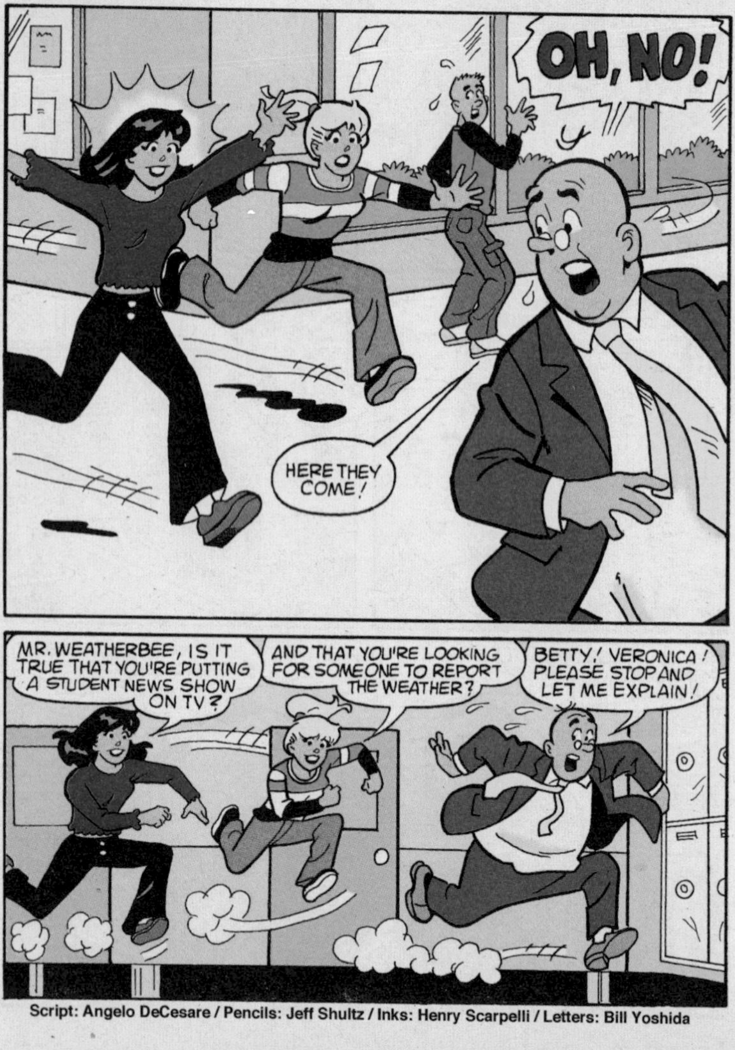

OH, NO!
HERE THEY COME!
MR. WEATHERBEE, IS IT TRUE THAT YOU'RE PUTTING A STUDENT NEWS SHOW ON TV?
AND THAT YOU'RE LOOKING FOR SOMEONE TO REPORT THE WEATHER?
BETTY! VERONICA! PLEASE STOP AND LET ME EXPLAIN!

Script: Angelo DeCesare / Pencils: Jeff Shultz / Inks: Henry Scarpelli / Letters: Bill Yoshida

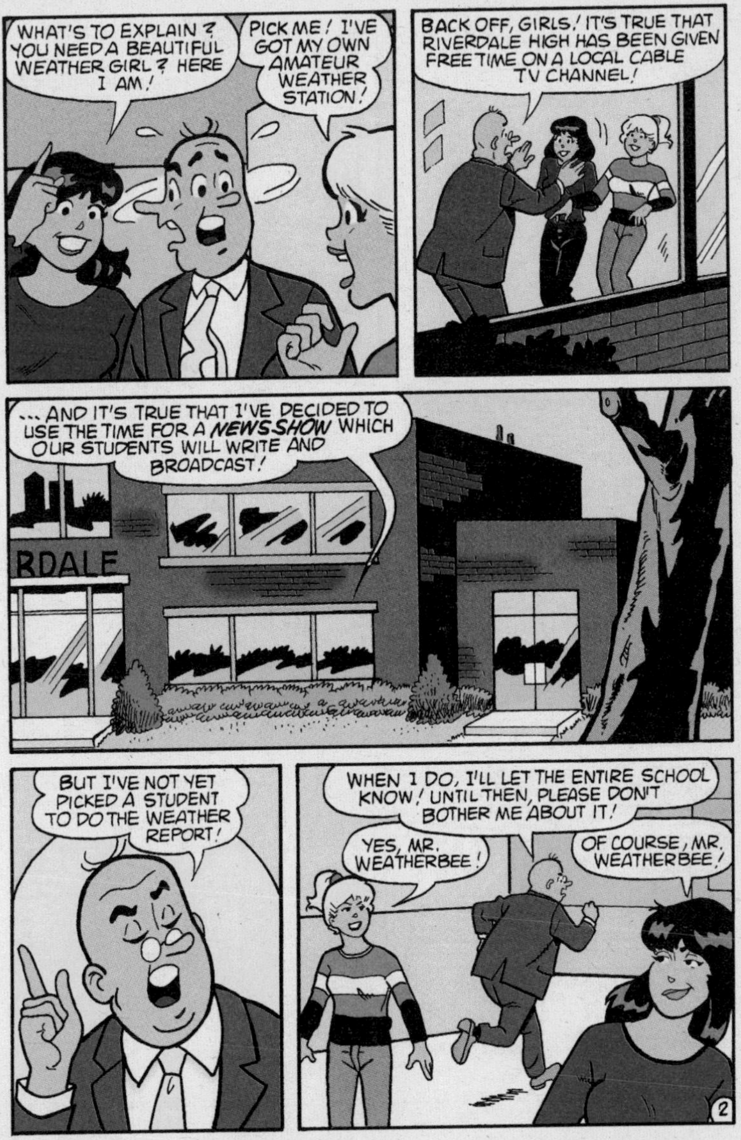
WHAT'S TO EXPLAIN ? YOU NEED A BEAUTIFUL WEATHER GIRL ? HERE I AM!
PICK ME! I'VE GOT MY OWN AMATEUR WEATHER STATION!
BACK OFF, GIRLS! IT'S TRUE THAT RIVERDALE HIGH HAS BEEN GIVEN FREE TIME ON A LOCAL CABLE TV CHANNEL!
... AND IT'S TRUE THAT I'VE DECIDED TO USE THE TIME FOR A ***NEWS SHOW*** WHICH OUR STUDENTS WILL WRITE AND BROADCAST!
RDALE
BUT I'VE NOT YET PICKED A STUDENT TO DO THE WEATHER REPORT!
WHEN I DO, I'LL LET THE ENTIRE SCHOOL KNOW! UNTIL THEN, PLEASE DON'T BOTHER ME ABOUT IT!
YES, MR. WEATHERBEE!
OF COURSE, MR. WEATHERBEE!
2

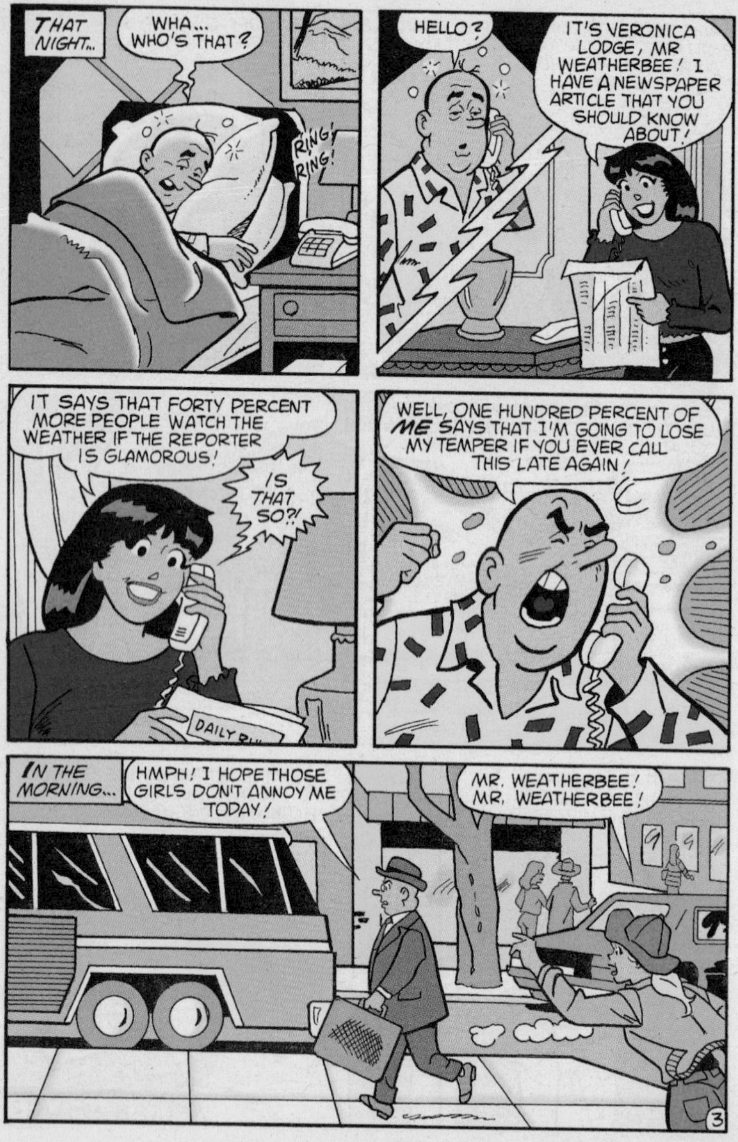
THAT NIGHT...
WHA... WHO'S THAT?
RING! RING!
HELLO?
IT'S VERONICA LODGE, MR WEATHERBEE! I HAVE A NEWSPAPER ARTICLE THAT YOU SHOULD KNOW ABOUT!
IT SAYS THAT FORTY PERCENT MORE PEOPLE WATCH THE WEATHER IF THE REPORTER IS GLAMOROUS!
IS THAT SO?!
WELL, ONE HUNDRED PERCENT OF ME SAYS THAT I'M GOING TO LOSE MY TEMPER IF YOU EVER CALL THIS LATE AGAIN!
IN THE MORNING...
HMPH! I HOPE THOSE GIRLS DON'T ANNOY ME TODAY!
MR. WEATHERBEE! MR. WEATHERBEE!

Betty: I SEE YOU DON'T HAVE AN UMBRELLA, SO I THINK YOU SHOULD TAKE THIS ONE!

Man: WHY IS THAT, BETTY?

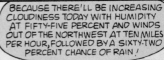

Betty: BECAUSE THERE'LL BE INCREASING CLOUDINESS TODAY WITH HUMIDITY AT FIFTY-FIVE PERCENT AND WINDS OUT OF THE NORTHWEST AT TEN MILES PER HOUR, FOLLOWED BY A SIXTY-TWO PERCENT CHANCE OF RAIN!

Man: YOU'RE WASTING YOUR TIME, BETTY! VIEWERS WANT BEAUTY, NOT *BOREDOM!*

Betty: OH, YEAH? WELL THERE'S NOTHING MORE BORING THAN WATCHING A MANNEQUIN READ THE WEATHER!

BUS

Veronica: I DON'T HAVE TO READ THE WEATHER! PEOPLE WILL WATCH ME IF I JUST *STAND* THERE!

Betty: YEAH, EVERYONE LIKES A GOOD LAUGH!

Mr. Weatherbee: STOP! I GIVE UP, GIRLS! SINCE YOU TWO ARE DETERMINED TO REPORT THE WEATHER, I'LL LET YOU *BOTH* DO IT!

Girl: BOTH OF US?

Girl: BUT, MR. WEATHERBEE...

Mr. Weatherbee: AND YOU HAD BETTER GET ALONG, OR I'LL GIVE THE JOB TO THE *SCHOOL MASCOT!!*

4

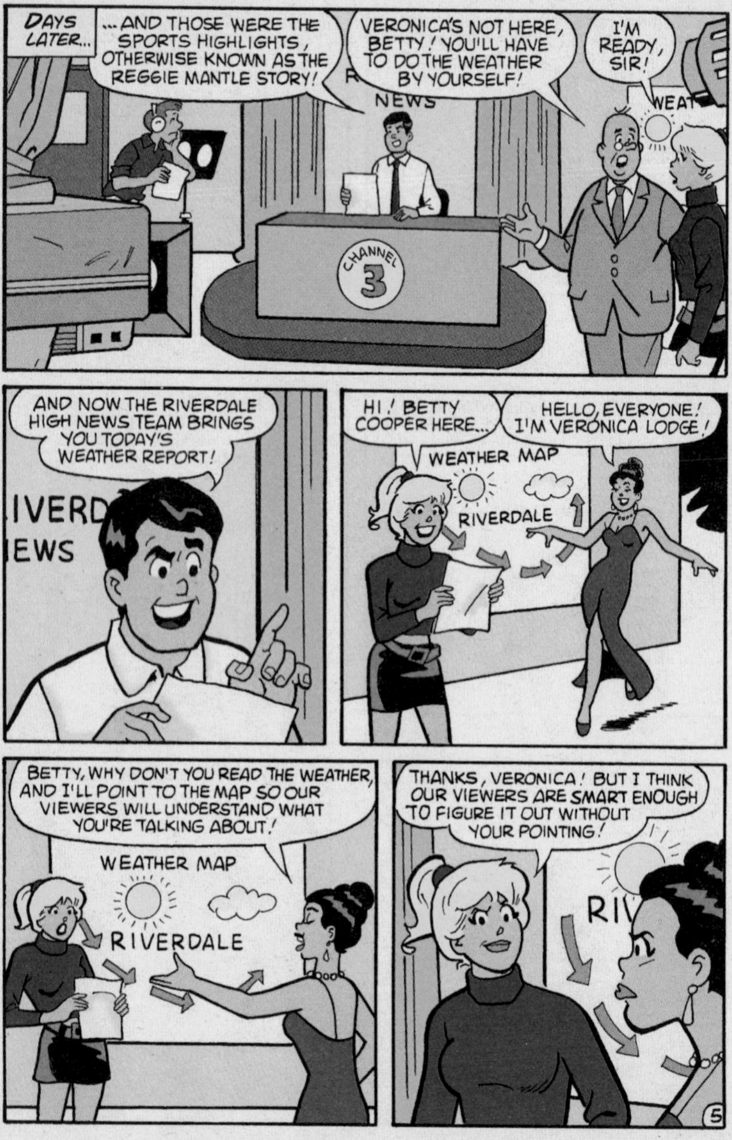
DAYS LATER...
...AND THOSE WERE THE SPORTS HIGHLIGHTS, OTHERWISE KNOWN AS THE REGGIE MANTLE STORY!
VERONICA'S NOT HERE, BETTY! YOU'LL HAVE TO DO THE WEATHER BY YOURSELF!
I'M READY, SIR!
NEWS
CHANNEL 3
AND NOW THE RIVERDALE HIGH NEWS TEAM BRINGS YOU TODAY'S WEATHER REPORT!
HI! BETTY COOPER HERE...
HELLO, EVERYONE! I'M VERONICA LODGE!
WEATHER MAP
RIVERDALE
BETTY, WHY DON'T YOU READ THE WEATHER, AND I'LL POINT TO THE MAP SO OUR VIEWERS WILL UNDERSTAND WHAT YOU'RE TALKING ABOUT!
WEATHER MAP
RIVERDALE
THANKS, VERONICA! BUT I THINK OUR VIEWERS ARE SMART ENOUGH TO FIGURE IT OUT WITHOUT YOUR POINTING!

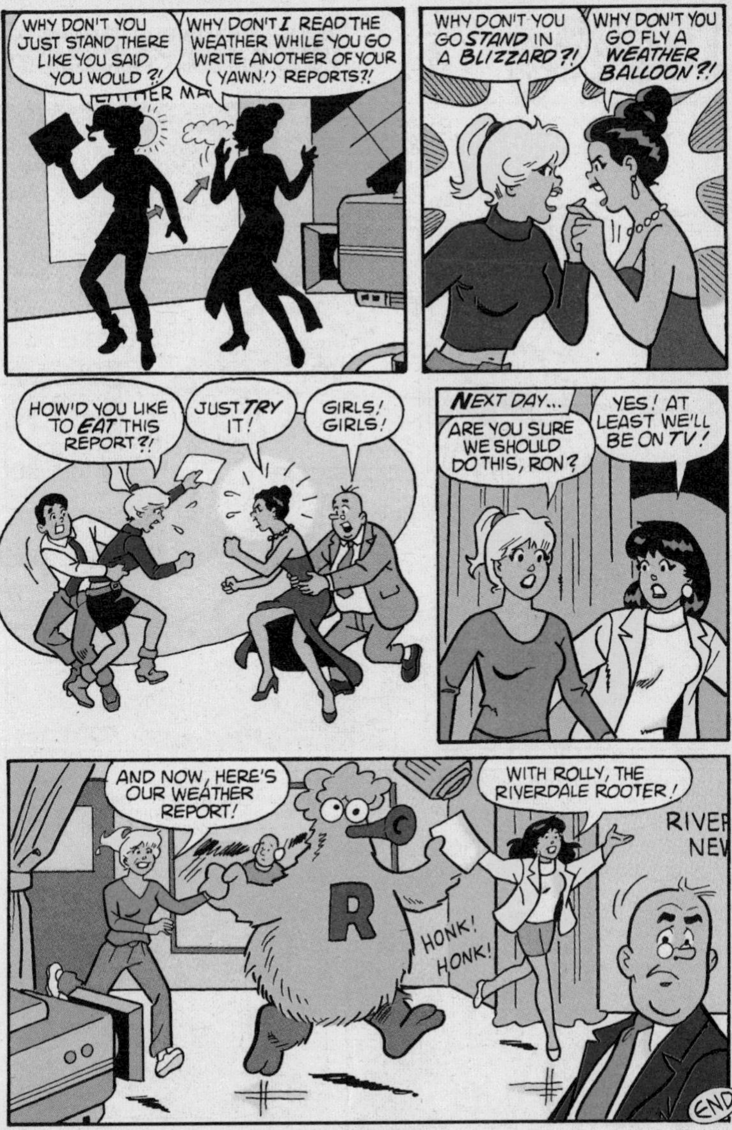
WHY DON'T YOU JUST STAND THERE LIKE YOU SAID YOU WOULD ?!
WHY DON'T I READ THE WEATHER WHILE YOU GO WRITE ANOTHER OF YOUR (YAWN!) REPORTS?!
WHY DON'T YOU GO STAND IN A BLIZZARD ?!
WHY DON'T YOU GO FLY A WEATHER BALLOON ?!
HOW'D YOU LIKE TO EAT THIS REPORT ?!
JUST TRY IT!
GIRLS! GIRLS!
NEXT DAY...
ARE YOU SURE WE SHOULD DO THIS, RON ?
YES! AT LEAST WE'LL BE ON TV!
AND NOW, HERE'S OUR WEATHER REPORT!
WITH ROLLY, THE RIVERDALE ROOTER!
R
HONK! HONK!
END

Betty in "No Comparison"

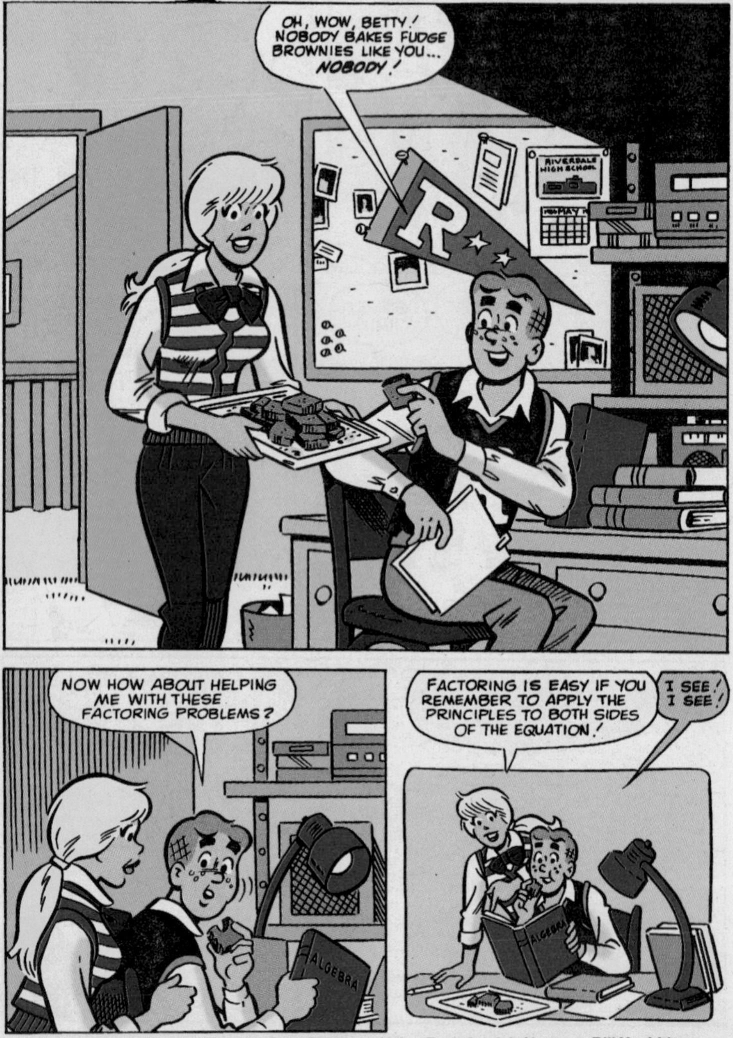
OH, WOW, BETTY! NOBODY BAKES FUDGE BROWNIES LIKE YOU... NOBODY!
R
RIVERDALE HIGH SCHOOL
NOW HOW ABOUT HELPING ME WITH THESE FACTORING PROBLEMS?
ALGEBRA
FACTORING IS EASY IF YOU REMEMBER TO APPLY THE PRINCIPLES TO BOTH SIDES OF THE EQUATION!
I SEE! I SEE!
ALGEBRA

Script: George Gladir / Pencils: Stan Goldberg / Inks: Rudy Lapick / Letters: Bill Yoshida

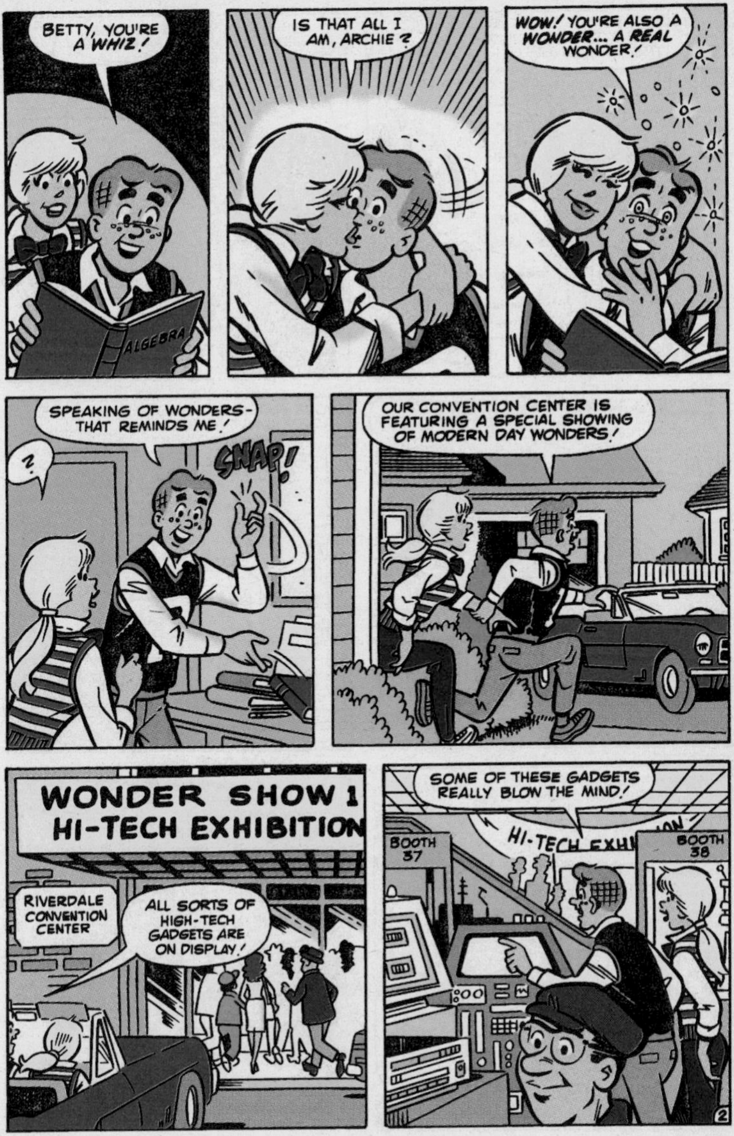
BETTY, YOU'RE A WHIZ!
ALGEBRA
IS THAT ALL I AM, ARCHIE ?
WOW! YOU'RE ALSO A WONDER... A REAL WONDER!
SPEAKING OF WONDERS- THAT REMINDS ME!
?
SNAP!
OUR CONVENTION CENTER IS FEATURING A SPECIAL SHOWING OF MODERN DAY WONDERS!
WONDER SHOW 1
HI-TECH EXHIBITION
RIVERDALE CONVENTION CENTER
ALL SORTS OF HIGH-TECH GADGETS ARE ON DISPLAY!
SOME OF THESE GADGETS REALLY BLOW THE MIND!
BOOTH 37
BOOTH 38
2

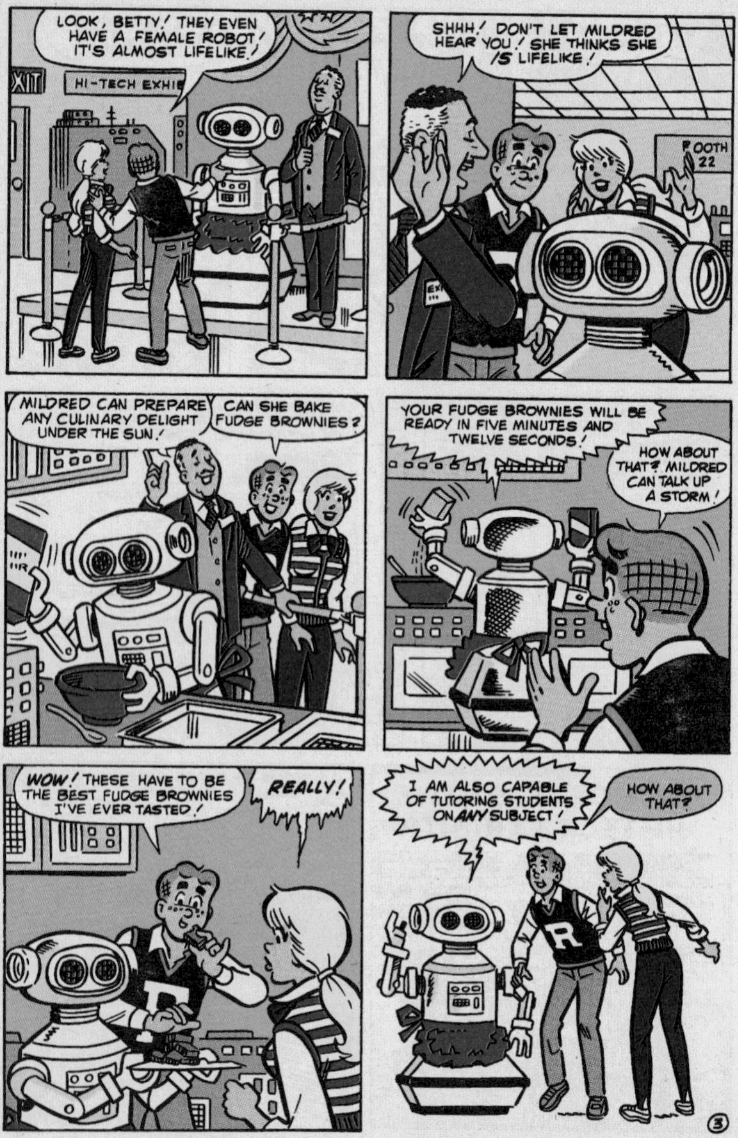
LOOK, BETTY! THEY EVEN HAVE A FEMALE ROBOT! IT'S ALMOST LIFELIKE!
HI-TECH EXHIB
SHHH! DON'T LET MILDRED HEAR YOU! SHE THINKS SHE IS LIFELIKE!
BOOTH 22
MILDRED CAN PREPARE ANY CULINARY DELIGHT UNDER THE SUN!
CAN SHE BAKE FUDGE BROWNIES?
YOUR FUDGE BROWNIES WILL BE READY IN FIVE MINUTES AND TWELVE SECONDS!
HOW ABOUT THAT? MILDRED CAN TALK UP A STORM!
WOW! THESE HAVE TO BE THE BEST FUDGE BROWNIES I'VE EVER TASTED!
REALLY!
I AM ALSO CAPABLE OF TUTORING STUDENTS ON ANY SUBJECT!
HOW ABOUT THAT?
3

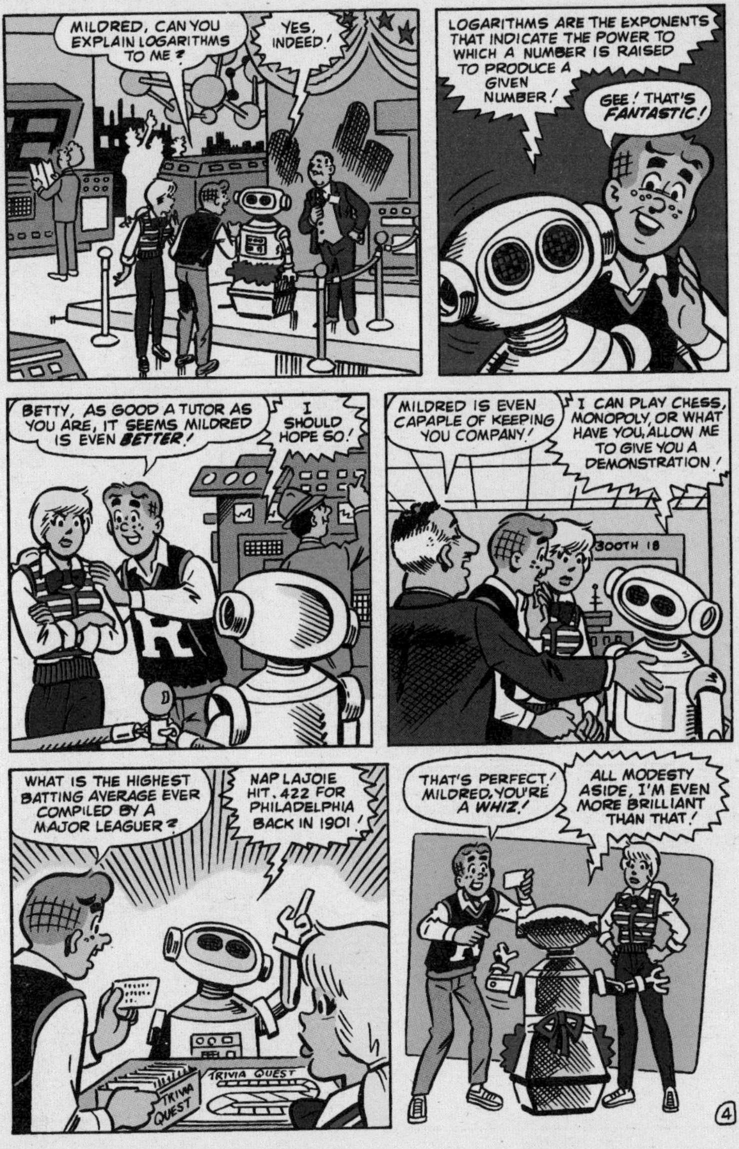
MILDRED, CAN YOU EXPLAIN LOGARITHMS TO ME?
YES, INDEED!
LOGARITHMS ARE THE EXPONENTS THAT INDICATE THE POWER TO WHICH A NUMBER IS RAISED TO PRODUCE A GIVEN NUMBER!
GEE! THAT'S FANTASTIC!
BETTY, AS GOOD A TUTOR AS YOU ARE, IT SEEMS MILDRED IS EVEN BETTER!
I SHOULD HOPE SO!
MILDRED IS EVEN CAPAPLE OF KEEPING YOU COMPANY!
I CAN PLAY CHESS, MONOPOLY, OR WHAT HAVE YOU, ALLOW ME TO GIVE YOU A DEMONSTRATION!
BOOTH 18
WHAT IS THE HIGHEST BATTING AVERAGE EVER COMPILED BY A MAJOR LEAGUER?
NAP LAJOIE HIT .422 FOR PHILADELPHIA BACK IN 1901!
TRIVIA QUEST
TRIVIA QUEST
THAT'S PERFECT! MILDRED, YOU'RE A WHIZ!
ALL MODESTY ASIDE, I'M EVEN MORE BRILLIANT THAN THAT!

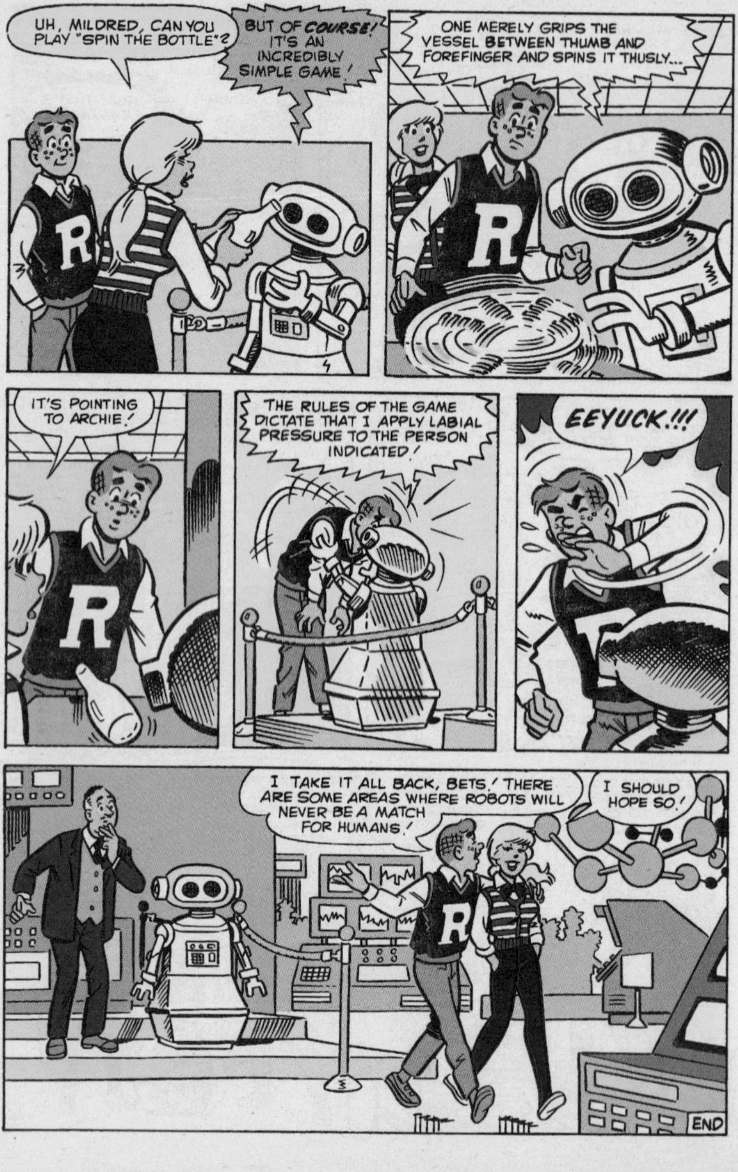

UH, MILDRED, CAN YOU PLAY "SPIN THE BOTTLE"?
BUT OF COURSE! IT'S AN INCREDIBLY SIMPLE GAME!
ONE MERELY GRIPS THE VESSEL BETWEEN THUMB AND FOREFINGER AND SPINS IT THUSLY...
IT'S POINTING TO ARCHIE!
THE RULES OF THE GAME DICTATE THAT I APPLY LABIAL PRESSURE TO THE PERSON INDICATED!
EEYUCK.!!!
I TAKE IT ALL BACK, BETS! THERE ARE SOME AREAS WHERE ROBOTS WILL NEVER BE A MATCH FOR HUMANS!
I SHOULD HOPE SO!
END

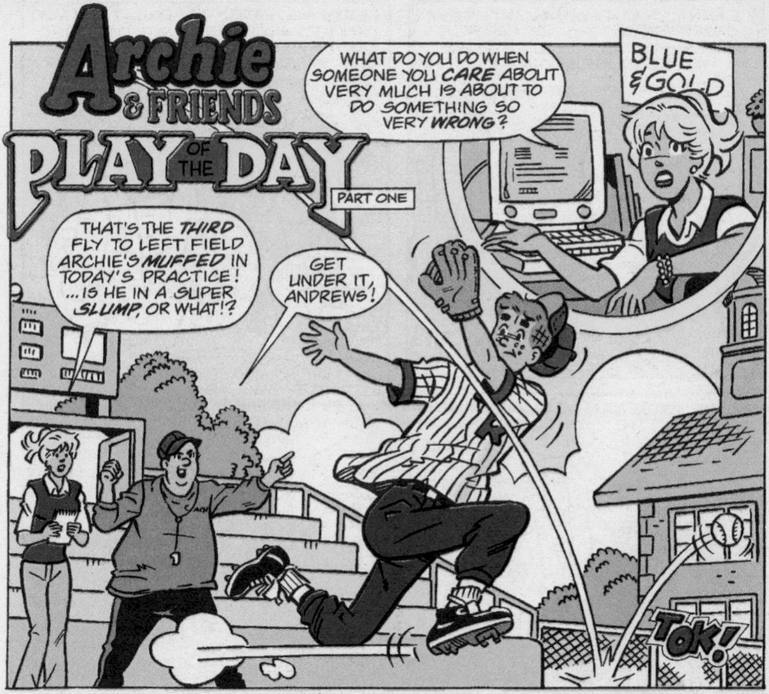
Archie & FRIENDS
PLAY OF THE DAY
PART ONE
WHAT DO YOU DO WHEN SOMEONE YOU CARE ABOUT VERY MUCH IS ABOUT TO DO SOMETHING SO VERY WRONG?
BLUE & GOLD
THAT'S THE THIRD FLY TO LEFT FIELD ARCHIE'S MUFFED IN TODAY'S PRACTICE! ...IS HE IN A SUPER SLUMP, OR WHAT!?
GET UNDER IT, ANDREWS!
TOK!

Script: Bob Bolling / Pencils: Rex Lindsey / Inks: Rudy Lapick / Letters: Vickie Williams

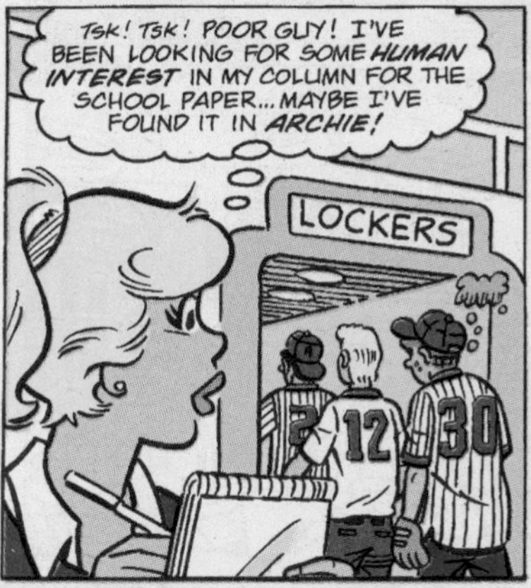
TSK! TSK! POOR GUY! I'VE BEEN LOOKING FOR SOME HUMAN INTEREST IN MY COLUMN FOR THE SCHOOL PAPER... MAYBE I'VE FOUND IT IN ARCHIE!
LOCKERS
12
30

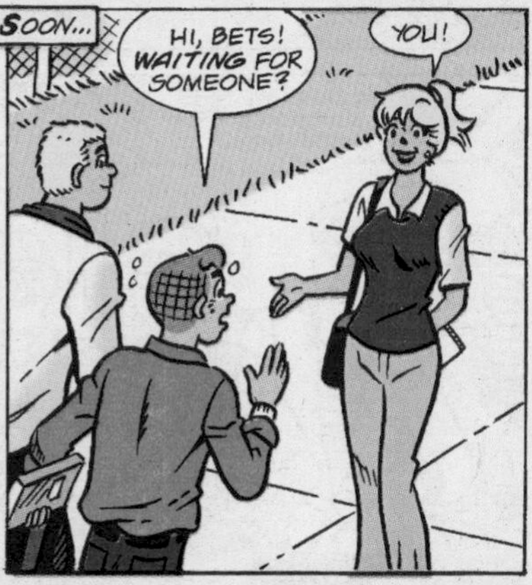
SOON...
HI, BETS! WAITING FOR SOMEONE?
YOU!

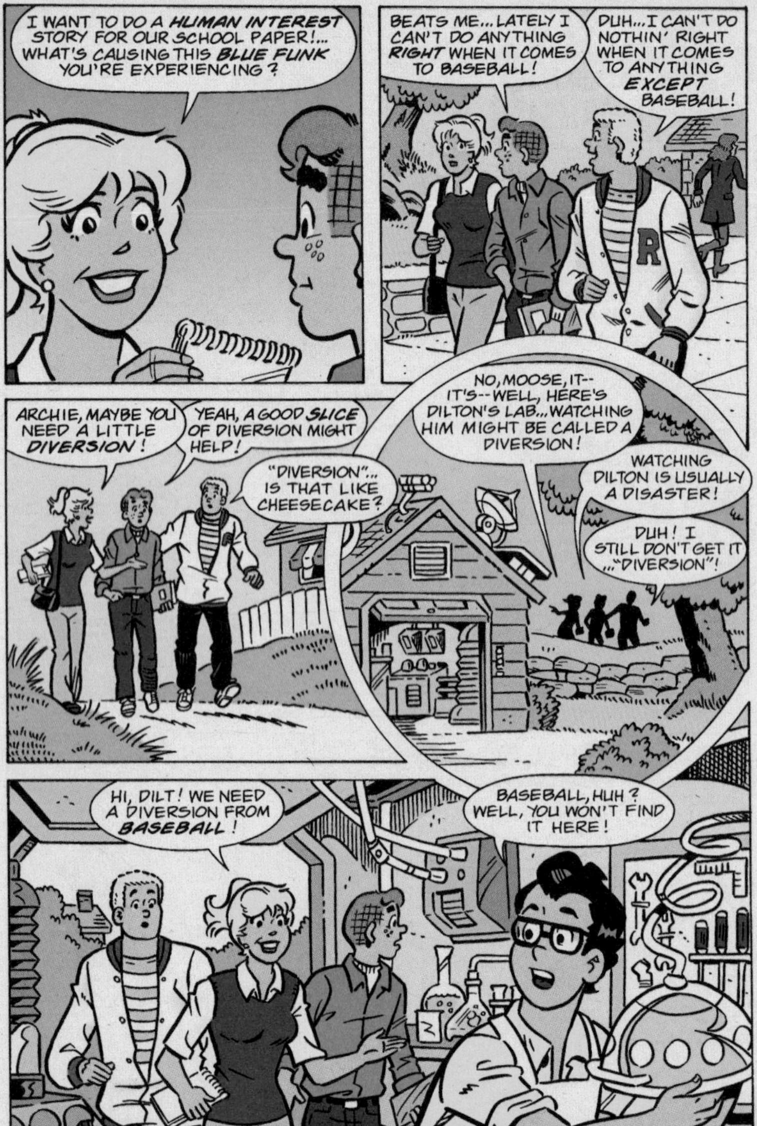
I WANT TO DO A HUMAN INTEREST STORY FOR OUR SCHOOL PAPER!... WHAT'S CAUSING THIS BLUE FUNK YOU'RE EXPERIENCING?
BEATS ME... LATELY I CAN'T DO ANYTHING RIGHT WHEN IT COMES TO BASEBALL!
DUH... I CAN'T DO NOTHIN' RIGHT WHEN IT COMES TO ANYTHING EXCEPT BASEBALL!
ARCHIE, MAYBE YOU NEED A LITTLE DIVERSION!
YEAH, A GOOD SLICE OF DIVERSION MIGHT HELP!
"DIVERSION"... IS THAT LIKE CHEESECAKE?
NO, MOOSE, IT-- IT'S--WELL, HERE'S DILTON'S LAB... WATCHING HIM MIGHT BE CALLED A DIVERSION!
WATCHING DILTON IS USUALLY A DISASTER!
DUH! I STILL DON'T GET IT ..."DIVERSION"!
HI, DILT! WE NEED A DIVERSION FROM BASEBALL!
BASEBALL, HUH? WELL, YOU WON'T FIND IT HERE!

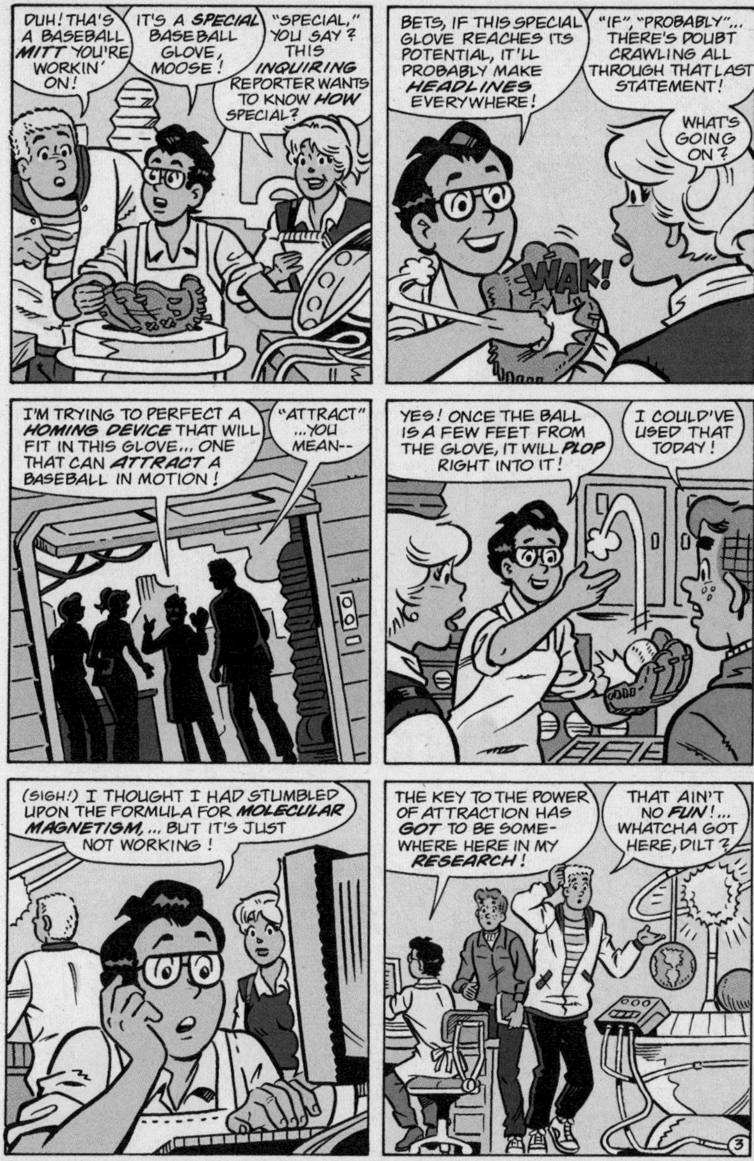
DUH! THA'S A BASEBALL MITT YOU'RE WORKIN' ON!
IT'S A SPECIAL BASEBALL GLOVE, MOOSE!
"SPECIAL," YOU SAY? THIS INQUIRING REPORTER WANTS TO KNOW HOW SPECIAL?
BETS, IF THIS SPECIAL GLOVE REACHES ITS POTENTIAL, IT'LL PROBABLY MAKE HEADLINES EVERYWHERE!
"IF", "PROBABLY"... THERE'S DOUBT CRAWLING ALL THROUGH THAT LAST STATEMENT!
WHAT'S GOING ON?
WAK!
I'M TRYING TO PERFECT A HOMING DEVICE THAT WILL FIT IN THIS GLOVE... ONE THAT CAN ATTRACT A BASEBALL IN MOTION!
"ATTRACT" ...YOU MEAN--
YES! ONCE THE BALL IS A FEW FEET FROM THE GLOVE, IT WILL PLOP RIGHT INTO IT!
I COULD'VE USED THAT TODAY!
(SIGH!) I THOUGHT I HAD STUMBLED UPON THE FORMULA FOR MOLECULAR MAGNETISM, ... BUT IT'S JUST NOT WORKING!
THE KEY TO THE POWER OF ATTRACTION HAS GOT TO BE SOMEWHERE HERE IN MY RESEARCH!
THAT AIN'T NO FUN!... WHATCHA GOT HERE, DILT?
3

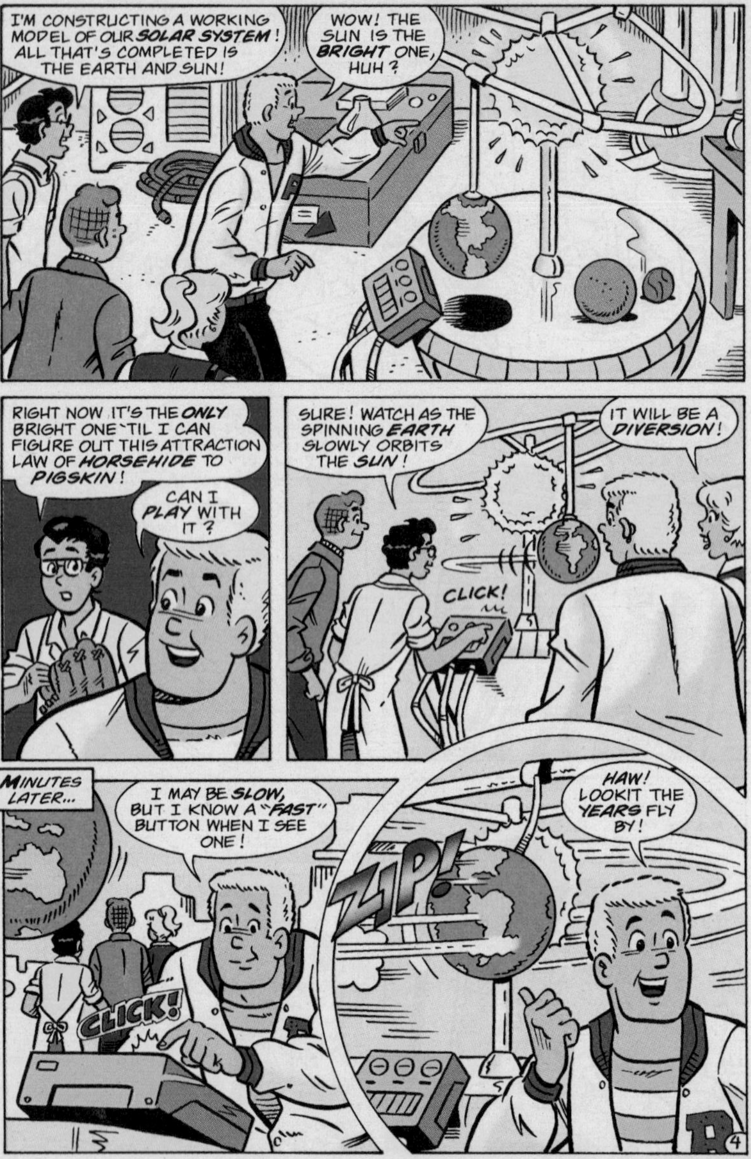

I'M CONSTRUCTING A WORKING MODEL OF OUR SOLAR SYSTEM! ALL THAT'S COMPLETED IS THE EARTH AND SUN!
WOW! THE SUN IS THE BRIGHT ONE, HUH?
RIGHT NOW IT'S THE ONLY BRIGHT ONE 'TIL I CAN FIGURE OUT THIS ATTRACTION LAW OF HORSEHIDE TO PIGSKIN!
CAN I PLAY WITH IT?
SURE! WATCH AS THE SPINNING EARTH SLOWLY ORBITS THE SUN!
IT WILL BE A DIVERSION!
CLICK!
MINUTES LATER...
I MAY BE SLOW, BUT I KNOW A "FAST" BUTTON WHEN I SEE ONE!
CLICK!
ZIP!
HAW! LOOKIT THE YEARS FLY BY!
4

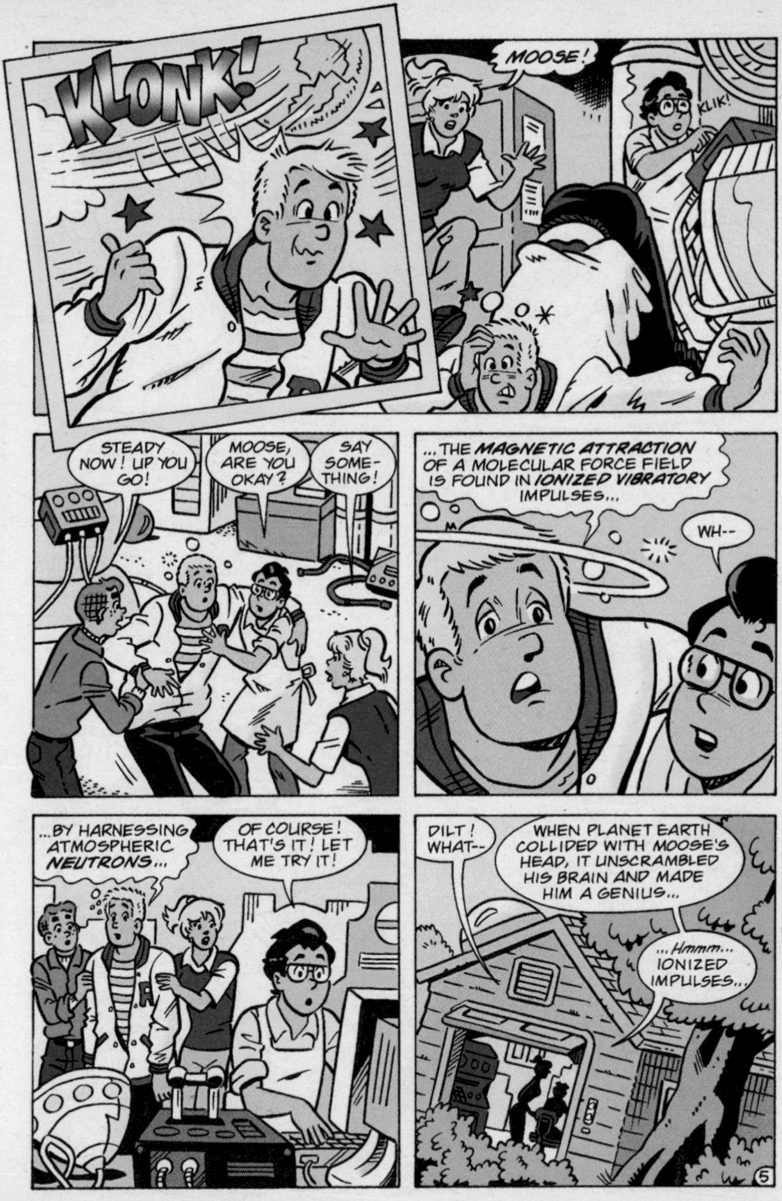
KLONK!
MOOSE!
KLIK!
STEADY NOW! UP YOU GO!
MOOSE, ARE YOU OKAY?
SAY SOME-THING!
...THE MAGNETIC ATTRACTION OF A MOLECULAR FORCE FIELD IS FOUND IN IONIZED VIBRATORY IMPULSES...
WH--
...BY HARNESSING ATMOSPHERIC NEUTRONS...
OF COURSE! THAT'S IT! LET ME TRY IT!
DILT! WHAT--
WHEN PLANET EARTH COLLIDED WITH MOOSE'S HEAD, IT UNSCRAMBLED HIS BRAIN AND MADE HIM A GENIUS...
...Hmmm... IONIZED IMPULSES...

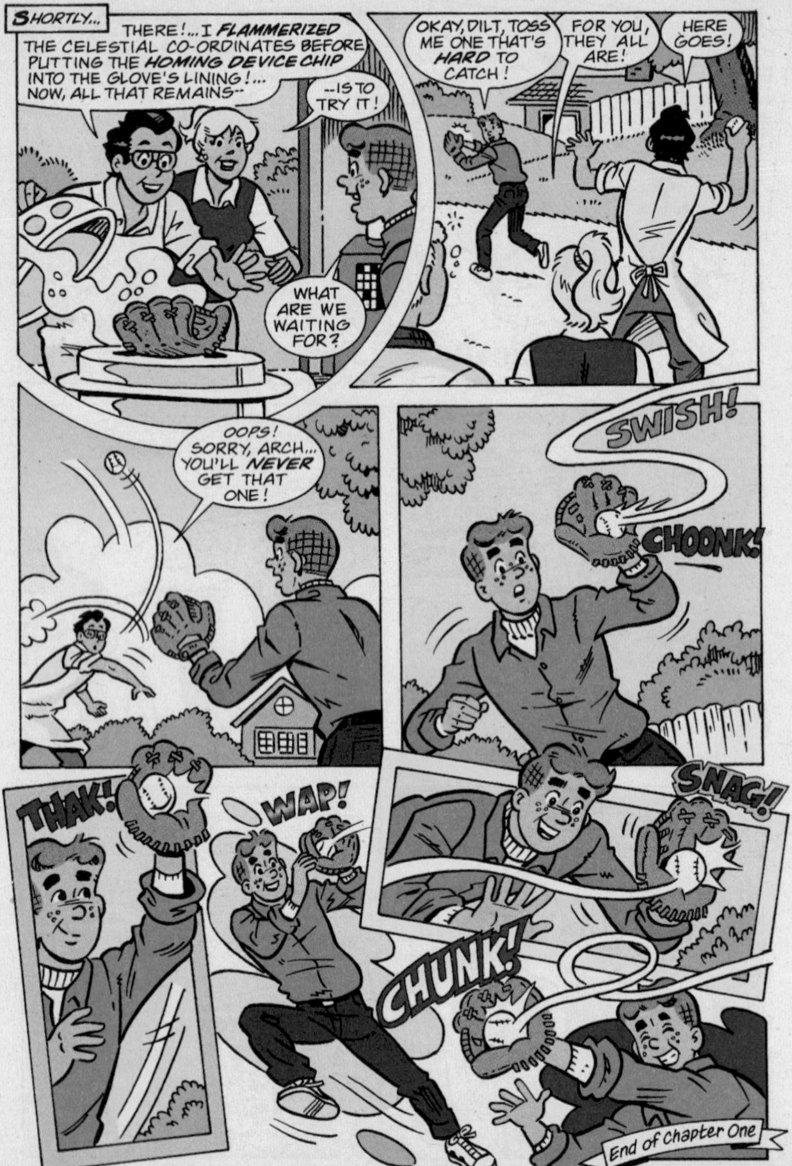
SHORTLY...
THERE!... I FLAMMERIZED THE CELESTIAL CO-ORDINATES BEFORE PUTTING THE HOMING DEVICE CHIP INTO THE GLOVE'S LINING!... NOW, ALL THAT REMAINS--
--IS TO TRY IT!
WHAT ARE WE WAITING FOR?
OKAY, DILT, TOSS ME ONE THAT'S HARD TO CATCH!
FOR YOU, THEY ALL ARE!
HERE GOES!
OOPS! SORRY, ARCH... YOU'LL NEVER GET THAT ONE!
SWISH!
CHOONK!
THAK!
WAP!
SNAG!
CHUNK!
End of Chapter One

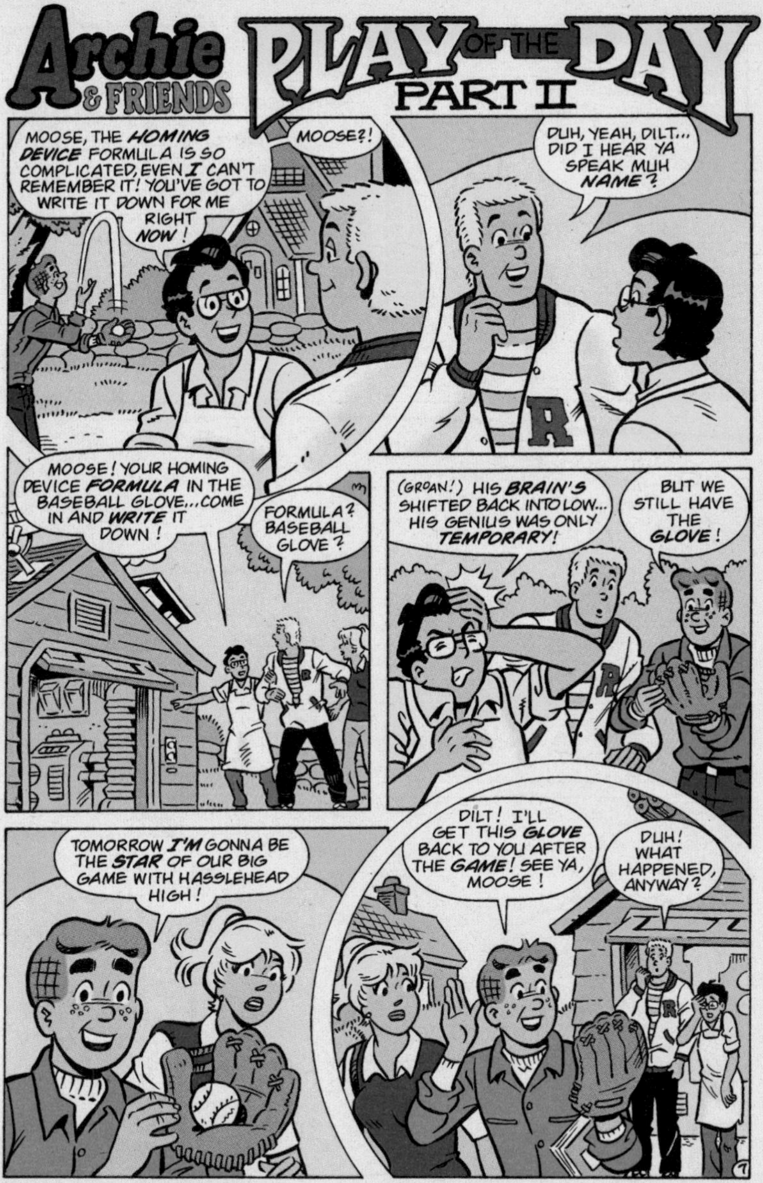

Archie & FRIENDS
PLAY OF THE DAY
PART II
MOOSE, THE HOMING DEVICE FORMULA IS SO COMPLICATED, EVEN I CAN'T REMEMBER IT! YOU'VE GOT TO WRITE IT DOWN FOR ME RIGHT NOW!
MOOSE?!
DUH, YEAH, DILT... DID I HEAR YA SPEAK MUH NAME?
MOOSE! YOUR HOMING DEVICE FORMULA IN THE BASEBALL GLOVE... COME IN AND WRITE IT DOWN!
FORMULA? BASEBALL GLOVE?
(GROAN!) HIS BRAIN'S SHIFTED BACK INTO LOW... HIS GENIUS WAS ONLY TEMPORARY!
BUT WE STILL HAVE THE GLOVE!
TOMORROW I'M GONNA BE THE STAR OF OUR BIG GAME WITH HASSLEHEAD HIGH!
DILT! I'LL GET THIS GLOVE BACK TO YOU AFTER THE GAME! SEE YA, MOOSE!
DUH! WHAT HAPPENED, ANYWAY?
7

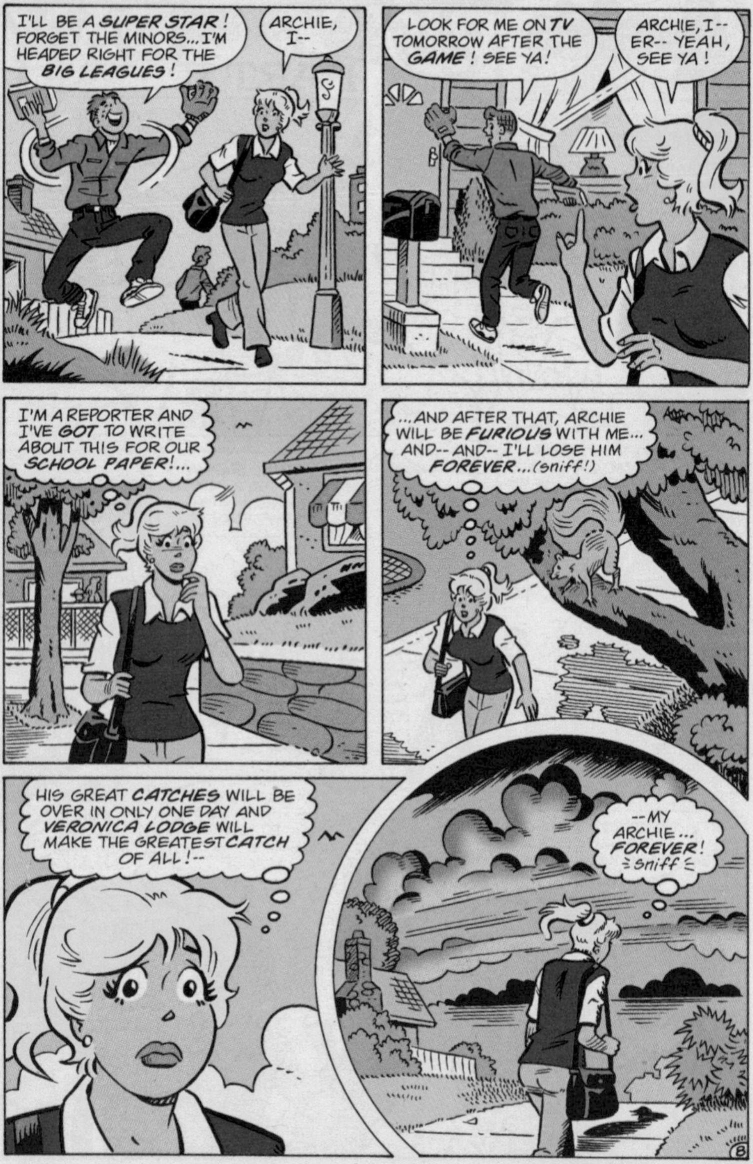

I'LL BE A SUPER STAR! FORGET THE MINORS... I'M HEADED RIGHT FOR THE BIG LEAGUES!
ARCHIE, I--
LOOK FOR ME ON TV TOMORROW AFTER THE GAME! SEE YA!
ARCHIE, I-- ER-- YEAH, SEE YA!
I'M A REPORTER AND I'VE GOT TO WRITE ABOUT THIS FOR OUR SCHOOL PAPER!...
...AND AFTER THAT, ARCHIE WILL BE FURIOUS WITH ME... AND-- AND-- I'LL LOSE HIM FOREVER... (sniff!)
HIS GREAT CATCHES WILL BE OVER IN ONLY ONE DAY AND VERONICA LODGE WILL MAKE THE GREATEST CATCH OF ALL!--
--MY ARCHIE... FOREVER! sniff
8

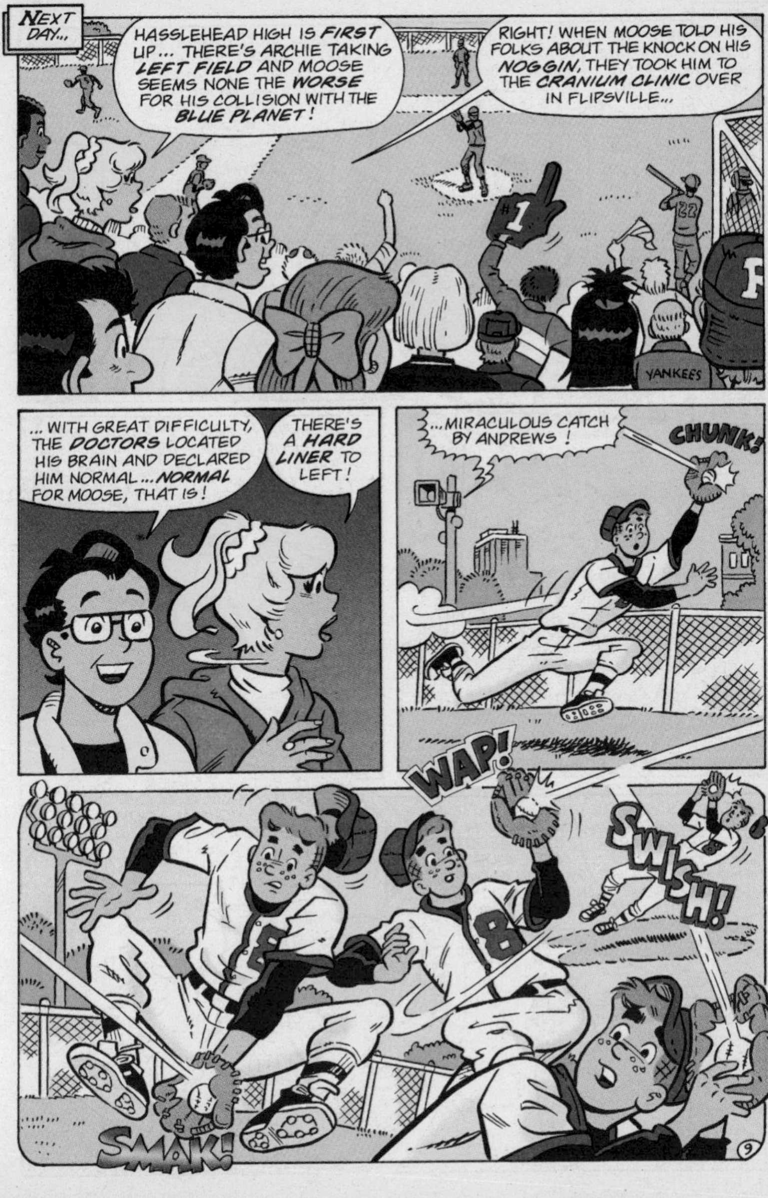

NEXT DAY...
HASSLEHEAD HIGH IS FIRST UP... THERE'S ARCHIE TAKING LEFT FIELD AND MOOSE SEEMS NONE THE WORSE FOR HIS COLLISION WITH THE BLUE PLANET!
RIGHT! WHEN MOOSE TOLD HIS FOLKS ABOUT THE KNOCK ON HIS NOGGIN, THEY TOOK HIM TO THE CRANIUM CLINIC OVER IN FLIPSVILLE...
#1
YANKEES
...WITH GREAT DIFFICULTY, THE DOCTORS LOCATED HIS BRAIN AND DECLARED HIM NORMAL... NORMAL FOR MOOSE, THAT IS!
THERE'S A HARD LINER TO LEFT!
...MIRACULOUS CATCH BY ANDREWS!
CHUNK!
WAP!
SWISH!
SMAK!

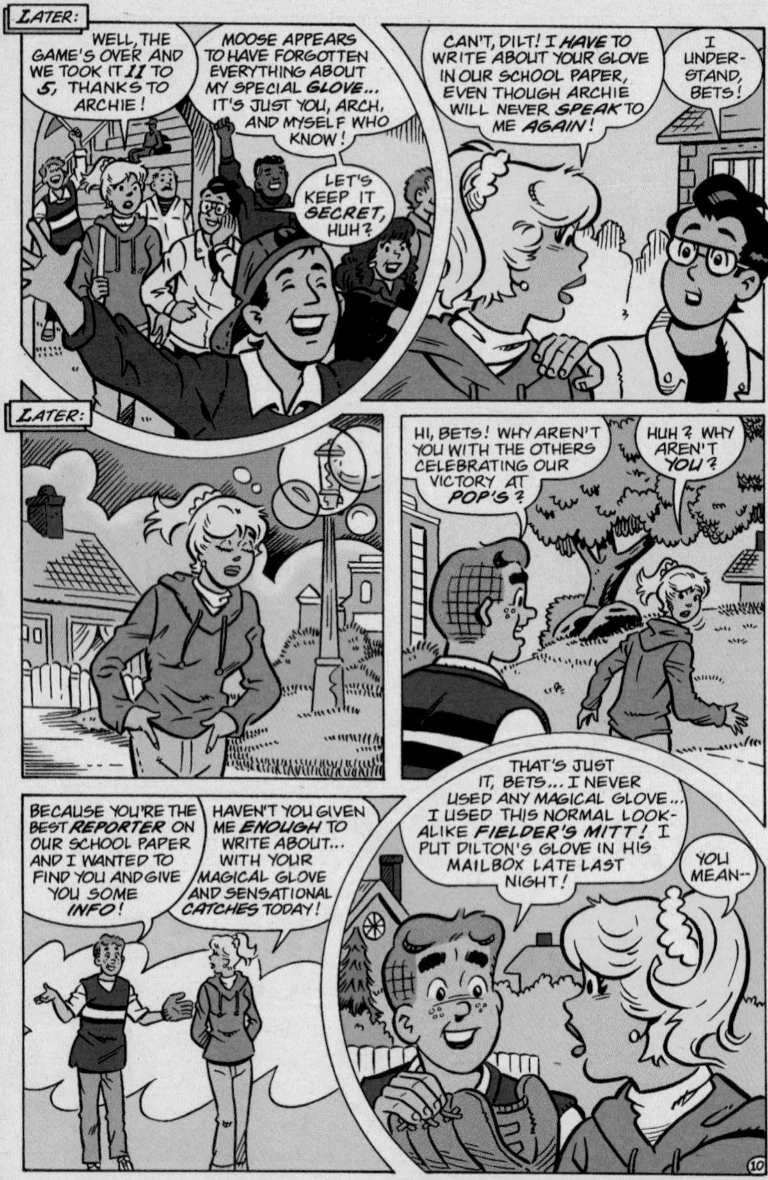

LATER:
WELL, THE GAME'S OVER AND WE TOOK IT 11 TO 5, THANKS TO ARCHIE!
MOOSE APPEARS TO HAVE FORGOTTEN EVERYTHING ABOUT MY SPECIAL GLOVE... IT'S JUST YOU, ARCH, AND MYSELF WHO KNOW!
LET'S KEEP IT SECRET, HUH?
CAN'T, DILT! I HAVE TO WRITE ABOUT YOUR GLOVE IN OUR SCHOOL PAPER, EVEN THOUGH ARCHIE WILL NEVER SPEAK TO ME AGAIN!
I UNDER-STAND, BETS!
LATER:
HI, BETS! WHY AREN'T YOU WITH THE OTHERS CELEBRATING OUR VICTORY AT POP'S?
HUH? WHY AREN'T YOU?
BECAUSE YOU'RE THE BEST REPORTER ON OUR SCHOOL PAPER AND I WANTED TO FIND YOU AND GIVE YOU SOME INFO!
HAVEN'T YOU GIVEN ME ENOUGH TO WRITE ABOUT... WITH YOUR MAGICAL GLOVE AND SENSATIONAL CATCHES TODAY!
THAT'S JUST IT, BETS... I NEVER USED ANY MAGICAL GLOVE... I USED THIS NORMAL LOOK-ALIKE FIELDER'S MITT! I PUT DILTON'S GLOVE IN HIS MAILBOX LATE LAST NIGHT!
YOU MEAN--

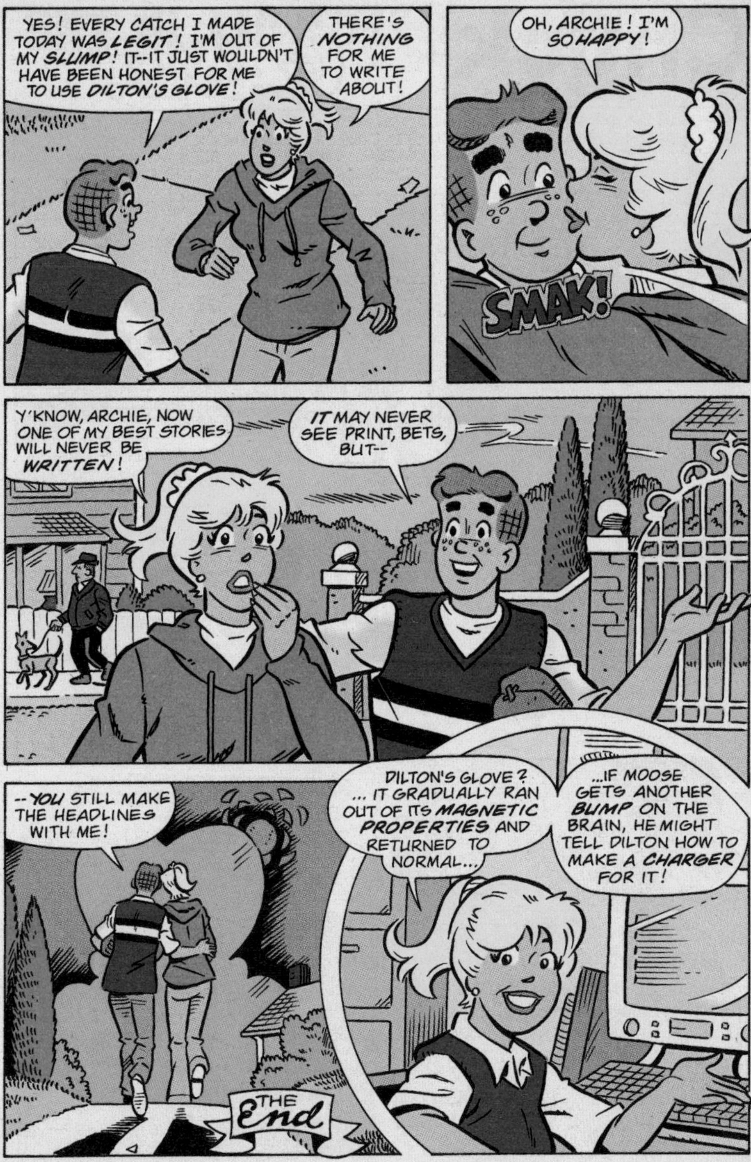
YES! EVERY CATCH I MADE TODAY WAS LEGIT! I'M OUT OF MY SLUMP! IT--IT JUST WOULDN'T HAVE BEEN HONEST FOR ME TO USE DILTON'S GLOVE!
THERE'S NOTHING FOR ME TO WRITE ABOUT!
OH, ARCHIE! I'M SO HAPPY!
SMAK!
Y'KNOW, ARCHIE, NOW ONE OF MY BEST STORIES WILL NEVER BE WRITTEN!
IT MAY NEVER SEE PRINT, BETS, BUT--
--YOU STILL MAKE THE HEADLINES WITH ME!
DILTON'S GLOVE? ... IT GRADUALLY RAN OUT OF ITS MAGNETIC PROPERTIES AND RETURNED TO NORMAL...
...IF MOOSE GETS ANOTHER BUMP ON THE BRAIN, HE MIGHT TELL DILTON HOW TO MAKE A CHARGER FOR IT!
THE End

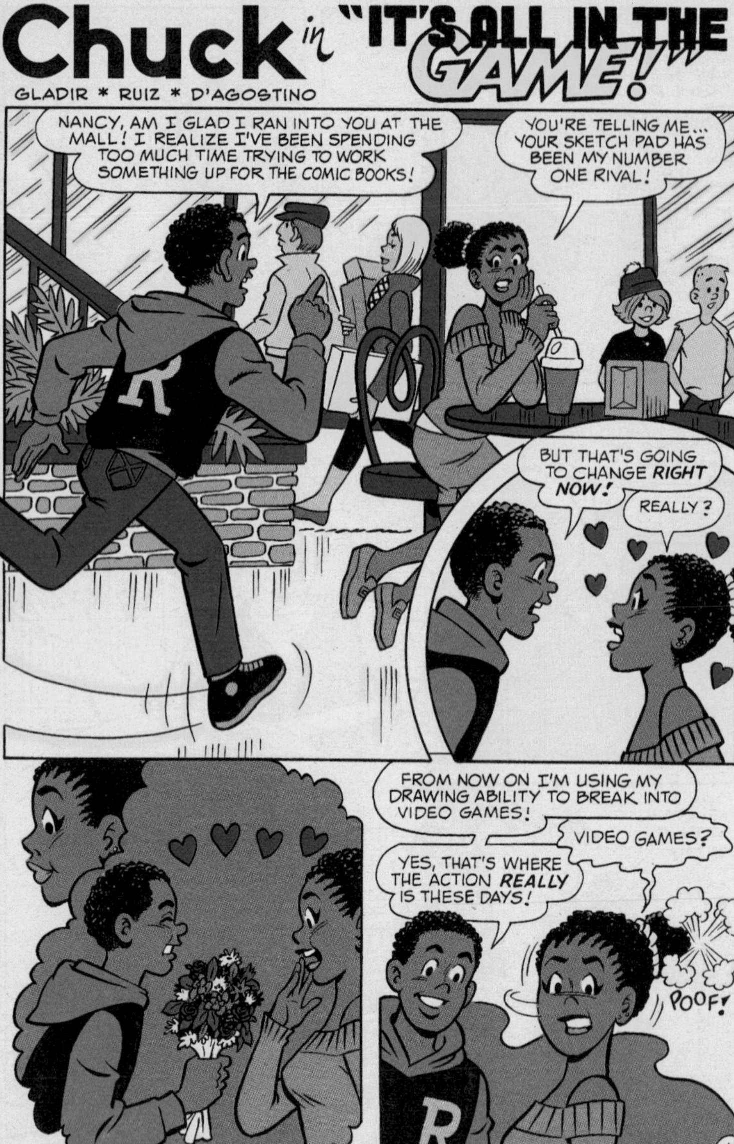
Chuck in "IT'S ALL IN THE GAME!"
GLADIR * RUIZ * D'AGOSTINO
NANCY, AM I GLAD I RAN INTO YOU AT THE MALL! I REALIZE I'VE BEEN SPENDING TOO MUCH TIME TRYING TO WORK SOMETHING UP FOR THE COMIC BOOKS!
YOU'RE TELLING ME... YOUR SKETCH PAD HAS BEEN MY NUMBER ONE RIVAL!
BUT THAT'S GOING TO CHANGE RIGHT NOW!
REALLY?
FROM NOW ON I'M USING MY DRAWING ABILITY TO BREAK INTO VIDEO GAMES!
VIDEO GAMES?
YES, THAT'S WHERE THE ACTION REALLY IS THESE DAYS!
POOF!
1

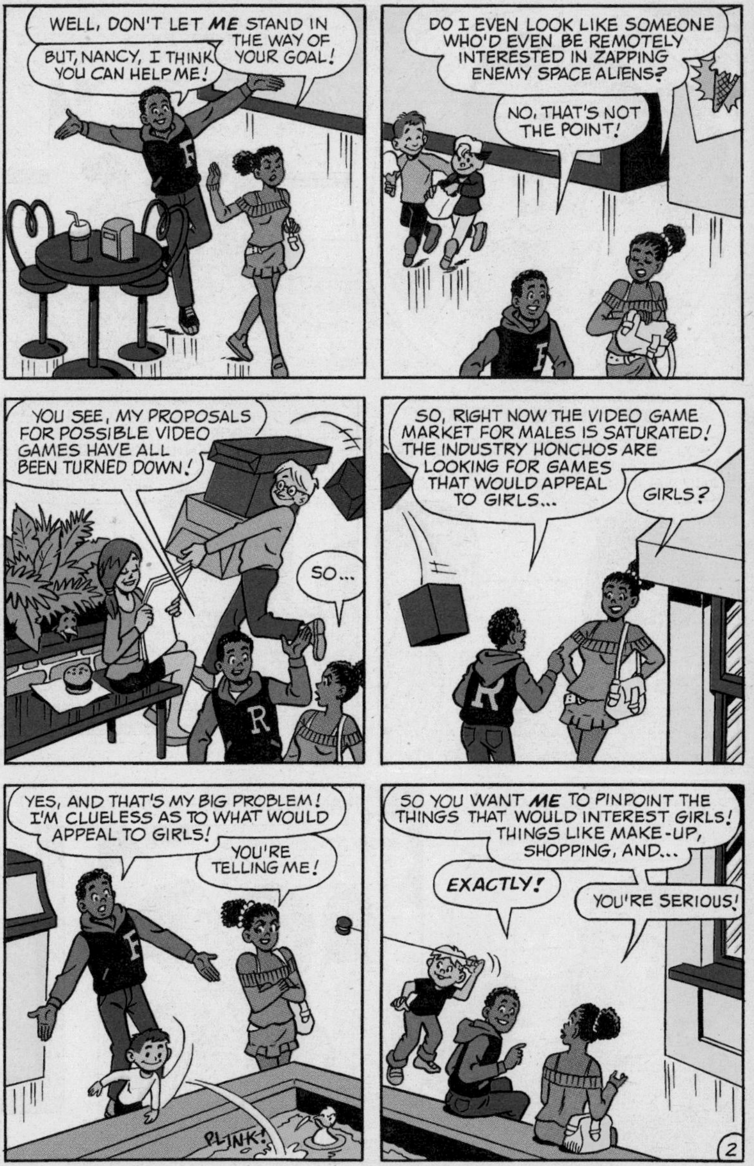
WELL, DON'T LET ME STAND IN THE WAY OF YOUR GOAL!
BUT, NANCY, I THINK YOU CAN HELP ME!
DO I EVEN LOOK LIKE SOMEONE WHO'D EVEN BE REMOTELY INTERESTED IN ZAPPING ENEMY SPACE ALIENS?
NO. THAT'S NOT THE POINT!
YOU SEE, MY PROPOSALS FOR POSSIBLE VIDEO GAMES HAVE ALL BEEN TURNED DOWN!
SO...
SO, RIGHT NOW THE VIDEO GAME MARKET FOR MALES IS SATURATED! THE INDUSTRY HONCHOS ARE LOOKING FOR GAMES THAT WOULD APPEAL TO GIRLS...
GIRLS?
YES, AND THAT'S MY BIG PROBLEM! I'M CLUELESS AS TO WHAT WOULD APPEAL TO GIRLS!
YOU'RE TELLING ME!
PLINK!
SO YOU WANT ME TO PINPOINT THE THINGS THAT WOULD INTEREST GIRLS! THINGS LIKE MAKE-UP, SHOPPING, AND...
EXACTLY!
YOU'RE SERIOUS!
2

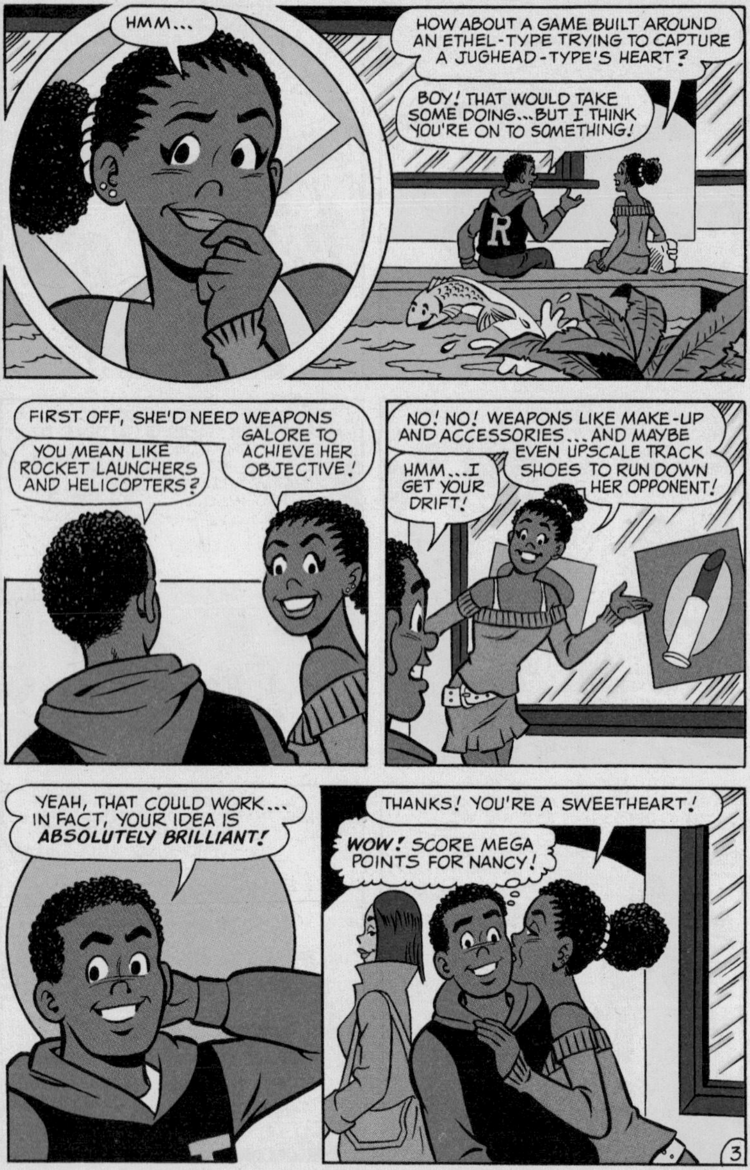
HMM...
HOW ABOUT A GAME BUILT AROUND AN ETHEL-TYPE TRYING TO CAPTURE A JUGHEAD-TYPE'S HEART?
BOY! THAT WOULD TAKE SOME DOING...BUT I THINK YOU'RE ON TO SOMETHING!
FIRST OFF, SHE'D NEED WEAPONS GALORE TO ACHIEVE HER OBJECTIVE!
YOU MEAN LIKE ROCKET LAUNCHERS AND HELICOPTERS?
NO! NO! WEAPONS LIKE MAKE-UP AND ACCESSORIES... AND MAYBE EVEN UPSCALE TRACK SHOES TO RUN DOWN HER OPPONENT!
HMM...I GET YOUR DRIFT!
YEAH, THAT COULD WORK... IN FACT, YOUR IDEA IS ABSOLUTELY BRILLIANT!
THANKS! YOU'RE A SWEETHEART!
WOW! SCORE MEGA POINTS FOR NANCY!
3

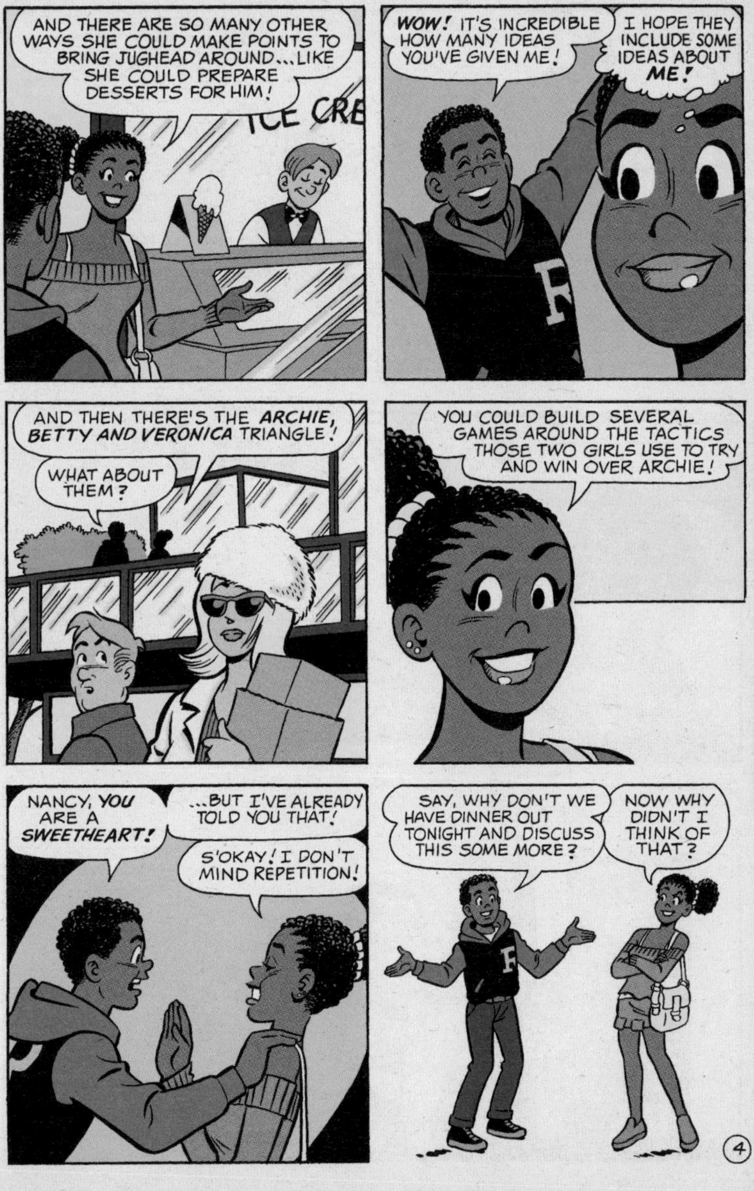
AND THERE ARE SO MANY OTHER WAYS SHE COULD MAKE POINTS TO BRING JUGHEAD AROUND... LIKE SHE COULD PREPARE DESSERTS FOR HIM!
ICE CRE
WOW! IT'S INCREDIBLE HOW MANY IDEAS YOU'VE GIVEN ME!
I HOPE THEY INCLUDE SOME IDEAS ABOUT ME!
AND THEN THERE'S THE ARCHIE, BETTY AND VERONICA TRIANGLE!
WHAT ABOUT THEM?
YOU COULD BUILD SEVERAL GAMES AROUND THE TACTICS THOSE TWO GIRLS USE TO TRY AND WIN OVER ARCHIE!
NANCY, YOU ARE A SWEETHEART!
...BUT I'VE ALREADY TOLD YOU THAT!
S'OKAY! I DON'T MIND REPETITION!
SAY, WHY DON'T WE HAVE DINNER OUT TONIGHT AND DISCUSS THIS SOME MORE?
NOW WHY DIDN'T I THINK OF THAT?

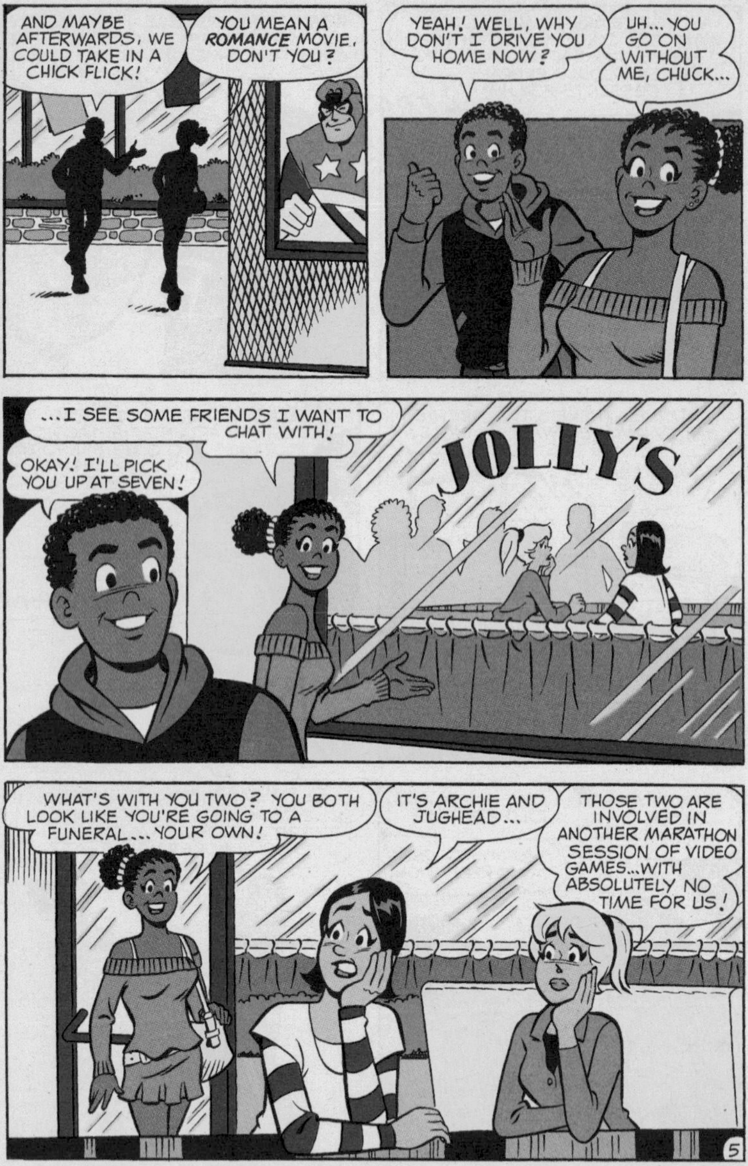

AND MAYBE AFTERWARDS, WE COULD TAKE IN A CHICK FLICK!
YOU MEAN A ROMANCE MOVIE, DON'T YOU?
YEAH! WELL, WHY DON'T I DRIVE YOU HOME NOW?
UH... YOU GO ON WITHOUT ME, CHUCK...
...I SEE SOME FRIENDS I WANT TO CHAT WITH!
OKAY! I'LL PICK YOU UP AT SEVEN!
JOLLY'S
WHAT'S WITH YOU TWO? YOU BOTH LOOK LIKE YOU'RE GOING TO A FUNERAL... YOUR OWN!
IT'S ARCHIE AND JUGHEAD...
THOSE TWO ARE INVOLVED IN ANOTHER MARATHON SESSION OF VIDEO GAMES...WITH ABSOLUTELY NO TIME FOR US!
5

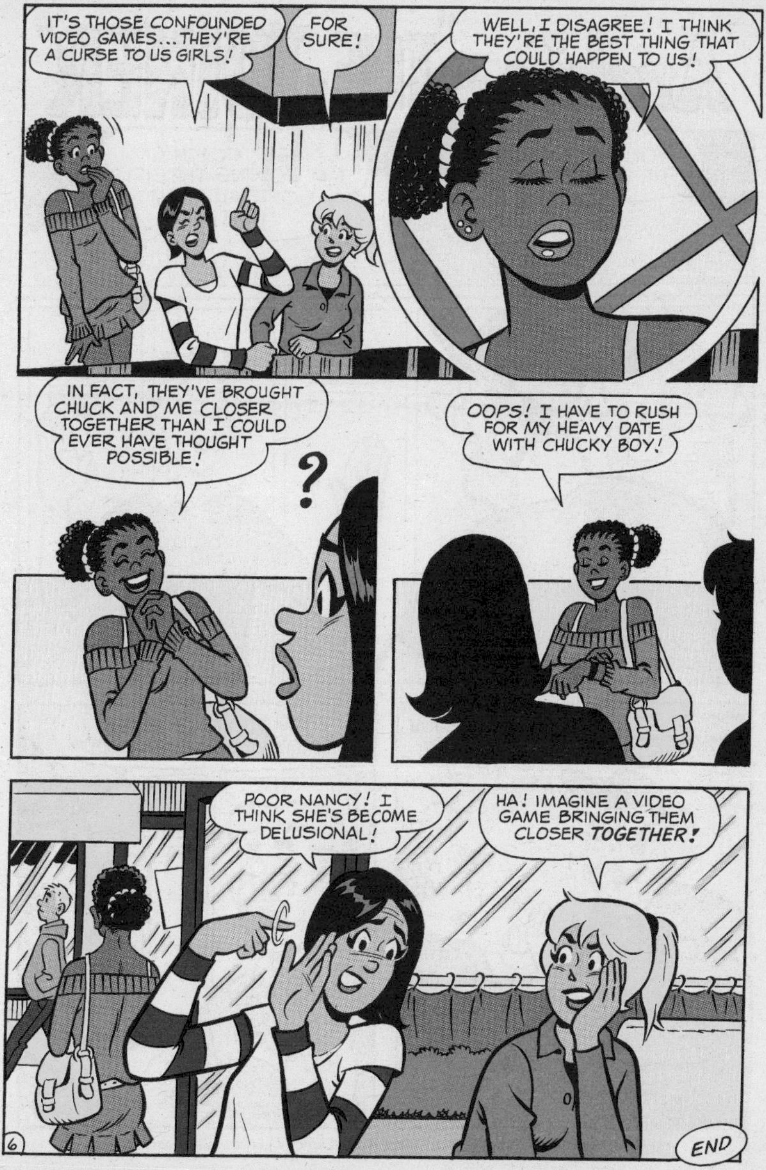
IT'S THOSE CONFOUNDED VIDEO GAMES... THEY'RE A CURSE TO US GIRLS!
FOR SURE!
WELL, I DISAGREE! I THINK THEY'RE THE BEST THING THAT COULD HAPPEN TO US!
IN FACT, THEY'VE BROUGHT CHUCK AND ME CLOSER TOGETHER THAN I COULD EVER HAVE THOUGHT POSSIBLE!
?
OOPS! I HAVE TO RUSH FOR MY HEAVY DATE WITH CHUCKY BOY!
POOR NANCY! I THINK SHE'S BECOME DELUSIONAL!
HA! IMAGINE A VIDEO GAME BRINGING THEM CLOSER TOGETHER!
6
END

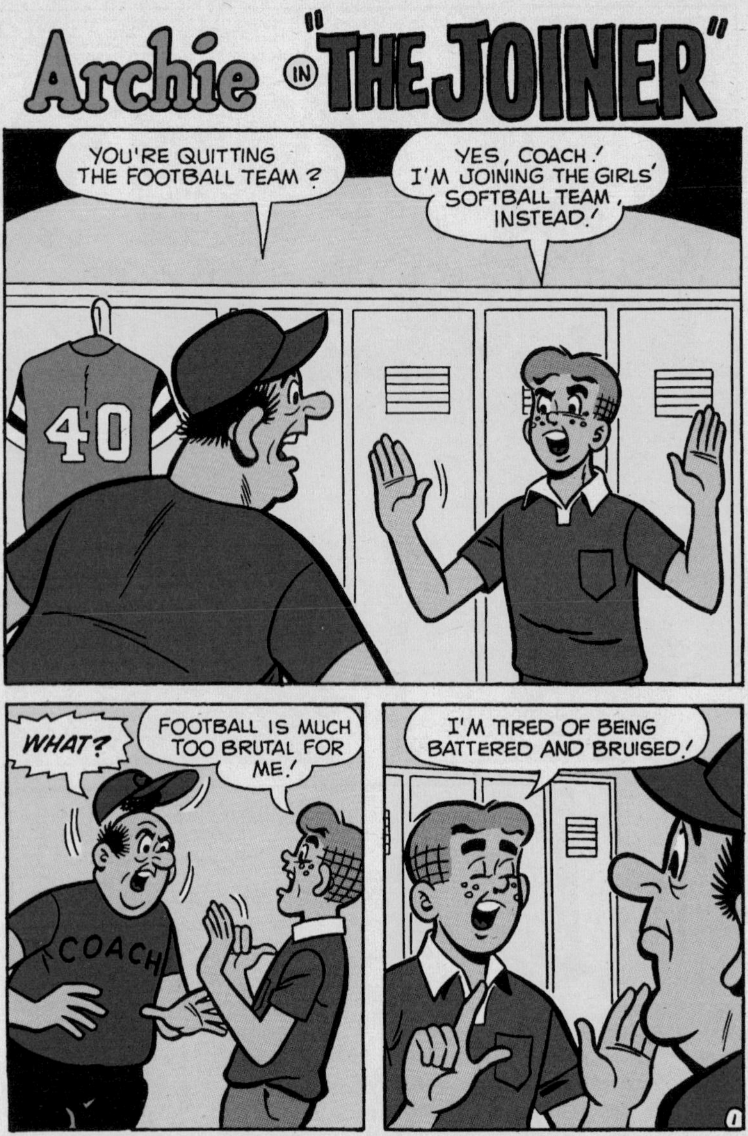
Archie IN "THE JOINER"
YOU'RE QUITTING THE FOOTBALL TEAM ?
YES, COACH! I'M JOINING THE GIRLS' SOFTBALL TEAM, INSTEAD!
WHAT?
FOOTBALL IS MUCH TOO BRUTAL FOR ME!
I'M TIRED OF BEING BATTERED AND BRUISED!
COACH
40
1

Script & Pencils: Dick Malmgren / Inks: Rudy Lapick / Letters: Bill Yoshida

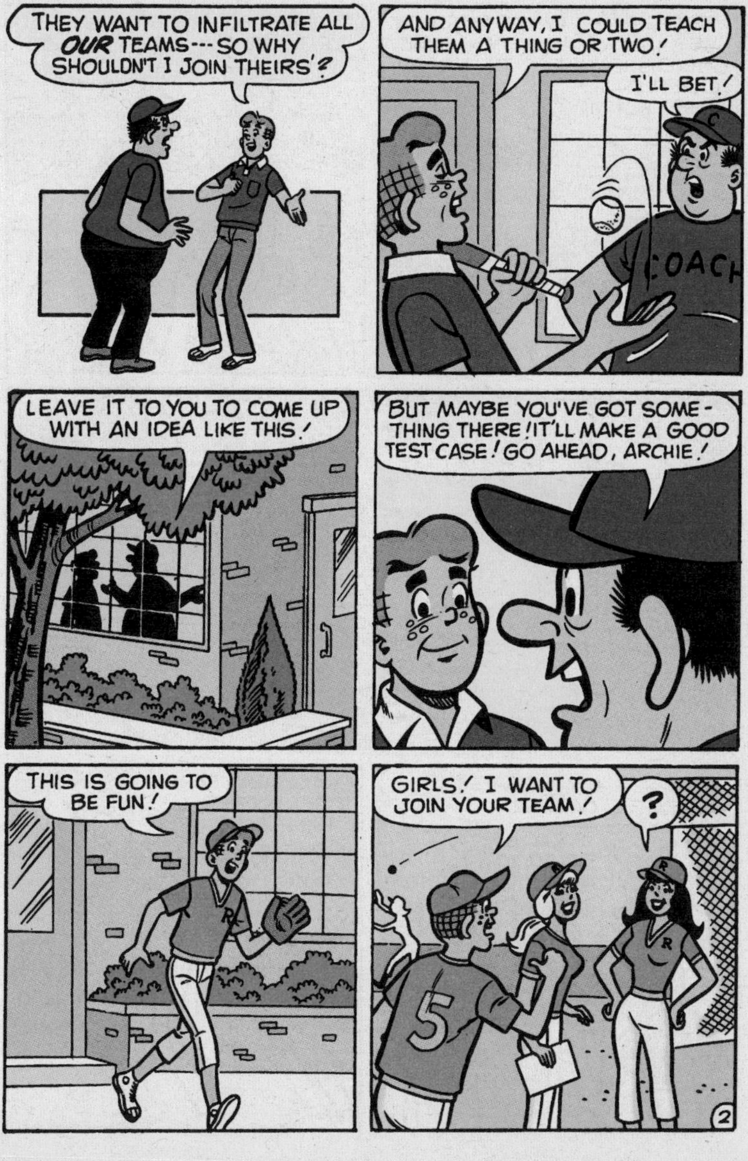
THEY WANT TO INFILTRATE ALL OUR TEAMS--- SO WHY SHOULDN'T I JOIN THEIRS'?
AND ANYWAY, I COULD TEACH THEM A THING OR TWO!
I'LL BET!
COACH
LEAVE IT TO YOU TO COME UP WITH AN IDEA LIKE THIS!
BUT MAYBE YOU'VE GOT SOME-THING THERE! IT'LL MAKE A GOOD TEST CASE! GO AHEAD, ARCHIE!
THIS IS GOING TO BE FUN!
GIRLS! I WANT TO JOIN YOUR TEAM!
?
5
2

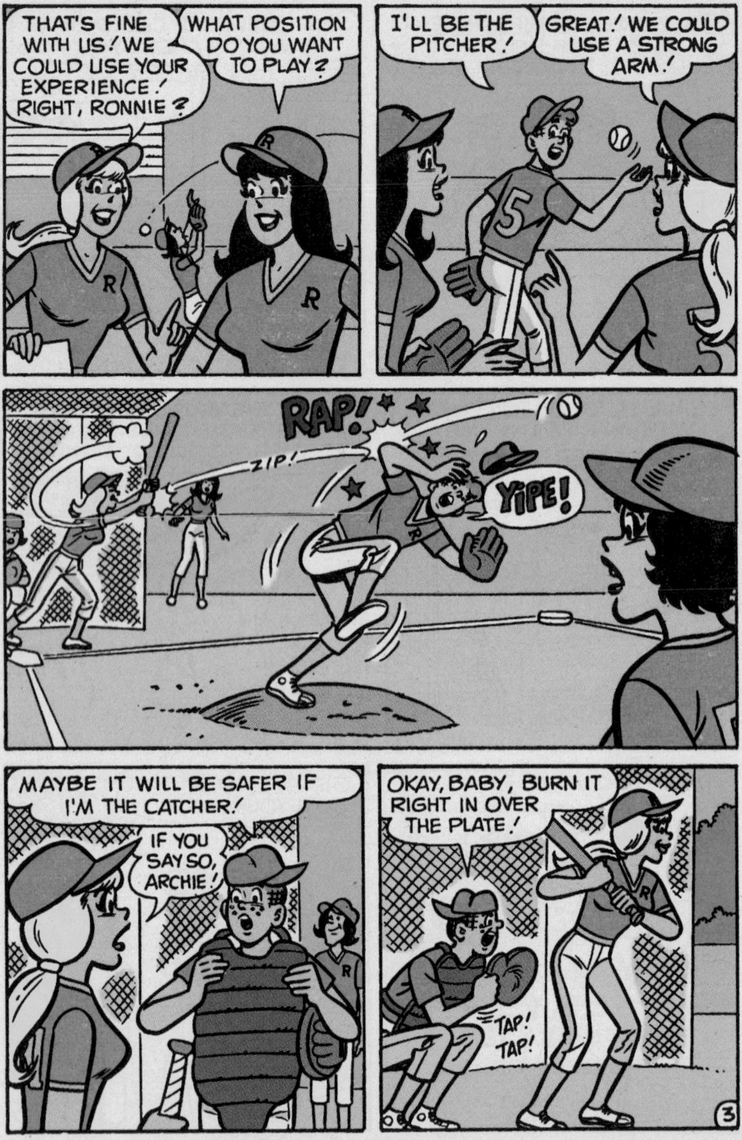
THAT'S FINE WITH US! WE COULD USE YOUR EXPERIENCE! RIGHT, RONNIE?
WHAT POSITION DO YOU WANT TO PLAY?
I'LL BE THE PITCHER!
GREAT! WE COULD USE A STRONG ARM!
RAP!
ZIP!
YIPE!
MAYBE IT WILL BE SAFER IF I'M THE CATCHER!
IF YOU SAY SO, ARCHIE!
OKAY, BABY, BURN IT RIGHT IN OVER THE PLATE!
TAP! TAP!
3

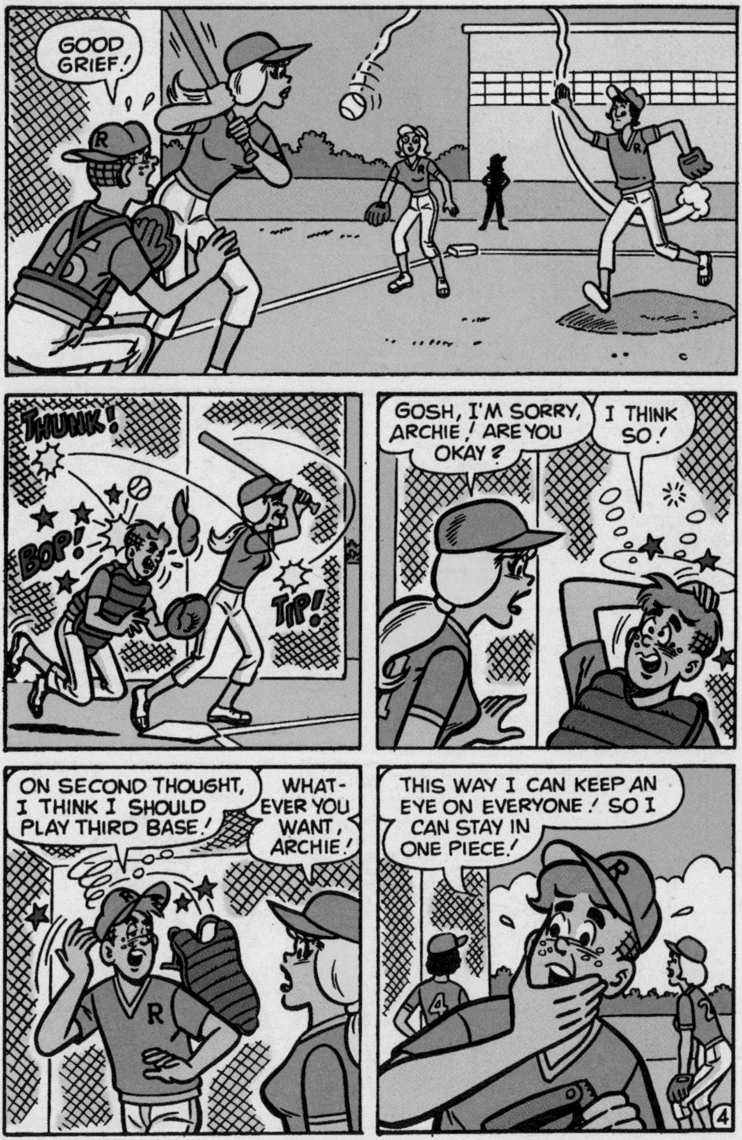
GOOD GRIEF!
THUNK!
BOP!
TIP!
GOSH, I'M SORRY, ARCHIE! ARE YOU OKAY?
I THINK SO!
ON SECOND THOUGHT, I THINK I SHOULD PLAY THIRD BASE!
WHATEVER YOU WANT, ARCHIE!
THIS WAY I CAN KEEP AN EYE ON EVERYONE! SO I CAN STAY IN ONE PIECE!
4

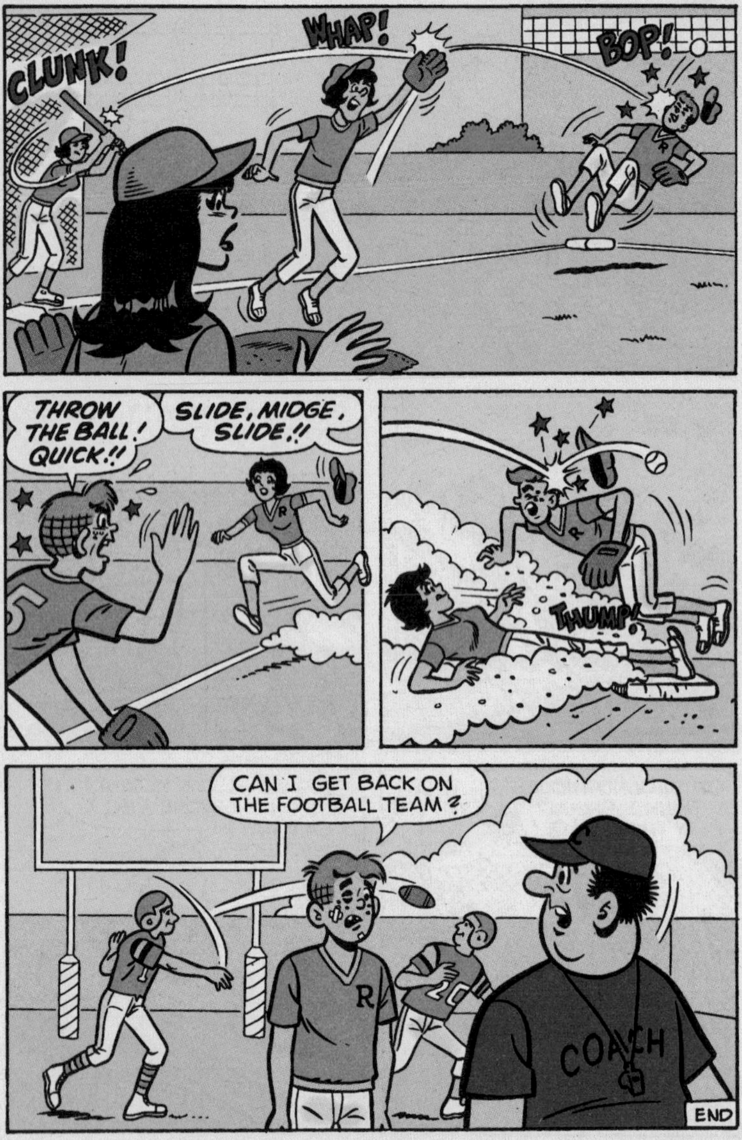

CLUNK!
WHAP!
BOP!
THROW THE BALL! QUICK!!
SLIDE, MIDGE, SLIDE!!
THUMP!
CAN I GET BACK ON THE FOOTBALL TEAM?
COACH
END

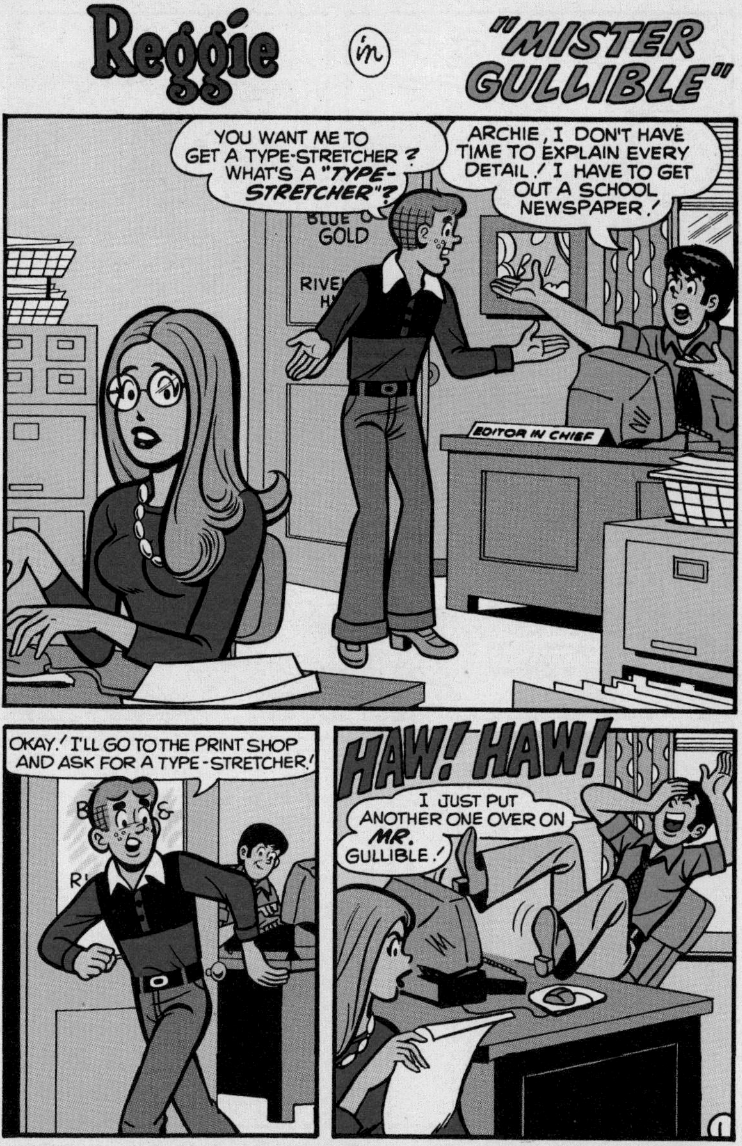
Reggie in "MISTER GULLIBLE"
YOU WANT ME TO GET A TYPE-STRETCHER ? WHAT'S A "TYPE-STRETCHER"?
ARCHIE, I DON'T HAVE TIME TO EXPLAIN EVERY DETAIL! I HAVE TO GET OUT A SCHOOL NEWSPAPER!
BLUE & GOLD
RIVE
EDITOR IN CHIEF
OKAY! I'LL GO TO THE PRINT SHOP AND ASK FOR A TYPE-STRETCHER!
HAW! HAW!
I JUST PUT ANOTHER ONE OVER ON MR. GULLIBLE!
1

Script: George Gladir / Pencils: Bob Bolling / Inks: Rudy Lapick / Letters: Bill Yoshida

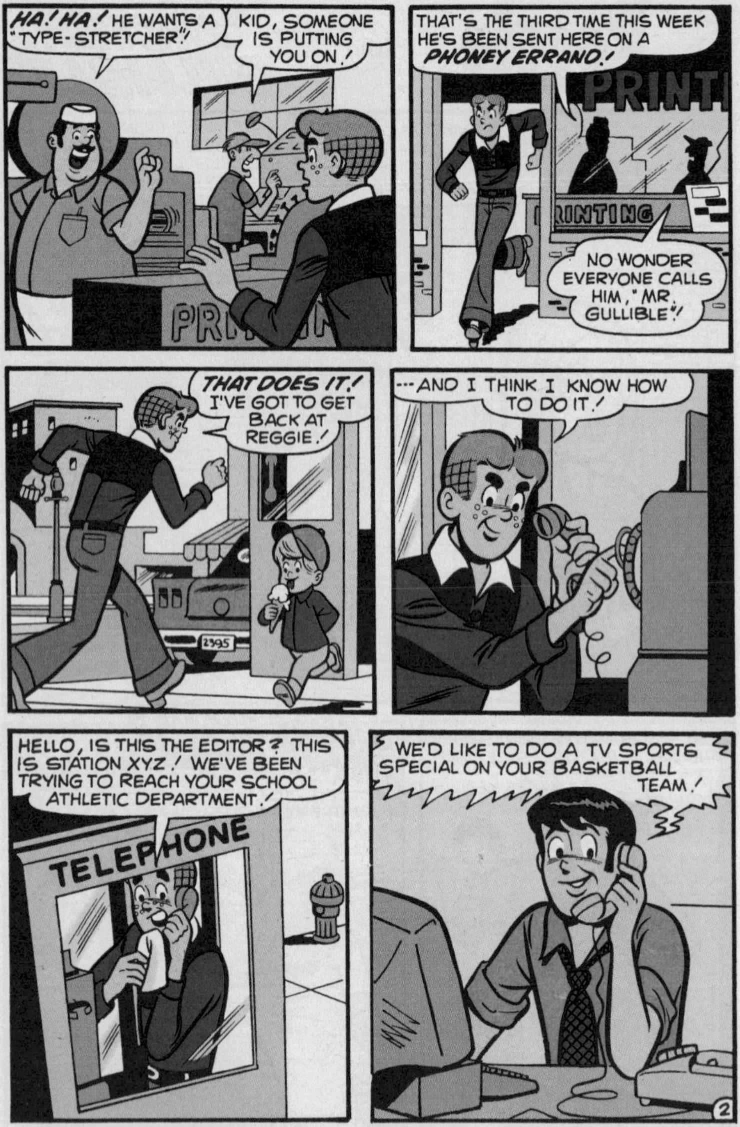
HA! HA! HE WANTS A "TYPE-STRETCHER"!
KID, SOMEONE IS PUTTING YOU ON.!
THAT'S THE THIRD TIME THIS WEEK HE'S BEEN SENT HERE ON A PHONEY ERRAND.!
PRINTING
NO WONDER EVERYONE CALLS HIM, "MR. GULLIBLE"!
THAT DOES IT! I'VE GOT TO GET BACK AT REGGIE.!
---AND I THINK I KNOW HOW TO DO IT.!
HELLO, IS THIS THE EDITOR? THIS IS STATION XYZ! WE'VE BEEN TRYING TO REACH YOUR SCHOOL ATHLETIC DEPARTMENT.!
TELEPHONE
WE'D LIKE TO DO A TV SPORTS SPECIAL ON YOUR BASKETBALL TEAM!
2

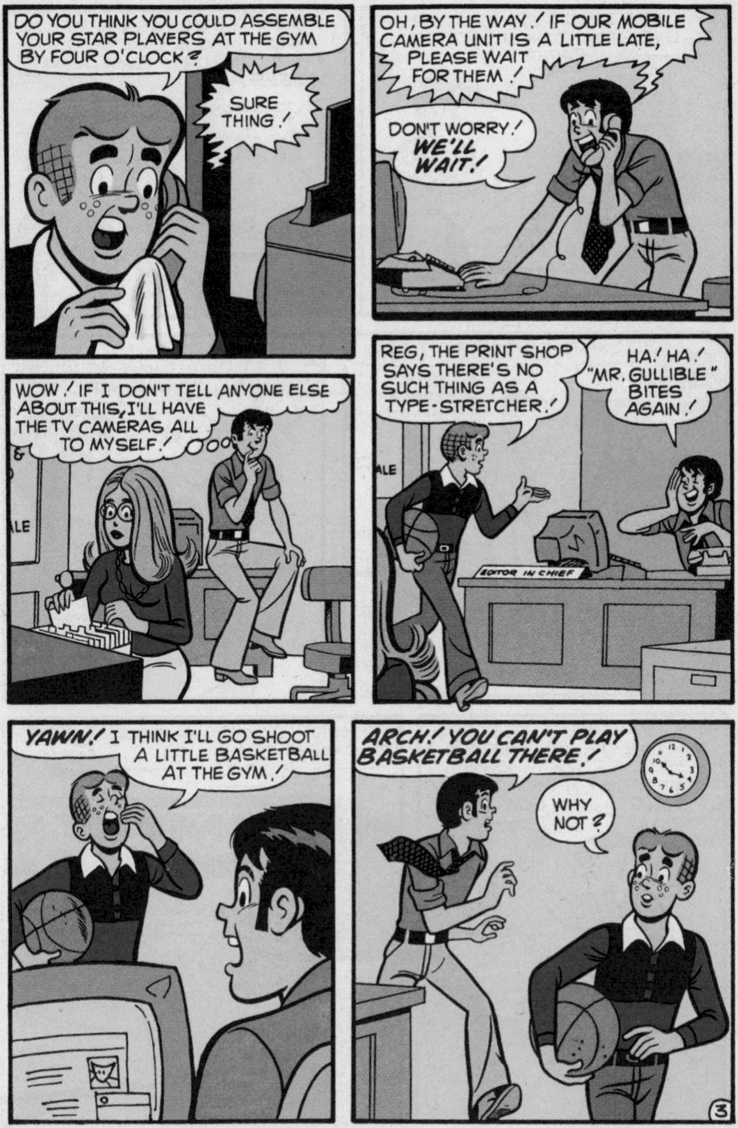
DO YOU THINK YOU COULD ASSEMBLE YOUR STAR PLAYERS AT THE GYM BY FOUR O'CLOCK?
SURE THING.!
OH, BY THE WAY.! IF OUR MOBILE CAMERA UNIT IS A LITTLE LATE, PLEASE WAIT FOR THEM.!
DON'T WORRY.! WE'LL WAIT.!
WOW.! IF I DON'T TELL ANYONE ELSE ABOUT THIS, I'LL HAVE THE TV CAMERAS ALL TO MYSELF.!
REG, THE PRINT SHOP SAYS THERE'S NO SUCH THING AS A TYPE-STRETCHER.!
HA.! HA.! "MR. GULLIBLE" BITES AGAIN.!
EDITOR IN CHIEF
YAWN.! I THINK I'LL GO SHOOT A LITTLE BASKETBALL AT THE GYM.!
ARCH.! YOU CAN'T PLAY BASKETBALL THERE.!
WHY NOT?
3

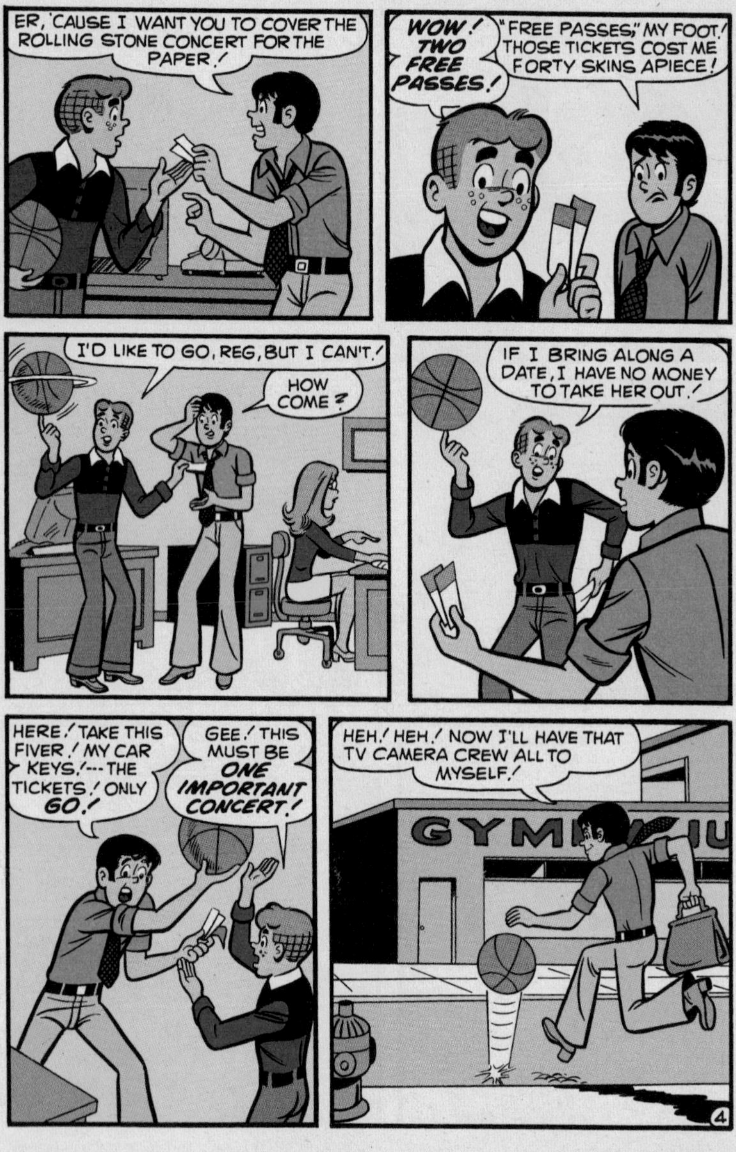

ER, 'CAUSE I WANT YOU TO COVER THE ROLLING STONE CONCERT FOR THE PAPER!
WOW! TWO FREE PASSES!
"FREE PASSES," MY FOOT! THOSE TICKETS COST ME FORTY SKINS APIECE!
I'D LIKE TO GO, REG, BUT I CAN'T!
HOW COME?
IF I BRING ALONG A DATE, I HAVE NO MONEY TO TAKE HER OUT!
HERE! TAKE THIS FIVER! MY CAR KEYS!--- THE TICKETS! ONLY GO!
GEE! THIS MUST BE ONE IMPORTANT CONCERT!
HEH! HEH! NOW I'LL HAVE THAT TV CAMERA CREW ALL TO MYSELF!
GYM

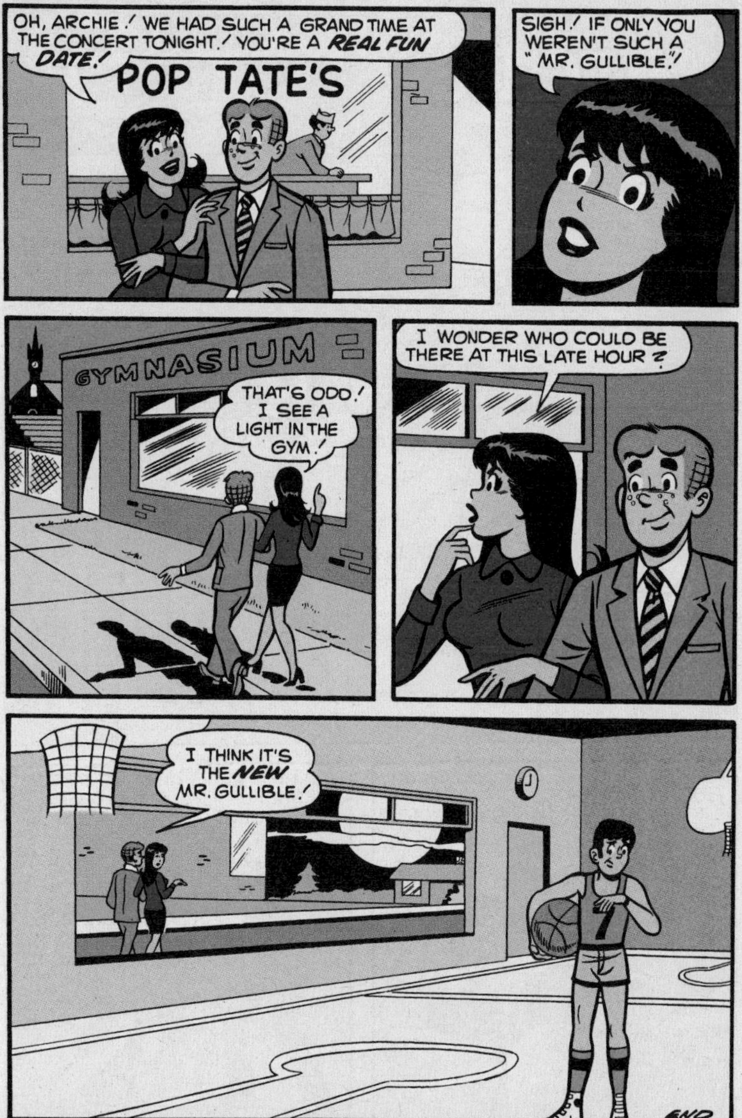
OH, ARCHIE! WE HAD SUCH A GRAND TIME AT THE CONCERT TONIGHT! YOU'RE A REAL FUN DATE!
POP TATE'S
SIGH! IF ONLY YOU WEREN'T SUCH A "MR. GULLIBLE"!
GYMNASIUM
THAT'S ODD! I SEE A LIGHT IN THE GYM!
I WONDER WHO COULD BE THERE AT THIS LATE HOUR ?
I THINK IT'S THE NEW MR. GULLIBLE!
7
END

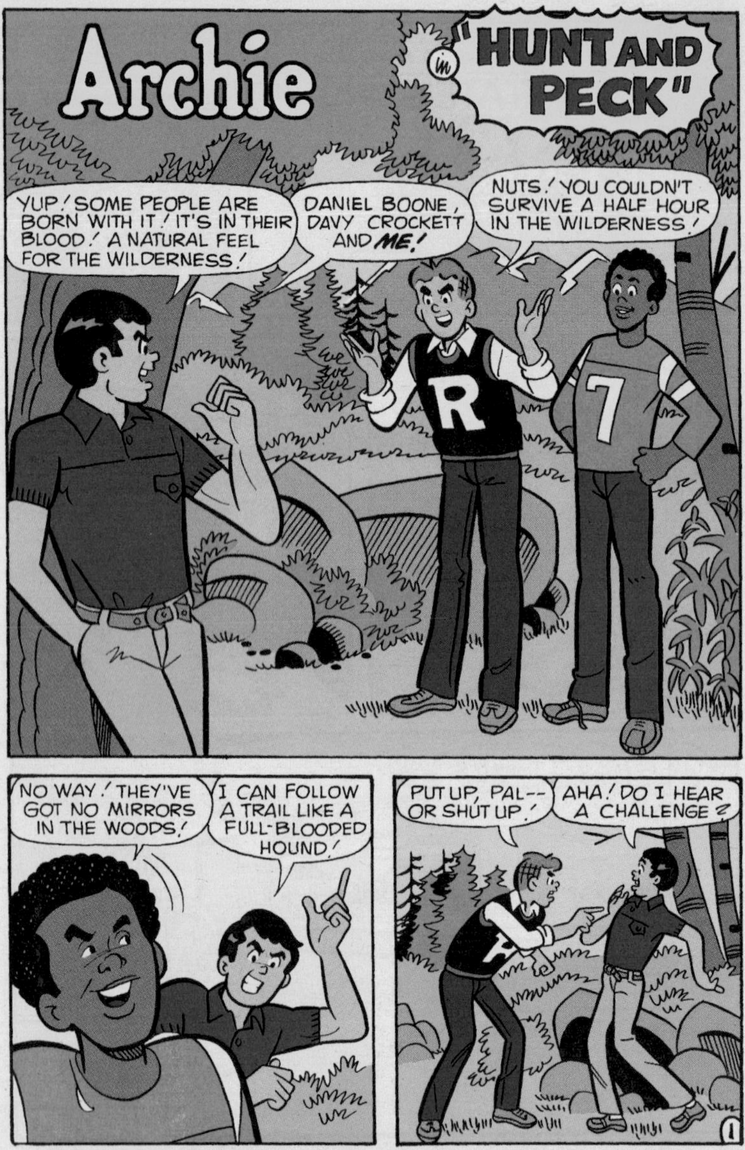
Archie
in
"HUNT AND PECK"
YUP! SOME PEOPLE ARE BORN WITH IT! IT'S IN THEIR BLOOD! A NATURAL FEEL FOR THE WILDERNESS!
DANIEL BOONE, DAVY CROCKETT AND ME!
NUTS! YOU COULDN'T SURVIVE A HALF HOUR IN THE WILDERNESS!
NO WAY! THEY'VE GOT NO MIRRORS IN THE WOODS!
I CAN FOLLOW A TRAIL LIKE A FULL-BLOODED HOUND!
PUT UP, PAL-- OR SHUT UP!
AHA! DO I HEAR A CHALLENGE?
1

Script: George Gladir / Pencils: Stan Goldberg / Inks: Mike Esposito / Letters: Bill Yoshida

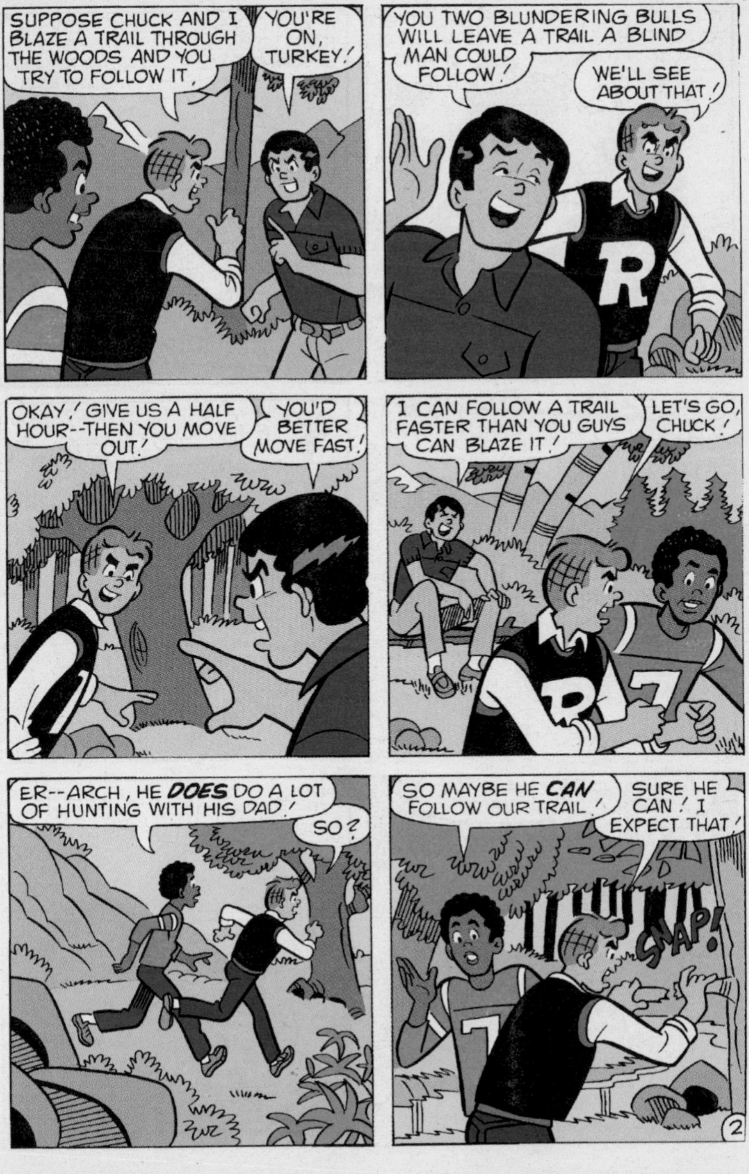
SUPPOSE CHUCK AND I BLAZE A TRAIL THROUGH THE WOODS AND YOU TRY TO FOLLOW IT,
YOU'RE ON, TURKEY!
YOU TWO BLUNDERING BULLS WILL LEAVE A TRAIL A BLIND MAN COULD FOLLOW!
WE'LL SEE ABOUT THAT!
OKAY! GIVE US A HALF HOUR--THEN YOU MOVE OUT!
YOU'D BETTER MOVE FAST!
I CAN FOLLOW A TRAIL FASTER THAN YOU GUYS CAN BLAZE IT!
LET'S GO, CHUCK!
ER--ARCH, HE ***DOES*** DO A LOT OF HUNTING WITH HIS DAD!
SO?
SO MAYBE HE ***CAN*** FOLLOW OUR TRAIL!
SURE HE CAN! I EXPECT THAT!
SNAP!

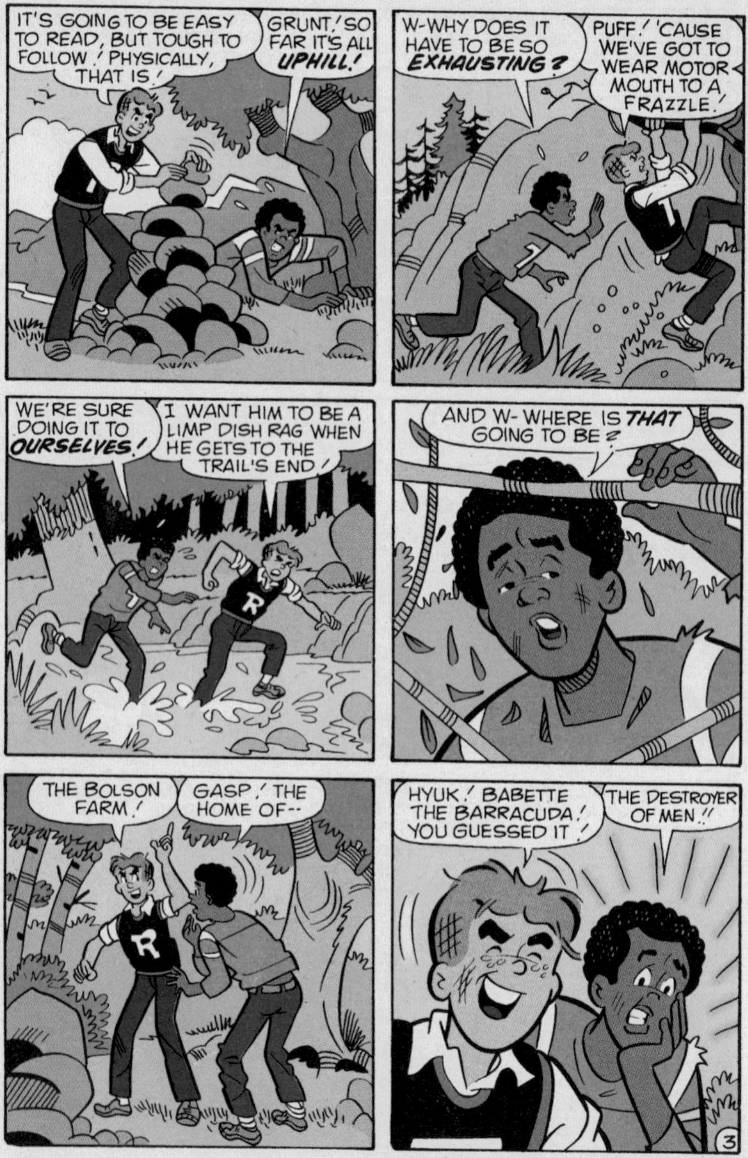
IT'S GOING TO BE EASY TO READ, BUT TOUGH TO FOLLOW! PHYSICALLY, THAT IS!
GRUNT! SO FAR IT'S ALL UPHILL!
W-WHY DOES IT HAVE TO BE SO EXHAUSTING?
PUFF! 'CAUSE WE'VE GOT TO WEAR MOTOR MOUTH TO A FRAZZLE!
WE'RE SURE DOING IT TO OURSELVES!
I WANT HIM TO BE A LIMP DISH RAG WHEN HE GETS TO THE TRAIL'S END!
AND W- WHERE IS THAT GOING TO BE?
THE BOLSON FARM!
GASP! THE HOME OF--
HYUK! BABETTE THE BARRACUDA! YOU GUESSED IT!
THE DESTROYER OF MEN!!

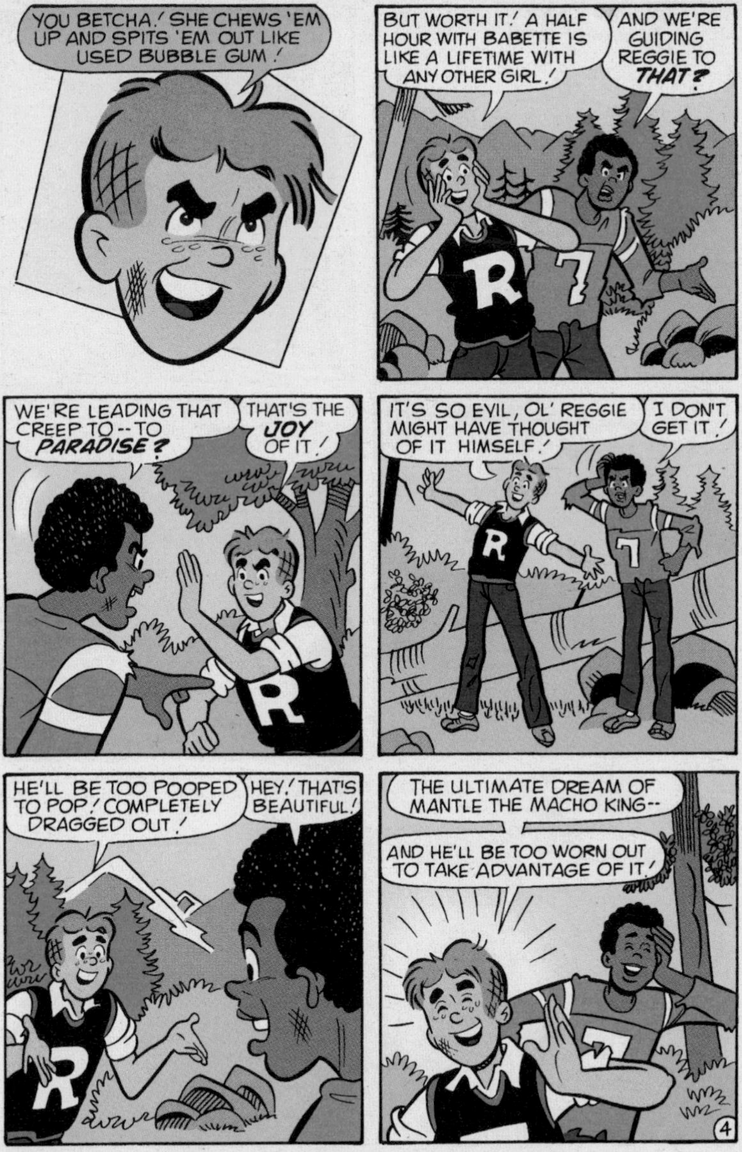
YOU BETCHA! SHE CHEWS 'EM UP AND SPITS 'EM OUT LIKE USED BUBBLE GUM!
BUT WORTH IT! A HALF HOUR WITH BABETTE IS LIKE A LIFETIME WITH ANY OTHER GIRL!
AND WE'RE GUIDING REGGIE TO THAT?
WE'RE LEADING THAT CREEP TO--TO PARADISE?
THAT'S THE JOY OF IT!
IT'S SO EVIL, OL' REGGIE MIGHT HAVE THOUGHT OF IT HIMSELF!
I DON'T GET IT!
HE'LL BE TOO POOPED TO POP! COMPLETELY DRAGGED OUT!
HEY! THAT'S BEAUTIFUL!
THE ULTIMATE DREAM OF MANTLE THE MACHO KING--
AND HE'LL BE TOO WORN OUT TO TAKE ADVANTAGE OF IT!
4

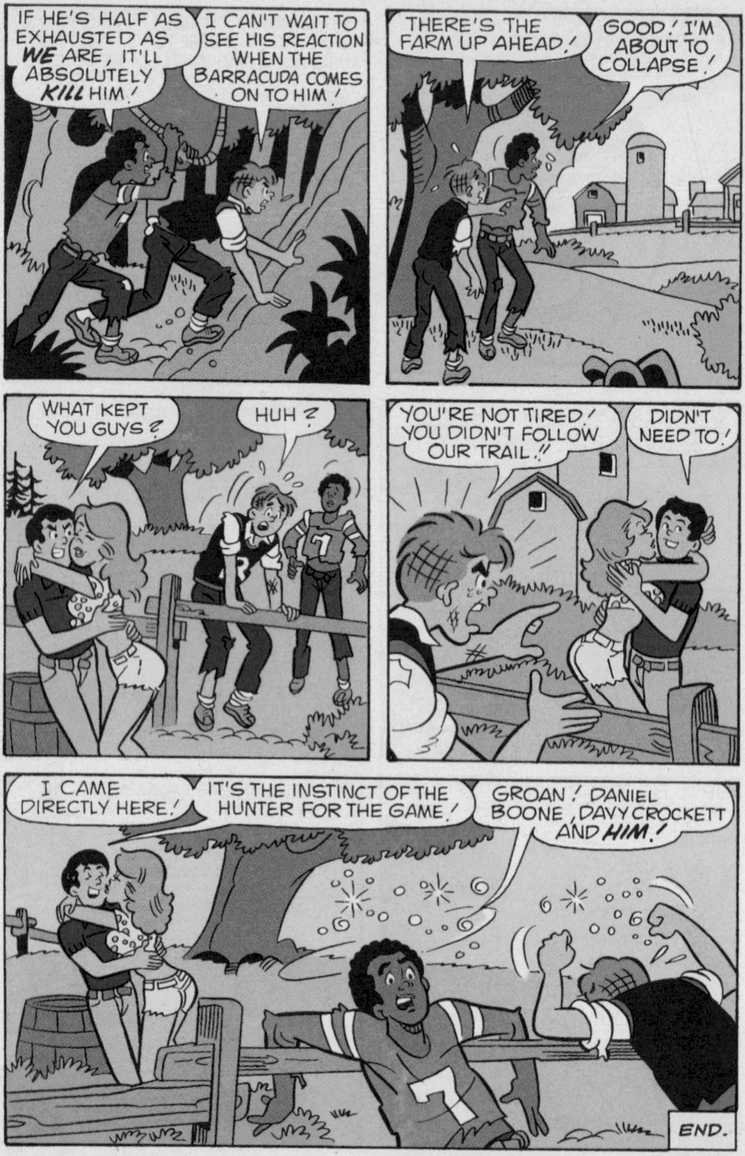

IF HE'S HALF AS EXHAUSTED AS WE ARE, IT'LL ABSOLUTELY KILL HIM!
I CAN'T WAIT TO SEE HIS REACTION WHEN THE BARRACUDA COMES ON TO HIM!
THERE'S THE FARM UP AHEAD!
GOOD! I'M ABOUT TO COLLAPSE!
WHAT KEPT YOU GUYS?
HUH?
YOU'RE NOT TIRED! YOU DIDN'T FOLLOW OUR TRAIL!!
DIDN'T NEED TO!
I CAME DIRECTLY HERE!
IT'S THE INSTINCT OF THE HUNTER FOR THE GAME!
GROAN! DANIEL BOONE, DAVY CROCKETT AND HIM!
END.